FATHER KNOWS
Last!

Psst!
Don't tell Father,
but he's in for a surprise....

Love and marriage don't necessarily go together.
When that happens,
Mother
might just have a little secret
that

FATHER KNOWS
Last!

Three complete novels by your favorite authors!

About the Authors

Candace Schuler—Popular author of over fifteen romance novels, Candace has lived in almost every corner of the United States. When she's not moving, traveling or writing, she's taking courses—the more offbeat the better.

Judith Duncan—Well-known author of a dozen novels, Judith has written some of the most compelling, passionate and controversial romance novels in print today. A dyed-in-the-wool Western Canadian, this mother of five is also a popular lecturer.

Shannon Waverly—An emerging star in women's romance fiction, Shannon is the author of almost ten romance novels. Her evocative, moving stories are often set in the New England area, where she lives with her husband of twenty-five years.

FATHER KNOWS
Last!

CANDACE SCHULER
JUDITH DUNCAN
SHANNON WAVERLY

Harlequin Books

TORONTO • NEW YORK • LONDON
AMSTERDAM • PARIS • SYDNEY • HAMBURG
STOCKHOLM • ATHENS • TOKYO • MILAN
MADRID • WARSAW • BUDAPEST • AUCKLAND

HARLEQUIN BOOKS

by Request—Father Knows Last!

Copyright © 1994 by Harlequin Enterprises B.V.

ISBN 0-373-20101-X

The publisher acknowledges the copyright holders
of the individual works as follows:
DESIRE'S CHILD
Copyright © 1984 by Candace Schuler
INTO THE LIGHT
Copyright © 1986 by Judith Duncan
A SUMMER KIND OF LOVE
Copyright © 1990 by Kathleen Shannon

CONTENTS

Desiree Weston has a secret—
a *five-month-old* secret named Stephanie!

DESIRE'S CHILD

Candace Schuler

1

"GO HOME," urged Dr. Craig gently when Desi just sat there, stunned at his news. "Give yourself a few days to think it over. But not too long. Just a few days and call me when you make a decision."

"You're sure?" was all Desi could say, her wide violet eyes raised hopefully to his.

"Well, the lab report could prove me wrong," he hedged, wanting to reassure her but not really able to, "but, yes, on the basis of my examination, I'm sure."

Desi's hand moved unconsciously to her stomach, feeling for the roundness that was not yet evident, an expression that mingled worry and wonderment creasing her smooth forehead.

"You really had no idea, did you, Desi?"

"Well . . . that's not *quite* true," she admitted, feeling like a prize fool at her seeming stupidity. "I mean, somewhere in the back of my mind I realized that it was a possibility. But that's all. Just a . . ." Her voice faded for a moment. "Just a very remote possibility. I know that must sound incredibly naive in this day and age, but—" she waved a graceful hand distractedly "—it just never occurred to me in any real sense! No, that's not true, either. I didn't *want* to see it. I made excuses. I mean, you know that I've never been very regular and I haven't been sick in the mornings or anything and . . . and it was only that once. . . ." Her voice trailed off and she colored in embarrassment because it had not been just one isolated incident as her words implied, but several uncounted times during one glorious abandoned weekend. That was what she had meant by "once"—one weekend.

Oh, Lord, how could she have been so incredibly stupid?

"I knew *something* was wrong, of course, but I told myself that it was probably just some sort of normal female problem," she said finally. "Or something terribly terminal. You know, like cancer or something!" She looked up then, her inborn irrepressible sense of humor coming to her aid. "In a way it's a relief. People don't usually die from being pregnant." She laughed, a bright, sharp sound, not at all like her usual warm chuckle. Hysteria hovered on the edge, waiting, and she stopped abruptly, refusing to let the emotion rise any further.

"Well, thank you for the extra time today, Dr. Craig," she said, rising, and slung the strap of a large, well-worn leather satchel over her shoulder.

Dr. Craig came around the desk and captured her hands as they fidgeted, adjusting the bright yellow scarf around her neck, smoothing the front of her bulky knit sweater over the still nonexistent swell of her stomach.

"Call me in a few days," he said. "You have to make up your mind quickly in a case like this. A few more weeks and it will be too late for abor—"

Desi shook her head, cutting him off. "No, I can't. I…it's…" She shook her head again, pulling her hands away from his. "No."

"Don't say no yet," he urged. "Think about it. You're young, Desi, with your whole life in front of you. It sounds trite, I know, but being trite doesn't make it any less true. Don't let one foolish mistake ruin your life."

"It wasn't a mistake," she flared, surprising them both with her vehemence. And she blushed again, feeling the heat rise from her throat, staining her pale redhead's complexion with betraying color. "It was foolish, I admit that, but . . ." She shrugged and reached for the doorknob. How could she explain to this kind caring man, who had known her all her life, what had happened?

She simply couldn't look at this pregnancy as a mistake. It would mean that everything leading up to it had been a mistake, too. And it wasn't! She had gone into it, grabbing at a dream, with her eyes wide open.

Well, almost wide open, she admitted ruefully, a small smile of self-deprecation curving her lips. Because not for one brief minute had she ever really considered the possible consequences. Very foolish.

But not a mistake. Never could she admit that it had been a mistake.

"Will the father...I mean are you contemplating marriage then?" asked Dr. Craig.

"Marriage?" Desi turned in the doorway, honestly amused, and a warm chuckle escaped her. "No, 'fraid not. He doesn't know and I'm not going to tell him."

"But surely, Desi, he has a right," Dr. Craig began, shocked through to his conventional core.

"Not in this case," she said gently. "No promises were made or expected. Not on either side. This is strictly my problem, okay?"

"Okay," he conceded reluctantly, recognizing the stubborn light in her violet eyes. Stubbornness, pride, willfulness—call it what you will. It had gotten her, uncomplaining, through childhood bumps and scrapes, broken bones and a long convalescence after a bad car accident in her teens. He hoped it would get her through this.

"Think about what I've said," he called after her. She half turned, smiled and shook her head, causing wavy tendrils of coppery hair to bounce gently against her pale cheeks. "Then see my nurse about a referral, you stubborn child," he said, turning back toward his office.

"A referral?" Desi frowned, her voice halting him.

"You still live in San Francisco, don't you?"

Desi nodded.

"Well, then, you're going to need a local doctor," he explained patiently. "Driving eighty miles for every appointment, especially during the last months, wouldn't be very practical. And you'll need someone close by in case of an emergency.

"Now don't start worrying, Desi," he added as she began to frown again, "There are plenty of good OB men in San Francisco—" he smiled encouragingly at her "—and you're young and very healthy. I don't anticipate any problems at all, but it's always wise not to take any unnecessary chances. And having your doctor eighty miles away is an unnecessary chance. Agreed?"

"Yes, agreed." Desi smiled and let him return to his office and his other patients.

She was given the name of two San Francisco obstetricians along with a prescription for vitamins, a calcium supplement and a list of dos and don'ts for supposedly fragile pregnant ladies. She stuffed them all into her satchel and went outside, heading toward the parking lot and her baby blue Spitfire convertible.

She didn't feel especially fragile, she decided as she struggled to put up the recalcitrant top on her car. On the contrary, she felt healthy as a horse, full of energy, strong. Physically, that is. Her emotions were another matter entirely.

Emotionally she felt stupid and foolish and incredibly naive. She simply had not considered this happening. Had not *allowed* herself to consider that it could happen. Pregnancy had seemed so far from that weekend. So removed from what was happening between them.

"Face it," she said to her reflection in the rearview mirror, "you were stupid. And now you're scared."

She surveyed herself in the narrow mirror. Yes, definitely scared. She could see her eyes reflected back at her. Wide and violet and uncharacteristically shadowed, with two creases furrowing the smooth surface between her brows. She wasn't prepared for this, she thought, a little wildly. She wasn't ready. It was too soon. She needed more time!

But there wasn't more time and, ready or not, it was most definitely happening.

She looked down at her hands, clenched tightly around the steering wheel, and slowly released her grip. *Coffee,* she thought. *I need a cup of coffee before I drive back.*

And maybe something to eat, she decided, thinking that lunch seemed as if it had been days ago instead of merely a few hours. She had been ravenously hungry lately and now she knew why.

She drove carefully, as if her belly were already protruding enough to hinder her movements, and parked in front of one of her favorite seafood restaurants, Stagnaro's on the Santa Cruz wharf. It was nearly empty and she chose a booth next to the plate-glass window, where she had an unimpeded view of the fishing boats tied up to the wharf.

She had always loved to watch the gulls and the pelicans swooping low over the water, bickering over the scraps of fish tossed to them as the fishermen cleaned their catch. Her father used to bring her there to lunch when she was a child. Grown-up lunches, just him and her. It had always made her feel important and special.

"I'll have coffee," she said when the waitress came to take her order. "No, make that tea," she amended. Pregnant women probably shouldn't drink coffee. "Hot tea and, oh, a bowl of clam chowder with extra butter for the sourdough, please," she added, thinking vaguely that dairy products were supposed to be good for you.

She sipped absently at the chowder when it came and drank the strong hot tea gratefully, feeling its warmth spread slowly through her body. As she sat there, pretending to eat, she tried to analyze exactly what it was that she was scared of. Exactly. No vague fears permitted.

Well, number one, she enumerated silently, what did she know about bringing up a child? Did she know how? No, that was too vague. Besides, everyone who has ever been pregnant has worried about that. Losing her job? No, the movie crowd she worked with would barely bat an eye. Although a few eyebrows might be raised at her decision to go through with it. Terminating the pregnancy would seem the more logical choice to most of them.

Well, she asked herself, wasn't it the most logical choice for a woman in her situation? It was still early enough, she was single and there was no one else—no man—involved. Not now, anyway, she thought wryly. So why not?

She tried to look at it logically and without emotion and failed. No, it was just not something she could do. And that left raising the child herself, because having a baby and then giving it up was also something she could never bring herself to do. No matter how logical or sensible it might seem.

But why change tactics now, she asked herself, a small smile tugging at the corners of her mouth, when nothing about this whole affair, from beginning to end, had any foundation in logic? Even being here, now, was not logical. Logic would have been seeing a doctor in San Francisco, where she lived. But she had been honestly worried, having fooled herself into thinking that there was something seriously amiss with her female "plumbing"—as her mother referred to it—and she had instinctively wanted the reassurance of the familiar and the trusted.

That meant, to Desi, Dr. Craig, who had tended to her medical needs all her life. So she had hopped into her Spitfire and driven the eighty miles south to her hometown of Santa Cruz.

And that was not only illogical, she thought, it was dangerous! Santa Cruz was a sleepy seaside town, at least in the wintertime when all of the tourists and summer residents had gone home. If anyone happened to see her who knew her mother—well, enough said. And almost everyone in Santa Cruz knew her mother, who was active in all the local women's clubs...or her father, who was a local attorney...or the youngest of her three brothers, Court, the only one of the four Weston children still living at home.

Almost anyone she might run into in town would know at least one of her family and would naturally mention that they had seen her. And then her mother would call, wanting to know why she had driven all the way down from San Francisco and not stopped by to see her family. And if not to visit her family, then why make the drive? All asked in the nicest way possible, of course, between bits of gossip and family news and with loving concern.

And Desi would have to lie. She wasn't a very good liar, but over the phone, away from her mother's eagle eye, she could do a convincing job of it. But it would be only a delaying tactic at best because, sooner or later, they would have to know.

How she hated the thought of telling them. Not that there would be a scene, no screaming or tears or "how could you do this to me's." Her mother would be all loving concern and her brothers, being of her own generation, would accept it as a part of today's morals, but she could already see the disappointment in her father's face.

She, as the only daughter among three sons, was the apple of her father's eye, and despite her twenty-four years, she knew that he still thought of her as his little girl. It would be different if her pregnancy was the result of a long-term relationship and if she was planning to marry the father. It would certainly be easier to explain!

But to say that this baby was a result of a virtual one-night stand! No, she couldn't do that to her father—to her parents. Even her brothers, not Ash or Court or even Zek, who moved in the same fast movie circles that she did, would understand that. Not in connection with *their* sister. A full and loving relationship outside the bounds of matrimony would have had, if not their outright approval, at least their understanding.

The waitress came by to offer more hot water for her tea and Desi, startled from her unhappy reverie, covered the cup with her hand, shaking her head. "Just the check, please," she said.

Rising from the booth, she collected her satchel and laid the appropriate amount of tip on the table. As she turned toward the exit, Desi caught sight of herself reflected faintly in the plate-glass window. A tall slim woman with flaming red hair caught up in a fashionably untidy knot on top of her head stared back at her.

She didn't look any different, she thought, than she had when she left home earlier.

Dressed up for her visit to Dr. Craig in a pair of soft tan cords tucked into deep forest green suede boots and topped by a bulky hand-knit sweater in a tweedy blend of greens flecked with yellow, she looked like the same woman who had stood in front of the bedroom mirror at one o'clock this afternoon telling herself that everything was going to be just fine. Dr. Craig wasn't going to find anything wrong with her.

Instinctively she turned sideways, looking for changes in her figure, and she found none that were readily visible yet. A thickening of her waist, an unaccustomed fullness and tenderness in her breasts was all. Signs that she would have recognized earlier—if she had been looking for them.

With a sigh she pushed on through the door and hurried out to her car, suddenly wanting very much to be home in her own cozy little apartment on California Street, where she could burrow down under the covers of her big brass bed and indulge in a good cry.

She only got as far as Scott's Valley before she turned the Spitfire around and retraced the thirty miles back to Santa Cruz—and her parents' house. They'd be at dinner about now, her parents and her youngest brother, Court. Just as badly as she had wanted to be at her apartment, she now wanted to see all of them. To tell them about her pregnancy now, before her courage failed her or before someone else could tell them first.

She wanted to share her fears and uncertainties with someone, yes. But even more, she realized, she wanted a chance to share and explore those faint stirrings of wonder and joy she had felt in those first few moments after Dr. Craig had confirmed her pregnancy. Those were the important feelings, the most real. Her first instinctive reaction to the news had been happiness.

A baby—his baby!—the tangible result of those two heavenly days.

"Hold that thought," she said to herself as she parked the Spitfire in front of her parents' house, a Victorian on West Cliff Drive with an unimpeded view of the bay.

She paused for a moment by the car to stare out over the cliffs at the sparkling blue sea. There were a few die-hard surfers sitting on their boards out past the breakers, talking and waiting for the perfect wave. Hardy souls, she thought with a smile, to be out there at all, even in their wet suits, because, despite the mild summerlike weather it was still only February and that water was *cold*. She knew because she had surfed off this point, too, in the days when she had been a young teenager determined to do everything her brothers did.

Lord, that suddenly seemed such a long, long time ago!

Sighing, she went through the front gate and walked around the house to the back door of her parents' home.

"Mom?" she called as she pushed open the screen leading into her mother's immaculate apple green-and-white kitchen. "Dad? Anybody home?"

"In here," her mother replied. Desi heard the scrape of a chair being pushed back as her mother rose and hurried toward the sound of her daughter's voice. "We're just finishing dinner, dear. Have you eaten yet?"

"Mmm-hmm, I had some chowder at Stagnaro's about an hour or so ago."

"Well, I hardly call that dinner," Mrs. Weston said, linking her arm affectionately through Desi's. They were much the same height, with Desi being perhaps a half inch taller and several pounds lighter. They had the same coloring, too, except Mrs. Weston's neatly coiffed hair was not so coppery a red as her daughter's, being liberally sprinkled with gray that she refused to color, and not nearly so wildly curly. The curls had come from Mr. Weston's side of the family.

"Come eat and tell us what we've done to deserve the unexpected honor of your company."

"Oh, Mom," she said, smiling. "Really. You'd think I never come home anymore."

"Not since Christmas," said her father from his chair at the head of the table, and Desi went around to kiss his cheek.

"Hello, Daddy."

"Sit down, Desiree," said her mother, "Courtland will get you a plate. Courtland, stop stuffing your face for a minute and get your sister a plate and some silverware before she wastes away right in front of our eyes."

Court grimaced at the use of his full name, but got up obligingly to fetch the requested items. "Here ya are, Desiree," he said, a subtle teasing stress on her full name. He knew she wasn't particularly fond of it, any more than he was fond of his. Or, in point of fact, any more than any of the four younger Westons were of their given names.

Mrs. Weston had a romantic streak that was apparently intensified by pregnancy, and each of her children had what she considered romantic names. As a result they all used a shortened version and only their mother—as mothers will—used their full given names.

"Thanks, Courtland," Desi returned, smiling impishly. She wondered briefly if her mother's particular brand of romanticism was hereditary. Would her baby end up as, God forbid, a Rhett or a Scarlett? The thought made her giggle.

"Share the joke?" asked her father.

"It's nothing, Dad. Just a passing thought," she said, but then went on. "No, that's not true. I was wondering if I'd be like Mom and give my baby some impossible name."

"Impossible!" her mother said with mock indignation. "You all have perfectly lovely names."

"Yeah," put in Court, "perfectly lovely. Just what a guy needs."

"Now, Courtland," Mrs. Weston began, but her husband, sensing something more beneath Desi's light words, silenced his wife with a slight shake of his head.

"What put that thought into your head, Desi?" he asked gently.

Desi put down her fork, violet eyes glued to her plate. "I drove down to see Dr. Craig today," she said softly, her voice almost inaudible, so that they had to strain to hear her. "I thought I was having some sort of female troubles. Something terrible. You know, like cancer."

"Desiree, darling." Her mother rose from her chair to lay a comforting arm around Desi's shoulders.

"But I'm not sick," she said, and her eyes sought her father's, pleading and defiance in their violet depths. "I'm pregnant."

There was a minute's stunned silence and then, "Lord!" said Court.

"Be quiet, Courtland," admonished Mrs. Weston automatically. "Desiree, are you sure? How long?" and then the inevitable question, "Do we know the father, darling?"

"When's the wedding?" asked Court.

"No wedding," said Desi firmly, her eyes still on her father's face.

"No wedding?" echoed her mother uncertainly. "But Desiree, a baby! Surely..." And then her face lit with compassionate understanding, and her arms around her daughter were fiercely protective. "Oh, darling! He doesn't want to get married, does he?"

Desi turned into her mother's embrace, returning the fierce hug. "Oh, Mom," she said breathlessly, hovering someplace between laughter and tears. "You're priceless! It's not that he doesn't want to get married. I don't!"

"You don't? But, Desiree—"

"Mom, he doesn't even know."

"You just found out yourself, of course! Yes, that explains it. When you tell him, then—"

"No, Mom, listen to me for just a minute. *I* don't want to get married. He doesn't know and...and I'm not going to tell him!"

"Not going to tell him!"

"Don't you think he has a right to know?" came her father's gentle voice, speaking for the first time.

"No, Daddy." She dropped her head, staring at her clenched hands. "He wouldn't want to know. He...we..." She struggled for the words, determined to be as truthful as possible now that she had started. "We don't have a relationship or...anything. It was something that just happened. But I'm not ashamed. I want you all to understand that. I wasn't coerced or...or drunk or seduced or anything like that. And I'm glad about the baby."

Her long artistic fingers unclenched and spread tenderly, protectively over her abdomen. "I want this baby," she said. "Very much."

She heard her father move, heard his chair scrape back as he pushed away from the table. *He's so disappointed*, she

thought miserably, her head still bowed, *that he can't stand
to look at me.*

But he hadn't left and she felt his hand brush her hair gently back from her face, and her eyes came fearfully up to meet
his. They were filled with loving compassion and concern for
his only daughter.

"One question," he said, "do you love him?"

"Yes," she found herself saying, although she had not admitted it before. Until this minute she had not dared to say it
out loud, even to herself. "Yes, Daddy. I don't want to, but I
do."

2

SHE HAD LOVED HIM, in a way, for years. Ever since that summer when her oldest brother, Zek, had used his influence and gotten her a temporary job on the movie he was working on.

The summer was supposed to have been a sorting-out period, a thinking time, before she went back to college in the fall. Her freshman year at UC Santa Cruz hadn't been very successful from an academic point of view. She'd changed majors three times and still hadn't found what it was that she wanted to do.

Her mother had suggested that she get her teaching certificate so that she'd always have "something to fall back on," but that didn't appeal to Desi. She was drawn to drama and other artsy pursuits, but she had no burning desire to act. The trouble was that she had no burning desire to do anything in particular, and she was floundering among all the choices that were made available to her.

She didn't know what she wanted to do yet, she'd told Zek, but she was fast finding out what she didn't want to do. And she most definitely hadn't wanted to go back to school the next fall to drift for another year.

So Zek, who was a cameraman, pulled a few strings and got her a summer job as a gofer on the set of *December Fire,* the picture he had been working on. That way, he'd said easingly, he could keep a brotherly eye on her, and she wouldn't be overburdened by the scope of the job while she did her heavy thinking.

She wasn't. A gofer does exactly what the name implies—goes for things. Goes for coffee, for cigarettes, for forgotten items of clothing or small props, for lost scripts, or anything that anyone might want. Not a taxing occupation, to say the

least, and not, especially when they were actually shooting
a very busy one.

Desi began hanging around the makeup artists, asking
questions and making herself useful and finding, suddenly
and decisively, what it was she wanted to do with the rest of
her life. As she watched these movie artists at work, subtly
aging the beautiful female lead, creating lines of debauchery
and hopelessness around the eyes of the male star, she knew
that this was what she wanted to do. Create magic with her
fingers.

And then *he* came on the set. The great Jake Lancing. He
wasn't the great Jake Lancing then, of course. He was a
twenty-six-year-old bit player with his first small speaking
part in an important movie. But he sizzled on the set. He
smoldered and struck sparks off of the cameras and the leading
lady. During his one major scene everyone stopped to
watch him, *really* watch him, and they applauded when it
was over, Desi included, awed at the magic he had created
with his voice and his dark eloquent eyes and his body.

He was given more lines and written into another scene and
the rest, as all the movie magazines said later, was history.
When *December Fire* was released the next year for the big
movie-going Christmas season, Jake Lancing became an
overnight success and a nominee for Best Supporting Actor
at Oscar time. He didn't get his golden statuette then, but two
years later he was nominated again, for Best Actor, and he
won that one.

Desi's career started that year, too. She hadn't gone back
to college after that fateful summer. Over the initial protests
of her parents, she had enrolled herself in beauty school, got
her cosmetologist's license and then attached herself stubbornly
to the same makeup artist whose work she had so admired
on the set of *December Fire*.

Evan Prince had laughed at her at first, amused by her
youthful determination and earnestness, but as a favor to Zoe
he took her on. He had never been sorry. Desi was hard
working and quick and very talented. When she struck out

on her own, nearly three years later, it added immensely to his prestige to have it known that she had been his protégée.

They still worked together two or three times a year. Whenever Evan was in charge of makeup on a particular movie, Desi was always his first choice as assistant. And if she was free, she was always more than glad to work for him. She hadn't enough experience or renown to head up the makeup department for a major movie yet. . . . But there was always next year.

"And then," she told Evan, laughingly, "I'll hire you."

In the meantime she worked free-lance, commuting from her home in San Francisco to Los Angeles when necessary and traveling, more and more often, to wherever the movies took her—and they had taken her to some pretty exotic places as well as some pretty dismal ones. She remembered Panama City as being a little bit of both. For six weeks one hot, humid summer she had applied and reapplied makeup that seemed to melt off the actors as soon as it was put on. But Vermont had been nicer, she thought, crisp and cool in the early fall.

She had not, by coincidence or divine intervention, worked on another movie with Jake Lancing, but she had followed his career with a rather proprietary interest over the years. They had, after all, started their careers on the same set.

She had seen all of his movies at least twice—because they were so awfully good, she told herself—and she tried never to miss one of his increasingly frequent appearances on Johnny Carson's or Merv Griffin's show. Only, of course, because he was so witty and knowledgeable and he made her laugh. But she was careful, for some deep and unacknowledged reason, to keep her interest in him from Zek and from Evan, either one of whom could have easily and quite happily arranged for her to meet Jake Lancing personally.

All of this interest and admiration had gone on safely, from afar, for almost six years, and then one misty night in late November, without any prior warning, there he was. Her

seatmate on the red-eye flight from Los Angeles to San Fran
cisco.

The flight was late taking off, which was unusual for thi
regular commuter run, and Desi moved restlessly in her sea
tired and longing to get home to her warm bed. Then th
cabin door opened, and the reason for the delay was sud
denly apparent.

Jake Lancing strode, confident and unconcerned, into th
airplane. Looking just as magnificently tall and whipcor
lean as he did on the movie screen. And more handsome now
at thirty-two, than he had been at the beginning of his ca
reer.

Desi saw, rather than heard, the stewardess gasp and the
giggle delightedly at some remark he made as she took h
ticket. His dark head bent to her blond one as he smiled h
famous thousand-watt smile, and he chucked her playfull
under the chin with one finger before he moved down the aisl
to his seat, seemingly unaware of the eyes that followed h
progress.

All except Desi's, that is. She, after one glance in his d
rection, was feigning sleep. Why, she couldn't have said. Sh
didn't know, except there were only three empty seats, or
of them next to her, and she was suddenly afraid that h
would read her eyes and see how desperately she wanted hi
to choose it.

Idiot! she chided herself silently. *He's only a man, after al
Don't be such a silly fool!*

She felt him sit down beside her, and an unwilling excit
ment flickered along her veins and then, incredibly, she fe
his hand on her thigh.

Her eyes flew open. "What—" she began indignantly ar
her eyes met his. Those dark dangerous eyes that had me
merized millions of movie-going women. The angry wor
died on her lips.

He smiled and her heart turned over in her chest. "I'
sorry," he said softly, and he really did look sorry. "I did
mean to wake you up." He made a motion toward her la
"But you have the other half of my seat belt."

Desi looked down at her lap, tearing her eyes away from his with difficulty. His seat-belt strap lay coiled across her thigh, partially under the magazine she held. "Oh, I'm sorry," she said, "I thought . . ." And then she blushed, the delicate telltale color stealing upward from the open V neck of her loose plaid shirt to stain her cheeks a fiery red.

"Yes, I know what you thought." He grinned disarmingly. "It always amazes me what dirty little minds you women have."

"Dirty minds! Well, I . . ." She sputtered and then stopped, because he was right.

"Did you, or did you not, think I was trying to play touchie-feelie?" he demanded, reaching again for the seat belt and fastening it securely across his lean middle.

"Well, yes, but . . ." Desi began.

"Then I rest my case."

"Now, wait a minute," Desi tried again, preparing to defend her sex. "What would you have thought if you woke up and I was groping *your* leg?"

He made a thorough survey of her upturned face, taking in the coppery red hair pulled into a loose, untidy knot on the top of her head and the true redhead's complexion, as pale and smooth as fresh cream, and the dark violet eyes, unusual in any case, but even more so when you expected them to be green.

"I'd have thought," he said solemnly with completely convincing, and therefore enormously flattering sincerity, "that I was a very lucky man."

And then his eyes, those melting brown eyes, dropped from his scrutiny of her face to touch lightly and briefly on the hidden curves of her slender body.

Not that he could see much, she thought, as covered up as she was in her loose "working clothes." Baggy stone-washed denim trousers, white sneakers with bright pink socks showing at the ankles and the oversize blue-and-beige plaid tailored tunic she wore loosely confined at the waist with a wide webbed belt from the army surplus revealed very little of her lithe figure.

But it didn't seem to make any difference that she was so covered up. She *felt* as if he were looking right through her clothes to the slim curves beneath. As if he could see right down to the little reddish mole on her left hip, the only mark on the otherwise creamy flawlessness of her pale body.

She felt herself blushing again, not only with embarrassment but with shy, pleased delight because she knew with unconceited feminine certainty that he liked what he saw. She lowered her eyes protectively, the thick reddish-gold lashes fluttering against her pinkened cheeks, afraid that he would read her reaction in her too-expressive eyes.

"A very lucky man," she heard 'iim say again, his deep voice soft and oh-so-seductive, seeming to ripple along her nerve endings with a sensation not unlike that of the finest silk being drawn over bare skin.

She shivered delicately and her blush deepened from pink to fiery red, causing her to silently curse the fair skin that exposed her emotions so easily. Never before had she wanted so much to appear cool and sophisticated and mysterious, and never before had she been so unable to do so!

Her suddenly uncontrollable emotions were fully revealed on her face, she knew. There for the whole world and Jake Lancing to see. Her delight at his obvious approval of her looks, her embarrassment at that delight. And, most damning, the sudden fierce desire that had flickered wildly through her body as his eyes had slowly assessed her, bursting into flame at the seductive caress of his deep voice.

A voice that had seduced millions, she told herself sternly, in a vain attempt to break the spell he seemed to have woven so effortlessly around her. *He knows what effect he has, don't think he doesn't,* her mind tried to warn her. *It's practiced, it's refined to an art, it's fake.*

But, somehow, she knew it really wasn't, despite what she tried to tell herself. His charm, his magnetism were as much a natural part of him as his monumental talent. Each enhanced and strengthened the other.

Besides, even if it had been fake, a practiced spell, it wouldn't have mattered. She wanted to be charmed by this man. There was no way she could deny that fact. Not to herself and, maybe, not to him.

All she could do was stare blindly, mutely at her lap, feeling the hot betraying color staining her cheeks and hope that, by hiding her eyes, she could keep him from knowing just how deeply and how completely he had affected her. How utterly, wickedly, deliciously shameless he had made her feel just by looking at her the way he had. Just by speaking to her.

You're acting like a silly fool, she told herself again, *like some dumb teenager groupie!* And, maybe she was, but she couldn't seem to help it.

"I've embarrassed you," she heard him say. "I'm sorry, I didn't mean to do that."

He reached out and touched her face lightly, almost experimentally. Desi felt herself take fire immediately as the backs of his fingers brushed softly against her cheek, feeling the heat of her blush. Then his hand slipped under her chin, urging her to look up at him.

"I *am* sorry," he said again in that deep seductive voice of his. "I really didn't mean to embarrass you."

Her lashes flew up at last, her wide-eyed violet gaze meeting the melting brown of his. "I'm not embarrassed," she said softly, almost on a whisper.

And she wasn't, not anymore. The heat of her face and body was no longer generated in any part by embarrassment. She had gone past that, somehow, when he'd touched her. It was fueled now only by desire. Sweet burning desire. Unchecked, unembarrassed and totally revealed in the darkening violet of her eyes as she stared up at him.

"No," he said then, taking in the message written so clearly in her face. "No," he repeated softly, incredulously. "I can see that you're not."

He still held her chin lightly, her face turned up to his, and his thumb moved to touch her full lower lip, pulling it down slightly, opening her mouth a tiny bit. Instinctively, her eyes still holding his, the tip of her tongue snaked out and delicately touched his thumb.

She felt him stiffen and gasp under his breath. His fingers tightened their grip, for just a second, against her rounded chin, and his eyes went from melting to smoldering as she watched. He seemed suddenly to be consumed by the same flame that had fired her, and she thrilled in feminine triumph at his reaction to her unintentional boldness. Deliberately his thumb stroked her lip again and, just as deliberately this time, her tongue flickered out to meet it in a brief, blatant caress.

They both seemed to hold their breath as questions were being silently asked and answered, and then Jake nodded decisively, just once. His hard long-fingered hand released her chin and traveled down the slim column of her throat to find the madly beating pulse at the base of her neck. Desi's eyes closed again, unable to bear the sudden scorching heat of his gaze without reaching out to touch him, too. She wanted, very badly, to touch him. But, despite her earlier boldness, she didn't quite dare to reach out for him.

Instead her head fell back a little to more fully expose the delicate line of her throat to his questing fingers, while her own hungering hands curled into fists on her lap. She managed, just barely, to stifle the excited, frustrated little moan that rose to her lips.

"Excuse me." Desi heard the stewardess's voice through a hazy fog as Jake's hand dropped reluctantly from her throat. "Would you like a drink, Mr. Lancing? Or coffee?"

"A drink?" he said, and Desi thought she heard a note of vague confusion in his deep tones as if he, too, had forgotten exactly where they were. As if, like her, he had completely lost touch with their surroundings and with time, and was as surprised as she was to suddenly realize that the plane was already airborne. But he seemed to recover himself quickly. "Yes, a drink would be fine. Brandy, if you have it."

"Certainly, Mr. Lancing. And you, miss?"

Desi looked up blankly, a little slower to respond to reality than Jake had been. It had been such a beautiful dream that she had been indulging in with him. Beautiful and all too brief. She was loath to let it go.

Jake's hand touched her arm lightly. "Would you like anything?" he asked.

Desi smiled at him, a soft, sleepy child's sort of smile, wholly charming and unconsciously inviting. "Yes, please, Jake," she said, and they both knew that she wasn't talking about a drink. "A Bailey's would be nice. On the rocks."

"You obviously know who I am," Jake said, turning to her when the stewardess had moved off down the aisle to take drink orders from the other passengers. "But I don't know who you are." His hand came up to gently tug at a wayward curl that had escaped from the knot on top of her head. "What's your name, pretty lady?" he asked, twining the coppery curl around his finger.

What do you want it to be, she wanted to say. *I'll be whoever you want, whatever you want.* But she said, "Desiree," not even aware that she had given him her full first name.

She was Desi to almost everyone else, she realized later, for him she wanted to be special and different.

"Just Desiree?" he questioned. His fingers released the curling tendril of hair and traveled lightly down her shoulder, along the length of her arm to the pale hand still clenched against her thigh. He lifted her hand in his as if to examine it.

The fingers were long and slender, the nails kept short and unpolished but buffed to a glossy sheen, so that they glowed like smooth flat pearls on the tips of her fingers. He touched each nail softly, almost wonderingly, and then turned her hand over in his and drew one hard brown finger slowly across her sensitive palm.

"No last name?" he said, still looking down at the slender hand in both of his.

"No," she said, "no last name."

This whole thing was *still* a dream, she thought. The stewardess hadn't succeeded in waking them up after all. To give him her last name, even though she already knew his, would somehow break the spell. She didn't know how it would, exactly, but she superstitiously didn't want to take the chance. To tell him that she was Desiree Weston might lead to talking about Zek, and from there to "Oh and do you know so-and-so?" and to the movie industry in general. All the mundane things that two people meeting for the first time would normally talk about.

But this meeting wasn't mundane or ordinary. It was fate, she suddenly realized. They were meant to meet like this. Strangers, instantly and fiercely attracted to each other. The way she had always secretly dreamed it would be.

"No last names, not tonight." She smiled up at him and her smile, soft and teasing, was like a promise. "Just Jake and Desiree."

He nodded again, that single characteristically decisive movement of his head. "Jake and Desiree," he agreed, and brought her hand to his lips.

His brown eyes held hers as he bent his head to kiss the palm, and he looked at her through the fringe of his short dark lashes.

What a beautiful man he is, she thought, *more beautiful than any man has a right to be*. Her eyes roamed hungrily, in open desire, over his face.

Those melting brown eyes with their thick lashes were dangerously seductive and knowing. The straight dark brows above them were marred, and thus made infinitely more interesting, by the tiny crescent-shaped scar slicing through the right brow. His nose was classically straight, his jaw strong and square with a hint of arrogance, his chin determined. A strong face, just saved from harshness by the softening effect of his dark hair, which was the color of rich, brown sable and so thick and shiny that Desi knew that she would need a whole hour just to run her fingers through it.

And his mouth, she told herself solemnly as she continued her painstaking inventory of his familiar face, his mouth was his best feature. An exciting, masculine mouth, rather hard and clean-edged, as if it had been chiseled by a sculptor. The bottom lip was just slightly fuller than the top, hinting at a softer, more tender and sensual side to his nature.

The side that he was showing to her now as those firm lips caressed her palm and kissed the tip of each slender finger. His eyes continued to hold hers, sending her silent, secret messages of his desire, so that she couldn't have looked away, even if she had wanted to. He was making love to her with his eyes, holding her a willing and eager captive in their bottomless brown depths.

Neither of them seemed to be aware, just then, of the people seated all around them in the dim, softly lit interior of the plane. People in front and in back and to the side, blocked out by the high seats and the curve of Jake's right shoulder as he sat turned toward her. It was almost as if they were alone. Almost, but not quite.

They were not nearly alone enough, she thought. And she wanted, more than she had ever wanted anything, for them to be really alone. For them to be somewhere where Jake's kisses could go beyond her hand.

It didn't occur to her that this was their first meeting. That, in reality, she hardly knew him and that she should not be allowing or encouraging his caresses. She felt as if she had known him all her life, wanted him all her life. As if his lips, moving so warmly against her palm and fingers and the tender inside of her wrist, had touched her before and would touch her again.

In a way it *had* happened before—countless times—in her deepest, most secret dreams. Dreams hidden even from herself, for Desi could never remember them in the morning, except for the feeling that they had been wonderful and the nagging wish that they had gone on just a little longer.

She was reminded now of the sweetness of those half-remembered dreams, and she wanted his lips to travel from her hand up to her shoulders and the pale line of her throat, across the curve of her cheek to, finally, claim her mouth. She wanted, desperately, for him to kiss her. And she knew, looking into his smoldering eyes, that it was what he wanted, too.

But the stewardess came back then, bringing their drinks. Jake didn't completely release her hand but instead placed it firmly on his thigh, pressing it down a little, as if to make sure that she would leave her hand there while he was busy with lowering the tray table.

His action was unnecessary because Desi couldn't have moved her hand even under the threat of dismemberment. It felt as if her hand was glued to his hard thigh by a strong current of electricity, and like someone receiving a tingling shock, she couldn't let go. Not that she wanted to anyway.

Jake handed her drink to her then, and his free hand came down to cover hers on his leg as if he, too, couldn't bear to break contact, even for a minute.

They touched glasses silently, toasting each other with their eyes, and sipped at their drinks. Jake reached up a long arm and switched off the overhead light, banishing their fellow passengers to formless shapes and surrounding the two of them in a cocoon of intimate darkness. With long hard fingers he deftly tore open the small foil package of smoked almonds that the stewardess had left with their drinks and popped one into Desi's mouth. She accepted it greedily, giggling softly from pure giddiness and anticipation.

They huddled together in the soft darkness, speaking of nothing in particular, neither seeming to feel the need, at least not then, to know any more about the other. They whispered and held hands and took turns feeding smoked almonds to each other, one by one, slowly and tantalizingly. Filling up the time until they could be alone.

The cabin lights came on unexpectedly, making them blink like two sleepy children, and the stewardess's voice came over the loudspeaker, advising them to extinguish all smoking materials and to fasten their seat belts for the descent into the San Francisco International Airport.

Since neither of them had any more than carry-on luggage—Desi with her favorite oversized satchel and a large soft-sided overnight bag and Jake with only one carry-on suit bag—they were able to bypass the sleepy irritable crowds around the baggage-claim carousels and go directly outside to hail a cab.

With a part of her mind Desi registered the looks that they, or rather, that Jake received, but no one came up to ask for his autograph. Maybe they thought it was too late, she speculated idly, or maybe they were warned off by his purpose-

ful stride and the way he looked neither to the left or right but
only at her.

"Hungry?" Jake asked as they waited for the cab to pull up
to the curb.

Instinctively Desi knew that he was offering her the opportunity, if she wanted one, to leave him without awkwardness. To keep from happening what they both knew was
surely going to happen if she went with him. If she said yes,
she was hungry, then he would take her somewhere very
public for a midnight snack, but if she said no . . .

Desi didn't even hesitate. The thought of refusing or hedging never even crossed her mind. And if it had, she would
have dismissed it without a second thought. She *wanted* what
was going to happen. Wanted it more than she had ever
wanted anything.

"No, I'm not hungry," she said as they settled into the back
seat of the cab.

He put his arm around her in the cab, holding her willing
body close to his side. But he didn't kiss her, not yet. And she
knew, again instinctively and with certainty, that he was
waiting until they were alone.

It didn't seem at all unusual to her that she should know so
surely what he was feeling . . . almost what he was thinking.
But she did. Or, at least, she felt that she did.

She snuggled against him, feeling warm and secure and
totally wonderful. In no hurry at all at this point. Content just
to feel his strong arm around her and his hand resting possessively on her shoulder. The subtle spicy scent of his after-
shave, the rich aroma of his leather jacket under her cheek,
the faint trace of brandy on his warm breath all combined in
her mind into one exciting sensation. The essence of man.
Jake. Forever after, those smells, separately or together,
would invariably remind her of this man and this magical
night.

He let go of her briefly to pay the cabbie when they pulled
up to the porticoed entrance of the Hyatt Regency Hotel. A
bellman snapped to attention when he recognized Jake, hurrying forward to help with the luggage. But he was waved

away with a smile and a brief, "No, thanks, we can manage it."

Jake took Desi's hand again, leading her onto the escalator that transported them to the lobby of the hotel. She followed him passively, almost like a sleepwalker, as if her actions were all taking place in a dream, and stood docilely and completely unembarrassed by his side as he checked in.

A tiny disinterested part of her mind noticed the looks they were getting—a bellman standing near the escalator who was looking their way, the surprised double takes of some of the hotel's other guests, the desk clerk's knowing smile as she handed Jake his key—but Desi put it down as attention paid solely to Jake Lancing, the actor, and in no way connected with herself.

In a way she was right, of course. Jake Lancing would attract attention wherever he went. He was, after all, an internationally famous, Oscar-winning actor. But she failed to take into account the attraction of her own flaming beauty and, more importantly, the soft love-struck expression on her face as she gazed up at the man at her side.

It was enough to make even the most hardened cynic smile a little to watch them as they walked toward the glass elevator; the tall, strikingly handsome man in tailored tan slacks and a black leather jacket possessively clutching the hand of the slender red-haired woman at his side. A woman who looked fragile and almost childlike in her fashionably funky clothes, with her huge violet eyes fixed firmly on her companion. Romance seemed to spiral around their heads like a beacon, unmistakable to even the most casual observer.

Jake, seemingly no more aware of anyone else than she was, opened the door to the room and stepped back, motioning for her to enter first. The door clicked behind them, a strangely final sound. They were alone.

After Jake turned from her to switch on a bedside lamp, he casually removed his jacket, tossing it on a nearby chair, and Desi felt a faint twinge of uneasiness, her only one since that first embarrassed moment of their meeting on the plane. Not at being in his room and not at her reason for being there. She

was not in the least uneasy or unsure about that! She had
never been *more* sure of anything in her life. But...what now?
she wondered vaguely.

*Am I supposed to just rip off my clothes and fling myself
on the bed? Do I wait for him to make the first move?* She
didn't know the protocol for a situation like this, and she
stood a little awkwardly in the middle of the room waiting
for him to give her a clue as to how they should proceed.

Jake reached out and took her satchel from her shoulder,
placing it on a chair, and she looked up at him, her violet eyes
wide with eagerness and trust and just the tiniest bit of fear,
had she but known it.

"Would you like a drink?" he asked gently. He didn't say
the word "first," but it hovered there, unsaid, between them.

"No...I..." she heard herself mumble, and thought, *maybe
he wants one and that's why he asked me. Maybe a drink first
is the way this sort of thing is done.* "But if you do—" her
hand fluttered up distractedly to nervously touch her neck at
the open collar of her shirt "—please, go ahead. I'll..." her
voice trailed off.

Wait, was what she had been going to say, but it would
have sounded so...coarse. And she couldn't think of anything else to say, not anything intelligent, with him looking
at her like that, with that smoldering look in his dark eyes.

"You go ahead and have one," she said, and her hands
fluttered again, moving from her neck to her hair, absently
pushing at the loose tendrils as if to tuck them back into the
coiled bun on top of her head. The upraised movement of her
arms pulled her shirt, loose-fitting as it was, against the soft
swell of her breasts, clearly outlining their shape and the
aroused state of her nipples, like hard little buttons pushing
against the confines of her shirt.

Jake made a low sound in his throat, a half-smothered
groan of desire, and he reached out, gently cupping his hands
around the tempting curves of her breasts, his thumbs just
touching her throbbing nipples.

Desi felt herself melt at his touch and would have fallen to
the floor in a trembling, molten heap, but somehow his arms

were suddenly around her, holding her up, molding her shaking, eager body firmly to his.

"I don't want a drink," she heard him growl, his lips at her ear. "I want you, Desiree."

She pushed at his chest almost frantically, and his arms loosened instantly as if he thought she was trying to get away. But, once her arms were free, her hands came up to touch his face, one pale slender palm resting tenderly on either side of his strong, angular jaw. Her eyes locked with his, their violet color darkened almost to black.

"I want you too, Jake," she said clearly, and offered him her parted lips.

He kissed her then—finally!—taking her offered mouth with a fevered eagerness that excited her already aroused emotions to an almost unbearable point. Her hands slipped from his face to the back of his neck, her fingers tangling joyfully in the thick brown hair that she had so longed to touch. It felt like silk against her palms just as, somehow, she had always known it would.

The feel of his hair under her hands, feeling so exactly right, made her suddenly hunger to touch him elsewhere. To run her fingers through the hair on his chest and to smooth her hands lovingly over the satin-hard muscles of his bare shoulders and back. But he was holding her too closely for that. Gently, passionately he ravaged her mouth with his teeth and tongue, while his hands burned through the barrier of her clothes, caressing her shoulders and back and, finally, cupped her small firm bottom to mold her as closely as possible to the hard arousal of his body.

Desi's fingers clenched in his hair, and she strained against him, making a small sound of unmistakable need. Jake's hands tightened on her buttocks, lifting her from the floor, and her slim legs locked themselves obligingly around his waist. He took three steps and then turned and fell backward onto the bed, taking her weight on top of his.

The short fall dislodged their lips and hands, and Desi lay still for a few moments, panting lightly, her hot face hidden in the curve of his neck. She felt his hands in her hair, removing the pins, and then he smoothed it through his fingers, down her back, stroking its silken length as if she were a purring cat. Desi could feel his heart beating heavily under hers, and as she lay there with her face pressed so closely to his neck, she became aware, once more, of the faintly spicy scent of his cologne mixed, tantalizingly, with Jake's own male scent.

Her tongue snaked out experimentally to taste him, and then her lips opened to feed greedily on that vulnerable place where his neck began to curve into his broad powerful shoulders.

Jake groaned and his hand stilled on her hair. He made a movement as if to roll over, trapping her under him. But Desi sat up abruptly, her wild hair foaming over her shoulders like a coppery cloud, and he lay still, waiting to see what she would do, staring up at her with hungry passion-glazed eyes.

"Desiree," he whispered almost pleadingly after a minute when she continued to sit there silently straddling his waist.

He's so beautiful, she was thinking, for the second time that night. *So beautiful and good and strong.* She didn't pause to wonder how she knew those things about him. She just did. He was all those things and more. And, for tonight at least, he was hers.

"What are you thinking?" he asked quietly, intrigued by the soft dreamy expression on her face.

"About how beautiful you are," she said simply.

"Good God, Desiree," he began. "Men aren't—"

"You are," she insisted, her fingers reaching out to cover his lips, "You're the most beautiful man I've ever seen." Then she smiled, a siren's smile of pure provocation. "And for tonight—all night—you're mine." Her hand trailed over his mouth and chin and throat to the top button of his shirt. "And I want to see more." She had the first button undone. "Much more," she said teasingly.

Slowly, then, and in a tense, tingling silence, she finished unbuttoning his shirt, running her fingers lightly over his broad furred chest as she went, and tugged it free from the waistband of his slacks. Her slim fingers hovered uncertainly over the buckle of his belt.

She could see the smooth muscles of his stomach tense in anticipation, waiting for her next move and, perversely, instead of doing what he expected her to, her hands went to the buckle of her own belt. She unbuckled it, tossing it carelessly to the floor and, in one swift movement—quickly before her wanton's courage failed her—she grasped the hem of her tunic in both hands and pulled it off over her head.

The peach-colored, lace-trimmed camisole she wore beneath her tunic, with tiny bows at the shoulders and between her breasts, was an intriguing contrast to the almost boyish appearance of her outer clothes. It served to emphasize the pale fragility of her shoulders and arms and, at the same time, to enhance the fullness of her breasts. It was as if she had been saving the real Desi, the feminine, inner Desi just for him.

Her hands went to the first bow between her breasts and pulled it loose. The look in Jake's eyes began to burn hotter. Not melting, now, or even smoldering, but a raging inferno of desire as he lay there, very still, watching her undress for him.

The look in his eyes scorched her, making her clever fingers suddenly clumsy with nervousness and trembling excitement. The second bow snarled, refusing to come undone, and Desi's hands dropped as she briefly considered pulling the garment off over her head.

"Don't stop, Desiree," he breathed raggedly. "You're driving me crazy!"

"You do it," she invited him, leaning forward so that he could more easily see the tiny bows. One hand held her hair back out of the way and the other touched the middle of his broad chest lightly, balancing herself as she leaned over him.

It took several seconds—an eternity!—to untangle the second bow, and she realized that his chest was heaving under her hand, as if he had run a long way, his heart thudding. A faint sheen of perspiration glistened across his powerful shoulders as he worked impatiently at the bow, fighting the urge to simply tear the fragile garment off her body.

Suddenly it came free under his fingers. Then there was only the third and last bow on the front of her camisole and the tiny ties on either shoulder. The silky garment slid slowly down her body as the last tie was released, revealing to his avid, hungry gaze the creamy perfection of her pale breasts with their small reddish-brown nipples puckered and straining for his touch, inviting him to explore their softness.

Jake needed no second invitation. He heaved his torso up from the pillows, fastening his mouth greedily to one hardened nipple, and twisted his body so that Desi was turned onto her back beneath him. He seemed frantic, suddenly, to have her completely bare. As his lips and teeth tenderly ravaged her breasts, his hands were busy peeling her, and himself, out of the rest of their clothes.

Desi helped him as best she could; kicking off her sneakers, lifting her hips as he tugged her slacks, and then her tiny bikini panties, off her hips and down the long slender length of her legs to toss them onto the floor on top of his own clothes.

He slid back up her body then, parting her thighs with his knees, and Desi received him into her as impatiently and eagerly and as passionately as he took her. There was no holding back for her with him. No coyness, no shyness, just an aching hunger and a desperate need to love and be loved by this man even if it was only for one night.

I love you, she wanted to whisper to him as he moved above her. *I love you, Jake.*

The words ran like a chant through her head, remaining unsaid because she knew that it was not what he wanted to hear from her. He wanted her passion and her heat, not her love, and she did her best to turn off the words running through her mind, giving him what he wanted.

Her thoughts, her desire, her very being were all focused completely on him at that moment—and for all the moments for the rest of that long lovely night. For all the mo-

ments of what turned out to be the almost forty-eight glorious
hours that followed it.

She had nearly two full days of love and laughter with him.
Two days of heart-stopping, head-spinning passion with the
man who had invaded her deepest dreams ever since the first
time she had seen him, nearly six years ago.

And it was enough, she told herself sternly, determined not
to cry when she woke up on that Sunday morning—alone—
and found only a scrawled note and the scent of him still lingering on the empty pillow next to her to reassure her that she
had not merely dreamed it all.

It had to be enough, she insisted, because it was all she was
ever likely to have.

3

"TEDDIE," Desi hollered, banging awkwardly on the front door with her elbow, trying to make herself heard over the music that was playing—loudly—inside. Pavarotti this morning, she noted with amusement. Nothing but the best for Teddie's plants. "Teddie, help!"

The music stopped abruptly and there was a pause, as if whoever was inside was listening to determine whether or not he had actually heard anything.

"Teddie, hurry up," she repeated into the silence. "It's me, Desi, and everything's starting to fall!"

The door swung open to reveal a slim young man in tight white jeans and a pale yellow cashmere sweater. His white-blond hair was cut short and carefully styled, and his feet were encased in well-worn Gucci loafers. A heavy gold chain lay against his tanned neck, and he wore a chunky diamond ring on the pinkie finger of his left hand.

Only the best for Teddie, too, Desi thought, suppressing a smile at the look of annoyance on his handsome narrow face.

"You could have made two trips," Teddie said, reaching out to take one of her grocery sacks from her.

"I *am* making two trips. There's more in the car," she informed him, nodding toward the practical yellow Rabbit that had recently replaced the more sporty Spitfire. "Be a darling and bring it up for me, will you please? While I get Stephanie unpacked."

Teddie's free hand reached out and touched the top of the tiny head nestled against Desi's breast—all that was visible of the sleeping baby in the navy kangaroo pouch strapped to Desi's front. "How is my little princess today?" he cooed, a foolish infatuated look on his face. "Did she enjoy her little outing?"

"Yes, she did," Desi answered for her infant daughter. "And now she's wet."

Teddie looked almost horrified. "Well, don't just stand there, go change her." He stroked the downy head again. "The poor darling might take a chill. And we can't have that. Go on—" he waved her up the stairs "—I'll get the rest of your groceries and put the car away." He held out his hand for the keys.

"In the car," she told him, moving on up the stairs to her second-floor apartment.

"Haven't we told you a million times how careless that is?" he began to admonish her almost automatically. "Anyone could just walk by and drive it away. And then where would you be?"

"Without a car?" she guessed, teasing him. "Oh, all right, Teddie. You're right. It is careless of me. I won't do it again."

He continued to glare up at her sternly.

"Okay, I'll *try* not to do it again," she promised, and he went out to get the rest of the groceries, muttering something to himself, she was sure, about how careless women should not be allowed to have charge of babies.

Honestly, since Stephanie had been born it was like having her mother—or a nursemaid—living in the apartment downstairs. Not that she was complaining, not really. Having Teddie and, to a lesser extent, his roommate, Larry, living so conveniently close and being so concerned about her and the baby was a godsend at times. And a comfort always.

He had been a bit uncertain at first when she had informed him that she was expecting a baby and asked him, as her landlord, whether or not he would prefer her to move out of her apartment on the top floor of his lovely Victorian. She knew that he and Larry had put a lot of work into restoring the gracious old house and thought that they might not be willing to put up with the eventual wear and tear, not to mention noise, that a baby living upstairs would mean.

"Let me talk it over with Larry," he'd said to her when she first approached him.

A few days later she was invited down to their apartment for a drink to discuss the terms of her continued occupancy. The mother-henning had started then, that very night, when she was given fresh orange juice instead of the cocktails they were drinking because, Teddie said, he had read that alcohol was bad for the developing fetus.

In the months to come they had more or less taken charge of her "delicate" health and would have, if she had let them, tried to run her entire life. It was Teddie who helped her paint the bright life-sized clowns and circus animals that marched around the walls of the baby's room and it was he, an interior designer who worked at home, who watched for the delivery truck that brought the new, snow-white nursery furniture.

Hardly a week went by when she didn't find another recipe for some vitamin-packed health drink or some informative article on prenatal care stuffed into her mailbox—the important parts always highlighted with a yellow marker pen.

It was Larry who had fortunately been at home that Sunday morning to drive her to Presbyterian Hospital when she started having labor pains nearly two months early. He had stayed on at the hospital during her surprisingly brief labor and was the one who called her mother with the news that there was another redhead in the family.

So much, in fact, did her two neighbors seem to enjoy their new, self-appointed roles as surrogate fathers that Desi's mother, who had come to stay with her for those first few weeks after the birth, had delicately tried to suggest that perhaps one of them was the father.

It was an idea that still made Desi chuckle delightedly because anyone, except for her dear, naive mother, would immediately know that it was highly unlikely that either of those two men would ever be anyone's father. Not unless they could find a way to adopt. And in San Francisco maybe that wasn't such a farfetched idea!

The thought made her laugh out loud, jiggling the baby enough to wake her.

"You slept through traffic jams and exercise class and Pavarotti," Desi accused her, smiling fondly as she unstrapped the carrying pouch to lay her child on the wicker changing table, "but *now* you wake up. Why is that, I wonder?" she asked the baby, who continued to stare up, following the sound of her mother's gentle voice with round, wondering eyes.

Jake's eyes, Desi thought, for the hundred-thousandth time.

They had lost that unfocused blueness common to most newborns within two weeks and were now a dark, Hershey-bar brown. Very definitely her father's eyes; bright and curious and meltingly sweet, in a tiny face that was otherwise a baby-sized replica of Desi's.

Desi sighed, resolving once again to put all thoughts of Jake out of her mind. He was no part of her life now. He had never been, really. But it was hard, so very hard, not to think of the man when she looked at the daughter he had given her.

"Come on, darling," she said, scooping up the now-dry baby. "Let's you and me go get us a little snack. All that exercise made me hungry."

She carried the baby down a short hallway papered with scattered sprigs of blue forget-me-nots and yellow primroses, and into the bright sun-filled kitchen.

Whatever else anyone might say about Teddie, she thought absently as she strapped Stephanie into her infant seat, they couldn't fault his excellent taste. The kitchen was a rather narrow room, more long than wide, high ceilinged like the rest of the apartment, the walls covered in brown-and-white checked gingham. White cotton-lace curtains fluttered at the bay window, and the gleaming golden-oak cabinets were glass fronted with blue forget-me-nots hand painted on the white ceramic knobs. A white wrought-iron chandelier decorated with twining green leaves and blue flowers hung over the table. Not strictly Victorian, but antique nonetheless and perfectly in keeping with the rest of the room.

The furniture and accessories in the apartment were Desi's own. Most of them were neither Victorian nor even truly antique. Somehow, though, her mixture of graceful white wicker, starkly modern chrome and glass, with a few pieces of early Americana and Art Deco thrown in for good measure made a pleasing, if somewhat eclectic, whole.

"Won't she be cold wearing just that?" asked Teddie, dropping the last load of the groceries on the blue-tiled counter.

Desi glanced over her shoulder to where Stephanie lay in her infant seat, staring with wide, fascinated eyes at a Boston fern as it slowly swayed in the warm breeze coming in through the half-open window. The "that" she was wearing was a clean diaper and a tiny neon yellow T-shirt with the words, Born to Boogie splashed across the front. A gift from her seventeen-year-old uncle Court.

"The fresh air is good for her," Desi said, suppressing a smile as Teddie tenderly and somewhat peevishly rearranged the T-shirt, smoothing it down over Stephanie's little round belly.

"She ought to have a sweater on at least."

"Sweaters are something babies wear when mommies—or in this case—uncle Teddies are cold," Desi informed him as she continued to put away the groceries.

It wasn't really the lack of clothes that Teddie was objecting to. It was the clothes themselves. His baby gift to her had been a very beautiful and far-too-expensive ivory lace christening dress, the sort that only royalty used now. Left to him, Stephanie would have spent these first six weeks of her life smothered in more of the same. To Teddie's way of thinking, baby girls should be dressed exclusively in pink lace dresses and ruffled bonnets.

"Well, I still think—"

"Teddie." Desi turned from the counter to face him. His concern was appreciated, and she was grateful for everything he had done for her and Stephanie, but sometimes all this unsolicited advice *did* tend to grate on her nerves a little. "Stop being such a worrywart, will you? She's fine."

"Well, you're her mother," he said, making it clear that he thought that particular circumstance to be an unfortunate state of affairs for the child involved.

Lord, now she had hurt his feelings! "Here," she offered, by way of apology, handing him the bottle of formula that had been warming in a pan of hot water. "Feed her for me, will you? I have to check my messages."

There was nothing Teddie seemed to like better than a chance to hold the baby, and Desi left them cooing and gurgling at each other while she went down the hall to her bedroom to check the telephone answering machine.

The phone must have been ringing incessantly all morning, she thought. Her mother with a "just checking" message, the pediatrician's nurse with a reminder about Stephanie's six-week checkup tomorrow, a couple of calls from Joanne at the agency about some possible free-lance assignments and, lastly, one from Evan Prince.

"Hello, luv. Got a job to discuss with you. Big one," his voice with its distinctly upper-class English accent boomed into the room. "Call me," he ordered, and reeled off a number with a 212 area code. That meant New York. She hadn't known Evan was in New York.

Desi switched off the recorder and flung herself back onto the blue-and-white patchwork quilt covering her modern brass four-poster. A job, he'd said. A big one. She stared up at the white plaster ceiling, her eyes absently following the detailed dips and swirls that had been so painstakingly restored.

A big one. The words echoed through her mind again, and a little thrill of anticipation snaked its way down her spine.

She was itching to get back to work. Stephanie was already a month and a half old, and because of a sudden case of toxemia, Desi had quit working full time much earlier than she'd planned, taking on only the occasional free-lance job through Joanne's agency when she was feeling up to it. Part-time work was okay; giving makeup lessons or doing up society ladies before big charity "dos" paid pretty well, and it was interesting—for a while. But it wasn't like working on a movie. Especially a movie with Evan.

A big one, he'd said. And if Evan, who had once referred to an invitation to the White House as a dreary social obligation, was excited enough about a new project to call it big, then it must be. Very big.

Her head began to whirl with possibilities. He meant big names, probably big money. She searched her mind for any bits of gossip or conversation she had heard in the last few weeks before she had quit working to have Stephanie, but could recall nothing out of the ordinary. Just the usual tripe about who was sleeping with whom and what names were on their way up or down. She had been more or less out of touch for—what?—almost four months now. A long time in this business. Anything could have happened. She sat up and reached for the phone.

"Sherry-Netherland Hotel," announced the voice on the other end of the telephone wire. "May I help you?"

"Evan Prince, please." Desi twisted the telephone cord nervously. "I don't know his room number."

Teddie poked his head around the bedroom door while she was on hold. "I've put Stephanie down for her nap," he said, and backed out as Desi silently mouthed her thanks.

"I'm sorry. Mr. Prince's room doesn't answer. May I take a message?"

"Yes, please. Tell him Desi..." She paused, glancing down at her watch. Almost two-thirty here. That made it about five-thirty on the East coast. "Could you page the bar for me, please?" she asked the operator. Evan never missed the cocktail hour. It was, he said frequently, the most civilized part of the day.

"Damn you, Evan," she swore without heat when he came on the line. "How could you leave a message like—"

"Ah, Desi, luv," he interrupted smoothly. "How nice to hear your lovely voice. How's our little mother doing?"

"I'm doing just fine, thanks. Evan—"

"And the baby? He's well?"

"She. Yes, Stephanie's fine, too. Now what does this message—"

"She. Yes, of course. How forgetful of me. You did send me a picture, didn't you?" he rambled on. He *knew* she was dying to know about this big new project of his. "Couldn't tell much from a photograph, though," he continued. "All eyes and no hair to speak of. Could have been a boy, if you ask me."

"Well, I didn't ask you," she retorted, stung by his last remark. Stephanie was very obviously a girl. "And she does, too, have hair. It's red."

"Another redhead for the world. How nice," he said with a sigh, and Desi could almost see his clipped gray mustache quiver as he did it. "Stephanie did you say her name was? Rather an unusual name, that. Goes well with Weston, though. Good theatrical sound to it."

Something in his voice changed, alerting her. Stephanie wasn't an unusual name at all and he knew it. Evan was fishing for something.

"I imagine that's why you picked it?" His voice rose on the last word, making it a question.

"I picked it because I like it," she said, shrugging carelessly as if he could see her through the telephone wires. "No special reason."

There was a special reason, though. Stephen was Jake's middle name. She had looked it up. Jacob Stephen Lancing, the father of her child. It had seemed a safe way, at the time, of forging a link, however small and invisible, between father and child. But now she wasn't so sure. Evan was not the first person who had tried to make something significant out of Stephanie's name.

Teddie and Larry had openly speculated about every man named Stephen that they, or she, knew even remotely. And Court had hinted about a boy named Steve that she had dated once in high school, clumsily suggesting that "maybe she had seen him lately?"

Everyone, it seemed, was trying to figure out who her baby's father was.

Well, let them try, she thought rebelliously, fire in her big violet eyes. She wasn't telling and there was no one else who knew. Not for sure.

"About this big job, Evan—" she tried again to change the subject "—what—"

"They're making a movie out of *Devil's Lady*." He announced it in a whisper, as if he didn't want anyone else to overhear them.

Desi lowered her voice automatically. "*Devil's Lady?* But that's . . ." Words failed her. *Devil's Lady* had been an immediate hit, the first novel by an unknown author. A stereotypical, grandmotherly little lady of eighty-odd years, as it turned out, who had written the most torrid bestseller of the year. Every major studio was after the movie rights, but so far as Desi knew Dorothea Heller wasn't selling.

Desi had seen her just last week on the *Tonight Show*. A proud and proper-looking woman, the kind who brings to mind old Boston wealth, in a rather plain black dress, demurely high necked and long sleeved, her snowy hair arranged softly around her lined aristocratic face. But she also wore a magnificently gaudy set of the most enormous rubies Desi had ever seen; necklace, earrings and bracelets on both wrists, with several rings on each of her hands.

"All real," she said. "Given to me by my late husband for . . ." And here her sharp black eyes slanted a coy look at the audience, "Well, I'd tell you, but this young man here says I can't say certain things on TV." She waved one jeweled hand airily. "It's all in my book," she said in her regal, cracking voice. "You'll just have to read it to find out, won't you?"

Her speech and accent were those of an educated and cultured woman of a bygone era, but some of her language was as salty as a sailor's and she flirted outrageously with Johnny and Ed and with Jake, who happened to be one of the other guests that night. It should have been a ridiculous performance, but it wasn't. It was thoroughly charming, totally captivating and the audience was delighted.

"Who bought it?" Desi asked excitedly. "What studio?"

It was public knowledge, at least in the industry, that Dorothea Heller was adamant about retaining some control—a great deal of control actually—over her work. It was her life story, she insisted, hers and her late husband's, and only she knew how it should be done. So far, no major studio had seemed willing to grant her, in writing, the amount of control she wanted. Given these circumstances, Desi half expected Evan's next words.

"No studio," answered Evan. "An independent producer walked away with the movie rights. First-timer who wanted it enough to promise her any amount of control she asked for."

"You're kidding! No, I know you never kid. Who?" she demanded.

"It's all still very hush-hush until negotiations for the female lead are made final. So I'm not free to tell you at this point," he said, his voice conspiratorial and smug. Evan loved a secret. "Your name could be on the credits for makeup," he tossed off casually. "Interested?"

"Interested! Evan...a credit? Me? But what about you? Aren't you heading this up? I mean...you know what I mean."

"Oh, we're going to think up a new title for me. Don't worry, luv, I'm not giving anything away. Not even to you."

"Oh, Evan." She could hardly believe it. "A credit! When do we start? Where do we start? In New York?" Would she be able to take Stephanie to New York?

"No, not New York. Haven't you read the book? The location shooting will be in the wine country, don't know exactly where just yet...some in San Francisco, too."

"Oh, that's wonderful!" she said, relieved. "I won't have to worry about Stephanie, then. I mean, I'd hate to be away from her for too long just yet—" Desi began to explain, afraid for a moment that Evan might not understand her concern for her child. She didn't want him thinking that she thought her baby was more important than her career. Stephanie was, of course, but nobody had to know that but her. Motherhood was not looked upon with indulgence in the movie industry.

"No need to explain," he said, cutting off her words, and then his voice became all business as he launched into what information he could give her at this time. "And needless to say, you won't whisper a thing to anyone yet. Not even that new redhead of yours, understand?"

"Yes, sir—" she smiled at his seriousness "—understood."

"See you in two weeks then," Evan said, and hung up without waiting for her goodbye.

Devil's Lady, imagine that! And *her* name was going to be listed on the credits. Her name! She felt goose bumps erupt on her arms just thinking about it. The book that every major moviemaker was after and some new and so far unknown producer had it. Unknown, anyway, to her, she amended. Desi wondered briefly whether Evan himself might be the producer. He certainly had the connections it would take to raise the necessary money.

But, she thought, if you were raising money from lots of backers, or maybe even just a few, you probably couldn't guarantee the author the kind of control that Dorothea Heller had been promised. That tended to point to one producer with his own money.

Who?

Desi got up from the bed and moved across to her desk, skirting around the sewing machine and the extra chair and the filing cabinet that had been moved into her room when her "office" had been turned into a nursery. It made her pretty blue-and-white bedroom a little cramped—cozy was the word she used when Teddie had commented on the new arrangement—but she somehow hadn't found the time to get rid of the furniture she no longer needed. She made another mental note to call the Salvation Army as she rummaged through the desk for her address book.

Finding it, she went back to the telephone by the bed and began to flip through the worn and lined-out pages, looking for Zek's new telephone number. She had to tell *someone* her good news. And Zek was the only member of her family who would really understand what this project was going to mean to her career. Maybe she could pump him a little, too. See if he knew or had heard anything about this independent producer who had bought *Devil's Lady*.

She put the phone down before it had rung once. Evan had said don't whisper a word to anyone. Anyone would mean Zek, too, she was sure. Evan would have her head on a plate if she let it out of the bag before he, and the producer, were ready for it.

She jumped up from the bed. She had to tell someone her wonderful news or she'd burst!

"Mommie's going to have her name up in lights, darling," she whispered next to Stephanie's tiny ear.

But Stephanie was sound asleep, lying on her stomach with her knees drawn up and her tiny hands curled inward toward her body. In addition to dressing her in a little pink stretch suit with feet, Teddie had also drawn the covers up over her as if it was midwinter. Shaking her head indulgently—she had told him and told him about too many covers—Desi rearranged the blankets, leaving the baby with only her sleepers as a covering. Her hand reached out, irresistibly drawn, to tenderly cup the back of her daughter's head for just a minute.

It was such a tiny head, covered with a fine soft fuzz of downy red. So innocent, so sweet, so utterly defenseless. Everything that was maternal in Desi welled up at the sight and the feel of her tiny sleeping daughter. She blinked, feeling foolish tears clog her throat and blur her vision. She had never thought it possible to love another human being as much as she loved Stephanie—with a love that was pure and sweet, untouched by lust or jealousy, totally maternal and giving.

Stephanie had been a seven-and-a-half-month preemie. Scarcely five pounds at birth but so perfectly formed, so utterly beautiful that Desi could not stop the joyful tears that slid helplessly down her cheeks when the doctor had laid her newborn daughter on her stomach. It was then, more than at any other time during her pregnancy, that she had most desperately wanted Jake. He should have been there to see the wondrous being that they had created, to hear her first indignant cries, surprisingly hearty for such a tiny creature.

And maybe, just maybe, it was her fault that he wasn't there when she needed him. If she had contacted him, met him in Ghirardelli Square last May, things might have been different. Now she would never know.

She had argued and argued with herself for months beforehand. She had even gotten dressed that morning to meet him, taking the fading note from the corner of her mirror to read it over—just one more time—as if she hadn't already memorized every word.

She repeated to herself now:

"You were wonderful, my mystery lady. We were wonderful together! I'll be back from Alaska in May. Meet me at the fountain in Ghirardelli Square. May 30, 12 noon."

That was all it said. No signature, no salutation. It could have been written by anyone, to anyone. Still, she was tempted. The urge to see him again was almost overwhelming. But she stood there in front of the mirror, the note still in her hands, and looked at the woman staring back at her. A pretty woman, perhaps, if you could see through the toxemia that had swelled her whole body—not just the six months' swell of her belly, but her ankles and hands and face as well—so that she looked like the Pillsbury Doughboy in drag.

What could she have said to him?

"Hello, Jake darling. Surprise, surprise!"

Oh, God, she could just see his face if she had done that! Murder flaming out of those big brown eyes. Anger narrowing that firm sensual mouth.

And, could she, in all honesty, have blamed him?

She asked herself that question now, as if she hadn't asked it a hundred times before. A thousand times before. Daily, almost hourly, starting from the first minute that she had known for sure that she had conceived a child. His child. Their child.

"My child," she whispered, leaning over to kiss the sleeping baby. "My beautiful little Stephanie."

She left the room quietly, pulling the door closed behind her.

The trouble, she acknowledged wryly to herself, was that, in a way, she did blame him. He had been there, too. He should have considered the consequences of that weekend, even if she hadn't. He should have tried to find her when she didn't show up in May. Like one of the heroes he played so well, he should have scoured the town for her, knocking on every door until he found the right one.

Never mind that he knew virtually nothing about her. Or that she was the one who refused to tell him anything about herself; where she lived, where she worked. To tell would have taken the experience out of the realm of dreams and risked crashing it against reality. And reality was too harsh. Looked at in the cold light of day, she was nothing but some overeager groupie he had picked up on an airplane and taken back to his hotel for fun and games.

He knew only that her name was Desiree. And that her hair was red.

"A redhead all over," she remembered him saying as they lay on the bed, naked together in the bright afternoon light. His big hands had run lightly over her slender body, touching her intimately, learning her responses. He smiled when his fingers finally made her gasp, her body stiffening against his caressing hand.

"Red curls mask the fires of hell, you know," he whispered in her ear. A line, slightly altered, from one of his movies. It made Desi laugh, as he had intended it to. And then, amid her delighted laughter and even more delighted gasps of pleasure, he made slow, languorous love to her all through the rest of that afternoon, until it was time to finally put some clothes on so that room service could bring up their dinner.

It was, curiously enough, memories like those that fed her resentment. If he had really cared at all, if he had really meant a word he had said, a caress he had given, he would have tracked her down. That he hadn't found her, hadn't even *tried* to find her, meant that he didn't care. And if he didn't care about the slim sexy Desiree he had left asleep in that hotel bed, just how would he have felt about the very pregnant Desi who might have waddled into the Square?

But why should he care about either Desi? she asked herself, fighting back sudden tears. She meant nothing more to him than a brief pleasant fling in a town he had just been passing through on his way to Alaska. Someone he had thought it might be fun to have another fling with in six months' time when he would be passing through again.

It was the same way she had meant to remember him. She had known from the first minute that it wasn't real. That it was just a dream and couldn't last. She *would* remember him that way eventually, she insisted stubbornly. He would be a fleeting memory of shared passion, nothing more.

If only she weren't reminded of him so constantly in the meantime; every time she turned on the TV or picked up a magazine, or looked into the innocent eyes of her daughter.

4

"NO, EVAN. No, no, no," Desi was almost frantic. "I can't! Don't ask me why. I just can't. I won't!"

Evan sat back in the upholstered pink armchair, one ankle crossed over the opposite knee, and let her rage. He was in no hurry to find out her reasons. Evan was never in a hurry. Besides, Desi in a rage was a truly lovely sight.

Her coppery red hair swirled wildly around her shoulders and back with each angry step. Her violet eyes were dark and stormy. Her pale redhead's complexion was becomingly flushed. A true titian beauty, he thought, with all of the fine bones and delicate lines of a Degas ballerina.

If only she wouldn't dress herself in those absurdly boyish clothes. Baggy khaki walking shorts rolled at the cuffs, and one of those knit shirts with the alligator on the chest. A hand-me-down from one of that horde of brothers she had, he speculated idly. It had been bright blue once and was too big for her, tucked in at the waist and secured with a webbed Army belt wrapped twice around her slender middle.

She looked remarkably like a child at summer camp, he thought, except, perhaps, for the firm unconfined breasts pushing at the front of her shirt and the long slender length of her legs left bare by the baggy shorts. Legs that ended in fine-boned ankles and narrow feet. No fool she, he thought, noticing the bright pink polish on her bare toes. She knows how attractive her pretty feet are.

All in all, he decided with purely professional appreciation, pregnancy had left her looking even better than before. Leaving her breasts a bit fuller, her hips a bit rounder without otherwise visibly marking her slender figure. Remarkable really, when you considered that just two months ago she had been as big as the proverbial house and about as graceful as a duck.

Evan glanced over at the baby on the floor, wondering again who the father was. They had certainly managed to produce a beautiful child, whoever the man.

As a general rule, Evan was not fond of babies, and he was not actually fond of this one, but he could admire beauty wherever he found it. And Stephanie was a lovely baby.

Still tiny, she lay on a pastel quilt in a warm patch of sunlight on the floor, her red fuzz a vivid halo around her little head, dimpled hands and feet kicking vigorously into the air. Her mother's child totally, except for the eyes. Wide and round and dark brown. Startlingly effective with her hair if it stayed that lovely color.

Impossibly tiny denim shorts and a scarlet T-shirt covered her busily squirming body. Obviously Desi was already dressing the child in the same style as herself.

How a woman who looked so delicate and feminine, and who chose to live amid satin-covered chairs and lace curtains in a Victorian house, could dress herself so carelessly was beyond him. A soft silk shirtwaist dress, pale pink and accessorized with a strand of pearls to set off her hair and skin, perhaps, or . . .

"Evan, have you heard a word I've said?"

He looked up to find Desi practically standing over his chair. Her bare feet were planted firmly on the faded Oriental carpet, her hands squarely on her hips and fire in her eyes.

"Yes, of course, luv," he said blandly. "You won't do it, you said, didn't you?"

"Yes . . . I mean no, I can't."

"So you see, I was listening." His glance flittered back over to the baby, who seemed to be becoming agitated, as if she sensed her mother's distress. "She looks remarkably like—"

"She looks like me," Desi snapped.

"No need to bite my head off, luv. I was only going to say how much a cherub she looks. Isn't that what every mother wants to hear?"

"You were sitting there trying to figure out who her father is," she accused him, "just like everyone else."

Evan shrugged. "It's a perfectly understandable thing to be curious about, wouldn't you say?" he countered reasonably, refusing, as always, to let anyone else's bad temper inflame his own. Evan prided himself, and quite rightly too, on never losing his temper.

"Maybe," she admitted grudgingly, "but I think it's disgusting the way everyone looks at Stephanie and at me and then at every man in the room, wondering if *he* might be the one. It's nobody's business but mine!"

"And the father's surely?"

Desi whirled away, hiding quick tears. "His least of all! Oh, now look what you've made me do," she said as Stephanie began to cry.

"It's all right, darling," Desi soothed, picking up the frightened baby. "Mommie's not yelling at you." She nuzzled her hot face against Stephanie's tiny neck, breathing in the baby-powder sweetness of her. "Shush, darling. Everything's okay." She bounced the quieting baby gently against her shoulder, whispering senseless words of endearment. "No more yelling, I promise. That's my good girl. Everything's fine. Everything's fine," she repeated, shielding her own teary face from Evan's sharp eyes by hiding it behind the curve of Stephanie's body.

Darn it! Tears came so easily, much too easily, to her lately. She rubbed her cheek gently against Stephanie's back.

"I'm sorry, Evan. Baby blues, I guess," she said, shifting the baby to her lap as she sat down in a corner of the rose-colored satin sofa. It was one of her Art Deco pieces, padded and luxuriously comfortable.

"Classic case of postpartum depression." She tried a careless smile, but it came off a little sheepishly. "Sorry."

Evan uncrossed his legs and reached for his sherry. "Think nothing of it," he said airily. "I understand."

"Oh, Evan, if you only did."

"Why don't you tell me about it, then, hmm?"

Desi shook her head stubbornly.

"Come on, luv," he urged. "Tell Uncle Evan. Why are you trying to turn down the biggest opportunity of your career?"

"Evan, please." She looked up at him, confusion and a faint shadow of pain visible in the depths of her wide violet eyes. "Just leave it. I can't work on *Devil's Lady* and there's no point in discussing it."

"I think you owe me an explanation at least."

"No."

He gulped down the last of his sherry—terrible way to treat fine sherry—and set the empty glass on a side table, rising to move slowly around the room. His fingers lingered for a moment on the lace curtains at the window, and then he stood for a minute, staring absently into the tall glass-fronted cabinet that housed Desi's collection of beaded evening bags and fragile fans.

Desi watched him as he moved, knowing he had not dropped the subject, but was only gathering his thoughts to make another, more concerted effort to find out what was troubling her. He looked so dapper, she thought, as her eyes followed him around the room. Just like central casting's idea of a well-to-do and quite proper English gentleman; impeccably tailored and fiftyish, with a military-school bearing. His neat cap of light brown hair was going a distinguished gray at the temples, and he wore a little caterpillar of a mustache on his upper lip.

He dressed as if he were in England, too. Sharply creased, gray twill pants and a tweed jacket over a crisp white shirt and an old school tie. Striped, of course. To look at him you would never know that it was an unseasonably warm September afternoon.

"Is it Dorothea Heller?" he asked, stopping in front of her. "I know she's a bit of an eccentric, but I felt sure you'd like her."

"I do! She's a wonderful, charming old lady," Desi said, and she meant it wholeheartedly.

They had met at the Tadish Grill for drinks and lunch, the three of them, just yesterday. It was supposed to have been four but Evan's other guest, this mysterious producer of his, was late and they were starting without him.

"You remind me of me when I was your age," Dorothea Heller told Desi, staring at her over the rim of a champagne glass, her black eyes sparkling with health and a sharp, biting wit. "Only I was brunette, of course, and had much more bosom. You young girls these days seem to have no bosoms at all! No hips either, come to think of it," she stated with characteristic forthrightness.

"Red hair, though, that makes up for a lot." She leaned toward Desi with the air of one imparting a priceless pearl of wisdom, "Most men do so admire red hair, dear girl. Remember that. You redheads can get away with a great deal where men are concerned if you handle it right," she rambled on. "They think it hides a passionate nature, poor fools. Even that good-looking devil, Jake, goes for redheads. He—"

Desi had stopped listening at the mention of Jake's name.

"Jake who?" she asked quietly when Dorothea paused for breath. But she already knew.

"Why, Jake Lancing, dear girl. Jake who, really!" She glanced sideways at Evan, smiling coquettishly. "I thought every red-blooded woman in the world knew who Jake Lancing was."

"Yes, of course. Jake Lancing. Is he on the picture?" Desi's voice shook a little as she asked the question.

"Why, he's the star, dear girl," Dorothea informed her grandly, "and the producer, of course. My dear, is anything wrong?" Desi's face had gone deathly pale. "Evan, quick, I think the poor child's going to faint."

"No, Dorothea, I'm fine, really. Please, Evan, sit down. I'm fine. It's just . . . I suddenly felt very weak. Maybe . . . maybe I'd better not stay for lunch. I think I had better go before—" She almost said before Jake gets here. "Before I get sick," she mumbled, grabbing at the first excuse that popped into her head.

She stood up and reached for her leather satchel from the floor by her chair. "It was very nice to have met you, Dorothea, thank you for the drink and...and I'm sorry I can't stay for lunch." She was almost running in her haste to get out of the restaurant before Jake arrived.

Jake, the producer! How could Evan have done this to her?

Simple, she answered her own question, Evan doesn't know. Or, he didn't know yesterday. But today? Oh, yes, before he left today Evan would know. He wouldn't leave until she'd finally told him the truth.

"Tell me something," she said then, untangling a lock of her hair from Stephanie's chubby fist. Her eyes were deliberately on her task, avoiding Evan's. Her voice was as casual as she could make it. "Did Jake Lancing know you were hiring me?"

"Not specifically. As art director I'm free to hire whatever staff I want. I doubt Jake has any interest in exactly who I hire? Why?"

"No special reason," she lied, feeling something inside her let go and relax. Jake didn't know that she was going to be on his picture. Her secret was still safe. She put a pink rattle in Stephanie's flailing hand.

"Jake," Evan said then with utter conviction, as if something had just that minute fallen into place.

Desi's eyes flew to his face, to ask him what he meant, even though she already knew. Evan's eyes were fixed firmly on Stephanie's pretty pixie face, as if searching for something in her big brown eyes.

"I didn't even know you knew him." His voice was faintly accusing and incredulous at the same time.

"I don't," Desi snapped, hoping somehow to head him off before he actually put it into words. If he didn't say it she could still pretend that he didn't know.

"Come on, luv. This is Uncle Evan, remember?" He sat down beside her and reached for her hand. "I don't know why I didn't see it before . . . those eyes. . . ."

"Her eyes are brown," Desi insisted. She pulled her hand away and stood up. "Just brown. Nothing unusual about that. My father has brown eyes. Even you have brown eyes."

She laid Stephanie back on the quilt. "Watch her a minute, will you? I'm going to make us some tea," she said, and escaped to the kitchen. Away from Evan's too-knowing eyes.

If Evan saw, who else would see? Jake's face, Jake's eyes were known all over the world. Would everyone know just by looking at Stephanie?

No, no, you're being paranoid, she told herself. *It's just that Evan knows Jake, and knows you.* And that silly performance at the Tadish Grill didn't help matters either. Running like a rabbit at the mere mention of Jake's name. That's what had started Evan thinking, not Stephanie's brown eyes.

Her reaction at the restaurant, her refusal to work on *Devil's Lady* without giving him a reason, her snappiness when he mentioned Stephanie's looks. Those things, altogether, were what made him guess, she reassured herself. And that's all it was, a guess. He couldn't have known just by looking at Stephanie.

If she had handled it better, given him a reason for not wanting to work on *Devil's Lady,* said she didn't like Dorothea Heller; anything except what she had—or hadn't—said.

"Jake's middle name is Stephen," Evan commented when she came back into the room with the tea tray.

"Yes," was all she said. It would be pointless to deny it now.

She added a squeeze of lemon to his tea and passed the fragile china cup across to him, then busied herself for a few minutes with her own. She took both milk and sugar, "nursery tea," Evan had told her once, fit only for the underdeveloped palate.

"Cookie?" she offered.

Evan waved the plate away. "Does he suspect?"

"I doubt he even recalls the incident," she said, a wry smile curving her full lips. "Oh, don't look like that, Evan. There's no need to pity me." She paused, biting into a cookie. "I don't pity myself. I knew exactly what I was doing." She chuckled and glanced over at Stephanie, asleep now on her blanket. "*Almost* exactly what I was doing," she amended.

"He should have been more responsible," Evan burst out, "than to run around, willy-nilly, seducing innocent young girls!"

"Oh, Evan, please," she said, laughing. "Don't play the outraged father figure. It doesn't suit you . . . and it doesn't suit me either. I'm hardly an innocent young girl."

"Well, I *am* outraged! Leaving you with an unwanted child to support. Getting off scot-free—"

"Now wait a minute, Evan," she flared, instantly on the offensive against anyone who might cast a slur upon her child. "Stephanie is *not* an unwanted child! She was unplanned, yes, but not unwanted. I wanted her from the very first minute I knew I was pregnant. If anything," she continued on a calmer note, "it's Jake who's the loser in all this."

"I don't see how." Evan's voice was still huffy.

"He'll never know he has a daughter," she explained. "He'll never get to see what a beautiful baby we made together. In a way, I almost feel guilty for keeping her from him."

"Why not tell him then?"

"No, Evan, I've already made my mind up about that," she said, her lips set in a firm, determined line. "It's better this way, believe me."

"But—"

"Do you think I haven't thought about telling him? I have! A million times. But the answer is always the same. No. Jake Lancing doesn't even like kids. I've heard him say so at least a dozen times and so have you. Every time he's on a talk show somebody brings up those two paternity suits and—"

"I happen to know that he was in Tangiers filming *Fly by Night* when that Phillips woman claims the deed was done. And he's been supporting Lisa Kendall's child."

"He is?" Desi was flabbergasted. "But I thought . . . she couldn't prove it was his, could she? She lost the case."

"It didn't get to court. She knew she didn't stand a chance of proving that the child was Jake's. It could have been the offspring of any number of men from what I've heard of the lady. And I use that term loosely," he said, grimacing mildly as if the word left a bad taste in his mouth. "A no-talent ambitious schemer is what she was, trying to get herself a free—"

"Then why is Jake supporting her child, if he isn't the father?" Desi wanted to know.

"*Was* supporting. He isn't any longer. She's since married—to another man who could also have possibly been the father."

"Yes, but why—"

"Oh, well, as to that." Evan seemed a bit embarrassed. "It was...possible that Jake could be the father. He'd been...ah, intimate with her at the appropriate time."

"Or inappropriate," Desi quipped irrepressibly.

Evan shot her a quelling glance. "Yes, well. In any case what I've been trying to say is that just because Jake has had a few indiscretions brought home to roost and was able to prove that they were not even *his* indiscretions, doesn't necessarily prove that he doesn't like children."

"No? Then what about the child he was supporting?"

"What about it?" Evan was plainly surprised that she should care.

"Does Jake...did he ever see it? It! Poor thing doesn't even have a sex or a name. Does Jake know or care about that?"

"Well, why should he? The child isn't his. That dratted woman admitted as much when she married."

"I suppose you're right—" Desi shook her head "—but I can't help feeling sorry for a child caught up in a mess like that. And I won't let it happen to Stephanie."

"Why should it? There's no doubt that she's Jake's daughter—" he paused infinitesimally "—is there? No, no, forget I said that. Of course, she's Jake's." He glanced over at the baby who still slept peacefully in her fading patch of sunlight, one small fist tucked under her chin. "You have only to look at her to know that."

"You can't tell by just looking at her, Evan. You guessed because of a number of things, the least of which is the color of her eyes. Stephanie looks like me, and like my mother, and that's all anyone sees when they look at her."

"Surely Jake would see his own eyes staring back at him," Evan protested, but the protest was feeble.

"Maybe yes, maybe no. And even if he did, Evan, he doesn't love the mother. Why should he love or want the daughter? No. He's never going to know she exists." Desi picked up the teapot. "More tea?" she asked, her eyes warning Evan that the subject was closed.

"Couldn't you . . ." he began anyway, waving away the offer of more tea.

Desi put the pot down with exaggerated care. What she wanted to do was bang it on the table—hard. But Stephanie was asleep. "No, I couldn't. Whatever you were going to say, the answer is no. Listen to me carefully, my dearest friend. And you are my friend or I wouldn't be telling you this. Are you listening?"

Evan nodded.

"As far as Jake Lancing is concerned, I am no different than Lisa Kendall. He was . . . intimate with me at the appropriate time, although—" her voice faltered a little "—I probably couldn't even prove that. Stephanie was almost six weeks premature. In any case, all he would remember—if he remembers—would be that he picked me up in an airplane and we went to his hotel room. Period."

"Desiree," Evan began. There was compassion in his face and a bit of something else. Shock, perhaps. He had not thought that Desi was the kind of woman who did that sort of thing. Go to hotel rooms with men she hardly knew. "I don't know what to say."

Desi patted his hand comfortingly. "I know you don't, Evan. And I'm sorry to disillusion you, but I *had* to make you understand why I can't work on *Devil's Lady*. You do see, don't you?"

"I'm beginning to." He picked up his cup. "I'll take that tea now," he said.

"You English and your tea," Desi teased, trying to lighten the conversation. She filled his cup and then her own. "It's England's national cure-all, I think."

"Nonsense," he replied after a minute, "just gives us something to do with our hands while we think."

"And what are you thinking?"

"I'm thinking," he said slowly, "that you should take this job."

Desi just stared at him, wide-eyed, over the rim of her tea-cup. Hadn't he heard a word she'd said?

"Now hear me out before you say no."

"I *have* said no." Desi's voice was firm.

Evan ignored the interruption. "This is the biggest opportunity of your career, luv." He leaned forward to emphasize his point. "The biggest! And it has come years earlier than you could have reasonably expected.

"Think for a minute," he urged her. "Think what it could mean to you. The chance to *head up* the makeup department of a major movie, recognition for your work, money. Desiree, my dear, it's what you've worked for all these years, handed to you on a silver platter. And you're actually thinking of turning it down!"

"Please, Evan. I know all that. Believe me, I do but..." She shrugged helplessly, unable to explain it any better than she already had. Nothing was as important to her as Stephanie. Not her career, not Jake, not anything. If she had to give up this chance to protect her baby, she would—gladly. There would be other chances.

She tried again to explain some of her feelings to Evan, but he cut her off brusquely.

"Protect Stephanie," he challenged her, "or yourself? How could Jake possibly harm Stephanie? He doesn't even know she exists and he won't know unless you tell him."

He leaned back on the couch, knowing by her shocked expression that he had finally said something that had gotten through to her. "I think you're afraid to face him," he went on before she could make any reply. "You're afraid that he might not remember you and you're afraid, too, that he might. Am I wrong?"

"No," she admitted after a minute. "No, you're not wrong." She looked at him with soft, stricken eyes. "I'm *ter-*

rified, Evan. I wouldn't know how to act. What to say to him."

"Don't say anything," he advised.

"Don't say anything? I don't understand."

"Play it by ear, luv," Evan explained. "Maybe you're right. I don't think you are, but maybe he won't remember you. In that case you won't remember either." He shrugged. "Problem solved."

"And if he does remember?" she asked.

"What will he remember? A lovely experience with a lovely woman. What harm could that do you?"

"Or a fling with a groupie?" Desi said crudely.

Evan winced at her words but went on smoothly, "Or a fling with a groupie," he echoed. "Not an admirable thing, I admit, but not so unusual either.

"What I'm trying to say, Desi, luv, is to take your cue from him. Play it cool if he does. Pretend you've not given him another thought from that day to this, if you want. There's no need for him to ever know about Stephanie. You won't tell him, and I won't," he said, letting it lie there, letting her come to the obvious conclusion by herself.

She did.

"Let me go make some fresh tea, Evan. This has gotten cold," she said, rising with the teapot in her hands. "And then you can tell me about how we're going to handle our part of *Devil's Lady.*"

5

OH GOD, how had she let Evan talk her into this!

It had seemed so easy, so sensible, sitting there in her cozy
apartment, sipping tea, while Stephanie slept peacefully on
her blanket.

"You're doing the right thing," Evan had told her, "the wise
thing." And she had nodded, finally agreeing with him.

But what was the right thing?

All of a sudden it didn't seem like it. She wished fervently
that she was back home in her apartment. Or at her parents'.
Or being tortured by enemy agents. Anywhere, as long as it
wasn't here in Los Angeles, waiting for Jake to arrive.

He would be coming through that door any minute. She
had heard his deep laugh just a second ago, responding to the
teasing inflection of Dorothea Heller's voice. The other people in the cavernous studio had heard it, too. The camera-
men, the people from wardrobe and makeup, the script girl,
the other actors—they all stood around, making idle conversation, but all eyes were on that door, waiting for him to
appear. The kick-off party couldn't start without him. Desi
got the impression that most of the people here thought it
wouldn't even _be_ a party without him.

Oh, I can't do it, she thought wildly. _I must have been out
of my mind to think I could._

Her hands were suddenly sweaty and her heart was beating erratically, fluttering like a caged bird against the wall of
her chest. She wiped her palms nervously on the seat of her
corduroy slacks and tried a few deep breaths. It didn't help.

"Evan, get me out of here!" She clutched his arm frantically. "I can't do it!"

"Steady now, luv," he soothed, patting her hands comfortingly. He seemed not to notice how her fingers dug into the tweed material of his jacket. "The hardest part will be over in a minute. Just hold steady, luv—ah, there he is now."

Jake had come through the big studio door. Making an entrance, as befitted his star status, with a woman on either arm. Dorothea Heller was on his right, looking aristocratic in a black Chanel suit, her snowy hair arranged in a regal-looking braid around her head and those huge gaudy rubies gleaming at her neck and wrists and on her gnarled hands. A brunette clung possessively to his other arm.

A gorgeous brunette, Desi noted before she dropped Evan's sleeve and whirled away, turning her back on Jake and his entourage as they slowly made their way around the room.

Maybe he wouldn't see her, she hoped, maybe he would just pass right on by. She fidgeted with the brushes and pots of rouge and Pan-Cake on the makeup table in front of her, moving them around so that they were lined up in neat, even rows. She shifted her stance a little, shielding her slim body behind the bulk of Evan's, all the while trying to watch Jake's progress around the room without turning her head to follow him.

He looked magnificent, as always. Taller somehow, she thought, harder, thinner maybe, and broader through the shoulders. His hair was cut shorter than she remembered—for this new role, she supposed. But it was a shame that it no longer curled onto the back of his neck and over the tops of his ears. His face seemed harsher without the softening effect of the longer hair. That jaw seemed even more determined, the planes of his face seemed sharper. But his eyes . . . his eyes were the same melting sensuous brown that she remembered.

Desi realized suddenly that she was staring into those eyes. Jake was standing right behind her, staring at her face in the makeup mirror.

Shocked recognition widened his eyes for a second, followed by a myriad of other emotions, coming so fast, one after the other, that Desi couldn't be sure what she saw. Joy, she thought, but maybe that was because she wanted to. Surprise, pain...anger. And then, consummate actor that he was, a shutter seemed to come down, and it was as if she were staring into the cold, unfriendly eyes of a stranger.

Follow his lead, Evan had said. Pretend if he does.

Desi turned around to face him.

"And this is Desiree Weston, our head of makeup." Evan was introducing her as if he didn't already know that she knew Jake far too well.

"My pleasure...Desiree, is it?" Jake's caressing voice held a polite question as if he hadn't quite caught the name.

"I prefer Desi, please," she said, and was amazed at the cool steadiness of her voice. The hand she held out to him was steady, too, and no longer damp with nervous perspiration.

Amazing, she thought, as his big hand closed over hers, *it's almost as if we've never met. I am actually going to make it through this without falling apart*, she congratulated herself.

And then Jake leaned down and his lips brushed hers in a brief, casual kiss—the kind of kiss that movie people are always giving one another.

"Welcome to our little family," he said. His voice was casual, too, as casual as his kiss had been, but there was a sting behind the words. Had he stressed the word "family" just a bit? Did he know something? Could he possibly know anything?

Desi felt the blood suddenly begin to race through her body. *I will not blush*, she told herself fiercely. *I will not!* But the inevitable heat rose from her chest upward, staining first her throat and then her pale cheeks a fiery red.

Even then Jake might not have noticed, for she had half turned away as he moved to be introduced to someone else, but then the brunette clinging to his arm—the gorgeous brunette—spoke up.

"You've made her blush, darling," she said, and Desi couldn't tell if she was being sarcastic or not. "I didn't know there was anyone left in this wicked business who still blushed."

Jake turned back to look at her again, his dark eyes raking her flushed face, missing nothing of her suddenly tongue-tied embarrassment. A memory flashed between them. A memory of other blushes, for other reasons.

"I'm sorry," he said, but this time he didn't look sorry. "I didn't mean to embarrass you."

Didn't you, her eyes challenged him, but he only stared back at her, an expression of bland innocence on his handsome face.

"Well, don't let it bother you," she managed to say at last. "We redheads tend to blush over the *least* little thing. It means nothing." She shrugged carelessly, hoping she didn't sound as hostile as she felt.

Apparently she did though, because when he smiled at her—a cool smile that didn't reach his eyes—she felt the force of *his* anger wash over her in waves.

What did he have to be angry about? she wondered vaguely. Nothing, that's what. Nothing at all. He was not the one who had been left to wake up all alone in a hotel room...left pregnant...left scared. He had walked away from it without ever knowing. And now he had the gall—the unmitigated gall!—to look at her like that. With anger! Almost, she could hate him.

"Jake," she heard the brunette say, her husky voice finally penetrating the silence that stretched between them. How long had they been staring at each other like that? "Jake, darling, there are others to meet."

"But you haven't met Miss...what did you say that last name was?"

"Weston," Desi supplied, "Desi Weston."

"Ah, yes." He performed the brief introduction. "Desi Weston, head of makeup, meet Audrey Ferris. Audrey is going to play the lead in *Devil's Lady.*"

"Yes, I know. I'm sorry I didn't recognize you sooner, Miss Ferris, but you're much more beautiful in person," Desi said pleasantly.

And she was. Much more beautiful. Audrey Ferris was a tall full-bodied woman with smooth tanned skin. She wore a stylish ivory silk wrap-front dress that exposed only a modest amount of cleavage. Her brunette hair was worn loose and full, curling to her shoulders in seeming abandon, her lips were glossed a rich rose, her nails were long and professionally manicured. An elegant woman; every sleek, feline, pampered inch of her. And she knew it.

"I watch *Night and Day* whenever I get the chance," Desi continued. "It's my favorite soap." She didn't volunteer the information that she had acquired the habit while sitting home, waiting for Stephanie to be born.

"Daytime drama, please," Audrey Ferris corrected her with a smile that didn't quite reach her big golden-brown eyes. They flittered back and forth between Jake's set face and Desi's, trying to decipher the sparks of tension that flashed between the two.

Cat's eyes, Desi thought, big, golden-brown, cat's eyes. She didn't think she was going to like the beautiful Miss Audrey Ferris even one little bit. Apparently the feeling was mutual because it was definitely not friendliness that she saw in the other woman's eyes.

What was it? Desi wondered. Dislike was too strong a word. Fear, maybe? Challenge? Uncertainty? Suddenly the brown eyes seemed to make a decision and Audrey smiled sweetly.

"It's very nice to meet you, Miss Wesley," she said, holding out a graceful hand, displaying long rose-tipped nails and the half a dozen slim gold bracelets that jangled on her arm.

"Weston," Desi corrected her dryly. She shook the offered hand, mentally contrasting the other woman's sleek manicured fingers to her own short unadorned nails. "But, please, call me Desi."

"Of course." Audrey smiled again and withdrew her hand to tuck it back into the crook of Jake's arm. "Desi." Her rich, theatrical voice seemed to taste the word. "It suits you, I think. Fresh, young, pixieish . . . almost boyish." She slanted a glance at the man beside her. "Don't you think so, Jake?"

"If you say so." Jake's voice was curt, then, "Come on, Audrey love, there are others to meet. Dorothea?"

Young, pixieish, almost boyish, indeed!

Desi glanced down at herself. She was dressed in her usual rather funky style. In fact, a little dressier than usual because of this opening-day cast party. Deep green corduroy trousers, pleated at the waist and slightly baggy, tucked into ankle boots of pale butterscotch-colored leather. A melon green knit T-shirt peeked out from under a tan-and-green tweed bomber-style jacket that, admittedly, had seen better days. Her long red hair was confined into a single neat French braid down her back, her creamy complexion was free of any trace of makeup.

Practical clothes, the kind she felt most comfortable in. The kind that allowed her to work without worrying about lipstick stains and makeup smears.

"Just when it was getting interesting, too!" Dorothea's aristocratic voice carried to every corner of the studio as she moved away on Jake's other arm. "I thought those two girls were going to start a cat fight over you." She shot a coquettish glance at him from her black eyes. "I can't say that I blame them, of course. You're far too handsome for your own good, dear boy."

"And you're a terrible flirt!"

"Terrible? And here I thought I was finally getting it right. Well," she said with a sigh, "I guess I'll just have to practice some more. But not right now. Right now, I am absolutely parched for some champagne, and I'm quite sure everyone else is, too. Come along, dear boy, we can't start drinking until you do."

"Bitch," Desi said to Evan when they had moved away.

"Who?" he asked, grinning at her, his soft brown eyes twinkling from under his shaggy gray eyebrows. "Dorothea?"

"Don't try to be cute, Evan. You know who I mean. Audrey Ferris." And then she grinned back at him. "Well, Dorothea, too. But she's a nice old bitch. Miss Ferris, however... Pixieish!" Desi's voice was indignant. "She's a class A, number one—"

"Don't say it." Evan covered his ears as she paused, searching for just the right word to accurately describe her feeling toward the movie's female star. "I hate to hear women swear."

"Actress," Desi finished. She opened her violet eyes wide and fluttered her lashes innocently. "What did you think I was going to say?"

"One never knows with you, luv."

She shrugged and smiled at Evan, and absently watched Jake as he opened the first bottle of champagne, pouring it ceremoniously into Dorothea's glass.

"It wasn't as bad as you thought it was going to be, was it?" he asked hopefully, all teasing gone from his kind face.

"Wasn't as bad as what?" she asked, her eyes still on the laughing group by the refreshment table.

"Seeing Jake again."

Was it? she asked herself.

In some ways, no, it hadn't been. A little awkwardness at first, a bit of embarrassment. Not too bad. But in another way it was even worse than she had expected. Far worse. In fact, it hurt like hell to have him look at her as he had, with that cold, unfriendly look on his face and the smile that never reached his eyes. As if they were total strangers. As if they had never shared that gloriously abandoned weekend that had resulted in the birth of a beautiful red-haired baby girl.

He didn't known that, of course, and maybe she was wrong to judge him. But he had judged her, she knew. Judged her and found her sadly wanting.

"Desi?"

She looked up to find Evan eyeing her with concern. "No, it wasn't as bad as I thought it was going to be," she reassured him.

"I'm glad," he said simply.

She reached up a small hand and touched his face gently. "I know, Evan, thank you." Her hand fell and she smiled brightly, showing him that she had sustained no lasting hurt. "Come on, let's go get some of that champagne before Dorothea drinks it all."

"Before I drink all what?" Dorothea came up to them, followed by a white-coated waiter.

"The champagne, what else?"

"Even I can't drink that much." Dorothea waved toward the buffet table and bar. "Though I have been known to try. Here. Take one of these," she ordered Desi, handing her a brimming glass of champagne from the waiter's tray.

"Are you sure you can spare it?"

Dorothea chose to ignore that remark. "You, too, dear boy. Drink up. Jake ordered bottles and bottles of the stuff, and it goes terribly flat if you don't drink it fast, you know." She watched approvingly while they each took a sip. "Jake has wonderful taste, don't you think?"

"Does he?" was Desi's softly murmured reply.

Dorothea's sharp eyes followed Desi's half-wistful glance. "A bit too obvious," she pronounced decisively after a minute. Audrey was still clinging to Jake, her voluptuous breasts pressed against his arm as she gazed up at him. "She ought to know by now that Jake appreciates a little more restraint in his women." Dorothea grinned wickedly. "At least in public."

Desi grinned back. Dorothea was such a sweet, aristocratic-looking little lady, grandmotherly almost, until you looked into those sharp black eyes . . . or she said something like that. And then, watch out! She was fast beginning to see how easily Dorothea could have written the torrid novel that she had. By now it seemed totally in character.

"Miss Audrey Ferris and I aren't going to get along, I'm afraid," Desi said dryly.

"Nonsense! Just ignore her," ordered Dorothea. "I intend to."

Desi sputtered into her champagne. "But, Dorothea, I thought you liked her! I mean, she was your first choice for the part, wasn't she?"

"She was," Dorothea agreed, nodding over her champagne. "The girl's a fine actress and she'll do me credit. Doesn't mean I have to like her, though. Most obvious little trollop I've ever met."

"Dorothea, really!" admonished Evan, in his most upper-crust English accent. "Remember your image."

"Oh, bother my image. You sound just like my late husband." Her sweet old face softened for an instant. "Richard always did say I had a mouth on me that would shame a dock worker. I'm usually right, though." Her eyes flashed back to Audrey for a second. "Oh, well, poor girl can't be blamed for trying to hang on to him." She stopped a passing waiter for another glass of champagne.

"You can go away now, Evan." She waved her free hand at him, the two huge square-cut rubies flashing in the lights. "Find one of those cute little actresses to amuse yourself with for a while. Go on. I want to talk to Desi—woman to woman—and you'd just be in the way."

Evan grinned and bowed jauntily from the waist, touching his hand to his head as if gallantly tipping a hat and went away, as ordered.

"Now, come here, dear girl. I need to sit down. Not as young as I used to be, you know. More's the pity." Dorothea led Desi a little way from the milling crowd and perched herself on the edge of a makeup chair. "I'd like you to indulge an old lady's curiosity."

"Certainly, if I can."

"Just how long have you known Jake Lancing and why are you both pretending that you don't?"

"Really, Dorothea!" Desi managed not to squeak. She glanced around to make sure that no one could overhear. "I don't know him at all," she denied, "except by reputation, of course. And that's quite enough."

"Really, Desi!" the older woman mimicked her. "Didn't your mother ever tell you that it's not nice to lie to little old ladies?"

"You're not old," Desi protested. "You're the youngest person here."

"Flattery, dear girl, is wasted on me," Dorothea informed her, "unless, of course, you're a good-looking young man."

"Or a good-looking old one," Desi quipped.

Dorothea sighed theatrically and sipped at her champagne. "That's too true," she admitted. "I never could resist one of those handsome devils, no matter what their age—" she glanced up at Desi from under her lashes "—always from afar, of course. At least after I was married. Richard would have beat me black and blue if it had ever gone beyond that. He wasn't jealous, mind you, just a bit possessive."

"Did it ever go beyond that?" Desi wanted to know. Somehow, she was sure that it had. Dorothea Heller seemed to her to be a woman who had always tested limits. Her own, and those set for her by others.

Dorothea laughed delightedly, a deep warm chuckle. There was a look of wistful remembrance in her black eyes. "Almost—once or twice. But it never got out of hand. I've always known how to handle men," she said confidentially, and then she laughed again. "Besides, Richard in a rage was always so terribly exciting. As Jake is, I imagine," she went on without pausing. "Isn't he?"

Desi shook her head. "You never give up, do you?"

"Never," she agreed, and then added after a minute, "Well, is he?"

"Is who, what?" Desi said, deliberately vague, her eyes on the empty champagne glass in her hand.

"Never mind now, dear girl. I think we're about to find out." Desi looked up, startled. Jake was weaving his way toward them. "Not that he looks in a rage, mind you. But definitely very stern. Oh, I do like a masterful man, don't you?"

"Ladies," he said pleasantly as he came up to them. He leaned down and kissed Dorothea's cheek, flashing a brief smile at Desi. But again the smile didn't reach his eyes. They remained shuttered and vaguely angry as he looked at her for that brief instant.

Why angry? she wondered again. He had no reason to be angry at her. No reason that he knew about anyway.

"Dorothea, my angel," he said as he straightened up. "I have someone who wants to meet you." A slight movement of his head summoned a young man who had been hovering just a few feet away. "Dorothea, this is Michael Ballard, he's going to play—"

"Tony," Dorothea said decisively.

The young man smiled, exposing attractive dimples in either cheek and very white teeth. "Yes," he said, holding out his hand, "but how did you know?"

"My dear boy, you look almost exactly like *my* Tony did. Same eyes, same smile."

Desi looked at him again with more interest. Not as young as she had at first thought. Early thirties, perhaps, instead of the twenty-four or -five she had pegged him. And he did indeed look like Dorothea's Tony. Or, at least, like her description of him in *Devil's Lady*. Light brown hair, hazel eyes, more green than brown, and an easy, charming smile. Tony was the man whom Dorothea had almost married before her dashing Richard had come along to claim her. Looking at Michael, Desi could almost see why. Jake's casting, so far, had been excellent she thought approvingly.

"I'm almost out of champagne," Dorothea said, sliding down from the high makeup chair. "And I really should have something to eat before it all goes to my head. Come along, Michael," she ordered, linking her arm through his. "Let's go see what's on that lovely refreshment table and you can tell me how you intend to play Tony. And I'll tell you some things about him that I *didn't* put in my book."

She glanced over her shoulder at Jake as they moved away. "Don't be too hard on her, dear boy," she warned him.

A small silence followed their departure.

"What did she mean by that?" Jake demanded harshly.

Desi looked up. His face was harsh, too, and angry.

"I don't know." She tried to keep her own voice low and even, her eyes gazing steadily into his. She couldn't let him see how his anger was affecting her. His anger and, suddenly, his nearness. Her lashes fell, hiding her eyes.

"Pretend," she could hear Evan saying. "Pretend if he does." Easy for Evan to say!

Jake was standing with his back to the rest of the room, close enough so that she only had to lift her hand to touch him. As close as he had stood that night at the Hyatt Regency when she had been so uncertain and his hands had reached over to cup her breasts.... *No, don't think of that! That's over! Finished!*

She felt his hand close around her arm and her eyes flew up to his face. "What did she mean by that?" he demanded. "What have you been telling her?"

Desi still couldn't understand why he was so angry and, besides, she was beginning to get angry herself now. Any minute, she thought, she would explode into a rage, despite all the other people in the room.

The trouble was, she hadn't expected this level of emotional reaction from him. Men like him—men used to lots of women—didn't usually waste any emotion on their casual bedmates. And that's what she had been, she told herself, just a casual bedmate. A woman he had picked up. A groupie.

She had expected indifference from him, if he remembered her at all. Or, possibly, even contempt for what he would consider her promiscuity. Neither of those emotions would have really surprised her. But this hot, harsh anger. The...the pain that lay hidden in the back of his eyes. Why?

"I don't know what you mean, Jake," she said softly, not realizing how naturally his name came to her lips. "I haven't been telling her anything—"

Her words were cut off as he shook her, his powerful hand around her upper arm, so that her fingers nearly slipped from the champagne glass she was holding.

"Jake, stop it!" she ordered. Her eyes darted around the room, but no one was paying any attention to them. From the back, she realized suddenly, it must look as if she and Jake were just having a friendly, private conversation.

"You can stop looking for your lover to help you. He's busy with Melanie, the script girl."

"My...my lover?" Desi echoed blankly, staring up into Jake's face. Her eyes were wide and puzzled, but her body tensed with an unwilling sort of excitement. Dorothea had been right. Jake in a rage was magnificent; his jaw tight, his eyes flashing warning sparks at her. Scary, but magnificent.

"Don't play innocent with me, Desiree." His voice made a mockery of her name. "You know who I mean. Evan Prince, your lover."

"Evan? My...my lover?" she whispered incredulously. "You're crazy!" But he seemed not to have heard her.

"That's how you got this job, isn't it?" he said almost conversationally, except for that faint hint of suppressed... something in his voice. She couldn't put a name to the emotion that he seemed to be struggling so hard to hide from her.

Desi yanked her arm from his grasp, backing as far away from him as she could. The makeup table came up against the back of her hips, stopping her. "I got my job strictly on my talents!" she told him indignantly.

"Oh, I know all about your talents." He moved forward, trapping her against the makeup table, one hand on either side of her body. "Very fine talents they are, too. And I should know, shouldn't I?"

His voice was as bland as if he was asking her opinion of a book she'd read or a movie she'd seen, but his eyes were hard and cold. She had never thought to see him look at her like that. She had not thought that his beautiful eyes could be so icy.

Desi's skin flushed a fiery red. Not with embarrassment or fear or even with pain at his harsh, unfair judgment of her— but with anger. A sudden explosive anger that matched his. How dare he!

"You bastard!" she swore at him through clenched teeth. "You dirty-minded bastard!"

She exploded then and her hand rose as if to hit him. He straightened, his hand coming up to block hers, and, suddenly, her wrist was swallowed in his firm grasp. "I have one thing to say to you, Desiree, and you'd better listen good. This film is important to me. Very important. Is that clear?"

She nodded slowly. Yes, she knew it was important to him. It would be important to anybody in his position. This film, if it was successful, would prove that Jake Lancing was more than a pretty face, that he could do more than display his handsome looks and body in front of a camera. It would make him a power to be reckoned with in the movie industry. But she wondered what that had to do with her.

"Is that clear?" he repeated when she didn't answer.

"Yes." She pulled her wrist out of his grasp. "It's clear." Her violet eyes were mutinous and hurt and angry all at the same time as she glared up at him. "So what?"

She saw his eyes blaze at her words. "I'll tell you what!" he said through clenched teeth. "Evan may or may not be your lover—"

"He isn't!" she denied again.

"It's immaterial to me one way or the other. Unimportant." He dismissed Evan with a wave of his hand. "What *is* important is this film. I won't let anything stand in my way. Not personalities, not emotions. Nothing." He seemed almost, she thought, to be talking to himself instead of her. That notion, however, was dispelled with his next words. "Certainly not some scheming little groupie."

Scheming little groupie! How dare he call her that? She forgot, in that charged instant, that she had called herself that very name. How dared he pass judgment on her? she thought indignantly. He had been there that night, too!

"And if I find out that your so-called artistic talent is lacking in any way," he went on, seemingly unaware of her seething anger, "I'll fire you so fast your head will spin!"

"I'm a fully qualified makeup artist!" she flung at him, stung by his slur on her qualifications.

She had been fighting that kind of innuendo for most of her professional life. *So-called artistic talent!* If makeup wasn't a talent, then what was it? How did he think he would look in front of the cameras without her so-called talent?

"Fully qualified!" she said again. "You can check my references if—"

She broke off abruptly, her eyes caught in the dark web of his gaze. They stared at each other for seemingly endless seconds, both pairs of eyes full of unasked questions. He made a half gesture with his hand, as if he was reaching to touch her face. Her lips, soft and trembling, started to silently form his name.

"Aw, damn!" The words were softly spoken but forceful. Full of suppressed emotion. He dropped his hand and walked away from her. Desi watched him glance around the room.

Like a . . . a hunter seeking prey, she thought.

He dropped his arm over the shoulders of a woman, one of the lighting technicians, and steered her toward the refreshment table. Dorothea looked up as they approached, and then her sharp black eyes flickered questioningly over to Desi.

Desi straightened, pulling away from the makeup table, and forced herself to smile at Dorothea, holding up one hand, thumb and forefinger circled, to indicate that everything was okay.

But she was far from okay. She was literally trembling with reaction. So much so that the empty glass shook in her hands. Anger, first and foremost. Anger that he would even dare to think, let alone say, what he had.

As if Evan would hire her for the reason he had suggested. As if she and Evan . . . He was disgusting, that's what he was! Disgusting, to suggest that she could even look at Evan in that way. He was one of her closest friends and, besides, he was old enough to be her father!

Still trembling, she placed her empty glass on the makeup table before she could give in to the urge to walk over and break it on Jake's head. How dared he say what he had to her! Disparaging both her morals and her talent in one breath.

She saw Dorothea look over at her again and then approach Evan. He looked over at her, too, a worried frown on his face, and began to move toward her.

She had to get out of here, quickly. The one thing she couldn't take right now was any sympathy or concern from Evan. The only thing holding her together was her anger and if Evan started talking to her, dispersing that anger, she would fall apart. Literally, in a crumbling heap on the floor at his feet. She picked up her satchel, heading for the door.

"Are you all right, luv?" he asked, intercepting her.

"Fine, Evan, really." She smiled up at him a shade too brightly. "I just want to get back to the hotel and call my mother. See how Stephanie's doing. It's the first time I've been away from her overnight," she admitted. "I think it's harder on me than it is on her."

"You're sure you're okay?" Evan insisted. "Jake didn't say anything to upset you, did he?"

"Him? No, of course not," she lied. "Just a few lewd suggestions. Harmless." She knew what Evan would infer from that. He would think that Jake had made a pass at her, but it was better than his knowing what disgusting things he *had* said.

Evan's forehead creased in a frown. "I've never known Jake to be lewd," he began and then stopped, realizing that she was in no condition to stand there and listen to him tell her what a fine man Jake really was. She looked, he thought, perilously close to breaking.

He patted her shoulder a trifle awkwardly, unable to offer any other sort of comfort. "See you at the hotel then." His lips touched her cheek briefly. "Drive carefully, luv, you know what these L.A. freeways are."

Desi nodded, unable to speak past the lump that was forming in her throat. She reached up to hug him fiercely for a second. "Thanks, Evan. I will."

The last thing she saw as she hurried out was Jake's disapproving glare. For her, she wondered, or Evan . . . or both of them?

IT HAD BEEN an exciting, exhausting month for Desi, and for everyone else on the crew, too. The actors and the dozens of technicians and craftspeople needed for the movie had spent the first six weeks shooting as many scenes as possible in a big studio in Los Angeles.

And now they were in San Francisco, doing location shots, and then it would be on to Sonoma where the bulk of the filming would take place. They would be using Dorothea's sprawling mansion and the surrounding vineyards. The very same house that Richard Heller had brought his bride to some sixty-odd years ago.

They were all driven relentlessly by Jake, who was the director as well as the producer and male lead of *Devil's Lady*. Somehow it did not at all surprise Desi to find that out. She had already half known it. He wanted everything perfect, everything exactly right and that meant, to him, doing it himself. Or as much of it himself as he could.

Jake had put up almost everything he owned to be able to make this picture—his reputation, his money, his talent—and there were people out there who were just waiting for the chance to pounce on his first mistake. To say "See, Jake Lancing's nothing but a pretty-boy actor. He should have stuck to acting."

But he would prove them wrong. Desi knew that already. *Devil's Lady* was going to be a blockbuster. A box-office smash. It had everything—sizzling romance, adventure, glamour, suspense—and Jake Lancing. His portrayal of Richard Heller was a masterpiece, and it would probably win him another Oscar nomination. But it was his direction that would make this picture great.

He had a quick, sure sense of just how it should be shot, and he was able to convey this sense to the people under his direction with uncanny accuracy and breathtaking results.

The whole crew worked extra hard for him, willingly doing take after take to give him what he wanted. The actors, the technicians, the wardrobe and makeup people, the stunt men; they gave him their all because that's what he gave back to them. They worked hard, long hours because they all seemed to know, instinctively, that it was going to be worth it. Jake made them believe that. He made them feel a part of something great, something magic.

Even Audrey Ferris worked hard for him. The role of Dorothea Heller was going to raise her from the level of a soap-opera queen to that of major-motion-picture star. Audrey knew it and was taking no chances.

Much as she hated to admit it, Desi knew that to be true, and she wholeheartedly admired and respected the way Audrey transformed herself into the young Dorothea Heller when Jake shouted "Action".

She still didn't like Audrey personally. She tried to tell herself it was because Audrey was unfriendly toward *her*— and perhaps that was partially true. But the real reason, whether she could admit it or not, was jealousy. Jealousy because Jake spent so much of his time with the beautiful actress; coaching her in her part, explaining her character's motivations, rehearsing her. And the love scenes...each time Jake took Audrey in his arms Desi had an uneasy feeling in the pit of her stomach.

Desi stood now, half leaning against the back of Dorothea's high canvas chair, holding a big black umbrella over both of them as she watched Audrey play out a scene with Michael Ballard as Tony. Jake seemed to hover around them as they enacted the scene, the lines of his lean body tense under the faded denim work shirt that he wore. Without actually moving, he gave the impression of circling the pair, encouraging, commanding and, in some way, of protecting them from the distractions of the crowd.

For, despite the cold drizzle and the brisk wind whipping up off the Bay, Fisherman's Wharf was crowded with curious onlookers. Tourists and locals alike pressed up against the police barricades to watch what was going on. But neither Audrey nor Michael, nor especially Jake, seemed to notice.

They stood there in the misting rain, Michael in a heavy pea coat and a Greek fisherman's hat shielding him from the elements, Jake in his work shirt and worn denim jeans, a script rolled tightly in one hand, and Audrey looking as lovely as a dew-kissed flower with her marcelled hair flattened to her head by the dampness.

"She plays me almost better than I did," remarked Dorothea, sniffling into her handkerchief.

"Hadn't you better do something about that cold? Like get in out of this rain?" asked Desi in a whisper. Jake was a fanatic about disruptions on the set. He had already jumped on her once for making unnecessary noise during a scene. He had jumped on everybody at least once. And once was enough. She had no desire to draw his wrath down on her head again.

"Nonsense, it's just a sniffle and it isn't *raining*, dear girl, it's only a light mist," Dorothea argued.

"Well, let me get you a cup of hot tea, at least." She handed Dorothea the umbrella. "I'll see if I can find some aspirin, too. You look a little flushed."

"Nonsense," Dorothea said again, stifling another sneeze, but Desi had already moved away. She was back in less than five minutes.

"Here, take these—" she handed Dorothea the aspirin "—and don't argue with me. Jake will have a fit if you get sick on him."

"I never get sick," Dorothea protested, but she took the aspirin and then wrapped her hands gratefully around the mug of steaming tea.

No rubies today, Desi noticed, glancing at the gnarled old hands wrapped around the mug. But then, rubies didn't really go with the wool slacks, chic though they were, and heavy coat that Dorothea was wearing today. Not to mention the red-and-white striped muffler around her neck and the jaunty red stocking cap pulled low over her ears.

That wind was freezing, Desi realized, hunching herself farther into her own heavy purple down coat. It was a wonder that Audrey hadn't already turned blue with the cold. That little fur-collared cloth coat she had on couldn't offer much protection against the bone-chilling cold of a San Francisco winter. And Jake's clothes weren't much better. No jacket, no hat. Somebody should do something about that.

"Cut," she heard him holler.

Audrey almost visibly dropped her character and began to shiver. Jake wrapped her in a big blanket, his hands rubbing briskly up and down her arms, heedless of the fact that he, too, was standing bareheaded in the rain.

And it *was* rain, Desi thought, even though Dorothea stubbornly referred to it as a light mist.

"That was great, Audrey. Great," Jake praised her. "You were perfect. You, too, Michael. Both of you were great." He propelled her toward the small trailer that served as her dressing room. "Go on inside. Get into some dry clothes. Have a cup of coffee while we get the next scene set up." He kissed the top of her head paternally and pulled the door of the trailer closed as she went in.

"Weston," he barked then, "get over here."

Desi sighed, handing the umbrella to Dorothea again. That's the way he had been toward her for the past two months. Unfailingly impersonal, unfailingly polite, unfailingly cold.

"Audrey's going to need a complete redo before the next scene," he told her, his voice sounding strained.

Desi looked up to tell him that she knew that, and then stopped. His eyes were showing the strain, too, and he looked tired. She wanted to reach up and massage his temples until the tenseness went away.

He ran his free hand through his hair and looked away from the concern in her eyes.

Almost, she thought, as if he was afraid to look directly at her for too long.

There had been no repeat of the explosive anger he had shown her at the cast party. In fact, she could almost have believed that she had imagined that angry scene between them. Because, for the past two months, he had been treating her as if he had no memory of it—or of the weekend they had spent together.

Except, she said to herself . . . except for the way he looked at her when he thought she wouldn't notice.

The first time it had happened she had thought, for a second, that he was looking behind her at someone else. Surely he couldn't be looking at *her* like that, with a sort of puzzled, almost wistful look in his dark eyes. She had actually turned around, that first time, glancing behind her to see whom he was looking at so . . . so longingly. But there was no one. When she turned back to him again, the look was gone and Jake was deep in discussion with his assistant director.

She thought, then, that she had imagined it. Seeing it because it was what she *wanted* to see. But it happened again several times.

But *this* time she knew it was directed at her. What she didn't know was why. *Why* was Jake looking at her like that? Why did his dark expressive eyes rake over her so covetously and what did it mean?

"Pay attention, Weston." Jake's voice brought her abruptly back to the here and now.

"I'm sorry," she said softly, her voice distracted. "What did you say?"

"Audrey needs her makeup redone. Give her fifteen minutes to get warmed up and then go on in. And try not to upset her this time, will you?" He turned away abruptly, dismissing her, to discuss camera angles for the next scene with his key grip.

He hadn't even given her a chance to defend herself against Audrey's latest complaint. Whatever it was.

"And just what did you do to upset our star this time?" Dorothea said, grinning impishly, as Desi flopped down into a canvas chair beside her.

"Beats me." Desi shrugged. "Probably not enough eye makeup again."

She glanced at her watch. She'd give Audrey *exactly* fifteen minutes to warm up, she decided, sipping at her cooling tea as she leaned back in the chair, and then she'd go on inside the trailer and try to redo the star's makeup without upsetting her too much in the process. Not that it would do any good. Everything she did seemed to upset Audrey Ferris. There was too much setting lotion in her marcelled waves. There wasn't enough kohl outlining her Betty Boop eyes. And on and on until Desi wanted to crack her over her lovely brunette head with the curling iron.

But she didn't. Having worked with so many actors and actresses, Desi knew that most of Audrey's complaints stemmed from insecurity—about her talent, about the fleeting nature of her beauty, about any of a hundred other things that the fragile actor's ego was heir to. So she restrained herself, smiling sweetly, refusing to be baited or lose her temper.

A cat fight with his leading lady would be all Jake would need to accuse her of unprofessionalism. To point out that she was too young . . . too inexperienced . . . too something to do her job right.

Not that he had actually mentioned her qualifications again, not after that first time. Because, she told herself, any fool—even Jake—could plainly see that she was good at her job.

"Damn it, Weston," she heard him roar, "why isn't Audrey ready for the next scene?"

Desi looked up from her mug of tea to find Jake bearing down on her, an impatient frown on his handsome face. Funny, she thought in that brief instant, that she should notice how handsome he was when he was obviously getting ready to berate her. But then, she always noticed how handsome he was. She sighed wearily and rose, setting the mug down on the pavement beside her folding canvas chair.

"Well?" He scowled impatiently, towering over her. His dark eyes pinned her to the spot where she stood.

"Really, Jake," Dorothea began, but Desi shook her head warningly, silencing her protest.

"You said to give her fifteen minutes to warm up, Mr. Lancing," she said evenly, emphasizing the Mister in the faint hope of pointing out his lack of courtesy when addressing her. She glanced at her watch. "It's only been ten."

"Don't be smart, Weston," he snapped. "I'm ready for her now. Move."

She stood there for a brief second, staring up at him with defiance blazing out of her narrowed eyes. It was almost too much. She was cold and wet, just like everyone else, and he had pushed her just about as far as she was willing to go.

"I said move," he repeated softly. "Now." The gleam in his eyes was almost anticipatory. He was just waiting for her to explode, she realized suddenly. Almost as if he relished the prospect.

Deliberately she unclenched her fists. Her eyes dropped. "Yes, sir," she said, falsely meek, and turned toward Audrey's trailer.

His big hand reached out and grasped her upper arm. "Where do you think you're going, Weston?"

Desi looked up blankly, not immediately responding to his question. What was he talking about? He knew where she was going . . . he'd told her to go! She opened her mouth to tell him so, in no uncertain terms, and then closed it again. He looked so haggard, with lines of strain clearly etched around his tired eyes, that she couldn't bring herself to add any more to the burden he already carried.

He doesn't mean to harass me, she told herself. He didn't mean it personally. He'd been under a lot of strain. A great deal of concentration and tension was required to make this movie. And, besides, he'd been a bear to everyone on the set. *It's not just you. So don't take it personally.*

Inside, though, she was seething with conflicting emotions. Indignation, hurt, compassion . . . and that terrible traitorous excitement that flickered along her veins at his nearness. She didn't *want* to tremble like this when he came near her, but she couldn't seem to help it. No more than she could help how she still felt about him. She didn't want that feeling, but there was nothing she could do about it.

"Where are you going?" he repeated. His voice was harsh and soft, angry and seductive, as if he didn't know what kind of response he wanted to provoke from her.

Her eyes lifted slowly to his face. Far from docile, they blazed up at him, confusion and hurt and anger in their violet depths, and something else. Passion, maybe. Or need. But her voice was still cool.

"To Audrey's trailer," she said evenly. She glanced down at his hand on her arm and back up to his face again. "Like you told me to. Remember?" Her voice was sweet and dutifully submissive, but her eyes still stared challengingly up into his as she added, "Sir."

His expression changed, the hostility fading suddenly from his eyes, and he smiled at her. That bone-melting, soul-shattering smile. "I've changed my mind. You can do my makeup first. It'll be faster that way," he said softly. "I'll meet you in my trailer in a minute." He nudged her gently in the direction of his trailer without, however, releasing his grip on her arm.

Desi couldn't move. Because he hadn't let go of her arm, she told herself later, even though he wasn't holding it so tightly now and she could have easily twisted away. But he *was* still staring down into her upraised face, holding her captive with the mere power of his gaze. That look was in his eyes again; questions, confusion, desire. She couldn't find the will to pull herself away from *that* so easily.

She felt herself melting helplessly at the touch of his hard fingers on her arm and the caress of his seductive voice and the suddenly hungry look in his smoldering eyes as they raked her face. A look that mirrored her own. It was as if he couldn't look away. Almost as if he was searching for something, she thought. But what? And why?

The defiant light faded from her own eyes, leaving only a soft sensual glow and her lips, firmed in anger, softened, too, and parted as if in breathless anticipation of his kiss.

They stood that way for several endless seconds, staring into each other's eyes, Jake seemingly as mesmerized as she was. Neither aware, for the moment, of anyone or anything else. And then Dorothea sneezed, breaking the fragile spell that held them immobile.

Jake tore his eyes away from hers, but his hand still held her upper arm, lightly now so that his touch was almost a caress, keeping her by him.

"What are you doing out in this rain?" he questioned Dorothea. "You should be in one of the trailers where it's warm."

"She's got a cold and I—" Desi started to say.

"I haven't got a cold," the old lady protested weakly, sneezing again.

"I'd like to know what you call it then." His voice was fond and indulgent. He let go of Desi, reaching out his hand to touch Dorothea's cheek and then her forehead. "You have a fever, too." He turned to Desi, motioning her to feel Dorothea's head for herself.

Desi's long fingers rested for an instant against the other woman's flushed face. It felt hot and dry, despite the misty air.

"I knew you were coming down with something," she said accusingly. "I told you to—"

"Get her inside one of the trailers right now," Jake interrupted. He glanced at his watch and then at the sky. "We'll shoot this next scene and then call it a day." An annoyed frown crossed his face. "It's almost raining too hard right now to get anything done." He strode away from the two women as he spoke, his tall, commanding figure somehow managing to hurry without looking the least bit rushed.

"I want you in my trailer in five minutes, Weston," he called over his shoulder.

Back to normal, Desi thought, a wry smile twisting her lips as she herded a protesting Dorothea into the nearest trailer.

"I thought for a minute there that you two were going to kiss and make up," Dorothea commented as Desi turned to leave the trailer.

Desi looked up sharply and Dorothea looked back at her, a false expression of innocent inquiry on her sweet lined face.

"What gave you an idea like that?" Desi asked carefully, her voice as expressionless and casual as she could make it. She thought she had succeeded in dispelling any notion that Dorothea might have had about her and Jake knowing each other but, apparently, she was wrong.

"He was eating you with those big brown eyes of his," Dorothea said almost enviously. "And you, dear girl, weren't protesting at all. Not at all. In fact, you were returning the favor. Not that I blame you, mind." Dorothea chuckled. "You'd be a fool not to—"

"You're letting your imagination run away with you again," Desi said firmly, but her eyes avoided Dorothea's.

"Humph!" Dorothea snorted derisively. "I don't know why you two think it's necessary to hide your feelings—especially when any fool on this set can see how it is between you." She shrugged. "But if you think you have to, well . . ." Her voice trailed off.

"Hide what feelings?" Desi started to say. What feelings had Dorothea seen with her sharp black eyes? Which of hers hadn't she been able to hide? What feelings had Jake shown besides the coldness and the polite indifference that was all Desi could see? *Were* there others? Could there possibly be others?

Jake's voice floated in to them over the noise of the rain coming down, hard now, on the metal roof. "Damn it! Where is Weston?" they heard him bellow. "I need her. Now!" There was the loud, resounding bang of a door.

Desi hurried from the warm, dry haven of Dorothea's trailer and ran across the wet, slippery pavement to Jake's. She turned the door handle and stepped inside without bothering to knock. Jake, after all, was expecting her.

"Glad you decided you could make it," he said, standing as he pulled up the zipper of a pair of blue dress slacks.

Desi stood stock-still in the open doorway, staring at him.
Obviously he was changing into costume for the next scene.
Obviously he had only gotten as far as the slacks. His feet,
beneath the hem of the blue pants, were bare and his
chest . . . his chest was bare, too. Desi gulped, a sudden vision of the last time she had seen him so scantily clothed
flashing through her mind.

He had been standing in the soft light of the morning sun
as it filtered through a curtained window, quietly pulling on
his clothes, trying not to wake her up. But she had been startled awake in spite of his efforts. More from the sense of being alone in the bed than by any noise he might have made.

She had reached for him in her sleep, coming abruptly
awake when her arms clasped only emptiness. *He's gone,* had
been her first panic-stricken thought as she lay there dreading to open her eyes. *It's Sunday morning and he's gone.
Without a word. Without even saying goodbye.*

"Jake." Her voice was soft, the word almost a moan, and
tears pressed against her closed eyelids.

"Go back to sleep," she heard him say quietly. "It's too
early for you to get up."

Her eyes flew open, focusing blindly on him as he came
around the side of the bed. The sun, she remembered, had
made a flickering pattern on his bare arms and shoulders as
it streamed through the loose-weave curtains of their hotel
room.

"Jake!" The word was a soft exclamation of joy. She sat up
in the middle of the big bed, heedless of the blankets that fell
away from her. "I thought you'd gone."

"Not yet." He sat down on the edge of the bed, his hands
moving to rub lightly up and down her bare arms. "But soon.
My plane leaves at 8:35."

"What time is it now?"

He glanced at the digital clock on the nightstand, his hands
never leaving her arms. "Six."

"Then you have two and a—" she'd begun, and then
stopped. No, she would not keep him. She knew he had to

leave this morning. It was no surprise. He was due on location in Alaska. He had to leave.

"Plenty of time," she heard him say softly. His voice had the lush, sensuous quality of a purring cat. A purring tiger. And his eyes—those dark, dangerous, mesmerizing eyes—were devouring her. "Plenty of time," he repeated.

Fascinated, she watched his eyes as his hands caressed the curves of her shoulders and neck. She felt his fingers whisper along the nape of her neck, his thumbs making slow, small circles just in front of her ears at the point where the delicate line of her jaw began. His eyes were hot, hot and burning with desire. His hands were hot, too, against her pale, willing flesh.

"Mmm, that feels good," she murmured. Her eyes closed and her head dropped back, like a flower too heavy for the fragile stem of her neck, inviting further pleasures.

Jake took the offered pleasures, ravishing her neck and shoulders and breasts with tender hands and a hot, avid mouth. And then he gave the pleasures back tenfold with the thrust of his body.

She had gone to sleep again, after their lovemaking, with her cheek against his chest and his hand slowly stroking her hair. When she woke for the second time that morning, he was gone.

"Close the door, Weston, before it's as wet in here as it is outside," Jake ordered.

Desi snapped back to the present with a start, her delicate complexion flushed with betraying color. She let the trailer door swing shut. "Sorry," she said, her voice low, her eyes looking anywhere but at him.

"Come on, Weston, get to it."

She looked up to see him sitting in front of the lighted makeup mirror. There was a white towel slung around his neck, startling against the bronze glow of his bare arms and the black mat of his hair-covered chest.

"We haven't got all day." His voice held the snap of impatient authority.

Desi nodded silently and hefted her makeup case up onto the counter, snapping it open with nervous fingers.

Stop it, she told herself sternly, rummaging around, head down, among the various pots and tubes for the appropriate Pan-Cake color. She'd made up his face innumerable times in the past two months. There was nothing different about this time. Nothing!

But, much as she tried to convince herself otherwise, there *was* something different about it. She was more aware of him.... No! Call it by what it was. She *wanted* him more than she ever had. She burned for him. She ached. She was, she realized, literally shaking with the force of her desire.

"Are you all right?" She heard Jake's concerned voice through a fog. "Desiree?"

She looked up at that, a makeup brush slipping from her nerveless fingers. He had called her Desiree.

Their eyes touched. Held.

"You're not coming down with Dorothea's cold, are you?" he asked, but his eyes held a different question. "You look flushed." His fingertips touched her cheek gently.

She closed her eyes against the question in his, shaking her head. "No." The words were barely audible. "I'm fine."

His fingers moved from her cheek, brushing an errant strand of hair behind her ear. "Desiree," she heard him say again and then, as if he couldn't help himself, his hands cupped her face and he was drawing her mouth down to his.

The touch of his lips was so tender, so incredibly sweet, so eager that Desi was overwhelmed by the tentative stirrings of hope. He had kissed her like this before. He had touched her face . . . just so . . . before. Maybe he wasn't as indifferent to her as she had thought. Maybe.

But then she ceased to think at all as the tenderness of his kiss turned to passion. Desi took fire immediately, her body feeling as if it were going up in flames, and she made no protest when he drew her closer. And closer still, until she was standing between his legs.

"Jake," she breathed when he released her lips for an instant. "Jake..." Her voice deserted her, and she couldn't form the words she had meant to say. She couldn't even remember what she wanted to say.

"I've thought about you," he whispered, his voice muffled against the softness of her breast. "About how you taste." He nibbled at her collarbone. "How you feel." His hands smoothed down her back, pressing her hips into his aroused body. Desi moaned softly. "About the little sounds you make." One hand touched the braid that fell down her back. "I've imagined your hair spread out on my pillow."

"Oh, Jake." She couldn't believe this was happening. That he was holding her, kissing her, loving her again. It was exactly as she had imagined it would be, dreamed it would be. Jake holding her tenderly as he declared his love....

Only, she realized suddenly, he hadn't said he loved her. He wanted her. And she...she hadn't said anything because—face it—because she was afraid that he wouldn't want to hear what she had to say to him.

He wanted her. She wanted him. It should be easy, it *would* be easy to fall into bed with him again. To give in to what they both wanted. But nothing had changed, not really. She still hadn't...wouldn't...couldn't tell him about Stephanie. And he had said, hadn't he, that first day on the set, that he wanted no emotion, no feelings? If that was true, then what was this? Just physical?

Oh, she was so confused!

And so weak. Because, she knew, if he pressed her now she would give in to him. Give in to herself.

"Jake." She put her hands on his shoulders, pushing herself away from him the tiny fraction that his encircling arms would allow. "Jake. The crew's waiting. I...I haven't made up Audrey yet."

Almost immediately, as she had feared, he let her go. If he had *felt* anything for her—anything besides physical desire—he wouldn't have let her go so easily.

"You're right," he said a little raggedly. "This isn't the time for indulging myself."

His arms slipped from around her body, and his hands on her hips put her away from him. Gently, but firmly and with a frightening finality.

"Let's just forget that this happened. It was a little madness on my part." He rubbed one hand across his face in a gesture of weariness or resignation. Desi couldn't tell which. "A little...flight of fantasy." He looked into her face, his eyes unreadable. "You'd better go do Audrey. Tell her I kept you if she gives you any grief."

"But . . . your makeup?" she said uncertainly.

"Tell Evan to come on in here and earn his salary. Go on." He turned away from her. "Get going, Weston."

_____ 7 _____

"WELL, YOU FINALLY DECIDED to show up," Audrey snapped as Desi pushed open the trailer door. "Where have you been for the last hour?"

"Sorry, Audrey," was all she said as she swiftly, if somewhat shakily, began to redo the makeup that would help to transform Audrey Ferris from a contemporary woman of the eighties into the audacious flapper that had been Dorothea Heller in the Roaring Twenties.

"More kohl," Audrey ordered, almost automatically. She said that no matter how much black liner Desi had used.

"You're going to have to put that cigarette down, Audrey," she said calmly, ignoring the complaint about the kohl as she held a lipstick brush ready in her hand.

Audrey took a few more drags on the cigarette before finally crushing it in the abalone-shell ashtray in front of her.

Desi suppressed the urge to smear the brilliant red lipstick all over the other woman's face. To run screaming from the trailer and never come back. Audrey's attitude, coming on top of what had just happened in Jake's trailer, was almost too much.

Audrey wasn't worth it, she told herself, breathing deeply to calm the turmoil that raged inside of her. She was not worth it. Stifling a sigh, Desi skillfully painted on the exaggerated Clara Bow mouth that had been considered so sexy during the twenties.

Someone tapped on the door. "Two minutes, Miss Ferris," a voice said.

Desi deftly penciled in a beauty mark just under the actress's left eye. "Finished," she said, standing back to critically survey her work. Audrey looked stunning, as usual. She would be beautiful no matter what style of makeup she wore, Desi thought.

Audrey stood up, running a professional eye over her mirrored reflection. "Thanks, Weston." She tossed the words over her shoulder as she left the trailer.

Ah well, Desi thought, shrugging at her reflection in the mirror, *that's the way it goes*.

The face that stared back at her was even paler than usual, the eyes seeming almost too big for her face, the lips colorless and pinched looking.

"You look sick," she said to her reflection.

"Well, I am," her reflection seemed to answer her. "Sick and tired of this whole mess. Sick and tired of pretending that I don't feel anything. Sick and tired of working on this lousy picture! Of Jake! Of Audrey! Of everything!" She stared into her own eyes. "I should just quit. Just pack up and walk off."

But she knew she wouldn't. There was too much at stake. The professional reputation that she had strived so hard to make for herself, her film credit, her future.

Oh, why did I let that kiss happen? Why did I have to make it harder on myself? Because now it would be. Every time she had to do his makeup she'd think of . . . *No, I won't!* she told herself.

Oh, yes, you will, said a little knowing voice inside her. *All he has to do is look at you like that . . . touch you. . . .*

Why *had* he touched her? she wondered then. *No emotion*, he had said. But what had happened in his trailer if not emotion? Raw, powerful, consuming emotion. She felt absolutely sure that Jake's passion had been real. He had wanted her as intensely as she wanted him. But—what was that he had said?

This isn't the time for indulging myself.

What had he meant by that? she asked herself. Other words, other things he had said began flashing through her confused mind.

What is important is this film. I won't let anything stand in my way. Not personalities, not emotions.

He seemed to think she would get in the way of his making this film. And, if he did think that, *why?*

She looked at her face in the mirror for a few seconds more, as if the answers to her questions might be found there, and then turned and went outside to watch the filming of the next scene.

Jake and Audrey—or rather, Richard and Dorothea—stood under the overhang of one of the big gray warehouses on the south end of the wharf. She was gesturing wildly, trying desperately to explain something to the man who stood there glowering at her, his arms folded across his big broad chest.

Desi wasn't quite sure which scene this was or where in the movie it would eventually belong. But then, she was never fully certain of where any of the scenes belonged. And she was always amazed at the actors' ability to keep the scenes straight in their own minds. Nothing was ever shot in sequence—or rarely ever—and it must take intense concentration, she thought, to summon up the proper emotions when, in one scene, you were supposed to be fighting with your lover and in the very next you were meeting him for the first time.

But then, that was not her problem, Desi thought absently, her mind still on other things, as she watched the two actors continuing their scene as quarreling lovers.

"He looks *exactly* like my Richard used to when he got angry," Dorothea said softly from behind her. "Exactly. Gives me goose bumps just to watch him."

"He's going to be angry for real when he sees you standing out here in the rain again," Desi warned her. She turned briefly toward the older woman, taking her arm with the intention of walking her back toward the trailer.

"Ah, now that *really* gives me goose bumps," Dorothea whispered, and Desi's head whipped around to focus again on the quarreling lovers.

It gave her goose bumps, too—or something, anyway, she thought as her stomach curled into a fierce, tight knot of what she stubbornly refused to acknowledge as jealousy.

Jake, or rather Richard—he *is* playing Richard, she reminded herself—had ended the quarrel by grabbing Audrey roughly by the shoulders and dragging her to him, his dark head bending to subdue her with a masterful kiss. The kiss seemed to go on for an endless time, Desi thought. Audrey-Dorothea struggled against it at first, beating against his shoulders with her clenched fists and then, slowly, she melted against him and, finally, her arms wound themselves tightly around his neck in total surrender.

Every woman on the set sighed rapturously, as if she was the woman in his arms—those on the crew as well as the onlookers behind the police barricade. At that very minute he could have made love to any one of them, Desi most definitely included.

Stupid, stupid, stupid, she berated herself. *It could have been you, for real. It could have been you loving him now in his trailer if you hadn't been so concerned about the might have beens. What he might think, might feel.*

"Cut," yelled the assistant director.

The two actors drew apart slowly, appearing reluctant to part. Desi watched, stricken with jealousy but unable to look away as they stood there still clasped in each other's arms. Then Jake grinned at Audrey and Desi saw his lips move.

"Good girl," he said approvingly to his female star. "Great scene," and then began to move with her, his arm still around her shoulders, toward the trailer.

He looked up at the group that suddenly surrounded him. "That'll be it for today, kids," he said.

Behind Desi, Dorothea began to sneeze again.

"Come on," Desi said, watching Jake escort Audrey to her trailer. "That's it for today. Let's get you back to your hotel before you catch your death," she said sternly to the older woman, turning away so that she wouldn't have to see whether he went in with Audrey or not.

By the time they had gathered up their things and driven to the hotel, it was obvious that Dorothea was in no condition to be left alone. Her face was flushed, her eyes red and watery, her nose stuffy, and she had developed a nasty sounding cough to go along with the sneezing.

"Haven't you got a thermometer?" asked Desi, standing in the middle of the pale green-and-blue hotel room, hands on her hips in an attitude of half-amused exasperation.

"Never needed one," Dorothea croaked.

"Well, sit down right there." Desi pushed her gently onto the bed and then rummaged around until she found a suitcase. Efficiently she began folding clothes into it. "You're coming home with me. And don't argue—" she held up a slim hand "—it won't do you any good. I'm not leaving you here alone," she said firmly. "A hotel room is no place to be sick. You need hot tea and aspirin and lots of tender loving care. And you're most certainly not going to get it from the hotel maid."

Dorothea tried feebly to argue, but she was feeling sicker by the minute and in the end made no more protests as Desi summoned a bellboy to deal with the luggage while she bundled Dorothea into the Volkswagen Rabbit.

Teddie came out to the foyer when they pulled up in front of the dove gray Victorian on California Street.

"Teddie—" Desi performed hurried introductions "—this is Dorothea Heller. Teddie Moffet, my landlord."

"*The* Dorothea Heller?" Teddie exclaimed. "The *Devil's Lady?*"

For once Dorothea was silent and allowed Desi to answer for her. "The very same," she said as they brushed past him to hurry up the stairs. "You'll have to excuse us now though, Teddie. Dorothea has come down with a nasty cold, and I want to get her straight to bed." She paused on the landing, leaning over the carved stair rail. "I'll be down to get Stephanie just as soon as I've got Dorothea settled, okay?"

"Sure thing, Desi." Teddie disappeared back into his apartment as Desi hustled Dorothea into hers.

"This way," she said, leading Dorothea toward her own bedroom. "Bathroom's right here. Fresh towels are in that cupboard. Now you get yourself into that bed, pronto, okay? I'm going to fix you something to eat."

"Anything but chicken soup," Dorothea called after her in a feeble attempt at humor.

Desi returned to the bedroom in a surprisingly few minutes to find Dorothea snuggled down under the blue-and-white quilt, coughing into a lace-edged handkerchief. She settled the footed tray on the bed securely over Dorothea's knees. No chicken soup, as requested, but a tempting light supper of fluffy scrambled eggs, toasted English muffins with blackberry jam and a small pot of hot fragrant tea. All very attractively served on delicate rose-strewn china with a pale blue linen napkin tucked under the fork.

"Open," Desi ordered then, popping a thermometer into the older woman's mouth before she could protest.

Dorothea glared at her silently.

"Who's Stephanie?" she asked as soon as Desi removed the thermometer.

"One hundred one," said Desi, ignoring her question. "Take these." She handed Dorothea two little white pills and a larger orange one.

"What are they?" Dorothea's voice was faintly suspicious.

"Aspirin and vitamin C. They won't hurt you." She stood over her reluctant patient, watching to make sure that the pills were taken.

"Who's Stephanie?" Dorothea repeated obstinately when she had swallowed the pills.

Desi glanced down at the woman on the bed and sighed. She'd have to tell her. There was no way to hide it now. Besides, she was tired of hiding it. Tired of never being able to show off pictures of Stephanie or brag about her daughter on the set like other proud parents because Jake might see them . . . might hear her. Sick and tired. Must be her day for it, Desi thought with a flash of humor. And besides, she was not ashamed of Stephanie.

"Stephanie's my daughter," she told Dorothea, her voice full of unconscious pride.

The older woman's mouth dropped open and the cup of tea nearly slipped from her fingers. *For once I've actually suc-*

ceeded in shocking her, Desi thought with perverse pleasure.

Dorothea recovered herself quickly. "I didn't know you
had been married," she said with admirable calm.

Desi sat down on the edge of the bed. "I haven't," she said,
"and before you ask, I'm not married now. I'm not engaged
or going steady or living with anybody either. That's all I'm
going to say on the subject. And I'd appreciate it if you didn't
say anything else, to *anyone,* either. Clear?"

Dorothea nodded. "Quite clear," she said and picked up a
toasted muffin. "Am I allowed to ask how old she is?"

"Yes, of course. Stephanie's almost four months."

Dorothea was silent for a moment, chewing on her muffin. "That's her?" Her sharp black eyes indicated the framed
picture on the nightstand. Desi nodded. "A very pretty baby,"
Dorothea said at last. "Looks remarkably like you."

"Thank you." Desi jumped up from the bed. "If you have
everything you need for a few minutes, I'll go down to Teddie's and get her." She caught the speculative look on Dorothea's face. "Teddie is my landlord, Dorothea, and my
baby-sitter. He works at home," she explained easily. "The
creative half of an interior-design business—and he's crazy
about Stephanie. But that's all he is. Okay?"

"Certainly," Dorothea said a bit huffily, "I never thought
he was anything else." She chuckled. "I could see *immediately* that you're not his type."

Desi grinned and hurried out of the room. She was always
so eager to see her baby at the end of the day. To find out what
miraculous new changes had taken place. She was acutely
aware of how fast Stephanie was growing and of how much
she had already missed by being away from her for most of
the day. But she loved her job, too, and she knew that she
made a much better mother for Stephanie because she had
something interesting and fulfilling to do during the day. Besides, someone had to make a living for them. Still, she reflected, it was hard.

"She's been an angel, as usual," bragged Teddie, bundling Stephanie up as if she would be traveling across town instead of just going upstairs.

Desi smiled lovingly down at the baby in her arms, and the tight ball of misery that had been forming inside her seemed to melt. Here was her salvation. Her daughter. The tiny being who made everything worthwhile. Everything better.

"Hello, darling." She kissed the silky cheek of her child, nuzzling the tender folds of the baby-scented neck. "Mommie missed you today."

She looked up. "Thanks, Teddie," she said, and impulsively she reached out to touch his arm. "I can't tell you how much I appreciate everything you're doing for us. How grateful I am for your friendship. You know if there's *anything* I can do for you...."

"Well, there *is* something," Teddie said slowly.

"Anything," she said eagerly. Teddie would not allow her to pay him anything for his loving care of Stephanie. "I'm home all day anyway," he'd said when she tried to make some sort of financial arrangement with him. He had accepted a new ficus tree, though, and she'd bought him the latest Pavarotti album as a surprise gift, but that was hardly enough, Desi thought.

"I'd like to meet Dorothea Heller. I just *loved* reading *Devil's Lady*," he gushed.

"Oh, sure. She'll probably be in bed for a few days with this cold, but as soon as she's better you and Larry can come up for dinner, okay? I'll make Mexican." She headed up the stairs with Stephanie in her arms. "I'll let you know when," she promised.

8

THE DINNER PARTY was a complete success, as Desi had been sure it would be. Dorothea and Teddie turned out to be sisters under the skin—so to speak—and had a truly marvelous time topping each other's outrageous stories. That they had little regard for the strict truth or the reputation of their victims only made it more fun. Desi found herself laughing until the tears flowed and she had collapsed weakly onto the floor in front of the fireplace. Even the quieter Larry had lost most of his reticence under the spell of Dorothea's warm charm—and the cold bubbling champagne that she insisted on buying as her contribution to the dinner party. She had overruled Desi's suggestion that a good Mexican beer, like Dos Equis, would go better with the planned menu.

"Nonsense," was Dorothea's characteristic reply. "Champagne goes with everything," she said, and ordered a whole case of the stuff.

"There's only going to be four of us," Desi tried to tell her when she came home from the set that evening.

"Well, we don't have to drink it all tonight, dear girl," Dorothea said reasonably. "Put some in your orange juice tomorrow morning." She skillfully opened a bottle and poured some into a fragile, etched wineglass. "Here, take this into the bath with you. It will get you in the mood for the party. And wear something pretty," she ordered, "not those old slacks of yours." She looked very festive herself in a heavy black satin caftanlike dress—a Halston, Desi thought—and, of course, it was adorned by all of her magnificent rubies and the snowy crown of her braided hair.

So Desi took her champagne with her into the bathroom and sipped at it as she bathed and powdered and perfumed and dressed herself, as ordered, in something pretty. A "lounging outfit" put together from special finds in local sec- ondhand shops. Satiny, loose-fitting pants with an elastic waistband and a tiny camisole-style top that, she was sure, had once been a pair of pajamas belonging to a slinky siren of the twenties or thirties. The material was a tissue-thin silk, and the color was the pale lavender of an orchid. Over this she added a floating, knee-length kimono wrap in a deli- cious shade of strawberry sherbet, delicately embroidered with a single exotic flower on the back, and more flowers scattered randomly down one sleeve.

She left her pretty feet bare, the polished toenails peeking out from under the floppy hem of the silk pants. Her face was expertly made up with smoky purple and lavender shadows highlighting her wide violet eyes, and a rose-tinted gloss ac- centuating the curve of her lips. She let her long coppery hair flow freely down her back, its wild curliness confined only by the enameled comb that held it up and back on one side.

She dressed Stephanie up for the party, too. Not in one of Teddie's lacy little gifts, but in a minuscule pair of buttercup yellow cotton pajamas purchased for less than five dollars in San Francisco's Chinatown. They had little red frog-type closings down the front and red piping around the cuffs and sleeves and a tiny mandarin collar.

"Pretty enough?" Desi questioned.

She stood framed in the living-room doorway, a slim young woman with all the grace of a dancer, in pink and lavender silks. The beautiful baby in her arms was gurgling delight- edly as she tangled one chubby fist in her mother's flaming hair.

"Lovely," said Dorothea sincerely, and then, almost to herself, "I do pity the man who's missing all of this." She made a sweeping gesture that took in the warm, inviting room and the even more inviting glow of the beautiful mother and child.

"He doesn't know," Desi said, coming into the room. "And what he doesn't know won't hurt him . . . or me. Right?"

Dorothea obviously did not agree, but before she could voice her opinion the doorbell rang; a triple chime that echoed throughout the apartment.

"Let them in, will you?" Desi put the baby on her quilt on the floor. "I'll go get the nachos."

Some ESP must have been working because Teddie and Larry had dressed for the occasion, too. Larry, as always, was the more conservative of the two in soft tan slacks, a burgundy velour pullover and no jewelry except for the ring on his left hand. He looked very much like the soft-spoken, high-school music teacher that he was. Teddie, however, with his flair for the dramatic and his faultless taste, was resplendent in pale gray suede slacks topped by a midnight blue velvet blazer. A silk ascot in a paisley print of blue and gray, with just the right touch of dark red, was tucked into the collar of a pale blue shirt that was the exact color of his eyes. It was secured by a diamond stickpin. Desi thought he looked like a young English lord from some silly romantic novel.

For once he seemed to approve of how Desi had dressed herself and, more importantly, Stephanie.

"She looks gorgeous," he complimented Desi when she came back into the room with the tray of nachos. "Just like a little princess. Don't you, my precious?" he cooed at the baby as he bounced her in his lap, totally unconcerned about the damage she might do to his immaculate suede slacks. Desi smiled at him indulgently and went to get the champagne.

Stephanie was put to bed about an hour later after being duly petted and praised, but the grown-ups stayed up much longer. It was, in fact, almost three in the morning by the time the party broke up. They had long since stuffed themselves with the plates of nachos and miniature tacos and Desi's homemade *chili rellenos* made with mild Monterey Jack cheese and served with fluffy Mexican-style rice. Dorothea had been right about the champagne. They drank nearly a third of what she had ordered.

Teddie and Larry moved with exaggerated care down the stairs to their apartment, giggling drunkenly as they went. Dorothea, however, was none the worse for wear. She had amazing stamina for a woman of her age—the short time it had taken her to convalesce from her rather bad cold attested to that fact. She was up at her usual time the next morning—just after the crack of dawn—and when Desi stumbled into the sunny kitchen a couple of hours later she found Dorothea and Stephanie happily communing over soft-boiled eggs and mashed bananas.

Desi poured herself a cup of coffee. "Dorothea, how *can* you?" She grimaced in the direction of the table and the revolting mess of food that the older woman was spooning into the baby's open mouth.

"She was hungry." Dorothea shrugged, pausing to sip her mimosa, a mixture of champagne and fresh orange juice.

"No, I mean the champagne!" Desi came to the table, smiling a good-morning at her daughter as she tickled the baby's bare tummy where it protruded from under the already too-small T-shirt. "I should think you couldn't even stand the smell of the stuff after last night."

"*I* wasn't one of those who overindulged," Dorothea reminded her.

"Hmm. You drank as much as anybody. More."

"Ah, yes, but I can handle it." She looked over at Desi and smiled smugly. "Apparently you young people can't."

Desi smiled back. "I'm beginning to think we young people can't handle half of what you do," she said, complimenting the other woman. She meant the words sincerely.

In the past few months Dorothea had succeeded in surprising her more than once, most especially during these three weeks when she had been sharing Desi's home. Not only had she gotten over her cold in record time and not only could she drink an unbelievable amount of champagne without ever seeming to feel the effects, but she had quickly become a favorite with Teddie and Larry, she had utterly charmed Desi's mother over the phone, and she was wonderful with Stephanie, too. She handled her as easily as Desi did, with none of the hesitancy or impatience that might be expected of a woman over eighty years old. And she hadn't said a word to anyone on the set about Desi's daughter.

"Have I told you how much I enjoy having you here?" Desi said impulsively, her hand reaching out to cover Dorothea's.

"A lot of bother," Dorothea responded quickly, coloring a little at Desi's warm words.

It was the first time Desi had ever seen her blush.

"No, I mean it," Desi hastened to assure her. "You've been wonderful with Stephanie. And you haven't told Jake—I mean, anyone on the set about her. I appreciate that. It's hard enough to maintain a professional image as it is, but if he...if they knew...." Her voice trailed off as Dorothea caught and held her eyes.

"Jake is Stephanie's father, isn't he, Desi?"

Desi stared back for a long, considering minute. "Yes," she said, then added, "Is it so obvious?"

Dorothea shrugged and spooned another mouthful of mashed bananas into Stephanie's open rosebud mouth. "No, not obvious. At least, not to just anyone. It's a lot of little things. Her name...I happen to know Jake's middle is Stephen," she explained. "Her eyes. But that didn't really click until recently. Mostly it's the way you look at him with your whole heart shining in your eyes. Even when he's bellowing at you like a maddened bull you look at him that way. I'm not so old that I can't recognize a woman in love when I see one." She paused reflectively. "Or a man, either, for that matter."

"Oh, no." The words were out before Desi could think. "He doesn't love me."

"Nonsense," snapped Dorothea. "That man devours you with his eyes every time he looks at you. He's possessive, too." She chuckled. "Doesn't even like Evan to come too close. If that's not a man in love, then I don't know what is," she declared. She looked up. "I thought, that day on the set a few weeks back, that you had both come to your senses."

Desi looked at her blankly.

"You spent a considerable amount of time in Jake's trailer, dear girl, and his makeup wasn't done when you came out."

"That's not love. It's lust." Desi attempted a brave, self-mocking smile and failed miserably. "Pure, old-fashioned lust . . . well, maybe not *pure*," she amended with a small smile, her sense of humor, as always, coming to her rescue.

"Lust can sometimes be the start of love," Dorothea said gently. "It was that way for my Richard and I, you know. He *wanted* me long before he *loved* me."

"Not in this case." Desi was horrified to find herself starting to cry. "I'm sorry, Dorothea. I'm not usually a crybaby." She wiped ineffectively at her eyes. "It's over with, anyway." She stood up and went to the sink, patting at her teary face with a cool cloth. She wrung it out and came over to the table to clean up Stephanie's face and hands after her breakfast.

"I have Stephanie, and I'll always be grateful to him for that even if he doesn't know it. But it *is* over," she said firmly, smiling down at the baby through her tears, "if you can call something that never really started over." It was a brave speech, but her hands trembled and her voice shook.

"It's never over, dear girl. Not if you still love him that much." She reached out and grasped Desi's hands, pulling her back down into her chair. "It might help if you tell me about it," she urged.

And suddenly Desi found herself pouring out the whole story. She told Dorothea about the first time she had seen Jake, so mesmerizing on the set of *December Fire*, and how she must have fallen in love with him then without fully realizing it. She told her how she had followed his career, almost obsessively, all those years and about the meeting on the plane, the hotel; his tenderness and sensitivity and her own total lack of shame concerning that weekend and, later, the resulting pregnancy . . . about her loneliness that Sunday morning, with only his brief note for company.

She talked unable to stop, it seemed, now that she had started, about how very much she had wanted the baby, how joyously she had looked forward to the birth, how rapturously happy she had been when Stephanie was put into her arms for the first time . . . and how desperately, how very desperately, she had wanted Jake then.

She tried to explain why she had let Evan talk her into working on Jake's film, what it would mean to her career and their future—hers and Stephanie's—and why she was now finding it so much more difficult to work with him than she ever imagined it would be. How hard it was to look at him each day and not tell him how much she loved him. To not just blurt out the news that he was a father.

And, now, how important it was to protect Stephanie from any of the publicity that would surely result if it was found out that she was Jake Lancing's illegitimate daughter. The one thing Desi would *not* do, she told Dorothea over and over again, was to subject Stephanie to the wrath of a father who didn't want her.

"How do you know he doesn't want her?" Dorothea asked when Desi's torrent of impassioned words finally ceased.

"His views on children are public knowledge," she said, in a voice still husky with tears, "those two paternity suits and his reaction to—"

"Nonsense," snapped Dorothea. "They obviously weren't his children. Just as Stephanie obviously is. Those paternity suits are irrelevant."

"Maybe." Desi unwillingly acknowledged the validity of Dorothea's argument. "But the main thing—the *relevant* thing—is that he doesn't love Stephanie's mother. I think…I think, maybe, he still *wants* me but—"

"Of course he wants you!" Dorothea interrupted.

"But he doesn't *love* me," Desi went on as if there had been no interruption, "and I won't subject Stephanie, or myself," she added truthfully, "to any kind of half life."

Dorothea's expression asked her to elaborate.

"I know enough about Jake to know that he's what you and Evan would call an honorable man. He . . . Evan told me that he supported Lisa Kendall's child until she got married, even though he didn't think the baby was his because . . . because it *could* have been. I don't want that from him, Dorothea. I couldn't take it if he ended up feeling about me the way he must feel about her. And even if he did believe that Stephanie was his . . . well . . ." she said stubbornly, her chin up. "I

wouldn't marry a man who didn't love me, even for the sake
of my child." She looked at Stephanie. "Especially for the
sake of my child."

"How do you know that he doesn't love you? He certainly
acts like a man in love . . . angry and jealous, certainly, but
definitely in love."

"That's not jealousy, Dorothea," she said almost bitterly,
"not in any real sense. He's just watching me to make sure that
I can do my job. He doesn't—or didn't—think I could, you
know. He thinks—thought—oh, I don't know!" She looked
up, her violet eyes swimming in tears again. "At the kick-off
party he actually suggested—no, he *said*—that Evan was my
lover. Evan! Can you believe that? Evan's like a father to me!
But Jake said that if Evan had hired me for other than my so-
called artistic talent that he'd fire me so fast that my head
would spin. Does that sound like a man in love to you, Dorothea? It doesn't to me."

The older woman hesitated, looking for the right words,
and Desi took her silence as an admission that she had no
answer for that.

"I'm really sorry, Dorothea. I didn't mean to cry all over
you . . . but, thanks for listening." She picked up Stephanie
from her infant seat, cuddling the tiny, precious body to her
breast. "Thanks for feeding Stephanie, too. I'd better get her
dressed." She glanced at the old gilt wall clock. "Me, too, if
we're not going to be late for work. Jake," her voice faltered
slightly as she said his name, but she squared her shoulders,
visibly struggling to control her tears, "Jake wants to finish
up this week in San Francisco as soon as possible."

Dorothea reached up and tenderly touched Desi's arm. "I
still think you should tell Jake, my dear. He's been under a
lot of strain lately, you know. This film is terribly important
to him. Terribly. He's trying to prove that he's more than just
a magnificent male animal, trained to do tricks in front of the
camera. Not that Jake would put it that way, but you know
what I mean. I think you should overlook his bad behavior
and give him a chance. Tell him about Stephanie," she urged.

"No." Desi's voice was firm and her eyes, though red-rimmed, were dry and clear. "No. I can't and I won't. Oh, please don't look at me like that, Dorothea. I know he's been under a lot of strain. You only have to look at his eyes to see—" She had a sudden stomach-wrenching thought. "You have to promise not to tell him either, Dorothea."

Dorothea nodded hesitantly.

"*Promise* me you won't tell him," Desi insisted.

"I promise I won't tell him," Dorothea said solemnly.

DESI WENT ABOUT HER JOB for the next few days with a vague feeling of apprehension hanging over her head. It wasn't that she didn't trust Dorothea—but Jake was such a favorite of the old lady's, and he reminded her so much of her beloved Richard. Add to that the fact that Dorothea felt that she—Desi—was doing the wrong thing....

It caused Desi to be apprehensive. Quite justifiably apprehensive, she thought. Especially when she caught sight of Dorothea and Evan, their heads together, as they conversed very quietly, glancing her way now and then. Evan didn't think she was doing the right thing either. He'd told her that more than once.

"You're underestimating him, luv," he'd said in that understated British way of his. "Jake's not the kind of man to turn his back on his responsibilities."

"I'm not his responsibility!" Desi shot back.

"No, but Stephanie is, or should be," he answered her with calm logic. "Besides, luv, don't you think that your daughter should know her father? One day she'll ask, you know, and then what will you say?"

But Desi had already resolved to face that problem when she came to it. It wouldn't happen for years yet. And, in the meantime, Evan and Dorothea had both promised not to tell. No matter what their personal feelings were they had assured her that they wouldn't say anything to Jake.

And she believed them. Still, she couldn't shake the feeling they were planning *something*.

"Weston!" Jake summoned her with his usual abruptness, and Desi took a deep breath, preparing to face him. To pretend. He hadn't referred to that afternoon again and, so, neither had she.

"Weston, where are you?"

"Here." She came up behind him, her sneakered feet masking the sound of her footsteps.

He turned to her, no sign on his handsome face to show that she had startled him, although she knew she had. She could tell by the tensing of his shoulder muscles when she had spoken from behind him.

"Have you got Audrey and Michael ready for this next scene?" he asked.

The question was totally unnecessary, she thought with a brief flash of irritation. Both Audrey and Michael were standing directly in his line of vision, not twenty feet away, talking over the scene with two other supporting actors and the assistant director while they waited for Jake to join them. He was in this scene, too. Any fool could see that they were ready!

Even Jake, she thought, a small grin suddenly dispelling her agitation.

"You find something amusing, Weston?"

Her grin faded, replaced instantly by the carefully blank look that she cultivated over these past couple of weeks to protect herself from him. And from her own emotions. Or, at least, she hoped it was blank. Dorothea had seen something, hadn't she?

"It's nothing," Desi said. He still scowled down at her. "Nothing to do with you," she lied. "Just a passing thought—"

"Everything on this set has to do with me," he informed her arrogantly. "You'd save yourself a lot of trouble if you learned that, Weston."

"Yes, sir," she said, suppressing the absurd desire to salute him. "I'll try to remember that, sir."

He grinned then, a curiously unwilling sort of acknowledgment of his own bad temper. "You do that, Weston," he said softly, his eyes roaming hungrily over her upturned face. He half raised a hand as if to touch her.

Desi felt her breath catch somewhere in her throat. She felt, almost, as if he was asking her a question. Lots of questions. *Ask me,* her mind urged him silently. *Ask me. Whatever it is, I'll say yes.*

"Is there anything else?" she said instead.

"No, nothing." He looked at his hand, suspended there halfway between them, as though he had no idea of how it had moved. It dropped to his side. "Just get out of my way," he said with no particular inflection or tone.

When she turned to go, he reached out again and touched her arm. "Look," he said haltingly, his long fingers pressing into the sleeve of her down jacket, "forget what I just said, okay? I've been a little touchy lately." He turned and strode briskly away from her.

"I wish I could hate him," she whispered to herself. "It would be easier if I could just hate him."

But she didn't. She loved him. Loved him more each day, it seemed, no matter what he said, or didn't say, or how he made her feel.

I must be a masochist, she thought, *to continue to want a man who doesn't want me.*

God, I don't think I can stand this until the picture is over. It gets harder and harder to look at him every day. Wanting him, loving him...and getting only indifference and the cold politeness of a stranger. Nothing, not even her first movie credit was worth it.

But in another month and a half or so it wouldn't matter anyway, she reminded herself. They would be finished shooting in San Francisco today, and then the whole company would be moved up to Dorothea's house in Sonoma to film the final scenes of *Devil's Lady.* Two months, at most, and it would be over. She would have done her job—gotten that all-important film credit—and if she was very, very lucky she would never have to work for or with Jake Lancing again.

She tried to smile at that, ignoring the fact that the thought gave her no pleasure. None at all.

She shrugged and turned away from the action going on in front of the cameras. This was the last scene for today, and when it was finished the technicians would start packing up for the move to Sonoma. She might as well start putting away her own equipment now. It wouldn't be needed until Monday morning—early—at the new location. As soon as she heard the word "cut" she would be ready to leave. She was looking forward to the weekend. Just herself and Stephanie, since Dorothea was packed and ready to leave for Sonoma after the day's shoot.

"I want to get a head start," she had told Desi, "see that the beds have been made up and the rooms aired properly and, of course, get enough of Richard's best champagne on ice. You, dear girl, will stay at the main house with me. No, no, don't argue. You are most definitely *not* going to a hotel," she insisted. "I simply won't hear of it! Not after I've imposed upon your generous hospitality for nearly a month. Aren't any decent hotels anyway," she added, as if that settled it. Which, as far as Dorothea was concerned, it did.

In the normal course of events Desi would have been eagerly looking forward to spending time in a turn-of-the-century mansion—and mansion she knew it must be. Despite Dorothea's casual references to a "drafty old house," she had also mentioned a cook and an upstairs maid and had said that not only would Desi be her houseguest but several others of the cast and crew as well.

"Bring some of your pretty clothes, dear girl," she instructed Desi. "We dress for dinner." Her black eyes twinkled wickedly. "Jake will look magnificent in evening clothes, don't you think?"

There was the rub, of course. Jake. He would be staying at Dorothea's house, too. Could she take twenty-four hours a day of Jake? Desi wondered fearfully. Working, eating, relaxing—or trying to relax—with him always there...sleeping under the same roof . . . with their shared memories and that hungry look that he sometimes got in his eyes? The same look that Dorothea said was in hers. Could she endure that without *something* happening?

Well, she could, she decided, because she had to. There was no other choice. After all, Dorothea would be there, and Evan. Jake wasn't likely to break down her door—no matter how hungrily he sometimes looked at her—not with a house full of people surrounding them.

But what about you? a little voice inside her whispered traitorously. *What's to keep you from creeping to his door in the middle of some long sleepless night?*

Even now, when he had just been so strange and abrupt with her, the thought of him sleeping under the same roof was unnervingly exciting. After the way he had been treating her, it shouldn't be. But, to her everlasting shame, it was.

"Cut!" The assistant director's voice carried through the open door of the trailer, where Desi was packing her equipment into a big, hard-sided, compartmentalized case. She snapped the metal clasps shut and hauled it off the makeup table, slinging her satchel over her other shoulder.

"See you on Monday," she called to Dorothea as she headed down the crowded street to her car.

9

"NIGHT, ANGEL," Desi whispered. She reached out to tenderly stroke the little red head and adjust the bunny-strewn blanket more comfortably over her sleeping baby.

Now she could have her own bath—or shower, rather—and then to bed. It had been a long day and tomorrow morning she and Stephanie were going to drive down to Santa Cruz to visit Grandma and Grandpa for the weekend. It had been a while since they'd all seen each other. A month or so at least.

She went into her bathroom, blue and white like the attached bedroom, and began preparations for bed; carefully creaming her skin of the day's grime, cleaning her teeth, shampooing her long hair under the piercing spray of the shower. She decided to give herself a hair-conditioning treatment—one of her little beauty rituals that had been inconvenient when Dorothea was sharing the bathroom with her. When that was finished she was no longer sleepy, so she decided to give herself a pedicure, too. There must be a good movie on cable tonight that she could watch while she pampered herself.

She blow-dried her hair, tying it back out of the way with a pink ribbon, and wrapped her creamed and powdered body in a silvery-sheened pink-on-pink kimono. Barefoot, she padded first to the kitchen for a glass of Dorothea's champagne and then into the living room. She switched on the portable television and settled back on the comfortable rose-colored sofa, her feet propped up on the coffee table in front of her. Threading a piece of surgical cotton under and over her toes to keep the polish from smearing, she then carefully began to paint the nails with the newest Revlon color.

"French lilac," the bottle said. Well, it sounded pretty, she thought, but it looked like plain old pink to her. She shrugged. Maybe French lilacs *were* pink.

Between sips of champagne and pauses to watch Fred and Ginger execute a particularly tricky dance number she got the requisite three coats of polish applied. She was settled back on the sofa, her feet still propped up on the coffee table and carefully crossed at the ankles, and was thinking about getting up during the next commercial to pour herself another glass of champagne when the doorbell rang.

Now who could that be? she thought with annoyance as she got up and walked—on her heels and slightly duck-footed because of the cotton—toward the front door.

"Teddie?" she said, peering through the peephole.

Not Teddie.

"Jake," she said in a small voice as she automatically opened the door.

"Hello, Weston," he said casually.

"Hello, Jake." She repeated his name softly, somehow unable to say anything else at the moment. Or even *think* of anything else. His appearance was such a surprise and yet . . . not a surprise. She had imagined him, so many times, knocking on her door. She had imagined what he would say, what she would say . . . but, just now, she couldn't seem to remember any of it as he stood there looking so tall and vital and incredibly sexy.

He was dressed much as he had been that first night. Slim tailored slacks, pale gray tonight instead of tan, his white shirt unbuttoned to a modest V but still managing to reveal an intriguing amount of dark chest hair. He had on the same black leather jacket, too, and the same tantalizing cologne.

Oh God, he looked so good and smelled so good and, despite everything, she was very glad he was there.

"You plan on keeping me standing here all night?" His deep seductive voice prodded her and his eyes—his dark beautiful eyes—surveyed her slowly, as she had unconsciously been surveying him.

One slender hand came up to nervously finger the neckline of her robe, adjusting the flat lapels closer together. "Uh, no, of course not," she said, a little breathlessly. "Please come in."

He brushed past her before she could step back, and his upper arm skimmed lightly against her silk-covered breasts. She felt the brief fluttering contact like a tingling jolt of electricity through her body, and she took a hurried step backward, still balancing awkwardly on her heels.

Jake's expressive face indicated concern. "You okay, Weston?" he said, reaching out for her elbow to steady her.

She backed away again, avoiding his touch. "I'm fine," she said, pointing to her toes.

He glanced down at her bare feet, and his expression changed immediately to one of half-amused curiosity. "What are you doing? Surgery?" he asked.

"Just polishing them," she informed him, unable to suppress a small answering smile of her own even though her insides were churning. What was he doing there? What did he want?

"Did you want me for something?" she said then.

"Not you," he denied, but his eyes gave lie to his words, caressing her with a look, touching her in a way that was almost physical. "I came to see Dorothea. Where is she?"

"Dorothea? She's gone to Sonoma already. She left after the day's shoot."

"Left?" He hesitated for a moment, uncertainty flickering across his face. "Already?"

"Yes, already." What did he want to see Dorothea for? she wondered. "She said she wanted to put some of Richard's best champagne on ice before we all descend on her," Desi added softly, her lips curving into a sweet smile in an unconscious effort to clear the frown from his face. "Was it important?"

"Was what important?" he asked absently, his eyes focused on her lips.

Desi took a step backward. "W-what you wanted to see Dorothea about. Was it important?"

"No," he said, still staring at her mouth. "I mean yes," he corrected himself, seeming to literally shake himself awake. He tore his eyes away from her lips with an effort.

"Yes," he said again, more firmly. "It's important. She said there was something in one of the upcoming scenes that she wanted to go over before we start shooting on Monday." He hesitated. An infinitesimal pause that would have gone unnoticed if she hadn't been watching him so carefully. "She asked me to come over tonight."

"Dorothea asked you to come over? Here? I don't believe it." Desi shook her head. "She knew she was leaving. She wouldn't—" She broke off, a terrible thought suddenly occurring to her. Dorothea most definitely *would*. It would be just like her to invite Jake over there for some trumped-up reason when she didn't plan to be there herself.

Oh Lord, surely she hadn't told. No, of course not. If she had told him, Jake wouldn't be standing there so casually. He would be raging at her and flinging awful accusations all over the room.

The room! Desi's eyes flew guiltily around the living room, looking for telltale signs of Stephanie. The pastel quilt lay folded over the back of a chair—but that was okay. It could be any quilt, not just one meant for a baby. Worse were the pictures of Stephanie displayed around the room.

But there were lots of other family pictures, she reassured herself; her parents, her brothers, Evan and even Teddie and Larry. Stephanie's were just a few among many. He wouldn't notice.

And if he did—if he did—she would just say that Stephanie was her niece. Besides, she would have him out of there in a few minutes. Simple.

"As you can see, Dorothea isn't here," she said. "She must have forgotten that she invited you over. I guess it will just have to wait until you see her in Sonoma." She made a subtle gesture, tacitly inviting him to leave.

He ignored the hint and moved farther into the living room, turning to face her where she still stood at the door, one hand resting on the ornate door handle. "Dorothea was really upset about that scene," he said softly, his dark eyes taking in her slender kimono-clad form from top to bottom. "Maybe she said something to you about it . . . ?"

His voice trailed off as he stood there, staring at the vision she made in her thin pink kimono. Her stubbornly curly hair was tied loosely back from her face, tumbling in coppery waves almost to her waist. Her eyes were wide and inviting, her pale skin flushed, and those ridiculous strips of cotton through her polished toes were somehow charmingly endearing.

"No—" Desi shook her head slowly "—she didn't mention it . . . I . . ." Her voice, too, seemed to desert her as she stared back at him, mesmerized by the smoldering gleam in his eyes.

Funny, she thought distractedly, how such dark eyes could shine so and still seem to get darker and darker. They drew her deeper into their hypnotic depths, leading her farther into something . . . someplace that she was more than willing to go.

Jake made a movement toward her, a barely perceptible lift of his hands, a tensing of his powerful shoulders under the leather jacket, as if he were reaching for her.

Desi hurriedly dropped her eyes, breaking his hold on her. "Maybe . . . maybe she left her script here," she suggested softly. "If you want to wait for a minute—" she glanced up, her eyes silently, unconsciously inviting him to stay "—I'll check for you."

Jake nodded his head once. That brief, characteristic gesture that she knew so well. "I'll wait," he said.

"If it's here, it's probably in the bedroom." She pushed the front door shut, its soft click sounding strangely final somehow, and motioned him toward the satin sofa. "Sit down, Jake. It might take me a few minutes to find it."

As he turned away from her, moving toward the sofa, Desi bent down swiftly and yanked the cotton strips from between her toes, bunching them into a ball in her fist. She straightened to find Jake eyeing her with knowing amusement. "I'll just be a minute," she stammered, escaping across the room to the hallway.

But she didn't find Dorothea's script in her bedroom because Dorothea had taken it with her to Sonoma. Desi knew that when she offered to look for it, but she *had* to get out of the living room for a few minutes—before she flung herself into his arms.

Because, even now, she wanted to feel Jake's arms around her, feel her arms around him. She wanted to wipe the strains of overwork and worry from his beautiful brown eyes in any way that she could.

Automatically, in an effort to give herself more time, she began opening her desk drawers, looking for the nonexistent script.

Why was he here? she wondered again. Had Dorothea really asked him to come over tonight, knowing she wouldn't be there when he did? Desi knew that Dorothea was capable of such a thing. There was no doubt of that. But she had promised not to tell him about Stephanie, and Dorothea was not the kind of person to break a promise, even indirectly. But, then, if she hadn't invited him over, why was he there? Had he really expected Dorothea to be there—or had he known she *wouldn't* be?

She remembered, suddenly, those looks she had intercepted on the set. The looks of confused desire, of longing and, lately, of a sort of grudging respect. She remembered, too, what had happened that day in his trailer. "Love sometimes comes from lust," Dorothea had said.

Was it possible? Could he have really come there tonight to see *her*? Was his story about Dorothea and the script just a ruse, an excuse?

Hope surged in Desi. A wild rush of joy that she tried, unsuccessfully, to stamp down.

Maybe he *had* come to see her!

And, then, so what if he had? It would make no difference. She still couldn't tell him about Stephanie.

She shut the last desk drawer, and then opened it again and picked up her own copy of the script. She had to have some reason for taking so long. She headed back into the living room, pausing briefly to check on Stephanie. Good baby that she was, she still slept soundly, her knees drawn up slightly under her, one small fist tucked under her chin. She had managed to kick most of her covers off, and Desi crossed the room to pull them up again.

"Your daddy's in the living room," she whispered to the sleeping baby. She reached out, resting her hand against the baby's soft cheek. It felt a little warm and the wispy curls at the nape of her neck were a bit damp. But she slept soundly, her breathing was quiet and even, so Desi simply smoothed her hair back and made a mental note to watch Stephanie more closely for the next few days. It was not impossible, she thought, that Stephanie could be catching Dorothea's cold.

"I couldn't find Dorothea's script," she said, coming into the living room, determined to be businesslike for the few minutes that he would be there. "But I brought my copy in case—" she began to explain, and then stopped. Jake appeared to be asleep.

He was sitting in the middle of the sofa, his long arms stretched along the back of it, his dark head resting tiredly against the rose-colored satin.

"She mentioned a scene," he said, opening his eyes as he reached out an arm for the script she held. "Maybe looking through it will give me a hint." He began flipping through it.

Desi stood apprehensively at the edge of the sofa, watching him as he looked for the proper scene. This wasn't how it was supposed to go. She had expected him to get up and leave when she couldn't produce Dorothea's script. Not sit there, idly thumbing through hers. Every minute he was here was dangerous. To Stephanie. To her. Mostly to her, she acknowledged silently. Just looking at Jake was dangerous for her.

Jake looked up suddenly. "Sit down, Weston," he ordered, "and quit fidgeting while I try to figure out what Dorothea meant."

"My name is Desi," she shot back, not bothering to stop and think about what she said, "or Miss Weston, if you insist, but I refuse to be called Weston like some upstairs maid in my own home!"

"Desiree, then," he said softly, and his eyes blazed up at her hotly.

"Desi," she insisted weakly. Not Desiree, please. Plain Weston was better than that. Desiree brought back those nights in his arms, the touch of his lips.

"Desiree," he said again, his eyes never leaving her face. He laid the script aside, and it slid off the sofa and onto the floor. Neither of them noticed it. "Come here." He patted the space next to him.

Desi hesitated uncertainly, traitorous desire and common sense at war in her slender body. It would be easy to forget these past few months, to forget his harsh words and unfair accusations, to just sink down beside him and lose herself in the smoldering depths of his dark eyes.

So easy.

But remember what happened the last time you blindly followed your instincts, she warned herself. *There's a four-month-old baby asleep in the other room if you need a reminder. A baby who was the direct result of the last time you allowed yourself to melt in this man's arms.*

Much as she loved her daughter, much as she could not now imagine a life without her tiny presence, she was not ready for another such experience. True, she was on the Pill now. Her obstetrician had prescribed it shortly after Stephanie was born, in an effort to regulate her erratic menstrual cycle. But that was no excuse for letting herself go.

And besides, she had more pride than that, she told herself fiercely. More pride and more self-respect! She would *not* be a slave to her desire for him. Nothing could come of it. Nothing except more pain.

"Desiree," he said again, and there was warm entreaty buried in the deep seductive tones of his voice.

I know a man in love when I see one, Dorothea had told her. *Jealous and angry, maybe, but in love.*

Was he? Desi wondered. Maybe he loved her just a little. Maybe Dorothea was right—lust did lead to love sometimes.

His dark eyes tempted her, and his hand reached out and lightly grasped one end of the sash that belted her kimono, pulling her slowly, inexorably, toward him.

She clutched at the sash, resisting him. "Jake, please," she stammered. "I . . . no . . ."

"Desiree," he repeated her name again, as if he knew how it affected her. How it set her insides to burning just to hear it on his lips. He continued to pull on her sash as he spoke, and she stumbled forward, sinking down onto the sofa beside him.

"No, Jake, please. Don't. . .don't kiss me." Her hands came up, pushing against his chest to hold him off. But it was only a halfhearted effort at best. She wanted him so much.

"Don't you want me to kiss you, Desiree?" he whispered seductively, his hands on her upper arms. "I want to kiss you," he said. "I'm dying to kiss you again! To make love to—"

"No." Desi stopped him from saying more. If he said any more, she would melt. "It wouldn't solve anything, Jake. It wouldn't change the way you f-feel about me." *Or the way I feel about you,* she added silently.

"I've already changed the way I feel about you," he murmured huskily. His hands continued to move lightly, hypnotically, up and down her arms.

"You have?" she said, going very still. Her mouth felt dry suddenly. "Why?" she whispered hoarsely. "When?"

"I've been watching you on the set." His gaze roamed hungrily over her face, touching briefly on her widely violet eyes, her flushed cheeks, her softly parted lips. He took a shaky breath. "You're good at your job. Very good. And professional. And I've come to realize that, whatever else he may have been to you in the past, Evan isn't your lover now."

"He never was my lover," Desi interjected softly, her eyes searching his.

"Never?" His hands slid up over her shoulders to her neck. His fingers curled around the pale slim column of her throat, tilting her head back, as his thumbs drew small drugging circles at her temples.

"Never," she repeated, a catch in her voice. "Evan's like a father to me. He's—"

"I'm glad." He bent closer. "So glad."

"Jake . . . Jake, this is ridiculous," she said, trying just once more, to reason with him—and herself—as his arms came around her. "We shouldn't."

"I know." He buried his face in the curve of her neck. "Oh God, I know." His voice sounded ragged, she thought, muffled as it was against her neck, but his arms were gentle around her. "But I can't seem to stop myself."

He held her close without seeming to restrain her in any way. Maybe if he *had* tried to hold her down she would have struggled against him, fought to be set free.

But he didn't. Through guile or cunning, or perhaps all unknowingly, he held her tenderly, almost reverently, as if she was infinitely precious to him. And Desi, overcome by her love and her need, let him hold her.

He sighed into the sweetness of her hair; a soft whisper of warm breath against her sensitive skin. "I just want to hold you," she heard him say. "It feels so good just to hold you. You're so warm," he said, a note of wonderment in his voice. His lips moved against the vulnerable curve of her neck, and it was all Desi could do to keep from crying out.

"So sweet," he murmured into her hair. "How can anyone be so sweet?"

Desi barely heard the muffled words he spoke, so enthralled was she by the feel of his arms around her and the touch of his lips on her neck. Her head fell back invitingly, exposing the long delicate line of her throat to his seeking lips. Her hands rested passively against the broad expanse of his chest. She could feel the heat of him through the thin material of his shirt and feel the steady thud of his heart under her tingling palms.

This was insane, she knew, totally, deliriously, deliciously insane. For both of them. It would solve nothing, change nothing. But it *felt* so right, so good to feel her body surge joyously in response to the experienced touch of his hard lips. They traveled down her neck to tease at the shadowy cleft between her breasts, and she could feel her blood racing madly through her veins, throbbing in her temples and setting the telltale pulse in her throat to dancing wildly in heated excitement.

It had been so long, was her last rational thought, so long since she had felt his fevered, fever-inducing touch.

Just this once more, she promised herself. Just once more.

"Jake," she whispered huskily, a throb of feminine need in her voice. Her hands came up to curl possessively into his rich brown hair, pulling his head up from the cleft of her breasts to silently demand his kiss. "Oh, Jake," she sighed, just before his lips closed hungrily over hers.

He tipped her backward onto the sofa, pressing her gently into the rose-colored cushions. Desi offered no resistance. She couldn't, not with his strong hands at her back and the feel of his lips and tongue so tenderly, sweetly ravaging her mouth. She slid her arms around the strong column of his neck, making sure that he followed her down.

It was suddenly as if the past eleven and a half months had never happened. As if they were still two lovers locked in that magical hotel room, hiding from the world and from reality. As if she hadn't experienced the pain, the emptiness of those long months, and as if he had never said any of those harsh, hurtful words to her.

It was only the two of them again. Each unable to turn away from the other. Seemingly compelled to touch and explore and murmur half-heard words of love and passion.

"I've thought of you like this. But I've already told you that, haven't I?" Jake said gruffly, as though the words were being dragged out of him, but Desi didn't seem to notice how unwilling an admission it actually was. She was lost in her love and need for him, overwhelmed by the fact that he seemed to be returning those emotions.

All she knew was that his lips were against her ear, his tongue lightly outlining the delicate curves, causing her to shiver deliciously under him.

"I've thought of your soft skin and the sweet fragrance of your hair." He raised himself up onto one elbow, his other hand reaching up and under her head, pulling loose the ribbon that bound her hair. He trailed her hair down and around her neck, so that it slithered silkily across the delicate skin of her throat, down her chest, and drew it slowly, tantalizingly, around the smooth mounds of her breasts.

"I've thought of how all that wild red hair curls so enticingly over your shoulders and down your naked back. Hiding you from me...." He let go of her hair, as if suddenly tired of his teasing game and his hot hard fingers nudged aside the silk of her robe, exposing one creamy breast to his avid gaze.

"You won't hide from me now, will you, my Desiree?" he growled, his breath burning against the silk of her still-covered breast. "Will you, Desiree?" he demanded.

"No," she whispered breathlessly. "No, Jake, I won't hide."

He nodded once, satisfied with her nearly inaudible answer, and then his big hand covered her exposed breast, thumb and forefinger teasing the nipple to rigid excitement. His head bent and his mouth closed over the other nipple, tonguing it through the thin silk of her kimono.

Desi moaned, deep in her throat, and arched her slender body against the almost unbearable pleasure of his skillful touch.

"Ah, Desiree," he breathed against her tormented flesh. "Tell me, Desiree. Tell me what you want."

"Please, Jake," she babbled incoherently. "Please ... ah, Jake!" The last was a cry wrenched from deep within her as he used his teeth to tug aside the damp material. His lips then closed gently over her nipple, causing an exquisite pleasure that snaked hotly down her flat stomach, tensing her insides into a tight, hard, burning knot of desire.

"Jake, please," she whispered again, almost mindless with the feelings he was so skillfully inducing in her and suddenly shy before the smoldering intensity in his eyes. The words seemed to stick in her throat. She could only murmur, "Please, Jake . . . please," and her hand came up to his on her breast, pushing it downward across her stomach.

He didn't make her ask again.

His hand paused at her waist, fumbling at the knot of her sash, and when it came loose he raised himself up off her, sliding to his knees beside the sofa. Almost reverently he opened the pink kimono, revealing the creamy perfection of her to his eager eyes.

Desi lay still for a brief minute, her violet eyes opened wide, watching his face as he gazed at the curves of her exposed body. He looked tender and puzzled at the same time, as if he couldn't decide whether to make love to her or not. Then his hand reached out, lightly skimming her from neck to knees, and the ambivalent look was gone, swiftly replaced by one of soul-searing, raging hunger.

Desi's eyes closed, then, and she gave herself up totally to his touch. She felt his hand skim lightly over her body again, just barely outlining the soft curves of her breast and hip and thigh. And then he moved, leaning over her recumbent form, and it was his lips she felt now, worshipping her body.

He started at her forehead . . . her eyes and cheeks and throat . . . moving slowly, ever downward, with little open-mouthed baby kisses . . . across her shoulders and breasts, her flat, quivering belly, her navel . . . the little reddish mole on her left hip.

"That's how I know you're real," he'd told her the last time, touching that mole. "You have a tiny imperfection. If I had imagined you, you would have been perfect."

"I have more than one imperfection," she'd laughingly tried to tell him. He had silenced her with a kiss, sliding her down from the pillows stacked behind her head.

"Ah, Jake . . . oh!" she'd said then.

She said it again now, over and over, as his mouth traveled back up her body to greedily claim a breast and his hand—his skillful, knowing hand—moved down, across her flat stomach to the flaming triangle at the apex of her thighs. All she could do was to murmur his name, over and over, like a chant, until she convulsed suddenly in a shattering climax. She bit her bottom lip, muffling the sound of her cries, and her hands clutched at his shoulders, frantically urging him to a final union.

His name was the only thing she seemed to be able to say.

"Tell me, Desiree," he urged, raising his head to look down into her passion-drugged face. "Tell me what you want."

"You," she managed to whisper then. "You, Jake."

She struggled to a sitting position on the sofa, shrugging her arms totally out of her kimono as she did so, and began hurriedly to unbutton his shirt. But her fingers were clumsy in their feverish haste, and Jake brushed her hands aside to finish the job himself. He slid the unbuttoned shirt off, pulling the tails from the waistband of his slacks, as Desi's hands reached eagerly for the buckle of his belt.

In minutes he was as naked as she and he moved swiftly, sliding over her body, parting her willing thighs with his knees. For a heartbeat or two it seemed as if he hovered, suspended, over her supine body, and Desi drank in the sight of his male beauty with greedy eyes. His lush head of dark hair, his beautiful smoldering eyes, his strong jaw, his powerful shoulders and arms, the muscles bulging as he held himself suspended above her. She devoured him with her eyes, visually caressing the hard broad wall of his hair-covered chest, his firm flat belly, narrow hips and turgid, virile manhood. And then her arms reached up to him. Her pale hands clutched at his shoulders to draw him down to her.

"Ah, Desiree!" she heard him moan raggedly as he thrust forward into her body.

She held him tightly as he strained against her, her fingers digging into the corded muscles of his shoulders as they climbed together toward the fire and fury of a mutual fulfillment that had been too long denied. And then her arms enfolded him, slipping around his back when the impassioned frenzy had passed, holding his trembling, sweat-sheened body to the comfort of her breasts while she was cradled in the tender haven of his arms.

"Jake," she murmured softly after a few minutes, planting moist, tender little kisses along his neck and jaw. "Oh, Jake...it was...I don't know how to describe it...you were..."

"*We* were great," he said, his deep voice still muffled in her cloud of hair. He raised himself up onto his elbows to look down into her face. "We've always been great together. Right from the first time," he said, and his voice was more normal now, no longer husky with passion or suppressed desire. "That's not something that happens too often." He brushed a few stray strands of coppery hair away from her face, and Desi had the distinct impression that he was finding his next words hard to say. "I didn't mean for this to happen when I came here tonight." He paused uncertainly.

"Neither did I," she murmured, waiting for him to continue.

"I'm not saying that I'm not glad that it happened." He smiled a little self-deprecatingly. "At least, I *think* I'm glad. But I was just going to talk to you tonight. To, ah, apologize to you for what I said about Evan. I was wrong about that." His eyes avoided hers. "And even if I wasn't. Well, it was none of my business anyway." His hand clenched in her hair. "I have no hold over you."

None that you know of, she thought, but said nothing.

"Anyway, what I'm trying to say, Desiree, is even though I didn't intend for this to happen, now that it *has* we ought to take advantage of it."

He untangled his hand from her hair and kissed her lightly, not seeming to notice the slightly stunned look on her face, and pushed himself up off her to sit on the edge of the sofa. He reached down for his clothes and began dressing.

Desi lay where she was, staring up at him. "Take advantage of what?" she said in a small careful voice.

"This. Us," he said, glancing down at her as he stood up to zip his pants. "There's an incredibly intense sexual energy between us that's very rare." He bent down to retrieve his shirt from under the coffee table. He went on casually, buttoning his shirt as he spoke. "Only one couple in a hundred—hell, in five hundred, maybe, can generate the kind of reaction we do together." He flashed her a quick grin; charming, boyish and comically lewd, all at once. "Be a crime to waste it."

Desi found that she couldn't return that grin. She didn't even try. She sat up, drawing on her rumpled silk robe, tying the sash securely around her slender waist. She felt suddenly hollow inside. Used and cheap.

Sexual energy, was that all he felt for her? The novelty and excitement of an intense sexual spark? Felt by only one of every five hundred couples?

It was obvious now that this encounter—soul shattering to her—was no more than a roll in the hay for him. An exciting, intense roll in the hay, to be sure—but no more than that. And it was also obvious that he thought she felt the same way about it.

Didn't it show on her face? Didn't any of it show? The love, the passion, the tenderness . . . and now the shame and the hurt? Couldn't he see it? Apparently not, because he stood there smiling down at her, an expectant look on his face.

"I'm sorry," she said, realizing that he must have spoken to her. "What did you say?"

"I asked if you'd like to drive up to Sonoma with me tomorrow."

Desi stood up. "Tomorrow?" Her voice was vague and then, "No, I'm sorry, but I can't," she said, just as if she had actually considered it. Fool! "We're—I'm driving down to see my parents tomorrow. I'm going to spend the weekend."

Jake shrugged, an odd look on his handsome face. Disappointment, she would have said if it had been any other man. But that was ridiculous in Jake's case!

"I'm sorry," she said again, edging toward the front door. Stephanie lay asleep in the other room, she remembered belatedly. A baby who might wake up any moment and start to cry. She had to get him out of here. Now. "I'd . . . I'd ask you to, ah, stay but I have to be up early tomorrow and well . . . it's late."

"Yes," he agreed. The odd look was gone from his face, re-placed by...what? Anger? Disappointment? Pain? She couldn't tell. "You're right. It's late." He looked around him. "Where the hell is my jacket?"

Definitely anger, she decided, feeling suddenly a little nervous of him, remembering another angry scene. Then her back straightened. *He* had no reason to be angry at her. *He* had used her, not the other way around. She was the one who should be angry!

Curiously, though, she wasn't. She couldn't seem to sum-mon up the energy to be angry. She just felt drained and empty.

"It's here," she said, bending to retrieve his jacket from under the edge of the sofa.

You were wrong, Dorothea, she thought. *Wrong. And I was right. It was lust, pure and simple.* A spectacular sexual attraction with nothing behind it, not on his side at least.

Do I still love him? she wondered, holding the leather jacket out to him. *Can I possibly still love him?*

She didn't know anymore, she told herself. She just didn't know.

"Desi?" he said, taking the jacket from her.

She looked up. It was the first time he had ever called her that. Not in the maddeningly seductive way he said Desiree, nor with the careless indifference with which he said Wes-ton. Just Desi.

"Yes?"

"Have a good time with your parents," he said softly, and then his hand reached out to cup her chin and he bent his head to kiss her. "See you Monday morning."

He was gone.

Desi stood with her forehead resting wearily against the closed door. Why had he done that? Kissed her like that? Not as a lover, exactly, nor as an enemy, but almost as a cher-ished friend.

It answered one question for her, anyway. She still loved him.

"DESI, MY DEAR GIRL. What a lovely surprise!" Dorothea rose from the piano bench where she had been sitting beside Michael Ballard, playing a silly child's duet, and hurried gracefully across the big cheery room, her hands outstretched in greeting.

She was wearing her black Halston again, Desi noted, but no rubies tonight. The glittering red stones had been replaced by pearls. A magnificent yard-long strand of large milky pearls. It was wound several times around her thin neck and the longest loop still fell to her waist.

"Welcome, dear girl," she said extravagantly, leaning forward to kiss Desi's cheek.

Desi returned the affectionate greeting, squeezing Dorothea's hands fondly. "You look marvelous, Dorothea," she said.

"Thank you." The older woman preened a little, fingering her pearls, and then linked her arm through Desi's to draw her into the living room. "I wish I could say the same for you but I can't," she added bluntly. "You look tired."

"I am," Desi admitted.

"Well, never mind. Come and sit down. We were just about to have coffee. That will perk you right up—especially with a little of Richard's special brandy in it. Jake, hand Desi that cup, please," she ordered.

"Thank you, no, Dorothea. I don't want any coffee," Desi said, trying unsuccessfully to ignore Jake as she took the cup that he held out to her.

She put it down on the coffee table in front of her without looking directly at him. She had glanced at him when she first entered the room, in that brief second before anyone was aware that she was standing in the doorway. Once was enough to imprint the image on her mind forever. He wore black tie; plain, unadorned and devastating.

"Brandy neat, then?" Dorothea questioned as Desi put the cup aside.

"No, thank you, Dorothea," she said again. "What I'd really like is a couple of eggs or a sandwich and then bed. I haven't eaten since lunch and I'm beat. I didn't get away from my parents' house until nearly four this afternoon."

"You drove all the way up here from your parents' house without stopping?"

"It's not that long a drive, Dorothea. Only about three hours. And I didn't drive straight through. I had to drop Ste—" She stopped herself, glancing furtively at Jake from under her lashes, but he didn't seem to have noticed her slip. "I stopped at my apartment," she went on, "to pick up a few things and give Teddie some last-minute instructions about my plants."

"Teddie?" He had picked up on *that* fast enough. "Who's Teddie?" he asked casually, but there was a frown furrowing his forehead.

"My landlord," she said, still not looking at him. "He lives downstairs and watches things for me when I'm not home."

"An interior designer, isn't that right, Desi?" Dorothea chimed in. "I met him, and his roommate, of course, while I was convalescing." Her sharp, black eyes darted back and forth between Jake and Desi. "Simply charming boys." She stressed the last word, smiling up at Jake with a significant look in her eyes.

Jake grinned, the frown disappearing immediately. "I see," he said dryly.

Desi continued to stare down at her hands, missing the byplay between Jake and Dorothea. She was glad that no one had thought to mention the fact that she had arrived about eight hours earlier than expected. Her original plan had been to stay at her apartment tonight and drive up to Sonoma early in the morning. Well, be grateful for small favors, she thought, because she wouldn't have wanted to explain why she had been in such a hurry to get here.

She glanced surreptitiously in Jake's direction. There was her reason. She had thought of him all weekend. Taking long walks on the beach while her mother happily monopolized Stephanie, she wondered and worried about how he would act toward her now, after their lovemaking of Friday night. About how she should react to him.

"Well, I'll just go see about that sandwich." Dorothea rose from her seat.

"I didn't mean for you to make it, Dorothea." Desi rose, too. "Just point me in the direction of the kitchen."

"Nonsense." She nudged Desi back to her seat. "I don't intend to make it myself. I'll just have Gerta, my housekeeper, fix you a little something on a tray and take it on up to your room. You can have a nice cozy supper in bed. Best thing for exhaustion. You just relax for a few short minutes," she instructed Desi. "I'll be back shortly to show you to your room."

"Did you have a nice visit with your parents?" Jake asked, sitting down next to Desi in the seat vacated by Dorothea. "Are they well?"

"Yes, a lovely visit," she said in a small voice. She didn't look at him, but she could feel him there, hovering at her elbow. "They're fine."

"And your brothers?" he prodded.

"Brother," she corrected him, wishing now that she had taken that cup of coffee so she would have something to do with her hands. "Court is the only one left at home. He's fine." There was a little silence. "Ash is at some mining camp in Nevada," she went on then, needing to say something. "He's an engineer. And Zek was still on location in New Orleans last I heard, doing that spy film. I expect they're both fine, too."

"Zek Weston? He's your brother?" Audrey spoke from her seat by the fire.

Desi looked across the room at her. She sat curled up in a corner of Dorothea's ancient wing-backed love seat, looking as sleek and self-satisfied as a cat. Her dress was another of those silky-looking wraparounds that she was so fond of. And rightly so, Desi admitted to herself. The color was flame red to flatter her hair and skin, and the wrap-front style showcased her spectacular figure in a ladylike way.

"Yes," Desi said finally, "Zek is my oldest brother."

"You don't look much like him," Audrey said. "Except for the hair."

"Yes, I know. Zek takes after my father's side of the family physically. They're all brawny men. But—" Desi smiled "—Mom managed to give her red hair to all of us."

She glanced toward the door, wishing that Dorothea would hurry up and come back for her. She felt grubby in her baggy, faded jeans and quilted purple down parka, especially when compared to Audrey's feline sleekness. And she was tired. Definitely in no condition to handle any of this tonight.

Not Jake, in this odd, friendly mood he seemed to be in. Not Audrey, who looked so cool and beautiful in her silky red dress. Not even Michael, who still sat harmlessly at the piano, absently picking out a popular tune.

"Where's Evan?" she said, realizing for the first time that he was missing from the group gathered in Dorothea's living room.

"Sick," Jake answered her. His voice was soft and pleasant and very close to her ear. She almost jumped out of her skin when she realized how close.

What *was* the matter with him? Desi wondered, looking up at Jake out of the corner of her eye. He caught her eye and smiled—a tender smile, almost—and Desi looked hastily away again. Was he planning on taking up where they had left off Friday night? she silently speculated.

"He seems to have caught the cold that Dorothea has been passing around," Jake went on.

"What have I been passing around?" Dorothea said, coming back into the room.

"Germs—" Jake grinned up at her "—to poor old Evan." He managed to imply, somehow, that she had given Evan the germs in a highly questionable way.

"Poor old Evan, indeed!" she countered with a chuckle, pleased by his teasing. "Lucky old Evan, I say, if he got them in that way."

"Point to Dorothea, I think," said Michael, looking up from the keyboard.

"Come along, dear girl," said Dorothea then, and Desi got up gratefully to follow her. "Gerta is whipping up a nice Spanish omelet for you. By the time you get yourself into bed, she'll have it ready." She glanced toward the front door as they entered the foyer. "Where are your suitcases?"

"In the car. I'll get them in the morning." She indicated the satchel slung over her shoulder. "I have everything I need in here. Really."

Dorothea eyed her satchel suspiciously. "You did bring some of your pretty things, didn't you?"

"Yes," Desi said with a smile as they started up the wide staircase.

A narrow strip of wine red carpet ran up the center of the staircase, and the polished hardwood treads exposed on either side gleamed with the patina of age and scrupulous care. The handrails were smooth and broad enough for a small child to use as a slide, and the newel posts, both top and bottom, were intricately carved pieces of art. Large clusters of grapes, Desi realized, leaning over for a closer look.

"This is a beautiful house, Dorothea," she said. "Simply beautiful. I can't wait to see it in the daylight."

"I'll give you the ten-cent tour tomorrow," Dorothea said casually, but there was a ring of pride in her voice. She opened a door leading off the long upstairs hall. "Here we are. My second-best guest room."

"Don't tell me. Let me guess," Desi teased. "Jake got the very best, right?"

"Naturally," she conceded, not the least bit embarrassed at being found out.

"Well, this is lovely, Dorothea."

And it was. Butter cream-yellow walls, defined with white
woodwork, gave the impression of lightness even at night.
The floor was highly polished hardwood, left beautifully bare
except where it was covered by a large oval rug spread under, and extending all around, the four-poster bed. The rug
was ivory with a pattern of soft green leaves and pale yellow
roses. The candlewick bedspread was yellow, too, with a
wide border of crocheted lace to match the curtains. There
was a Queen Anne armchair upholstered in pale green bro-
cade in front of the window, delicate pressed-flower prints
on the walls and two of the newest bestsellers on the nightstand by the bed.

"If this is your second best I can't imagine what the best
might be like."

"Bigger," said Dorothea, "and it doesn't share a bath. You
share a bath with Audrey, by the way," she said, and grinned
impishly when Desi grimaced. "Right through that door."
Dorothea pointed it out for her. "Why don't you go get into
your nightclothes before your dinner gets here?" She nudged
Desi toward the bathroom.

Desi washed her hands and face, brushed her teeth and
slipped into a white nightshirt that had originally been a
man's silk dress shirt. Not much to look at on a hanger, but
the effect on Desi was one of innocent sensuality.

"You are such a pretty little thing," Dorothea said in exasperation when Desi came out of the bathroom, hairbrush
in hand. "I can't for the life of me see why you dress yourself
like a boy."

"I have three brothers, remember?" Desi said, getting into
the bed Dorothea had turned down for her. "I used to wear
all their hand-me-downs when I was a kid. They're comfortable. I must admit that Mom wasn't too thrilled about my
clothes either," she said with a fond smile, "but it was a losing battle." Desi shrugged. "She finally had to give up and
let me wear what I wanted. Besides, it's easier to dress this
way for my job."

"How is your dear mother?"

"Just fine. She sends her love," Desi said, snuggling back against the fat pillows behind her.

"And Stephanie?"

"She has a bit of a cold—"

"She caught my cold, too! Oh, dear."

"It's nothing," Desi hastened to reassure her. "Just a sniffle. I wouldn't have left her with Teddie if I thought it was anything serious. Don't worry, she'll be fine."

There was a knock at the door.

"Gerta with your supper," Dorothea said, moving to open it.

But it was Jake instead. He stopped there in the hallway in his faultlessly correct evening clothes with a tray in his hands. "I told Gerta I'd bring this up for her," he said, walking into the room, "since I was coming up myself, anyway." He placed the tray over Desi's knees.

For a minute his eyes were on a level with hers and he smiled. A warm knowing smile, caressing her face and her upper body in the flimsy nightshirt. Desi flushed slightly and had to stifle the cowardly impulse to yank the bedclothes up to her chin. She put her hands on the tray instead, steadying it.

"Thank you," she said, looking at a point somewhere around the level of his black satin bow tie.

"Looks delicious," he commented in that deep seductive voice of his, and they both knew that he wasn't talking about her Spanish omelet.

"Yes, it does." Desi looked up into his face for an instant. She wasn't talking about the omelet either.

"Come along, dear boy," Dorothea spoke up then. "Let's you and I go away so Desi can eat her supper while it's still hot."

Jake straightened and dropped a long arm affectionately around Dorothea's shoulders. "Whatever you say," he teased her.

"Whatever I say, indeed! Whatever I say only when it pleases you to do it, is more like it." They started toward the door, bantering with each other as they went.

"Dorothea?" Desi halted them with her voice. There was something she had to know—now. "Stay a minute, will you?" she said when they both turned to look at her. "I, ah, have something I want to talk to you about." She paused, glancing at Jake from under her lashes. "Privately."

Jake accepted the dismissal with a smile. "Sweet dreams, Desiree," he said as he pulled the door closed behind him.

Dorothea came back over to the bed. "What is it?" she said, a conspiratorial gleam in her black eyes as she hitched up her caftan to sit down.

"Well . . ." Desi plucked at the yellow candlewick spread, her eyes downcast. If she asked the question, then Dorothea would want to know *why* she had asked it. But she had to know. She raised her eyes to Dorothea's. "Did you invite Jake over to my apartment last Friday night?"

"No, I didn't. Why? Did he pay you a visit?"

"Yes, he did." Desi's eyes blazed with sudden joy. He *had* come just to see her! Dorothea and the script had just been an excuse!

"And?" Dorothea urged.

"And, ah, nothing." Desi shrugged, feigning indifference.

"Nothing, my eye!" Dorothea huffed with mock indignation. "I wasn't born yesterday, you know, dear girl. Far from it." She leaned forward, her soft blue-veined hand cupping Desi's chin. "He made love to you again, didn't he?"

Desi's face flamed scarlet. "Yes."

"Well, that's nothing to be ashamed of, my dear. Quite the reverse, in fact." She gave Desi's chin an affectionate squeeze and stood up. "No wonder he's been strutting around here like a peacock," she said, half to herself. "As proud of himself as if he'd just won another Oscar. I *knew* something had happened. I just knew it. And if you don't mind my saying so, dear girl, it's about time, too!"

"It really doesn't change anything, Dorothea. Or prove anything, either," she warned.

"Nonsense! It proves he still wants you, doesn't it?" She grinned. "And wants you enough to tell little white lies in order to get to you, too. That's what he did, isn't it? Told you that I had invited him over so you'd let him in?"

"Uh-huh, but I let him in before he told me that," Desi confessed, laughing in spite of herself.

"Well, of course you did! You're a sensible girl." She slanted a teasing glance at Desi. "Most of the time," she said, and then her tone became serious. "I take it that you haven't told him about Stephanie yet?"

Desi shook her head.

"Well, my dear, I wouldn't put that off for too much longer," she advised solemnly. "It's the kind of news that gets harder to tell the longer you wait to tell it."

"I still haven't decided whether I'm *going* to tell him." There was a stubborn light in her violet eyes. "Just because we made love doesn't change anything. Oh, he *said* that he was wrong about Evan but—"

"Well, there, you see. He is changing his opinion."

"But he *still* thinks of me as just a casual bedmate." Her fingers curled around the edge of the tray. "Someone to share an 'intense sexual energy' with."

"Well, I think you're wrong, my dear. Dead wrong. But what I think isn't important. It's what you think that counts. And the only person who can change your mind is Jake—if you give him a chance to change it." She leaned over, patting Desi's hand where it gripped the tray. "Well, enough of that. Eat your dinner, dear girl, before it gets cold. I've got other guests to see to."

She crossed the room, reaching for the doorknob as she spoke. "You really should give him a chance," she said, closing the bedroom door behind her.

Desi released her death grip on the tray and slowly picked up her fork. She took a bite of her omelet, washing it down with a sip of hot black coffee. Thank you, Gerta, she thought, distracted for a minute by the delicious combination of fresh eggs made spicy with onion, tomato and bell pepper.

What had brought about this startling change in Jake? she wondered again when she had finished the last bite of her omelet, the last piece of toasted sourdough bread. Could

Dorothea be right? Could it be just because he had made love to her again? She remembered, all too well, how angry he had been when he'd left her apartment Friday night. Or so she had thought. But he *had* kissed her goodbye like . . . Like what?

She shook her head in bewilderment. Was he just trying to get back into her bed? she wondered. Maybe he had decided that this new, friendlier, more tender self would be the right track to that end.

Oh, no, please don't let it be that!

She heard water running in the bathroom and realized that Audrey must be getting ready to turn in. Leaning over, she put the tray on the floor beside the bed and switched out the lamp on the nightstand. Snuggling down into the crisp sheets, she pulled the covers up over her shoulders and tried to go to sleep.

She woke the next morning very late, coaxed gently awake by the unaccustomed sound of the birds bickering outside the bedroom window and the sun shining on her face. She glanced at the clock on the bedside table and sat up with a gasp. Nine-thirty! Jake would have her hide!

She rose quickly, stepping over the tray on the floor, and knocked quietly on the bathroom door. No answer. Either Audrey was not up yet or, more likely, she was already up and gone. Desi pushed the door open and went in.

Pinning up her hair, she took a quick, refreshing shower and then slipped back into her nightshirt. Her robe and clean clothes were still in the suitcases in her car.

She wondered if she should wait for someone to bring them up or get back into the grubby clothes of last night to go down and get them herself. The thought of yesterday's jeans and T-shirt was distasteful, but she didn't have time to wait around for someone to remember she was there, waiting for her luggage.

She went back into the bedroom and was already slipping out of her nightshirt before she saw him sitting there in the Queen Anne chair by the window. Her eyes opened wide for a shocked second, taking in his tall form as he lounged, completely at ease, in the delicate chair.

The sun glinted off of his dark hair, making it shine, and he was dressed more casually than Desi had ever seen him. He wore snug-fitting jeans that neatly encased his lean hips and legs and a ratty blue sweatshirt with a stretched-out neckline and faded gold lettering that proclaimed him to be the property of the UCLA track team. Battered sneakers worn without socks completed his outfit. He looked more rested and at ease than she had seen him in weeks.

"Looks delicious," he said, grinning at her.

"Jake!" Desi whirled away from him, pulling the night-shirt back up over her shoulders, hurriedly buttoning it. "What are you doing in here?"

"I heard you moving around, so I brought in your suit-cases." He motioned toward the two canvas bags standing at the foot of the bed.

"What were you doing?" she asked suspiciously, turning to face him. "Lurking in the hall?"

"As a matter of fact, yes," he said, surprising her.

Desi's eyes opened even wider. "Why?"

"I wanted to talk to you—privately," he replied, rising la-zily from the chair to move toward her.

Desi backed away a step or two, still clutching the front of her nightshirt. "You could do that anytime. You didn't have to invade my bedroom."

"This house is full of people," he informed her easily.

"And you think they don't know you're in here?" she scoffed, taking false courage from his mild demeanor.

He smiled again and took another step toward her. Desi hastily backed away. "Not unless you tell them," he said. "Everyone's at breakfast. Outside on the sun porch. It's a beautiful day, in case you hadn't noticed yet."

"Isn't it a little late for breakfast?" she said. "Shooting was supposed to start hours ago...." Her voice trailed off. Dumb, she thought, to call his attention to her own lateness.

"No filming today," he said, surprising her again.

Jake was suddenly full of surprises. She was beginning to think he had taken some mood- or mind-altering drug. He had never before been so lighthearted about a delay—if it was a delay—in the shooting schedule. Time is money, he was often heard to yell, my money.

"Why?" she asked.

"Why what?" he asked vaguely, his dark eyes beginning to wander over her face and her pinned-up hair in a way that left her breathless.

"Why no . . . shooting?" she managed to stammer.

"One of the vans broke down about halfway between San Francisco and here last night. Couldn't get anybody to work on it until this morning," he said as if it didn't bother him in the least. "So today we're all playing hooky."

"Oh," she said. "How . . . nice."

"Yes, isn't it." His hand reached out then and touched her neck, just at the place where it began to curve into her shoulder, too close to the telltale pulse that had begun to beat wildly. "Very nice."

Desi clutched her nightshirt tighter and stepped back again, instinctively seeking to protect herself from his maddening touch. She always melted when he touched her. She couldn't melt again. Not now. Not here, in Dorothea's house.

The backs of her knees hit the edge of the bed, halting her, and she was forced to sit down abruptly. Jake's body followed her, pushing her back into the rumpled sheets.

"Jake, please," she began, struggling to sit up, trying to pull down the hem of her nightshirt at the same time.

"Please what?" he teased her.

He held himself propped up on one elbow, holding her down by the simple expedient of placing his other hand on her shoulder. She couldn't kick or struggle, she realized. She was naked under the brief shirt.

"Jake, stop it," she said as sharply as she could manage. It came out in a mere whisper.

"I haven't done anything yet," he said reasonably, and she dared to look up into his face. He was smiling down at her, a strange, almost tender, look in his eyes. "But I will if you keep looking at me like that," he said, low.

"Like what?" Her soft voice, her eyes, invited him.

"Like my Desiree," he said, and then he leaned down, the hand on her shoulder slipping around her back to gather her close. "Sweet Desiree," he murmured, and kissed her.

It was like the kisses he had given her that very first time. Tender kisses. Kisses that explored and cajoled and coaxed rather than demanded. His tongue sought entrance to her mouth, outlining her lips with sweetness and patience until she opened to him like a blossoming flower.

She felt him sigh into her mouth—a soft shuddering sigh—and she turned to him, molding her mouth more closely to his, twining her arms helplessly around the strong column of his neck, her fingers feasting greedily in his thick hair.

His hand was on the outside curve of her thigh, sliding up her leg under the nightshirt. Gliding slowly, sensuously, up over her rounded hip and the surprisingly lush inward-sloping curve of her waist, to close tenderly, adoringly over her breast.

He seemed content for the moment just to hold her thus, making no effort to arouse her further, as yet. He kissed her as if that was his sole purpose, as if he had all the time in the entire world, drinking in her intoxicating sweetness, giving her back an intoxication of his own unique making.

Suddenly his hand stilled on her breast and he raised his head.

"What is it?" she began groggily.

"Shush," he said against her lips, listening, and Desi stilled, listening too.

There were noises coming from the adjoining bathroom. Loud noises. Water being run into the porcelain sink. The door of the medicine cabinet being opened and closed.

Audrey.

"Jake," Desi said, squirming under him. "Let me up."

"Why?" He began to tease her. "You ashamed to be seen with me? Oh, all right. All right. I came up here to talk anyway." His hand slid slowly from her breast, across the flatness of her stomach, to stop at the mole on her hip. He sat up and leaned over, placing his lips for a brief instant on the tiny mole. "To remind me where to start later," he said, smooth-

ing her nightshirt down as far as it would go. He sat up on
the edge of the bed, pulling her upright with him.

"There isn't going to be a later," she said, blushing.

"Oh, yes there is," he stated firmly. "Lots of laters." He
reached out to touch her again, brushing back the loose,
straggling hair from her face.

Desi jumped to her feet. "No, Jake," she warned him off.
"No more . . . I don't know what got into me to allow you
to—"

"What *almost* got into you," he corrected her, grinning
comically.

"Jake!" she admonished, trying to convince him—and
herself—that she was shocked by his teasing words, but
showing them both only how excited he made her.

She turned away, hiding her red face from him. "You said
you wanted to talk to me," she reminded him.

"Yes, so I did."

She heard the bed creak as he got up and then felt his hand
on her arm, turning her to face him. "Look at me, Desiree,"
he commanded gently, his hands on her shoulders holding her
still in front of him.

"Desi," she corrected him.

"You'll always be Desiree to me," he told her and then said
once more, "Look at me."

She looked up into his face. There was that odd look again.
Tender, friendly, a little uncertain, perhaps, with the desire
still in his eyes.

"I've been doing some heavy thinking since Friday night,"
he said seriously. "Since before then, really. And I realize that
I've been wrong about you. Evan isn't your lover and he never
has been."

"Yes, you told me that already," she pointed out.

"So I did." He ran one hand distractedly through his hair.
"You're obviously very good at your job, too," he said. "A
total professional."

"Well, thank you," she said archly, and he had the grace to
look a little shamefaced. "But you told me that, too."

"Look, I don't pretend to know *why* you went to bed with me so...quickly," he continued as if she hadn't spoken. "But it's obviously not for the reasons I thought. Not at first and not later, either. You're not some sort of groupie. Even I can see that—now."

"Not at first?" What did he mean, not at first? "What do you mean—" she started to say, and then was stopped by his next words.

"Desiree, I misjudged you in the worst way possible," he said, intent on saying it all now that he had started. "And I know that I've been almost impossible to work with." He turned to the window, his fingers raking through his hair again.

Desi could hardly believe it. Could this be the great Jake Lancing? The man who had been such a bad-tempered bear on the set, apologizing? To her? A smile began to turn her mouth up at the corners.

"I'd go down on my knees to apologize if I thought it would do any good," he went on, his back to her. "If I thought it would help you to forgive me for being such a thick-headed..." He groped for a word.

"Ass," she supplied, unable to stifle the sudden glee that bubbled to the surface.

He whirled around, trying to read her expression. Was she angry? Hurt? Resentful? No, her eyes were laughing and she was having trouble suppressing a smile.

"All right," he agreed with a grin. "I was behaving like a thickheaded ass." He moved quickly across the width of carpet that separated them and gathered her close in his arms. "Do you think we can start over?" he said, serious again. She felt his lips brush her hair. "See if there's a real relationship here? Something beyond this." His hand caressed her buttocks briefly. "Not that this isn't extremely nice, of course, but..." His lips nibbled playfully at her ear.

"You haven't apologized yet," she said, trying hard not to laugh yet, not to throw herself into his arms in glorious abandon. His warm lips were wreaking havoc with her senses, and there was a bright bubble of happiness rising up

from deep inside her, making it very difficult for her to keep
a straight face. "On your knees, I think you said."

"Witch," he growled, but he started to slide to the floor.

"Oh, no, Jake, I was only teasing!" she said as he began to
sink to his knees in front of her. "Get up!" She tugged him to
his feet. "I forgive you," she said, wrapping her arms around
his neck to pull his head down to hers.

Dorothea was right, she thought. Lust could turn into
love—or, at least into liking. It was up to her now to turn it
into something lasting.

She should tell him about Stephanie, she thought guiltily.
Start out today with a clean slate. But not now, she told herself. Not this minute when she was so joyously happy. Later,
when they had had time to build a firmer foundation of trust.
When she had found just the right moment, the right words
to tell him that he had a baby daughter. Words that would
make her deception understandable.

"I forgive you anything . . . everything," she murmured
fervently, just before his lips closed over hers.

I only hope you can forgive me as easily, she prayed.

11

JAKE LIFTED HIS HEAD a long moment later. "We'd better stop this," he said, and then immediately voided his words by nuzzling his face against the soft curve of her neck.

"Why?" Desi wanted to know.

"Because—" his lips were against her ear "—everyone is waiting for us on the sun porch—I told you we're all playing hooky today. Well, Dorothea has plans to conduct a tour of her wine cellars. Total participation is mandatory, she says—" he kissed her closed eyelids "—so she sent me up here to get you out of bed."

Desi's eyes opened reluctantly, and she leaned back in the warm circle of his arms. "Do you mean to tell me that the entire household knows you're up here?"

"Yep." He grinned, his expression as playful and loving as it had been in that hotel room in San Francisco.

"You beast." She pushed against his chest. "I thought you said that nobody would know you were in this room unless I told them! I think you've deliberately ruined my reputation." She tsked. "What's Dorothea going to think?"

"That I've come to my senses, probably, and am doing what I should have done months ago. How does she put it in her book? A rowdy, rollicking tumble under the covers?"

"You haven't been up here long enough for that—" Desi began, her face beginning to turn a delicious shade of pink.

"Plenty long enough," he corrected her, pulling her back into his arms for another kiss. "Since your reputation is already ruined," he suggested, lifting his mouth from hers, "what do you say we finish what we started?" He began edging them back toward the bed.

"Oh, no, you don't." Desi resisted him, digging in her heels, and he stopped to look down into her face.

"Why not? They already suspect the worst."

"They may *suspect* the worst," she admitted, twisting lightly out of his arms, "but I can still look Dorothea in the eye with a clear conscience."

"Dorothea doesn't care about a clear conscience. Haven't you read her book?" He made a move to recapture her.

"Oh, no, you don't," she repeated breathlessly, a little catch of laughter in her voice as she retreated to a far corner of the room. "You have to get out of this room. Now," she ordered, pointing at the door. "Go on. Out! I have to get dressed. We're supposed to be touring the wine cellars, remember?"

"I could help," he offered, grinning suggestively. "I'm very good with buttons."

"Lot of help you'd be," she jeered, laughing at him. "Now go."

"All right." He admitted defeat, "I'll go." He paused with his hand on the doorknob. "But I'll be back for you later," he warned, disappearing into the hall. "When it's dark." His head reappeared around the edge of the door. "When you're alone. Asleep and unprotected. No one will hear your screams for mercy," he promised her.

"That's because I won't need to make any," she shot back.

"We'll see," he said. "We'll see." The door closed behind him, and she heard him whistling as he moved down the hall.

Desi hugged herself rapturously, doing a happy little dance step as she moved across the bare floor to toss her suitcases onto the bed.

It was going to be all right, she told herself joyously. It was all going to work out fine.

"You were right, Dorothea," she said aloud. "You were right!"

Unlocking the suitcases, she began to rummage through them for something to wear. Nothing seemed appropriate. None of her usual jeans and cords, loose boy-styled shirts and T-shirts seemed exactly right for today. She felt light as air, beautiful, ethereal, loved. Though he hadn't actually said the word, that's how she felt—loved. And she wanted to look that way. Too bad it wasn't dinnertime, she thought longingly. If it had been, then she could float down the stairs in her pastel silks with her hair curling down her back.

Jake had a thing about redheads, Dorothea said once. "That's wonderful—" Desi laughed aloud, as if she had only just realized it "—I'm a redhead."

She slipped out of her nightshirt, tossing it onto the clothes in her open suitcase and dug around until she found her favorite, most enticing set of underwear. Silky, powder blue string bikini panties and a flimsy little camisole top, whisper sheer, that stopped, deliberately short, at the level of her navel.

She might look like a boy on the outside, but underneath she would be all enticing woman. And maybe, she giggled, just maybe, if she worked it right, Jake would see that, too. There were lots of places in a wine cellar where two people could *accidentally* get lost for a half an hour or so. Simple.

She stepped into the panties and pulled the wisp of sheer lace over her head. She'd wear her hair loose, too, she decided suddenly, instead of pinning it up into its usual topknot or neat braid. After all, she wasn't working today—and Jake liked her hair down. He'd said so.

"I've thought of how all that wild red hair curls so enticingly over your shoulders," he'd said, his voice husky with passion, his eyes dark and smoldering.

Desi shivered in remembered delight and anticipation and reached for a pair of knee socks. She tugged the fuzzy blue-and-pink striped socks on, pulled on a pair of jeans and slipped her arms into a navy-and-powder blue plaid shirt. She brushed her hair, head down, until the unruly mass glowed like a shimmering coppery wave. Standing, she tossed its length over her shoulders and surveyed herself in the mirror.

A tiny frown creased her forehead. Something was missing. She stood, considering her image for a second or two, and then an impish smile curved her lips. Daringly she undid two more buttons than was usual for her, exposing the lacy edge of the pale blue camisole.

"Not bad, Weston." She smiled at her reflection. "Not much, but not bad."

Suddenly her eyes caught those of her mirrored reflection and the smile faded from her face.

What are you so happy about, those violet eyes seemed to ask her. *Nothing's really changed. You still haven't told him about Stephanie.*

"I will," she said out loud. "I will."

She turned away from the mirror abruptly, unable to face what she saw. She *would* tell him. Soon. As soon as they had had more time together. As soon as she was sure he loved her. As soon as . . .

But how will he feel? she asked herself, trying to be honest. How will he react, say a week or a month from now, after you've developed this relationship he was talking about and *then* you spring it on him? How will you break the news to him that he's a father?

"Oh, by the way, Jake. There's just one little thing I forgot to mention."

No! She had to tell him. And soon. Today or . . . or tomorrow. Yes, certainly tomorrow! She would give herself today to be happy. Today to bask in the glory of his warmth and tenderness and passion. And tomorrow she would somehow find the words to tell him.

She picked up her dinner tray from the floor to take it downstairs to Gerta.

"Everyone's still on the sun porch, waiting for you, Miss Weston," said the housekeeper when Desi handed her the tray. "It's out toward the back of the house." Gerta waved her out of the kitchen.

Desi wandered into a couple of wrong rooms—a banquet-sized dining room, then a library—before the sound of voices finally drew her in the right direction. She took a deep breath before pushing open the door to the glassed-in sun porch.

"Good morning, dear girl. I hope you slept well."

"Yes, fine. Thank you, Dorothea." She glanced around the table quickly. They were all there. Dorothea, charming in a chic red pantsuit. Michael, casual in jeans and cowboy boots.

Audrey, looking elegant and beautiful in a pair of cream-colored raw-silk pants and a matching sweater. And Jake. Her eyes met his briefly, skittering away at his look of secret delight. "Morning everyone. Sorry I'm late."

"Well, come and have some coffee so we can get started," Dorothea ordered. "Or would you prefer tea? Evan brought it up with him, so I assume it's probably drinkable."

"Tea, please, Dorothea." She moved around the table, a pleased smile curving her lips. "Hello, Evan," she said, bending down to kiss his cheek. "I didn't see you sitting there when I came in. When did you arrive?" He looked a little pale but very English in his correct country tweeds, and she was glad to see him. "How are you feeling?"

"Just in time for breakfast," he answered her, "and I'm feeling quite the thing now. Quite." He looked up at her with fond concern in his brown eyes. "How are you, luv?"

"Fine," she told him, stealing a shy glance at Jake in his seat across the table. He grinned at her and patted the empty chair next to him. Suddenly her doubts were completely forgotten. "I feel just wonderful, Evan."

12

THE WINE CELLARS weren't dark today, not as they had been yesterday. It was crowded now and people seemed to be everywhere; setting up lights and cameras, making sure that props were exactly where they were supposed to be. A far cry from the quiet, secret hiding place it had been.

It was Jake, and not Desi, after all, who had managed to separate them from the rest of the group touring the shadowy cellars. He had used the simple but effective expedient of putting her with him behind one of the high wooden shelves of wine just as everyone else was moving away.

"Shush," he said, silencing her instinctive cry of surprise with his lips. It was several long breathless minutes before she could speak.

"What a lovely idea," she said with a sigh. "How did you ever think of it?"

"It's in Dorothea's book," he whispered. His hands were already busy with her buttons and hers had moved up under his sweatshirt, eager to caress the smooth bare skin of his back. "It drives me crazy, the way you dress," he growled. "Like a tomboy on the outside, but all morning I could see that little bit of lace peeking out from the top of your shirt. Teasing me. You do it on purpose, don't you?"

"Yes." Desi giggled softly—and then she gasped as he pushed aside the material of her shirt, his hand brushing against her belly and up under the tiny blue camisole, to close possessively over one soft breast.

"Desiree," he breathed against her open mouth as his other hand sought the roundness of her hips, pulling her to his hardness. "You make me feel like a crazy teenager." He laughed, gently mocking himself and her and the situation in which they found themselves.

"We're going to get caught like teenagers, too," she warned him, breathless laughter in her own voice.

But neither of them heeded the warning. Instead they pressed closer together. Kissing and caressing feverishly like two lovesick teenagers in a parked car.

"Desi? Jake? Where are you?"

They heard Dorothea's voice and froze, stopping the helpless laughter against each other's necks.

"They must be around here somewhere," Dorothea said, her voice raised. She knew full well where they were and was giving them enough time to put themselves to rights before the whole group descended on them.

Jake moved quickly then, turning their bodies so that Desi's back was to the wall, shielded from view by the broadness of his. "You'd better hurry," he suggested in a voice choked with passion and laughter, as Desi fumbled with her buttons. "They're coming."

"Well, if you'd stop helping!" She slapped at his hands, trying to push her hair out of the way at the same time. "Jake . . . Jake, darling," she said breathlessly, trying to stifle her giggles. "Stop it now!"

"Jake?" Dorothea's voice was closer. "Desi? Are you there?"

They could hear the click of Audrey's heels on the stone floor. "They were right behind us," she said.

"Are you buttoned up yet?" Jake whispered, and his tongue snaked out, tickling her ear.

She pushed at his chest. "Yes, I think so." She giggled. "No thanks to you. Is it buttoned straight?"

"You look beautiful," he assured her, taking hold of her hand to draw her out of their hiding place. "Desi had, ah, something in her eye," he explained to the group, clearly not expecting anyone to believe him, and clearly not caring whether they did or not—because there was obviously nothing wrong with Desi's eyes.

They were wide and happy and sparkling, and they gazed up at Jake with adoration. She looked, in fact, like a woman who had just been very thoroughly and enjoyably kissed and one who, furthermore, had very thoroughly kissed back. Jake's smooth, sable hair was ruffled, and his dark eyes had that triumphant and rather smug look common to men who had just had a very satisfactory amorous encounter.

"Come along, children," Dorothea said then, "on to the wine tasting." She linked her arm through Desi's, pulling her a little ahead of the group. "You ought to learn how to dress yourself," she whispered.

Desi glanced guiltily down at her shirtfront, blushing prettily as she rearranged the mismatched buttons.

"Much better," Dorothea said. "Are we allowed to congratulate Jake yet?"

"Congratulate?"

"On being a father, my dear girl."

"Oh, no, Dorothea. Not yet. I . . . I haven't told him yet."

Dorothea looked at her almost disapprovingly. "I'd suggest you tell him soon. It wouldn't do to have him find out from someone else, would it? Especially not now."

"No . . . no it wouldn't."

Desi sighed. Dorothea was right. It wouldn't do, not at all, to have Jake hear it from someone else. She had to be the one to tell him. If only she could find the right words, the right time.

She had tried, later that night, when Jake had tiptoed across the hall to her room after everyone had turned in for the night.

"I told you I'd come after you when it was dark," he said teasingly to her, slipping out of his robe and under the covers, pulling her warm willing body into his arms. He was naked, but then, so was she. She had known he would come to her and she was ready for him. "No one will hear your screams for mercy," he whispered against her breast.

"I won't make any," she whispered back.

But she did. Little cries and moans that were wrenched from deep inside her. No one heard them but Jake, and he gloried in the soft, womanly sounds she made.

In the morning, as the pink cloudy dawn slowly changed to yellow sunshine, he made love to her again. Slow, languorous love that reminded her of another joyous daylight encounter. When he finally left her, tiptoeing back across the hall, pretending that no one would know where he had spent the night, she still hadn't told him about Stephanie.

Today, she promised herself again, absently applying the finishing touches to Audrey's makeup. Today, when they had finished shooting, she would tell him. No matter how hard it was, she would tell him. She had to.

"Hey, watch out! You nearly jabbed that thing in my eye."

"Sorry, Audrey," she said automatically.

"Hurry it up, would you? I want a cigarette before this scene starts."

Desi put down the lip brush she had just picked up. "You'd better have it now, then. I'll do the lipstick afterward."

"Fine." Audrey lit a cigarette and got up to pace around the cramped set, waiting for the technician to finish setting up the scene. She stepped over thick cables as she picked her way around the small corner of the cellar.

She's really nervous, realized Desi with a small start of surprise. Funny, she hadn't thought that a single nude scene would unnerve Audrey like this. Or partial nude scene, rather.

This particular bit being shot today was a crucial scene in the movie. The one where Richard has finally had enough of Dorothea's teasing, gadabout ways and he drags her away from the party upstairs, down to the deserted wine cellar.

"Where he had his way with me," Dorothea had said, chuckling reminiscently.

The nude scene would come when Audrey-Dorothea tried to twist away from her lover and he reaches out to grab her, tearing her fragile red chiffon dress down the front, leaving the actress bare from the waist up.

"Except for the pearls," Dorothea had reminded them during rehearsals. "If I close my eyes I can still feel the pearls pressing into my back," she said outrageously.

Audrey was wearing those pearls now. Looped twice around her neck, they fell nearly to the hem of the skimpy little flapper dress. She had a matching red chiffon scarf tied around her forehead with the ends trailing down to one shoulder.

"I was considered very wicked in those days," Dorothea informed them gleefully. "Fast, they called it then."

"Yeah, and you're still fast," Jake teased her and she glowed.

"Okay, clear the set," Jake hollered, and everyone who wasn't absolutely necessary for the filming of the scene began filing on up the stairs. He went across to Audrey, patting her shoulder reassuringly. "Ready?"

"Ready as I'll ever be." Audrey crushed out her cigarette and Desi was there immediately, before either of them could call her, to apply the finishing touches to the stars' makeup. She painted on the exaggerated Clara Bow lips with flaming red gloss and then pressed a powder puff briefly against Audrey's forehead, nose and chin to tone down the nervous shine.

"Jake?" she said.

"Oh, all right," he said impatiently, his mind on the upcoming scene. "Just a dab." He bent down a little to allow her to pat his face lightly. It was all he needed.

He looked absolutely magnificent, she thought, in his snowy dress shirt and the distinguished black tuxedo with the real pearl studs down the front. His lush dark hair was slicked back in the twenties fashion giving him a dashing, rather gangsterish look that complemented Audrey's audacious flapper to perfection.

They made a spectacular couple, Desi admitted unwillingly.

"Quiet on the set," bellowed the assistant director, "and . . . action!"

Suddenly it was Richard and Dorothea standing there, not merely two actors. He dragged her, protesting vehemently, into a dark corner of the cellar.

Our corner, Desi thought as the action continued.

The couple argued. He demanded. She refused and began to turn away. He reached out for her and the fragile dress came apart in his hands. She stood there before him; scornful, proud, refusing to cower or hide herself from his eyes. She said something, taunting him, and with a hungry moan, he reached for her again.

Desi turned away. That moan of desire, that look on his face had turned him back into Jake for her. Not Richard. It was Jake she saw now, reaching hungrily for Audrey, pressing her to the floor. Jealousy tore at her insides. Blind, unreasoning jealousy.

How dumb, she scolded herself. Dumb, dumb, dumb! Jake's professional life, his screen persona, had nothing to do with his private life. He was just doing his job, kissing Audrey like that. Just doing his job. She knew that and yet...and yet she kept her face turned away, unable to watch him making make-believe love to the half-naked woman in his arms.

"Cut!" the assistant director yelled.

Jake levered himself up immediately, hauling Audrey to her feet to wrap her in the terry-cloth robe that someone handed to him. There was no lingering kiss this time, no long second look at his co-star. He was the total professional, but Desi didn't see that. She had already started for the stairs.

"Great job," she heard him say. "Audrey, honey, you were wonderful."

"You made it easy, darling." Audrey's voice was husky and still shaking a little from the emotions she had called forth to do the scene. It gave her casual words more intimacy than she had perhaps intended. "You always make it easy."

Jake and the crew laughed at that, treating it as a joke, but Desi couldn't. In her mind's eye she could still see the other woman locked in Jake's arms.

"Break for lunch," Jake said then, and everyone began trooping up the stairs behind Desi, heading for the sun porch and the cold buffet that Gerta had set up.

"Desi." Evan drew her aside before she reached the buffet table. "You've got a call. It's Teddie. He's worried about Stephanie. Been holding for the last ten minutes."

"Stephanie? Is she all right? Where's the phone?"

Evan headed her toward the library. "It's more private in here."

"Teddie," Desi said worriedly into the phone. "What is it? What's the matter with Stephanie?" She listened intently for a few minutes, the phone pressed tightly to her ear. The sound of Stephanie's crying was clearly audible to Desi. "Have you called her pediatrician? Dr. Marshall. His number is on the emergency list by the phone." Another short silence. "No, no, it's not your fault, Teddie. It's mine. Stay calm. I'm on my way."

She hung up. "Stephanie's cold has gotten worse," she told Evan, looking up at him with guilt-stricken eyes. "At least, he thinks it's a cold. He says she's been screaming all morning. She sounded so . . . so sick. Teddie says her temperature is one hundred and two! Oh, Evan, I never should have left her! My baby is sick and I'm here in Sonoma making . . . making movies." Making love, she had almost said. Behaving irresponsibly, with never a thought for her child. Guilt washed over her in waves. "I've got to get home."

"Now, Desi, luv, you couldn't have stopped her from getting sick, you know. It would have happened whether you were with her or not."

"But I'm her *mother*," Desi insisted. "I should have been there. I *knew* she was coming down with something. Sniffles, I told Dorothea. Nothing to worry about. My poor baby. She's so little." She hurried out of the room. "I've got to pack, Evan. Excuse me."

Evan didn't try to stop her as she raced up the stairs, taking them two at a time. She pulled her suitcases out from under the bed and began haphazardly tossing her clothes into them. She dashed back and forth between the bed and dresser and bathroom, throwing her things any old way into the open suitcases, berating herself as she did so.

Stupid! To leave Stephanie when she was so sick, she told herself, completely forgetting that even her own mother had said it was only a sniffle. *But, no, you had to be a career woman. Run off to do your job...run off to a man.* That was the worst of it, she thought frantically. She had left her sick baby to chase after a man. A man she didn't even know for sure wanted her. Not on any permanent basis, anyway.

She had been so happy yesterday and last night, she remembered guiltily. So happy, with never a single thought for Stephanie. Except to wonder how she was going to explain her daughter's presence. Explain her! As if she were something to be ashamed of!

Nothing she could think of to call herself was rotten enough.

"Evan told me that Stephanie was sick." Dorothea hurried into the room, a worried frown on her face. "Is she all right?"

Desi snapped her cases shut. "I don't know," she said, her violet eyes shimmering with frightened tears. It was the first time that Stephanie had ever shown any signs of illness and she was scared. "Teddie said she has a high fever...I could hear her crying over the phone. He said he can't seem to make her stop. Oh, Dorothea," she wailed, "I didn't know she was so sick!"

"Of course you didn't, dear girl." Dorothea embraced her fiercely for a moment. "You're too good a mother to have left her if you had known."

"If anything happens to her, I'll...I'll..."

"Nonsense!" Dorothea squeezed her once more, hard, and let her go. "Nothing is going to happen to her. It's probably just one of those childhood things that all babies get. You wait and see," she reassured the frightened young mother. "She'll be just fine. Why, by the time you get home you probably won't even know that she's been sick."

"Thanks, Dorothea." Desi gave her a wan smile. "You always manage to make me feel better." She dragged her suitcases off the bed, heading for the open bedroom door.

"What do you want me to tell Jake?"

"Tell him—" Desi paused in the doorway, adjusting the strap of her satchel over her shoulder "—tell him the truth."

"The truth? Are you sure?"

"No, I guess the news that he's a father should come from me, shouldn't it?" She thought a minute. "Tell him that there's been a sudden illness in my family... that way you won't be lying." She headed toward the stairs, Dorothea trailing along in her wake. "Tell him I'll call."

THE DRIVE seemed interminable to Desi. Especially when all the way home she was tortured by visions of Stephanie taking a deathly turn for the worse. Stephanie in the hospital. Her tiny fragile body in one of those backless hospital gowns. Breathing tubes. Needles. Doctors shaking their heads sadly.

Stop it, she told herself sternly. *Stephanie's going to be fine. Dorothea's right. Everything will be okay when you get home. She'll be sleeping peacefully. Teddie will feel foolish for having called you. You'll feel foolish for having panicked.*

But it wasn't all right. At least it didn't seem to be. She could hear Stephanie's fretful crying as she ran up the stairs to her apartment.

"Thank goodness you're home!"

Teddie surrendered the screaming baby thankfully as Desi reached out for her. She cradled Stephanie lovingly, peering down into the little screwed-up face, red from her crying. "How's her temperature?"

"The same, hasn't budged either way. Is that good, do you think?" he asked hopefully.

"Well, at least it hasn't gone up any more. So that must be good, I guess. Did you call Dr. Marshall?"

"He was no help!" Teddie said with disgust. "Said it could be any one of a dozen things—all perfectly normal—but that if she was like this tomorrow to bring her in."

"He didn't think it was serious?" she said, glancing up at Teddie as she sat down in the big cane rocker and began to rock gently back and forth. Without conscious thought she offered Stephanie the knuckle of her little finger as a pacifier.

Almost immediately, the baby's cries changed to little whimpers and then ceased altogether. She seemed to nestle happily against her mother's breast, sucking contentedly on Desi's bent finger. "That's my good girl," Desi soothed in a gentle singsong voice. "That's my angel."

"She stopped crying!" Teddie said in real amazement. "What did you do? She's been crying on and off all day and I felt so helpless." He stood looking over Desi's shoulder at the now-quiet baby.

"I don't know. Maternal instinct?" she ventured to guess. "Or maybe she just wanted her mommie." She looked down at the baby. "Is that it, angel? Did you just want your mommie home? Well, Mommie's home now. It's okay. Hey, wait a minute." Her voice changed, the look on her face going from meltingly loving to alert. Her finger probed gently inside Stephanie's mouth. The baby seemed almost to purr with contentment, as if she welcomed the gentle pressure on her gums. "I think she's cutting a tooth!" she said.

"A tooth? Getting a tooth can make her sick?"

"Some babies, yes. Makes them feverish and fretful," Desi explained, beginning to feel much, much better now that she knew what was wrong with her baby. "Besides, she has a little case of the sniffles, too. That's bound to make her feel all the worse." She leaned down and tenderly kissed the baby's head. "Isn't that right, angel? You feel rotten, don't you?" Now that she knew Stephanie wasn't in any grave danger she could become her usual relaxed self. "Have you given her anything?"

"A dose of that liquid baby aspirin you have in the bathroom. Your doctor said it might help the fever."

Desi nodded. "When was that?"

"About, oh—" Teddie looked at his watch "—four hours ago. I tried to feed her then, too. I thought it would be better if she had something on her stomach but she didn't eat much. Only about half a jar of that strained green glop, so I put the leftovers in the fridge."

"Thanks, Teddie." Desi looked up at him. "I really appreciate all the trouble you've been put to. I know it couldn't have been much fun for you."

"No trouble." He waved aside her thanks and reached down to touch one finger to Stephanie's flushed little cheek. "Well, not much, anyway. Anything for my princess. I'm just glad that she's feeling better."

"Well, your princess appreciates it," she insisted. "And her mother appreciates it, too. All I can say is that I'll try to see that you never have to go through this again." She cuddled Stephanie closer to her. "From now on we travel together, or we don't travel," she said firmly. She stood up, being careful to keep her knuckle in Stephanie's mouth. "I'm going to give her another dose of aspirin and try some of that Ambesol stuff on her gums. It's supposed to numb them a little. Then maybe she'll be able to get some sleep." She smiled at Teddie. "You should try to take a nap, too. You look like you could use about eight hours."

"Need anything before I go downstairs?"

"What? Oh, no, nothing. Thanks again, Teddie," she called after him as he left her apartment.

"Come on, angel. Let's go take care of that nasty old tooth."

She got another dose of aspirin down Stephanie, and the numbing medication seemed to make her less fretful and cranky. Enough so, at least, so that Desi was able to get her to eat the rest of "that strained green glop," as Teddie called it, along with a full jar of strained pears. Stephanie loved strained pears.

"Now, how 'bout a bottle, angel, and then a nice long nap? Hmm?"

But Stephanie didn't want to sleep. She didn't even want to be put down. Every time Desi tried she became fretful again, crying weakly, obviously tired but unwilling, or unable, to drop off to sleep.

"All right, darling, all right." Desi finally quit fighting it and sat down in the cane rocker. Crooning soft off-key lullabies, she slowly rocked back and forth until Stephanie quieted again and finally dropped off into an uneasy sleep.

Desi stopped rocking and sat quietly for a few minutes, one slim finger tenderly stroking the baby curves of Stephanie's soft flushed cheek. The baby didn't stir.

"Come on then, angel." She rose carefully from the rocker. "Let's get you into your crib."

She had just closed the nursery door and was on her way to her own room, worn-out and half-asleep herself, when the doorbell began to chime insistently, as if someone was leaning on it. She hurried from the hall to answer it before whoever it was could rouse Stephanie from her fretful sleep.

"Jake."

She stood there, staring at him around the edge of the half-opened door. What was he doing here in San Francisco when he was supposed to be filming? And then, a terrible, heart-stopping thought occurred to her. Someone must have told him about Stephanie!

That was the only reason she could think of for his leaving Sonoma in the middle of filming. Certainly, he hadn't followed her just to yell about her own abrupt departure from location.

Oh, God, what was she going to do now? What could she say to him? How could she make him understand?

"Jake," she said again as he stood there looking down at her.

"Can I come in?" His voice was low, the words softly spoken, and the look on his face was almost pleading.

But Desi was too agitated to see that. She stepped back quickly, holding open the door. "I'm sorry. Yes, come in." She gestured toward the rose-satin sofa. "Sit down."

He sank down onto the sofa, his head falling back to rest against the low back, one hand going up to absently massage the bridge of his nose.

He looked tired, she thought. Tired and a little stunned.

Well, wouldn't you, she asked herself, *if you had just found out that you had a nearly five-month-old daughter?*

"Can I . . . can I get you a drink?" she offered hesitantly, wondering why he hadn't said anything yet. Why he hadn't asked about Stephanie. "Or a cup of coffee?"

Would you like a drink? The words echoed eerily in her head. He had said those words to her once. In a hotel room to ease her obvious uncertainty and shyness. Well, she wasn't shy with him now but she was still uncertain. Now, more than ever.

I should have told him, she thought. As soon as she had known she was pregnant she should have contacted him, somehow, and told him.

"Coffee, please." He lowered his massaging hand to look at her. "I want to keep a clear head."

A clear head, yes. They would both need clear heads.

"Wait a minute." He started to rise from the sofa. "I'll help you."

"No, thank you. Really. I . . . it's okay. My kitchen is so small and . . ." She realized that she was babbling and turned, fleeing to the kitchen, praying that he wouldn't follow her.

He didn't and Desi was allowed a precious ten minutes to pull herself together. She busied her hands making sandwiches while the coffee was brewing. She had missed lunch today and, probably, so had Jake. The dinner hour had come and gone unnoticed, too, and—surprisingly—she was hungry. Besides, she reasoned, a small flash of humor coming to her aid, a full stomach was said to make a man more reasonable.

Taking a deep breath, she shouldered open the door and came out into the living room with the laden tray. Jake jumped to his feet immediately, taking it from her to place it on the low coffee table in front of the sofa and then, before she could sit down, he took her hands in his.

"I know that now isn't the time," he said, very gently, pulling her down to sit on the sofa beside him. "I know you're worried sick about your mother. But I had to come. Had to be here with you." He dropped one of her hands and reached up to brush a strand of hair back from her face, tucking it gently behind her ear.

"You're surprised, I know," he said in answer to the incredulous look on her face. A wry smile curved his lips. "But not half as surprised as I am, believe me. When you left Dorothea's house in such a rush, I suddenly realized just how very much you mean to me. Realized *why* the sex was so great between us. Why I couldn't forget you." His hand cupped her cheek and his dark eyes were soft as he stared intently into her wide violet ones. "It's because I love you."

Desi still said nothing, just gazed up at him with that disbelieving, incredulous look on her face. Her mother? What did he mean about her mother?

"Desiree, are you listening to me?" His other hand came up to cradle her face. "I've just said that I love you."

"Yes, I'm listening," she said, blinking slowly as his words finally penetrated her fogged brain. *He said he loved her!*

"Oh, Jake," was all she could utter. Tears threatened, turning her eyes to pools of liquid amethyst, as she smiled tremulously up at him. "Oh, Jake, I . . ."

"Well, it's nothing to cry about, is it?" he asked, tenderly kissing the lid of each eye, touching his lips softly to each pink cheek. "Is it, Desiree?" The words were a mere whisper.

Oh, if he only knew how much there was to cry about. "No...no, it isn't.... Oh, Jake." Her eyes closed as his hands slid around to the back of her head, holding her willing captive under the force of his gentle soul-searing kiss.

Their mouths clung for endless seconds. Lips and tongues and teeth tenderly probing and tasting and nibbling at the sweetness that each so freely offered the other. Desi's arms twined around the strong column of his neck, her body boneless as a rag doll as she melted against him in total surrender.

She felt his hands slide down her back to encircle her pliant body. For a second they tightened almost painfully, convulsively, crushing her to him, and she gloried in the force of his desire for her.

"Desiree." The word was a ragged sigh against her mouth as he lifted his lips from hers. "Sweet Desiree." His lips touched her cheek again. "I don't know why I kept you at

arm's length for so long. Why I couldn't admit how I felt."
His mouth traveled to the delicate curve of her ear.

"You had a lot on your mind," she ventured softly. "The
film. No . . . no emotion, you said, and I . . . I know how important it is to you."

"The film. Yes, the film." She felt him smile against her
cheek. "But not more important than you. Never again more
important than you." He leaned back a little to look into her
face. "When you left so suddenly I was angry—furious—that
you went without saying anything to me. Because of the
filming I told myself, at first."

"At first?"

"And then Dorothea told me how upset you were. That
someone—your mother—had taken a turn for the worse and
you had to get home. I realized then how much you meant to
me. All I could think of was being with you, comforting you.
I was nearly frantic, trying to find you." His lips gently caressed her temples, and he drew a deep shuddering breath
against her cheek. "There was no answer at your parents'
house when I called—I thought you would have gone directly there. And . . . the hospitals couldn't tell me anything
either. But then I remembered that Dorothea had mentioned
how close you were to your landlord, so I came here." He
pressed his cheek against hers again, hiding his face in the
cloud of her copper hair as if his emotion embarrassed him.
"You'll never know how relieved I was to see your car in the
driveway."

"But, Jake, it isn't my mother that's sick. Dorothea didn't
actually tell you it was my mother, did she? No . . . no, never
mind. It's not important." She squirmed in his arms, trying
to get her hands up to his face. She had to tell him. Now.
"Jake, look at me."

His beautiful brown eyes gazed questioningly, lovingly into
hers, his arms cradled her tenderly. How would he look at
her, hold her, when she told him?

"Well, maybe Dorothea didn't actually say it was your
mother," he began, "I may have misunderstood her but—"

Desi shook her head, silencing him. "My mother's not sick, Jake. It's...oh, I don't know how to say this! How to tell you! I should have told you, Jake," she said earnestly, bravely holding his gaze, even though tears glistened on her lashes now. "I should have told you months ago. But I couldn't. I didn't know how. It's—" she stumbled over the words "—it's my daughter that's sick, Jake. Not my mother."

"Your daughter?" He didn't seem to quite take it in. "You have a daughter?"

"Yes, Jake." She paused, taking a deep breath. "And she's your daughter, too."

He stilled, his body gone tense, his face uncomprehending, incredulous...blank.

"My daughter?" His eyes, even his very skin under her hands, began to cool. "What do you mean, *my* daughter?"

Desi's hands dropped from his face to clench in her lap. "Just what I said, Jake, your daughter."

He stood up. "Just what are you saying, Desiree?"

She stared down at her hands. "I'm saying that I got pregnant last...last November. I'm saying that I had a baby." She looked up at him. "Your baby." Her eyes dropped again, unable to face the look in his. He looked as if he had been hit on the head with a sledgehammer and still hadn't come to yet. "A little girl," she said softly. "A beautiful little girl. I...named her Stephanie. Stephanie Louise."

"Am I supposed to be pleased?" he asked then, in a hard voice.

She could feel him standing over her, his presence menacing, stern, unyielding. "No...no, I didn't expect you to be pleased," she said, her head still bowed. "I don't know what I expected. No, that's not true." She sighed. "I expected anger, I guess. Shock, maybe. I—"

He grabbed her by the shoulders, pulling her roughly to her feet. "Anger, you guess! Shock, maybe!" He looked as if he would like to shake her and then thought better of it, letting her go as he turned to pace the room. "Why in hell did you wait until now to tell me? Why?" He passed a hand through his thick hair and turned to face her from across the room.

She shrank back from the look that had come into his eyes.
The eyes that only minutes ago had been filled with such love
and tenderness.

"Did you think it was safe to tell me now that you had me
hooked? Now that I'd admitted how I feel about you?"

"No!" Her denial was shocked and vehement and totally
unfeigned. If he hadn't been so wrapped up in his own pain
and bewilderment, he might have seen that. "No, Jake, I—"

"Did you think I'd just say 'Gee, isn't that nice.' A daughter!" His voice rose harshly on the last word, echoing through
the room.

"Please, Jake." Desi's hand went out to him warningly.
"She's asleep."

But the warning came too late. They both heard the thin
wail that came from the other room. Desi stilled for a minute, holding her breath. Maybe she'd fall back to sleep. But
no, the whimper became a full-fledged cry for immediate attention.

"I have to go to her. She's teething." Desi hurried past Jake
into her daughter's room.

"There, there, darling," she soothed, lifting the crying baby
from her crib. "Hush, darling, Mommie's here." She held the
baby against her shoulder, gently rubbing her back in an effort to quiet her tears, all the while desperately fighting tears
of her own. When that didn't work she turned Stephanie,
cradling the baby in the crook of one arm, and applied gentle pressure to her irritated gums. Almost immediately the
crying stopped as Stephanie began to suck contentedly on her
mother's finger.

"Poor little angel," she crooned softly. "You need some
more medicine on those sore gums, don't you?" Desi turned
from the crib with the baby in her arms to see Jake standing
in the doorway, silently watching her.

She almost quailed before the look on his face, but then her
shoulders stiffened and she crossed the room, brushing past
him on her way to the bathroom for Stephanie's medication.
He followed, watching as she sat down on the edge of the
bathtub to apply the numbing cream to the baby's gums.

"She looks like you," he said after a minute.

"Yes, she does." Desi's voice was as controlled as his but she didn't look up. "She has your eyes, though."

"Does she?" He folded his arms across his chest as he leaned against the doorframe. Almost, Desi thought, as if he was afraid he might reach out to touch one of them, if he didn't. "I don't see the resemblance myself."

"I didn't think you would," she murmured. She gave Stephanie another dose of liquid baby aspirin and stood up. Again, Jake followed her as she returned to the baby's room to put Stephanie back into her crib.

"What did you say her name was?" he asked from behind her as she smoothed a light quilt over the drowsy baby.

Desi's hand touched her daughter's head briefly, brushing back a few curling tufts of red hair that were still damp with fever-induced perspiration. The baby's face was lightly flushed from crying, and she looked incredibly sweet and angelic.

"Stephanie," Desi said softly, her eyes on her daughter.

"Stephanie what?"

She glanced over her shoulder at him. "Weston," she said firmly.

"And who did you put down as the father?"

He meant the birth certificate, she realized. That was still a very sore point with her. She had hated to do what she did, but at the time it had seemed like the best thing to do. Putting the name Jake Lancing down as her baby's father would have resulted in unbearable publicity. Birth certificates were a matter of public record, if anyone cared to investigate. It would have made the front page of every scandal sheet in the country.

"Well—what name?"

"Unknown," she said softly, still looking down at her daughter.

"What?" He made her repeat it.

"Unknown." She looked up at him defiantly. "I wrote, 'Father unknown.' What else would you expect? You know what would have happened if I'd put your name on it!"

There was a strange, cold smile on his face that didn't reach his eyes. "Well, that solves one problem, at least."

"What's that?" she asked suspiciously, not trusting that smile.

"It will save me the trouble of going to court to have it changed."

He didn't believe her! He didn't believe Stephanie was his daughter! So, okay, what else had she expected? She drew herself up proudly.

"It will save you any trouble at all," she said. "It may have escaped your notice, but I haven't asked you for anything!" She turned away quickly, heading for the nursery door, and so missed the momentary expression of confusion, or doubt, that crossed his face.

I will not cry, she told herself, fighting tears. *I will not cry or explain or plead.* She turned back to face him when they reached the living room. Her eyes were dry. "I think you'd better go, Jake."

He didn't make a move toward the door. "Not until I know what you're up to."

"I'm not up to anything! I told you that. If I was up to something, wouldn't I have made my move long before now? Stephanie is almost five months old. Five months, Jake! The time for me to bring the paternity suit you're so obviously afraid of was when she was born, not now."

"When *was* she born—exactly?"

"July 10," she answered him absently, anxious to get back to what she considered a more important question. "I don't intend to bring suit, Jake, I . . ." Her voice trailed off.

She could almost see him doing the calculations in his head. A look of something very like disappointment crossed his face for the merest instant, but it was replaced almost immediately by anger. Anger and a frighteningly cold sort of contempt.

"So you were already pregnant when you picked me up that night on the plane." There was complete conviction in his voice.

"No!" she denied automatically, forgetting her resolve not to explain or plead. "Stephanie was premature. Six weeks premature." But she could see that he didn't believe her.

"Did you plan it all?" he wanted to know. "Did you intend to use me? Or was it just a spur-of-the-moment idea? An opportunity too good to pass up? Hmm?" he said with a curl of his lip. "I'd be curious to know just how you planned to work this out."

"I didn't plan anything," she denied. Her voice was a mere whisper. "You've got to believe me, Jake. I never used you. Stephanie *was* premature—"

"Just how stupid do you think I am?" he exploded. "My God, Desiree, that's one of the oldest tricks in the book!"

"It isn't a trick," she insisted, but she knew it was no use. Jake wasn't listening to anything she had to say. He was too angry to listen. Maybe he would always be too angry to listen.

"Did you really expect me to just take your word for it? Be so overjoyed that you had supplied me with a daughter that I wouldn't ask any unpleasant questions?"

If you only knew what I'd thought, she wanted to say but she didn't.

"You should have done your homework better," he taunted. "That particular little scheme has been tried before. And by more experienced hustlers than you!"

Desi covered her ears with her hands. "That's enough, Jake. Enough!" She lowered her hands, and her fists clenched tightly at her sides. She could feel the smooth ovals of her nails digging into her palms, but it didn't seem to matter. All that mattered at this moment was making him understand a few important facts.

"Stephanie is your daughter," she said slowly, carefully enunciating each word so that he would be sure to understand. "You can believe that or not. I don't care one way or the other," she lied.

"You can bet I don't believe it!" he cut in savagely.

"Fine!" she shot back. "As far as I'm concerned, it's your loss. Not ours." She turned away again, trembling now. Her self-control was almost at an end. "I'd appreciate it if you'd leave now, Jake."

"Not until I know what you plan to do."

"I told you what I plan to do. *Nothing* is what I plan to do!" She turned back to face him once more. "Are you listening, Jake? Nothing! My daughter's name is Stephanie Weston. It will stay Weston! We don't need you," she flung at him, struggling with her tears. "We don't want you. Just go. Please!"

"Desiree," he said, a strange note coloring his deep voice. His hand reached out and touched her shoulder.

She shook him off, moving away from his dangerous touch. If he stayed any longer she would break down and do what she had promised herself she wouldn't do. She would start to cry and explain and plead.

"Please go," she repeated. "There's nothing more to say."

He went, closing the door softly behind him. Desi stood where she was in the middle of her comfortable living room, holding herself together by sheer effort of will. She heard his footsteps on the stairs and then the outermost door slammed shut.

Something in her broke then. Whatever it was that had been holding her together during this past year finally gave way. She had held tight through the long lonely months of her pregnancy, through the complicated birth and the early fears for her premature baby, through these last tension-filled months on the set, pretending that Jake was no more to her than an employer. But, suddenly, she just let go.

Desi crumbled into a chair, racked by sobs. Deep wrenching sobs that came up from her stomach, making her gasp for each breath, until there were simply no more tears left to cry.

To have what she had wanted, had dreamed of, for so long. To hear Jake say those three wonderful words. And then to lose him again, all in the space of a day. To see his eyes go from warm and loving to cold and contemptuous. To hear him say those hateful things. Liar, he had called her. Why, oh why, hadn't she told him sooner? Why? But there were no answers in the silent room. None.

She got up from the chair, wiping her eyes with the back of her hand, and went in to look at Stephanie. She needed to see her baby . . . her anchor.

"Well, your daddy didn't want us," she said to the sleeping baby. "But don't worry about it, angel. We can get along just fine without him. We have so far, haven't we?"

13

DESI STRUGGLED UP from the depths of sleep, her one thought to stop the noise, quickly, before it woke Stephanie. She reached out groggily to shut off the alarm, and her hand hit against the tray of cold coffee and uneaten sandwiches. For a minute she was disoriented and then she remembered. She was on the sofa, curled up under Stephanie's quilt. The noise wasn't her alarm, it was the doorbell.

It sounded again, louder this time it seemed, and she jumped up, wrapping the quilt around her shoulders, and stumbled toward the door.

"Hold it down, will you. The baby's asleep," she rasped as she pulled open the door. She pushed the hair out of her eyes with one hand, peering out into the dim hall with tear-swollen eyes.

"Go away," she said, trying to close the door on him.

His foot stopped her. "Desiree, we have to talk."

"We've talked." She pushed against the door. "Now go away."

Please go away, she pleaded silently. *Let me start getting over you again.*

"We've got to talk," he repeated.

Desi remained silent, leaning her full weight against the door but he didn't budge.

"I'll stand here all night if I have to."

Wearily she heaved herself away from the door, swinging it open, and stared up at him. "So talk," she said rudely.

"Can I come in?"

"You're in, aren't you?" Quickly she turned away, hunching herself farther into the pastel baby quilt, before her hands could disobey her and reach out to touch him.

He looked tired—as tired as she felt—and there was a shadow of stubble on his lean jaw. His beautiful dark eyes held an expression she couldn't read. Good, she didn't want to read it.

I don't care, she told herself. *I don't care.* But she did, and God help her, she probably always would.

"What do you want?" she said, throwing the words over her shoulder as she moved across the room, away from him, to stand staring sightlessly out the window at the moonlit San Francisco night.

"To talk to you."

"About what?" She knew she sounded rude and nasty, but that seemed to be her only defense against him. She turned from the window and found him standing right behind her.

He reached out one hand and gently touched her tear-streaked face. "You've been crying," he said softly. His thumb caressed her cheek.

For just a second, the space of a heartbeat only, she allowed herself the tenderness of his touch, and then she jerked out of his reach as if he had burned her. In a way, she thought, he had.

"My tears surprise you?" she said.

She glared defiantly up into his face for an instant and then quickly looked away. It was a mistake to look too closely into his eyes. There were questions there and a strange expression that bordered on pain. She didn't want to know about his pain. Not now. She had enough pain of her own.

"What did you expect?" she said then, moving to the safety of the cane rocker. She sat down, wrapping the quilt around her bent knees. "It's not every day that someone calls me a hustler—" her voice began to shake "—and a liar." She flung the words at him bitterly.

Jake made a sound like a groan, running a hand through his hair. "I'm sorry for that, Desiree. I'd give anything to have those words unsaid."

There was a long silence as she stared down at her pink-tipped toes, where they peeked out from under the edge of the enveloping quilt. "Is that what you came to say?" she said finally. "That you're sorry?"

"Among other things."

"What other things?"

"Desiree, we've got to talk! I've been driving around the city for hours. Thinking. Going over everything...over and over again...in my mind. We've got to talk this out. Reasonably. Calmly—"

"Talk what out?" she said, deliberately misunderstanding him.

"You. Me. Stephanie."

"No!" She jumped to her feet, leaving the chair rocking wildly behind her. The quilt fell unheeded to the floor. "No. I've said all I'm going to say about that. Stephanie is your daughter. I'm not going to beg you to believe me. I'm not going—"

Suddenly his hands were on her shoulders, shaking her into silence. She stared up at him, her eyes wide and tear-filled again.

I won't cry, she told herself fiercely, closing her eyes against him. *I won't cry!*

"Desiree, look at me."

She opened her eyes slowly, willing the tears not to fall. He was staring down into her face, devouring her, feature by feature, with agonizing thoroughness. She could see the questions in his eyes again. See him doubting her.

"Why didn't you meet me at the fountain?" he said, as if that question was more important to him than anything else.

"The fountain ...?"

"I waited for you in Ghirardelli Square, Desiree. And I came back the next day in case we'd gotten our wires crossed. But you never showed up."

"You waited ...?"

"Like a fool, for hours. I kept telling myself that you'd be there. That you were special. *We* were special. That it hadn't been just another one-night stand." He shook her again. "Why didn't you come?"

"I wanted to," she replied softly, gazing up into his eyes as if her life depended on it, willing him to believe her. Her life *did* depend on it. "I wanted to. I even got dressed, but . . ."

"But what?" he prodded her, his voice raw and savage.

"I was more than six months' pregnant and . . . and as big as a house," she blurted out. "I had toxemia by then and I'd swelled up like a balloon. I . . . I didn't know what I could say to you. How you'd react. If you'd even be there!" She paused, gulping for air, and the tears spilled over, coursing unheeded down her cheeks. "I was fat and ugly and . . . and I thought you'd hate me for getting pregnant!"

His arms went around her shoulders, pulling her close, one big hand pressing her wet face into his chest. "Women!" he said softly, incredulously. She could feel the tension drain out of him as easily as if someone had pulled a plug, and she felt his chest heave under her cheek as if he was stifling a laugh . . . or a sob.

"I could never hate you, Desiree. Don't you know that?" he said into her hair. "I can only love you."

She stood stock-still against him for a minute, doubting what she had heard. She wanted, so very badly, to believe those words that she feared her ears were playing tricks on her. Hearing what they wanted to hear.

But he was still holding her, she realized, so it must be true. Somehow. His hand at her head was tenderly stroking her hair. His other hand was biting, almost painfully, into the soft flesh of her hip, as if he feared she would try to move away from him. She felt his lips against her ear.

"You could never be ugly to me, no matter how pregnant you got."

He *was* laughing now, she was sure of it. She didn't know why—whether it was relief or real amusement, or both. But that was okay. As long as he held her like this he could laugh till doomsday and she wouldn't object.

"I'd have loved to see you pregnant," he said then, the laughter suddenly gone out of his voice. There was a pause. "With my daughter," he finished softly.

Desi twisted her head to look up at him. His daughter, he'd said! "Oh, Jake, are you sure? You believe me?"

"I believe you." He was smiling down at her. A look of tenderness was on his face, and his beautiful brown eyes were unclouded by uncertainty or doubt, though unshed tears shimmered in their depths. "Deep down I've always wanted to believe you. From the minute you told me, I wanted to believe that Stephanie was mine. Because *not* believing was tearing the heart out of me. And because I knew, deep down inside of me, that you weren't the sort of woman to lie about a thing like that. I *knew* it but . . ." He shook his head and the next words came out haltingly, as if he hated to say them. "But there were the memories of those two other times. Those women who said that their babies were mine, and I guess I went sort of crazy for a little while, remembering."

"Oh, Jake." Her arms went up around his neck, pulling his head down to hers so that she could plant tiny healing kisses all over his face. "Oh, Jake, I'm sorry. I'm so sorry. I should have told you. As soon as I knew I was pregnant, I should have told you."

"Yes, you should have," he agreed. "It would have saved us both a lot of needless grief. A lot of wasted months when we could have been together."

"I wanted to tell you. I did! But I was scared."

"Of me?" His hands captured her face, holding her still.

"No . . . not exactly, but of . . . of, oh, I don't know how to say it! It was just that I had loved you for so long. Ever since *December Fire*, I think and—"

"Since *December Fire*? But you couldn't have been more than a teenager then. You didn't even know me."

"Yes, I did. In a way. I worked on *December Fire* as a gofer. Zek got it for me as a summer job. And I guess I just . . . fell in love with you then. I *know* it sounds stupid, but—"

"I don't remember you at all," he said incredulously, shaking his head.

"There's no reason you should. We never even spoke to each other," she admitted. "I told myself that it was just a crush. That I'd get over it, but I never did and then suddenly, there you were on the plane and . . . later, when you'd gone, I was afraid that it was just a one-night stand for you even though it meant so much to me. I *knew* you'd think I was just some dumb groupie."

He winced. "Can't you ever forgive me for that?"

"There's nothing to forgive," she insisted. "What else could you have thought? I picked you up on that plane. I went to your hotel and . . . and, well, you know." She looked down, embarrassed, as the fiery color stained her cheeks. "There was nothing else you *could* think."

"I never, not for one minute, thought that," he denied. "Not that weekend, anyway. That weekend all I could think of was how good it was. How *right* it felt to hold you and love you. And for six long months, in the wilds of Alaska, it was the thought of you that kept me from freezing to death. All I could think about was getting that movie over with and getting back to you!"

He smiled down into her wide shimmering eyes, his own brimming with love and tenderness. "You were too shy to be a groupie. Too uncertain about what you were doing. Groupies are bold little tramps, and they like to brag about their exploits. I couldn't even get you to tell me your name!" he teased.

"But later?" she prompted, remembering what he had said to her in Dorothea's second-best guest room.

"Later what?" he said absently, watching the delicate color come and go in her cheeks.

"That first day on the set and—" she shrugged "—you know—later."

"You surprised me," he answered quietly. His lips touched her cheek, feeling the warmth of the blush that seemed to so intrigue him. "By that time I had convinced myself that I would never see you again. That you didn't mean anything to me. And then, there you were. With Evan, I thought. Cool as a cucumber and looking just as sweet and beautiful as I remembered." His hands made lazy circles against her back as he talked and Desi leaned into him, only half listening to his words. "I was angry and hurt," he went on, his lips against her ear, "and so jealous I couldn't see straight. I just said the first thing that came into my head."

Desi arched away from him a little to look up into his face. "Were you really jealous?" she asked him, a delighted little half smile curving her lips.

"Damn right I was!" he said and then added, "You like that idea, don't you, you little witch?"

Desi nodded, rubbing her cheek against his chest. "Only because I was so jealous, too. It's nice to know I wasn't alone in my misery."

"Jealous of whom?" He seemed genuinely puzzled.

"Of Audrey," she admitted.

"Audrey!"

"Yes, Audrey! She's so beautiful and sophisticated. More your type than I am and ... every time you kissed her on the set I just—" Desi blushed, lowering her eyes "—just wanted to tear her hair out!"

"But that's just part of my job—"

"That's what I told myself but—"

"Hell, I don't even like her much." He slanted a glance down at Desi's face. "You'd have been more on the mark to be jealous of Dorothea."

Desi giggled. "Oh, she'd love to hear that. It would make her day. I'll have to..." Her voice trailed off as she caught the look in his eyes. Her eyes closed of their own accord, her head fell back ... waiting.

He kissed her then. Sweetly, at first, teasing her lips with his tongue even after they had opened to him.

"Oh, Jake," she breathed, straining upward to bring her mouth closer to his. "Jake, I love you. I'll never hide anything from you again. Never! No matter what it is. I—"

"Be quiet, woman," he growled, molding his mouth more firmly over hers. His tongue invaded her mouth, hungrily, demandingly, and she felt his hand move up her body to close possessively over her breast, kneading the soft flesh gently through her shirt. Desi melted against him helplessly, her body gone pliant in his arms.

He lifted his mouth from hers for a brief instant. "You will marry me, won't you?" he whispered against her lips. "Give Stephanie a father?"

Marry him! Desi felt joy surge through her and, then, his last words echoed through her head. *Give Stephanie a father*, he had said. Was that what this was all about? He wanted to marry her because of Stephanie?

"Desiree?" He pulled back slightly to look into her eyes. "Will you marry me?"

"Oh, Jake . . . I—" her voice trembled piteously "—I don't know . . . I . . ."

"You don't know! What do you mean, you don't know?"

She looked up into his face, a stubborn look in her violet eyes, despite the shimmer of tears. "I won't marry you just to give Stephanie a legal father! It wouldn't be good for her, or me . . . or you, either!" She tried to explain. "You'd just end up hating us both and—"

Jake's left hand came up to cover her mouth. "Be quiet," he ordered.

"But I—"

"Quiet, I said. Now, I'm only going to explain this once, so you'd better listen." He took his hand away when she nodded her head. It slid around her back and he pulled her to him. Hard. His beautiful brown eyes bore steadily into hers.

"I love you, Desiree," he said softly, slowly. "If I didn't love you I wouldn't have asked you to marry me. I would be willing to provide for Stephanie financially, but I wouldn't tie myself to a woman I didn't love. Not even for my daughter. Is that clear?"

"Yes, Jake," Desi murmured obediently.

"Good. Now—will you marry me?"

"Yes, Jake!" she sighed rapturously. "Oh, yes!"

His mouth took hers again, devouring all the sweetness she so eagerly offered. They began to edge blindly toward the sofa, stumbling into the coffee table in their feverish haste. Jake stopped what he was doing with his hands and mouth to lift her into his arms.

"The bedroom?" he said, his voice low and husky with passion.

"That way," she whispered, pointing toward the hall. "To the left. Second door."

He stopped by the bed, letting her body slide slowly down the hard length of his until her bare feet touched the floor. Without a word being spoken, she began to unbutton her shirt—one slow button at a time. The shirt dropped to the floor and she reached for the snap of her jeans, sliding them down her legs to the floor and kicking them aside.

She held his eyes all the while, unwrapping herself like a gift until she stood there covered only by a wisp of lilac silk across her hips and the flaming copper hair that curled to her waist.

Jake reached out with both hands and lifted her hair, pushing it back behind her shoulders. His fingers lingered on the creamy skin of her neck, then trailed lightly across her fragile collarbone and down to her breasts to cup their enticing fullness in his palms.

"It always amazes me," he said, a note of wonder in his deep voice, "how very female you are under your boy's clothes."

His hands left her breasts then, following the curves of her waist and hips. His fingers slid under the lilac silk and continued their slow tantalizing trek downward as he caressed her slender thighs and calves and delicate, fine-boned ankles. Obligingly Desi stepped out of her panties when he reached her feet, one hand reaching out to his shoulder to steady herself as she did so.

Jake leaned back on his heels. "You're absolutely perfect," he murmured. His hot dark eyes surveyed her again from the top of her flaming head to her bright pink toenails. "Imagine hiding all this magnificence under those baggy jeans."

"I have one fault, remember?" she said teasingly, but her voice was shaking and her body had begun to tremble.

"Ah, yes. The beauty mark."

"Mole."

"Beauty mark," he insisted, teasing her. He leaned forward suddenly, catching her off guard. His arms went around her waist, pulling her to him, and his mouth moved, moist and hot, against the little reddish mole on her left hip.

"Jake!" she gasped. Her hands clutched his shoulders to keep from falling as his mouth wandered tantalizingly from her hip to her navel and beyond, making her weak-kneed with rapturous delight.

From the next room the baby began to cry softly. They both stilled, listening, hoping she would settle down again, but the whimper rose to a steady wail. Desi began looking around for her robe.

Jake rocked back on his heels, his hands on Desi's hips, and levered himself to his feet. "You stay here," he said in a voice not quite steady. "I'll go to her."

"Don't be silly. She'll probably need changing and, besides, she's teething. You might have to rock her back to sleep."

"You think I can't handle one little baby?" he asked in mock indignation.

"No," she answered him honestly, her violet eyes alight with laughter and tenderness.

"Don't bet on it. My older sister has four kids. I'm an expert baby rocker."

"And diaper changer?" she said dryly.

"Anybody can change a diaper." He grinned. "It just takes a strong stomach." He put one big hand between her breasts and toppled her backward onto the bed. "Wait for me right there," he ordered. "I'll be back."

Desi smiled up at him. He'd be calling for her help soon enough. She'd give him five minutes, at most.

She heard the door to Stephanie's room creak open and then the baby's crying quieted abruptly, presumably as Jake picked her up. She heard the deep, muffled sound of Jake's voice as he talked to his daughter, but there was no frantic appeal for her help. Maybe he *could* change a diaper.

Desi got up from the bed and pulled back the quilted spread and the crisp powder blue sheets, fluffing the pillows before she crawled back in it to wait, as ordered.

It was just as if they were already married, she thought, hugging herself happily. She, waiting there in their bed, keeping it warm, while Jake took his turn with the baby.

"I'll make him happy," she whispered aloud, to no one in particular.

She made herself comfortable under the covers, listening to the muted music of father and daughter in the next room. Jake seemed to be talking to the baby, and there were pauses, as if she was answering him. Desi closed her eyes, smiling at the picture that conjured up. The internationally famous heartthrob, Mr. Jake Lancing, babbling gibberish to a five-month-old baby girl. It was enough to bring foolish tears to her eyes.

"YOU DIDN'T WAIT for me." Jake's breath tickled her ear as he snuggled down into the bed beside her.

Desi's eyes flickered open, focusing groggily on the bare, hairy chest in front of her. "I guess I fell asleep," she said. She wrapped her arm around his waist, burying her face against his furred chest as if waking up to find him naked in her bed was the most natural thing in the world. "You took long enough," she complained sleepily.

"Stephanie wanted to talk."

Desi rubbed her cheek against his hair-roughened chest. "She's too young to talk."

"She is not," he informed her, a ring of fatherly pride in his voice. "We decided that she's going up to Sonoma with us tomorrow to finish the picture."

Desi rolled over onto her back to look up into his face. "She is, is she?"

Jake nodded.

"I thought you didn't like kids."

"Who told you a lie like that?"

"You did—indirectly, anyway."

He looked at her quizzically, one eyebrow raised in mute question.

"Those paternity suits," she explained, "and a couple of things you said in interviews and on the *Tonight Show.*"

"I never said I didn't *like* kids. I just said those particular two weren't mine."

"Oh," Desi uttered softly, not knowing what else to say.

"In fact, I'm crazy about kids." His arms cradled her. "Especially little redheaded kids. I'd like to have at least as many as my sister." He peered down into her face. "Did I tell you that she has four?"

"Ah, yes." Desi nodded against his chest. "Four." She felt his hands moving slowly on her body. "That's quite a large . . . ah, family, isn't it? I mean—" she squirmed as his fingers explored her navel "—for a working couple. That's a lot of . . . um, responsibility and, um . . ." She was becoming incoherent as his hands continued their tantalizing journey over the curves of her slim body.

"Don't worry about it." He spoke against his ear, his tongue teasing the lobe. "We'll get a nanny and they can travel with us. I'm rich, unless this film flops and then—"

"It won't flop!" Desi interrupted loyally, propping herself up on one elbow. "It's a great film and it'll be a box-office hit! I know it will."

"Hey," Jake said, a slow, sexy smile on his face, his dark eyes alight with love and tenderness and passion. "Do you really want to talk business? Now?"

Desi's smile matched his. "No-o-o," she said, a little breathlessly.

"Then kiss me," he ordered, rolling her over so that she was trapped under the welcome weight of his hard body.

Her arms came up, pulling his head down to her searching mouth, and her slender body arched under him, inviting his most intimate possession. He shifted eagerly as her legs opened, taking what she so freely and so sweetly offered.

"Desiree!" he groaned, straining forward into the honeyed warmth of her body.

Desi's fingers clutched convulsively at his shoulders, and she murmured his name softly, over and over, like a chant. It was the only thing she seemed able to say as he took her beyond coherent thought with the thrusting heat of his muscled body and the sweet, exciting love words that he whispered hoarsely against the dampness of her neck. It was those words, as much as what he did to her with his body, that finally drove her over the crest.

"Jake!" She nearly screamed as an intense pleasure washed over her in waves. "Oh, Jake, my darling," she murmured again as she felt him stiffen in her arms.

He lay there for several long minutes, holding her trembling body close, as they both drifted back to reality. Slowly she became aware of the sheets rumpled under their sweat-sheened bodies, of the comforter that had slipped to the floor, of the distant sound of the constant city traffic, and the weight of Jake's body above her—all things that had gone completely unnoticed during the act of love.

Jake shifted his body then, relieving her of his weight, but keeping her close still, with his arm around her shoulders and her head on his chest.

"I think you were right," he said, his voice soft and gruff from somewhere above her head.

"About what?" She lifted her head a little to peer up at him.

"Stephanie does have my eyes," he told her, a note of pleased conviction in his voice. He pressed her head back down to his chest with his free hand.

"Oh, you!" She punched him lightly in the ribs in retaliation and was rewarded by a soft oomph of laughter.

His hand stroked lazily down the length of her back. "Go to sleep, my Desiree," he said. "We have a long day tomorrow." His voice sounded fuzzy and far away as if he, too, was drifting off to sleep. "Drive up to Sonoma. Get *Devil's Lady* in the can before Christmas. Shall we have Christmas with your family, sweetheart? We could get married then."

He paused, in case Desi wanted to speak, but she remained silent, cuddled contentedly against his side. "It should be a small wedding, don't you think?" he went on, not really waiting for, nor expecting, an answer. "Just immediate families. Will your parents mind arranging a wedding on such short notice? Or should I have my secretary take care of it?"

"Mmm," Desi mumbled against his chest.

Jake jiggled her a little. "Hey, we're planning a wedding here. Pay attention, woman."

"Mmm," Desi said again, drowsy with love and contentment. "It sounds wonderful. I'd love a Christmas wedding, and my mother will have a ball."

They had almost dropped off to sleep when a sudden thought brought her upright. "Oh my goodness!"

"What?" Jake heaved himself up onto his elbow, concern in his eyes. "What is it?"

"My mother."

"What about your mother? Don't you think she can handle the arrangements for the wedding?"

"No, that's not it." Desi was giggling now. "Mom and dad will be *overjoyed* to arrange the wedding, believe me. It's just that their future son-in-law is going to come as a real shock. They have no idea that there's even a man in my life." She lay back down against the pillow and smiled up at him mischievously. "Let alone a man like you. The great Jake Lancing," she teased. "Mom will be the envy of her bridge club."

Jake raised a skeptical eyebrow, ignoring her teasing. "Surely, they must know there's *someone*," he said dryly, his head cocked toward Stephanie's room.

"But that was nearly a year ago." Her smile widened into a grin.

She lifted her hand and touched his face softly, trailing the tips of her fingers across his eyebrows, down his nose, over the curve of his upper lip. Her grin faded.

"That time should have been yours, too, Jake," she said seriously. "You had a right to know that you were going to be a father, and I shouldn't have let pride and hurt feelings keep me from telling you." Her other hand came up and cupped his face between her palms. "I'm so sorry, Jake. Can you ever forgive me for being so selfish?"

Jake turned his lips into her palm, too moved, for a moment, to speak. "We've both done some things and said some things we should be sorry for, Desiree. But that's all in the past. Tonight—" he turned his head, kissing her other palm "—tonight we start with a clean slate, agreed?"

"Agreed," she whispered. Her hands curved around his jaw to the back of his head, her fingers threading through his dark hair. Her lips parted softly, her lashes lowered over eyes as dark as amethysts, as brilliant as diamonds.

He resisted the pull of her arms for just a moment. "You want to seal it with a kiss?" he said, his eyes smoldering with love and passion and teasing laughter.

"Several kisses." Desi tightened her arms around his neck, lifting her head to his. "Lots of kisses," she murmured as their mouths touched.

Jake's arms slid under her then, hugging her body to his. He pressed her down into the pillows, tilting his head so that their kiss was deepened. Desi's lips opened wider, eagerly accepting the sweetness of his seeking tongue. She wrapped her arms more tightly around his neck, needing to hold him as close as possible. Closer. She moaned softly.

Jake freed his mouth for just a moment. "A lifetime of kisses," he said solemnly, and bent his head to taste her lips again.

Natalie Carter has been keeping a secret for almost
eleven years—and his name is Patrick!

INTO THE LIGHT

Judith Duncan

CHAPTER ONE

THE REST STOP at the side of the road overlooked a narrow green valley wedged between two mountain ranges, the distant jagged peaks now muted by a soft purple haze. Coniferous forests clung tenaciously to the steep slopes, their growth rooted in shallow infertile soil, their survival dependent on heavy rainfalls. Farther down the valley, avalanche trails lay barrenly exposed, their never-changing paths scoured clean during countless winters by thundering snow slides.

The destructive forces of nature were dormant now, their ravaging power sedated by the potency of the summer sun. But even in the summer, this remained a hostile wilderness, cloaking itself in a menacing stillness.

She stood alone, her arms resting on top of a cairn as she stared across the valley. At first glance, there was an almost puritanical plainness about her. Her ash-blond hair was pulled back from her face and twisted into an austere chignon, and she wore little, if any, makeup. She was dressed in a long-sleeved white silk blouse and a pair of steel-gray slacks, and had a matching gray cardigan draped around her shoulders.

Everything about her was subdued, but there was something unusually compelling about her, too. As she stood there motionless, her eyes fixed on some distant point, a lone eagle skimmed overhead, its eerie screech echoing in the silence of the noonday heat. She looked up, one hand shielding her eyes against the brightness. As she watched the soaring, wheeling flight of this magnificent bird of prey, her

impassive expression dramatically altered and a look of
elation blazed in her eyes. And for that split second, it was
as if she and the eagle were one, and she was experiencing
the same untamed freedom, the same soaring flight. There
was another echoing scream and the golden bird plum-
meted from sight, its talons outstretched as it prepared for
a kill.

As quickly as it came, her excitement died, leaving behind a haunting emptiness that darkened her wide gray eyes.
As if a shadow suddenly crossed her face, her expression
changed. Her finely sculpted features were marked by tension and her soft mouth compressed into a taut line. She
shivered and pulled her cardigan more snugly around her.
Her trial by fire had begun.

Natalie Carter leaned against the cairn and dispassionately looked out over the valley. It was not as she remembered it. The ugly bald scars left by excessive logging were
no longer evident, and where there had once been only
graying stumps, young forests were beginning to flourish.
And the air, once polluted by the foul haze belching from
the stacks of the pulp mill, was now clean and unspoiled,
free of the acrid stench she remembered so well. It had always been there it seemed, that stench. Heavier than the thin
alpine air, it had been trapped in the valley by the mountains that surrounded the town.

Folding her arms in front of her, she tried to stifle the
dread that was settling like a rock inside her. She had left
eleven years ago, and she had never been back. And if it
wasn't for Doc, she would have never come back to Can-
ada, let alone to this remote area of British Columbia. If it
wasn't for him, she wouldn't be within a hundred miles of
this isolated valley in the wilderness. But he needed her now,
and no matter how deep her apprehensions were, she could
not turn her back on the man who had salvaged a scrap of
humanity so many years ago—the man who had become a
father to her during the ensuing years. He had given her a
means of escape, and she owed him her life for that.

After Natalie's mother had died, Doc had taken her to his widowed sister in California, and from that day, Aunt Bea and Doc had become her family. They had given her a secure home, provided for her and educated her, and she cared for them more than words could ever express. But especially Doc. She owed him everything. He had been her guardian, her mentor, her provider. But now, at sixty-eight, he was suffering a stretch of very bad health. He'd had to be hospitalized a few weeks earlier, and Aunt Bea had come. His doctor had told Bea that Doc's severe problems with high blood pressure and diabetes were acutely compounded by an improper diet. He was very frank; Doc was not looking after himself, and if he didn't start, his condition would worsen rapidly. He was, in sober terms, playing with his life.

Deeply concerned about his welfare, both Natalie and Aunt Bea tried to pressure him into moving to California, but he refused to even consider it. He said that he could never rip up the roots he had put down in the dying, depression-struck town that had once been the thriving center of this narrow valley. He could never leave the lush forests of his beloved mountains; he could never leave the people who had been his friends for forty years. He was like an old Douglas fir, he said—he would die from transplant shock if they tried to move him to new soil.

Even though she didn't share his feelings about the valley, Natalie could understand them. He had been a vital part of the community for a long time. He was a pharmacist by profession and had opened up the first drugstore in that part of British Columbia shortly after he emigrated from Ireland. In the beginning there wasn't a doctor within a hundred miles, so he was automatically the authority everyone turned to for advice if there was a sickness. It was only a matter of time until Patrick James Alexander Patterson was known to everyone simply as "Doc."

But in a different way, this man had served an even more essential role in the town. He had been the kind of man anyone could go to in times of trouble, and no one would ever know for certain how many dozens of people he and his wife had quietly helped over the years. And most of those people remembered the Pattersons' kindness. When his beloved Nell died fifteen years ago, people had come from all over the country to attend her funeral.

Natalie knew Doc's many friends would never neglect him, but it worried her to death when Aunt Bea had come back home and he was left alone. As soon as she could arrange it, she took her four weeks of holidays and two weeks' leave of absence. She had come to take care of him, but while she was there, she was also going to try to persuade him to go back to California with her, at least for a few months. She could not stand the thought of his being alone and uncared for.

The cool mountain breeze finally penetrated her sweater and Natalie sighed and straightened, then turned and started back toward her car. Her unwillingness to complete the final leg of her journey was becoming more and more intense. She had known that going back to the town that had been her childhood home would be an ordeal, but now that she was actually facing it, she realized it was going to be much worse than she had anticipated. Somehow she had to find the courage to get back in the car and force herself to drive down that winding road, a road she had not traveled since that chilling rain-slashed night more than a decade ago—a route she swore she would never travel again—one that would lead her back to that which she most desperately wanted to forget.

She met only two transport trucks on the road, one following the other, their diesel engines straining with the loads they were hauling from the coast. Navigating a hairpin turn, Natalie crossed a trestle bridge that spanned the rushing waters of a river. Shadows from tall spruce stretched across the pavement as she passed through a dense stand of trees, then rounding a sweeping turn, she entered an open area and the pulp mill came into view.

It was closed now, the weathered buildings deteriorating in their abandonment, the steel link fence locked against intruders. Shrinking international markets had had dire effects on the lumber industry in British Columbia, and since the mill had been the major source of employment in the valley, its closure had hit the town very hard. But somehow the town and its people had managed to survive. Many of the younger workers had left, hoping to find better opportunities for employment elsewhere. But most of the older ones had stayed, a few finding work in the independently owned sawmill at the edge of town, some taking laborer jobs with the railway or the Department of Highways, some eking out a living on traplines, and some of the luckier ones landing good-paying jobs in a mine that had been reopened forty miles away.

Slowing to obey the speed limit, Natalie shut off the air-conditioning in the car and rolled down her window. A distinctive fragrance wafted in. The scent of rain-dampened forest, freshly sawn cedar stockpiled by the railway, crisp mountain air all mixed together in a fresh, clean bouquet. She had forgotten how beautiful, how invigorating that fragrance was. She crossed the river again, only now its wild downhill rush had slowed and she was able to see the rocky bottom through the crystal-clear water. The road led across a railway crossing, then made another sweeping turn.

Before her was Main Street.

In all those years, it had hardly changed. The two-story hotel had been painted and a new neon sign advertised Goldie's Bar, but there were only a few other alterations: new aluminum siding and a minor remodeling job on the town office; a set of traffic lights at the main intersection; a new post office. It was as though time had stood still, and Natalie didn't like the feeling. It threatened her with familiar impressions, familiar memories—and she didn't want to remember any of it.

Turning on her signal light, she waited for a half-ton pickup to pass, then made a left-hand turn at the Sears

Catalog Order Office. That was something else she had forgotten about. The area was isolated and it was several hours' drive to a major center, so catalog shopping was a way of life in the valley. From clothes to winter tires, to material, to appliances—the catalog had it all, and the order office used to do the steadiest business in town. Brides had been married in Sears wedding dresses, babies had been brought home in Sears blankets and nearly every kid who started school had started in a new Sears outfit. The Christmas *Wish Book* was the ultimate in catalogs, and was probably fully memorized by every youngster in the valley.

The lines of anxiety on Natalie's face were softened by a look of amusement. Catalog shopping was a little like playing Russian roulette. There was always that chance that the girl she disliked the most would show up at school one day in the same outfit. But then, it had the added advantage that she and her best friend could get identical clothes, and dressing the same was the visible evidence of their absolute loyalty to each other.

Natalie turned down a street that led toward the river and smiled slightly when she approached a group of children gathered at the side of the road. It was still the same—summer holidays, and it was up to the kids to amuse themselves. There were no elaborate sports complexes to provide equipment and facilities, nor were there any specially trained recreational directors to develop a long list of structured activities. But maybe that wasn't the terrible disadvantage Natalie once thought it was. Maybe the kids here had retained that wonderful sense of adventure she had grown up with.

She drove past the small white church and a house with a For Sale sign stuck haphazardly in a patch of grass by the front walk, then slowed as she approached a yard surrounded by a slightly overgrown hedge. Natalie pulled into the graveled driveway and parked behind the small four-wheel-drive station wagon. This must be the new vehicle Doc had raved about in his most recent letter. He loved nothing better than investigating all the old abandoned logging roads in his never-ending search for the ultimate in trout streams, and she knew this new car was his concession to that passion. She suspected he bought a four-wheel-drive because he'd had to walk out of the bush once too often, stubbornly refusing to believe there was a road anywhere in the valley he couldn't navigate.

A sudden bout of nervousness hit her, and Natalie closed her eyes and made herself take some deep, even breaths. She most definitely did not want to be here. If only Doc had agreed to come to California. But that was such pointless thinking, and it changed nothing. He didn't want to go, she was here and that was that. She'd better make the best of it. Resolutely lifting her chin, she picked up her purse and got out of the car.

She found Doc in the garden at the back of the house staking up some delphiniums that had blown over in the wind, and she smiled when she heard his familiar Irish brogue as he muttered to himself, "These damned intolerable flowers aren't worth Paddy's spit."

Her drawn expression changed to one of deep affection as she watched him wrestle with the tall stalks. "If you hate them so much, why don't you just chop them off?"

There was an obvious struggle with stiff muscles and an arthritic back as he straightened and slowly turned around. His eyes mirrored his disbelief when he saw her standing there, then his craggy face creased with profound pleasure. As he made his way across the large garden he fumbled with the side of his sweater and managed to find his pocket and shove in the wad of twine he'd been holding. He was so flustered by her unexpected arrival that he plowed through a row of peas and trampled his precious strawberry patch in his haste to get to her.

With his arms open wide he exclaimed loudly, "Faith and begorra! I never expected to find you planted in my garden."

As he enfolded her in a hearty bear hug, she fought back a sudden rush of tears, then said unsteadily, "Well, since you wouldn't come to us, I decided I'd better come to you."

"Bless you, lass, bless you. You are a sight for these tired old eyes." He held her away from him. "Here, now let's be havin' a look at you." Pursing his lips, he nodded his head in approval. "You look fine. Just fine."

"You'd say that even if I was covered with warts."

There was a touch of devil in his faded blue eyes as he chuckled. "And you'd look just fine with warts, too."

Natalie made a face at him, then slipped her arm through his as they started walking back toward the house. "You lie with such finesse."

He patted her hand. "I'm sure you'll manage to do a passable job yourself. I can't wait to hear the load of rubbish you're going to feed me when you start explaining why you're here."

She laughed. "Would I do that to you?"

"Unquestionably, if you thought you could get away with it."

"I just came for a visit."

"Balderdash. You came to boss me around and to play nursemaid."

"I came," she said firmly, "to make sure you're following doctor's orders and to see that you're sticking to your diet."

"Same thing."

She thought about it for a minute, then answered, "You're right. It is the same thing."

Doc chuckled as he opened the screen door for her. "I can see my sister's hand in this. My guess is you have orders to bring me to heel, come hell or high water."

Natalie grinned. "Well, she never mentioned anything about hell or high water."

He snorted. "Damn woman. She does love to meddle."

"You love it and you know it."

He didn't answer, but Natalie saw the twinkle in his eyes as he stomped through the sun porch and opened another screen door that led into the living room.

When Doc had built the house for his new bride decades before, he had constructed it to take advantage of the spectacular view of the river his property afforded. Consequently, the whole design was basically back to front, and one entered the living room through the back door.

As a child, Natalie had loved this house, and walking into it was like coming home. She had to wait a moment for her eyes to adjust to the dimness of the interior before she could take it all in. He had a few pieces of new furniture—a sofa and two easy chairs—but there was still much that she remembered. His old leather easy chair, an ancient rolltop desk, the beautiful old cherrywood dining-room suite, his favorite floor lamp with the brass stand. And on the table by his chair was a humidor and a rack of pipes. The familiar smell of his tobacco permeated the room, and Natalie inhaled deeply. She loved that smell.

"Would you like a cup of tea?" he asked as he took off his garden shoes and put on his slippers.

"I'd rather have something cold, if you have it."

There was a flash of dry humor. "Then how about a cup of cold tea?"

She laughed as she set her purse on the desk. "Sounds great."

Still smiling, she followed him into the kitchen. Hugging herself against the cool breeze from the open window, she leaned against the cupboard and watched him fill the battered copper kettle. His white hair was still thick, and as usual, it was in a disheveled mess. He was tall and thin, and for some reason, he always reminded Natalie of a stork. Maybe it was because of his long neck and his long legs. Or maybe it was because of the way he marched along with his head thrust forward. The exact reason was forever elusive.

As she scrutinized him, she realized something she had never been consciously aware of. Doc was aging. With each passing year he was getting a little more stooped, a little stiffer. She hated the thought of him getting old, but she took comfort in the fact that he still moved with the brisk-ness of a man who liked to walk. And Natalie knew that he still walked a great deal. Doc knew the high country like the back of his hand, and she doubted if there were many trails around that he hadn't hiked at one time or another.

Knowing that he took heated exception to anyone com-menting on how he managed in his home, Natalie watched him fix her tea in silence. But she had to bite her lip to keep from laughing. Doc's idea of iced tea was to use the dregs of what was still in the pot from lunch, pour it over some crushed leaves ripped from the potted mint plant on the windowsill and throw in a few chips of ice. He slapped the drink he'd prepared on the counter, as if he was silently daring her to try it. Natalie took a wary sip. Expecting it to taste like mint-flavored lye, she was surprised by the re-freshing flavor, and without thinking, she nodded her head in approval.

"Surprised you, didn't I?"

She grinned. "Never."

He snorted and waved his hand toward the living room. "Let's go sit in there."

"What about your tea?"

He gave her a disgruntled look, then responded tartly, "My new nursemaid can fix it for me when the kettle boils."

Natalie managed to keep a straight face, but her dancing eyes gave her away as she stared back at Doc. He muttered something about her being cheeky as he sat in his comfort-able old chair. He pretended to ignore her as he selected a pipe, but she could see the corner of his mouth twitch as he filled the bowl. It was an old game they played, this father-daughter routine, but there was an element of truth to it. No daughter could have loved him more.

Doc's expression became deeply thoughtful as he care-fully tamped the tobacco. There was a lengthy silence be-fore he lifted his head and stuck the stem between his teeth.

Natalie sat on the hassock in front of him and took a long drink from her glass, then set it on the table by his chair.

Watching her steadily over the rim, he put a burning match to the bowl and continued to draw in until the tobacco glowed red, then he shook out the flame and dropped the burned match in the ashtray. "I never expected to see you sitting at my hearth, Natalie," he said quietly.

Tucking her hands beneath her thighs, she watched the thin thread of smoke spiraling up from the charred match, her face showing signs of strain. When she finally met his gaze, her gray eyes were solemn. "I never intended to come back, Doc. You know that."

"But you came back because of me."

She held his steady gaze for a second, then nodded.

Leaning forward, he reached out and laid his bony hand on her shoulder. "That means a great deal to me, lass— knowing that you'd do that for me."

The affection she saw in his eyes touched her deeply. She tried to smile at him, but unshed tears suddenly burned her eyes and she abruptly looked away. "You're my family," she said simply.

"I know that, lass. I know that." Grasping her shoulder, he gave her a reassuring little shake, then leaned back in his chair and reflectively puffed on his pipe. Several quiet moments passed before he spoke again. "How long are you staying?"

She swallowed against the tightness in her throat, then looked up at him. "I've a month's holiday and I've taken a two-week leave of absence."

He pursed his lips together and studied her with wry amusement. "With orders from Bea to bring me back with you."

Natalie managed a smile. "Come hell or high water."

He chuckled, then fell silent as he nursed his pipe, lost in reflection. Cradling the bowl in his hand, he stared into space, his brogue touched with melancholy. "'Tis been my home for forty years, lass. I cannot leave."

There was empathy in her eyes as she said softly, "I know you can't, Doc. I don't think either Bea or I ever really believed you would. You can't leave here for the same reason Bea can't leave there."

"Except her ties are even stronger. All her children and grandchildren are there." He raised his finger in a gentle admonishment. "You're not to worry about me, Natalie Carter. I'm content with my life." He took another pull on his pipe, then said absently, "Do you know, lass, I've always hated California in the summer." He spoke in a tone of voice that held a certain bafflement, as though he knew he was out of step with the rest of the world and didn't understand why. "I couldna abide to live there, you know."

There was a spark of humor in her eyes as Natalie responded in a flawless Irish lilt. "Bea would rip your heart out, lad, if she heard such blasphemy cross your lips."

His shoulders shook with silent laughter as Doc nodded in absolute agreement. "That she would, lass. That she would."

Natalie smiled at him with affection, then restlessly stood up. She wandered around the room, stopping to study the collection of photographs on the piano, pausing to examine a group of paintings on the wall. But there was an air of distraction about everything she did. Slipping off her cardigan, she hung it on the back of a chair and went to the window. Staring out, she didn't say anything for the longest time, then folding her arms tightly in front of her, she said softly, "I can't believe I'm actually here."

Doc watched her with concern as he rested the stem of his pipe against his bottom lip. "Perhaps it won't be as bad as you think. You've been gone a long time."

"I wish I could believe that." She leaned her shoulder against the window frame, her head resting against the cool pane. It was a long time before she could make herself ask about the past, and her voice was strained when she spoke. "What did you tell everyone...after I left?"

With studied care, he laid his pipe in the enormous ashtray by his elbow. Sighing heavily, he lowered his head and laced his fingers across his chest. "I simply told them you were in the car when your mother had the accident, only you were thrown free. It was obvious you couldn't possibly be at her funeral because you'd been so badly injured yourself."

"Did anyone ask why I never came back?"

A hard glint of Irish ire appeared in Doc's eyes and his voice had a bitter ring to it. "It was obvious you had nothing to come back to after your stepfather burned the house to the ground. In the drunken state he was in, it was a wonder he didn't burn up with it." Doc's hands were trembling and an unhealthy flush darkened his face. "I know she couldn't cope with all the pressures after your father died, but I'll never understand what she saw in that scoundrel of a Carl Willard."

Natalie suddenly had to fight for breath as a heaviness pressed upon her chest, and her knuckles turned white as she clenched her fists against the terrifying feeling. "Don't, Doc," she pleaded desperately. "Don't even mention him."

The grandfather clock in the corner sounded out the half hour, and Natalie made herself focus on it, the familiar chime echoing in the charged silence of the room. It was very strange, but the chime of that grandfather clock was one sound that was crystal clear in the confusion of Natalie's jumbled memories. She could recall it so clearly. And it was a memory that held no menacing overtones. It was a safe one to hang on to.

It seemed like an eternity passed before Doc broke the silence. "It's all in the past, Natalie. No one ever knew the real reason why you left."

Without thinking, she responded with a grim smile. "And no one cared."

"That's not true, lass, and you know it," he scolded her gently. "The lad was near frantic when he couldn't find you. It was a terrible hurt you inflicted on him."

"I had no choice—"

"You should have at least told him about the babe," he interjected. "You'll live to regret that, lass. You denied him the right that was his. And you denied the boy his father."

She took a deep, unsteady breath before she spoke, her voice low and taut. "I know what I did was wrong, Doc, but I couldn't face him then." Her voice broke, and she pressed her hands tightly together. "And because I didn't face him then, I could never do it now."

Doc sighed. "I know, lass. I know. It's easy for me to say what was right and what was wrong."

Her eyes darkened by tormenting memories, she nervously fingered the chain around her neck, trying to scrape up the courage to ask. "Have you heard anything about him recently?"

Doc hesitated, then said, "There was a write-up about him a few months ago in a news magazine—I've got it tucked away in some cranny. He was about to leave for South America to start filming another wildlife documentary." Doc wearily rubbed his eyes, then tipped his head back. "I sometimes wonder what would have happened if your mother hadn't had that accident."

She turned to face him, her expression suddenly inflexible, her face ashen. "Her death was no accident, Doc."

His age seemed to have doubled as he slowly lifted himself out of the chair and went to her, his shoulders more stooped than usual. With compassion lining his face, he put his arm around her and drew her against him, trying to give her some measure of comfort. "We'll never know what was going through her mind that night, lass," he said gently. "And it will serve no purpose if we start wondering now."

Her body was stiff with tension as she stared numbly out the window. He was right. What good would it do to know for certain that her mother had abandoned her by taking her own life? All she wanted to do was put that nightmare out of her mind, once and for all. Maybe by coming back, by facing the past, she would be able to put those old ghosts to rest. Maybe. She closed her eyes as she slowly massaged her temples with her fingertips, trying to erase the dull ache that throbbed in her head. With a heavy sigh, she turned to look at him. "One reason I've dreaded coming back was because of all the questions."

There was a sudden haggardness about him as Doc dragged his hand across his face. "If anyone starts asking, tell them you don't remember."

She gave him a grim smile. "I *don't* remember." Her eyes were like ice as she turned and again stared rigidly out the window. "At least I don't remember anything after I was admitted to the hospital. I doubt if I'll ever forget what happened before."

"You must quit tormenting yourself, lass," Doc said gently. "I sometimes think that beneath the disgust and ugliness of it all, you unconsciously keep blaming yourself for what happened, and it wasn't your fault."

There was a heavy silence as both of them became lost in their own thoughts. When Natalie finally spoke, her voice had lost some of the bitterness. "In my logical mind, I know that. But whenever it all rises up to haunt me, there's always guilt associated with it. There's always that awful feeling I must have done something, that somehow I was to blame for everything that happened. If it hadn't been for me, mother wouldn't have done what she did."

"You can't think like that, Natalie," he said firmly. "What happened was out of your hands." Sensing how much this conversation was disturbing her and knowing nothing would be gained by continuing it, Doc wisely changed tack. "I hear the kettle boiling. Come make my tea and tell me how that fine lad of yours is doing and how you're doing. Bea wrote and said you had another promotion."

Grateful for his insight, Natalie was more than willing to follow his lead. Turning from the window, she gave him a look that was laced with perverse humor. "It seems to me that you've adapted to the idea of a nursemaid awfully fast."

He chuckled. "If the truth be known, lass, there isn't a man alive who doesn't like to be pampered now and again. But being the strong, hardy providers we are, we aren't supposed to let anyone know it."

Natalie knew his game and didn't take the bait. Picking up her glass from the table and following him into the kitchen, she retorted dryly, "This could be interesting. I've never looked after a sixty-eight-year-old boy before."

"A new challenge, lass. Look upon it as a new challenge."

"I don't need any more challenges in my life. Patrick gives me plenty of those."

"He's a fine lad, lass. He'll do you proud."

Natalie smiled ruefully. "If he doesn't do me in first."

"He has some life in him, that one. His letters always make my day." Doc rinsed out the teapot. "One of my favorites was the one he wrote telling me about his big adventure when he went deep-sea fishing with...what was his friend's name? Gary, wasn't it? I laughed for days over that."

Natalie smiled and nodded as she opened the cupboard door Doc pointed to. "He was so excited about going that he nearly drove me crazy. He had his suitcase packed two weeks in advance."

"I'm glad that boy had a chance to go along. He'll remember that weekend for a good many years."

"He really will. He had a fantastic time." Setting two mugs on the countertop, she passed Doc the canister of tea, and added absently, "Gary's father took a picture of Patrick hauling in his very first catch." She grinned. "Seeing there's a fish in the picture, I thought you might like to have a copy, so I got the negative and had an enlargement done for you."

"That's a fine gift, lass. I'll be putting it on the piano with the others." Doc flung some tea in the pot and slapped the lid back on the canister. "How come he didn't come with you?"

Natalie shot her mentor a quick glance, but his expression was bland. She knew very well that he was skirting the question he really wanted to ask. For years Doc had wanted Natalie to let Patrick spend part of his summer vacation with him, but Natalie would never let him come. She was afraid her son might be put in a very awkward situation and asked questions he didn't have any answers for. And Natalie didn't want that to happen. This time, though, she had relented to Patrick's badgering, but she still had some very deep misgivings about it.

Her tone was introspective when she answered, "He's going to come later. I'd promised him he could go to camp this year with some of his friends, so Aunt Bea's going to put him on a plane as soon as he gets back."

Doc bowed his head and frowned, his face creased with concern. Natalie studied him intently for a moment, then glanced away. "What is it, Doc?"

He kept turning the teapot lid over and over in his hand, then he looked at her and sighed. "His coming will raise a few eyebrows, lass. I would have dealt with the gossips if he had come alone, but with you being here, you could be put on the spot, you know."

"Eyebrows can raise all they want, Doc," she said tersely. "Patrick is the one thing in my life I'll never ever apologize for."

"As long as you realize what's apt to happen."

She gave him a warped smile. "Oh, I know." And she did know. Yet as skeptical as she was about Patrick's coming, her guilt had finally outweighed her reluctance. It didn't seem fair to deny the boy the chance to spend a summer vacation with his adopted grandfather because of her own apprehension. Her voice was low when she said, "He's so excited. He's wanted to visit you for ages."

"Good. I've wanted him to come. Now I can take him fishing."

She gave Doc a pointed look. "You can take *me* fishing."

He chuckled and nodded. "As good as done, lass. As good as done. We'll explore all the old spots."

For some reason his comment hit a nerve, and Natalie kept her head averted so he couldn't see her face. She didn't want to explore the old spots. She didn't want to do anything that might arouse old memories. But her mental barriers had been weakened. The picture of Patrick she brought for Doc took shape in her mind, and even though she tried to block it out, another image slowly superimposed itself on Patrick's. And a deep ache started to unfold. There were memories she wanted to forget, and there were others she didn't dare remember.

CHAPTER TWO

THE NEXT FEW DAYS slipped by quietly. Doc took her for several drives along some of his favorite logging roads, and if the mood hit them, they did a little fishing along the way. Mostly though, they stayed at home. Doc had a house-keeper who came in twice a week, so there was little for Natalie to do in that respect, but meals were another matter altogether.

Natalie was determined that Doc's health was not going to deteriorate any further because of sheer neglect. She thoroughly studied all the information about the strict diet Doc was supposed to be on, and with him grumbling about bossy women, she implemented a dietary regime that would make a nutritionist cringe. His days of eating what he felt like eating were definitely over, and he accepted that with a certain acerbic equanimity that made Natalie want to laugh.

It had not all been sunshine and roses for her, though. They had gone downtown twice: once for groceries and once to get some fishing gear for her. And both times they had run into neighbors. Without consciously being aware of it, she had been very cool when questions about her mother and stepfather had arisen. In both instances the women realized that she didn't want to talk about it and had tactfully let the matter drop. Natalie honestly didn't know how she would have handled the situation if they hadn't, and that uncertainty unsettled her nearly as much as the meetings had. She would give anything if she could simply avoid further confrontations, but that was going to be impossible.

Especially with the major local event that was planned for the upcoming week.

The town council had organized a homecoming to celebrate the seventy-fifth birthday of the town, and the entire community had become involved. The businesses had awarded prizes for the most beautified storefronts, the streets had been decorated and the Chamber of Commerce had organized a parade. The celebrations were to take place the second weekend she was there, and the kickoff event was a community dance that was to be held in the hockey arena on Friday night. She desperately wanted to steer clear of the whole thing, but she knew that Doc was counting on her to attend with him, and she could not let him down.

Right from the beginning, the homecoming had all the makings of a roaring success. Former residents were coming back by the scores. By late Friday afternoon, tents, truck campers, holiday trailers and motor homes were everywhere, and the usually quiet streets were bustling with activity. It didn't seem like the same town.

Natalie felt a near giddy sense of relief when it dawned on her that if she was going to come back, she couldn't have picked a better time to do it. Everyone assumed she had come back for the reunion, and there were so many other people who had returned for the same reason that she ended up safely lost in the crowd. This was a celebration. No one cared about what had happened eleven years ago; they were too intent on making the best of a good time now. And it wasn't long before she was actually enjoying herself.

She was even looking forward to the dance. Natalie was tour coordinator for a national travel agency and her job demanded a certain amount of socializing, but except for those instances, she seldom attended adult functions. Aunt Bea's two sons and their families considered Natalie and Patrick part of the clan, so most outings were family oriented. Maybe she was simply caught up in the general excitement and enthusiasm, but whatever the reason, she found herself in youthful high spirits as she dressed that evening.

She took extra time choosing her clothes and applying her makeup. She always wore her hair up and drawn severely back in a chignon because it was neat and easy to manage, but without consciously realizing it, she had selected a style that suited her perfectly. The dramatic simplicity did incredible things to her face. It gave a classic look to her delicate features and sharply emphasized her wide eyes and long slender neck. But tonight she spent more time on her hair, and instead of the simple bun, she did it up in an elaborate woven style, which highlighted her blondness. On Natalie, it was sheer elegance.

The dress she chose added to the effect. It was made of a fine cotton, the simple design a perfect style for the gauzy material. It had long, very full sleeves that were caught at the wrists in wide cuffs, and a full skirt that was topped by a wide belt, which accentuated her narrow waist. The wispy fabric made her seem even more slender and willowy, but what added the ultimate touch was the color. It was a deep pink that was shot with mauve, and it intensified the color of her eyes and added a faint blush to her skin. She was utterly feminine and looked as delicate as an orchid.

When she entered the living room, Doc stopped filling his pipe and stared at her. After a long silence he said, "You look lovely, lass. You do me proud."

She smiled at him. "You aren't so bad yourself. You look very spiffy." Doc was wearing gray flannel slacks and his navy-blue legion blazer with its red, white and gold silk crest embroidered on the left pocket. And he did indeed look spiffy. The collar of his white shirt was slightly twisted, and Natalie stepped behind him to fix it. She smoothed the lightly starched fabric down over his tie, then brushed a piece of lint from the shoulder of his jacket as he turned to face her.

"Tell me, do I pass inspection or do I look like I dressed in the dark?"

She laughed and patted his shoulder reassuringly. "You most certainly pass inspection. And I don't even have to check behind your ears or see if your fingernails are clean."

There was a large crowd already gathered when they arrived at the arena, and Natalie glanced around as the young man at the door took Doc's tickets and stamped the backs of their hands. Some of the tables and chairs had been cleared out of the combined lounge and cafeteria, leaving an enormous space for an informal reception area. Glancing through the row of windows that separated the outer room from the sports complex, Natalie could see that the floor of the arena had been covered with boards for the event.

Doc had told her that the steering committee had decided to organize a Community Showcase. It would feature various arts and crafts from former and current residents of the community. Through the crowd, she caught a glimpse of the displays set up at the near end of the arena. At the far end a space had been kept clear for a dance floor, which was already jammed with people. She could see the live band on a makeshift stage, and over the din she could hear the beat of a snappy polka. The party was in full swing.

Even in the crush of milling people, she could pick out several familiar faces, and Doc raised his hand in greeting as someone in the crowd called to him. For some strange reason she experienced an acute nervousness, but she buried that feeling behind a smile as Doc guided her toward a large group.

"For gawd's sake, it's Natalie Carter!" A buxom woman worked her way through the crowd and raised her arms in an expansive gesture of welcome.

Natalie's face lit up as the redhead moved toward her. Stella Ralston. She most certainly had not changed. If anyone else had ever dared to dress the way this woman did, it would look cheap and garish, but for some weird reason, Stella Ralston managed it with a very earthy kind of style. Her slinky black dress had a slit up the side that revealed a startling amount of thigh, the plunging neckline exposed a daring amount of cleavage and what little there was of the satin material clung graphically to every curve.

Somewhere in bygone years, Stella had cultivated a mind-boggling walk that made her full hips roll provocatively. Her shoes, which had two rhinestone-studded straps across the toes and extremely slender high heels, exaggerated her hip-swinging strut. As always, she wore her coppery red hair piled on top of her head in an elaborate upsweep that was stiffened with hair spray and adorned with rhinestone combs. Her theatrical makeup was liberally applied, the crowning touch being incredibly long, thick false eyelashes that weighed her eyelids down in a sensuous droop. The whole effect was a lush and lusty sensuality. And that was exactly the effect that Stella wanted.

The redhead finally reached her, and with an extravagant sweep of her arms, clutched Natalie against her voluptuous bosom in a smothering embrace. Natalie laughed and hugged her back.

Releasing her, Stella took Natalie's face in her beringed hands and gave her an affectionate shake. "Gawd, don't you look marvelous! It is so damned good to see you!" Grasping Natalie's hand, she turned to Doc. "Why didn't you tell me she was coming?" she scolded testily, one hand on her thrust-out hip.

Stella's perfume was a bit overwhelming and Natalie moved downwind as she laughingly interceded on Doc's behalf. "He didn't know. It was a surprise." She squeezed Stella's hand, her eyes sparkling. "You look terrific, Stella. You haven't changed at all." Stella did look terrific. Her age could have been anywhere from thirty to fifty, and Natalie was one of the selected few who knew the truth. Nearly eleven years—it didn't seem possible, but this woman was in her early fifties. Knowing her old co-worker the way she did, Natalie was willing to bet a month's salary that she was publicly swearing she was still thirty-nine.

Stella managed not to look too pleased as she snorted, "Gawd, child—I'm ten years older. Of course I've changed. My boobs are sagging down to my—"

"Stella!" blustered Doc. "We don't want specifics of your anatomy here and now!"

Stella grinned and patted him on the cheek with an airy gesture that showed off her long scarlet nails. "Don't be such a prude, Doc. You'd think you were a virgin the way you huff and puff."

It was impossible for Natalie to keep from laughing as she watched the two of them in action. Stella had worked in Doc's drugstore for years, and she always seemed to get some sort of perverse enjoyment out of trying to shock him. She might have the compassion of an angel, but she also had the vocabulary of a truck driver, and with frequent and deliberate regularity, Stella would scandalize her boss. Doc, on the other hand, always seemed to enjoy tormenting Stella with tantalizing bits and pieces of gossip. While she was going to high school, Natalie had worked part-time for Doc, and she had idolized the flashy and glamorous Stella with an adolescent awe. But beneath her exterior glitter, Stella was a warm and caring person who viewed life with a mixture of skepticism and dry humor. And she was loyal to the core. Natalie was genuinely glad to see her.

Stella turned back to Natalie and pursed her mouth in a skeptical twist of humor. "Why in hell did you ever come back to this dump, Natalie? What ever possessed you to leave the high life, tinsel town, the razzle-dazzle dazzle, the gorgeous male bodies on the beach for this godforsaken country?"

Natalie's amusement was written all over her face as she tilted her head toward Doc. "He's been misbehaving again, so I thought I'd better get back here and whip him into shape."

Stella gave Doc a pithy look. "Good luck. That should keep you busy for the rest of your life."

"Don't talk as if I wasn't here, Stella," Doc responded loudly. Then muttering to himself, he added, "I should have fired her twenty-five years ago."

Stella made a face at him and grinned as she slipped her arm through Natalie's. "How long are you here for, Chicken?"

"Six weeks, unless I can persuade Doc to go back with me."

"Did you bring Patrick with you? I'm dying to meet this kid of yours."

Natalie's expression became suddenly guarded as she shot Doc a questioning look. He nodded his head, wordlessly reassuring her. Stella hadn't missed the silent exchange and she raised one eyebrow in an expression that was mildly disdainful. "Really, Natalie. Of course he told me about the kid. I mean, I could hardly miss the several hundred photos he has stuffed in his wallet, could I? He brags about him so much it's disgusting. He's ten times worse than a real grandfather, you know."

Natalie laughed, but her discomfort was visible and she had trouble meeting Stella's steady gaze. "I'm sorry, Stella. I don't know quite how to handle this, I guess."

"Honey, you don't owe one damned person in this hell-hole an explanation," Stella said firmly. "What you've done or not done with your life is none of their damned business." She tightened her arm around the younger woman's waist and gave her a bolstering hug. "If anyone gives you a hard time, you tell them to go to hell." She gave Natalie another squeeze and grinned. "Now tell me about this boy of yours. Am I going to get a chance to check this kid out?"

"He'll be here later on. He's in camp right now."

"Well, as soon as he gets here, I want to meet him." The effervescence beneath Stella's breeziness faded and she became serious. She lowered her head, a small frown appearing as she absently toyed with her gaudy rings. When she finally looked up, her eyes were unsmiling and she stared at Natalie with a strange intentness. "If you need a friend or need to talk, Natalie, don't hesitate to call on me," she said quietly. "I'm always available."

Natalie had the strangest feeling that Stella had a certain insight that she lacked and that there was something darkly significant about her offer. It was disconcerting. But Stella never gave her time to dwell on it as the redhead grabbed Doc and Natalie by the arms and swept them off in a whirlwind of socializing.

For the next hour Stella was firmly in charge and acted a little like a mother hen, never letting either one of them out of her sight. They were shepherded from one group to another until Natalie was lost in an avalanche of names and faces and was beginning to feel slightly giddy. Needing a bit of a breather from all the commotion, she unobtrusively slipped away from yet another mob and went into the arena.

The Community Showcase had been well organized and the caliber of homegrown talent that was featured was surprisingly good. There was everything from paintings to needlework, from woodworking to silversmithing, and as Natalie moved slowly from one display to another, she became more and more engrossed. She had a deep respect for anyone who had the ability to create, probably because she had a strong creative streak herself. But because of the demands and financial responsibility of being a single parent, what talent she possessed had never been nurtured. At one time, long ago, she had dreamed of enrolling in art school, but that was just another dream that had died from neglect.

Natalie approached the final exhibit but the display was obscured by a crowd of people. Not wanting to push her way through, Natalie was about to bypass it and go back to Doc and Stella. As she moved behind the audience, she caught bits and pieces of what the woman behind the table was saying, and with mild curiosity, she paused to listen. "It was very generous of him really. He donated all these books, and the entire proceeds from the sale of them goes toward our library fund."

That awful feeling of having walked into a bad dream washed through Natalie, followed by a chill of premonition. She wanted to run but was drawn by an overpowering need to know. With certain dread, she slipped through the crowd. The voices around her faded into a distant drone, and her heartbeat was spurred to a frantic gallop as she screwed up enough courage to pick up a book from the top of the stack. It was one of those expensively bound, carefully produced showpieces of photojournalism that allowed the reader to view the subjects and the scenes through the eyes of a master craftsman.

She didn't even need to open it. She could recognize one of his photographs among a thousand others, and the incredible shot on the dustcover of a lynx poised on a rocky overhang was distinctively one of his. The shock of finding a display of his books in the Community Showcase was paralyzing. It shouldn't be affecting her this way. It wasn't as though his work was unfamiliar to her; she had seen several of his wildlife documentaries on TV, and she'd bought two of his books for Patrick. But she had never once considered coming face-to-face with a new volume of his work here.

And that was stupid and unthinking. After all, this was where his career was launched, where it had all began.

With trembling hands Natalie opened the book and felt suddenly suffocated by the overwhelming potency of the photograph on the inside fold of the cover. It was one of those rare pictures that fully captured the vital element of the subject, creating a powerful study of the man. He was leaning against a tree with one hand resting on his hip, the other holding two cameras by the straps. The wind was ruffling his hair. One foot was balanced on an exposed root, and he was gazing off in the distance, intent on something in the sky. Even in repose, his muscled athletic body hinted at the animal power that was not unlike the sleek wildcats he so often photographed. His aura was dynamic, virile, magnetic, but there was something more, something indefinable. It was a candid black-and-white shot, and the lights and shadows across the chiseled masculine face created an illusion of strength and sensitivity. The photo exposed his raw vitality, but it also subtly revealed a deeper, darker element, something very poignant, something haunting. Something that filled her with profound sorrow.

In a weak attempt to avoid confronting the feelings that were beginning to smother her, she made herself concentrate on reading the author's profile. "Adam Rutherford began his illustrious career as a photographer of wildlife in the Canadian Rockies when he was still a university student..." But the list of his impressive credits was lost on Natalie. Buried memories were painfully unearthed. She remembered only too well how his career had been launched.

He'd had a summer job with the provincial government on a reforestation project. A carelessly attended campfire had started a forest fire that had raged out of control for days, razing thousands of acres of prime forest. He had been working on a firebreak along a small lake, and he had taken a single roll of film of animals taking refuge in the water from the roaring flames and the blinding smoke. They were sensitive, gripping pictures that had eloquently captured the terror and destruction. The local newspaper had run some of his shots, which were eventually picked up by a national wire service. One thing led to another, and within a matter of months, those same photographs were used for a massive public awareness campaign for the prevention of forest fires. His genius had been discovered, and from that point on, he had never looked back professionally.

But all that happened so long ago. More and more memories came flooding back, and the nearly forgotten grief slammed into her with such force that she didn't think she could endure the pain.

Forgetting the volume she had clutched against her, she whirled, desperate to elude the old feelings that were bombarding her, but her path of escape was blocked. She glanced up and suddenly every muscle in her body was paralyzed, and for an instant she couldn't breathe. She was trapped, and Adam Rutherford was watching her with steely eyes, his expression inflexible. And she could tell by the look on his face that he had been watching her for some time.

WHEN STELLA REALIZED that Natalie was no longer with them in the lounge her anxiety became plainly visible and she scanned the crowd. A frown appeared on Doc's weathered face as he watched her. He knew Stella very well; if she was anxious, she had every reason to be. "What is it, Stella? What's troubling you?"

She pursed her lips in exasperation, still searching with a worried desperation. "Adam Rutherford is here. I saw him earlier in town, and I saw him come in the door a few minutes ago." She placed her hands on her hips and stared at Doc, a shrewd look in her eyes. "I don't know the whole story, Doc, and I figured you had damned good reasons not to tell me, but any bloody idiot can add." She gave him a wry smile. "I don't think I'd be taking a big risk if I bet my life that Natalie's kid is also his. And I don't think I'd be taking much of a risk if I said he doesn't know a damned thing about it, either."

Doc gravely studied her for a minute, then slowly shook his head. "No, he doesn't."

"Well, isn't that just peachy keen," she muttered. "This could turn into a real stinker if he finds out. You know what he was like after she disappeared. He was ready to tear this whole damned town apart."

He sighed heavily, his sudden weariness weighing heavily upon him. "I know, Stella, I know. Now all the things she's refused to deal with have finally come home to rest. She can't evade the past forever." His brogue was thick with sadness as he stared off over Stella's shoulder, caught by some deep reflection. "Natalie's been living in a vacuum for years, Stella—pushing the past into the dark recesses of her mind. She's become a shell of what she once was because of it. I've seen it coming for a long time, this moment of truth. It fills me with dread, but I know that she's reached a crucial point in her life. She can't get on with her life until she deals with what went before." There was a deep sorrow revealed in the old man's eyes as he finally met Stella's compassionate gaze. "She's caught in a terrible maze, Stella. She cannot go forward any further until she goes back the way she came." He shook his head sadly as she stared across the room. "And the terrible truth is, she has to do it alone."

CHAPTER THREE

HE STOOD IN THE SHADOWS of the darkened vestibule of the side exit to the lounge, the ever-present camera and equipment bag slung over his shoulder. There was an air of introspection about him as he folded his arms in front of him and leaned against the wall. He stared at the crowd within, his expression unfathomable.

He was no stranger, yet he was. Gone was the free and easy youth; in its place was the cool and collected man. He had the quiet confidence and polish that comes with experience, and it was apparent to even the most casual observer that this man would be as much at ease in an exclusive country club as he was here. His clothes were expensive; his light brown shirt and slacks were complemented by an off-white suede jacket, and his suede boots were handmade. His shirt was open at the neck, exposing corded muscles and a deep tan. His dark blond hair, which was heavily streaked by the sun, was brushed back from his chiseled face. Broad cheekbones accentuated dark hazel eyes. Overwhelming masculinity enhanced the image of success and sophistication, but there was an underlying hardiness about him that warned the image was only a veneer and that this man was as tough and rugged as he looked.

But there was an emotional upheaval taking place in Adam Rutherford that was eroding his calm veneer. It was insane how her memory had come back to torment him after so many years. There had been long periods of time when he'd gone for months without thinking about his youth, but for some incomprehensible reason that had all changed within the past year. Now something as insignificant as the words of a song would summon up disturbing memories of her. And those memories would haunt him until, out of sheer desperation, he'd immerse himself in his work and drive himself so hard that he'd eventually hit a point of exhaustion where he couldn't think at all.

There had been a time when Adam honestly thought he could substitute success for happiness, but he finally came to terms with the fact that all the success in the world could never fill the vacuum in his life. And his life was indeed empty. After Natalie, he'd initially been very guarded about the types of relationships he developed with women, vowing he'd never let anyone get that close again. But eventually the pain had eased, and when he'd been able to get on with his life, he found that his work was of primary importance, and he simply didn't want a permanent relationship tying him down. There had been plenty of women during the past few years, but no one really special. Nobody he could see himself spending the rest of his life with. Nobody who could fill the emptiness. Nobody like Natalie.

And that was a little unnerving, to think that maybe he had been unconsciously making that kind of comparison all along. His only logical explanation for his recent preoccupation with her was that he had, in fact, burned all his bridges. He'd reached a point in his life when he'd started doing some very serious evaluating. He had attained all his professional goals, and what lay ahead held few challenges. There was nothing in his future but more emptiness. Maybe that's why he was preoccupied with the past; his life had been so full and promising in those golden days.

With all the old memories reactivated, he knew he was taking a tremendous risk when he decided to come back to his hometown, but he was impelled by some self-destructive force that overrode his common sense. His parents had moved from the valley five years ago, and after they left, he'd had no reason to return. He had tried to justify his coming back now with the excuse that this was the best possible location for the filming of his proposed television documentary on the cougar. But now that he was here, with her memories all around him, he realized there was a damned sight more to it than that. Ever since he had come back from South America, he'd been fighting against an inexplicable compunction to return to his boyhood home. And as he stood in the shadows, he knew it was her ghost that had drawn him back.

To his way of thinking, there was something abnormal about this obsession with faded memories of a sixteen-year-old girl, especially when he hadn't laid eyes on her for eleven years. It was as though it was an insidious disease he had no immunity against. He strongly suspected that there was some deep-seated flaw in his personality that prevented him from recovering from that first poignant affair. Yet he knew with absolute certainty that if he was ever going to find any peace of mind he would have to drag up those ghosts—and that meant he was going to have to talk to Doc. He was hoping that once he finally dealt with all the unanswered questions, he could put her and everything associated with her out of his mind for good. Maybe then he could stop being the cynical bastard he was and finally get on with his life. Maybe.

And then maybe not. His facing it didn't seem to be making one bit of difference now. The moment he had arrived at the arena, he was swamped with stifling recollections of her. He had been fighting with himself for the past hour, but he was getting nowhere.

Shaking his head in self-disgust, Adam straightened and entered the hall. For a brief moment he stood at the edge of the crowd and stared out the row of windows at the arena floor. That was a big mistake. It seemed as if it were impossible to escape her ghost in this place, and everywhere he looked he was reminded of her. Even when he let his glance sweep across the shifting crowd, his attention was immediately drawn to a blond woman—the color of her hair, her slenderness, the way she held her head—it was all too damned familiar. And if it hadn't been for the fact that he had promised the steering-committee chairman he'd be available to autograph copies of his book, he'd have gone back to his trailer and drunk himself into a stupor.

With an uncompromising set to his mouth, he went into the arena through one of the sets of double doors and worked his way down the steps to the floor, heading in the direction of the display area where his books were. He'd get this over with as fast as possible so he could get the hell out of here. As determined as he was to clear his mind of memories, he couldn't keep his eyes off the blonde as he wound his way through the crowd. Drawn like a moth to the proverbial flame.

She stood out so distinctly from the rest of the crowd, like some fragile mountain flower clinging to a rocky windswept slope. A subdued elegance, an unstudied grace, that incredible glossy silver-gold hair—she looked like a delicate, lithesome dancer in that dress. He had a sudden image of her twirling in slow motion, her pliant body arching like a ballerina's as she slowly raised her arms, the deep pink fabric flaring out around her like a gossamer cloud. Adam felt as if he were trapped in a bad dream. She too closely resembled the real thing, and her likeness awakened all the disturbing feelings he had been trying to forget. He was about to turn away when the person beside her moved and he was able to get a good look at her profile. The shock of recognition hit him with a devastating force.

This was no dream.

For a moment he felt completely removed from reality. But as he stood there staring at her, a newly ignited resentment about the past slowly spread through him. Nearly eleven years and he'd never really gotten over the stunt she'd pulled. Those long, unbearable months after she disappeared when he'd tried to convince himself that it was only an adolescent infatuation, that it was only his injured pride that wouldn't let go. Those months of trying to deal with the knowledge that she had been able to dispassionately walk away without so much as one single word. Eleven long years, and feelings were emerging that he thought he had put behind him. He didn't like it one damned bit.

When she lifted her head and saw him, she froze, her eyes widening with shock as the color drained from her face. For a moment he thought she was going to faint, then she whispered, "God, no."

For some reason her response riled him. When he realized how much his presence had rocked her, he experienced a weird disconnected sensation that only added to the conflicting feelings warring within him. There was a part of him that wanted to turn around and walk away, but there was another part of him, a long-forgotten part, that desperately wanted to touch her.

Her lips parted as if she was going to speak, but instead she closed her eyes and took a deep unsteady breath. When she looked up at him, she had regained a thin veneer of control, but it was obvious that she was badly shaken. Taking another deep breath, she clutched the book even tighter. "I—Adam, I—"

"Hello, Natalie. I never expected to see you back in this part of the country." His voice was cool and impersonal as he stared at her, his expression impassive.

She was gripping the book so tightly her knuckles were white, and the pulse in her neck was throbbing frantically as she avoided his gaze. For a moment Adam expected her to simply escape this exceedingly difficult confrontation and disappear into the crowd, but she held her ground. Her body was stiff and unnatural, and there was a nervous tremor in her voice when she answered evasively, "I hadn't planned on coming to this... It was more circumstance than anything." She hesitated, and as though bracing herself to face some formidable ordeal, she hauled in a shaky breath and looked up at him. "Your work is incredible, Adam. I didn't think it was possible, but it's even better." She swallowed hard, then unable to hold his gaze any longer, she looked down, her movements jerky as she fingered the volume. "I know how much you wanted this and how hard you've worked. And I just wanted to tell you that I think you really deserve your success.''

A nerve in his jaw twitched as Adam stared down at her lowered head. After so many years, why would she think it mattered to him what she thought? He didn't want to continue this pointless, awkward conversation; there was nothing she could possibly say that would interest him in the slightest. His manner was one of complete indifference. "Thank you." He motioned toward the table where his books were displayed. "Now if you'll excuse me...." With one last stony glance, he turned and walked away. He was halfway across the arena before he realized how angry he was. He was filled with resentment. He had never expected that seeing her again would arouse such hostile feelings. He didn't think she had that power over him anymore. But she did. Damn it, she did.

ADAM DIDN'T COME OUT of his trailer for the next two days. He had lost count of how many bottles of rye he'd gone through, but no matter how much he drank, he could not erase the fact that she was here. Whether he liked it or not, that was an unalterable fact.

With his shoulder braced against the metal frame and a drink in his hand, Adam stood in the doorway of his trailer staring out, his haggard, unshaven face ravaged by tension and fatigue. The sky was tinged with the first streaks of dawn, silhouetting the jagged top of the forest against the deepening shades of mauves and pinks. The exquisite color made him think of Natalie's dress, and clenching his jaw against the sudden twist of pain, he slowly drew in a deep breath to try to ease it.

What was it about her that had such power over him? In the space of a few minutes she had eradicated the years that separated them, and he was experiencing the same devastating sense of loss, the same sense of betrayal, the same frantic helplessness he had felt when she had disappeared.

And that was utter madness. He couldn't let her screw up his life again, especially when there was a damned good chance she had probably taken off sometime during the past two days. Disappeared again.

Somehow he was going to have to attain a certain degree of objectivity about what had happened. Somehow.

His eyes became bleak as he thought about their meeting. She hadn't changed much. She was slimmer and she had a certain maturity and poise about her now—but that inner sparkle was gone. He wondered why. He tossed back the remainder of his drink, then angrily crushed the plastic glass in his hand. This was getting him nowhere.

As if suddenly doused in cold water, a random thought cut through the fog of too much booze and too little sleep. There was a very real possibility that she was married and had a family, and that disturbed him more than he liked to admit. He frowned, trying to recall if she'd had rings on, but he couldn't form a total image. He could picture only her stricken face, and that image was one he wanted to forget.

His frown deepened as he went over the details of the confrontation in his mind and uncovered something he hadn't recognized before. There was more behind that look than shock. When he stopped to think about it in the cold light of day, he could also identify a deep apprehension, an apprehension that bordered on panic. It was almost as if she were afraid of him, and that made him wonder. What did she have to fear? But there could be another explanation for her alarm: what did she have to hide?

Swearing softly through gritted teeth, he slammed his hand against the doorjamb in frustration. This was so damned senseless. This marathon of sleeplessness had netted him nothing, except he had definitely decided to drive into town to see Doc. He didn't know what purpose that would serve, but it was something he had to do. And feeling as though he was beaten before he started, Adam wearily straightened and went into the trailer.

It was midmorning when he finally drove down the quiet street to Doc's house. He felt like hell and didn't look much better. He desperately needed a few hours of uninterrupted sleep, but he knew he wouldn't get a moment's rest until this was behind him. Adam wasn't looking forward to this meeting with the old druggist for more reasons than one.

Ever since he could remember, he and Doc had hiked the back country together. They both had the wilderness in their blood, and in many ways, Doc had been a mentor and teacher to Adam. He had trusted Doc and honestly believed that there was a solid bond between them. But that adolescent confidence was brutally shattered when Natalie disappeared without a trace. Adam suspected that Doc knew far more than he let on, and he had gone to him on more than one occasion trying to find out what had happened. But Doc would tell him nothing, and to a twenty-year-old kid whose world had just come crashing down, his silence was like salt in an open wound. Adam had viewed it as an outright double cross, and he had sworn he'd never forgive the old man for that. The whole mess had ended with one nasty scene in the drugstore when he'd told Doc exactly how he felt.

Subdued by those unpleasant recollections, Adam silently vowed that no matter what transpired today, he would not lose his temper like that again. He slowed as he approached the hedge, prepared to pull into the driveway. But there was already a small car parked there with California plates, so he drove past and parked his mud-splattered Bronco on the street beside the front walk.

Hunching forward, Adam rested his arms on the steering wheel and stared out the window. Obviously Doc had company, and under the circumstances, Adam really didn't want an audience. Now was not the time, it seemed, nor the place. He was just about to turn on the ignition and drive off when the white-haired man came out the side door of his garage carrying a spade. Without giving himself a chance to reconsider, Adam quickly climbed out of his truck.

Doc turned when he heard the door slam, and with a solemn expression etched into his wrinkled face, he watched the young man walk up the gravel driveway toward him. It was apparent that the old gentleman was not at all surprised to see him there, and that struck Adam as very strange. Why was he expecting him? There was something about the way the old man was watching him that made Adam suspicious. What was going on here?

A knot of apprehension settled in his gut, but somehow Adam managed to keep his voice devoid of all expression. "Hello, Doc."

Doc tipped his head in acknowledgment as he stretched his hand toward the newcomer. "Hello, Adam. I heard you were in town."

Adam shook the pharmacist's thickly veined hand, mildly surprised by the firmness of the grip, then stuck his hands in the back pockets of his jeans. A sudden gut feeling hit him, and without taking time to consider it, he played out his hunch. "I'd like to talk to Natalie, if you don't mind."

Doc didn't say anything as he looked away, his face set as he squinted against the sun. From the older man's calmness, Adam deduced his hunch was wrong. Then Doc turned his attention back to him and spoke. "She's in the house." He seemed to be weighed down by some invisible burden as he slowly turned and motioned toward the back door. "I'll take you in and tell her you're here."

The unexpectedness of this evoked a host of conflicting feelings that really caught Adam off balance, but he had long since mastered the ability to mask every trace of emotion. When he met Doc's worried glance, his expression was completely unreadable, and he said nothing.

As he followed his old companion up the steps and into the porch, he found himself questioning the rationale behind this visit. What did he hope to gain by all of this? It wasn't as if he could look back on their time together dispassionately. His feelings had been too strong. On the other hand, it had been made acutely clear to him that Natalie's feelings had been pretty damned shallow; if she had cared about him at all, she never could have done what she did.

Catching the screen door so it wouldn't slam shut behind him, Adam entered the living room. Doc motioned to a chair. "Have a seat, lad. I'll get her. She's in the kitchen."

Adam acknowledged the offer with an abrupt nod, but remained standing as Doc left the room. His edginess left him feeling like a caged cat. Needing something to focus on, he went over to the piano and idly glanced at the framed photographs arranged on top. There were quite a few: two old ones of Doc's wife, another large faded photo of a group of young men wearing World War II air-force uniforms and standing beside a Lancaster bomber, and a couple more of people he didn't know. But the one that arrested his attention was a studio pose of Natalie. His expression hardened as he stared at it for a moment before deliberately focusing on the two remaining photographs. They were encased in brass frames that were hinged together, and driven by some sort of morbid curiosity, Adam picked the unit up.

One was a candid shot of Natalie standing under a tree, holding a small boy in her arms. The other was a color photo of the same boy, only in this one, he was several years older. A sensation similar to claustrophia suddenly washed through him, and he was only vaguely aware of the sound of Doc departing by the other door.

There was no doubt about it—the kid was Natalie's. The eyes were a dead giveaway. He set the frame down with a slam and went to stand rigidly before the window. He stared out, his face cast in harsh lines. He had sensed she had something to hide. Now he knew what it was. He had a nearly uncontrollable urge to drive his fist through the wall as his anger took on a new dimension. He intended to bloody well find out what her story was. And the way he was feeling, he didn't give a damn what he had to do to get it out of her. The questions would all be answered, one way or another.

"Doc said you wanted to talk to me."

Adam took a minute to get a grip on his temper before he turned to face her. When he did, his hazel eyes were as brittle as emeralds. "I thought it might be a good idea." He moved toward the piano, and his cutting tone was dripping with sarcasm as he went on. "There are one or two things about your disappearance I've been mildly interested in."

"Adam, I—"

He indicated the photographs. "Your son, I take it?"

Natalie went deathly pale. Again he sensed the apprehension that bordered on panic, and he pressed the issue. "Well, is he your son?"

She folded her arms tightly in front of her as though she was suddenly cold, her eyes darkening. In a nearly inaudible voice she answered, "Yes, he's my son."

Adam picked up the pictures and studied them. "You work fast, Natalie," he said curtly. "I'd say he was nine or so."

She didn't respond and he looked at her as he replaced the pictures, his eyes narrow. She had started to tremble; her fear was visible. Adam had seen that same fear in wild animals that had been cornered. By some sixth sense he knew she was still hiding something. It was pretty obvious from the age of the boy that she'd become involved with someone shortly after she'd disappeared. The idea of that happening ignited his fury and a streak of ruthlessness emerged. He wanted confirmation of her duplicity, and he wanted it now. "How old is he, Natalie?" he ground out.

She still didn't answer, and he glanced at her left hand. No rings; she wasn't married. He knew Natalie well enough to realize that even if her marriage had collapsed, she very likely would still wear a wedding ring, especially when there was a kid involved. So what did that mean?

He studied her intently as he tried to make something out of all this. What was she hiding? His voice was ominously soft as he repeated the question. "How old is he?"

Her voice was barely a whisper. "He's ten."

Ten. That meant she'd had to pick up with someone else within a matter of weeks after she left, and the thought sickened him. There was, however, another possibility. She could have been involved with someone else even before she disappeared, right after he'd left his summer job to go back to university. That thought really rocked him. He had been so much in love with her, so sure of her, and he'd never once doubted how she felt about him. Not until she disappeared. A sense of betrayal nearly choked him. "When did he turn ten, Natalie?"

She had a trapped look about her, and he could sense her desperation. And he knew. Before she even answered, he knew that she had violated his trust long before he'd thought she had. He braced himself for her answer. Her voice was wrought with tension when she finally choked out, "His birthday's in April."

Adam stared at her, his anger overridden by disbelief. Born in April. Conceived in July. He felt as if she had just yanked the rug out from under him, and he continued to stare at her. Not once in all the time that had passed between then and now had he ever considered this as even an outside chance. But he knew by the look on her face that his deduction was right.

The kid was his.

The shock of it numbed him, and with his face looking as if it had been carved out of stone, he turned back to the window. His mind was in a turmoil. He had been so damned careful with her—except that very first time—that first time when their feelings overwhelmed every shred of common sense, and an uncheckable passion carried them off like leaves in a storm. The memory of that very special afternoon clawed through his numbness and unearthed a deep, empty ache. The consummation of that passion had been so intense, so incredible that he'd never been able to erase it from his mind. And it was then that she'd conceived . . . his son.

And she never even had the decency to tell him. He had a son who was ten years old, a son she had deliberately kept from him. Anger began to build in him until he felt as though he couldn't contain it. There wasn't one single reason she could give him that could even come close to justifying what she'd done. His wrath was infused by a cold, calculating vindictiveness. He'd be damned if she'd walk away again unscathed. This time he'd call the shots, he thought bitterly, and one way or another, he was going to even an old score. He'd hurt her as much as she'd hurt him, and he knew exactly how to do it.

He continued to stare out the window as he spoke, his voice low and grating. "Why in hell didn't you tell me? Why didn't you have the decency to tell me you were pregnant?"

Her voice was very low. "I didn't... I wasn't sure until after I left."

Natalie had never been able to lie worth a damn, but knowing that she wasn't telling the truth really didn't matter now. There were other things that were far more important. "I want to see him."

She didn't answer and he turned around, his eyes filled with contempt. She was sitting in a big leather armchair, her body hunched forward, her head lowered so he couldn't see her face. He felt nothing but fury. "I said I want to see him."

She looked up at Adam, her eyes dark and tormented. Then, as if daunted by the look on his face, she quickly glanced away. She swallowed hard before she whispered brokenly, "He's at camp for the summer—"

"That's not good enough, Natalie. I want to see him, and I won't be put off by some damned lame excuse." His voice was like ice as he gave her an ominous warning. "You'd better bloody well produce him, lady, or you're going to regret it."

She lifted one hand in a beseeching gesture, her eyes pleading with him as she whispered unevenly, "Please don't involve him in this, Adam. Don't hurt him because of me—"

"Don't play games, damn it!" Adam went to stand before her, his voice shaking with rage as he bent over the armchair. "He's mine, Natalie, just as much as he's yours. And if you don't cooperate, I'll have you in court so fast it'll make your head swim. I'll bring in the best damned lawyers in the country, and I'll challenge you. Just give me an excuse and I'll do anything I have to to gain full custody of him." With his eyes narrowed menacingly, he pointed his finger at her, his tone harsh and threatening. "And don't try anything cute. Another stunt like your last one, and I'll track you down, Natalie, and I'll make damned sure you never see him again."

He was breathing heavily, his pulse pounding from the violent anger that was consuming him. She had kept the knowledge of his son from him for ten years, and if he hadn't met her again through sheer chance, he very likely would have never known about the boy. And the fact that she had made that conscious decision, that she had withheld that piece of information from him, enraged him like nothing ever had. For years he had been trapped in a web of lies. He had remembered only her gentleness; until she'd vanished he'd known nothing of her deceptiveness. He turned and went back to the window, and with his expression steeled by rage, he braced his arm against the window frame and stood glaring out.

A son. His own flesh and blood. A son he knew absolutely nothing about. How could she be so damned hard, so damned unfeeling? It was a long time before the strangling feeling of full-blown fury eased, and his pulse rate slowed to an even beat. Adam slowly drew in a deep breath in an attempt to regain a semblance of control before he faced her again.

His voice was devoid of emotion. "I don't even know what his name is."

Natalie lifted her head and looked at him, her eyes dark, her ashen face scored by strain. "Patrick. I named him Patrick—" Her breath caught as a tremor quivered through her. She clenched her hands tightly together, her knuckles turning white. "Don't do anything to hurt him, Adam." Her voice broke and she looked away. "Don't punish him because of what I did."

Adam stared at her for a moment, then snorted in disgust. "Do you really think I'd stoop to those kinds of tactics?" His smile was twisted by malice. "But be forewarned, Natalie. I have every intention of taking him away from you, but by the time I'm finished, it will be Patrick's decision to leave. You won't have a damned thing to say about it."

"Adam—"

"Drop it, Natalie. You just make damned sure he gets here." His voice took on a sinister tone. "And don't try any tricks. You'll be sorry if you do."

There was a tense silence, and she knew he meant every word. Her face seemed paralyzed when she whispered, "He's finished camp this Friday. He'll be arriving in Calgary on a direct flight from Los Angeles on Sunday."

He studied her suspiciously, his fury abating. "Why Calgary? Why not Vancouver?"

"I work for a travel agency, and I could get a much cheaper rate with the Calgary flight." Her level gaze held his, and he knew she was telling the truth.

"What time does the flight arrive?"

"I'll have to check to make sure it's on time, but if it is, it's due late in the afternoon."

Absently stroking his bottom lip, Adam assessed her with cold detachment. He had no intention of letting her pick up the boy alone—he didn't trust her for a minute. It was a little more than a six-hour drive to Calgary, which meant they could leave in the morning and still be there in plenty of time to meet Patrick's plane. He watched her like a hawk as he spoke in a tone that dared her to argue. "We'll both go to get him."

That was the last thing she wanted and he knew it, but she also knew he had her backed in a corner, and she didn't have the energy or strength to fight her way out. It seemed to take a massive effort for her to nod in unwilling assent. Her hand was shaking badly as she brushed back a loose tendril of hair, and it was this unsteady movement that drew his attention to the long ragged scar along the left side of her jaw. That hadn't been there before. He frowned slightly as he scrutinized her. There was something else that hadn't been there before, and that was the finely veiled tenor of fear. The scar was probably from the accident she'd been in when her mother was killed, just before she dropped out of sight. Where, he speculated silently, had the fear come from? His hostility and anger faded as he stared at Natalie intently. There were other scars, he sensed, scars that went deeper and were more disfiguring than the one on her face.

Irritated by the direction his thoughts were taking, Adam tore his eyes away from her stricken face and directed his attention to the pictures on the piano. His expression softened. He was a good-looking kid, he thought with the first glimmer of paternal pride. The boy had the kind of face he liked to photograph: good bone structure, an animated expression, an engaging smile. A flicker of recognition punctured his thoughts, unmasking a staggering revelation. The smile, he realized, was a carbon copy of his own. This one identifiable likeness drove home the irrefutable fact that this was, without a doubt, his child.

He wanted to ask her what he was like, to find out everything about him, but anything she told him would have little meaning. She had denied him the knowledge of his own son, the special memories, the chance to be an important part of his child's life. She had denied him all that, and he could never reclaim that which was lost to time. He could never forgive her for that.

A peculiar heaviness settled in his chest as he stood totally self-absorbed, trying to cope with the host of new feelings that were slowly unfolding. The incredible miracle of conception and life were biological phenomena that filled him with reverence and awe, and knowing that a part of him had gone into the creation of this boy meant more to him than anyone would ever know.

As if drawn by a force that was too powerful to deny, he reached out and touched the pictures of his son with an unspoken longing, his finger slowly outlining the shape of the boy's face. There was something in that one lingering gesture that hinted of an immeasurable hunger, a certain poignancy that provided insight into the man. He was a complex, sensitive human being; he was also a solitary figure, alone and bitter. Unwittingly he had allowed his defensive barrier to slip, exposing the deep feelings and the even deeper passions of the man he had become.

"He's very much like your family," Natalie said softly.

An unaccustomed tightness in his throat made it difficult for him to talk, and his words were strained when he finally spoke. "In what way?"

Adam's question was met with a tense silence and he turned toward her. She was watching him with dark, fearful eyes, and he realized her comment had been an impulsive response. It goaded him, knowing that she held the only key to his finding out about the boy, and his anger reignited with a vengeance. But as quickly as his fury flared, it died. He loathed himself for letting her get to him. And he loathed her even more for having the power to do it. He jammed his hands in his back pockets as he stared at her, his jaw set in rigid lines. She stared back at him, her finely sculpted features as colorless as wax. She knew how close he'd come to losing control. And that knowledge had obviously frightened her, but for some strange reason, he sensed his reaction hurt her a hundred times more than it scared her.

Adam experienced a certain amount of grim satisfaction, but that feeling was pathetically short-lived. The pain he had inflicted on her was obvious; she abruptly turned her head, tearing her eyes from his riveting gaze. But he had already seen the awful anguish in those gray depths.

As if by some telepathic osmosis her pain became his, and Adam was suddenly swamped by the most intense need to shield her from whatever was tearing her apart. Again his memories betrayed him. As though it were yesterday, he remembered how intoxicating it was to hold her supple body tightly against his and to envelop her slender form in his strength. He remembered her warmth, her softness, the fragrance of her, how she moved beneath him in the night. And he remembered in living detail the scorching fever of needing her.

His response was overpowering. He didn't try to analyze it, he didn't try to rationalize it. Instead he fought to stifle it, but it was unrelenting. His bitterness and anger were being seduced by ghosts that had haunted him forever. Feeling dangerously exposed, Adam turned away, his hands curled into tight fists.

It felt as though his chest was in a vise and he couldn't breathe. Damn it, what was happening to him? His feelings were so volatile, so unpredictable, and they were boomeranging from one end of the emotional spectrum to the other. The anger he understood, the bitterness he understood, and he certainly understood the whole range of responses in between, from loathing to a sense of betrayal. But what was throwing him more than anything was this feral protectiveness she still aroused in him. That was not expected. Nor did he understand it. Especially after the gaping hole she'd left in his life; especially after finding out she'd chosen to keep the existence of the boy from him for so many years. He should feel nothing but anger. Anger was a clear-cut, definable emotion, one with definite parameters. And it was an emotion he could control and nurture with black memories. But the feelings he was experiencing now were uncontrollable; they had a will of their own.

Adam was unconscious of passing time, and he had no idea how long he had stood staring numbly out the window. But the long shadow from the garage had shrunk to a thin line by the time he finally dragged his thoughts from his personal turmoil. It took a lot of self-discipline for him to grasp some semblance of dispassion. It had been a long time since he'd lost his cool like he had, and he couldn't afford to lose it again. Now, more than ever, he had to use his head. Threatening her had been a stupid move, and the only thing he was apt to accomplish with threats was to drive her back into hiding. And she was the one existing link to his son. His son.

Turning slightly, he rested his shoulder against the wall and looked at her. His tone was low and expressionless when he finally spoke. "Are you going to try to stop me from spending some time with him?"

It was a challenge she could have probably evaded if she'd wanted to, but Natalie didn't even attempt to dodge the issue. Instead she met his piercing gaze with unwavering directness. "No." There was a haunting bleakness in her eyes that seemed to reach down to her very soul, and Adam detected the glisten of tears before she lowered her head. "I know you aren't going to believe this, but I never wanted to keep him from you, Adam." He saw her try to swallow, and it seemed to be very difficult for her to speak when she finally continued in an uneven whisper. "There was never a conscious decision not to tell you."

Adam narrowed his eyes as he studied her, silently searching for some tiny clue that would either support or refute her sincerity. But he was unwilling to trust his instincts. A gut feeling warned him that now was not the time to delve into her reasons for doing what she did. Not when the accessibility of his son was at stake. This time he was forced to give her the benefit of the doubt, whether he liked it or not. His calm, rational mind told him that it had all happened a long time ago, and that she had been little more than a child herself when she'd been faced with an unexpected pregnancy. Then there had been her mother's fatal accident on top of it. Who was he to sit in judgment?

But his rational self was submerged beneath a part of him that did not respond to logic. He had been torn apart by her callous rejection, and there was no explanation on earth that could ever excuse what she'd done.

The emotional battle was draining him of what little energy he had, and Adam was suddenly bone tired. Wearily rubbing the back of his neck, he went to the armchair nearest Natalie's and sat down. He slouched his shoulders, stretched his long legs out in front of him, then rested his elbows on the wide arms and laced his fingers together across his chest. Those feelings that tied him to the past would have to wait. What he had to do now was make sure she wouldn't balk at letting him see the boy. And until that was assured, he was totally within her power. He didn't like it, but that's the way it was.

He studied her as he tried to assess all the angles. One thing he had going for him was that Natalie had always been a lousy liar. As long as he asked all the right questions, he should get all the right answers. He frowned slightly as he considered his best line of attack, then spoke in a deliberately passive tone. "I'm not asking you to tell him who I am right off the bat, Natalie. All I'm asking is a chance to spend some time with him. I think you owe me that."

She was huddled in the large armchair with her feet tucked under her, her profile muted by shadows. She had always sat like that when she was troubled about something, and the sudden exposure to that long-forgotten mannerism of hers jarred him more than he liked to admit. In some ways, she had changed so little.

There was a slight softening in Adam's expression as he solemnly watched her. She was the same, yet she was a stranger. Physically, she had changed little, but there was a remoteness about her now that was utterly foreign to the girl he remembered, and there was that element of fear he had sensed. And something else that he couldn't quite put his finger on. It was almost as though some inner flame had gone out and part of her had died. He found that analogy grimly disturbing.

Abruptly realizing that his idle reflections were leading him toward treacherous ground, he forcibly closed his mind against her. He could not, no matter how strong the temptation, lose sight of the cold hard fact that she had deceived him once, and she'd do it again if given the chance. There was now too much at stake to take any risks. Even being fully aware of the kind of person she was, it took every ounce of self-discipline he had to drag his attention back to the issue of Patrick. Somehow he managed to marshal his resolve, and when she lifted her head and looked at him, his face was without a trace of emotion.

She seemed to have nothing left to fight with—no energy, no spirit, no desire—as if she was completely spent. Her voice was lifeless. "I won't try to keep him from you, if that's what you're worried about." She finally looked at him, her eyes as lifeless as her voice. "The only thing that I ask is that you give me some time with him before I tell him . . . who you are. I'd like to prepare him a little."

"Has he ever asked about me?"

"Yes."

"What did you tell him? Or did you take the easy route and tell him I was dead?"

Natalie wearily leaned her head against the high wing of the chair, an air of absolute defeat about her as she stared into space. "No, I didn't tell him you were dead," she said quietly, her voice a monotone of resignation. "But I've never encouraged him to ask too many questions."

Adam silently considered her response, trying very hard not to let his emotions gain the upper hand; he couldn't risk making a mistake because his temper got the best of him. It was imperative that he shut down any avenues of escape she may have. "I plan on going with you when you go to get him, Natalie," he said flatly.

She looked at him, anxiety etched in her face. "It would be best for Patrick if I could spend some time alone with him before you see him."

He gave her a cynical smile, his eyes riveted on her. "It won't wash, Natalie. I'm not as blind and trusting as I used to be. There would be absolutely nothing stopping you from picking him up and taking off." His voice was cutting with sarcasm. "You are, after all, very good at disappearing."

She met his disdainful look, silently begging him to relent as she raised her hands in an imploring gesture. "I promise I'll bring him back, Adam. Just let me go get him alone."

He snorted derisively. "Do you honestly think I'm stupid enough to let you out of my sight? I've everything to lose and nothing to gain." He folded his arms across his chest, his expression unyielding. "You know damned well I don't have any kind of information on you. It would take a while to track you down if I let you get away from me. And you also know that my only source of information would be Doc—and we both know he won't open his mouth if you tell him not to." He gave her another cold smile that was warped with bitterness. "You forget that I've been through all this once before with you."

Natalie managed to remain unmoving beneath his hostile gaze for only a moment, then she stood up abruptly, her body unnaturally stiff. She moved to the piano and gently touched the photos of her son. Adam never took his eyes off her. He sensed she was struggling with a decision concerning his demands and he watched her through narrowed eyes, trying to read something from her expression. She turned, and with her face drawn by tension, she went over to the ancient rolltop desk and opened a handbag that was lying beside a stack of books. She took out something and came back to where Adam was sitting. Deliberately avoiding his gaze, she held out her wallet to him.

At first he didn't comprehend, then the significance of what she was doing registered; she was handing him the most concise source of information about her life that any detective could hope to find. Glancing up at her face, he wordlessly took the wallet from her and opened it.

Her driver's license, one general credit card and one for an oil company, a card for medical insurance, two pink insurance slips for her car, one of which was out of date. There were other pieces of identification relevant to her day-to-day living—a wallet-size copy of her birth certificate, a library card, a picture of Patrick—all revealing a great deal about one Natalie Anne Carter.

In a side pocket Adam found several of her business cards, and on the back of one was written a name, an address and two telephone numbers; beneath these details was a printed record of some dates and locations. His edginess eased a little when Adam realized he was holding all the information about Patrick's camp in his hand. So now, at least, he knew where the kid was. He couldn't have asked for more.

Natalie opened her mouth to protest when he slipped the picture of Patrick, the expired copy of her car insurance and the business card with the details of Patrick's camp in his shirt pocket. He could tell by the horrified look in her eyes that she realized she had unwittingly trapped herself. Not only did Adam have access to her vehicle registration, her home address and her place of employment, but he now had something she had no intention of giving him—Patrick's present whereabouts. With an insolent smile, he gave her a level look that dared her to challenge him. She hesitated, then abruptly turned away, her eyes filled with stark comprehension. They both knew he had her cornered. If she didn't play his game, he could get to Patrick, on his own.

Feeling adequately defended against anything she might have considered, Adam started replacing everything he had taken out of her wallet. As he went to slip her plasticized birth certificate back in a side pocket, an identically sized card separated from the back of it. "The Province of Alberta, Division of Vital Statistics." For a moment he thought it was a duplicate of her birth certificate, but when he looked at it more closely, he realized it was Patrick's. Adam frowned as he glanced at the statistics. Place of birth: Calgary. Why Calgary? He read it again, only this time he noticed every detail. And he was in for another shock, one that would haunt him for many nights to come. Registered name: Adam Patrick Carter.

His son carried his name.

CHAPTER FOUR

FROM THE TIME HE LEFT Doc's until he parked the Bronco at the campsite, Adam wasn't aware of anything—not of driving through town, nor of turning onto the old forestry road. Nothing. The accidental discovery that Natalie had named the boy after him had really shaken him. He couldn't figure out why she'd done it. It seemed to him that naming the kid after a lover she had left without a backward glance didn't make much sense. But then, nothing was making much sense.

Adam was contemplative as he climbed out of the truck and slammed the door, then turned toward the river. He kept searching for explanations that didn't exist, kept digging for the slightest clue when there wasn't one, and the more he mulled it over, the more tangled his thoughts became. He was reaching for answers but was only uncovering more questions. If only he could summon up the energizing fury he had felt earlier. Without it, he was so damned exhausted he could hardly think—and he had to think. He had a lot to sort out.

For once oblivious to the siren's call of the untamed country that surrounded him, Adam walked along the rocky riverbed until the river narrowed and the dense bush crowded against the mountain stream as its rush to the sea became more turbulent. A huge chunk of granite had been heaved up by some ancient force of nature, it's stony mass warmed by the heat of the sun. Sitting down beside it, Adam leaned back against the smooth face of the rock, his forearm resting on his raised knee as he stared across the sparkling water, squinting against the glare.

When he'd first found out about Patrick, Adam had been trapped in a war of opposing emotions. But now that he had a chance to look at everything in a more rational light, he found he was doing some very heavy soul-searching. He felt oddly out of touch, as though some force had altered the course of his life and he was left scrambling to catch up. For the past few years he had been a man alone, a man on the move, but still a man who had an ever deepening and unsettling awareness of his own mortality.

But now, in the space of a few hours, all that had changed. He learned he had a son, his sole link with continuation, his only provision for the perpetuation of a part of himself. It was a sobering discovery. And he also felt a deep sense of fulfillment, and as he thought about the boy, a strong paternal instinct was unearthed that he didn't even know he possessed.

Now that he was finally able to dissect his thoughts and feelings with some objectivity, he came up with one unalterable conclusion. And that was that he very much wanted this kid. This resolution had nothing to do with vindictiveness, nor did it have anything to do with his feelings about Natalie. It did, however, have everything to do with one of the things he had wanted out of life, and that was a generation to follow him. Now he had it. And he wasn't going to take any chances of losing it. This time he was going to protect his back.

He went back to the trailer and immediately drove into town to make the phone calls. The first was to the headquarters of the summer camp to confirm the information he had found on the business card, and to find out for certain that Patrick was enrolled in the program. The second call was to a prominent lawyer he knew in Los Angeles who represented the television network that aired his documentaries. The purpose was to arrange for a tail to be put on Patrick. By the following morning, the boy would be under the surveillance of one of the best private investigation firms in the country. He was not taking any chances, not with Natalie's track record.

Using his telephone credit card, Adam made the calls from the pay phone that was still located in the cubbyhole he remembered in the deserted hotel lobby. After he completed the calls, he crossed the dingy foyer and entered the brightly lit coffee shop. He couldn't honestly remember when he had eaten last, and he was beginning to feel the effects.

Straddling one of the rust-speckled chrome stools, he sat down at the counter and took the ketchup-battered menu from its place behind the napkin holder. Adam scanned it as a disinterested gum-chewing, pony-tailed waitress ambled over and gave the chipped blue Formica an indifferent swipe, then listlessly waited for him to order. For the first time in days, a spark of humor lit Adam's eyes as he studied her profile in the mirror backing of the glass shelves behind the counter. He would love to photograph her just like that, with the harsh light and the long empty counter providing an unfocused background. She was a perfect study of absolute, utter, total boredom.

He had placed his order and was drinking coffee when someone sat down on the stool beside his. "Are you going to buy me a coffee, or are you going to sit there like a dummy and ignore me?"

He turned to find Stella Ralston, one eyebrow cocked in a mocking expression. He grinned lopsidedly, his eyes lighting up with a warning that he was going to try to get a rise out of her. "Stella," he said in deliberately provocative tones, "I'll buy you anything you damned well want."

She grinned as she signaled for a cup of coffee. "I'll settle for a one-way ticket out of this dump," she responded dryly. Taking a deep drag on her cigarette, she propped her elbows on the counter and stared at him through a haze of blue smoke. "What in hell are you doing here? I thought for sure you'd be one of the smart ones who'd have enough sense not to come back."

The gleam in Adam's eyes grew more mischievous. "I couldn't stay away from you any longer, Stella."

Stella gave him a long level stare, her mouth twisted in a tart expression. "God, you're a lousy actor. If you expect me to believe that crap, you're a damned sight thicker in the head than I thought."

The lines around his eyes crinkled as he laughed and shrugged slightly. "It was worth a try." He paused as he reached down the counter to the bowl of sugar cubes she had motioned to, then met her steady gaze as he passed it to her. "Actually, I was looking for a location to film the next TV segment, and thought some of that country northwest of here might work well."

"So you'll be around for a while?"

"Very likely."

She obviously had something on her mind as she slowly unwrapped the sugar. "I saw you at the arena the other night, but you disappeared before I had a chance to talk to you."

Adam's expression immediately became shuttered as he hunched forward, his attention focused intently on his coffee mug. He absently traced the crack in the handle with his thumbnail. "I didn't stick around," he said curtly.

Stella had been watching him closely, her lips pursed in a thoughtful expression as the silence stretched between them. She took another drag on her cigarette and exhaled slowly, her eyes narrowed in contemplation. "Where are you staying while you're in town?"

He continued to pick idly at the crack. "I haul a trailer when I'm out scouting locations. I'm parked down by the river just off the old forestry road."

"Why don't you come for dinner tonight? I'll cook you a real meal instead of this crap."

Adam finally looked up and gave her a lopsided grin. "That's an offer I can't refuse."

Stella glanced at her watch, then crushed her cigarette in the battered metal ashtray. "I've got to run or I'll miss the bank." She stood up and slipped the strap of her handbag over her shoulder. "I'm still living in the apartment above the drugstore. Make it around seven, okay?"

"Sounds great."

Stella Ralston had a reputation for being one of the best cooks in the valley, and it was a reputation well deserved. But she was also an excellent hostess—funny, entertaining and with a view on life that was definitely ribald. During dinner, she brought Adam up to date on all the happenings in the community, and by the time they reached the liqueurs and coffee, he was more relaxed than he'd been in months. He couldn't remember the last time he had enjoyed an evening more or laughed so much.

They had moved into her living room, and he was sitting on the sofa, his legs stretched in front of him, his elbow propped on the wide arm. Stella was seated in an armchair across from him, absently swirling the brandy in her glass, her expression settling into one of thoughtfulness. She looked at him intently. "What's the real reason you came back, Adam?"

Adam stared at her, then drained his glass. With studied care, he set it on the table beside him, his expression suddenly unfathomable. "Was this entire evening a setup, Stella?"

"Partly."

His gaze narrowed on her, and she gave him a rueful smile. "There are some things I think you ought to know, and there are some things I want to find out." She frowned as she slowly ran her finger around the lip of the crystal brandy snifter. "And you look like you bloody well need a friend right now."

He held her gaze for a minute, then looked away. There was a heavy silence before he said, "I sure in hell need something."

"You saw Natalie, I take it."

His voice was gruff. "Yes, I saw her."

Setting her glass down, Stella drew a cigarette from the inlaid silver case sitting on the table and tapped the end of it on the polished surface. "Look, Adam, I know it's none of my business, but what in hell happened between you two? I would have bet the farm on you kids."

Several moments passed before Adam raised his head and looked at her, his mouth twisted in a humorless lopsided smile. "Don't ask me, Stella," he said stiffly. "I hadn't heard from her for four or five weeks, so I came home from university to find out what was going on."

"Hadn't you heard anything about the accident?"

He continued to stare at her for a minute, then sighing heavily, he looked down at his feet. "My folks were away visiting my sister in Ontario that fall, so I didn't hear a damned thing until I came home. Tim Watson was at the bus depot when I arrived, and he told me her mother had been killed in a car accident a month earlier, and that Natalie had been badly injured. But no one I talked to seemed to know anything—where she was, how badly she'd been hurt—nothing. I damned near turned this town inside out, but I still couldn't find out anything, and to top it off, I couldn't find hide nor hair of Natalie's stepfather."

Adam would never forget the awful helplessness he had felt that day. It was a desperation he had never known before, and it was one he'd never known since.

"How did you find out?"

"I finally tracked Doc down. His neighbor told me he'd been away but that he was due home that night, so I was sitting on his doorstep when he arrived."

Stella toyed with her glass as she dissected this bit of information. She had been away on a buying trip for the small gift shop Doc ran in one section of the drugstore, and she didn't know a thing about the tragedy until she arrived home the day after Jean Willard's funeral. But there had always been something about the whole mess that didn't quite sit right with her. She could never put her finger on exactly what it was that made her suspicious.

She was still frowning slightly as she asked, "What did Doc tell you?"

"Not a hell of a lot. He said that Natalie and her mother were on their way back from Calgary when the car went out of control. Apparently it rolled before it plunged over the edge of the enbankment, and that's when Natalie was thrown clear." His voice was heavily strained when he added, "Unfortunatey Mrs. Willard wasn't so lucky."

Resting his head against the high back of the sofa, Adam stared off into space, his mind caught up in dark recollections. "Tell me about it, Adam."

He glanced at her, then looked away, his face scored by the agony of remembering. His voice was very quiet when he began to speak. "It was a hell of a night, Stella. I borrowed Tim's car, and after hitting nothing but dead ends, I parked in Doc's driveway waiting for him to show. I couldn't figure out for the life of me...I couldn't figure out why someone...why Doc hadn't had the decency to notify me about the accident, especially since Natalie had been injured. She could have been killed and I wouldn't have even known."

No words could ever explain the panic he felt that night. After enduring countless hours of wondering and waiting, Adam had been almost frantic by the time Doc showed up.

Looking back, he realized he had handled that meeting very badly, but he'd been nearly crazy with worry and so damned desperate to find Natalie, he had simply overreacted. It had in fact, been pretty ugly.

"What happened when Doc showed up? What did he tell you?"

Adam sighed and dragged his hand down his face. "Doc told me the details about the accident—when it had happened and where. But when I asked him why Natalie and Jean Willard had been traveling from Calgary in the first place, Doc had said he didn't know. I don't know why, but

I started to suspect Doc was holding something back. And I was pretty upset." Which was putting it mildly. But it wasn't until Adam's sense of utter helplessness turned into fury that the situation started to come apart. He had been trying to find out if Natalie had been moved to a hospital in Calgary, or if she had been taken somewhere else when Doc finally leveled with him.

Now that he could look back with a certain amount of objectivity, Adam realized that Doc had tried to soften the blow, but for a twenty-year-old kid who had stars in his eyes, the blow was devastating. Natalie had been discharged two weeks earlier and had gone to live with an aunt somewhere in the United States. Without a word. After all they had shared, she had been able to leave without one single word. Nothing could ever describe how betrayed he felt, but at least now he knew why she'd gone. She had obviously left to keep him from finding out about Patrick, and that was almost as devastating as her betrayal had been.

The redhead watched Adam intently as she lit her cigarette, a frown of concentration furrowing her brow. "When did Doc finally tell you that Natalie wasn't coming back?"

"That night."

"Did you believe him?"

There was a watchfulness about Adam as he met Stella's gaze with a warped, mocking smile that was filled with self-disdain. "It's a nasty habit of mine. I have to bang my head against a few brick walls before I accept the facts, Stella."

Adam's eyes narrowed as he watched his companion's face. "He told me how the accident happened, and he told me Natalie wasn't coming back, but that was it. I still don't know why Natalie and Mrs. Willard were in Calgary in the first place."

Stella exhaled a cloud of smoke, then absently rolled the tip of her cigarette around the edge of the ashtray by her elbow. "I can answer that. Jean was having bad back problems, and there was a doctor in Calgary who had a new treatment. Her doctor here made the appointment for her."

Adam's eyes narrowed even more. "Then what was the big deal? Why didn't Doc tell me that?"

The redhead shrugged. "Your guess is as good as mine. Doc was damned closemouthed about the whole mess."

"What happened to Carl? I tried to track him down that fall and he'd disappeared."

"You knew about the fire, didn't you?"

Adam shifted his position and gave her a quizzical look. "I heard that he'd gone to bed and left a cigarette burning. A stack of newspapers caught fire and they barely got him out before the entire house went up in flames."

"Yeah, well, that's what happened all right. Except he was so drunk, it took him two days to sober up. In fact, I don't think he drew one sober breath after Jean died." She took another long drag of her cigarette before she continued. "He took off right after the fire. That was the last anyone heard of him." It was obvious that she was agitated as she flicked the ash into the ashtray and shook her head in disgust. "Good riddance to bad rubbish. Carl Willard was a louse from the word go."

Adam gave her a warped grin. "Well, he sure didn't like me hanging around."

"He didn't like anyone hanging around," Stella added sardonically. "Carl Willard was nothing but an arrogant, self-centered loudmouth."

Leaning forward, Adam poured himself another brandy from the decanter sitting on the coffee table, then rested his shoulder against the arm of the sofa as he studied Stella. "You said there were things I should know... Or was that just a ruse to get me talking?"

Deliberately avoiding his gaze, she emptied her glass, consuming the potent drink as though it was some kind of fortification.

There was a long, tense silence before Adam prodded her. "Spit it out, Stella."

Her brow creased as she pursed her lips in an expression of consternation, and her bosom heaved as she exhaled sharply. Her eyes were filled with apprehension when she finally looked at him. "Have you been to see Natalie?"

He stared at her woodenly. "Yes, I have."

"Did she say anything to you?"

Adam drained his own glass and set it on the table, then folded his arms across his chest. It was unquestionably a defensive gesture. "Like what, Stella? What was it she should have told me?"

She met his cold glare with a steady calm. "Did she tell you she had a son?"

"I saw his picture."

Stella was finished hedging around, and she snorted in exasperation as she set her glass down with a solid slam. "Just how thickheaded are you, Rutherford? I mean, I can add and subtract. It didn't take a genius to figure it out."

"So?"

She shook her head in disbelief. "So! So since the kid has been such a deep dark secret, I thought maybe she hadn't told you," she snapped, irritated by his offishness. "I thought maybe you didn't even know about him, that's all."

The hardness in Adam's eyes changed to bleakness as he answered quietly, "I didn't."

Stella sighed heavily. She rested her arm on her crossed knee and laced her fingers together. "When did you find out?"

"This morning."

"Wonderful," she said succinctly.

"Yeah." Restraint showed on his face as he sat up and poured himself another drink. "How did you know about him?"

"Doc. He has pictures of him in his office at the drugstore." She picked a piece of lint off her slacks and idly rolled it between her fingers, her mood contemplative. "Are you going to get a chance to see him?"

"He's flying into Calgary on Sunday, and Natalie and I are going to pick him up."

She watched him closely, her shrewd eyes assessing as she tried to read his face. "It must have been one hell of a shock, finding out you had a kid."

"Shock doesn't even come close." His expression became reflective, and there was an air of vulnerability about him as he stared at the glass in his hand. "I was so damned furious at first, I couldn't see straight. A kid—and she never even had the decency to tell me."

Stella butted her cigarette, brushing an ash off the arm of her chair as she asked, "Did she give you a reason *why* she didn't tell you?"

"She said she didn't tell me because she didn't find out that she was pregnant until after she left."

"Sounds like a crock of crap to me."

Adam gave her a halfhearted grin. "It sounded like a crock of crap to me, too." He averted his eyes and the muscles in his face tensed. "Did you know his name was Adam Patrick?"

Instantly alert, Stella responded, "How did you find that out?"

"I saw his birth certificate."

"Does the kid know about you?"

"No."

"Did you ask her why she named him Adam?"

"No."

There was exasperation in her voice when she asked, "Well why in hell didn't you?"

Adam's expression was suddenly guarded as he looked at her. "What difference does it make? Maybe she did it out of guilt—who knows? All I know is that it's going to be a damned sight easier for everyone concerned if we don't even see each other, let alone talk."

"If that's how you feel, your trip to Calgary could prove interesting," retorted Stella dryly.

Adam sighed heavily, as though he didn't have the energy to speak. "I wish I trusted her enough to let her go alone."

Stella frowned and tilted her head to one side. "Why don't you trust her?"

"I really don't know. I just have this gut feeling that there's a hell of a lot she's not telling me. And if she disappeared once because of it, she could disappear again."

Stella thoughtfully tugged at her bottom lip as she mulled that over in her mind, and her eyes narrowed as she murmured more or less to herself. "I wonder what in hell she's hiding?"

SUNDAY MORNING, and the final countdown. Adam had hardly slept during the past few days, and when he had managed to sleep for a few hours, his rest had been punctuated by disturbing dreams. If it hadn't been for Stella, he didn't think he could have made it. As it was, he was sure he couldn't have taken much more of the tension or the endless hours with nothing to do but think.

The shrill drone of his rechargeable razor sliced through the distinctive hush of early morning as he stood in the minuscule bathroom of the trailer, his mind wandering. Patrick's flight was due in at 3:40 P.M. In little more than nine hours he would meet his son, and for the first time in years, Adam had butterflies.

If he had managed to accomplish anything during the past few days, it was to separate his negative feelings about Natalie from his awakening feelings for the boy. He had made up his mind to be careful not to do or say anything that might alienate Patrick. The kid was bound to have deep-seated loyalties toward his mother; it was only natural. And regardless of how Adam felt about Natalie, he would not use Patrick as a weapon to even an old score.

He shut off his razor and replaced it in its case, then pulled the towel from around his neck and tossed it in the sink. Absently rubbing his hand across his naked chest, he stared at his reflection in the mirror, trying to see himself through a stranger's eyes—his boy's eyes. What if Patrick wanted to have nothing to do with him? What then? With a grim expression lining his gaunt face, he swore and turned away.

What he put on was never a big deal for Adam. His wardrobe was certainly adequate, but he wore even his most expensive clothes with the same kind of detachment he did blue jeans and a faded plaid shirt. But today he found himself selecting his clothes with unaccustomed care. He kept telling himself it was only a kid, but that did nothing to calm the butterflies.

The sun hadn't yet risen over the mountain to touch the valley floor, but that first soft breeze of daylight was rustling through the trees by the time he reached the Patterson house. The neighborhood was still early-morning quiet, except for the far-off barking of a lone dog.

When he had phoned Natalie the day before to make arrangements for the trip, she had once again tried to persuade him not to go with her, but Adam refused to compromise. He did relent when she had asked to take her car. He suspected that was a kind of thin assurance for her that she had some control over what was happening, that she wasn't completely within his control. It didn't matter to him how they got there, only that they did.

Climbing out of the truck, Adam picked up a small duffel bag, a camera case and his camera from the passenger seat, then closed the door. He slung all three straps over his shoulder, and thrusting his hands in his pockets, he walked into the backyard. Doc had a fantastic view of the river, and for a few tranquil moments Adam savored the raw beauty of the panorama that opened up before him.

The breathtaking backdrop of the jagged gray fortress of haze-clad mountains, the impenetrable denseness of the verdant forest, the rushing, crystal-clear stream—it was like a majestic cathedral, more awe-inspiring than any structure built by man. This wilderness was in his blood, and no matter where he went it called out to him like some possessive mistress. He could never rid himself of that relentless attraction.

The sound of a screen door closing shattered his reverie, and he turned. Natalie was coming down the back steps carrying a small soft-sided case and a handbag. She had on steel gray slacks, with a matching cardigan draped around her shoulders, the shade exactly the color of her eyes. There was a glint of silver chains against the pristine whiteness of her silk blouse, and her thick, flaxen hair was drawn back in an austere chignon. Her girlhood loveliness had evolved into a classic beauty and an ethereal remoteness.

His face was unreadable as he moved toward her. "Good morning, Natalie."

She had trouble meeting his gaze, and she toyed nervously with the car keys in her hand. "Good morning."

He took her suitcase, aware of her reluctance to let it go, and turned toward the car. She cast him a nervous look as she followed him, her small face drawn with fatigue and strain. He kept his voice impersonal as he asked, "Did you phone Patrick last night?"

"Yes. He was so excited about finally getting to come. He wants to go trout fishing in the worst way."

"I'd like to take him with me when I go back into the high country, if you don't mind." His tone of voice suggested that it didn't matter if she minded or not, he had every intention of taking his son with him.

In an unsteady whisper she answered, "He'll like that."

As they reached the car, Natalie looked up at him as though she was about to speak, then changed her mind. He sensed that she longed to try to dissuade him from going with her, but after seeing the tenacious set to his jaw, she knew better than to try. Adam opened the passenger door of her small car and swung her suitcase, his duffel bag and camera case onto the back seat, then set his camera on the console separating the bucket seats as he climbed in. Adjusting the seat to accommodate his long legs, he did up his seat belt and rolled down the window. He watched Natalie as she took her sunglasses out of her handbag and put them on, then selected the proper key. Her hands were trembling as she put the key in the ignition. This was going to be one hell of a long trip, he thought darkly as he tossed his own sunglasses on the dash. She was a wreck and so was he.

Adam fell asleep within the first half hour, his arms folded across his chest, his head resting against the door. Natalie couldn't have been more relieved. The drive to Calgary along twisting mountain roads was an endurance test at the best of times, but having Adam sitting there in brooding silence would make the six-hour trip nearly unbearable.

And her nerves were nearly shot as it was. Ever since Adam had appeared at Doc's, she had been going through an agony of indecision about how she was going to tell her son about his father. It was a confrontation she was dreading. Patrick had always been very sensitive and troubled about the absence of his father, and when he discovered he had a father like Adam, somebody he'd idolize, she realized he could end up hating her for what she'd done. She didn't know what she was going to do; she didn't know what she was going to say. And she was alone in this. Alone and scared.

To make matters worse, her sleep had been repetitively broken by shadows in the night. Shadows of old memories, shadows of remembered dreams.

When she had first left the valley, she had relived every moment of that incredible summer with Adam so often and with such detail that every second spent with him was indelibly engraved in her mind. In those black days after Doc had taken her away, those beautiful memories had been her salvation. She had been able to block out the horror of her mother's death with those memories. She had been able to block out the ripping pain that filled her whole body as she fought for her life and that of her unborn baby's, and she had been able to block out the revulsion, the loneliness, the grief, the guilt.

But in time, the specialness of those memories turned on her, and she honestly didn't know how she bore the anguish when she finally had to admit that it was truly finished. Those same memories became a self-inflicted torture, and she tried to hold them back. But they always came. If it hadn't been for Patrick, and knowing that he needed her, Natalie knew she wouldn't have survived.

A rough spot in the highway jerked her back to reality, and she made herself relax her white-knuckled grip on the wheel. Her shoulders and arms hurt from tension, and her fingers were numb and unresponsive. Her nerves were as taut as a drawn bow.

Orange warning signs told of construction ahead and Natalie slowed to the posted speed. Around the next curve, heavy equipment was ripping up a portion of the highway and she stopped behind the other vehicles that were lined up, waiting for the flagman to wave them through. Resting her arm on the open window, she turned to look at Adam. The racket outside was almost deafening, but he didn't move a muscle, and his breathing remained deep and even.

He had been twenty when she'd left and he had remained twenty in her memories, but now she had a chance to study him and fully absorb the changes that had matured him.

And there had been changes. The boy in her memories had worn his blond, slightly curly hair fairly long. But that had changed. It had darkened to a rich tawny color that was heavily streaked by the sun, and was shorter and brushed back from his face.

The years had left their mark in other ways. The boyish face had lost its smoothness and had become more chiseled, more weathered, more durable. There were lines around his eyes and creases around his mouth that hadn't been there before, and his cheeks had hollowed out beneath broad cheekbones. His jaw had always jutted forward, but now it had a more pronounced and determined set to it, and his mouth had lost much of its softness. His thick eyebrows had darkened and were bushier, but she could see that his eyelashes, which fanned out against his cheeks as he slept, were still tipped with the remembered gold. It had become such a strong masculine profile, and Natalie realized that she would never be able to call up the image of the boy she had known without calling up this new image, as well. And she felt a haunting sense of loss.

But it wasn't just his face that had matured. Adam had always been muscular, but he had filled out even more. He was wider through the shoulders and broader through the chest, and there was a nuance of sheer brute strength that hadn't been there before. But he still moved with that same fluid athletic grace she remembered so well.

Within this man was the familiar twenty-year-old, but other changes had turned him into a stranger. He had become remote and uncommunicative. And hostile.

Those changes hurt her most of all, and Natalie looked away, blinking rapidly against the threat of tears as her hands curled tightly around the steering wheel. Had she done that to him, or had living the life he had turned him into that kind of man? The line of vehicles started to edge forward, and Natalie put her car in gear and followed, the ache in her chest worsening. One thing was certain. He despised her now, and of all the changes that had taken place in this man, that was the hardest one of all to bear.

With the exception of that brief stop at the construction site, Natalie drove nonstop for three hours, and she was beginning to feel the lack of sleep. There was a mining town up the road a mile or so and she planned to stop there for a coffee and gas. Adam had stirred a couple of times, but he was in a deep sleep and she was grateful for that.

She found that the magnificent scenery was a soothing balm to her distressing thoughts, and she was lulled into a floating detachment, as though she had become suddenly divorced from the trauma of the previous week. She didn't want to let go of this unexpected sense of calm, but the steady hum of the tires on the pavement and the heat of the sun beating in through the window were drugging her, and she had to make a conscious effort to stay awake. It was definitely time for a break.

ADAM HAD OFFERED TO DRIVE after they'd stopped for breakfast, and much to his surprise, Natalie had unresistingly handed him the keys. She had been silently staring out the window for some time and Adam shot her a quick glance. Her head was resting against the door and Adam realized she had fallen asleep. Unaware that a sudden frown lined his brow, he turned his attention back to the road. He had been following a logging truck for several miles, and when the narrow highway finally widened into a passing lane, he swung out to pass.

Propping his elbow on the open window, Adam rested the back of his hand against his mouth, a troubled expression darkening his eyes. This whole thing with Natalie was getting out of hand. He had been half-asleep when they pulled up in front of the coffee shop, and there had been a split second when their eyes met and he nearly reached out and touched her. He'd been caught with his guard down, and he had been more vulnerable than he liked to admit. He had to be careful it didn't happen again, especially when he knew he was playing with an undefendable weakness. His shield of rage was gone. It had come as something of a shock when he realized his anger had burned itself out, and he was left with nothing but a gnawing emptiness. . . .

"Where are we?"

He dropped his hand and looked at her. "Just a few miles this side of Banff."

Straightening, Natalie tucked a loose strand of hair back in place, then glanced at her watch.

He knew she was thinking of Patrick. "Has he ever traveled alone?"

"No. He's always gone with someone. But at least this is a direct flight. He should be fine."

But Adam could tell by the tone of her voice that she wasn't at all comfortable about him traveling by himself. There was a hint of a grim smile around Adam's mouth as he considered Natalie's concern. Even though she was uneasy about him traveling alone, Adam doubted that she would feel any more secure if she found out that Patrick had been under the watchful eye of a private eye for the past week.

"Adam?"

"What?"

"You will give me a chance to talk to him first, won't you?"

Adam's jaw stiffened, his eyes becoming hard behind his sunglasses. She looked so scared. So damned scared. And suddenly there was a very large chink in Adam's protective armor; he no longer wanted to bring her to her knees. He couldn't stand the thought of Natalie being afraid of him or afraid of what he might do. At least not the kind of soul-destroying fear he saw in her eyes. Never that.

There was a tightness encasing his chest when he finally responded. "I said something in anger that should never have been said, Natalie. I don't want to hurt him or confuse him." He met her gaze with forthrightness. "And I won't ever try to turn him against you." His tone was still low, and there was a quality to it that let her know he was not prepared to play any games. "But on the other hand, I expect some cooperation on your part. I don't want to be shut out of his life any longer." He stared at the road, his expression altering as a muscle in his jaw twitched and his voice became flat and emotionless. "Of course, there is the possibility that he won't want to have anything to do with me."

"Adam," she said softly, as though she was chiding him for being so absurd. "That isn't even a remote possibility."

It wasn't so much what she said that surprised him, but how she said it. It was clear that she felt certain Adam would become a major influence in Patrick's life, but what surprised him the most was that she seemed to approve. And that approval put them on neutral ground. Adam felt some of the tension ease from him, and he was finally able to ask, "What's he like?"

Bracing her elbow on the open window, she rested her head against the back of her hand, a touch of amusement in her voice. "He's a little taller than average, he has an energy supply that never seems to deplete, loves sports, hates girls and drags home every stray animal he can find."

Adam grinned lopsidedly. "He sounds like a normal boy to me. Does he like school?"

"So far. He's not allowed to watch very much TV, so he reads a tremendous amount, and he's in the swim club." She smiled wryly, affectionately. "He's a total loss at neatness, but he does excel in math. And for the most part, he's really easy to get along with."

When he spoke again, it was almost as though he was thinking out loud. "It must have been tough, raising a kid on your own."

She laughed softly, a rueful tone in her voice. "It's had its moments. But the travel agency where I work pays well, so that makes a big difference."

"How did you get into that business?"

"I started out as a clerk, but I took night courses and I worked my way through the ranks. Then a little more than four years ago, I was given the job of tour coordinator."

Adam suddenly remembered her always saying that someday she would see the world. "Have you done much traveling?"

"No. I didn't like leaving Patrick, and it wasn't really required of me."

Adam became lost in thought and there was a brief silence as he turned something over in his mind. Finally he looked at her and asked, "Did you ever consider giving him up for adoption?"

There was a sudden steeliness about her as she sat up abruptly, defiance flashing in her eyes as she met his gaze. Her response was fiercely adamant. "Never."

For some reason Adam felt compelled to push. "There was nothing stopping you. You could have even decided not to have him. An abortion wasn't unheard of then."

"That was absolutely out of the question," she said, her voice brittle. Adam frowned, unsettled by her obvious agitation. Her body was stiff and her face was unyielding, and she had laced her fingers together in a white-knuckled grip. Adam said nothing more as he vainly tried to focus his full attention on the winding, treacherous road that had been blasted out of the side of a mountain.

What had happened in the past to leave such wounds? It was obvious he had touched a raw nerve, and Adam had the most uncanny feeling that she had been, for one reason or another, heavily pressured to terminate the pregnancy. There had been plenty of gossip about her mother's accident, and it was a well-known fact that Natalie had been with her. Adam considered the possibility that the older woman had known about Natalie's pregnancy, and that knowledge had something to do with the crash. One explanation started to take form in his mind, but it was too grisly to even consider. Surely it hadn't been deliberate.

Keeping his voice calm and devoid of expression, he said quietly, "For what it's worth, I'm glad you made the decision you did—to have him and keep him."

Natalie's eyes flew to his face, and Adam held her gaze for as long as he dared. But he caught the unmistakable glitter of tears before she turned away. If there had been any anger left in Adam, it would have died then. This was a tormented woman. And for whatever pain she had inflicted, she had paid the price many times over.

THE LONG DRIVE had left its mark, and by the time they got off the elevator, Natalie was so pale, she was beginning to look ill. Adam was starting to wonder if it was just nervousness or if there was something really wrong. She had hardly eaten anything when they had stopped for breakfast, and she seemed to be constantly cold. Even as warm as it had been in the car, she had kept her sweater either on or wrapped around her.

The adjoining rooms they had been given were the ultimate in comfort, and Adam laid his camera on the desk, then hung up his jacket as the bellboy opened the drapes and adjusted the air conditioner. After the uniformed young man unlocked the separating doors between the two rooms, Adam tipped him and quietly pocketed both keys.

Adam closed the door, then glanced at Natalie, who was standing at the window looking out, her body a silhouette against the outside brightness. "We have a couple hours before we have to leave for the airport," he said. "Why don't you try to get some sleep?"

She shook her head as she slipped her sweater from her shoulders and dropped it on the small sofa. "I doubt if I can."

"Would you like me to have something sent up from room service?"

She shook her head again. "No thanks." Pensively, she began caressing the chains around her neck and his attention was drawn to her hands—slender and graceful, so delicately expressive—and they still held a deep fascination for him. They could be so gentle, so tender, so unbelievably sensual....

He jerked his eyes away and clenched his jaw as he turned abruptly, trying to beat back the sudden recollection of how it felt to have her hands caressing his naked chest and thighs. He could clearly remember the sensation she induced when she softly stroked him, arousing a pulsating ache that he could barely contain. And he could recall the paralyzing excitement when their bodies were finally welded together in a searing, impassioned need that equaled no other.

The room was suddenly hot and airless, and Adam felt as if he were slowly suffocating. He could feel beads of sweat dampen his skin as he clenched every muscle in his body against the debilitating empty ache of wanting her. His pulse was thundering in his head as he said raggedly, "I'm going to have a shower."

CHAPTER FIVE

A LONG LINE OF CABS was parked along the arrival ramp of the airport, and the traffic was heavy. Realizing he'd never get a metered parking spot in front of the building, Adam dropped Natalie off at the entrance doors and made another circuit to the parking lots.

Inside was just as bad. The place was congested with summertime traffic, and the minute he strode through the sliding doors he was caught in a steady stream of holiday travelers. Crowds of people gathered around the luggage carousels on the lower level, and it was apparent by the flight numbers displayed on the huge screens that two flights had just landed, disgorging their loads of passengers among the swarm of people already there.

It took him only a moment to spot Natalie in the crowd. She was looking up at the TV monitors that displayed all the updated departure and arrival times. Adam had phoned just before they'd left the hotel to make sure that Patrick's flight was on schedule, but obviously Natalie wanted to make sure there had been no changes since then. For a moment he stood watching her. Again he was struck by her uniqueness. And once again, he experienced feelings he dared not acknowledge.

He picked his way through a group of travelers to get to her. "Still on time?"

"So far." She glanced up at him, her anxiety beginning to show. "I wish he didn't have to clear customs by himself."

"They aren't going to hassle him," he said quietly. "And besides, a flight attendant will help him through." He glanced at the huge information signs suspended overhead, then motioned toward the escalators. "Let's get out of this crowd. There's an observation deck on the next level. We may as well find a decent place to wait since we have a half an hour before his flight's due in."

"Where's customs?"

"On this level. But we'll have plenty of time to work our way back once they announce the flight arrival." She hesitated a moment, then nodded and fell into step with him.

The second level, where the arrival gates for all the domestic flights were located, was just as busy as the lower level, and they had to pick their way across the congested concourse to get to the spacious lounge on the far side of the terminal.

Adam dropped his suede jacket on an empty chair, then motioned to the coffee bar that was located down the mall. "Would you like anything while we're waiting?"

She didn't meet his eyes as she shook her head. "No, I don't think so."

His expression was contemplative. "You haven't had anything to eat all day, Natalie."

She shrugged, still refusing to meet his eyes. "I couldn't eat anything right now."

Natalie was a fairly readable person and Adam knew she was very worried about telling Patrick the truth; he also knew it wasn't going to be an easy thing for her to do. And in spite of everything, he did want to take the pressure off. His voice was quiet when he said, "I told you I don't expect you to tell him right away, and I meant that. And if you'd rather, I'll tell him."

"No, I'll tell him. It has to come from me." She turned away, and Adam's expression was inflexible as he watched her walk over to the massive windows overlooking the runway approach. Ever since that afternoon, a hole had been punched in his resistance, and it was becoming more and more difficult to remain detached. She seemed so damned defenseless.

Needing something familiar to do to help him relax and regain his composure, Adam checked the reading on the light meter attached to his camera strap, then made some adjustments to his lens settings.

The routine was such a deeply ingrained habit that he never even thought about it. He had packed photography equipment for so many years that his cameras had become an extension of himself, and he very rarely went anywhere without one. Early in his career, his initial fascination with wildlife and landscapes had expanded to other types of photography, and the subject he now found most rewarding was character studies of people. Acquiring exceptional photographs of wildlife took sound knowledge, hard work and painstaking patience. But with people, the most incredible shots could turn up anywhere.

Adam removed the lens cover and focused, and for a reason he didn't stop to analyze, he focused on Natalie. She was standing with her shoulder resting against the glass, her face profiled against the light from the windows. There was something very poignant about this solitary figure alone in the crowd, her pensiveness a nearly tangible thing. She had her head tipped slightly as she watched a flock of pigeons arch skyward, the muted light angling across her finely sculpted features and casting her solemn face in a compelling study of light and shadows.

It was a portrait of aloneness. A haunting study. And even as he shot several frames, Adam was grimly aware that this would be one batch of photographs he should have never taken.

His face suddenly hardened as he slung the camera strap over his shoulder and sat down. Leaning forward, he clasped his hands together and rested his arms across his thighs as he stared at the floor. Only his eyes revealed the bleakness of his thoughts. He didn't like the feeling that he was walking a narrow line of self-control. He didn't like it at all.

The minutes crawled by and Adam must have looked at his watch a hundred times before it was finally time to return to the lower level. Never in his life had he felt the nerve-racking kind of anxiety he experienced as he followed Natalie to the waiting area outside customs. This waiting game was over, and in a few minutes, he'd see his son for the first time. It seemed to take forever before passengers started straggling into the area visible behind the glassed-in partition that separated the Canadian Customs's final checkpoint from the rest of the terminal. Unable to get a clear field of view, he moved forward until he was standing behind Natalie, his body a shield for hers against the buffeting from the milling people who were beginning to gather around them. She looked up at him, then with a flustered movement, turned away.

They were standing with their bodies lightly touching when a laughing flight attendant appeared from behind a partition with a grinning blond-haired boy in tow. Adam felt Natalie react, and suddenly his butterflies were back. But he only caught a quick glimpse of his son before the pair disappeared behind another partition. A short time later they reappeared, and Patrick was dragging a large suitcase that matched the one Natalie had brought.

Adam was aware of nothing except this small blond boy. This was his flesh and blood. A part of himself, his son.

Just then, Patrick spotted his mother on the other side of the glass wall, and he grinned broadly and hiked up his shoulder bag before giving her an excited little wave. Natalie waved back then glanced up at Adam, her eyes bright with unshed tears, communicating her wordless appeal. He tipped his head, silently indicating that she was to meet the boy alone. She only hesitated a moment.

Seeing this kid of his for the first time was having one hell of an effect on Adam, and he desperately needed time to deal with these new, intensely gripping feelings. The boy and the flight attendant came through the door, and as if compelled by some reflex action, he automatically reached for the familiar security of his camera. Safe behind the anonymity of his equipment, he recorded it all: Patrick's face lighting up as he approached his mother, the sheer joy in Natalie's eyes, the way she fought back the tears as she knelt and hugged her son. But the photographs were unnecessary; it was a scene Adam would never forget.

It all seemed to happen in slow motion, but finally Natalie gave Patrick another quick hug, then stood up, her eyes no longer bleak as she smiled down at the boy. She spoke to the flight attendant, then laying her hand on Patrick's shoulder, she leaned over and said something to him.

With her hand still against his back, she guided him toward Adam. "There's someone special I'd like you to meet, Patrick," she said quietly, and Adam shot her a sharp look. Surely she wasn't going to tell him here.

Patrick looked up, and for a moment he didn't react. Then his eyes widened and his mouth sagged open in an expression of incredulity. He stared at Adam a moment, then as though he was unsure of what he was seeing, he glanced at his mother. She smiled and nodded, and Patrick looked back at Adam, his face suddenly flushed. He swallowed hard and whispered in awe, "Are you really Adam Rutherford—you know, from 'The Wilderness Beyond'?"

It had never once entered Adam's head that Patrick might be familiar with his wilderness shows, and it came as a bit of a shock when the boy recognized him. Knowing that he wasn't a complete stranger to the boy did, however, help to take the edge off his tenseness. Smiling crookedly, he stretched out his hand and nodded. "Yes, I am. I'm glad to meet you, Patrick."

Still staring at him in wonderment, Patrick dazedly shook his hand. "I've watched every one of your specials, but I like your books even better. My mom bought 'em all for me, and they're my favorites. I like the one about jungle cats the best."

So Natalie had bought his books for Patrick. That was a
bolt out of the blue, and Adam shot Natalie another penetrating look. What had possessed her to do that? If she had
purposely not told the kid who his father was, why had she
purposely chosen to expose Patrick to his work? Natalie
deliberately evaded his eyes, her discomfort becoming more
pronounced as he continued to scrutinize her, his eyes narrowing contemplatively. None of the information he was
receiving seemed to jigsaw together, and he was still coming up with more questions than answers.

Aware that Patrick was watching him closely, Adam
managed a smile. "I have a new book out, Patrick. I'll give
you a copy."

"Will you autograph it for me?"

The boy's gray eyes were wide with wonder—so much like
another pair of gray eyes, and Adam found that very disturbing. His voice showed signs of strain when he answerd,
"I'd be happy to."

Another passenger paused to speak to Patrick, and Adam
shifted his gaze. The newcomer was a medium-size nonde-
script man in his early forties, the kind of person who would
be easily lost in a crowd. But as soon as Adam got a good
look at his eyes, he realized that that first impression was a
carefully nurtured image.

"This is Mr. Dickson," explained Patrick. "He sat with
me on the plane." Shyly, the boy indicated his mother.
"And this is my mom."

Mr. Dickson grinned at Natalie as he ruffled Patrick's
hair. "This is quite the boy you have, ma'am. He was good
company." He looked down at the boy as he grasped his
shoulder. "You have a good holiday, Pat. And you be sure
and catch a few fish for me."

"I will, sir. You have a good holiday, too."

Raising his hand in a friendly gesture of farewell, the man
turned to leave, but as he turned he very pointedly caught
Adam's eye. Adam acknowledged the wordless message
with an almost imperceptible nod, and with that silent dis-

missal, Mr. Dickson's responsibility as the investigator tailing Patrick was completed. Adam suddenly felt like a traitor for hiring him in the first place. It had been a cheap shot and an unnecessary move. He knew that now. Unable to meet Natalie's gaze, he picked up Patrick's suitcase and indicated the doors. "Why don't we get out of this crowd?"

NATALIE WATCHED HER YOUNG SON rummage through his suitcase, an uneasy feeling grating away at her already shaky composure. Something was definitely wrong. He seemed strangely alienated and had been uncommonly quiet on the drive back from the airport. She'd caught him watching Adam with an intentness that was definitely unsettling, and she suspected that he was trying to figure out why this man was suddenly so involved in their lives. He had given his mother a strange, quizzical look when Adam had slid behind the wheel of the car, and he'd given her another one when they'd arrived at the hotel and it became apparent that this stranger was lodged in the adjoining room.

Patrick took a flat box out of his suitcase and stiffly laid it on the bed, and Natalie's stomach did a sickening nose dive when she recognized it. So Bea had found it. Natalie clasped her arms in front of her, suddenly chilled by a strange reluctance. She should have left it where it had been hidden, in the top back shelf of her closet. Having it here was a mistake—a very big mistake. She glanced at the box, then quickly looked out the window, feeling suddenly trapped. On a foolish impulse, she had asked Bea to send it, and now that it was here, she didn't know what to do with it.

It was a photograph album. A photograph album that carefully chronicled Patrick's life from the time he'd been born to the present. And it had been Natalie's way of evading reality for a very long time. It had been her escape, her consolation, her atonement to Adam.

Because the album was for Adam. Right from the beginning, it had been for him.

And she had taken such comfort in that, especially in the beginning. When she had been almost unable to cope with the horror, the guilt, the utter despair, the photograph album had been her source of comfort. It was her way of clinging to that part of her life that was so very special, and by carefully tending the picture journal of their small son, she was able to hang on to that shattered dream.

When her day of reckoning finally came, when she finally had to face the fact that she'd been living in a warped fantasy and that Adam could never again be a part of her life, she had wanted to die. If it hadn't been for Patrick, she would have never survived.

And now it was here. Lying on the bed.

Trying to take a deep breath to ease the awful ache in her chest, Natalie pulled herself back from the brink of those disturbing thoughts and turned to study her son. His face was pale and the set to his jaw forewarned her of his mood.

Her own face was drawn as she went over to the bed and sat beside him. Clasping her hands tightly together to keep from turning him to face her, she asked quietly, "What's the matter?"

He didn't look at her. "Nothing."

"That's not true, Patrick. You've hardly said ten words since we picked you up, and that's not like you."

He didn't say anything for a minute, then he finally met her gaze steadily, an accusing look in his eyes. "You never told me you knew him. You bought me his books and everything, and you knew how much I liked his shows, but you never told me you knew him from before."

There was not a single thing she'd said that could have possibly revealed she had known Adam "from before," and her son's unexpected astuteness left her groping for balance. "What makes you think I've known him for very long?" she countered softly.

"I can tell."

Her apprehension became more acute as she realized that she would not be able to put off telling him the truth about

Adam, even for a few days. The thought scared her to death. Patrick would have every reason to turn on her.

"Aunt Bea packed this box in my suitcase, and she said you asked her to get it from home." Natalie stared at him uncomprehendingly, confused by his change in direction and even more confused by his agitation. His mouth started to tremble as he continued, his voice becoming more strident. "So I looked in it and there was a photograph album and it was full of pictures of me. I've never seen it before, and I wondered and wondered why you had it."

It was as though an invisible hand forcefully squeezed the air from her lungs and the room began to swim as panic crawled up her throat. Her hands were trembling as she reached for him. "Patrick—"

He stepped away, his eyes glistening with angry tears. "But now I know. You had it hidden so I wouldn't find it because it was a big secret. And you never keep secrets, except about my dad. So it has to be for him. He's my dad, isn't he?"

She had never dreamed that he would figure it out on his own, and the awful shock paralyzed her as she stared at him, her face suddenly deathly white, her heartbeat echoing dully in her head.

"Isn't he?" he demanded shrilly.

"Patrick, let me explain—"

He twisted away from her, his hands balled into fists, his white face streaked with tears. "Isn't he?"

Damn, she had wanted to spare him this. Natalie felt like she was condemning him to some horrible fate as she answered in a tortured whisper, "Yes, he's your father."

He stared at her, his small body shaking with suppressed sobs, then he whirled and made a blind dash for the door. "I hate you!" he cried. "I hate you! I hate you!" He was in the hallway before Natalie could catch him, and like a wild thing, he fought his way out of her grasp. He was running blindly.

Adam, who was just coming up from the lobby, stepped off the elevator just as Patrick bolted from his mother, his racking sobs echoing hollowly in the long corridor. One glance at the stricken look on Natalie's face, and he knew something was desperately wrong. Reacting on pure instinct, he crouched, intercepting the boy's wild flight. Holding this sobbing, hurting, angry child in an enveloping embrace, Adam experienced a rush of feelings that went beyond anything he'd experienced before. For the first time he was holding his son in his arms. And for the first time in his life, Adam Rutherford felt the agony only a father can feel.

His voice was shaking badly from this onslaught of emotion as he murmured against Patrick's hair. "It's okay, son. It's okay."

Patrick tried to fight his way free as he sobbed, "Let me go! Let me go! I hate her!" He twisted and struggled, but Adam's hold was unbreakable. Eventually realizing his fight was in vain, he collapsed against his father and wept bitterly, his thin arms in a stranglehold around Adam's neck. "Why couldn't you come before? Why?"

Why. Forty-eight hours ago, the heartbreaking pain he heard in that one muffled question would have evoked a seething rage in Adam, but now it only made him feel impotent. How could he find the right words to give comfort when he didn't know the answer himself?

He purposely kept his eyes averted from Natalie's as he stood up with the boy in his arms, strangely reluctant to see what kind of anguish Patrick's words had inflicted on her. On one hand, she deserved the attack for deliberately keeping father from son, but on the other hand, Adam was beginning to suspect that something dark and sinister had driven her to do what she had. Her reasons were obscure but they were genuine, and he had a gut feeling whatever they were, they were directly related to her mother's accident.

The heavy door had swung shut behind Natalie when she had gone after Patrick, and they were automatically locked out of the room. Bracing the weight of his son on his thigh, Adam fished a room key out of his slacks' pocket and handed it to Natalie as he talked quietly to Patrick, who had his face buried in his father's shoulder. His deep sobs seemed to be torn from his small body, and Adam felt every sob.

Once inside, he carried Patrick over to the sofa and sat down, the distraught child clinging to him with a desperate strength. Gently stroking his fair head, Adam said softly, "It's okay to cry, Patrick. Get it out of your system, and we'll talk later. It's okay, son." He finally looked at Natalie and nearly winced when he saw the effect this was having on her. And he wondered if Patrick had any idea just how much pain he'd inflicted when he told his mother he hated her.

It took awhile for Patrick's stormy outburst to subside into the occasional deep, shuddering sob. Natalie appeared with a glass of water and a cold cloth and wordlessly handed them both to Adam. His face was taut with worry as he took them, fervently hoping that Patrick would suffer no permanent scars from this. Both his mother and his father carried too many as it was.

He gently eased the boy away, and the tension lines around his mouth deepened when he saw how the violent weeping had ravaged his son's face. His eyes and mouth were so swollen, he looked as though he'd been physically battered. With infinite tenderness he wiped Patrick's face with the cool cloth, then pressed the glass into his hand. "Have a drink, Patrick. Then we'll talk."

Patrick had a sip, then Adam set the glass on the table by his elbow. Hooking his knuckles under his chin, he lifted his son's face and gently forced him to meet his sober gaze. The boy's eyes were identical to Natalie's, and that uncanny likeness aroused some feelings that were extremely hard to handle. Especially now.

A tear slipped down Patrick's cheek, and Adam gently wiped it away with his thumb. "I want you to tell me why you're upset, Patrick," he said softly. "I need to know what you're thinking right now."

Patrick stared at his father for a moment, a slightly rebellious set to his mouth, then he lowered his head and nervously twisted his fingers in the front of his T-shirt. "I don't know."

Adam studied Patrick's bowed head, his eyes extremely thoughtful. Finally he asked, "Do you wish I was someone else?"

Patrick's head flew up, his eyes wide with sudden alarm. "No!" He held his father's steady gaze for a moment, then he looked down again, suddenly embarrassed. "No, I don't wish that," he whispered into his chest.

"Don't be afraid to say what you're thinking, Patrick. You have every right, you know."

The boy didn't respond, but sat huddled forlornly on Adam's lap, his misery clearly evident. After a long silence he finally lifted his head, his gray eyes again swimming with tears. "I used to think about what my dad would be like ... after I went to bed and it was dark. I thought something must've been really wrong with him—or maybe he was even dead—because Mom would never talk about him. So I pretended sometimes." He wiped away the tears with the back of his hand as he hesitated, struggling valiantly to sort out his thoughts and feelings. Suddenly his composure crumbled and he started crying again, and Adam cradled his head against his shoulder. "I wished and wished you'd come. That someday, I would come home from school and you'd be there. Then I could go to school and say I had a dad, too. I wanted you so bad," he sobbed out. "Why didn't Mom tell me? Why did you have to wait so long to come?"

The angry threat Adam had flung at Natalie when he'd found out about the boy's existence, the threat about taking Patrick away from her, came back to haunt Adam now. He knew that if he wanted to turn the boy against his mother, all he'd have to say was, *She didn't tell me about you. I would have come if I had known.* Adam glanced up at Natalie, and she was watching him with naked fear in her eyes, her body rigid. They both knew he had the weapon to hurt her as much as she'd hurt him.

An eternity passed as they stared at each other across the shadowed room, but eventually Adam severed the tension-charged connection and looked down at his son. "There were reasons why. Believe me." He tried to convince himself that the desperate, fearful look on Natalie's face had nothing to do with his split-second decision to fabricate an answer. One thing he was absolutely sure of was that he'd do anything to protect this kid—it was as simple as that. "At first there were reasons she couldn't tell me about you, Patrick," he said gently. "Then later, she was afraid that I wouldn't want you, and you'd be hurt."

His hastily concocted explanation seemed to give Patrick some measure of comfort, but the effect it had on Natalie was something else altogether. The jolt she received seemed to throw her into a state of shock, and every speck of color drained from her face. Adam stared at her, wondering what was going on. It took a few moments for everything to sink in, then the significance of her reaction finally dawned on him; his invented excuse was no invention. He had unwittingly stumbled onto some answers. At least the vaguest of answers, which meant he was one step closer to the whole truth. He forced himself to drag his eyes away, an intent frown creasing his brow. The truth. But what, exactly, was that? What were the reasons that had prevented her from telling him about her pregnancy? He was still no wiser than before. No wiser, but definitely a little closer.

It took considerable self-discipline to haul his attention back to the small boy who was so hurt and bewildered. His voice had a heavily strained timbre to it as he murmured against his son's hair, "I know you're upset right now, but don't be mad at your mom, Patrick. Sometimes things happen that change our lives, and we can't do much about it."

Something compelled Adam to glance up, and his gaze locked with Natalie's. She was standing with her arms pressed against her chest as though she was experiencing excruciating pain; never in all his life had he witnessed so much anguish in another person's eyes. Fleetingly he wondered how she was able to endure it. All this emotional duress was beginning to get to him, and he could feel his resistance beginning to weaken. But he could not allow that to happen, not at any cost. From some inner reserve, he had to find the strength of will to remain detached. He tightened his arms around his son, reinforcing his resolve. Patrick was all that mattered.

Suddenly drained by the tension, he nestled his son closer, wearily leaned his head against the high back of the sofa and stared at the ceiling. His strong survival instincts were warning him he didn't dare allow his feelings toward Natalie to soften. The very last thing he needed was to let himself get involved with her again, even remotely. He had to keep reminding himself that she had messed up his life before, and she could mess it up again if he let her slip past his emotional defenses. And he had no intention of letting that happen. Ever.

Patrick stirred and pushed himself away from his father's chest, his tears finally spent. Adam experienced a kind of protective tenderness he hadn't felt for a very long time. His eyes softened as he cupped his hand around Patrick's head and drew his thumb across the boy's puffy cheek. "Do you want to talk, or do you want to leave it for a while?" he asked gently.

Patrick kept his eyes averted as he furtively slid off Adam's lap and stood between his knees, suddenly embarrassed by the arrangement. There was a knowing look in Adam's eyes and a hint of a smile around his mouth as he gazed down at the boy's lowered head. He knew exactly what had prompted Patrick to move. A boy of ten was much too big to be indulging in something so babyish as sitting on someone's knee. Now that he had a child of his own to relate to, it was surprising how clearly he remembered those same feelings from his own childhood. Adam half expected Patrick to pull out of the circle of his relaxed hold, but he remained, self-consciously fidgeting with the hem of his T-shirt.

Sensing the boy's uncertainty, Adam said quietly, "Don't sweat it, Patrick. We've got lots of time to talk later."

Patrick lifted his head and met his father's gaze with a steadiness that Adam found slightly disconcerting. He could read the reluctance in his son's eyes; he didn't want to talk. Not now, at least. Adam grasped the boy's shoulder and gave it an empathetic little shake as he nodded his head in silent understanding. Patrick lowered his head again and an uneasy silence stretched between them. Finally the boy eased out of Adam's arms and without looking at anyone, went into the other room. Adam watched him go, his eyes dark with concern, then he glanced at Natalie, who was standing in front of the window. Her back was to him, but he could tell by the stiffness in her stance that this thing with Patrick was tearing her apart.

He felt at a total loss. When he had first found out about Patrick, he had been so outraged by the injustice of what she'd done that he'd vowed to get his revenge and make her life as miserable as he could. He'd leveled some cruel and malicious threats. But now that Patrick had actually turned on his mother, Adam discovered it was the last thing on earth he wanted.

Looking squarely at Natalie, he rested his arm on the back of the sofa, his expression grave. "He didn't really mean what he said, Natalie," he said firmly. "He just needs some time to get used to the idea."

She turned and looked at him, then gave him a bleak, twisted smile. "He means it."

"He thinks he means it because he's upset, but he'll get over it."

She pressed her hands against her head as though she had a bad headache, then she tilted her head back and rubbed the back of her neck. She looked at him, her eyes dominating her pale face, her voice filled with gratitude. "I appreciate you...prevaricating for me. It—you so easily could've told the truth."

With a penetrating stare, he waited for her reaction. "But then I wasn't really lying, was I?"

Natalie looked away abruptly. Adam saw her tense, her eyes darkening as she stared numbly across the room. He shifted his gaze and found that she was staring at Patrick, who was standing at the foot of the bed with what appeared to be a very thick photograph album in his grasp. Natalie's voice was an agonized whisper that cut through the charged silence. "No, Patrick. Not now."

But the boy never even so much as glanced at his mother as he moved across the room, his small face pinched, his mouth trembling. He swallowed hard, then held the book out to Adam. "This is for you," he whispered unevenly.

Adam cast a questioning glance at Natalie. She was visibly shaking, but she refused to meet his gaze. Adam looked back at his son, who was watching him with wide, uncertain eyes. It was as if he was silently begging his father to accept the gift he offered. Without saying anything, Adam took the heavy album from the boy, sensing that this was a very significant offering. Adam lifted his head to look at Natalie, but she pushed past the chair and left the room. Adam frowned, silently wondering what was going on. He felt as though he was a player in a game in which he didn't know the rules, and he felt oddly out of step.

Curiosity overcame Patrick's hesitancy and he moved closer and leaned against Adam, his fair head resting against his father's shoulder. Adam's attention was instantly dragged back to the boy and the gift he'd brought. An unaccustomed ache tightened in his throat as he shifted his position and slipped his arm around his son, deeply touched by Patrick's unquestioning recognition of him as his father. Bonds forged by blood. Only a child's unconditional trust could readily accept something like that. And only a child could forgive so easily.

Unable to speak, he tightened his arm around his son and opened the thickly padded cover. On the fly leaf, in beautiful flowery script was written, "Adam Patrick," and beneath it was neatly printed Patrick's full birth date. Adam found it increasingly hard to breathe as he turned the page and saw a photograph of a newborn baby, and mounted underneath it was the hospital nursery card. At that moment Adam knew why he had sensed this was such a significant offering. It was more than significant; it was momentous. He was holding the pictorial journal of his son's entire life.

It took a while for the stunning effects of this latest bombshell to wear off, then Adam rapidly flipped through a few pages to verify his suspicions. It was all there, even down to Patrick's old report cards. He stared at it numbly, trying to figure out what all of this meant.

His voice was very unsteady when he asked quietly, "How come you brought this, Patrick?"

The boy shrugged. "Mom had Aunt Bea put it in my suitcase. I'd never seen it before then." Patrick kept turning pages, obviously engrossed by the contents, then said excitedly, "Hey, look. Here's the page with my footprints on it."

"What do you mean, you'd never seen it before then?" Adam asked abruptly.

Patrick quit turning pages and looked up at his father. "I didn't. Not until I looked at it after Aunt Bea put it in my suitcase. I didn't even know Mom had it."

Trying to ignore the implications behind Patrick's response, Adam groped for a logical explanation. "Maybe your mother was keeping it for you."

"No. I've got my own at home. I put my old swimming badges and birthday cards and stuff like that in mine." He shrugged again and said with childlike conviction, "This is for you." With that, he calmly dismissed the issue and started leafing through the album again.

Adam's face had lost considerable color as he firmly closed the book, then turned Patrick to face him. "How do you know it's for me, Patrick?" he asked, his mouth suddenly very dry.

Patrick met his father's intense, questioning look, then lowered his head. "That's how come I knew you were...you were my dad," he whispered unsteadily. "I didn't know what was in the box when Aunt Bea put it in my suitcase, and she was so secretive about it—said it was something Mom asked her to send. And the only thing my mom ever kept secrets about was my dad. So that night after Aunt Bea went to bed, I looked." He raised his head and met his father's gaze, his eyes filled with apprehension. "I didn't know for sure what it meant until you...until you came with us." He lowered his head again, his voice barely audible. "And that's how I knew you must be my dad. Because Mom had wanted the photograph album. And because your name is Adam, too."

Adam had the funny feeling that he was getting mixed signals, and he watched Patrick intently. "Did you tell your mother all this *after* she told you about me, or before?"

"Before. She asked what was bothering me so I told her."

So the kid had put it all together. And Patrick had clobbered her with his deductions before she even had the opportunity to tell him. Adam winced as he drew his son against him in a secure embrace, trying to put everything into some sort of perspective. He rested his chin on the top of the boy's head and stared across the room. He sighed, then murmured, "Don't hate your mom, Patrick. She did what she thought was best."

Patrick abruptly pulled away from Adam, suddenly hostile and very disturbed. "I always watched your shows when they were on TV, and she knew how much I liked your books. She knew I really admir—admir—liked you, and she could have told me you were my dad." He roughly wiped his eyes. "She *should* have told me," he mumbled brokenly. "She should have told me."

Adam could feel the boy struggling to suppress his tears, and he slowly rubbed Patrick's back, trying to give some measure of comfort to his son. He felt so damned helpless. Patrick twisted his face against his father's shirt, then mumbled, "Did you know about me?"

Adam's eyes were bleak as he reluctantly answered, "No. I didn't know about you, Patrick. Not until a few days ago."

The boy burst into ragged sobs again, his small body shaking. "Why? Why didn't she tell?" There was so much hurt and bewilderment in Patrick's anguished query, and for an instant, Adam's anger flared. Damn Natalie. Damn her for making such a shambles of their lives. But then a recollection of her dark, tormented eyes took shape in his mind, and as abruptly as it flared, his anger died. Whatever her reasons, she had paid a heavy price.

Again resting his head on top of his son's, Adam stared unseeingly across the room, his face haggard. This was enough to take the heart out of anybody, he thought dully, and especially a kid. But then, he'd never once thought that Patrick would hold his mother responsible, nor did it ever enter his head that the kid could turn on her. There were too many raw wounds over all of this. Too many.

Patrick finally grew quiet in his father's embrace, and Adam gently lifted his face. "Feeling better?"

His mouth and eyes were puffy and his nose was running as Patrick self-consciously looked up and nodded. Adam's expression softened and there was a touch of amusement in his eyes as he reached into his pocket, then handed his young son a tissue to blow his nose. "Then how about us looking through the album together? You'll have to fill me in about all the pictures, you know."

Patrick gave him a wobbly grin. "Okay. If I can remember."

Looping his arm around the boy, Adam opened the large bound book. A strange poignant sensation slowly spread through him as page by page, he saw for himself the gradual development of his child. Each picture had been carefully selected and mounted, and he had the feeling that this was never meant to be a typical family album, but was intended to be a painstakingly detailed record. He wondered why she'd kept it. Patrick was convinced it was for Adam— for his father—but was it? What if it was? What did it mean? And he realized with a touch of alarm that he desperately wanted Patrick to be right, that the album was for him.

The sudden dead weight of Patrick leaning heavily against him dragged his attention back to his son. Adam smiled lopsidedly as he glanced at the child, who had dropped off to sleep, his hand resting limply on his father's thigh. Pushing the album onto the sofa, Adam gathered the boy in his arms and carried him to the bed, deriving a quiet paternal pleasure from holding his sleeping child. He could remember his own father carrying him up to bed in exactly the same way, and he could still call up the smell of pipe tobacco clinging to his father's favorite sweater. The ache in Adam's throat intensified. He wanted so badly to give Patrick those kinds of special boyhood memories.

As he laid him down, Patrick stirred and fought against the weight of sleep to open his eyes. He smiled at his father, then slipped his hand into Adam's as he whispered sleepily, "You really are my dad, aren't you?"

Tightening his hold on the small hand lying in his, Adam smiled softly. "I really am, Patrick."

"Then I can call you Dad, can't I?"

Adam had to fight to contain the fierce surge of emotion that gripped him, and his voice was very strained as he answered, "I'd like that, Patrick." The boy smiled drowsily, then with a satisfied sigh, rolled over onto his side and drifted off to sleep again. Adam gazed down at him, and there was a deep ache in his chest as he gently straightened Patrick's legs. Such a miracle, this child was. Part of him self, part of Natalie, conceived in love but born in a shroud of secrecy.

Lightly brushing his knuckles against the sleeping child's cheek, Adam straightened, then felt oddly ill at ease when he realized Natalie had been watching him from the door. He stuck his hands in his pockets as he tipped his head toward Patrick. "I think he's had it for a while."

Her voice was a soft, husky whisper. "I'm not surprised." She slipped past Adam and carefully removed Patrick's runners, then pulled the corner of the spread over him so that he was protected from the draft from the air conditioner.

Adam watched her with solemn eyes, intuitively aware that her tending of Patrick came from the basic need to touch her child. Very gently, she smoothed Patrick's tousled blond hair back from his face as she gazed down at him with immeasurable tenderness, her deep love for this child revealed in every soft, eloquent gesture. Adam saw tears well up and gather in her long lashes as she bent over and kissed Patrick softly on the temple. Struggling to contain her anguish, she reluctantly straightened, her face drawn with the kind of exhaustion that sleep would never cure. She looked so alone and so vulnerable, and Adam found himself fighting the response she was evoking in him.

As if sensing his scrutiny, she raised her eyes and met his dark, unwavering stare. Adam felt as though he was caught in some unbreakable spell, an empty ache suddenly tightening his gut. He was so close to her that he could smell her soft fragrance, and his body responded as the ache intensified. Her lips parted and he heard her breath catch on a ragged intake of air, then as though she was overwhelmed by some galvanizing emotion, she closed her eyes.

She was hurting and alone, and Adam couldn't take it any longer. He desperately wanted to pull her into his arms. He never knew he could want anything as badly as he wanted that, and the pain of that need was almost more than he could endure.

The temptation was agony. A single step, that's all it would take, and he could gather her against him. A single step, and he would once more know the feel of her body warm and soft against his.

A single step. His face looked like it was chiseled out of hard cold granite as he turned and walked out of the room.

CHAPTER SIX

THUNDERCLOUDS WERE BEGINNING TO AMASS against the impregnable palisades of the mountains, a menacing bank against the rocky peaks. The air was deadly calm and thick with heat, and not a leaf trembled as the muted rumble of thunder warned of the approaching storm.

Adam parked the Bronco in front of Doc's, then rested his arms on top of the steering wheel and watched the lead-ing edge of the storm move closer, the dark furling clouds shadowed with ominous colors. The cumulus mass could remain there, trapped against the barrier of the mountains, or the prevailing winds could eventually roll the rain-laden clouds over the granite fortress, setting the squall free to ravage the valley.

As a small boy, Adam had experienced an untamed ex-hilaration each time he witnessed the awesome power of a mountain storm, and he still felt the same way. To him, it was like a shot of adrenaline, and he liked nothing better than being in the high country when a front moved in.

Exhaling a weary sigh, he dropped his hand and took the keys out of the ignition, then climbed slowly out of the truck. He felt so drained that every movement seemed to take a concentrated effort. Slamming the door, he stuffed the keys in the pocket of his jeans, then walked up the gravel driveway, his mouth compressed in a determined set. It had been one hell of a week, and he was beginning to suspect that the upcoming one wasn't going to be much better. Maybe what he needed was a pilgrimage, to head into the wilderness and find a solitary place. Except that he knew that wouldn't work. Not this time.

The week that had passed since he and Natalie had gone to pick up Patrick felt like a lifetime. Her presence was getting to him, and he was beginning to feel as though he was trying to slog his way through an endless bog. Patrick was the only bright spot. Adam made a point of having his son with him for a good portion of every day, and getting to know his child meant more to him than he could have ever imagined.

Not wanting to be confronted with any more unexpected lapses in his resistance, Adam had deliberately avoided seeing Natalie since they'd returned. But even staying away from her didn't help. He'd lie awake nights thinking about her, wondering why she'd done what she had. Then old memories would creep in, bringing with them a terrible, tormenting emptiness.

The unexplained existence of the photograph album, which was now on his bed in the trailer, haunted him, and night after night, he'd try to figure out why she'd kept it. And then he'd remember standing in that hotel room aching to touch her, yet somehow finding the strength to walk away. It was damned hard, this constant battle to shut her out.

He only hoped he could avoid her again today. He had just finished hauling the trailer to a beautiful secluded spot he'd discovered up in the mountains, and the move had taken much less time than he'd expected. Consequently, he was two hours early.

He would have waited until it was time to pick Patrick up, but with the storm moving in, he couldn't afford to take the chance. Patrick was going to be spending the next few days with him at the new location, and they planned on doing some exploring in the back country. With the poor condition of the abandoned logging road that accessed the site, Adam was concerned that a heavy rain would make it impassible. He wanted to collect his son and move out before the storm hit.

Normally, he'd phone just before he left to pick up Patrick, and the boy would be sitting on the front doorstep waiting for his father. But when he called today there had been no answer, and he had to assume that everyone was outside, trying to find some relief from the cloying heat. Attempting to dredge up some energy, Adam steeled himself against the possibility of seeing Natalie. He had too damned many weak spots as far as she was concerned, and he knew it.

But his luck finally ran out. Just as Adam rounded the corner of the house, Natalie came out the back door and started down the steps. The instant they saw each other, both stopped dead in their tracks. She stared at him wide-eyed for a second, then glanced at her watch.

His stomach twisted into a hard knot, and in an attempt to conceal his sudden edginess, Adam rammed his hands into the back pockets of his jeans. "I'm afraid I'm early," he said, his tone unnaturally gruff. "With the storm moving in, I thought I'd better pick him up early."

It was obvious he had caught her off guard, and it took her a second to recover. "He's not here right now." He saw her grip tighten on the handrail as she took a deep unsteady breath. "He's gone with Jimmy from next door. His dad was going to pick up a Roto-tiller, so the boys went with him."

"Do you know when they'll be back?"

It was apparent that she was also feeling the strain, and her voice had a nervous quaver to it when she answered, "They left about half an hour ago, so they should be back soon."

Adam studied her thoughtfully for a moment, then turned to leave. "Tell Patrick I'll be waiting at the coffee shop in the hotel. He can give me a call there when he gets back." With that, he started walking away, and he was about to turn down the driveway when he heard his name. He stopped and turned, his tension compounding.

Her face had gone very pale and she was standing stiffly on the step, her hands clasped tightly together as she watched him with apprehensive eyes. It seemed to cost her an enormous effort when she asked shakily, "Would you like to wait here? He really shouldn't be that long."

Adam stared at her for a second, trying to gather the strength to walk away, but this time he was unable to do it. His face was heavily carved by strain as he nodded, then silently he followed her up the steps. He knew it was a big mistake, but he had no will to fight the fatal attraction. At least not now.

The shades were pulled in the living room to keep out the heat, and he paused until his eyes adjusted to the dim interior, acutely aware of her nearness. As though suddenly very unsure of herself, Natalie moved across the room. "Would you like some iced tea? I just made a fresh pitcher."

"That'd be fine," he answered, the sound of his own voice seeming oddly distant. She stood looking at him for a moment, then turned abruptly and disappeared into the kitchen. Adam moved around the room with a caged restlessness. How in hell was he going to manage to stay in the same room with her without coming undone?

"Adam."

He turned. She was standing behind him, and without speaking he took the tall glass she offered him. Needing to put some distance between them, he went over to Doc's old easy chair and sat down, stretching his legs out in front of him. Natalie sat down in the chair opposite, and an awkward silence filled the room, a silence that was oddly grating.

Several tense moments passed and then she spoke, her voice so soft he could barely hear her. "I know this won't change anything, but I don't blame you for feeling the way you do. Keeping Patrick from you was an unforgivable mistake." Her voice broke and she whispered raggedly, "I never meant to hurt you, Adam."

He looked up at her sharply, never once expecting this kind of overture from her. He stared at her for a moment, then his face hardened as he looked down at the glass in his hand. The old bitterness was fermenting inside him, and his voice was biting when he asked, "Then why did you do it, Natalie? Not even one damned word." His anger ignited, fueled by the sense of betrayal that had stayed with him all those years. "You didn't even have the damned decency to offer an explanation. Nothing." He raised his head and stared at her coldly.

She met his hostile gaze with a kind of stoic courage, as though this ordeal of finally facing him was something she felt compelled to do. But her desolation seemed to consume her strength as she whispered, "I was wrong, Adam. I should have tried to explain."

She looked away, her thin veneer of calm taxed to the limit as she struggled to hold back tears. Adam's eyes narrowed in intense contemplation as he stared at her profile and stroked his bottom lip. He said very quietly, "Why don't you try to explain now?"

Natalie's gaze flew to his face, and it was apparent by her confused expression that this response was not at all what she had expected from him. She had expected anger. Natalie stared at him numbly, then as if it finally registered that he was waiting for an answer, she looked down at her hands. She didn't say anything for the longest time, then in a hushed tone, she started to speak. "I thought my decision was the best one—the decision not to tell you. But I was so young and so inexperienced in dealing with anything, let alone an unexpected pregnancy—" She hesitated, then looked up at him with a steadiness that said more clearly than words that she was telling the truth. "And I didn't want to drag you into something you weren't ready for," she added softly, almost reluctantly.

His face was expressionless as he stared at her. "And why did you think you'd be dragging me into something?"

She held his gaze for a minute, then she rose and went to the screen door. She stood staring out, her back to him. There was a long silence, then she said, "Do you remember Jack and Leanne Baker?"

Puzzled by her strange query, Adam frowned as he tried to think back. "Do you mean that couple on the hill you used to baby-sit for?"

"Yes, that's them." She folded her arms in front of her as she leaned against the doorjamb, her manner introspective. "I had to go over there one night—I'd left a textbook there the day before and I went to pick it up. Jack was working overtime so Leanne was home alone, and she was really upset when I arrived. I guess they'd had a fight before he went to work, and she needed someone to talk to."

"What's this got to do with you leaving?" he interrupted curtly.

Her shoulder still against the doorjamb, Natalie turned to look at him, her face grave. "Apparently Jack was a very talented hockey player. Doc said he had more natural ability and hockey sense than any juvenile he'd ever seen. He'd been scouted by several of the professional teams, and everyone assumed he'd make it in the big time."

Natalie straightened, and avoiding his gaze, came back and sat down. Thoughtful, she leaned forward, her folded arms resting across her knees. There was a peculiar quietness in her voice as she continued. "Jack was only seventeen when Leanne got pregnant, and apparently both sets of parents went wild when they found out. It was such a mess and everyone was so irate about it that Leanne and Jack felt they had no other choice except to get married. At that time rookies had very little job security, so Jack got a job in the mill to support his new family, and his dream of playing professional hockey went out the window."

She met Adam's gaze, and he felt a contraction in his chest when he saw the bleak look in her eyes. "He never threw up to her what he had sacrificed, and he was a good father and he loved his kids, but he'd had to turn his back on his lifelong dream. And both Jack and Leanne had to live with that. He had to spend the rest of his life tied to a job he hated. And every time he watched a game on TV, he was reminded of how much he'd lost.''

There was a touch of anger in Adam's voice. "And you thought I'd feel that way?"

She studied him for a minute, then slowly shook her head. "No. You would have picked yourself up and got on with your life." She became intent on her hands as she laced her fingers together. "It was how *I* would have dealt with it. It would've affected me the same way it affected Leanne." She looked up at him again, the pain in her eyes starkly real. "I couldn't do that to you, Adam. I'd have spent the rest of my life feeling guilty for ruining a chance of a lifetime for you." Her voice broke, and she abruptly looked away as she swallowed hard. A strained moment passed, then she continued unsteadily. "Your success with those posters was a once-in-a-lifetime chance. I couldn't take that away from you."

Adam's eyes narrowed and there was an unyielding thrust to his jaw as he said tersely, "They didn't approach me about using my photographs for the campaign until long after you disappeared."

She met his steely gaze with unwavering directness. "I know. Four months to be exact."

Her response caught him by surprise, and he welded his full attention on her as he assessed everything she'd said. Something was happening here he didn't quite understand, but he sensed she was more or less leveling with him. "Then I have to assume that something else happened to influence your decision."

Her voice was flat and without expression. "Yes, something else did."

Adam remained silent as he studied her, wondering how far he could dig before she'd clam up on him. He felt as though he was on dangerous ground when he asked, "Did it have something to do with your mother's accident?"

She gave him a startled glance, then looked away, her expression instantly guarded.

Adam could feel her withdrawing into herself, withdrawing from him, and it was suddenly imperative that he didn't let her shut him out. Willing her to look at him, he leaned forward, his voice low and urgent as he spoke. "Talk to me, Nat."

It had been an unconscious slip, his calling her that, a half-forgotten habit that had stuck with him after all those years. Natalie looked at him, and he could tell that his slip hadn't gone unnoticed. She was so close. So damned close. Finding it nearly impossible to speak, Adam said huskily, "Just talk to me, Natalie."

She raised her hand in an expressive gesture, silently beseeching him to understand. "I can't, Adam," she whispered.

There was something about how she said it, something about the tormented look in her eyes that triggered a new level of comprehension in Adam, and he experienced a flash of insight. It was suddenly all so clear. It wasn't that she was refusing to tell him; instead, it was something so emotionally shattering she was incapable of dealing with it. What, Adam reflected soberly, had exactly happened in that accident? What had scarred her so deeply?

Intent on his thoughts, Adam absently took a drink then set the glass on the table by his elbow. His expression was solemn when, compelled by the need to know, he asked a question that had been chewing at him ever since they came back from Calgary. "Was Patrick right? Was the album really for me?"

She glanced at him, then swallowed hard and quickly looked away. "Yes, it was for you."

His undivided attention was suddenly glued on her profile. Trying to ignore the disturbing sensation her barely audible answer evoked, Adam leaned forward and rested his arms across his thighs, his hands clasped between his knees. He hadn't realized until she answered him how vitally important her response was, and he found it difficult to keep his voice level when he finally spoke. "Why did you do it, Natalie? Why did you bother to keep that album for me when you made it so damned clear you wanted me out of your life?"

She met his gaze, her distress clearly revealed in her tormented eyes. "I didn't want you out of my life, Adam. But I had to get out of yours."

A current of intensity bound them as Adam stared at her, never shifting his attention for even a second. Finally he spoke. "Are you ever going to tell me why?"

She held his gaze for a moment, then looked down at her hands, her voice breaking as she whispered, "I—I don't know."

The sound of someone racing up the back steps broke the thread of tension, and Adam clamped his mouth shut, a nerve twitching in his jaw. Ten minutes. If only he'd had ten more minutes alone with her.

Patrick burst in, letting the screen door slam loudly behind him as he greeted his father. "Hi, Dad. How come you're here so early?"

It was a hard thing for Adam to do, to tear his attention away from Natalie and focus on his young son. Patrick was wearing only a pair of shorts, but his face was still flushed and his darkly tanned skin was filmed with perspiration. Adam could smell the clammy sweat that was radiating from the boy's wiry body as Patrick leaned against the arm of his chair and grinned up at his father. His freckled nose had peeled, leaving a patch of pink skin amid the golden brown. There was a smear of grease on one cheek, and his hair was tousled and clinging damply to his head. Adam experienced a surge of emotion—he did love this kid.

Patrick was looking at his father with a slightly quizzical expression in his wide gray eyes—Natalie's eyes. And a numbing realization slammed into Adam. Yes, this son of his had filled a gaping hole in his life, but not simply because Patrick was his own flesh and blood. The real truth was that he loved this child because Patrick was so very much a part of Natalie. He had her eyes, her hair, her sensitivity and warmth. This child—their son—had been created by the two of them, but he had been borne, nurtured and protected by her. It was no longer deeply significant to Adam that the seed had been his. What mattered above all else was that his seed had found fertile ground within this woman, and she had willingly harbored it.

There was a strange poignant hollowness in Adam as he forced a smile and lightly ruffled the boy's sweat-dampened hair before resting his hand on Patrick's bare shoulder. "The road up to the trailer is in bad shape, and I thought it might be wise if we made tracks before the storm hit."

"Oh, okay. I've got my stuff all packed." Patrick grinned at his father as he gave him an affectionate thump on the shoulder, then bounded off toward the hallway that led to the bedrooms. "I'll go get everything." Adam watched Patrick disappear around the corner, then stretching his long legs in front of him, he slouched back in the easy chair and glanced at Natalie.

She, too, had been watching Patrick. Adam didn't know if it was something he read in her eyes or if it was simply something that he sensed, but he was acutely aware of how much she was hurting right then. And it didn't take a genius to figure out that most of that hurt had been caused by their small son.

Adam experienced a twist of guilt. He'd been so intent on his own emotional upheaval, he'd never given much thought to what was happening between Natalie and Patrick. But with a sudden flash of insight, he was forced to admit that wasn't exactly the truth. The real truth was that he hadn't wanted to know what was happening. Because of his shaky defenses, Adam had deliberately avoided even mentioning Natalie to Patrick, let alone openly talking about her, and without realizing it, he had very likely sent some strong signals to the boy. Because of that lack of communication, Patrick probably continued to blame his mother for the years of separation.

And that was wrong. Adam knew he should have done something days ago to defuse the resentment Patrick harbored. But his ability to reason wisely had been hopelessly distorted by warring emotions, especially at the hotel when Patrick turned on Natalie. Adam had decided right then and there that it would be best if he could establish a closer relationship with Patrick before the two of them ever dared talk about Natalie, or what she'd done, or how each of them felt about it. Adam had really believed he'd been totally objective when he rationalized his decision to let things ride for a while, but now he realized he'd been less than honest with himself. It hadn't been only Patrick's emotional welfare he'd been concerned about. Not by a long shot.

The harsh lines around Adam's mouth had softened when he finally lifted his head and looked at Natalie. "I take it he's still packing a grudge because you never told him about me."

There was a brief silence before Natalie met Adam's steady gaze. She stared at him for a moment, then nodded, her expression one of concern. "He has a right to be upset." She glanced away and Adam saw her take an unsteady breath before she looked at him again. "He really idolizes you, Adam." Her voice broke and she quickly turned her head away. "All he talks about is you and what you're going to do together."

It wasn't all that long ago that her admission would have given Adam a certain amount of grim satisfaction, but now it only made him feel like a heel. It didn't seem fair that he had so easily garnered Patrick's loyalty and affection. At least not at Natalie's expense. He was about to speak to her, to try to right a wrong when Patrick bounced into the room, the expensive backpack Adam had bought him slung over his shoulders. Patrick had put on a pair of jeans and hiking boots, which Adam had also purchased for him, and in his hand he carried an old camera of his father's. Adam inwardly winced when he realized what he'd done. There was no way Natalie could compete with the money or the time Adam was able to spend on Patrick, and it must have been like a slap in the face for her when Adam had immediately become the major influence in her son's life. Now Adam realized that in some ways, he'd had an unfair and unearned advantage.

"What's the matter, Dad? Aren't we going to go now?"

Feeling suddenly even more drained, Adam leaned his head back and exhaled sharply. He looked at Patrick and nodded. "Yes, we're going now." Unable to meet Natalie's eyes, Adam stood up, and placing his hand on Patrick's shoulder, aimed him toward the door. "I'll have him back in a couple of days."

"That's fine." Natalie touched Patrick on the arm, her voice very soft. "Have a good time, Patrick."

Patrick jerkily nodded his head, deliberately avoiding eye contact. "I will," he mumbled, then bolted out the door.

Adam wanted to say something that would breach the awkward silence that Patrick's abrupt departure left, but what could he say that wouldn't make matters worse? There was a haggard look in his eyes as he rested his hand on the handle of the screen door. As if drawn against his will, he glanced at her. She was standing with her back to him, and suddenly Adam felt he had betrayed her in the most unforgivable way. His voice was very low when he said, "We'll see you in a couple of days."

She only nodded.

Patrick had already stowed his gear in the back of the Bronco and was waiting in the cab by the time Adam got there. Engrossed in the stack of maps Adam carried in the truck, Patrick didn't look up when his father climbed in. There was a stern set to Adam's jaw as he started the vehicle and put it in gear. He checked his side mirror for traffic and made a sharp U-turn, the wheels spewing a hail of gravel. But this time his anger was directed at himself. He was abandoning her, and never in his life had he felt so damned low.

They were at the outskirts of town when Patrick asked, "What's the matter, Dad?"

Adam glanced quickly at his son and swore under his breath when he saw the anxious look on the boy's face. Without giving himself a chance to reconsider, Adam pulled over and parked beside a huge shade tree. He stared at his hands for a moment, then leaning against the door, he turned to face his son. His voice was nonthreatening when he asked, "Are you still mad at your mom?"

Patrick held his father's gaze for a moment, then stared at the floor. "She should have told me. I think what she did was mean."

Adam reached across the seat and gently lifted Patrick's face until their eyes met. "Don't be mad at her, Patrick. She's been a good mother to you, and she did what she honestly thought was best." Adam studied the boy's pinched face, uncertain about how far to go. He didn't want to lay a guilt trip on the kid, but on the other hand, he couldn't allow Patrick to nurture this grudge any longer. Somehow he had to walk the narrow line in between. "Don't hurt your mom, Patrick. She's feeling very badly right now, and it must make her feel even worse when I can go out and buy you things she can't afford to get you, and we're out doing things together, and she's left alone."

Patrick tried to pull away as his mouth began to quiver and his eyes filled with tears. With his own emotions creating a tight ache in his throat, Adam took Patrick's hand in his. "Don't stop loving your mom because she made one mistake, Pat," he murmured huskily. "No matter what, she'd never stop loving you, you know."

Patrick took a racking breath, then buried his face tightly against his father's chest. His words were muffled when he sobbed out, "Why couldn't we have been a real family? Why did I have to wait so long for you?"

Adam had to swallow heavily before he could speak. "I don't know why. But I do know she loves you a lot, and I know she never meant to hurt you."

Patrick remained in the circle of his father's arms until he stopped crying, then he pulled away and looked up, his face smeared with tears. There was a stricken look in his eyes. "I never said goodbye to her, Dad. I should have said goodbye."

Taking Patrick's face in his hands, Adam tenderly wiped the last of his son's tears away with his thumbs, then smiled reassuringly. "Then I guess we'll just have to go back, won't we?"

Patrick nodded and gave him a wobbly smile. At least one hurdle had been cleared.

When they pulled up in front of Doc's, Patrick gave his dad a slightly sheepish look. "Will you come with me?"

Adam studied his son, then nodded. "If that's what you want."

Patrick grimaced, obviously embarrassed. "Yeah, I think you should come."

There was a glint of amusement in Adam's eyes as he climbed out of the truck and walked around to where Patrick was waiting for him. Neither of them spoke as they walked up the drive.

Patrick stopped short when he rounded the corner of the house, then as if seeking direction, he looked up at Adam, his uncertainty visible. Natalie was standing beneath a huge poplar tree staring across the river, her shoulder resting against the rough trunk, her arms folded in front of her. And her face was wet with tears.

Seeing her like that cut Adam to the quick. He tried to keep his face from revealing what he felt, and because of his constraint, his expression was rigid as he gave Patrick a gentle push in the direction of his mother.

The boy once again looked up at his father, his ashen face dominated by his dark eyes, and Adam nodded his encouragement. With his body stiff and his gait awkward, Patrick went toward his mother, his voice taut with anxiety. "Mom? I forgot to say goodbye, Mom."

Natalie jerked back from the tree and turned away from her son, quickly wiping away her tears with the back of her hand. By the time she faced him, she had an unsteady smile in place. "That didn't matter, Patrick," she said huskily, trying to reassure him with her smile.

Patrick stared at her, then with a muffled sob, he flung himself into her arms. "It does matter." His voice broke as he gave way to his tears. "I'm sorry, Mom. I'm really sorry. I don't want you to think I'm still mad at you."

With her son clasped in her embrace, Natalie dropped to her knees, her face twisted by pain. She squeezed her eyes against the flood of tears that slipped relentlessly down her face. It was obvious that she was going through some private hell, but she never made a sound. She contained the sounds of her weeping, contained the pain, the anguish, the grief.

Because of Patrick, because she didn't want him to know what she was experiencing right then, she somehow managed to hold it all in. As he watched her battle for control Adam grasped the depth of her feelings for their son; she'd sacrifice anything and everything for Patrick. Unable to cope with the gripping emotions that were threatening him, Adam had to walk away.

He went back to the truck to wait for Patrick. His face was carefully schooled as he braced his legs and leaned against the front fender of the mud-spattered vehicle. Hooking his thumbs in the front pockets of his jeans, he stared at the ground, vaguely aware that the storm had moved closer. No matter how hard he tried to keep his mind empty, he was unable to shut out the image of Natalie as she knelt before their son. So much pain. He felt so damned helpless, so trapped by sheer circumstance. There were too many unanswered questions, too many doubts, and no matter how much he might have wanted it otherwise, he could not pretend all that did not exist.

Adam caught a glimpse of color out of the corner of his eye, and inhaling slowly, he lifted his head. Patrick and Natalie were coming down the driveway toward him, and he watched them approach with a solemn stare. On the surface it appeared that all was well, but as the pair came closer, Adam could detect a forced brightness in Natalie that was very alien.

He tried not to think about it as he glanced down at his son. "Ready to go, Patrick?"

Patrick looked up at his mother, and Natalie smiled back. Adam could tell that her stiff smile had been dredged up to reassure her son, and apparently it did exactly that. Patrick grinned at his father and nodded. "Mom says there's gonna be enough thunder and lightning to scare even me."

Adam's own smile was forced as he opened the truck door for his son. "Is that a big deal—thunder and lightning?"

Patrick climbed into the vehicle and waited until his father slammed the door before he answered. "Mom hates storms so I bug her about it sometimes. She says someday I'll get mine."

The impact of Patrick's offhand comment stopped Adam cold. Natalie hated storms? Since when? Thinking it had to be some sort of private joke, Adam shot Natalie a questioning look. She was staring at him with a numb expression, her wide dark eyes dominating her ashen face. And suddenly Adam felt as though he had stumbled onto something acutely significant.

As their gazes locked and held, a crystal-clear recollection crowded into his mind: Natalie and him soaked to the skin as they huddled under the overhang of a rocky ledge. The rain was beating down around them in a chilling torrent, curtaining the mountainous landscape in gray. She was sitting between his upraised knees, her back pressed tightly against his chest as she shivered in the shelter of his arms, but her body taut with anticipation. Her rain-drenched face was lifted to the blackened skies as she sat transfixed with an impassioned awe, watching the jagged slashes of lightning rake the mountain peaks. As the storm raged around them, she was caught up in the savage drama. An almost sensual excitement radiated from her as the deafening thundercracks reverberated down the valley, shaking the ground with their violence. There had been no fear then, no fear at all.

In that electric moment as they stared at each other, Adam somehow knew that she was also remembering. He could see it in her eyes: the pain, the awful longing to recapture the love and laughter and happiness they had once shared. Unable to tear his gaze from hers, he found his will to resist the haunting sadness in her eyes was no longer there. And he was lost. Something gave way within him, and suddenly, in the space of a heartbeat, all the inner barriers he had erected to shut her out came crashing down. Everything he had restrained for so long broke loose, catching him undefended. All the feelings he'd ever felt for her were surging inside him, but now they were magnified tenfold. The impact was paralyzing. For all that had gone before, in spite of the hurt she had inflicted, in spite of what she'd done, he still loved her. He had never stopped.

CHAPTER SEVEN

THE HEAT SMOTHERED EVERY SOUND and trapped the usual neighborhood noises in its humid cocoon. A deep rumble of thunder rolled across the mountains, breaking the silence that was as suffocating as the heat.

"Come on, Dad," Patrick interjected as he squirmed impatiently on the seat. "Let's go. It's hot in here."

Adam had the strangest feeling as he stood there, his eyes still riveted on Natalie. It was as though he had been in a dream, trying to photograph something far off in the distance, but the image was blurred, indistinct. Then, as if released from some invisible bond, he was finally able to bring the shadowy image into sharp focus, making everything so profoundly clear.

"Are we going, Dad?"

It was all Adam could do to drag his attention away from the slender blond woman and look at his son. His elbows hanging out the open window, Patrick rested his chin on his folded arms and watched his father, squinting thoughtfully. From that look, Adam could well imagine the questions going through the boy's head—questions he didn't want to deal with, at least not yet.

Pushing away from the fender, he went around to the driver's side of the vehicle, opened the door and climbed in. The interior was stifling and the heat from the seat burned through his clothes as he put the key in the ignition. He glanced up and Natalie's face was framed in Patrick's window. Her hair was pulled back in its usual style, but some curls had slipped free of the pins and were lying damply against her neck. She looked so hot and exhausted as she stood there with that forced smile on her face.

As much as he wanted to stay, common sense told him there were other considerations. With Patrick sitting there watching, Adam didn't dare create a situation that carried the risk of emotional repercussions. He wasn't playing any more games with himself; he knew that if it hadn't been for Patrick's presence, he would have made some kind of overture toward her right there and then. He would have at least tried to talk. But he didn't want an audience, not even his son, when he finally bridged that gap of eleven years.

Even though he was aware of this, it was the hardest thing he'd ever had to do when he started the truck, put it in gear and pulled away. It was as though he was physically connected to her as he watched her diminish in the rearview mirror. He felt as if he was abandoning her, and that feeling deepened when he turned the corner and she was lost from view.

They had driven through town and across the bridge, then turned onto the old forestry road that eventually intersected the narrow trail that led up to the campsite. The dark clouds hadn't yet obscured the sun, and the long dark shadows and bright splotches of sunshine flipped by as they started to climb through the thinning forest. The fragrance of fir and cedar wafted in, and above the noise of the truck, Adam could hear the wild rush of the river that was now below them.

Patrick hooked his heels on the edge of the seat and wrapped his arms around his legs. He sat hunched in silence, the breeze from the open window ruffling through his hair as he stared out, obviously lost in thought. With his bottom lip caught between his teeth he finally turned to study his father. An anxious look on his face, Patrick tipped his head to one side and asked hesitantly, "Do you still like Mom?"

Unconsciously, Adam tightened his grip on the wheel as he tried to contend with the host of disturbing feelings that one innocent question aroused. How could he explain to this small boy that he felt as though he'd torn himself in half when he'd driven off and left her standing there? How could he explain that he had just come fact-to-face with something he'd been trying to evade for years? How could he put all that into words this child could understand?

His voice was rough and unsteady when he said, "Yes, I do...very much."

Patrick turned under the restraint of the seat belt, then rested his chin on his upraised knees. "She still likes you, too," he said, the anxious look suddenly gone. Not receiving any comment from his father, he continued, "She said you were special."

Adam's stomach nose-dived as he was hit with an electrifying mixture of fear, excitement and hope—the kind of reaction that made it nearly impossible to breathe. He cast a sharp glance at his son. "When did she say that?"

"The other night—after you took me canoeing."

His pulse pounding heavily, Adam had to fight to keep his tone casual. "How come you were talking about me?"

Patrick shrugged and leaned back against the seat. "I was telling her about all we did, and she said I was a lucky kid, that you were really special. She looked like she was gonna cry when she said it, like it made her feel bad." He turned to look at his father, a perplexed expression on his brown face. "Why would she say it like that, like it made her feel real sad? Do you know why?"

His face suddenly drawn, Adam was gripped with an intense rush of emotion, and his knuckles turned white on the steering wheel as he braked, a cloud of dust enveloping them as they slid to a stop. Bracing his arm on the open window, he clenched his jaw as he covered his eyes with his hand. If there had been room on the narrow mountain road to turn around, he would have done it. He couldn't handle this empty feeling, knowing he had left her there alone.

"What's the matter? Are you sick?" Patrick's eyes were wide with alarm, and his hands were awkward as he hastily fumbled with the buckle on the seat belt. He moved toward his father, his small face pinched with concern as he looked at Adam. "What's wrong, Dad?" he asked, a tenor of fear in his voice. "You look so funny."

Adam didn't think he could get a full breath past the excruciating tightness in his chest, but he slowly inhaled, then lifted his head and looked at his son. His voice was gruff. "Nothing's wrong, Pat." He made his body relax as he slouched back in his seat, his face suddenly very haggard. He took another deep breath, then said unevenly, "How about we go back and get your mother?"

Patrick stared at him for a second, then his anxious expression changed and lightened, as if he finally figured out the deeper meaning behind his father's words. "She won't like it up here if there's thunder and lightning," he said finally. "She gets all nervous in a bad storm." There was an air of uncertainty about him as he moved away from his father. It was obvious he was mulling something over as he sat back on the seat, raised his knees and locked his arms around them. He frowned slightly, then began absently picking at a scab on his leg. Finally he looked up at his father. "Besides, could we maybe talk, Dad?"

"About what, son?"

Patrick hesitated for a moment, then shrugged self-consciously as he deliberately avoided Adam's gaze. "You know. About you and Mom . . . and everything."

Adam considered that for a moment, realizing that some of Patrick's unanswered questions had to be dealt with before anything else. He switched off the ignition, then undid his seat belt and leaned back against the door, one arm loosely draped across the steering wheel. There was a note of quiet reassurance in his voice as he asked, "What exactly do you want to know?"

Patrick fiddled with the cuff of his jeans before he looked up, then squirming a little under his father's steady scrutiny, he lowered his head again. "Did you used to like each other a lot?"

Adam sensed this was something that was vitally important to Patrick's sense of security, to know that his mother and father really cared about each other. Adam's voice was very low when he said, "I loved your mom very much when we were young, Patrick." He looked out the window, waiting for the aching constriction in his throat to ease, then said softly, "And those feelings don't change easily, Pat. I still do love her."

Patrick's voice was a barely audible whisper. "I don't think she knows that, Dad. Are you going to tell her?"

The constriction became more painful. Adam leaned his head back and closed his eyes. His voice was ragged with emotion when he said softly, "Yes, I am."

IT WAS MORE THAN AN HOUR later when Adam and Patrick pulled into the clearing by the trailer. And it had been a very difficult hour. When Patrick was finally given the chance to open up and ask questions, Adam was dumbfounded by the kinds of queries the boy had made. Not only about Natalie and Adam, but about Patrick's paternal grandparents, Adam's boyhood and a range of other topics. He seemed to have an insatiable thirst to find out everything he could about his parents. And the more Patrick asked, the more Adam understood just how much this boy had bottled up.

They had climbed out of the truck and were walking through a thick stand of fir trees on their way to the lake. Patrick slipped his hand into his dad's and swung around. "What do Grandma and Grandpa Rutherford look like?"

"Well, your grandmother's tall and has hair about the color of mine. She really likes to swim and play tennis, and she and your grandfather both learned how to sail after they moved to the coast."

"Does she work?"

"She used to teach school, but now she works part-time in a craft store."

"And Grandpa?"

"Well, everybody says we look a lot alike. He was a foreman at the mill when we lived here, but he retired when they moved to Victoria. He's really big and he laughs a lot." Adam glanced down at his son and smiled reassuringly. "You'll like them, Patrick. Your grandparents always made time for kids."

"Are we going to visit them pretty soon?"

Adam considered the question briefly, then answered, "I don't see why not. We'll have to check with your mom."

Patrick scuffed his feet through the thick layer of dried needles and leaves, then looked up at Adam. "Can she come?"

Adam tried to keep his voice neutral when he answered. "If she'd like, sure."

"Do you want her to come?"

He experienced that same aching tightness in his chest when he answered softly, "Yes, I want her to come."

Reassured, Patrick squeezed his hand and grinned up at him. "Can we go fishing now?"

Relieved that the inquisition was temporarily set aside, Adam grinned back. "I think it could be arranged."

The small secluded valley where Adam had parked the trailer was particularly beautiful, and he couldn't believe his good fortune when he'd discovered it. He'd been exploring old roads, looking for good filming locations and happened on this spot strictly by chance.

A few years before, some of the locals had tried to start up a guide and outfitter's association, and this site had been part of their development. There were two small cabins, a corral and a shelter for pack animals, and a small wooden dock that angled out into the lake. The developers had also installed a septic tank and built a cistern that filled from a nearby stream. Since everything in the trailer ran off either propane or batteries, all Adam had to do was install a large propane tank and rig up a pump to get water from the cistern into the trailer. The cabins had their windows broken, the doors were missing and the roofs leaked, but it would take very little work to make the necessary repairs. The location had everything he wanted, especially the peace and serenity that was an integral part of this wilderness valley.

The cabins and trailer were situated on a slight rise of land at the north end of the lake, the natural clearing heavily dotted with clumps of alder, white birch and pine, and farther back the verdant forest crowded down the mountainside. The crystal-clear alpine lake that was cupped in the valley was the headwater for the sparkling mountain stream that bordered the campsite. At the far end of the lake, the small valley folded open to a larger one that offered a magnificent view of the rugged purple mountains. It was one of the prettiest spots he had seen in a long time.

But now there was a strange hush as the storm clouds trundled over the mountain peaks, darkening the sky and eventually covering the sun. And suddenly the ominous quiet was split by a roll of thunder, which echoed for miles along the blackened heavens.

Patrick had managed to catch one small lake trout before Adam suggested they'd better head back to shore if they wanted to beat the rain. They had just finished beaching the canoe and putting the fishing gear away when the first drops of rain fell, leaving large wet splotches on the dusty ground.

The pewter-gray lake was beginning to get rough with whitecaps, the agitation forecasting a strong wind. Adam checked to make sure everything in the camp was secure before he followed his son into the trailer, the huge drops of rain spotting his blue denim shirt. He had turned to close the door behind him when a vehicle pulled up beside the Bronco, and he frowned slightly when he recognized the car was Doc's.

Adam had ambivalent feelings about the old man. Part of him deeply resented his intrusion, and part of him recalled the hours the two of them had spent hiking these very mountains. But the resentment won out and his voice was tense as he said, "Your grandfather's here, Patrick."

Patrick let out a whoop of approval as he brushed past Adam and jumped out of the trailer, then started running toward Doc. Adam followed, his face wiped clean of any expression, an uncompromising set to his chin. Sticking his hands in the back pockets of his jeans, he nodded to the old pharmacist. "I didn't expect to see you up here, Doc."

Doc read the underlying implication beneath Adam's cool greeting, and the warm smile he'd greeted Patrick with faded as he steadily met Adam's gaze. "I need to talk to you, lad." Realizing Patrick was watching them with an anxious look, he ruffled the boy's hair as he grinned down at him. "And I had to see if the fish were biting, young Patrick. I had my mouth all set for a good feed of lake trout."

The spattering of rain was picking up momentum, and a gust of wind whipped dust and dead leaves into a blustery whirlwind. Patrick caught Doc's hand and started dragging him toward the trailer. "Come on, Grandpa. Hurry up, or we're going to get wet." With their heads bent against the wind, they crossed the clearing and entered the trailer. As Adam pulled the door firmly shut behind them, the boy scrambled up on one of the padded seats by the small table and grinned at Doc. "I only caught one fish before we had to come in, but we can share it, Grandpa. Dad said he's going to have steak instead."

Doc held back a smile as he looked at the very small fish lying in the sink, and said dryly, "Then your father is an eminently wise man."

His eyes were twinkling as he looked at Adam. There was something about the amused look in the old man's eyes that neutralized Adam's annoyance, and he found himself grinning back. "I take it I could interest you in a steak, too, Doc."

"You could indeed, lad. You could indeed."

As the sky grew darker and the wind picked up tempo, Adam set about preparing a meal for them all. It took him back in time to watch Doc with his son. The old man still wove the same spellbinding stories that Adam remembered so well from his own youth, stories that were based on woodsmanship and a far-reaching knowledge and understanding of the wilderness. Their appeal had not lessened over the years. Adam found himself wondering if Doc had ever considered putting them on paper. Properly illustrated, they would make a fantastic children's book. It was something worth thinking about.

By the time they'd finished eating, the sky was black and the wind was gusting so strongly it was rocking the trailer, yet the heavy rain hadn't come. But Adam knew the cloudburst wasn't very far away. It was obvious that Doc had planned to stay the night, so when Patrick finally curled up in the corner and fell asleep, Adam picked him up and carried him back to the small bedroom at the back of the trailer. The table in the kitchen folded down and the seats pulled out, making another very comfortable double bed where Doc could sleep.

Quietly closing the folding door that separated the bedroom from the rest of the trailer, Adam went to a cupboard above the tiny sink and lifted out two mugs. "Would you like coffee, Doc?"

"If you please, Adam." He fished his pipe out of his pocket and nodded his thanks as Adam slid an ashtray across the table to him. Adam set both steaming mugs on the table, then slipped into the seat across from the old man. Leaning against the wall, he stretched his legs out on the long seat, then flexed one knee and draped his arm across it. Absently he took a sip of coffee, his eyes narrowing as he watched Doc go through the ritual of filling his pipe.

As the old gentleman put the flaring match to the bowl, the expression in Adam's eyes changed. There was an edge to his voice when he reminded, "You said you wanted to talk."

Doc glanced at him sharply, then fixed his attention on the match as he lit his pipe. A cloud of fragrant smoke screened his face as he drew in until the tamped tobacco glowed red, then he carefully shook out the match and dropped it in the ashtray. He took another puff, and cradling his pipe in his hand, he leaned back and met Adam's unwavering stare.

"Yes, lad, I do want to talk."

"About what?"

Doc rested his arms on the table and, avoiding looking at Adam, he fingered the elaborate carving on the bowl of his pipe. "I know it's none of my business, Adam, but I'd like to talk to you about Patrick."

That was unexpected, and Adam studied Doc, trying to figure out what the old man was leading up to. He expected him to bring up Natalie, not Patrick. "What about Patrick?" he asked flatly.

Doc's expression was grave as he stared at him for a moment, then answered, "I was wondering what arrangements you're considering for the lad."

In a stall for time, Adam took another sip of coffee, then cradled the mug in his hands as he slowly rubbed his thumb against the rough pottery texture. His mouth was taut when he finally spoke. "You think I'm planning on keeping him with me, don't you?"

Doc heaved a sigh then tipped his head. "Natalie has been deeply troubled ever since Patrick arrived, and I've wondered what's been weighing so heavily on her. I thought perhaps there had been some discussion about the boy. She hasn't that much longer before she has to go back to her job, and she's been so quiet. I thought it had something to do with him."

Adam leaned his head against the wall, his face drawn as he stared at the ceiling. "I told her I wouldn't try to take Patrick away from her." He turned and looked at his companion, his eyes revealing more than he realized. "I don't want to hurt her, Doc. And I haven't a clue what I'm going to do. I know she'll be leaving in a couple of weeks, and we haven't even talked about . . . anything." A feeling of defeat settled on Adam. What was he going to do if she decided to leave again? How in hell was he going to handle that?

Wearily rubbing his hand across his face, he straightened and looked at the white-haired gentleman sitting across the table from him. Doc's head was lowered; he was obviously deep in his own thoughts. He stroked his bottom lip with the stem of his pipe, his brow creased with a heavy frown. Suddenly it became important to Adam that he clear the air about what had happened so long ago.

"I acted pretty damned irresponsibly eleven years ago, Doc. I realize now you were caught in a bind, especially when Natalie didn't want me to find out she was pregnant."

Doc dismissed his apology with a wave. "You were hurting, lad. I knew that."

The wind rocked the trailer, and a crack of thunder sounded overhead, finally splitting the skies. The rain came lashing down, drumming heavily on the aluminum roof. The racket echoed hollowly in the trailer, and both men fell silent under the deluge, the smell of rain and wet forest seeping in through the closed windows.

Adam emptied his mug and set it back on the table, then laced his fingers around his upraised knee and turned his attention back to Doc. After a moment of deliberation he asked, "What exactly happened in the accident, Doc?"

An unusually alert expression appeared in Doc's eyes. Adam frowned slightly, and some gut feeling pushed him on. "Something happened to Natalie in that accident that left some damned deep emotional scars, and I think it had something to do with her mother finding out she was pregnant."

Adam watched Doc like a hawk, and a feeling of expectation cut through him when he saw how tightly the older man was clamping his pipe between his teeth. He'd struck a nerve. Adam pushed a little more. "I also think that the accident was no accident. I think Jean Willard drove off the cliff deliberately."

His arms still folded across his chest, Doc dropped his head and fixed his gaze on the ashtray in front of him as he puffed agitatedly on his pipe. He was carefully calculating his answer, and Adam tried to assess the real meaning of his reaction. His tone curt, Adam prodded, "I think you owe me, Doc. I want to know what in hell happened to make Natalie run. There was more to her disappearing than Patrick, that's for damned sure. She's admitted that much."

A brilliant flash of lightning sliced the darkness, followed eventually by a sharp crack of thunder that rolled menacingly along the heavens until it disappeared in a distant grumble. An unnerving tension started to build as Adam watched Doc, waiting for an answer. But as the tension grew, Adam's senses became keener. A sobering feeling of premonition sent a chill down his spine, and every muscle in his body reacted as his pulse rate increased. He was carefully disciplined as he persisted quietly, "I want to know about the accident, Doc. I want to know exactly what happened."

The silence was so thick he could have cut it with a knife, and Adam kept clenching and unclenching his jaw, fighting to maintain a veneer of calm. But it was a thin veneer. He forced himself to remain motionless, but he was poised and waiting. He sensed he was finally going to get answers to questions that had tormented him for years. It seemed like an eternity passed before the old man lifted his head and looked at him. Adam was caught completely off guard. Doc looked like he had aged twenty years in a space of moments. And it unsettled Adam even more when he realized there were tears of distress in the old man's eyes.

Doc's voice quavered. "Natalie wasn't in the car accident, Adam. She was already in the hospital in Calgary when her mother drove off that cliff."

Adam had been prepared for a bombshell, but nothing on earth could have prepared him for this. There was a moment, one split second of time before he could even think, let alone respond. He stared dumbfoundedly at Doc. "What in hell are you saying?"

"Adam, it's not a pleasant—"

"Damn it, just tell me what in hell happened to her! I need to know." He had a nearly uncontrollable urge to shake the answer out of Doc as a sickening dread started building in him. His voice carried an undercurrent of threat as he ground out, "For God's sake, answer me, Doc."

Their eyes locked, and Adam was unnerved by what he saw. Suddenly he was very cold. Like a nightmare in slow motion, he waited for the answer.

"She was raped, Adam. That bastard of a stepfather raped her."

There was a moment of frozen disbelief, then something exploded in Adam. Unable to contain all the feelings that were tearing through him, he stumbled to his feet. Like a wounded animal that was racked with pain, he started pacing back and forth in the confined area, his whole body braced against the agony of finally knowing the dark, ugly truth.

"Adam . . . Adam, lad," Doc soothed as he stood up and grasped the younger man by the shoulder. "Don't do this to yourself, lad. She wouldn't want it, you know that."

Adam turned away abruptly, and gripping the sink, he lowered his head, his body shaking with violent spasms. His voice was ragged when he was finally able to whisper, "Tell me everything, Doc."

There was a pause before Doc answered, his voice infinitely weary, his Irish brogue suddenly thick. "She wouldn't tell you, lad, because she was terrified you'd kill him. She didn't want you to have blood on your hands because of her. She loved you too much for that."

Doc's softly spoken words were like an injection of ice water, and Adam slowly straightened, his body trembling with shock. Numbness claimed him as he turned to stare at the white-haired man who was hunched over the table. "I would have," he whispered hoarsely. "I would have ripped him apart with my bare hands." It was no idle threat, and anyone hearing him or seeing the look on his face wouldn't have doubted him for a minute.

"She knew that, lad. She told me the night it happened. She said, 'He'd end up in jail, Doc. He'd go to jail because of me.' She couldn't bear that, Adam. She was trying to protect you, lad."

Praying that this cold, immobilizing numbness held until he heard the whole story, Adam went back to the table and sat down, his face drained of color, his hands unsteady as he raked them through his hair. "I want to know the whole story—from the beginning."

Doc puffed on his pipe then rested his elbows on the table and stared at the ashtray, quietly recalling the details. "Jean had been sent to Calgary to a specialist because of her back, and Natalie knew her mother would be gone for a few days. The lass suspected she was pregnant, but she thought that with her mother gone, it would be a perfect opportunity to find out for certain. She'd taken a bus out of the valley and went somewhere else so no one would find out. She'd been so careful not to give anything away, but somehow Carl found out."

Adam felt utter revulsion rising up in him again as he whispered, "So he went after her."

"No, he didn't—not right away. Maybe if he'd confronted her that morning when he found out, things wouldn't have turned out the way they did. But from what I gathered later, he'd spent all day drinking in the hotel and brooding about it. Being the kind of man he was, he ended up in a dirty mood. Old Mike Barnes was in the bar when he left, and he said that he'd never seen a man in such an ugly mood. It was seven o'clock when he left the bar, and it appears that he went straight home."

"And Natalie was there alone."

Doc leaned forward, his face heavily lined, his eyes bleak with remembering as he murmured gruffly, "Yes, the lass was there alone."

The muscles in Adam's face were hard and his body was rigid with restraint as he slid out of the seat, stood and opened the cupboard door above the table. He brought down a bottle of rye and a small stack of plastic glasses, then unscrewed the top and poured himself a drink. He sat back down and stared at the glass a moment, then tossed the entire contents down in one shot. His hands were very unsteady as he poured himself another drink. "Go on," he said hoarsely.

"I don't know much about what happened after he got home, Adam," the old man continued softly, trying to ease the horror. "She would never tell anyone what all he did to her. All I know is that he showed up in a foul rage, told Natalie he knew she was carrying your baby and that he was going to make damned sure she'd never carry it to term."

A shudder coursed through Adam's body and his head shot up, his face white with shock. "What are you saying, Doc?"

Doc reached across the table and covered Adam's fists with his hands, his face haggard with sorrow and compassion. "He nearly beat her to death first, Adam. I couldn't believe how battered she was when she showed up at my door. He'd smashed her jaw, several ribs were cracked, her elbow was dislocated, her pelvis was broken—" Doc wiped his eyes with the back of his hand, then clasped both hands around his empty mug as if to stop their violent shaking. His voice was so strained it was nearly inaudible when he went on. "He'd used his belt on her. Her body was a mass of welts. I hardly recognized her when I opened the door."

Adam knew a rage like he'd never known before—a still, cold and deadly rage. What kind of a bastard was Willard to do that to her? What kind of twisted mind could create such punishment? Adam felt sick to his very soul, knowing Natalie was the helpless target of a perverted bloodlust that was warped beyond rationality, the victim of the most revolting savage violation. Even though it happened so long ago, he still wanted to kill him.

And when he was finally able to speak, his voice held a deadly ring. "What did she tell you?"

Doc slowly shook his head. "She only told me what he said when he first came home. And she told me that he raped her. But beyond that, she refused to say. All the months she was in the hospital, she would freeze up and panic the instant anyone tried to uncover exactly what had happened that night. All I know is that it was seven o'clock when Carl left the bar, and it was just after nine-thirty when the lass showed up at my place."

Two and a half hours. Alone and defenseless. She was subjected to that kind of inhuman brutality for two and a half hours.

Doc's voice droned on in a weary monotone. "I called George Johnson over—he was still practicing medicine then. He said she had to have a damned good surgeon and the very best of care, so we decided to get her to a major medical center. He knew her lung had been perforated by a broken rib, so he put in a chest tube and patched her up enough so that she could tolerate the trip. It was a terrible night, storming badly and low cloud cover, but the weather was clearing to the east so Calgary was accessible. And her mother was already there. So George made arrangements for a float plane to meet us at Catherine Lake."

The old man sat back and folded his arms across his chest, his eyes solemn with this grim reminiscence. "During that drive to the airplane, George and I agreed that it would only make things more unbearable for Natalie if anyone found out what that bastard had done to her, so we decided to start laying a smoke screen. If we could help it, no one would find out what had happened that night."

The steady drone of Doc's voice had been oddly subduing and Adam was able to ease some of the rigidness in his body. In an attempt to get a grip on himself and block out the ugly images that were pressing in on him, he concentrated on the sound of the rain on the roof. It was frightening, the price she'd paid for loving him. How had she endured it all?

Adam knew the only way he could keep from losing control was to focus on the facts. He poured himself another drink and looked at Doc. "What happened when you got her to Calgary?"

"She went directly to surgery." Doc fumbled a handkerchief from his sweater pocket and roughly blew his nose, then stuffed it back in his pocket. Picking up his pipe, he clamped it between his teeth before he went on. "It was touch and go for a few hours. They wanted to take the babe, to abort him—but Natalie went hysterical when they approached her on it. She said she'd rather die than lose the babe."

Propping his elbows on the table, Adam rested his forehead on his tightly interlaced fingers, obscuring his tortured face from Doc's view. "Dammit, Doc," he whispered unevenly, "she was only sixteen. She was only sixteen."

"I know, lad. She was no more than a babe herself. But she was determined to have that child. It was the only thing that kept her going all those months. I don't know what would have happened to her if she'd lost it."

Adam's shoulders were shaking, and unable to watch the younger man's anguish, Doc slowly got up, his movements slow and stiff as he stooped and picked up Patrick's jacket off the floor. His words were somewhat muffled when he continued to speak in that same quiet monotone. "It was hard for me not to tell you the truth when you came to me, Adam. But I was afraid that her worst fears would come true if I did tell you, and she was so...fragile. And on top of everything else, there was what happened to her mother. I didn't think she could take it if anything happened to you." Bracing his hand on his thigh, he slowly straightened and looked at Adam. "I knew what you were feeling, lad. But I had to do what was best for her." He dropped the jacket on the counter, then stood in the soft glow from the light above the sink, his head lowered in reflection. "She put up a long fight, the lass did. She wasn't discharged until after Patrick was born."

Dragging his hands down his face, Adam sat back and closed his eyes. "So that explains why Patrick was born in Calgary." But then, it explained more than that. Hauling in a deep breath, he turned to look at Doc. "What about Jean's car accident? Or was it an accident?"

Doc lifted his head and shrugged. "We'll never know, lad. We'll never know. Natalie believes it was deliberate."

"What happened?"

"We had to contact Jean at her hotel so she could meet us at the hospital—she had to sign the release form for Natalie's surgery. At first, she wouldn't believe us when we told her what happened."

"What changed her mind?"

Doc came back to the table and wearily sat down. "When they were getting Natalie ready for surgery, they discovered that she had a piece of material still clutched in her hand. It was a piece of Carl's plaid shirt, and Jean recognized the pattern."

Adam felt like he'd received so many crippling blows that he couldn't react to anything else, but he reacted to that. A sudden picture formed of a nurse bending over Natalie's bruised and battered body, carefully prying open her hand. He pushed on. "What did Jean do?"

"Not much then. She sat in the waiting room, staring straight ahead, not a trace of expression on her face—frightening, in a way. It was late in the afternoon of the following day when the doctor said he was feeling fairly hopeful about the lass. Jean excused herself to go to the rest room. That was the last time I saw her."

"How did you find out about her accident?"

"George had flown back with the plane. He called me at the hospital when he got word that she was dead. That's when he came up with the scheme to tell everyone that Natalie was in the car with her mother."

Another gust of wind rocked the trailer, driving the rain loudly against the metal exterior as another crack of thunder sounded overhead. The dampness was beginning to pervade the warmth of the trailer, bringing with it a chilling clamminess.

Realizing how cool it was, Adam got up and went into the bedroom to check on Patrick. As he gazed down at his sleeping son, a strangling knot of emotion expanded in his chest. And with a sudden stab of awareness, he realized the price Natalie had paid to give him this child. His hands were unsteady and very gentle as he drew the quilt up and tucked it around the boy.

Doc had relit his pipe and a cloud of smoke was curling around his head as Adam quietly closed the folding door. Slowly rolling his shoulders to try to work out the aching tension in the muscles across his back, Adam slid into the seat. Resting one elbow on the table, he leaned back against the wall and looked at Doc. "There wasn't one leak to give your story away. And God knows, I was sure trying to dig up something. How did you ever manage to keep the lid on this?"

Doc drew in deeply, sending another curl of smoke upward, then smiled wryly. "Oh, I had a little help from my friends."

"How many people knew the whole truth?"

"Myself, George Johnson, and now you."

Adam rested the back of his hand across his mouth as he continued to watch the old man. "I take it there was never any discussion about going to the cops?"

"No. Never. Natalie didn't want it. If she was unable to bring herself to tell the doctors what had happened, she certainly could have never managed it in a court of law." His brogue was more pronounced than ever when he said quietly, "She couldna do it, Adam. It would have been an unbearable humiliation for her to face Carl *and* the town . . . especially without her mother. And it would have changed nothing."

The sounds of the thunder squall intensified, and in an attempt to disconnect the treadmill of his thoughts, Adam concentrated on the storm. The fir trees behind the trailer were moaning loudly as the wind cut through their heavy, swaying boughs. And he knew from the torrent outside that the narrow rutted track would already have deep trenches cut from the deluge washing down the mountain. There was another blinding flash of lightning, closely followed by a crack of thunder that shook the ground. He turned his head and listened, expecting to hear some noise from the bedroom. But Patrick slept on, unafraid. Unafraid.

Suddenly Adam remembered what Patrick had said when they'd stopped to talk. *"She won't like it up here if there's thundering and lightning. She gets all nervous when there's a bad storm."* He had wondered why, but now he knew. It was chillingly apparent why Natalie had developed such an irrational fear of storms. Only it wasn't irrational. It was part of her nightmare. And she was all alone.

Propelled into action by that grim realization, Adam nearly knocked the table off its wall brackets, sending Doc's ashtray and the bottle of rye crashing to the floor. The old man's head jerked up, his eyebrows raised in a startled expression. "What's the matter, lad? Is something wrong?"

Adam yanked open a small storage space beside the fridge and started pulling out his gear. Determination was stamped into every line in his face. "I'm going back to town."

Doc's expression turned to one of incredulity. "Don't be daft, man. You can't go back down that road in weather like this. It isn't fit for man or beast. You'd be taking a terrible risk. You could slide into the canyon!"

Ignoring Doc's plea, Adam rammed his feet into boots, then grabbed his slicker from the hook by the door and put it on. "I'm not leaving her in there alone," he said grimly. "Patrick made a few comments about her being terrified of storms. At the time I wondered why she'd developed an aversion to them, but now I know. You said it was storming the night it happened, didn't you?"

"I did, lad. But you're daft to try to get off this mountain now."

Adam picked up a large battery-operated light, a hatchet and a thick coil of yellow rope. Slinging the rope over his shoulder, he went to the door. "If Patrick wakes up, tell him I've gone for his mother."

"Adam, wait—"

But Adam ignored the old man's entreaty and stepped out into the storm, slamming the door shut behind him. The rain felt like sleet against his skin and the wind caught his breath as he struggled through the drenching blackness, his head down against the driving force. Lightning zigzagged across the sky, and in that instant of illumination he was able to see deep puddles gathering on the ground and the trees bending and twisting in the wind. In seconds his jeans were drenched and clinging to his legs, the rain runneling down his neck. Adam shivered and yanked up the collar of the slicker, then hunched his shoulders against the gale.

But he was barely aware of what was happening around him. The only thing he could think of was Natalie and this compelling need to get to her. There was a crack of thunder, and an eerie chill crawled up the back of his neck. Damn, he wished she wasn't all alone.

CHAPTER EIGHT

THE STORM CONTINUED to assault the earth as the rain beat down, the torrent cutting deep gashes in the narrow winding road and turning the brown clay soil into treacherously slick mud. The conditions were so severe, Adam doubted if he would have even made it out of the campsite without a four-wheel-drive vehicle. Regardless of the terrible conditions, his sense of urgency drove him to the brink of recklessness as he pushed on through the slashing rain, his need to get to Natalie fueled by anxiety.

That compulsion nearly overrode his common sense when he rounded a bend and found the road blocked by a fir tree that had been uprooted by the storm, its sweeping boughs creating an impenetrable barrier. Ready to explode with frustration, Adam fought down the urge to abandon the truck and walk out. He knew rashness was the last thing he could allow to govern his actions. Swearing under his breath, he gritted his teeth and grabbed the hatchet and rope from the back seat, then climbed out of the truck into the chillingly wet night. Even at the speed he worked, it seemed to take hours to clear a path wide enough for the vehicle. And by the time he could proceed, he was soaked to the skin and nearly frantic.

The thunderstorm had moved down the valley by the time Adam drove into town. Lightning zigzagged across the sky, thunder detonated overhead with a deafening crack and the rain pounded down even harder. Water several inches deep gathered along the curbs, the downpour too heavy for the drains to handle, and branches lay broken and twisted in the deserted streets.

As Adam turned down the road that led to Doc's, the lights along the route went out, the electrical service abruptly disrupted by the storm. His anxiety escalated as the sudden darkness seemed to swallow him up, and all he could think about was Natalie alone in that house with no power. The headlights barely penetrated the gray curtain of slicing rain as he drove down the blackened street and turned into the driveway. He could feel his heart hammering wildly against his ribs as he grabbed the battery-powered light and sprang out of the mud-encrusted truck.

The thin beam of light cut through the blinding torrent as Adam sloshed through a huge puddle of water, then took the stairs at the back of the house two at a time, the rain pelting against him. His jeans were clinging to his legs and his blond hair was plastered against his head when he entered the porch. Stripping off his slicker and boots, he banged on the door leading into the main house, his apprehension growing by the minute.

Thunder rattled the windows, drowning out the sound, and he knocked again. He paused for a moment, waiting for a response, but there was none. He called out, then tried the door. With a strange feeling of caution, he entered the living room, the light in his hand creating ominously shifting shadows. The room was empty and he paused again, trying to detect some sound that would tell him where she was. But the only sounds he could hear were those of the storm and his own frantic heartbeat.

"Natalie?"

Nothing.

Drawn by instinct, he turned toward the hallway that led to the bedrooms. "Natalie, it's Adam."

He thought he heard something, but it was so indistinct he wondered if he'd only imagined it. Straining to hear above the sounds of the storm, he followed the shaft of light down the black tunnel of the hallway and paused at the first doorway he came to. Slowly he swept the light around the room. It was furnished with a single bed and a dresser, and was obviously the room that Patrick was using. And it was empty.

"Natalie, where are you?"

But the only answer was the rain pounding on the roof and the wind rattling the windows. Adam shone the light down the hall, the beam moving across a closed door at the very end. Walking silently through the darkness, he grasped the knob and pushed the door open. It was Doc's study, and for a moment, Adam thought it was empty, as well. But as he moved, the shaft of light focused on Natalie, pinning her against the far wall.

Dressed in a blue-and-white striped nightshirt, she was standing in the corner by a heavy old-fashioned wooden filing cabinet, her body rigidly pressed against the dark oak, her eyes wide with alarm. A hideaway bed was situated beside the cluttered oak desk, and from the rumpled state of the covers, he assumed she had been in bed.

Adam stood by the door, his wet clothes clinging to him. "I didn't mean to frighten you, Nat, but I was worried when you didn't answer the door." She didn't move a muscle and Adam took another step toward her. As he moved, there was a flash of light against metal, and he froze, dumbfounded by what he saw.

She clutched a long flat letter opener, the blade thin and lethal. His eyes flew to her face, and it hit him that the expression he saw in her eyes went beyond simple alarm—this was paralyzing terror. He finally grasped what was happening. Her deep-seated fear of thunderstorms had gained control, and she was reliving the horror that had been inflicted on her years before. She was so overwrought that anything—a sound, a movement, a single careless act—could push her into reacting. Adam had never felt so ill-equipped in his life, yet somehow he managed to keep his voice calm when he spoke. "Don't be afraid of me, Natalie. I won't hurt you. I just came to talk."

There was not even the slightest indication that she had
heard him. Desperately trying to break through her wall of
fear, he moved a step closer and cautiously stretched out his
hand and murmured softly, "Give me the letter opener,
Natalie. I won't touch you or come any closer, I promise.
Just give me the letter opener."

Her hand moved, the gleaming blade shifting dangerously. Adam realized he dared not move an inch closer.
Slowly he withdrew his hand and backed away, his eyes
glued on the weapon as he frantically tried to think of some
way to reach her. He thought of Patrick. He tried to keep his
voice steady and nonthreatening. "Patrick was worried
about you—he said you'd be afraid of the storm."

There was only the slightest response, but it was there. He
saw it in her eyes. But then the fear was back and she shrank
away and it suddenly hit him that her terror was magnified
by the fact that she had no idea who was behind the light.
He didn't even want to think of the terrifying thoughts that
were going through her mind right then, but he knew he had
to say or do something that would penetrate her fear.

He was still searching for solutions when the lights came
back on. The lamp by the bed was small and sent out a
muted glow, but it was enough to illuminate Adam's face.
And with his expression taut with anxiety, he watched her,
desperately longing to go to her, knowing he didn't dare. His
voice was hoarse and heavily strained. "Please let me have
the letter opener, Nat. I'll leave if you want me to, but just
give me the letter opener."

For one awful moment, she continued to stare at him,
then as if waking up from a horrible dream, her expression
changed. A violent tremor shuddered through her, and she
whispered his name as she closed her eyes, her knees slowly
buckling beneath her.

Adam caught her before she went down. Holding her
around the waist in a viselike grip, he grasped the letter
opener, but she wouldn't let go. He caught her wrist and
drew her arm away from her body. "Let me have the letter

opener, Nat," he whispered gruffly. "You have to open your hand."

Natalie shivered again, then turned her face into his shoulder, her voice shaking so badly he could barely understand her. "I can't."

She was in such a state of shock she couldn't relax her muscles, and Adam had to pry her fingers from the carved ivory handle. As soon as he worked it free, he threw it amid the clutter on the desk, then gathered her into his embrace. An enervating rush of relief poured through him, and every muscle in his body went weak as he locked his arms around her, his heart slamming against his ribs. Suspended in the aftermath of fear, he began to tremble as he pressed her head against his shoulder, his face haggard. For a moment she remained stiff and unyielding, but then as though her strength suddenly evaporated, she melted against him.

Adam squeezed his eyes shut, and his breathing became labored. This was the first time he'd touched her, and the feel of her body against his unleashed a storm of sensations. He felt the kind of fulfillment he hadn't experienced for a very long time, and he savored that. This is what he'd been aching to do for so long—to hold her, to feel her warmth, her softness. He buried his face against her hair as he tightened his arms around her, longing to absorb her body into his.

Both of them were emotionally raw as they clung to each other, their bodies molded tightly together. But somewhere in the passage of time, Adam became aware of the fact that Natalie was still shivering. The last thing he wanted to do was let her go, but his common sense told him she should be wrapped in a warm, dry blanket, not getting more chilled from his wet clothes. Very reluctantly he forced himself to loosen his hold on her. But when he tried to ease her away from him, she wouldn't let go.

Her voice was barely audible as she whispered, "Please, Adam. Please. Don't go."

Her plea destroyed what little resolve Adam had, and with infinite tenderness, he gathered her tightly against him and murmured softly against her hair, "You're shivering, Nat, and I'm wet. You're going to get so cold." Hooking his thumb under her chin, Adam gently lifted her face. She looked absolutely ravaged, and her eyes were still haunted by fear. Only now it was a different kind of fear—the fear of what was yet to come.

He began to caress her back with long soothing strokes, his eyes bleak as he stared into the shadows. His touch was firm, yet each motion was slow and gentle. He waited until she was lulled into a state of calm before he said, "Doc told me the whole story tonight. That's why I came."

It seemed to take a second for his words to register, then she pulled away, trying to break free of his hold. Adam held her fast as her body stiffened, then a choked sound was torn from her as she twisted again. He cradled her closer and felt an awful tension build in her.

"No," she whispered brokenly. "He gave his word he would never tell you."

Adam pressed his cheek against the fragrant silk of her hair. "Don't, Nat. Don't feel that way. Nothing you can tell me is going to change how I feel about you."

He felt her tense, then she became stiff and unmoving. After a nerve-grating silence, she lifted her head and looked at him. Her eyes were dark and tormented as she met his steady gaze, searching for answers to her unspoken questions. He understood her uncertainty, her need for reassurance. Adam tenderly caressed her jawline. "I love you, Natalie. I've never stopped. And nothing is ever going to change that."

She stared at him numbly, as though unable to comprehend, then suddenly her eyes filled with tears, and she opened her mouth to speak. Adam covered her trembling lips with his thumb, afraid that she was going to say something to revoke those feelings. "Shh, Nat. Don't say anything now."

Natalie slipped her arms around his neck and clung to him as harsh sobs were wrung from her. Murmuring softly, Adam picked her up and carried her to the bed, then lay down beside her. His face was drawn as he tucked the quilt around her, holding her tightly as she finally vented the years of accumulated pain.

His hands were unsteady as he gently stroked her hair, his embrace all encompassing as he whispered, "It's all right, Natalie. Get it all out. Everything's going to be okay."

The only indication that she heard him was that she clung to him even more desperately. She wept until Adam didn't think he could stand it any longer, this tortured outpouring of a tortured soul. It was agony to witness.

The storm had moved down the valley and there was only the soft tattoo of rain against the windows when she eventually exhausted herself.

Adam held her for a while longer, then kissed her softly on the temple and murmured, "Don't be upset with Doc because he talked to me, Nat. He's been really concerned about you, and he decided it was time I knew what had happened."

She stirred weakly in his arms, her breath warm against his neck. "I don't think I could have ever told you. I wanted to, but I didn't know how. I still don't know how."

He stroked her hair, then let his hand rest against her neck. "Just start talking," he said quietly. "And tell me everything."

She didn't say anything for the longest time, then her voice low, her expression frighteningly impassive, she told him exactly what happened that night. There were times when Adam had to fight to keep from being physically sick, and there were times when his fury was so murderous he could barely contain it, but Natalie never knew what he was experiencing as she talked about the twisted and perverted degradation she had endured. He wanted to beat Carl Willard to a bloody pulp for the atrocities he'd inflicted on her; he wanted to destroy the man who had violated her so brutally, but somehow he managed to suppress those savage feelings. He could do nothing more than hold her and listen as she dredged up the horror of that night. At long last, she was dealing with the ugliness, the pain, the sickening revulsion, the awful sense of helplessness she had suffered at the hands of her stepfather. It became an excruciating kind of purge as she finally told it all. Every ugly, brutal, sordid detail.

Natalie's story only went as far as her arrival at Doc's, and sensing she had reached her limit, Adam didn't press her to go on. When she stopped talking, he simply gathered her closer against him and kissed her lightly on the temple. Slowly, almost hesitantly, she slipped her arms around his neck and pressed her face against his shoulder, and he could tell by her ragged breathing she was struggling to contain her emotions. Gently he stroked her trembling back, aware of the fine, delicate bone structure beneath his touch. It was, he realized with sickening clarity, a miracle that she had survived at all.

The dampness from his clothes had penetrated Natalie's thin garment, and she began to shiver again. Very carefully, Adam eased her away and wrapped the blankets more snugly around her. He brushed back the loose hair that was clinging to her face, savoring the smooth texture of her skin beneath his fingertips. She looked up at him, her eyes so hollow it made his chest ache to look at her. He wanted to lock his arms around her and crush her against him. He wanted to respond to the sudden rush of desire she aroused in him, and he ached to feel her naked body beneath his—warm, soft, yielding. But he battled those feelings, knowing now was not the time.

His voice was low and very husky when he finally spoke. "You're cold, Nat, and my clothes are wet. I think maybe I should get up—"

She turned her face against the curve of his neck as she implored, "Please stay."

An ache of tenderness surged up in him, awakening a fierce protectiveness that obliterated all else. All he was aware of was Natalie. Softly, so softly, he touched her face, and it was all he could do to keep from leaning over her and covering her soft mouth with his own. He could feel his pulse quicken and become thick and heavy as he lost himself in the mesmerizing depths of her eyes. A throbbing hunger unfolded in him. She was so lovely, and he wanted her so damned much. His life had been so empty and meaningless without her, and now that he had her back, he wanted nothing more than to lose himself in her and the galvanizing sensations she awakened in him. But he only caressed the lines of her face. The rest would come later.

Very gently he cupped her cheek in his hand and whispered unevenly, "I didn't meant to frighten you when I came in, Nat. I was in such a panic to get here, I never thought. I'm sorry."

Tears gathered along her lashes as she shook her head, then laid her hand on top of his. It was such a little thing, her touching him like that, but it drove the strength out of him. God, but he did love her.

"It wasn't just you, Adam," she whispered, her mouth trembling. "It was the storm. I'd been sleeping, and the thunder woke me. Then I heard you come in, and I didn't know who it was, and my imagination got the best of me." She closed her eyes and pressed her face against his hand. Her voice was so rough with emotion that her words were a shaky murmur. "I can't believe you came. It was like a dream when I realized it was you."

Her voice breaking on a sob, she turned her face against his shoulder, and Adam gathered her tightly to him. In spite of the hell they had just been through, he experienced an overwhelming sense of relief. Without realizing she'd done it, she had let him know that he still mattered to her, and he felt like someone had just lifted an enormous weight off his back.

He cradled her head on his shoulder, and the huskiness in his voice revealed how deeply he'd been moved. "I love you, Nat. You'll never know how much I've missed you. There was always a part of me that was so damned empty, and I hated you for doing that to me, for ripping my life apart." Cupping his hand against her neck, he turned his head and gazed down at her, his eyes solemn. "I should have known you'd never leave unless you'd been driven to. I doubted you, and that was the worst mistake I've ever made in my life."

With a choked denial, Natalie laid her fingers against his mouth, her eyes brimming with tears. "No, Adam, no," she pleaded. "Don't blame yourself. You couldn't think anything else."

Adam could tell by the panicky tone in her voice that she was on the verge of coming apart again, and with his hand on her jaw, his fingers thrust into her hair, he nestled her head more securely against the curve of his neck. "That's all behind us, Nat," he murmured softly as he rubbed her back, his strokes firm and comforting. "We can talk about it tomorrow. I'm taking you back with me, and we can spend some quiet time together up in the mountains." Deliberately keeping his voice soft, he continued to talk to her as he slowly massaged her back. It wasn't very long before her body relaxed heavily against his, and her breathing became deep and even. With his chin resting on the top of her head, he stared into the shadows across the room, keenly aware of the woman who lay sleeping in his arms. It was going to be a long, sleepless night.

THE MORNING was clear and bright, the droplets of moisture on the rain-drenched grass glistening in the early-morning sun. Adam stood looking out the kitchen window, his hair still damp from his shower, a steaming cup of coffee in his hand. He rested his shoulder against the wide window frame as he took a sip, his eyes darkly reflective. He had managed to get a couple hours sleep, but that was about all, and he was really feeling it.

The night had been an unusual kind of ordeal. Having Natalie so close yet in so many ways unreachable, had strained his willpower to the limit. The morning sky had just started to show the first colors of sunrise when he realized he had to get away from her before he gave in to desire. It was so hard to let go of her, but he had gently eased her out of his arms, then carefully covered her. She would never know what it cost him to walk out of that room.

Adam took another sip from the earthen mug, then exhaling heavily, he straightened and turned from the window. He went over to the stove and was refilling his cup when there was a sound behind him. He turned around to find Natalie standing in the kitchen doorway. She was still wearing the blue-and-white striped nightshirt, and Adam frowned when he recognized anxiety in her eyes.

Setting his cup on the counter, he went to her. He laid his hand against her jaw, his thumb caressing her ear as he murmured softly, "Hey, what's the matter? You look like you've had another scare."

She stared up at him for a second, then weakly rested her forehead against his chest. "I woke up and I was alone... and I thought you'd gone."

Drawing her into his arms, he held her securely, his expression darkening when he realized she was shivering again. He held her until the trembling stopped, then caught her face between his hands as he gazed down at her, his eyes solemn. "I'm not going to leave you," he said quietly. "If there's anything in this world you can be sure of, it's that I'm not going to leave you."

"Oh, Adam—"

Shaking his head slightly, he slowly stroked her bottom lip with his thumb, his gaze tender. "We're going to see this thing through together, Natalie. Something that happened eleven years ago can't be allowed to control our lives forever."

She looked up at him, her eyes glistening, and for the longest time they stood caught in their own private space, his hands warm and gentle against her face. Finally she closed her eyes, her breath catching raggedly. "Oh, Adam, is this really happening?"

He lowered his head and kissed her closed eyes, her tears warm against his lips. "It's happening. Years too late, but it's happening."

She tensed suddenly and pulled away from him. Folding her arms tightly in front of her, she turned her back to him, her hands tightly gripping her arms. Confused by her actions, he watched her, wondering why the sudden remoteness. "What's wrong, Nat?" he asked quietly as he went to stand behind her. She only shook her head. With the awful feeling that he was losing her, Adam grasped her by the shoulders and turned her to face him. "Don't shut me out, Natalie. I need to know what you're thinking."

It was a long time before she lifted her head to look at him, and Adam felt the first stirrings of dread when he saw her expressionless face. He knew if he didn't get her talking, she would withdraw completely. His voice was harsh and edged with alarm. "Damn it, talk to me! Don't do this to me again."

She met his gaze for a moment, then with an unnatural stiffness, she turned and walked away. She went to stand before the window, her arms still clutched around her. Her voice was devoid of expression when she finally spoke. "I left because I was afraid you'd kill Carl, that you'd destroy your life because of me. If I stay, I could end up destroying you myself."

"What in hell are you talking about?"

She turned, her face so pale it appeared waxen. She met his gaze with a steadiness that made him feel even more uneasy. "I don't think you want to know."

He stared at her, trying to determine how best to deal with this alien woman standing before him. He realized he would have to stay calm if he was going to get her talking. In an effort to camouflage his tenseness, he stuck his hands in the pockets of his jeans and leaned against the cupboard. "I do need to know, Natalie," he said quietly. "It's my life at stake, too, you know."

She held his gaze briefly, then she turned back to the window, her slender body silhouetted against the morning light. Suddenly, she seemed very vulnerable and alone. He longed to go to her, but he reluctantly held his ground. She had put distance between them, and he sensed it would be a foolish move to violate it. And he didn't want to make any stupid mistakes, not when their future happiness was at stake.

Finally she spoke, and her voice had a strange quality to it, as though she was thinking aloud. "No one will ever know what it was like for me that night. And that victim's complex will stay with me for the rest of my life. My own body repulses me now, and I feel dirty and soiled. I feel contaminated, as if I'm carrying some vile disease."

She fell silent for a moment, then she turned to face Adam. "I feel like that all the time, Adam. I've tried to conquer that feeling but it's always there." She looked down and absently started breaking away the brown edges on the geranium plant that was sitting on the window ledge. When she looked up at him again, he could see the bleakness in her eyes, and he realized how hard this was for her. There was a slight tremor in her voice when she finally continued. "But there's more to it than that. I've tried to develop a normal attitude about a relationship, but I can't." Her voice broke and she abruptly turned back to the window, her nails digging into her flesh as she grasped her arms. "The minute a man touches me, I remember Carl's hands all over me, and I want to be sick. That revulsion's always going to be there, Adam. Nothing can erase it. Even an examination by a doctor is an unbelievable ordeal for me, and I can't remember the last time I had a medical."

Feeling as though he'd just had the rug yanked out from under him, Adam stared rigidly at the floor. His anger ignited as he grimly digested this latest revelation. So the bastard had destroyed that, too—that intoxicating sensuality of hers that used to make his blood boil. She used to be so responsive, so electrifying, and now she couldn't even stand to be touched. He could kill Willard for that alone.

When her sexual self-esteem had been so debased, how could he ever convince her that she meant more to him than a bed partner? What argument could he use to make her realize she wasn't giving herself a decent chance? He stared bleakly at the floor, unaware that she was watching him. When he lifted his head, he caught a glimpse of the agony in her eyes before she quickly looked away. It was the same look she had when she was telling him the ugly details.

Feeling as though his body weighed a ton, he pushed himself away from the counter and went over to her. She resisted briefly when he tried to make her face him, but eventually, as though she dreaded meeting his gaze, she looked up. He touched her face and experienced a thin ray of hope when she didn't draw away. "How many people have you told about what happened that night?"

She frowned slightly, thrown off balance by his question. Wanting to make sure she didn't misunderstand it, he rephrased it. "Who knows exactly what he did to you?"

"Just you," she said softly.

"Why did you tell me, Nat? Why would you tell me and no one else?"

She shook her head, refusing to look at him.

Adam hooked his knuckles under her chin and raised her head. "Do you trust me, Natalie?" he asked, his eyes locked on hers.

She stared at him numbly for a second, then the dark haunted look in her eyes lightened almost imperceptibly. Her voice was trembling when she answered, "Yes, I trust you."

"Did you tell me because you trusted me?" Every muscle in his body tensed as he waited for her reply.

"Yes."

He grasped her face between his hands, his voice strained with urgency as he whispered, "Then trust me now, Natalie." He could see her waver, and his hold on her face tightened, his need to reach her vitally important. "Don't shut me out again. Needing you means more to me than just sex, Nat. And I know we can handle this if we want to. You trusted me before, now trust me about this."

There was so much longing in her eyes, but there was so much uncertainty, as well. She was a woman torn in two; her heart was pulling her one way, her mind was pulling her another. He could feel her start to tremble as she struggled with her warring emotions. She opened her mouth to speak, then closed her eyes as she took a ragged breath. When she looked at him again, he could see how close she was to yielding. "I can't do that to you, Adam. What if I can't deal with those feelings? What if they never change? I can't expect you to live the life of a monk."

Tension left his face as he gently brushed a lock of hair behind her ear, then smiled warmly. "And what if you can? And what if they do?"

"Oh, Adam...."

His expression altered and became very somber. "We'll deal with it one day at a time. And I promise you, we'll only go as far as you want—I'll never force you, Nat." His voice took on a new intensity as he whispered, "I love you, and I need you with me. I want to have my own family—you and Patrick. I want us to build a life together."

Natalie's eyes were almost black as she whispered, "I'm so scared."

Profound feelings—tenderness, compassion, love—filled him, and he found it very hard to speak. "I know," he said softly.

"I don't want to make you unhappy, Adam. I've hurt you so badly already."

Ever so gently, he caressed her face, his touch more eloquent, more poignant than words could ever be. His voice was husky with emotion when he spoke. "Nothing could hurt me more than having you leave again. Nothing could hurt worse than that."

There was a charged silence as she gazed up at him, then with her eyes brimming with tears, she whispered his name and stepped into his arms.

Adam felt as though his chest was going to explode as he enveloped her in a fiercely tender embrace, his control strained to the limit as wave after wave of emotion slammed through him. She had reached out for him, and that had been a conscious choice. Last night she had come to him out of fear, but today she'd come to him because that's where she wanted to be, and that was all that mattered to him. She was finally back. After so long she had finally come back. He felt so whole again, and so alive.

He didn't know how long they stood there, their bodies molded together in a clinging embrace, but he could have remained like that forever. But eventually he caught her by the shoulders and eased her away from him. Taking her hand in his, he silently led her toward the living room.

But as he sat down on the sofa, she pulled her hand free, and there was an anxious look in her eyes. In a nervous gesture, she pressed her hands against her thighs. Her voice was not very steady when she asked, "Why did you get up before me this morning?"

Adam stared at her for a second, then sighed heavily as he reached up and captured her hand again. He would never play games with her. It would be easier to lie, but that would get them nowhere. His expression was solemn. "You know why, Nat."

Adam watched her like a hawk. He saw her swallow and he saw the terrible look of uncertainty dull her eyes, and he could sense her shrinking inside herself. He knew she was struggling. He tried to pull her toward him, but she resisted, her face drawn. She swallowed again, then opened her mouth to speak, but he never gave her the chance. He tightened his hold as he said quietly, "Look, Nat, I said before that there was more to my needing you than sex, and I meant that. I'll admit it isn't easy not to respond, but if I have to choose between you and sexual satisfaction, it's going to be you."

Unaware that she was even doing it, she gripped his hand with a panicky strength that transmitted her fear, her guilt. "But I'm inflicting my... inability to function on you."

Ignoring her resistance, he drew her closer until her legs touched his. "Natalie, if you only knew how much pleasure I get from simply holding you. That alone gives me a kind of contentment I can't find anywhere else." His voice became very husky as he stroked the back of her hand with his thumb. "I couldn't sleep last night, partly because I really wanted you, but mostly because I wanted to be conscious of every second. I like having you in my arms." His eyes were warm and inviting as he slid his hand up her arm, then murmured, "And I really want to hold you now, Natalie." Unable to stand the vibrating tension any longer, Adam reached up and slipped his arm around her, then gently but firmly pulled her down.

Natalie melted weakly against him as he gathered her slender body across his lap. She buried her face in the curve of his neck, her breath warm against his skin. There was no need for words. Adam nestled her closer and shut his eyes, savoring the heady sensations she aroused in him.

It was a long time later that Natalie finally spoke. "I can't believe this is really happening, Adam. If you only knew how many times I thought about you holding me like this, especially when I was still in the hospital."

A haggard expression appeared on Adam's face as he opened his eyes and stared across the room, thinking about how much she had endured. In spite of how badly she was injured and how much pain she must have suffered, she still fought to have Patrick. He didn't know how to express his feelings or what words to use, so with his voice heavily strained by emotion, he simply said, "Thank you for having my son."

Bracing her arm against his chest, Natalie raised her head and looked at him, her eyes soft and misty as she whispered, "Thank you for giving him to me."

Her answer created another storm of emotions in Adam, and his eyes were smoldering with intensity as he smoothed his hand across her shoulder and up her neck. There was a tight ache in his throat as he traced the curve of her cheek. "Doc told me how you fought to have him, Nat. You could have so easily given in and had an abortion, but you didn't, and I'm so damned grateful you didn't." His voice broke roughly as he pressed the heel of his hand against her jaw. "He's such a terrific kid."

As though she was trying to erase the hard lines around his mouth, Natalie gently trailed her fingers along his lips. Her voice was just as gentle when she said, "He was the one thing I had that was yours, Adam. I was able to block everything else out as long as I could hang on to that thought."

Adam studied her face, his expression very grave. "Doc said you became hysterical when they suggested it would be safer for you if they performed an abortion." He hesitated, then went with his gut instinct. "There was more to it than simply losing the baby, wasn't there?"

Natalie stared at him, then she looked down at her hand, avoiding his penetrating eyes. In the softest of voices she whispered, "Yes."

He tightened his hold on her, trying to give her the courage to answer. "Tell me, Nat. I need to know."

A tremor shuddered through her, and Adam realized he had unwittingly confronted her with something that really upset her. He didn't expect her to answer, but she did. She kept her eyes averted, and her voice was riddled with humiliation. "It was all so ugly, but the worst was when...was when Carl was on top of me. I thought I was going to go out of my mind, it was so repulsive and awful, and there was so much pain. There aren't words disgusting enough to describe how filthy, how defiled I felt."

She lifted her eyes and looked at him, and a cold, murderous fury seethed in Adam when he saw how deep and how destructive her shame was. *The bastard,* he raged inwardly. *He should be tied down and castrated for what he did to her.* But he managed to keep those violent feelings from showing as he met her tormented gaze. As devastated as she was, there was still a thread of defiance in her trembling voice. "The only thing that I could hang on to that kept me sane was that your baby was growing in me, and no matter what he did, my womb was inviolate. He had the physical strength to force me to submit, he could do the most disgusting things to my body, but he could never make me pregnant."

Adam's insides convulsed into a hard sickening knot and he had to clench his jaws together to keep from reacting. His face felt numbed by shock as he stared at her, then with a low groan he hugged her tightly against him. If he had been able to keep his hands off her, if he hadn't got her pregnant in the first place, Carl Willard probably would have never assaulted her. And Adam had to live with the fact that he had been indirectly responsible for Natalie's attack.

Her touch was cool and gentle as she took his face between her hands and made him look at her. "Don't, Adam," she whispered huskily. "Don't start blaming yourself."

He had forgotten how adept she was at reading him, and he gave her a contemplative look. There was a smile in her eyes as she brushed back his hair with the same tender, maternal gesture he'd seen her use with Patrick. "Don't look so surprised," she admonished softly. "I spent too many years following you around when I was a kid not to know how you think, Adam Rutherford."

Adam found himself smiling back at her. "And a gawky little kid at that." She made a face at him, and the sickening sensation caused by her confession slowly eased as amusement lit up her eyes.

It was true. Natalie had trailed around behind him for a good many years. But Adam had never paid much attention to the girl who lived down the street. It wasn't until he'd been away at university for a couple of years and Natalie had a chance to grow up that he started taking notice. Only it was more than a simple case of noticing; it was more like getting hit by a train. The big discovery came during the annual raft races. It was just before one race was to start, and Adam and his crew were on the dock waiting to find out what heat they were in. He got their assignment and turned to go. And there she was.

His eyes alight with amused recollection, he leaned his head against the back of the sofa and stared off into space. "I'll never forget what a shock I got the first time I saw you after I got home from university that summer."

Natalie laughed and gave him a wry look. "I'm sure Mrs. Marshall never forgot what a shock *she* got, either."

"Yeah, that was great. She was such a cow—she was always giving somebody a hard time. I think the whole town cheered when she went in the drink." He looked at Natalie, his expression a mixture of tenderness and amusement. "There I was, minding my own business and I just happened to look up... and there was little Natalie Carter on another raft." His voice got husky, and his eyes darkened as he gazed at her, clearly recalling every detail. "Only it wasn't *little* Natalie anymore. She had on a sexy red harem costume and her hair was all bound in jewels, and she nearly blew my mind." The laugh lines around his eyes crinkled as he continued. "Since we were Viking warlords, I figured it would be very appropriate if we kidnapped her."

Natalie laughed and shook her head, her expression disbelieving. "Then would you please explain how Mrs. Marshall ended up in the river?"

Adam grinned. "I was so busy looking at you I didn't see her standing behind me, and I must have upended her with that big shield I was carrying. The funny part was, I was so intent on getting you off that raft that I honestly didn't realize what I'd done, at least not until I'd grabbed you and was heading to our own raft."

Natalie's eyes were still sparkling with laughter, and there was also a nostalgic glow that came from a very special reminiscence. "I couldn't figure out what you were up to when the five of you came swarming into the river. I was so surprised I couldn't even react when you grabbed me, threw me over your shoulder and carried me off."

"That's what warlords do."

"And I loved it." She became solemn, and the expression in her eyes softened as she touched his face. "And you took me to the dance that night, and you brought me star flowers to wear in my hair."

He was watching her with a heady intentness as he spoke, his voice very husky. "And you wouldn't dance with anyone else." For a moment they were caught in a spell of their own, then unable to handle the overwhelming tenderness that unfolded in his chest, Adam thrust his fingers in her hair and pressed her head against his shoulder. And for a long time, neither said a word.

Finally he sighed and combed his hand through her tousled hair. "We have so much to catch up on, Nat," he said with a touch of wishfulness. "It's been such a long, long time."

"And there's Patrick," she added softly.

"And Patrick." His expression changed as he looked at her. "Tell me about the photograph album."

She shrugged self-consciously and began toying with a button on his shirt. "I suppose it was my way of avoiding reality. As long as I was working on the album, I could keep you a part of my life." She looked up at him, her eyes darkened by the pain of remembering. "While I was in the hospital I was able to make believe that everything would be as it was before. But when I was discharged and Doc took me to live with Bea, I had to face the fact that I'd never see you again."

He frowned slightly. "If you thought you'd never see me again, why did you keep it up?"

She smiled again, her mouth trembling and her eyes suddenly brimming with tears. "Because I couldn't stop hoping."

Adam's hand wasn't quite steady as he brushed the tears from her long lashes, then kissed her gently on the corner of her mouth. He didn't know why it had become so vitally important, but he had to pick up where they had left off so many years before. "Marry me, Nat," he whispered softly against her mouth. "Marry me as soon as we can arrange it."

CHAPTER NINE

IT WAS MIDAFTERNOON when Adam and Natalie arrived at the trailer. Adam spotted Doc and Patrick down by the lake and it was apparent that neither of them heard the vehicle pull into the campsite. The old man and the young boy were standing on a rocky point just on the other side of the pier, and the way Doc was gesturing with his arms, it was obvious that either the fish were biting or he was telling one of his many fish stories. Adam grinned and glanced across the cab at Natalie. "He never changes, does he?"

She was looking toward the lake, the sunlight slanting across her face and neck. The brightness caught in the fine strands of hair that had been pulled free by the breeze whipping in from the open window, and her face was framed in a soft golden halo. There was an inflexible set to her shoulders that was unusual, and her hands were grasped together in her lap.

He leaned over and separated her hands, then laced his fingers through hers as he watched her profile. His tone was quiet when he said, "Let's hear it, Nat."

For a second she didn't respond, then Natalie turned to look at him, her finely sculpted face still showing signs of strain. She was wearing a dark blue cotton shirt and slacks, and the shade accentuated the dark shadows under her eyes. She looked exhausted. Her hold on his hand tightened when she met his gaze. "I don't know what to say to Patrick."

Leaning closer, he reached out with his free hand and brushed back a wisp of hair that was clinging to her cheek, then asked softly, "Why are you worried about it?"

She stared out the windshield, her expression bleak. "He was so upset in Calgary when he found out about you. How's he going to feel when we show up together? He's only little. He's going to wonder why it couldn't have always been this way, instead of his spending the first ten years of his life without his father."

Adam caught her chin and forced her to turn her head. His smile was warm and full of reassurance. "We've already had a talk about you, and I know for a fact you're crossing bridges that aren't even there."

The expression in Natalie's eyes changed as she watched him closely. "When was this?"

"Yesterday, before the storm."

Her voice was very strained. "What, exactly, did you talk about?"

"Everything." He turned so his legs were wedged between the bucket seats, then he hunched over and rested his elbows on his thighs. Taking both of her hands between his, he looked at her, his eyes darkening as he recalled the details of his talk with Patrick. "He asked me if I still liked you," he paused, his tone growing husky, "and I assured him I did—very much."

The intimacy between them became so charged that Adam couldn't hold her gaze any longer, and he lowered his head and began stroking the back of her hands with his thumbs. "I wanted to go back and get you right then and there, but he wanted to talk. He had a thousand questions that needed answering, but the thing that was most important to him was how we felt about each other. He needed to know that I cared about you and you cared about me. When I told him I still loved you, he said he didn't think you knew that, and he wanted to know if I was going to tell you." Adam finally looked up at Natalie, his eyes holding hers with a magnetic intensity. "When I said I was going to tell you how I felt, his whole attitude changed and he made it very obvious he wanted us together."

Natalie seemed dazed and her voice had a tremor of wonderment in it when she whispered, "You mean you'd decided on coming to get me *before* you knew what happened?"

"Yes."

Natalie stared at him for a minute, then she weakly leaned her head against his, her grip on his hands so tight that her nails dug into the backs of his hands. "Oh, Adam, you don't know what that means to me."

Extracting his hands from hers, Adam slipped his arms around her shoulders, his expression becoming grim when he felt how tense she was. She'd had about all she could take, and somehow he had to find a way to take the pressure off. Filled with an aching tenderness, Adam cupped the back of her head with his hand and nestled it in the curve of his neck. He kissed her temple, the fragrance from her hair filling his senses. "Come on, Nat," he teased softly. "You had my number when you were still practically in diapers. You must have known I'd be back."

He felt her take a shaky breath, then she raised her head and looked at him. There was laughter behind the tears clinging to her long thick lashes. "I was *not* in diapers."

He grinned at her as he dried her eyes with the side of his hand. "I had to see if I could get a rise out of you, that's all." He gave her another fleeting kiss, then said quietly, "Let's go see our son."

The sound of doors slamming carried to the lake, and Doc turned stiffly toward the small rise where he had parked his car. It was only a short space of time before Adam and Natalie appeared through the scattering of trees, walking hand in hand.

The old man felt as though a tremendous darkness had been lifted from his soul, and he experienced a profound gladness as he watched them. A hint of a smile played around Doc's mouth. Natalie looked at her companion, and Doc saw Adam lace his fingers through hers in a secure grip as he drew her closer to him. It was unquestionably a protective gesture, and Doc's expression altered as he took a closer look at her.

She looked as though she had been through a terrible ordeal. She was very pale and drawn, and Doc felt a sudden rush of concern. Perhaps it hadn't gone entirely as he had hoped. But he made sure his voice did not betray his anxious thoughts as he said lightly, "Trust the luck, Patrick. As soon as the fish are biting, we can count on someone horning in on our spot."

Adam grinned and pointed to the fishing rod Doc was holding. "If this is your spot, how come that gear looks so familiar?"

"A wee oversight," said Doc, a twinkle in his eyes as he turned to Patrick. "Shall we share our catch with them, lad, or shall we keep it for ourselves?"

But Patrick hadn't heard a word he said. He was standing stock-still, his eyes fixed anxiously on his parents. He licked his lips and nervously scrubbed his free hand against the seam in his jeans. "Hi," he said, his voice quavering.

Adam's attention was focused on his son. "Hi. So you're having a streak of luck, are you?"

"Yeah. We caught six trout already." Doc watched Adam and Patrick, realizing that the real exchange was unspoken, transmitted by sight between father and son. As though the silent message had been received, Patrick looked at his mother. "Would you like to use my rod, Mom?"

Doc could see how hard Natalie was fighting not to break down, but he wasn't the only one who was aware of her battle. Adam put his arm around her and pulled her against him. "I think your mom would rather watch for a while, Pat."

Patrick nodded and stepped back onto the flat rock he'd been standing on, his movements suddenly stiff and awkward as he cast his line. He started to reel it in, then stopped, his voice muffled. "I tangled it again."

Adam's face was showing signs of enormous strain as he gave Natalie a reassuring squeeze, then went over to his son and crouched beside him. He took the rod from Patrick and started unwinding the tangled line as the child remained standing rigidly beside him. Doc heard him murmur something to the boy, but Patrick made no response. Adam said something else, and the boy turned toward him and with a muffled sob, threw himself into his father's arms. Doc glanced at Natalie, but looked away again when he saw the naked anguish in her eyes. She had endured so much.

Adam picked up Patrick and started toward her. "It's okay, Patrick," he heard him whisper against the boy's hair. "Everything's going to be okay." As Adam crossed the rocky point with his son in his arms, he never took his eyes off Natalie, his expression taut with concern. Shifting Patrick's weight onto his hip, he reached for her, and like a magnet to metal, she went to him. Everything he was feeling was rawly exposed on Adam's face as he held them both in a crushing embrace. He was unmistakably a man shielding his own. Natalie shuddered and pressed her face against his shoulder. There was another stifled sob, and Patrick dragged one arm free and slipped it around his mother's neck. At long last, father, mother and son were united. And with his vision blurred, Doc walked away, leaving these three special people alone in this very private and moving reunion.

ADAM WAS AMAZED at the resilience of his son. Half an hour after that first emotional encounter, Patrick was acting as if it was the most ordinary thing in the world to have his mother and father together. But Adam was also aware of the many times Patrick stopped whatever he was doing and visually checked on them both, then continued on in obvious high spirits.

Natalie, however, was a different story. She was so drained she hardly had the energy to move. Remembering a hammock he had stored in one of the compartments in the trailer, Adam dug it out and strung it between two enormous poplar trees near the shore of the lake. Without giving her a chance to protest, he picked Natalie up and dumped her in it. Patrick thought that was great. The idea of someone being big enough and strong enough to put his mother to bed delighted him to no end.

Realizing that his son would soon grow bored with nothing to do, Adam decided to build a fire pit not far from where he'd hung the hammock. As they started hauling slabs of shale from the edge of the lake, Doc set about cleaning the fish for supper and a quiet harmony settled on them all.

The bright blue sky was cloudless, providing an unblemished background for the gray and purple fortresses of the distant snowcapped mountains, the dark green forests creeping densely up their granite slopes. It was such a calm, clear day that it was hard to believe there had been a violent storm the night before. Because of the location of the isolated little valley, the campsite had been relatively protected. The only evidence of the violence was a new crop of pinecones lying on the ground beneath the trees, and a few small broken poplar branches scattered across the clearing.

A light summer breeze sighed through the leaves and ruffled the surface of the lake, sending brilliances of sunlight dancing across the surface and small waves lapping at the shore. A birdcall rang clearly through the trees, the shrill notes seeming to hang suspended in the crystal-clear air. Adam noticed it all. There was nothing like it, this deep sense of oneness he had when he was in the high country.

With his hot, flushed face streaked with grime, Patrick dropped the last rock beside his father, his bare torso clammy with sweat. "Are we finished?"

"That should do it, I think."

Patrick crouched and watched his father work the flat slab into place. He absently brushed a mosquito from his forehead then scratched a bite on his arm. "Mom's asleep."

Wiping his hands on his jeans, Adam looked at the hammock, and then at his son. "I know."

"Is she sick or something? She never sleeps in the afternoon."

"Your mom has been under a lot of pressure lately. She just needs some quiet time."

That answer seemed to satisfy Patrick. He picked up a rock and threw it in the lake, then sat watching the ripples spread. "Where's Grandpa gone?"

"I think he's gone for a walk along the creek."

"Oh." Patrick pulled out a handful of grass and made a little pile, then picked up a twig and started drawing circles in the dust.

Adam leaned back and rested his hands on his thighs, a touch of knowing amusement in his eyes as he studied his son. "What is it, Pat?"

Patrick fidgeted some more, then looked at his dad. "Are you and Mom really getting married?"

"Don't you think it's about time we did?"

Grinning broadly, Patrick stretched out on his stomach, his head propped in his hand. "Yeah, well. But not many kids get to go to their parents' wedding."

"Yeah, well," Adam responded dryly.

"Will my name be Rutherford after?"

"Do you want it to be?"

Patrick let out a sigh of exasperation. "You answer questions with questions just like Mom does."

Adam grinned as he stood and reached for his shirt, which was hanging on a bush. "Well, what do *you* want?"

"Rutherford."

"Then that's what it'll be."

Patrick rolled over on his back and watched the leaves turning and twisting overhead. "Will we live here?"

"That's something the three of us are going to have to talk about, Patrick. If your mom wants to keep working, we'll settle in Los Angeles, and if not, we may go somewhere else. We might even decide to stay here." Adam did up a few buttons on his shirt and tucked it in his jeans before he asked, "Would it really bother you if you had to move away from your friends in California?"

"If we moved, we could go back for visits, couldn't we?"

"Definitely."

Patrick looked up at his dad, and it struck Adam again how much his son's eyes were like Natalie's. The boy moved his head in a gesture of approval. "Then that's okay." Patrick brushed another mosquito off his face, then pulled out a long stem of grass and chewed the end. "Will you be gone lots? Like when you go to Africa and South America and places like that?"

Adam braced his arm against the rough trunk of a tree as he gazed solemnly at his son. "I'm not going on any long shoots unless you and your mom can come, Patrick. I want you with me, not left at home."

Patrick's eyes lit up. "Hey, you mean I might get to go to Africa?"

"Very likely."

"Wow," he breathed, his eyes wide with wonder. He fell silent as he watched the sunlight dancing across the lake, a faraway look in his eyes. Several minutes passed, then he sat up and drew up his knees. Grass and dead leaves were clinging to his damp skin and tangled in his blond hair. With jerky little movements, he started pulling single blades of grass from a clump of sod that had been dug from the hole for the fire pit. "Dad?"

"What?"

He wouldn't look at his father as he continued to pluck nervously at the grass. "I'm really glad . . . about you and Mom and everything."

There was a brief silence before Adam spoke, his voice very husky. "So am I, Patrick."

As if he were trying to avoid any more awkward conversation, Patrick scrambled to his feet and picked up the small collapsible spade they had used to dig the fire pit. "I'll go put this back with your backpack."

Adam smiled knowingly as he ruffled his son's hair. "If you bring me back my big brown camera case and the camera I gave you, I'll teach you how to use the telephoto lens."

"Oh, boy," Patrick exclaimed, and he raced off toward the trailer.

Adam watched him dodge through the trees, then sticking his hands in the back pockets of his jeans, he went over to the hammock. Natalie was still asleep, her chest rising and falling shallowly, her lips parted. She had her head turned toward him, the side of her face resting on her hand, her long lashes fanning out against her cheeks. Her fair hair was pulled back in the usual chignon, but the movement of her head against the coarse weave of the hammock had loosened the pins and strands had pulled free.

Sunlight winked through the fluttering leaves, dancing across her face in patches of light and catching in her hair. She looked very delicate as she lay sleeping, a soft flush coloring her cheeks. Adam's gold-flecked eyes absorbed every detail. Drawn by a need to touch her, he gently traced the long scar along her jaw and wondered what other scars her body carried. As he lightly brushed the back of his knuckles against her neck, she stirred and slowly opened her eyes.

For an instant she stared at him, then she smiled sleepily and covered his hand with her own. "Hi," she murmured drowsily.

It was all Adam could do to keep from responding to a sudden rush of desire. Her mouth was so damned tempting, and he ached to lean over and cover it with his own and experience the intoxicating moistness. He could remember her clinging to him and moaning softly, her mouth hot and yielding, and he could remember how she'd move beneath him, her body seeking the rhythm of his. He could remember it so vividly....

"What's the matter?" she whispered, her eyes suddenly alert.

Curling his fingers around her hand, he forced himself to smile down at her, his voice slightly gruff. "Nothing's the matter, Nat. I was just remembering, that's all."

"Remembering what?"

His expression softened as he gazed at her. "You," he said simply. And unable to resist any longer, he bent over and cupped his hands around her face, then kissed her softly on the corner of her mouth, the contact testing his endurance to the limit. Adam didn't know if he would have had the strength to draw away if he hadn't heard Patrick coming. But he doubted it.

His heart was pounding violently, and he inhaled very slowly, then straightened. "I was going to turn Patrick loose with a camera. Would you like to come?"

Natalie's voice was unsteady. "I'd love to." Grasping Adam's outstretched hand, she let him pull her out of the hammock and onto her feet. She straightened her shirt, then raised her arms to tidy her hair.

Adam caught her wrists and held them. Loose wisps of hair framed her face and curled against her neck. It was soft and feminine and utterly appealing. "Don't," he whispered huskily.

She stared at him blankly for a moment, then looked away, a light blush coloring her cheeks.

Patrick came tearing across the small clearing, the camera bag slamming against his legs, another small case around his neck, and a plastic bag clutched in his hand. "I got it, Dad. I brought my camera case, too." His chest heaving and his breath coming in deep gasps, he stopped in front of his father. He set the larger case on the ground, then he lifted the other strap over his head and set that case down beside his father's. He wiped the palm of his hand on his jeans as he looked up at his mother. "Are you coming too, Mom?"

Natalie nodded, then indicated the large bag of shelled sunflower seeds he was holding. "Where did you get those?"

Patrick grinned as he held the bag up for his father to see. "Grandpa was in the trailer making tea, and he said you'd lash him to death with your tongue if you caught him eating these. He made a mistake and got the salted ones, so he said I'd better take 'em." He opened the bag and took out a handful, then funneled them into his mouth. "He said the chipmunks and squirrels would like them."

Natalie raised her eyebrows in skepticism, then commented dryly, "Not to mention yourself."

With a look of utter innocence, Patrick held out the bag toward her. "Want some?"

Biting back a smile, Natalie narrowed her eyes at him as she reached into the bag. Patrick offered the seeds to his father, then squatted and opened the Velcro fasteners on the camera cases, removing a camera from the small one.

Wiping his hands on his jeans, Adam crouched beside the boy and took the camera Patrick handed him, then opened a padded compartment in the large case and lifted out a long-barreled lens. Patrick watched intently as his father removed the regular lens from his camera and placed it in the compartment. Adam attached the telephoto lens, then handed the assembled equipment to Patrick. "I think that's going to be too heavy for you to hold steady, Pat. You'll likely have to use a tripod so your pictures aren't blurred."

Patrick nodded, then listened intently as his father explained the basic mechanics and showed him how to use the lens. The boy asked a few questions, then tried to focus on a weathered stump that was sticking out of the water. Leaving Patrick to do some experimenting, Adam lifted out another camera from the case, then picked up both bags and slung the straps over his shoulder. "You'd better stick that insect repellent in your pocket, Patrick, and put on your shirt. With the rain last night, the mosquitoes will be thick in the bush."

"Oh, okay." Patrick did as he was told, then held the bag toward his mother. "Will you carry this, Mom? I'll need both hands."

She took it from him, then shook her head ruefully as she brushed his sweat-dampened hair off his dirt-streaked face. "You certainly are not the cleanest kid I ever laid eyes on."

Patrick gave her a pained look and groaned. "Aw, Mom. It's summer holidays."

Adam was laughing as he held out his hand toward Natalie. "Give it up, Mom. A little bit of dirt gives him character."

"Yeah, Mom," echoed Patrick, an impish grin splitting his face as he danced along the trail in front of them. "It gives me character."

Taking Adam's outstretched hand, Natalie gave him a loaded look. "I hope you remember this when his ears rot off."

"If they haven't rotted off by now, I think he stands a good chance of hanging on to them."

Patrick's eyes were sparkling mischievously as he turned around to look at them. "And I really need 'em if I ever have to wear glasses, right, Dad?"

Adam laughed again. "Among other things."

"Does all this mean you're going to wash them?" Natalie asked, trying not to smile.

"Oh boy," said Patrick, woefully shaking his head.

The deer trail emerged from the trees and ran along the lakeshore for a short distance. Patrick picked up a small rock and threw it in the lake, the ripples radiating along the smooth surface of the water.

Adam squinted and gave Natalie a calculating look, a definite gleam in his eyes as he said very casually, "Speaking of washing, how about the supper dishes?"

She gave him a puzzled look, then a light began to dawn in her eyes as he bent over and picked up a smooth flat pebble. He handed it to her. "Supper dishes?" he said again.

Her face lit up and she took the pebble from him. "Supper dishes," she agreed with a grin.

Patrick had been watching his parents, a totally confused look on his face. "What? What do you mean 'supper dishes'? I don't understand."

"A long time ago, your mom and I used to have contests skipping stones. We'd make certain deals, and if I lost, I had to do whatever she'd challenged me to do, and if she lost, she had to do whatever I'd challenged her to."

"Hey, that's neat."

Adam thought so, too. That was how he'd finally managed to get Natalie to go skinny-dipping with him the first time. And as he'd recalled, he'd never skipped stones like that before, and he certainly had never done it since. That was some afternoon.

He was smiling to himself as he remembered that episode in living color. Natalie's soft laugh interrupted his musings. He glanced at her and found her watching him with an amused, knowing look. And he could tell by the gleam in her eyes that she had tuned in to his thoughts. "But then, Adam," she said heartlessly, "there was the time that you ended up painting three hundred feet of fence."

He laughed, positioned the pebble on his fingers and made a smooth side-arm pitch. The stone skipped five times. "Beat that lady, or you do dishes."

"That's not fair," she protested. "I haven't done this for years. I need a warm-up."

"No dice. Put up or shut up."

She gave him a menacing look, then carefully selected a rock. Aiming for the best reflecting angle, she bent to the side, and the pebble kissed across the surface, disappearing after six hits. Natalie laughed and clapped her hands, then made a doleful face at him. "Poor Adam. Has to do the dishes."

Undaunted, Adam picked up another pebble and slammed it into her hand. "Supper."

"Supper," she agreed.

Patrick straddled a piece of driftwood, an impish look on his face. "Popcorn," he challenged.

Adam and Natalie laughed, and his father handed him a rock. "You're on, kid."

They skipped stones until they lost track of who was to do what for whom, and the grand finale was a niner by Adam, who asked Natalie if she felt like a swim.

She gave him a pithy look, and he laughed. Firmly clasping her hand in his, he drew her beside him as they started walking again, wending their way through the trees.

Like most small boys, Patrick was enthralled with bugs. With the help of his father, he managed to photograph a colony of ants, a spider weaving a fragile deadly web between some slender reeds, and two water beetles walking across the still water of a small stagnant pond, their hairlike feet leaving minute dimples in the water. Patrick was fascinated as his father explained the role each insect played in nature, and was obviously awed by how much his father knew.

They had happened on a secluded clearing where the stream burbled into a clear mountain pool and the soft golden sunlight filtered through the trees in shafts. A thick growth of ferns spread beneath broad trunks of giant fir trees, the delicate fronds rimming a small lea that ran along one side of the creek. The grass grew lush and green in the shallow hollow, the humus soil retaining moisture from the spring flood. Wild lupine grew thickly, their stocks of blue flowers swaying lightly in the breeze, and just beyond the grass, before the ferns dominated, a path of yellow violets grew among their shiny heart-shaped leaves. On the other side of the creek, a thicket of wild dogwood bushes crowded against a rocky outcrop.

Adam showed Patrick where the long grass in the middle of the thicket was flattened, explaining that some wild animal, probably a deer, had lain there. Dragonflies flitted through the clearing, their blue gauzy wings glinting opalescently in the rays of light.

Patrick squatted and watched intently as one lit on a branch near the ground, its fragile wings outstretched. "What do they eat, Dad?"

"Mosquitoes, mostly." Adam checked the light meter attached to his camera strap, then pulled the tripod from the side strap on the camera case. "With the angle of the light, the colors in the wings should show up. Do you want to try it?"

Patrick nodded, and he and his father prepared to photograph. Natalie watched them for a moment then wandered deeper into the clearing. Adam noticed her move away and thought how perfectly she fit into this enchanted little dell in the wilderness. He could have watched her indefinitely, and a little reluctantly, he dragged his attention back to his small son.

Patrick had photographed the dragonflies and was focusing his attention on a furry caterpillar when a familiar sensation crept up the back of Adam's neck and he turned his head.

Natalie was standing motionless at the edge of the clearing, her hand outstretched. Downwind, and camouflaged in the shadows, were a doe and her fawn. All eyes and ears, the deer watched Natalie as she started talking to them in soft singsong tones, coaxing them toward her with the hypnotic lure of her voice.

Adam had forgotten her rare gift to instill trust in animals. Ever since she was a small child, she seemed to possess some magical power that enabled her to communicate with them, and tame or wild, they seemed to know she'd never harm them. It had amazed him the first time he'd seen her do it, and it amazed him now. Moving cautiously, he reached over and took the camera with the telephoto lens from Patrick's hands. Adam's actions caught his son by surprise, and Patrick turned to protest. Adam clapped his hand over his mouth to silence him, then pointed toward Natalie.

Patrick turned, his mouth dropping open. Adam caught him by the shoulder and held him immobile. "Watch, Patrick," he said in a barely audible whisper. "She'll get the doe to come right up to her." Patrick glanced at his father, not quite believing him, then he looked back at his mother. She was standing very still, her hand outstretched, and Adam realized she was holding a handful of sunflower seeds. She kept talking in the same quiet tone, and slowly the adult deer came a step closer, then another, and another. The doe hesitated, then stretched out her neck and very daintily nuzzled the sunflower seeds from Natalie's hand.

Patrick's eyes nearly fell out of his head. He stood rooted to the spot as the animal licked the salt from his mother's palm. Adam shot several frames, then wanting to get a close-up of her, he zoomed in on Natalie's face. Intent, expressive and so lovely. And carrying a long jagged scar along her jaw.

Adam's insides twisted into a hard knot as he suddenly recalled one particularly sordid and graphic description Natalie had numbly related the night before. He clenched his teeth, fighting to contain his anger, his frustration, his bitter sense of helplessness. He grimly wondered what he would do if he ever came face-to-face with Carl Willard. Would he be able to keep from killing him? He doubted it.

That grisly thought stuck with Adam for the rest of the day, and he became quiet and withdrawn. At supper he was aware that Natalie was watching him, her eyes anxious, but he couldn't snap out of the dark introspective mood that had settled on him.

He knew he needed some time alone, so as soon as Doc and Patrick were ready to go to bed, he took his bedroll out to one of the cabins. But sleep eluded him as his mind focused on one particular realization; he had to face some hard cold facts about himself. He was the kind of person who did not forget easily. And because of this characteristic, he now had to face the fact that the anger, the frustration, the sense of helplessness he felt about Natalie's assault would always be there, and those feelings would rise up to haunt him at the most unexpected times. Like this afternoon. She had been stuck with the horror and brutality, the pain and suffering; he had been stuck with the haunting aftermath.

The sounds of night filtered through Adam's bleak thoughts. The dilapidated cabin was near the lake, and through the paneless windows he could hear the gentle lap of water against the rocky shore. The leaves rustled softly overhead, and an owl hooted in the distance. There had been a threat of rain when he had left the trailer, but now the night sky was sprinkled with a canopy of stars, and a spectral wisp of cloud drifted across the moon.

The chill of the alpine air touched his skin as Adam stared out the rectangle of the door, the solitude of darkness laying an eerie stillness on the forest. He lay on his back, his fingers laced behind his head as he peered into the night, trying to ward off disturbing thoughts of Natalie. Today was the first time he'd really seen her as Patrick's mother. He had caught glimpses of her in that role when they'd gone to Calgary, but the situation had been so strained and unnatural, he hadn't seen the true picture.

It could not have been easy for her raising a son on her own. Especially a son like Patrick, who had an endless store of energy. Adam was aware that the boy could have easily ended up being one of those kids who approached everything at full speed without taking the time to follow through on anything. But Natalie had used the boy's natural curiosity to channel that energy, and consequently he had turned out to be a bright, intense kid who had been encouraged to develop a broad range of interests. She had done a remarkable job of raising him. And Adam wished like hell he'd been a part of the process.

Feeling suddenly very empty, he stared unseeingly into the darkness, trying to block out other images of Natalie that threatened to inundate him. Images he didn't dare let develop.

HE DIDN'T KNOW how long he'd been asleep. The night was still smothered in darkness, but something, some foreign sound had penetrated his sleep. With his senses suddenly alert, he opened his eyes and turned his head toward the door. His voice was thick with sleep as he said softly, "Natalie?"

The shadow at the door moved and slipped soundlessly into the cabin and dropped to his side. He reached out toward her, his hand touching her bare arm. He could feel her shivering. "What's the matter?" he murmured as he raised up on one arm.

She exhaled slowly, as though she was trying to make herself relax. "Nothing. I—I just wanted to make sure you were all right. It got so cold."

Adam slid his hand up her arm and across her back. "Come here, Nat. Let me hold you." He could feel her resist as he threw back the sleeping bag that covered him. "I just want to hold you," he said softly as he overrode her resistance and drew her down. He pulled the sleeping bag around her, then lying back down, he cradled her tightly against him. "Now tell me what's wrong," he whispered against her hair.

"Nothing's wrong, Adam," she said as she pressed her face against his neck, her breath warm against his skin. "I woke up, and for a minute I didn't know where I was. And I had this awful feeling that I had been dreaming this."

Quietly savoring the feel of her in his arms, he started to massage her back. "But there was more to it than that, wasn't there?" he asked astutely.

She lay so still he couldn't even feel her breathing, then she moved her head, and he knew she was staring off into the darkness. "Yes, I guess there was."

"Like what?"

She didn't say anything for a moment, then she answered quietly—too quietly. "So much has changed, Adam, and I know that nothing will ever be as it was."

There was an undertone there that made him uneasy, and his own voice was strained. "What are you driving at, Natalie?"

Again she hesitated before she answered, only this time he could hear the apprehension. "What if we can't work things out, Adam? What if I never get over my...inhibitions?"

Relieved that her fears were not his own, he cuddled her closer and whispered, "I told you before not to cross bridges, Nat. Given enough time, I know we can overcome anything."

"But how much time?" He detected a thread of fear as she continued, her voice so taut it was trembling. "You can't be expected to stand around waiting while I decide whether I can come to terms with my problems or not. It's too much to ask."

"Don't doubt my feelings," he admonished gently.

"Oh Adam, I don't. But what scares me more than anything is that you could end up loathing me."

He slid his hand up the nape of her neck, his fingers tunneling into her hair as he pressed her head against his shoulder. "That isn't going to happen—ever," he said, his voice low and sure.

Raising up on one elbow, Natalie laid her hand against his jaw, her long slim fingers caressing his neck. The moonlight from the door make it possible for him to see the shadowy outline of her face as she leaned against him. Her voice was husky and soft. "I know you, Adam. I know how much you need the physical aspects of a relationship." Her hand pressed against his face and her voice became very uneven. "I knew exactly what you were feeling this afternoon when you woke me up. I could feel that sexual tension in you the minute you touched me. And how long can I expect you to go on denying your own masculinity because of me?"

Adam didn't know. He really didn't know. And now was a hell of a time to consider it. With her so soft and warm against him, with him fighting to clamp down on the hunger she aroused in him, with his body responding to the nearness of hers.

He inhaled slowly, trying to calm his laboring heartbeat, then whispered raggedly, "We'll work it out, Nat. We have to. I need you in my life." And somehow, he had to keep believing that they could work it out. Because he didn't know how he would survive if they couldn't.

CHAPTER TEN

ADAM CAME OUT of the office at the back of the drugstore and started walking up the side aisle between the display racks of greeting cards and paperback novels. He was wearing tight jeans, hand-tooled cowboy boots and a plaid shirt that was open at the neck. His tawny sun-streaked hair was windblown and he was darkly tanned, and his heavily tinted sunglasses added a touch of mystery to his very masculine face. Moving with the saunter of an athlete, he came toward the front of the store, a preoccupied look on his face as he rolled back the cuffs of his sleeves.

Stella had been busy restocking the supply of cigarettes at the front counter, but she stopped what she was doing and watched him come toward her. Her eyes narrowed with appreciation. Here was a man who bloody well knew what being a man was all about. His masculinity was so blatant, he may as well have had Virile stamped on his forehead. With a dramatic sigh, she took the gum out of her mouth, dropped it in the wastepaper basket and shook her head in awe. "Gawd, you should be flexing your muscles in underwear ads. Give us poor underprivileged women a chance to drool over your body."

Adam gave her a suspicious look, as if he thought she'd just lost her mind. There was a wicked gleam in her eyes as she raised her gaze to the ceiling, beseeching some greater power. "Why wasn't he born twenty years sooner? I ask you...why?"

Adam grinned and took off his sunglasses. "You know somebody always screws up the logistics, Stella." He was standing with his feet apart and his legs locked, and his shirt pulled taut across his shoulders as he folded his arms across his chest.

She gave him another wistful glance, then sighed again and raised her hands in a gesture of futility. "Ah, well. Maybe next time around." She broke open another carton of cigarettes, then crumpled up the wrap and threw it in the garbage. She started filling the slot in the showcase. "Did you finish your phoning?"

Adam nodded and dropped a handful of bills on the counter. "Yeah. This should cover the long-distance charges."

Stella eyed the money then gave him a cynical look. "Where did you call—China?"

His smile didn't quite reach his eyes as he shook his head. "Not quite."

She studied him. "Where *did* you call?"

Adam was straightening the rolls of breath mints that were displayed in a rack on the front of the counter, the sunlight from the window highlighting the blond hair on his darkly tanned arms. "I phoned Vital Statistics in Alberta to find out how we go about getting Patrick's name changed."

"And?"

He glanced up at her, his expression relaxing slightly. "It's a lot less complicated than I expected. Both Natalie and I have to make a statement in writing that Patrick's my son. Once the bureau receives that, the existing records are changed, registering me as his natural parent. After the legalities are completed, a new birth certificate is issued in the name of Adam Patrick Rutherford."

Stella frowned as she leaned against the counter. "You mean Natalie didn't list you as his father?"

"She wasn't allowed to unless I had acknowledged in writing that Patrick was mine."

Stella raised her eyebrows in an expression of mild surprise. "I didn't know that." She squinted as she watched Adam's face, then she casually tidied the countertop. "And who else did you call, Adam?'' she asked a little too innocently.

He looked at her sharply, his expression guarded. Stella took a calculated guess. "By any chance, you didn't try to track down Carl Willard, did you?"

Adam stared at her, then he glanced away, his jaw rigid. "As a matter of fact, I did."

She snorted. "I take it it wasn't a social call to invite him to the wedding." Adam made no comment, and Stella studied him intently as she absently tapped the glass top of the display case with her long scarlet nails. "So," she said very softly, "Natalie wasn't in the accident after all."

Adam's gaze riveted on her. She gave him a mirthless smile. "Don't look so stunned, Adam. Something never sat quite right with me when Jean died, but I had no choice but to take the whole story at face value. But ever since you blew back into town, it's been bugging the hell out of me. The whole thing just seemed too... tidy."

Adam's eyes were flashing as he looked away. Stella continued, her attention focused on his profile. "After both you and Natalie turned up, I started thinking about it again. The more I thought about it, the more holes I could see. There seemed to be only one logical explanation, and I thought I'd better do a little quiet digging so I could head you off at the pass if I had to." She hesitated for a moment and glanced down, mulling something over. When she looked up, her eyes were very sober. "I found out Carl Willard's in a nursing home in Ontario," she said quietly. "He had a bad stroke six years ago that left him partially paralyzed and unable to speak."

It was a long time before Adam turned to face her, but when he did, his eyes were cold and his voice was harsh as he ground out, "I could kill him, Stella. I could break his neck with my bare hands."

Stella's tone was caustic. "And put that son of a bitch out of his misery? Don't be stupid." Her expression softened as she came around the counter and went over to him. Laying her hand on his arm, she said earnestly, "Leave it, Adam. A higher power has already dealt with him. He could spend the next twenty years locked up in that body, unable to speak, unable to move. Just think about it—it's a punishment worse than death. So leave it be. Get on with your life."

Adam still wouldn't look at her. "How did you figure it out?"

"Gut instinct, I guess. He always bothered me, and then there was the way he dropped out of sight after the fire. He wasn't the type to walk away from a good job. And Doc would get so riled if anyone mentioned his name." She gave Adam's arm a little shake, trying to snap him out of his grim mood. "Don't dwell on it, Adam. He can't ever hurt her or anyone else again, and that's all that matters."

Adam looked down at her, his eyes bleak, then sighed heavily. "I don't know if I'll ever be able to think about him without wanting to kill him."

"You will. In time, you will."

Tipping his head back, he wearily massaged the back of his neck. "I sure hope you're right."

"Of course I'm right." She gave him another pat, then went behind the counter. "Now wipe that hangdog look off your face and look sexy. Natalie's coming across the street."

Adam gave her a rueful grin. "Lord, but you're bossy."

Stella waved her hand in an airy gesture. "It's from working with Doc all these years. It just doesn't seem right without him in here every day, giving orders."

"I thought he'd retired."

Stella shook her head. "Not really. He still owns the business, and he wanders in here from time to time to make sure I haven't run it into the ground."

The bell on the door jangled and Natalie entered. Stella would have dropped dead before she'd ever admitted it, but underneath her cynicism and flippant manner, she was a dyed-in-the-wool romantic. And seeing these two people together left her feeling very misty-eyed, especially when she noticed how the expression on Adam's face softened when Natalie smiled up at him.

Blinking furiously, Stella blew her nose then plastered a bright smile on her face. "Well it's about time you got here. I'm going to take you two to lunch."

Natalie grasped her chest and grimaced. "You mean you're going to make us eat at the coffee shop?"

Stella pursed her lips and gave Natalie a very dry look. "Serves you right. I've had to put up with Mick's cooking for years. You can stick it for one lousy meal." Mick and his brother owned the hotel, and Mick ran the coffee shop. He was an excellent chef, but for some reason, both Natalie and Stella had always got some sort of perverse delight out of giving him a hard time.

Adam was grinning as he held the door open for the two women. "I think I'm going to clue poor old Mick in on how you two deride his cooking."

Stella sniffed. "Ha. I could teach him a thing or two."

"Oh, I'm sure you could," Adam said smoothly. "And not just about cooking, either."

The redhead gave him a long narrow look, then directed her attention to Natalie. "Any change in plans for the wedding?" she asked hopefully.

Natalie slanted an amused look up at Adam, then turned to her old friend, a tone of warning in her voice. "There aren't going to be any plans, Stella."

Stella let out a heavy sigh. "Damn, I wish you kids would let me organize a do. It doesn't seem right, just five of us at the church, especially when you both grew up here. I don't know why you won't go along with an open house at least."

"It wouldn't be right without Adam's parents here," Natalie responded.

"I hope they disown you both when they find out you got married without them," Stella said peevishly. "They lived in this town for most of their life, and they have so many friends here. And you know how Hilda loves weddings. And to think Gordon has given the toast to the bride to half the married women in this town. They will be so disappointed about this.'' Stella really would have liked to organize something for them, but she did understand. Adam's parents were on a fishing trip in the Northwest Territories, and there was no way of reaching them. And she suspected that Natalie was using the Rutherfords' inaccessibility as the excuse for a very private ceremony.

Adam, she guessed, was using his family's inaccessibility for entirely different reasons. This way, there was no delay; if he couldn't contact them, he wouldn't have to wait for them to arrive. And he had made it very clear that he did not want to wait.

Gordon and Hilda Rutherford had thought the world of Natalie, and Hilda especially had been very upset when Natalie had left town without so much as a goodbye. Stella couldn't help but wonder what their reaction would be when they found out that Adam and Natalie were married.

And that they already had a ten-year-old son.

THE FOLLOWING DAY, at seven o'clock in the evening, Natalie and Adam were married in the old stone church. It was a simple ceremony with no bridal march, no organ music, no flowers at the altar. There was only Doc, Stella and Patrick to watch them exchange their solemn vows and their plain gold bands.

Outside the open door, the long shadows of early evening fell as robins twittered in the still, clear air of dusk, and the soft breeze carried a fragrance of stocks, roses and freshly mown grass. The last golden blaze of sunlight slanted through the stained-glass window behind the choir loft, the diffused rays glancing across the altar in muted shafts of light.

With the soft sounds of dusk infiltrating the old church, Natalie and Adam made their eternal commitment to each other. Natalie, with dainty starflowers in her hair, stood beside Adam, the floating blue chiffon of her dress brushing against his slacks as she placed her right hand on his.

The contours of Adam's face became even more pronounced as he closed his hand around hers and looked down at her. His intense gaze never wavered and his voice was filled with conviction as he made his pledge. He promised to love and comfort her, honor and keep her. The depth of feeling in his quietly spoken words overwhelmed Natalie, and she held his compelling gaze, her eyes brimming with unshed tears. And with her voice trembling with emotion, she repeated the vows that would bind them together. The rings were exchanged, and after years of separation and heartache, they were finally proclaimed husband and wife.

As the tears spilled over and slipped down her face, Natalie whispered his name. Adam's eyes darkened as he raised her hand, then solemnly kissed the gold band he had just placed on her finger. Wordlessly they stared at each other, then drawing a deep unsteady breath, Adam took her face in his hands and whispered unevenly, "Natalie. My Nat."

Drawn to her by the enraptured glow in her eyes, he lowered his head and kissed the corner of her mouth. Her whole body shaking, Natalie moved her head until their mouths met, and with a tremor coursing through him, he gathered her into his arms. For the space of that brief, galvanizing embrace, the overpowering storm of emotions was so strong it broke down the dark barriers in her mind. For that one senseless moment, Natalie's fears were overridden by sheer need. Adam held her, wondering how he was ever going to let her go.

It was twilight when Adam and Natalie returned to the trailer. The sky still held the fading colors of sunset, the jagged outline of the mountains silhouetted against a muted orange. As though the setting sun was drawing the color from the darkening sky, the orange diminished through a spectrum of shades until finally it blended with the faded light of dusk. Each vibrant shade was perfectly mirrored in the still, silvery surface of the lake, the reflections adding to the subtle hues. The stillness seemed to magnify the eerie spell as the melancholy cry of a loon echoed across the water.

Adam leaned against the fender of the truck, his arms folded in front of him as he watched Natalie. She had been very quiet during the drive up the mountain, and he had sensed she was dreading arriving at the campsite. He couldn't really blame her; he had been dreading it himself. He didn't know how he was going to handle being by themselves tonight, especially after that one staggering encounter in the church. That had rocked him...badly. It was one thing to exercise control when she was distressed. It was an entirely different thing to exercise control after she'd blown his discipline to bits.

But now that they were here, he hoped she would be temporarily distracted by the haunting beauty and the peace that surrounded her. The air was cool, and he saw her shiver. Feeling as though every muscle in his face had petrified, he stripped off his jacket and draped it around her shoulders. "Come on, Nat. We'd better go in before you freeze."

The ground was uneven, and the fading light made it difficult to see. Adam took her hand in his, his grasp firm as he led her silently toward the angular shape of the trailer. He could feel her shaking, but he wasn't sure if it was from the cold or from nerves.

Once inside, he turned on the small light mounted on the wall by the door, then moved away from her, determined not to touch her. He couldn't touch her; he didn't dare. Feeling as though he was suffocating, he roughly stripped off his tie and undid the top buttons of his shirt, his expression inflexible.

"Adam?"

He dropped the tie on the table, then turned to face her. She was watching him, her body so stiff she appeared almost breakable, the anxiety in her eyes dominating her face. Suddenly her shoulders sagged and she clutched her arms in front of her in a gesture of anguish. "Oh, Adam, what have I done to you?"

He reacted. She closed her eyes, her breath catching a tortured sob as he pulled her against him, encircling her slender form. He cradled her head against his shoulder, his face pressed against her hair as he whispered hoarsely, "Shh, Nat. Don't cry. It's okay."

"Adam—"

"Don't try to talk," he interjected raggedly. "Just let me hold you."

It helped—being able to hold her. Her warmth soothed the hollow ache in him, and the firmness of her body against his helped dull his unsatisfied hunger. She filled up the emptiness, and that eased the tension that gripped him. He closed his eyes, savoring the delicate scent of her perfume, the sensuousness of her silky dress against her bare back, the weight of her arms around his shoulders. Yes, it did help.

He held her for a long time, unaware of the deepening night or of the breeze eddying in through the open door or of the moths fluttering around the dim light. He held her until his heartbeat steadied and until her trembling stopped.

Finally she stirred in his arms, and easing away from him slightly, she looked up. Her eyes darkening, she took his face in her hands and drew his head down, her mouth moving lightly against his in a tormentingly gentle kiss. It was all Adam could do to keep from crushing her against him.

With a sigh, she slowly opened her eyes as she pulled away, her hands still warm against his face. There was a misty glow in her eyes as she whispered, "I do love you, Adam."

Moved beyond words, he swallowed against the ache in his throat as he caressed her back, his eyes absorbing every detail of her. When he was able to speak, his voice was painfully husky. "I've been waiting all my life for today, Nat." Feeling raw and exposed, he closed his eyes and tightened his arms around her. "I need you so damned much."

Holding him tightly, she slid her hand into his hair, her embrace protective. When she felt his tension ease, she began to slowly stroke his head, her touch soothing and gentle. "Just think, Adam," she whispered, her words tinged with quiet wonder, "today is the beginning of a whole new life."

Adam kissed the curve of her neck, then raised his head. He trailed his finger across the fullness of her bottom lip, his expression softening. "Then maybe we should break open a bottle of champagne to launch it."

Natalie narrowed her eyes in a very skeptical look. "Is that a genuine invitation or merely an idle thought?"

The fine laugh lines around his eyes deepened as he grinned. "A genuine invitation."

Not quite convinced, she asked suspiciously, "Is this some of Doc's dreadful potato champagne, or is it the real stuff?"

"Definitely not the best, possibly not even very good, but certainly the real stuff."

Natalie laughed, and Adam was completely captivated by her. She looked so lovely standing there with flowers in her hair and her eyes so full of life and laughter.

"What's the matter, Adam?"

She was watching him with a puzzled look, and he smiled softly as he caressed her cheek. "Do you know how much I love to hear you laugh?" he asked gruffly.

She laid her hand on top of his and met his warm gaze. "Do you know how happy I am?"

There was an amused gleam in his eyes. "Patrick's right. You do answer questions with questions."

She smiled, then sighed and shook her head. "He's going to run wild at Doc's, especially with Stella indulging him."

"Good. Every kid should have a chance to run wild and be indulged once in a while."

"That's easy for you to say."

He grinned. "You're right. It easy for me to say." Adam lost all sense of time and place as he gazed down into her wide gray eyes, her physical closeness testing him to the limit. Knowing he had little resistance left, he caught her shoulders and eased her away. "I'll get the champagne," he murmured unsteadily.

Adam had brought a small suitcase of Natalie's with him when he had come back to get dressed for the ceremony, and he had laid it on the settee at the end of the trailer. He heard her open it as he took the chilled bottle out of the fridge. Closing the refrigerator door with his elbow, he picked two glasses out of the cupboard and went over to her. He knew something was wrong when she didn't look up at him.

"What's the matter?"

She nervously fingered a garment still packed in the suitcase, then turned to look at him. All the vibrancy had drained out of her face.

Sensing she did not want him to touch her, he very carefully set the bottle and glasses down, then stuck his hands in the pockets of his slacks and leaned against the cupboard. His expression was solemn as he encouraged her, "Talk to me, Nat."

Her voice was weak. "My feelings are all over the place. One minute I'm so happy I can't believe it, and the next minute I'm so scared I can hardly think. And mixed up with that is so much guilt, it seems I'll never get out from under it."

"What happened just now? What frightened you?"

She averted her gaze and folded her arms stiffly in front of her. There was some inner struggle going on; that was evident by the look on her face. And it was evident by the brittleness in her voice when she finally spoke. "It's obvious that we didn't make arrangements to be here by ourselves so we could sleep in separate beds."

It sounded so harsh, but he recognized the sharp undertone as one of self-contempt, and Adam waited, a heaviness settling in his stomach. She gave him a taut smile. "When you went to get the champagne, I wanted to say something a new wife would say, like 'Why don't we take it to bed with us.' I wanted to be able to do that, but the minute I started rehearsing it in my head, I started freezing up.

And I remember—'' She turned away abruptly, her body rigid as she gave a forced, bitter laugh. ''Isn't this a wonderful, unforgettable experience, Adam? A honeymoon with a paranoid wife?''

Adam had never felt quite so impotent in his life, but he knew he had to make her say it all. ''Why the guilt, Nat?'' he asked quietly. ''What makes you feel guilty?''

At first he thought she wasn't going to answer, then she turned, stared at him for a long time and finally whispered, ''You make me feel guilty.''

She may as well have slapped him. The muscles in his face stiffened. ''How?'' he asked tautly.

''Because, Adam,'' she answered. ''Because I sometimes feel as though I've trapped you. If it hadn't been for finding out about Patrick, would you have ever come back after you talked to me that first time? And if it hadn't been for Patrick, would you be stuck with a woman who is so sexually warped she panics when somebody touches her?''

Adam suddenly felt as though he didn't know this slender woman with the haunting eyes who stood before him. His voice was cold as he said, ''So you resent having him.''

''No!'' Her face went white with shock as she caught his arm, her eyes beseeching him to understand. ''Heavens, no. I don't resent him, Adam. He's my son, and I love him.'' Her eyes suddenly filled with tears and she turned away. ''Don't you see? If you hadn't found out about Patrick, you would have left town and never looked back.''

And finally, Adam did see. Somehow he was going to have to make her understand. ''I might have left town, Nat,'' he said solemnly, ''but I most certainly would have looked back.''

Natalie faced him, her brimming eyes revealing the look of someone desperately wanting to believe. He met her gaze with a steady stare. His tone was without censure as he said softly, ''I told you once before not to doubt my feelings. I'm here because I want to be.''

Brushing away the tears with her fingertips, she clasped her arms around herself and whispered, more to herself than to him, "But are you going to want to stay?"

It annoyed him that she had so little faith in the sincerity of his feelings, and his voice had a steely edge when he demanded, "And what in hell is that supposed to mean?"

She was struggling to hold back tears and she tried to swallow. Unable to speak, she shrugged her shoulders in a helpless gesture, and he felt like a bastard for hurting her. He wanted to stop this ordeal, but he didn't know how. It wasn't something he could simply walk away from. Not now. Deliberately avoiding her eyes, he slowly undid the cuffs of his sleeves and rolled them back. "How else do I make you feel guilty?"

It took her a moment before she could answer, and even then he could barely hear her. "I know you so well, Adam. We spent so much time together, and I know—" Closing her eyes, she tipped her head back, as though she was utterly spent. "You said there was more to a relationship than sex." She looked at him, her expression solemn. "Those are fine words, but how long can a relationship last under that kind of strain?"

She stopped him as he opened his mouth to answer. "No! Don't say anything," she pleaded. "Let me finish. Please let me finish." She made a gesture of frustration with her hands then clenched them into fists, her expression tormented. "I think I've relived every moment we spent together at least a thousand times. And if I learned anything that summer, it was what a very physical person you are." She hauled in a deep breath and pressed her hands tightly against her thighs. Her voice became very strained as she whispered huskily, "I know how much pleasure you derive from that intimacy, and I know how little it takes to arouse you. And I know what you were feeling in the church, and I know what you were feeling a few minutes ago. I know these things, Adam." Her voice broke, her desperate unhappiness apparent. "And do you know how much I want to give you that pleasure again, and what I'd give to be able to lose myself in that incredible passion we used to share? Do you know?" Tears were slipping down her face, and she had her arms clutched in front of her.

Adam was rooted to the spot, his own face haggard as her unbearable pain became his. But somehow he managed to speak, his voice ragged. "Have you any idea how empty and meaningless my life has been? Do you know the times I would have endured anything just to be able to wake up in the middle of the night and find you sleeping beside me?"

She kept her distance for a moment, then with a low sob, she was in his arms, clinging to him with desperate strength. Clenching his jaw against the strangling ache in his throat, Adam crushed her against him. "If I have to choose, I'll take the frustration over the emptiness anytime," he murmured hoarsely. "Anything is more tolerable than that."

"Adam—"

"No. No more, Nat," he said firmly, gently. "No more self-recriminations or doubts. I know it isn't going to be easy, but we're damned lucky to even be together." He closed his eyes and rested his head against hers, waiting for the ache in his chest to ease.

Neither of them spoke again, and he stroked her back until he felt her body relax. Finally he eased her away from him and smiled down at her. "I have this bottle of questionable vintage and even more questionable quality, and I have every intention of getting you slightly drunk."

He could sense her inner struggle to hang on to her shaky composure, but like sunshine through the rain, she smiled at him through her tears. "It sounds wonderful." The tears spilled down her face, but the smile stayed as she suggested unevenly, "Why don't we take it to bed with us."

The lights went on in Adam's eyes, and his face creased into an engaging grin. "Sounds like one hell of an idea." He gave her a quick hug then caught her by the wrist. "Come on."

She resisted and he glanced down at her. She looked just the way she did when she was sixteen—shy, uncertain, a little scared—and he suddenly felt the loss of the intervening years. "What?" he asked softly.

The pulse in her throat was fluttering wildly, and it was obvious she was nervous as she slipped her hand out of his. "You go ahead. I'll be in in a minute."

He gazed at her for a moment, then nodded, and picking up the bottle and glasses, he went into the minuscule bedroom and quietly closed the door.

The room was stuffy from being closed up all day, and Adam set the bottle and glasses on the shelf at the head of the bed, turned on the small lamp mounted on the wall, then cranked open all the windows. A soft night breeze wafted in as Adam stripped off his jacket and shirt and hung them on a hook. His expression was very thoughtful. He had a number of silent conversations with himself as he removed the rest of his clothes, but none of them got him anywhere.

She had to change clothes; that was obvious. And because she wouldn't want to provoke him by wearing something soft and feminine, she would put on something practical. Adam wished it could have been different, but that's the way it was. Leaving his underwear on as a concession to her, Adam threw back the covers and climbed into bed. With an air of preoccupation, he stacked the pillows behind his back and drew up the sheet. His face still solemn, he reached for the bottle and began peeling off the foil wrap.

The folding door opened, and Natalie came in. Adam froze, his full attention glued on her. What she had on was anything but practical. Seductive? Yes. Provocative? Absolutely. But practical? Not even close.

He could feel his heavy pulse accelerate as he scrutinized her. She still had her hair up, exposing the long column of her neck and her naked shoulders. But that was only half of it. She had on a deep mauve negligee that accentuated every curve, and the lace bodice revealed tantalizing amounts of cleavage and bare skin. The long skirt molded to her and when she moved, it seemed to erotically caress her.

His heart was hammering so hard he could barely breathe, and it felt as if it would slam through his chest as he absorbed every intoxicating detail of her. When he was able to speak, his voice was low and velvety and textured by a smoldering sexuality. "Nice. Very nice."

She was trembling and uncertain, but her gaze was riveted on him, her eyes dark and smoky. Leaning forward, Adam caught her wrist, his expression serious as he drew her to him. It cost him a heavy price not to touch her the way he wanted to, but he simply pulled her down and gathered her against him. Holding her like that felt so good, but he wanted so much more. Every nerve in his body was on fire, but he clamped down on the heated excitement that was pounding through him, determined to control the incredible fever of wanting her.

It seemed to take an eternity for that initial burst of desire to pass, but eventually his pulse steadied and the ache abated. Still very shaken, he smoothed his hand across her back. "Thank you," he whispered, his lips moving against the soft curve of her shoulder.

Raising herself on one elbow, she looked at him. "For what?"

He caressed her neck with the back of his hand, his eyes dark as he slipped his fingers under the strap of her negligee. "For trusting me enough to wear this."

A light flush colored her cheeks and she shrugged self-consciously. "If we hadn't talked before I never would have had the courage." Her expression changed as she absently combed her fingers through his hair, her eyes deeply troubled. "What's wrong with me, Adam? Why can I go this far but no farther? Why—"

"Don't, Nat. Tonight we simply enjoy being together." He loosely wrapped his arms around her back, and there was a glint of amusement in his eyes as he looked at her. "Don't worry about it. It takes me a while to calm down, but my grandmother used to swear that denial was good for the soul.''

There was a smile in her eyes as she propped her head on her hand, her other arm resting on his chest. "That sounds like a lousy way to develop character."

He laughed. "I always thought so." He shifted his hold on her, and the silky material of her negligee moved against her skin. The expression in his eyes softened as he smoothed his hand up her back. "It does feel so damned good to hold you."

A gleam of mischief appeared in her eyes and she grinned down at him. "What you really mean is that under the circumstances, holding me is only slightly less trying than throwing yourself in front of a moving train."

His smile was lopsided and he gave her a wry look. "Something like that." He shifted his shoulders to a more comfortable position, then adjusted his hold on her as his smile broadened. "Besides, I want to talk."

She laughed and gave his chest a playful slap. "Now that's a new twist. And such a *good* line, Adam."

He grinned up at her. "Glad you like it."

The sparkle in her eyes softened as she slowly trailed her finger across his bottom lip. "Do you know how much I love you, Adam Rutherford?"

He kissed her fingertip as he tightened his arm around her. "I think I could stand to have you tell me, Natalie Rutherford."

Her tone was teasing as she said, "I thought you were going to get me drunk."

"I think I'm drunk already," he said, his gaze smoldering.

She wove her fingers through his hair and laughed softly. "Cute, Adam, but definitely clichéd."

"Married three hours and a critic already."

Her eyes dancing with laughter, Natalie caught his ears and gave his head a shake as she groaned in frustration. "Just pour the wine, Adam. Pour the damned wine."

Adam laughed and hugged her hard, then hauled himself into a sitting position. With Natalie sitting cross-legged beside him, he opened the bottle, the plastic cork leaving a dint in the roof when it exploded, before ricocheting off the walls. The champagne fizzed down the side of the bottle onto his bare chest, and Natalie made some smart comments when it collected in his navel. It set the mood for the rest of the night. They emptied the bottle, they talked, they laughed, and they talked some more. There were no shadows, no grim reminders. Instead, it was a time of incredible closeness; it was a time of a very special kind of sharing. The sky was starting to lighten when Natalie finally drifted off to sleep, her head on his shoulder, her arm draped across his chest. And as he watched her sleep, Adam didn't think it was possible for him to love anybody more than he loved her.

CHAPTER ELEVEN

IT WAS THE THIRD NIGHT in a row that Adam had quietly left his bed, leaving Natalie alone as she slept. He had gone down to the lake, trying to find relief from the agony of wanting her, but fighting his natural instincts was a hopeless battle. Especially at night.

During the day, he could discipline himself to a certain degree, and he made certain he tested that discipline as little as possible. But at night, when she was lying so close to him, his mind rebelled and he'd lie there in the dark, trying to ignore the consuming hunger that inflamed him. He'd hit a point where he had to leave, the fever of desire finally unbearable. And he was beginning to wonder how much longer he could maintain the facade of calmly coping with the situation when he was, in fact, quietly going out of his mind.

A log in the fire charred through and the burning wood shifted, sending a shower of sparks skyward. Adam was lying in the hammock with his hands behind his head, staring unseeingly at the black canopy of densely interwoven branches. The fire snapped and crackled again, sending up another eruption of sparks, and he turned his head to watch the dancing flames, his expression solemn. The night sky had lightened slightly and he could see the lake, its surface mirror smooth in the stillness of approaching dawn, the jagged outline of the mountains barely visible against the fading blackness.

The firelight cast flickering shadows against the trunks of the trees, and Adam watched the play of light and darkness, trying to focus his thoughts on something other than

the unsatisfied ache that was gnawing at him. Unable to remain motionless any longer, he swung out of the hammock. He checked the fire, then turned toward the lake. His
boots echoed hollowly on the wooden dock, then he reached
the end and stood staring out. There was a raft anchored a
short distance from the shore, and he could just make out
the dark outline of it against the faint gleam of water. He
hesitated a moment, then started stripping off his clothes.

The water was so frigid it knocked the wind out of him,
and he had trouble catching his breath when he surfaced. He
finally hauled in some air, and with dogged single-
mindedness, set out toward the raft in a clean fast crawl.
Adam did laps from the end of the dock to the raft until his
body was nearly paralyzed with cold, but he continued to
push himself on, trying to dull his senses with sheer exhaustion.

He was on his way back to the dock when he caught a soft
glimmer of satin and realized that Natalie was standing on
the weathered wooden structure watching him. The mauve
nightie shimmered as she moved toward him, and she looked
like some shadowy illusion emerging from the darkness. As
she stopped at the end of the pier, a sudden breeze billowed
through the lustrous fabric, swirling it around her, and her
hair whipped across her face, the faint light touching it with
a silver sheen.

Placing his hands on the wooden surface, he hoisted
himself out of the frigid water, the muscles across his
shoulders rippling. Water sluiced down his naked body as
he stood up, his skin gleaming. Silently he reached for his
jeans, which were draped over one of the air mattresses
leaning against the pilings.

Her presence disturbed him, and he was even more disturbed when she reached out and touched him—a touch that
was like liquid fire as she slowly brushed beads of moisture
from his chest. As though scalded, Adam reacted. Catching her wrist, he pulled her hand away. "Don't, Natalie,"
he said, a taut edge to his voice.

"Let me," she whispered unsteadily.

Adam felt as if his chest was caving in, and he clenched his jaw against the rush of heat that pumped through him. He loosened his hold on her slightly, keenly aware that he could feel her rapid pulse beneath his fingers. His voice was hoarse when he spoke. "Don't, Nat. Don't make it worse than it is."

She moved closer, and her hair feathered across his chest with tantalizing lightness as she smoothed her other hand up his torso. "This time you have to trust me, Adam," she murmured. Then very lightly, she moved her hand downward.

Clamping his teeth together, Adam tried to choke back a groan as the intimacy of her caress set off an explosion of white-hot heat, a surge of desire searing through him. He couldn't breathe, and an incapacitating weakness slammed into him as she lightly stroked him, driving him senseless with her touch. He ground out her name and roughly grasped her wrist. "Please, Nat. Stop. For God's sake, stop."

Weakly she leaned against him, her face against his chest. "Hold me."

Adam felt as if every drop of his blood was engorging his groin. Shaken and fighting for breath, he released his grip on her wrists, then gathered her against him, his face buried in her hair. Natalie was trembling as she slipped her arms around him, and when she spoke her voice was low. "I want so badly to touch you the way I used to. Please let me, Adam."

He tried to think, tried to regain some control over his scorching desire that had sensitized every nerve, but he was lost. The only thing he was conscious of was Natalie, and the unbearable ache of wanting her. She turned her head and slowly brushed her mouth against his. "Please, Adam." She caught his arms and pushed them away, then she sank to her knees in front of him.

But before she could touch him, he grasped her head and held her immobile. The last of his strength deserted him, and with his legs too weak to support him any longer, he sank down in front of her. Tightening his grip on her face, he spoke, his voice raw and unsteady. "I love you, Nat. And I don't want you to do anything simply because you think you should."

She didn't answer. Instead, she caressed his jaw, then leaned forward and kissed him softly. With his heart slamming against his chest, Adam opened his mouth and responded hungrily, urgently, his body famished for the sustenance of hers. He felt her tense, then she tightened her hold on him and pulled away. Taking a ragged breath, she whispered unevenly, "Let me love you, Adam. Let me do it my way."

He understood what she was asking, but he didn't know how he was going to keep from responding. But somehow, he had to. Closing his eyes, he turned his head and kissed the palm of her hand, his voice chocked. "I won't do anything to frighten you, Nat. I promise."

The air mattress was cold and damp, but Adam was unaware of everything except the weight of her on top of him and the soothing hardness of her against his groin. His breathing became more labored and his pulse went wild as she began to work her spell. Adam thought he was going to go out of his mind. Her mouth was warm and moist against his skin, and her hands slowly explored the planes of his wet body, as though she was committing every inch of him to memory. He wanted to move against her, to find the driving rhythm that would bring relief from the torment, but he remained immobile, his body braced against the throbbing agony she aroused.

A low sound was wrung from him as Natalie eased her weight off him, the thick heavy ache no longer soothed by the pressure of her body. Unable to endure it, Adam was about to roll over on his stomach, but she gently grasped him, and he had to grit his teeth to keep from crying out. He was so inundated with fevered sensations that he didn't fully comprehend her intent when she straddled his body, but when she guided him into her, he reacted. Roughly clasping her arms, he pulled her down against him, his voice ragged and weak. "Nat, you don't have to—"

But she moved against him and he was unable to go on, his body paralyzed with wild excitement. She bracketed his face with her hands and kissed him softly, then whispered huskily against his mouth. "I want to, Adam." Her weight shifted, and Adam's breath caught as shock waves of heat ripped through him, every movement tormenting him even more. She disengaged his grip and pressed his arms down, then tightly lacing her fingers through his, she slowly started to move against him.

She stroked him to a frenzy, slowly drawing away, then engulfing him, her body moist and tight around his. The hunger in him continued to build to an agonizing pressure, and he felt as if she were dragging him inside out each time she drew away. Finally he hit the peak of his endurance, and he groaned and twisted under her as the liquid heat finally erupted from him with a devastating force. The scalding release was so violent, so exquisite that he was senseless to everything else. Everything except the woman who lay trembling in his arms. And turning his face into the tumble of her hair, he held her with immeasurable tenderness, a dull ache suddenly encasing his chest.

ADAM AWOKE THE NEXT MORNING to sounds of rain on the roof and an outside world that was shrouded in a gray drizzle. He was lying on his stomach, a sheet draped loosely across his hips, his body drugged by a warm, languid sensation. But the drifting sense of contentment was roughly dispelled when he recalled what had happened on the dock only hours before.

And he became wide awake. The encounter had shaken Natalie badly, and she had really gone to pieces afterward. She had trembled as though she was in shock, and he had carried her back to the trailer and put her to bed, a sick feeling twisting in the pit of his stomach when she continued to cling to him, yet refused to talk.

Now, in the cold light of day, that same sick feeling hit him. Adam closed his eyes, his face drawn. How was he going to face her, knowing that she'd forced herself to do what she had because of guilt. His eyes flew open and he stared at the empty pillow beside him. And where was she? Suddenly apprehensive, he pushed himself out of bed.

Just then the folding door slid open, and Natalie came in carrying two mugs of coffee. Adam's attention was instantly riveted on her face. She seemed unwilling to meet his gaze as she came around the end of the bed and set the cups on the ledge by his head. There were taut lines around his mouth as he caught her wrist. "I know it doesn't really help much, but I am sorry about last night."

Natalie looked at him, her eyes glistening with unshed tears as she turned her wrist and slipped her hand into his. Her grip was tight as she murmured, "Don't be sorry." Her mouth was trembling, and she looked so vulnerable. But suddenly she smiled through her tears, and with a soft sob, she slipped into his arms. "Don't be sorry, Adam. If you only knew how special last night was for me."

With his hands tangled in her hair, Adam caught her face and gently raised it until he could see her eyes. His expression was grave. "But was it, Nat, or was it just an exercise to please me?"

She pulled away from him, and brushing aside her tears with the back of her hand, she gazed down at him, her eyes dark and misty. "I was so scared, Adam. I wanted so badly to touch you, to make love to you the way I used to. But I didn't know how far I could go. But knowing how much you needed me—" She glanced away and swallowed with great difficulty, fighting hard to suppress her raw emotions. It took her a while to regain control, but finally she drew in an unsteady breath and continued, her voice even more husky.

"Knowing you needed me somehow gave me the courage to go on."

Adam slowly caressed her face, his eyes troubled. "But it wasn't that good for you, was it?"

Sitting up, she took his hand between hers, and he sensed the emotional upheaval she was struggling with as she stared down at their joined hands. She finally looked at him, her voice breaking beneath the stress. "I know you won't really understand it, but whether it was good for me or it wasn't didn't really matter. It wasn't important."

"It's important to me, Nat," he said quietly.

Her eyes intent, she whispered, "Do you know how special it was for me to be able to give you that kind of pleasure? I was so afraid I couldn't follow through, but I did, Adam, and that meant so much." Fresh tears slipped down her face. "The fact that I didn't have a climax *wasn't* important, but the fact that I could share something like that with you was. Don't you see, Adam, that I took an enormous step forward?"

Adam studied her, then looked down at her hands as he toyed with her wedding ring, an odd tenor to his voice. "But in other words, I still have to keep my hands to myself."

Pulling free of his grasp, Natalie lifted his chin, forcing him to look at her. "Don't feel that you're cheating me out of anything, Adam. Please, don't feel that way. It meant so much to me."

His gaze was penetrating. "If that's true, why were you so upset afterward?"

Her eyes clouded and her uneasiness was apparent. She looked away, the pulse in her neck beating wildly. He touched her cheek to turn her face toward him. "Why, Natalie?"

Her breath caught, and she nervously clasped her hands together, her expressive eyes revealing her distress. "I don't know how to explain it."

"Try."

She stared at him for a moment longer, then she looked away, her face pale. "For the first time in eleven years, I felt clean inside. That awful tainted feeling was gone, and I don't think I can ever find the words to explain how good that feels." His hand was still against her cheek, and she covered it with her own as she looked at him again. "I know you're having trouble with what happened," she whispered, "but if you only knew how vitally important it is to me to simply feel touchable again, you wouldn't question what happened last night."

A painful contraction tightened Adam's chest, and without speaking he slipped his hand to the back of her head and pulled her down. Closing his eyes, he wrapped his arms around her and gathered her securely against him, his face set in somber lines. He should have been more than satisfied with her explanation, but for some reason it left him feeling very hollow.

The soft patter of rain on the roof filled the silence as he held her and stared off into space. Finally he dragged his thoughts back, and sighing softly, he began to stroke her hair. "I don't want you doing anything, especially going to bed with me, simply because you think you owe it to me, Nat," he said quietly.

She raised her head, her eyes smoky. "I love the feel of your body, and I like to touch you. And just because I didn't experience the same thing you did doesn't mean it wasn't enjoyable for me." Her voice became unsteady as she softly caressed his lips. "You gave me the space I needed last night, and that made me feel so special."

Brushing her tousled hair back behind her ear, Adam let his hand rest against her neck, his eyes serious as he stroked her jaw with his thumb. His voice was husky when he murmured, "If only you knew how hard it was to keep from touching you. You arouse me until I can hardly think, and it's so damned incredible and exciting. I just want to be able to arouse the same feeling in you."

Her trembling fingers against his mouth, she struggled to contain her feelings. "Don't," she whispered brokenly. "Don't think about something that might never be. I might never be able to put the entire nightmare behind me."

"Nat—"

But she didn't give him a chance to speak. She caught his head, her fingers buried in his hair as she covered his mouth in a soft pliant kiss. His response was instantaneous, and he shuddered as the heat of desire rushed through him. Hauling in a ragged breath, he twisted his head free, his pulse pounding as he murmured hoarsely, "Nat . . . don't."

But she found his mouth again, her hands curved around his neck, her hold on his face secure. "I want to, Adam," she whispered against his mouth. "Don't fight me."

And Adam felt as if he was paralyzed as she moved on top of him, her body molded tightly against his, her softness inflaming his senses. He was lost, trapped in the fire that she aroused in him.

THE NEXT WEEK was almost perfect. There were times, though, when Adam was deeply bothered by the feeling he was using her, but for the most part those days were truly golden ones. They had the time and the privacy to redevelop the special closeness they had once shared, and each savored every minute of it.

Even the weather was perfect, but it turned scorching hot, and in an attempt to beat the heat, they had gone for a swim. The mountain lake was freezing, and they only managed a few laps to the raft and back before Natalie decided she'd had enough and hauled herself onto the dock, the water from her hair cascading down her back. She picked up a towel and dried her face and arms, then started toweling her hair.

Hooking his arms on the edge of the pier, Adam watched her. "Don't tell me you're quitting already."

Her lips blue with cold, she confirmed, "I'm quitting already."

He laughed as he hoisted himself onto the dock, then wiped the water from his face. "I told you not to tell me that."

Natalie shivered, her teeth chattering. "I think you're trying to do away with me, Adam Rutherford. If that water was one degree colder, it would be ice."

He grinned at her as he took the towel out of her hands. "What a baby."

She made a face, then checked the position of the sun before she moved one of the air mattresses. "I don't care if I'm a baby or not. It's still going to take me at least two hours to thaw out."

She stretched out on her stomach, then resting her head on her arms, she turned her head toward the sun and closed her eyes. Adam tossed the other air mattress down beside her. Lying on his back, he, too, shut his eyes.

Her voice was slightly muffled. "Why, may I ask, are you lying here? I thought you intended on swimming another eight or nine miles."

"Don't get smart," he warned, "or I'll throw you in again."

"I'd sink your canoe."

"You can't sink that canoe, Natalie."

There was amusement in her voice. "Why? We've done it before."

Adam started laughing. "I'd forgotten about that. Dad's brand-new canoe and we rip the bottom out going through the rapids." Squinting against the blinding sun, he turned his head to look at her, his face creased with a grin. "Lord, did I catch hell for that."

She opened her eyes and gave him a reproachful look. "You did not. Considering he lost his new canoe and we nearly drowned in the whirlpool trying to find it, your dad was really decent about it."

"He might have been decent about his canoe, but he sure in hell wasn't decent about my taking you through those rapids in the first place. Even Mom got into it. For days afterward, every conversation was peppered with pointed little references about assuming responsibility."

Dragging her hand from under her head, Natalie reached over and patted his shoulder. "Poor Adam," she said without a shred of sympathy.

"You could show a little remorse, you know. Especially since it was your damned idea in the first place. 'Take me white-water canoeing, Adam. It'll be so much fun,'" he mimicked.

She grinned and slapped his chest. "It *was* fun." Bracing herself on her elbows, she leaned over and kissed him on the cheek. "And you were an angel not to tell your parents I pushed you into it."

He gazed up at her, his eyes dancing with amusement as he softly caressed her shoulder. "They wouldn't have believed me anyway. As far as they were concerned, you were a blameless innocent. Their only concern about us spending so much time together was the four-year difference between us. They felt it was such a big gap at that age." His eyes developed a wicked gleam as he added, "And they were concerned their golden-haired boy would lead you astray."

Natalie slanted an amused look down at him. "And who says parents are blind." Her expression grew pensive as she began tracing invisible patterns on his darkly tanned chest. "It was funny, but just before Patrick was born, it was your mom I wanted with me most. I was so scared, and she was always so calm and unflappable. She always seemed to know what to do or what people needed." Natalie looked at him, her expression troubled. "I really missed them when I left. In fact, if they'd been home the night it happened, I would have gone to them first."

Tightening his hold on her shoulder, he said softly, "They thought a lot of you. I know you're worried about facing them, but I know for a fact they're going to be so glad to have you back." He smiled with affection as he trailed his finger down her cheek. "Come on, Nat, can't you picture it? Mom will have a little cry, and Dad will get all blustery and gruff and overprotective.''

She shrugged self-consciously, a touch of apprehension in her eyes. "I guess the big thing is Patrick. What are they going to say?''

He gazed at her for a minute, then grinned. "I *know* what they're going to say. Dad's going to give me hell for leading his blameless innocent astray, and every conversation will be peppered with pointed little references about assuming responsibility.''

That made her smile, and she shook her head at him. "You're awful, do you know that?''

"I know.''

Propping her head on her hand, she began to trace patterns on his chest again, not quite sure how to approach him. She finally looked at him and said unevenly, "How would you feel about me getting pregnant right away?''

He watched her intently. "How about defining 'right away.' ''

She gave him an anxious little half smile. "Like maybe already.''

He stared up at her, feeling a little like she'd dropped him in the lake with that one. When he finally surfaced from the jolt, he realized she had a very worried expression on her face. Shifting his position, he slipped his arms around her, his gaze tender. "I think I could learn to live with it," he said gently. "As a matter of fact, I kind of like the idea.''

She exhaled in a rush and relaxed against him. He slid his hand around her neck and hooked his knuckles under her chin, then lifted her face. "Hey, Nat," he admonished gently, "I'm not the only one to be considered here. How about you?''

She gazed down at him, and when she assured herself he was being completely honest, her face lit up with gladness. "I'd love it.''

The warm expression in his eyes held a hint of amusement. "How do you think Patrick would feel about us having another kid?"

"I think he'd love it, too. He's totally sick of being an only child. He'd see a new baby as the big liberation. I'd have somebody else to fuss over, and maybe I'd get off his case."

Adam grinned. "Sounds like a hell of a deal." There were beads of water from her hair clinging to her shoulders, and Adam wiped them away with his hand. Unable to resist the texture of her skin, he lightly caressed the nape of her neck, then tunneled his fingers into the wet tangle of her hair.

Natalie's eyes darkened and she slowly smoothed her hand across his chest, her touch deliberately provocative. He caught her hand and kissed her palm, then said gruffly, "It's too hot, Nat."

"But I'm cold, Adam," she whispered as she cupped her hand beneath his head and leaned over him.

She was still chilled from the swim, and her wet swimsuit was cold against his skin as he turned to face her. Gathering her against him, he began to stroke her back. Right then, he would have sold his soul to be able to strip off the wet barrier of fabric that separated them and experience the intoxicating sensation of her naked body against his. Natalie began to caress his shoulder, and Adam braced himself on his elbow as he gazed down at her. The warmth in her eyes hypnotized him as she caught him by the back of the head and pressed him down.

It was a gentle searching kiss that knocked the wind out of him, but he felt even more breathless as she opened her mouth under his. With his senses drugged by a rush of desire, he responded with a blistering, thirsty kiss. That contact completely shattered his control, and without thinking, he crushed her against him, his arms like a vise as he pulled her beneath him. For a split second Natalie remained pliant in his fierce embrace, then suddenly she was twisting frantically, trying to fight him off.

Jerking her head away, she pushed against his chest, her voice filled with panic. "No! Don't!"

Her reaction stunned him, and Adam froze. His face was suddenly expressionless as he stared down into her terror-filled eyes, then averting his gaze, he stiffly withdrew his arms and rolled to his feet. His eyes were steely and the muscles in his jaw were twitching as he stood at the end of the dock and stared rigidly across the lake. The fault was his; he knew that, but even recognizing that fact, her reaction had still stung. Maybe what wounded his pride more than anything was the fact that she had, for that brief flash, replaced him with the ugly recollections of her stepfather. And that realization left him cold.

He heard her get up, and every muscle in his body tensed as she paused beside him and laid her hand on his arm. Her voice was shaking and very weak. "I'm sorry, Adam. That was an unforgivable thing to do to you."

He turned his head and stared down at her, then answered tautly, "Yes, it was." He snatched the other towel off the piling, then turned and left her standing there.

He knew he was handling this all wrong, but he couldn't stop himself. Realizing that she reacted to him the same way she must have reacted to Carl Willard filled him with a sickness he couldn't describe. He felt as though she'd stabbed him in the back.

Entering the trailer, he flung the towel on the counter, then opened the top cupboard and took out a bottle of rye. He picked a glass out of the sink and went into the bedroom, his face like stone as he slammed the folding door shut behind him. He poured himself a drink and tossed it back, then changed into his jeans.

Adam had just finished pulling on his boots when he heard Natalie enter the trailer. He poured himself another drink and stood with his back toward the door, his mouth compressed into a hard line.

The door slid open, and a soft breeze stirred the curtains. There was a tense silence, then Natalie spoke. "I don't blame you for being angry, Adam. What I did to you out there was the worst insult I could have ever leveled at you. I know it's not enough to say I'm sorry, but I am."

He took a stiff drink, then turned to face her. "Under the circumstances, I can't see any point in discussing it."

Natalie was standing in the doorway, her hair hanging down her back in a wet tangle, her swimsuit damp against her body. There was an air of inevitability about her as she met his hostile gaze. "Would it be better if I left?"

He responded coldly, "Do you want to leave?"

She had seemed so self-possessed, but it wasn't until she looked away that he realized how stark her expression was. "What I want, Adam," she said carefully, "is to not hurt you anymore." She cast him a quick glance, then turned and walked out of the tiny room.

Swearing in frustration, Adam slammed his glass down and went after her. He caught her by the arm and whirled her around. "Where in hell are you going?"

She tried to pull free of his grasp. "Just let me go," she said brokenly.

He eased his grip on her, but his expression was still uncompromising as he stared down at her. "I have no intentions of letting you go," he snapped.

"Anybody home?"

Adam tensed, and Natalie weakly closed her eyes. "It's Doc."

Adam swore under his breath, then let go of her arm. "Go change," he said curtly, "and I'll go talk to him."

Doc was almost at the trailer when Adam went to the door. But he was not alone. There was another man with him who was wearing the uniform of a park ranger.

Doc raised his hand in greeting when he saw Adam. "Sorry to intrude, lad, but we have a wee bit of an emergency on our hands."

Adam opened the screen door and stood back as the two men entered the trailer. Doc turned stiffly to introduce the man who had followed him in. "This is Doug Clifford,

Adam. He's the park warden at Andrews Lake." As they shook hands, Adam scrutinized Doc's companion. The warden was in his early fifties and had the weathered look of a man who had spent most of his life outdoors.

Andrews Lake was the name the locals tagged a nearby provincial park that covered several hundred square miles of some of the most rugged terrain in the province. This year, the area had been extremely dry and there was some concern about the wildlife. Adam wondered if that problem had something to do with the warden's visit.

He motioned them toward the settee. "So what's this emergency?"

Doug Clifford sat down wearily, then took off his hat and wiped his brow. "We have a group of five young hikers who are trapped in the box canyon at the south face of Hoodoo Mountain. We had a fire break out in that area last night. There wouldn't have been too much to worry about, but we had a wind change early this morning, and the fire's moving across the mouth of the canyon."

Hooking his thumbs in the loops on his jeans, Adam leaned against the cupboard. "Can't you get in there with helicopters?"

The warden shook his head. "The visibility is zero with the smoke, and the winds are really gusting. And you can count on strong downdrafts there even at the best of times. That canyon's hell to get into even in perfect conditions. We could put somebody on the top of Hoodoo, but there's no way we can get in at the bottom."

Doc picked up an ashtray off the counter, then sat down at the other end of the settee. "Doug heard that I knew of a route down the west face that bypasses the overhang, and he came to see me about it." He scraped out his pipe and emptied the ashes in the ashtray, then looked up at Adam. "As you remember, lad, that area below the overhang has been off limits to hikers for the past fifteen years. But Doug says the erosion has deteriorated that whole base even more during the past few years, and everyone knows it's dangerous. Consequently, no one among the park staff is very familiar with that side at all." Clamping the stem between his teeth, he leaned back and folded his arms across his chest, his expression earnest. "Unfortunately, the only way they can get those boys out of there is either straight up the south face or bring them across base and hike them up the west side. The south face is out of the question because none of them are experienced climbers." He paused and pursed his lips, then fumbled in his pocket for his pouch of pipe tobacco. "The problem is, lad, that we need somebody who knows that old route."

Adam was very thoughtful as he stared at the old pharmacist. "That's a long time ago, Doc, and how old was I? Thirteen or fourteen? I don't know if I can remember it that well."

Doc nodded his head in complete confidence. "You knew that whole canyon like the back of your hand, lad. You'll remember once you're there."

Adam narrowed his eyes in contemplation as he looked at the warden. "You're certain you can get a helicopter to the top of Hoodoo?"

Doug nodded. "That won't be a problem, but whoever goes in is going to have to dangle. That fire's traveling damned fast, and if it gets into the canyon, we could be in big trouble."

Adam lifted his head, and he felt oddly disquieted when he realized Natalie had been standing in the narrow entrance to the bedroom. It was obvious by her expression that she had been listening for some time, and she was more than a little concerned. That didn't make Adam feel any better, and he looked away, his face inflexible.

Doug leaned forward and rested his arms across his legs, then thoughtfully rubbed his chin. "How much time would it take to go in that way?"

Adam made himself concentrate on the warden. "It's a good six-hour hike down the west side, and then probably another two hours to get to them. There's no way we can make that climb out of there in the dark, so it'll be the better part of two days. I can cut some time off that going in, but the climb back out will take longer. And if the fire moves into the canyon, the wind will be against us, and we'll be fighting smoke the whole time."

Doug Clifford was watching Adam closely. "Then you'll go in?"

Adam gave him an intent look. "Didn't you want me to?"

Doc chuckled and started tamping his tobacco into his pipe. "Of course they want you to, lad. We wouldn't have driven in over that terrible excuse for a road just to have a little chat. But one of the senior bureaucrats with Parks was a tad disturbed that we were going to ask the famous Adam Rutherford to head up a rescue mission. He felt that we had an uncommon amount of cheek to even *think* about asking you. Said something about it being like asking a brain surgeon to paint the town hall."

Adam grinned wryly as he straightened. "Well, if I had a choice, I'd rather paint the town hall."

Doug Clifford rose and tucked his hat under his arm. "How soon can you be ready to go? I don't know how the reception will be from here, but I can try to radio out so there's a chopper waiting for us in town."

"Twenty minutes. I need to get my gear together."

Doc stood up slowly, his legs obviously stiff, then his face lit up. "Well, Natalie, I didn't see you standing there."

Her smile was slightly forced, and there was tension in her shoulders as she came forward and kissed the old man on the cheek. "Hello, Doc. Didn't Patrick come with you?"

"No, lass, he has better things to do. Stella's put him to work at the drugstore and he's having a grand time."

A strained awkwardness still stretched between Adam and Natalie, and Adam's manner was slightly aloof as he introduced her to Doug Clifford. Feeling more disturbed about the rift between them than he liked to admit, he deliberately avoided looking at her as he went to the door. "I'll get my gear together. I have everything stored in one of the cabins, so it'll take me a few minutes."

Doug Clifford followed him. "And I'll see if I can scare up somebody on the radio."

"While you're at it, see if they can scare up a good topographical map of Hoodoo and the immediate area. I'd like a chance to refresh my memory." Adam glanced up as he was about to leave the trailer, and his gaze connected with Natalie's. For one tense moment, they stared at each other, then with his mouth set, Adam stepped out into the blinding sunshine.

He had his gear laid out and was kneeling on the rough floor of the cabin packing a small backpack when a shadow fell across him. He looked up and his face tightened when he saw Natalie standing there.

She sat down beside him. "I brought you a change of clothes and the first-aid kit."

He continued to pack, his tone deliberately impassive. "I want to travel with a small pack, so I won't have room for the clothes."

She went through the stack of folded garments she had laid on her lap, then handed him a pair of socks. "At least take these. You'll need a dry pair."

Natalie was experienced enough to realize that this venture was no hike in the woods, and he could tell by the strained quality of her voice that she was concerned for his safety. And in spite of everything, he did not want her worrying about him. Nor did he want to leave her with this air of restraint hanging between them. His expression softened, and he stopped what he was doing and looked at her. "Don't worry, Nat," he said quietly. "It isn't going to be that risky."

Natalie looked up at him, her eyes dark with distress. She didn't say anything for the longest time, then she murmured unsteadily, "It's not just the rescue mission, Adam. I am so sorry about what happened earlier. I know it doesn't change things, but it wasn't a conscious reaction." She swallowed hard and looked away.

Adam's anger evaporated and he gazed at her profile, his expression grave as he reached across and slowly brushed her hair back. "I'm sorry, too," he said softly. He smoothed his hand along her cheek as he stared at her with obvious concern. Very gently, he turned her head so he could see her face, then he leaned over and kissed her lightly on the mouth.

With a choked sound, she slipped her arms around him and held him tightly. "Be careful, Adam. I don't know what I would do if anything ever happened to you."

Adam closed his eyes and pressed his face against the soft skin of her neck. "I'll be back before you know it," he whispered huskily. "And that's a solemn promise."

CHAPTER TWELVE

THE SILENCE WAS STIFLING. Natalie was completely motionless as she stood beside Doc's leather chair, her face drained of color. The jolt had been so traumatic, she felt as though every ounce of breath had been driven out of her body. With a weird detached sensation, she watched Doc fumble for support, then grasp the arm of his chair and slowly lower himself into it, his skin suddenly an unhealthy gray. Agitated, he looked at Doug Clifford and said sharply, "What do you mean—Adam never made it back?"

Dropping his hat on the table, the warden slowly sat down, his face showing the effects of long grueling hours with very little sleep. "When the helicopter went to pick the bunch of them off Hoodoo, there were only four hikers there. Seems that one of the kids fell and broke his leg pretty bad. They'd made a stretcher and were carrying him out, but the fire moved into the canyon and it looked like their route to the west could be cut off. Adam found a cave that he figured would give them some protection, and they were all going to hole up there. But the kid who was hurt was no dummy and he realized the fix they were in. He told Adam to leave him there and get the others out."

"My God," Natalie whispered, her eyes wide with alarm. "You mean Adam's down there alone—with no help, and an injured man to bring out?"

Leaning back in the chair, Doug Clifford dragged his hand through his thinning hair in a gesture of weariness, the worry lines deepening. "I'm afraid so, ma'am. I guess Adam was concerned about the direction of wind, and he figured he had to make a choice. Either get four out for sure, or stay and maybe take a chance that they'd all be trapped. So he brought the four out, then went back for the one they'd left behind. One of the kids we rescued was able to pinpoint the location of the cave. We've had the water bombers hitting that area pretty heavy, but it's so dry it's like a pile of kindling down there. With the mountains so close, the planes don't have much room to maneuver, but they're trying their damnedest to get as close to Hoodoo as they can. Your husband had a hand-held portable radio with him, but in this terrain, you can almost spit farther than they'll receive and send. Unless a plane is right overhead, they won't pick up a signal. The only reason he had it with him in the first place was to bring in the chopper once they hit the ledge on Hoodoo."

Natalie looked at Doc, then swallowed against fear, she turned her attention back to Doug Clifford. "I take it you've picked up no transmission?"

There was a disturbing somberness about him as he answered quietly, "No, ma'am. Nothing." His exhaustion seemed to weigh him down as he drew his hands across his eyes. When he raised his head to look at Doc and Natalie, his expression was bleak. "I'm afraid it looks pretty bad, Mrs. Rutherford. We're making every effort we can to locate them, but the fire's right at the base of Hoodoo, and there aren't a whole lot of places he could have gone."

Still in a state of shock, Natalie numbly turned and went to stand before the window, her arms clasped tightly around her. Staring out, she tried to fight through the numbness of disbelief. Like a tormenting dream, she suddenly remembered Adam giving her his solemn promise that he would be back soon, and with a cold shiver, she dragged her mind back to the grim present. "Have you considered sending someone down the west side?"

There was an air of defeat about him as the warden stared at her. "No, ma'am, we haven't. If you know Hoodoo at all, you'll remember that the ledge where we land isn't that wide. The smoke is heavy, in fact it's sitting in that canyon like soup, and we need good visibility so the chopper pilots can get in under that flat ridge on the upper part of the mountain."

"How long do you think it will be before you can?"

Doug Clifford picked up his hat and began turning it around and around in his hands as he considered her question. "It's hard to say. Unless there's a radical change in the wind or we get a gully washer of a rain . . . two, maybe three days."

She turned to look at him, her face drawn. "Are there facilities at Andrews Lake where I can stay?"

He stared at her briefly, then leaned forward and rested his arms on his legs. "There's not a whole lot there right now, but we could put you up in one of the staff quarters. We're moving in a trailer camp for the extra men." There was a heavy frown on his face as he began fidgeting with his hat again. "You may want to reconsider about going up to Andrews, Mrs. Rutherford. Somehow word leaked out that your husband had gone in on a rescue mission, and the place is swarming with reporters. We even have some from a TV network out of Los Angeles. They could make it pretty tough on you."

Who cares, she thought frantically. *Who gives a royal damn about reporters.* Aloud she assured him, "I'll manage."

The warden pursed his lips and shook his head, then heaved himself to his feet. "I can take you with me now if you like."

The shock was beginning to wear off, and Natalie suddenly felt very unsteady, and her voice revealed what she was feeling. "Thank you, but no. I want to talk to our son before I go, and I'd prefer to have a vehicle there." She went to the desk and made a notation on a slip of paper. "Adam has a phone in his truck, so you can either reach me here or on the radio telephone." She went over to him and handed him the paper. "Here's the mobile-call sign."

Doug Clifford took it, his manner preoccupied as he carefully folded the paper and tucked it in his breast pocket. "I want you to know that we're going to do our damnedest to get him out."

Natalie clasped her hands tightly together as she forced a tight smile. "I know you are, Warden."

Doc stood up and wearily clapped the warden on the back. "We have to keep faith with the lad, Doug. He uses his head, Adam does. And he'll come through this, you can be sure of that."

The warden sighed heavily, his expression anxious. "I hope so." He put his hat on as he went to the door. "We have the area sealed off, but I'll leave word at the gate that you're coming in, Mrs. Rutherford. And if something changes in the meantime, I'll get word to you."

Natalie nodded. "That will be fine."

He stared at her for a moment, as though he wanted to say something else. But he shook his head instead and opened the door. "The damned weather is against us, that's for sure. We had such a dry fall last year, and we haven't had much rain up there yet. Seems strange. Only eighty miles from here to Andrews Lake and it's as different as night and day. But maybe we'll get lucky and have a downpour tonight." He shook his head again, then touched the brim of his hat in a gesture of farewell. "We'll see you later, ma'am."

Doc followed him into the porch and as soon as the two men disappeared, Natalie sank into a chair, her strength suddenly gone. She felt strangely disconnected, as though her body were somewhere else. The sensation added to her growing alarm, but as fearful as she was for Adam's safety, she was determined not to give in to panic. She simply had to believe that he was still alive.

"I don't think it's a good idea for you to go up there, lass. The reporters could become an enormous drain on you."

Natalie looked up at Doc, her ashen face set with determination. "I can deal with it."

He sat back down in his chair, his shoulders even more stooped than usual. "You'll serve no purpose by being there, Natalie," he reasoned gently.

No purpose. She met his worried gaze with an unyielding stare, her voice low and inflexible. "I will personally walk every square foot of that canyon if I have to, but I will not leave until we find him."

It was obvious by her tone that absolutely nothing would change her mind. Doc had seen her like this once before, and that was when she was sixteen years old and the doctors had tried to convince her to terminate her pregnancy. She had not given in then, and he knew she would not give in now. Feeling very tired, he rubbed his temple with his fingertips. "What are you going to tell Patrick?"

"The truth—that his father has gone back in to bring an injured hiker out." She met Doc's gaze square on, the look in her eyes daring him to challenge her. "He'll understand why I want to be there."

"Natalie, lass, you have to be realistic about the possibility that—"

"No!" Her eyes were flashing as she abruptly stood up. "No. Don't even think it, Doc. He's going to be all right. He has to be." She turned away quickly, and Doc saw her shoulders start to shake. "He has to be," she said again. And the undercurrent of sheer panic he heard in her voice was also grimly familiar. It was too much the same, this ordeal she was facing, and there was little he could do to give her comfort. Especially when he was well aware of just how critical the situation was. He slowly rose, then went over and patted her shoulder. "I'll go for Patrick, lass, while you pack your things."

THE COMMAND POST at Andrews Lake was bedlam. Men and equipment were being moved in, along with the supplies and services to support them. The fire, which was raging out of control, was consuming hundreds and hundreds of acres of prime forest, and if not contained, would consume thousands more. That in itself was tragic enough, but to make matters worse, a well-known wildlife photographer was missing on a dangerous rescue mission, and the media were having a field day with that.

Doug Clifford was right about them. They had latched on to Natalie the moment she arrived. But their persistence only made her more determined to maintain a calm, confident front, regardless of the fact that with each passing hour, her fears for Adam's safety mounted.

The sky was unnaturally murky and the sun burned like an eerie red globe through the smoke, the outline of the mountains barely visible through the gray haze. The water bombers reloaded on Lake Andrews, and the drone of them taxiing across the lake as they took on water seemed almost continuous. The smell of burning timber insinuated itself on her senses, and the acrid odor of smoke clung to her clothes and hair.

The first night in camp was never-ending for Natalie. Camp units had been hauled in for accommodations, and she had been put up in the trailer provided for the women. But she never closed her eyes. During the day, as long as she didn't have time to dwell on it, she could keep her confidence up.

But it was a different story at night. As she lay staring into the darkness, she tried to battle the awful realization that there was every possibility that Adam was already dead. And as some sort of masochistic punishment, her mind turned on her, and she was tortured with grisly mental scenarios of Adam trapped in the fire. The stark horror of knowing those scenarios could be deadly accurate awakened a cold sickening feeling in her, and she experienced a new level of fear. As she stared into the darkness, she tried not to think about what life would be like without him. Instead, she tried to call up the warm secure feeling of going to sleep in Adam's arms, but it eluded her, and only the smell of smoke infiltrated her senses.

As soon as the sky started to lighten, Natalie left her bed. She had a shower in the campgrounds' shower and bathroom facilities, then went over to the kitchen to help with breakfast. Shortly after her arrival, Natalie realized they were desperately shorthanded in the kitchen. Needing something to do to take her mind off the endless waiting, she had volunteered to help. The cook had put her to work, and Natalie had spent hours making sandwiches and packing lunches.

The warden came in just as she was pouring herself a cup of coffee. She poured a second cup and took them over to his table.

He glanced up as she set the mug before him. "Why thanks, Mrs. Rutherford." He watched as she sat down, a worried look in his eyes. "You're sure not expected to help out here, you know. You're going to be dead on your feet if you keep that up."

She gave him a small smile. "Keeping busy helps, Warden. You don't have so much time to think." Avoiding his eyes, she tidied the arrangement of salt and pepper shakers, napkin holder, then moved the cream and sugar to the side. "Have you had any reports yet this morning?"

He hunched over his coffee as he stirred in the cream, then raised his head. His eyes were red-rimmed, and he looked as though he hadn't slept in days. "Only by radio, and those reports aren't going to give us anything about your husband. Another hour and it'll be light enough for the water bombers to take off. We'll know more then."

Natalie's expression was carefully schooled as she looked at him. "You said last night that one of the helicopters would make a sweep over Hoodoo this morning."

"Yes, ma'am, as soon as it's light enough."

"I want to go."

He stared at her for a moment, then looked down at his coffee. "I think maybe it would be better if you stayed on the ground, ma'am," he answered gruffly.

Reaching across the table, she laid her hand on his wrist as she pleaded with him. "Please, I have to go. I need to see it, Warden. For my own peace of mind, I have to see that canyon."

He raised his eyes and looked at her, his expression grim. "It isn't going to do a hell of a lot for your peace of mind, ma'am. I can assure you of that."

Three-quarters of an hour later, Natalie was a passenger in the Bell helicopter that was making the reconnaissance flight. The noise in the machine was deafening, and Doug Clifford had given her headphones so she could hear the conversation between him and the pilot.

They were skimming along a few hundred feet above the ground, the rocky surface slipping dizzily below them. Suddenly they crested a ridge and the earth dropped sharply away, and spread below them were miles and miles of burning timber. The pilot's voice crackled hollowly on the intercom. "We'll be turning north in a minute here, Mrs. Rutherford. We have to fly around that ridge to the west before we have a clear shot of the canyon."

They swept around the ridge, and their destination came into view. It was a long narrow canyon that was hemmed in by mountains, the far end blocked by the eerie, looming fortress of Hoodoo. And it was a trough of flames. There wasn't a square inch that had escaped the inferno. At the throat of the canyon, there was the charred, smoldering remains of a virgin forest, and at the other end, there was a raging wall of fire licking at the base of Hoodoo. Squeezing her eyes shut, she weakly leaned her head against the window as a cold sweat hit her. Not even in her worst nightmares had it been this bad.

The warden had been watching her over the back of his seat, and he shook his head when he saw the expression on her face. "I think she's seen enough, Mike. You'd better head back."

Natalie was vaguely aware of the return flight, but she felt numbly disoriented when she realized they had landed. Her senses dulled by shock, she went through the motions of taking off the headset and undoing her seat belt like a robot. The minute she emerged from the doorway, TV cameras focused on her and reporters moved closer. Realizing that she was functioning in a daze, Doug Clifford pressed her head down as they ran out from beneath the whirling blades.

Somehow she got through the cluster of reporters, and somehow she made it back to the camp. Once clear of any onlookers and Doug Clifford's deep concern, she stumbled into the bush like a wounded wild animal going to ground. Her numbness cracked like crystal as the reaction set in, and she was violently sick. She could play all the games she wanted to, but sheer logic told her that no living thing could have possibly survived that canyon fire. She desperately wanted to run, but there was no place for her to go.

The rest of that day passed in a numb blur. By the following day, she was so exhausted she could barely stay on her feet.

On the third morning, relief finally came when the winds changed, and the fire was driven back on itself. And Natalie knew with a deep cold dread that it was only a matter of hours until her waiting would be over.

That end came early the next morning. The helicopters had taken off at first light, and it was just midmorning when Doug Clifford appeared in the cook house. One of the men turned to speak to him, but he held up his hand and shook his head, then quickly scanned the room. He stopped looking when he spotted her, and Natalie's stomach dropped sickeningly as he wound his way through the tables to her, his expression tense.

Tightly grasping the edge of the counter, she watched him approach, her body braced for bad news.

"One of the choppers has something, Mrs. Ruthford, but we don't know what. The pilot's been having trouble with the radio the past couple of days, but the transmission was really breaking up bad today. We could only make out the odd word. All's we know for sure is they found something and they're headed back. They should be on the pad in twenty minutes." He took his hat off and ran his hand through his hair, then looked at her, his eyes very solemn. "I wouldn't get my hopes up if I were you," he warned gently. "You know what that area was like."

She swallowed hard, then looked away, her voice strained. "Yes, I know."

A sudden hush fell in the kitchen, and for an instant, all eyes were riveted on Natalie. Then as though they didn't want to intrude on her private hell, they averted their eyes. The only sound came from the far corner as two photographers quietly eased away from the table, collected their equipment and left the room. The silence became oppressive, and finally Natalie broke it. "I'll be down at the landing pad if you want me," she said very quietly.

The sky was heavily overcast and there was a mugginess in the air that warned of an impending storm. Natalie stood removed from the others, unable to endure the claustrophobic confinement. Her mind was a jumble of disjointed thoughts as she stared numbly at the leaden sky.

She heard the approaching helicopter before she saw it. Then it shot out from behind a ridge, skimming above the trees, and Natalie experienced a flurry of dread as she watched it come closer. The aircraft made a sweeping turn into the wind, then briefly hovered, the pitch from the turbine changing as it slowly lowered to the ground. The downdraft kicked up a flurry of dust, and Natalie shielded her eyes and turned her head from the machine-made whirlwind. The minute it settled on the gravel pad, Doug Clifford and two other uniformed men headed for the plane, ducking to miss the whirling rotor blades.

They slid open the side door and Natalie experienced a frightening heaviness in her chest as the warden climbed in. It was as though she was looking through a long thin tunnel, her attention welded on that open door. For one agonizing moment there was nothing. Then a rescue cradle was lifted out.

The warden crouched beside the stretcher, and Natalie felt as if every drop of blood suddenly drained from her body as she saw him shake his head. Her view was blocked as some photographers moved in, and panic started to build in her when she couldn't see. Desperate to find out who was in the stretcher, she started to run. The ground was rough and she stumbled, her muscles anesthetized by fear. A photographer turned and let out a whoop of excitement, and a cheer went up from those waiting at the sidelines. It took a minute for it to sink in that the person in the cradle was alive. Her heart started slamming frantically in her chest, and she could hardly breathe as she was hit with an incapacitating mixture of fear and hope. Just then, one of the flight crew who had been standing in the doorway stepped aside, and Natalie could see the other passenger.

Adam Rutherford ducked through the helicopter door.

There were no words to explain how she felt. She couldn't think. She couldn't breathe. She could barely absorb the fact that he was there. Aware of no one but him, she stared across the space that separated them, feeling as though she was finally waking up from a long and horrible dream. He was back, and he was safe. Then the aftermath of fear hit her, and she knew if she moved one single muscle, she would start to shake so badly she wouldn't be able to stand. He had somehow managed to escape that scorching fury.

And from the look of him, it had been a vicious struggle. He was filthy and caked with mud, and every inch of exposed skin was blackened by soot. His smudged face was streaked with sweat and a rough beard covered his jaw. His eyes were bloodshot and glazed with exhaustion, and he moved as though he was ready to drop. He looked as if he'd been to hell and back.

Orders were being shouted, and the warden pointed to the stretcher, then motioned to the helicopter, and the reporters started moving away from the aircraft. Adam crouched beside the cradle, his expression intent as he spoke to the injured hiker, then patting the young man on the shoulder, he slowly straightened. He helped reload the casualty on the helicopter, then spoke briefly to the medic who had followed the stretcher on board. As he closed the door, the warden shouted at Adam, and Adam turned abruptly and looked in Natalie's direction. The pitch of the rotors changed and the engine's whine accelerated as Adam ducked and headed toward her.

Natalie started to shake, but somehow she found the strength to move. He reached for her and she stumbled blindly into his arms, unable to contain the unbearable surge of relief any longer. When they came together, Adam's arms were like a vise clamping her against him. He turned his face into the curve of her neck and whispered hoarsely, "God, Nat, I'm so damned glad to see you."

He smelled strongly of smoke and sweat, and Natalie squeezed her eyes shut as she inhaled the living essence of him. She was trembling badly and her voice was ragged. "Adam . . . Adam—I was so scared."

"I know, love," he whispered roughly. "I know."

His hand in her hair, he pressed her head against his shoulder, cradling her body in an enveloping, protective hold.

"We'd like a shot of Mr. Rutherford if you don't mind. Could you turn for the camera?"

Adam swore. Drawing a deep shuddering breath, Natalie lifted her head and he gently eased her away from him. His throat was raw from smoke, and his voice was very hoarse when he asked, "Are you okay?"

Not trusting herself to speak, she nodded and wiped her eyes with the side of her hand.

He touched her face and said softly, "Just a few more minutes, and we can get the hell out of here, Nat. Can you hang in there for a little longer?"

She answered with a shaky smile. The expression in his eyes softened, and he lightly touched her face. He gazed at her a second longer, then assured she was able to deal with the final hurdle, he slipped his arm around her shoulders and turned to face the cluster of reporters.

Natalie felt him sway slightly, and she looked up at him, her expression suddenly anxious. He was so exhausted he was on the verge of dropping in his tracks. Slipping her arm around his waist to give him what support she could, she matched her stride with his as they started walking toward the camp.

A reporter who had a reputation for being pushy hurried ahead of them, then turned to face them. Walking backward, he held out the mike of his tape recorder and started quizzing Adam. "Tell us how you felt being trapped down there."

Adam gave him a cutting look and answered dryly, "Unhappy."

Natalie looked up at him, the worried look in his eyes giving way to a glint of amusement. He winked at her and she grinned, and suddenly he didn't feel so damned beat.

"And how did you finally manage to get out?"

The reporter's manner started to irritate Adam and he stared at him coldly. "Luck," he answered tersely.

Realizing he'd get nowhere with Adam, the pimple-faced young man made the grave mistake of shoving the mike at Natalie. She stumbled as she tried to avoid it, and with lightning speed and his eyes flashing fire, Adam knocked the mike out of his hands. "Stick that in her face again," he said through clenched teeth, "and I can assure you you'll eat the damned thing."

With the main attraction obviously in no mood for interviews, everyone quietly faded away, and Adam and Natalie covered the rest of the distance in silence. It was all Adam could do to keep putting one foot in front of the other. His eyes felt as if there was gravel in them, his throat was burned raw from smoke, his tongue felt like leather, and he was so tired he could go to sleep standing up.

When they got to the kitchen, Doug Clifford was waiting for them at the door. "Sorry I had to take off down there, but I had to let the other units know we got you out."

Too weary to answer, Adam nodded in acknowledgment, then reluctantly withdrew his arm from around Natalie so she could precede him. Once inside, he sank into the first chair he came to, tipped his head back and closed his eyes. Somehow he would have to find the energy to tell the warden what happened.

"Adam?"

He lowered his head and slowly opened his eyes. Natalie was standing beside him with a large glass of water in one hand and a frosty glass of milk in the other. Feeling as though his arms weighed a ton, he took both glasses from her and managed a feeble smile, "You're reading my mind again."

The water was ice cold, and he downed it thirstily. Natalie took the empty glass from him and set it on the table. She stood behind him, her arms draped loosely around his neck. Her hands were cool and soothing against his skin as she pressed him back. Experiencing a poignant rush of gratitude, he wearily leaned his head against her abdomen.

Doug Clifford pulled out a chair and sat down. "I know you're wiped, but I'm afraid I have to bug you for a couple details. We have these damned reports that have to be filed."

Adam took a long drink of milk, then fixed his bleary gaze on the warden. "What do you need to know?"

The warden gave him a warped smile. "How the hell you walked out of that inferno."

Adam finished the milk, then covered one of Natalie's hands with his. "If it hadn't been for the accuracy of those water bombers, we would have been fried three days ago. They gave me the time and the room I needed to get from the cave to the base. And from there I packed the kid up onto the overhang." Adam managed a weak grin. "Then I prayed that the erosion at the base of it wasn't really as bad as it looked."

The warden appeared stunned. "Dammit, man, that's one hell of a climb."

Adam nodded, a spark of humor in his eyes. "It sure in hell is."

"How did you ever lug that kid up there?"

"I piggybacked him. Fortunately he was small and light. I never would have made it if he'd been any heavier. As it was, my legs nearly gave out on me."

The warden shook his head, his expression dazed. "I don't know how you managed it. I really don't."

Adam's tone was dry. "A forest fire licking at your heels gives you plenty of incentive, Warden."

The man shook his head again, then looked at Adam. "So you holed up on the overhang," he said, his voice tinged with amazement.

"When the wind turned, I decided I'd better move out while I had the chance. We were on the ledge when the chopper spotted us."

Doug Clifford mulled that over for a moment, then frowned as he studied Adam. "How bad is the kid?"

"He has a bad fracture in his ankle, and I suspect he has some torn ligaments in his knee. He was in a lot of pain, and four nights on a mountain with no shelter doesn't do anyone much good, but he's young. He'll come out of this okay."

Leaning forward, the warden stared at the floor for a moment, then he raised his head, his expression grave. "It doesn't seem like enough to say how damned much we appreciate what you did for us here. Five young kids can thank their lucky stars you were around."

Adam met his serious gaze. "Anytime," he answered quietly.

There was a silent exchange between the two men, then the warden slapped his knees and stood up. "I think you'd better hit the sack before you fall asleep right here. There's some empty beds in the bunkhouse."

Adam managed a weak grin and shook his head. "If you don't mind, I'd just as soon get the hell out of here."

The warden frowned. "The minute you step out that door, those media guys are going to be all over you."

Natalie smoothed her hand across Adam's shoulder. "I'll take him out the back." There was a touch of cynicism in her smile. "None of them would be caught dead in a kitchen."

"Well, if you're smart, you won't go back to Doc's. That pack out there will follow you to the ends of the earth." He paused and rubbed his chin thoughtfully. "If I were you, I'd head for that trailer of yours."

Natalie glanced down at Adam, who was leaning heavily against her, and a deep ache tightened in her chest when she saw that he was already asleep. The warden was right. Adam needed a few hours of undisturbed rest, and the trailer would be the only place he'd get it. She gently stroked Adam's coarsely bearded face, her voice suddenly husky, "Would you contact Doc and explain? Tell him Adam's fine but I'm taking him back to the trailer for a while."

"I'll have to radio, so I'll give you a half hour head start before I contact him just in case a wise ass is monitoring the radio channels." He tipped his hat back on his head and motioned to Adam. "Now let's get him out the back door."

Adam was out like a light the minute he settled into the comfortable reclining bucket seat in the Bronco. The next thing he was aware of was Natalie bending over him, a cool breeze against his face. "Come on, Adam," she said softly. "We're home." It took him a while before he could fight his way through the heavy fog that clogged his mind. When he was finally able to focus, he realized that Natalie had driven the truck right down to the trailer instead of parking it where they normally did. He rubbed his face, then looked at her. The front of her pale pink shirt was smeared with dirt, and there was a smudge of soot along her neck and across her jaw. He realized the grime was from him, and he also realized just how damned filthy he was. Suddenly he desperately wanted a long hot shower.

He wearily climbed out of the truck and closed the door. "By any chance, did you leave the propane on when you left?"

She grimaced guiltily. "I'm afraid I did. I never even thought to shut it off."

He gave her a lopsided grin as he laid his arm across her shoulders. "A wise mistake, Nat. That means there's a whole tankful of hot water."

"Don't you want something to eat first?"

There was a flicker of humor in his eyes. "Not if it's anything I have to chew."

Natalie opened the door, then looked up at him, a smile pulling at her mouth. "Can you manage something really taxing, like swallowing?"

"Maybe. And maybe not."

The trailer was hot and stuffy from being closed up for so long, and Natalie opened all the windows and vents, then went to the fridge. While Adam was shaving, she fixed a tall mixed fruit drink with crushed ice, and Adam doubted if he'd ever drunk anything that tasted so good. He was badly dehydrated after five days in that heat with closely rationed liquids, and his throat was so sore, something cold and wet was all he wanted.

Natalie stood by the cupboard as she watched him drink. "Are you sure you don't want anything to eat? I can fix you something light, like an omelet."

He handed her the empty glass as he shook his head. "Maybe later. Right now all I want is a long hot shower and a bed."

Adam stayed in the shower until he drained the hot water tank. When he finally got out, the heat had sapped what little strength he had. He made a halfhearted effort to dry his hair, then wrapping a towel around his hips, he went into the bedroom. Natalie had folded the bed down and there was another tall glass of fruit punch on the ledge behind the bed.

"Is there anything else I can get you?" she asked softly.

Adam turned. She was looking up at him, her eyes so dark they seemed almost black. He reached out and slowly caressed her cheek. "All I need right now is a few hours' sleep."

She looked down quickly but not quick enough, and Adam caught the gleam of tears. He hooked his knuckles under her chin and gently raised her face. "What's the matter?"

"I saw that canyon," she whispered unevenly. "And to think you walked out of that...."

He wanted to put that ordeal behind them, and he tried to lighten the mood. "Didn't Doc ever tell you that close calls don't count, Nat?" he said softly.

She stared at him for a moment, then with her breath catching on a choked sob, she was in his arms. He hugged her tightly against him, his cheek pressed into her hair. "I'm sorry, Natalie," he murmured huskily. "I shouldn't treat it lightly. It's just that there were too damned many hours when I really wondered if I'd ever see you again." He tightened his arms around her and his voice became even more gruff. "There was one point when it looked really grim, and I would have given anything to have one last chance to tell you how much I love you."

Hauling in a ragged breath, she caught the back of his head, and with a sound, she covered his mouth with her own. There was a staggering amount of emotion in that kiss—fear, relief, but beneath it all, there was a fire of passion. And Adam's response was instantaneous. Like a starving man, he moved his mouth against hers, famished for the warmth and moistness she was giving him. An incredible energy flooded through him, the feel of her body against his washing away the utter exhaustion. He couldn't move; he couldn't think. All he could do was feel, and galvanizing sensations coursed through him with a blinding intensity.

But suddenly a sliver of sanity penetrated the fever and he realized what was happening. Grasping her by the shoulders, he pushed her arms away, roughly severing the scalding contact. He was fighting for breath as he buried his face in the curve of her neck and whispered hoarsely, "God, Nat. I'm sorry."

She seemed almost frantic as she caught his head, her mouth hot and liquid against his neck. "Don't, Adam. Please, don't stop. Don't stop." She found his mouth and moaned against it, her desperation tearing at her. "Please, Adam . . . please."

A groan was wrung out of him, and widening his stance, he locked her against him, his need out of control. She responded to every move he made, and a searing passion possessed them, welding them together in a white-hot heat. And much as he wanted to be gentle with her, he could not relax his hold on her. He felt as if he would go out of his mind if he severed that electric contact, even for a second.

Natalie made a low throaty sound of protest as he caught her hips and held her motionless. Then with shaking fingers he undid her slacks, and slipping his hands against her naked skin, he pushed her jeans down. As though she couldn't stand the separation, she clasped his head between her hands and kissed him with a blistering heat as he unbuttoned her shirt.

Groaning against her mouth, Adam experienced the agonizing pleasure of their naked bodies locked together, and from somewhere he found the strength to drag her down on the bed beside him. Natalie cried out as he drew her beneath him, her body moving frantically against his, searching for the rhythm that would carry them even higher. He took her, and she arched against him, her body convulsing around his and drawing from him a hot, liquid eruption that paralyzed him. And they clung to each other, fused by a blinding release.

IN THE FIRST DRIFTING STAGE of consciousness, he felt oddly displaced. Slowly he became aware that he was lying on his stomach and there was a cool breeze against his skin. The sound of a light drizzle on the metal roof penetrated his sleepy stupor, and he slowly opened his eyes. The curtain on the open window lazily billowed, and drops of rain slid down the foggy windowpane. And it was so unbelievably still.

The heaviness of sleep weighed him down, but somehow he summoned up enough strength to turn his head and look at Natalie. But she wasn't there. Instantly awake, he levered himself out of bed. He swayed slightly, his body still drugged by the residue of a very deep and heavy sleep, and shaking his head to clear the fog, he went to the bedroom door.

The trailer was empty and silent, and Adam suddenly had a very hollow feeling in the pit of his stomach. He turned to get dressed, intending on going after her. But before he could move, the door opened and Natalie came in, wearing nothing except his yellow slicker. He felt welded to the floor as he watched her, his apprehension nearly suffocating. How would she react to him after the blaze of passion? Had that encounter dredged up ugly memories, or had it overpowered them?

Pulling the door shut, she kicked off her shoes and looked up. Adam felt as if his life were hanging by a thread. For a split second, they simply stared at each other, then she smiled and brushed the rain from her face. "I remembered I left the windows of the truck open." She grimaced a little sheepishly. "I thought I might get away with one goof over the propane, but I would never get away with two."

Adam had a hard time easing a breath past the strangling ache in his chest. Most of her hair had pulled free of the pins, the loose strands framing her face, and tiny beads of moisture were caught in the disheveled tangle. The slicker hung open, exposing a long narrow strip of her naked body, and the whole combination was totally alluring and very,

very sexy. But what captivated him more than anything else was the soft glow in her eyes.

It took a tremendous effort for him to speak, and his voice was very husky as he murmured, "If that's what you wear to roll up windows, you can leave them down in a hurricane if you want."

Her eyes darkened and she moved toward him, holding his gaze with a mesmerizing intensity, her mysterious half smile very provocative. She stopped in front of him, seducing him with her eyes as she slowly smoothed her hands across his pelvis and up his chest. "I like that, Adam—a man who knows his priorities."

Her touch set off shock waves of sensation, and closing his eyes, he crushed her against him. The smell of rain clung to her hair, and he breathed deeply as he pressed his face into the silky tumble, his deep feelings for her nearly overwhelming him. "God, Nat," he whispered hoarsely, "when I woke up and you weren't there, I thought for sure I had come on too strong."

She caught his head and forced it up so she could see his face, then with trembling fingers she stroked his mouth. "Nothing can ever equal the kind of cold paralyzing dread I had when you were missing, Adam. And my other fears were so insignificant compared to that." Her voice became more strained and her eyes darkened. "You overpowered my senses, Adam, and I couldn't think of anything but what was happening between us."

Feeling raw and exposed, Adam lowered his head and kissed her softly. Her mouth slackened beneath his, and became hot and yielding as the kiss deepened into a scalding explosion of desire. Running his hands across her shoulders and down her arms, Adam stripped the slicker from her slender body, then picked her up and carried her to the bed. Her eyes were glazed with passion as he leaned over her, then with a soft sob, she tried to pull him down on top of her.

Resisting the pressure, he thrust his fingers into the tangle of her hair and slowly stroked her cheek with his thumb. He smiled softly. "No, Nat," he murmured huskily. "I've waited a damned long time to really make love to you, and I want to make it last. I want to savor every sensation, and I want time to savor every inch of you." He smoothed his hand along her thigh and let it rest on her midriff, his smoldering gaze locked on hers. Then in an agony of tension, he slowly moved his hand higher.

Her reaction was explosive, and her breath was driven out of her by the force. Twisting her head to the side, she closed her eyes as a heavy tremor coursed through her. A galvanizing hunger spread through him while he caressed her, his senses reeling as he watched her respond. Another tremor shuddered through her, then she slowly opened her eyes and looked at him, her fevered gaze intoxicating. Her eyes locked on his, she reached up, caught his head and drew it down. Moaning softly, she arched against him as he touched her sensitive flesh with his mouth, and as she responded to his intimate caress, his rigid control caved in around him.

The agony of the past was finally behind them. He had led her out of the shadows, and now he would lead her into the light.

EPILOGUE

A VIBRANT AUTUMN SUNSET lit the western sky, tinting the cloud formation a blaze of colors, and each vivid shade was perfectly mirrored on the smooth surface of the lake. The smell of burning leaves drifted up on the crisp autumn air, and sounds of laughter echoed across the still water.

Adam leaned back against the trunk of a tree, the rough bark penetrating the thickness of his heavy fisherman-knit sweater. Flexing one knee, he rested his arm across it, lazily watching the dancing flames of the bonfire through half-closed eyes.

Just three days earlier he had finished filming the main background material for his documentary about the cougar, and this chance to relax was a treat. He still had to get more close-up footage, but that would have to be done in the spring and summer months so he could record the development of the cubs, providing, of course, that the female he'd been tracking did him the favor of having some. It had been a good shoot, and he was experiencing the deep satisfaction he always did at the end of a project. But then, he had a lot to feel satisfied about.

It was the Thanksgiving weekend and Stella and Natalie had organized a massive buffet that was both Thanksgiving dinner and a windup bash. They had packed everything Friday afternoon, and as soon as Patrick got home from school, they moved out to the lake for the long weekend. Adam's parents had driven in from the coast in their motor home, and Pete, the sound man, had somehow managed to wheel the huge network remote unit up the mountain road.

Adam had fully restored one cabin, and Doc, Patrick and three of Patrick's friends had moved into that. Stella had scandalized Doc by closing the drugstore Saturday, stating very loudly that she had no damned intention of missing all the fun. And Stella, being Stella, spent the night wherever she had her last cigarette. It had been a fantastic weekend so far, and Adam was glad they still had another day.

Shifting his shoulders to a more comfortable spot, he grinned as he watched his father and Doc whipping the pants off two members of the film crew in a game of horseshoes. Stella and his mother were sitting in lawn chairs on the other side of the fire, and Natalie was on the ground in front of them, her arms locked around her knees.

His expression became sober as Adam considered his parents. They had been terrific about everything. When he had taken Natalie and Patrick out for the first visit, Adam's mother had welcomed her new daughter-in-law as though Natalie had never been away. They had been absolutely enthralled with Patrick, and he with them. Natalie had really surprised Adam the first night they were there. They had been sitting around the kitchen table having coffee, recalling the time Natalie and Adam sank Gordon's brand-new canoe. They had laughed about it, and a few other episodes were remembered.

There had been a comfortable silence, then Natalie had spoken up, her voice shaking. "I want you to know that the reason I left had nothing to do with me being pregnant." And then in an unsteady voice, she told them, without getting into the sordid details, what had happened. It was almost eerie to watch his father's reaction. It had virtually been a duplicate of his own.

"Are you sleeping or are you just hiding behind your eyelids?"

Adam opened his eyes to find Natalie crouched beside him, a steaming cup of coffee in her hand. He grinned as he took it from her. "I'm hiding. I had a hard day."

"What you had was too much turkey and pumpkin pie," she said succinctly.

Adam took a sip and choked, his coffee slopping over the edge of the cup. Biting back a grin, Natalie shrugged, her tone almost reproving. "It's only a little brandy."

"A little!" he rasped, his eyes watering. "And whose 'little'—yours or Doc's?"

"Actually, it's Stella's. But I'm just trying to keep your blood circulating."

He gave her a long steady stare as he said suggestively, "There are other, much more satisfactory ways of keeping my blood circulating, Natalie."

There was laughter in her eyes as she leaned over and gave him a quick kiss. "You can tell me all about them later."

Adam caught her around the waist and pulled her on top of him, then shifted her weight so she was sitting between his legs with her back against his chest. "Let's talk about them now," he murmured against her ear.

She was smiling as she leaned back against him, and Adam tightened his arm around her and snuggled her closer. "What we need to talk about," she said firmly, "is the fact that Pete and his gang are now at the picnic table teaching Pat and his gang the fine art of playing poker."

Adam took another sip of coffee, then laughed softly. "Don't worry about it. By the time Pete finishes explaining the rules, Patrick and his gang will have graduated from high school."

Pete's soft Louisiana drawl came out of the shadows. "Oh, I think we could move that projection up a year or two. That kid plays poker just like his old man." Squatting beside them, he took a long pull of his beer, then started picking at the label. "I just thought about something I meant to ask you when we first came up. I heard you had a bit of a run-in with Deek McCarthy."

Adam frowned and shook his head. "I don't know a Deek McCarthy."

There was a devilish grin on Pete's face. "Sure you do. That pimple-faced mouth that does locations for the network."

"Never laid eyes on him."

The grin broadened. "Well that's not how he tells it. Seems that you pitched a five-hundred-dollar mike of his over a cliff because he crowded your little lady here."

Adam's tone was cryptic. "He was damned lucky I didn't pitch him over a cliff."

Pete studied the two of them. "Yeah," he said thoughtfully "I'd say he was." Pete had worked with Adam Rutherford for a good many years and he knew him pretty well. And knowing Adam Rutherford the way he did, he wouldn't give two cents for anyone who ever laid a hand on Natalie.

Patrick came tearing up and dropped on his knees in front of his parents. "Hey, Dad, can I have your Buck knife? Aunt Stella has a big bag of marshmallows for us to roast, and Grandpa's going to take us to some willow sticks. And we need a sharp knife."

Holding Natalie securely, Adam twisted and undid the leather case he wore on his belt, then handed the knife to Patrick. "Which Grandpa's going with you?"

Patrick scrambled to his feet. "Both Grandpas. Grandpa Patterson is going to show Grandpa Rutherford where he caught that big trout." He smiled broadly as he scrubbed his nose with the back of his hand. "Grandma says that scales will start popping out on their arms any day now."

Natalie took a Kleenex out of her pocket and handed it to him. "I hope you'll remember that, Patrick. Your grandmother is a wise woman."

He gave his mother a long-suffering look then blew his nose. "Grandpa Rutherford is going to teach me how to play chess. He says he's going to get me some books to read so I can learn all about it." Patrick wiped his nose again, then wadded up the tissue and dropped it on the ground.

"This isn't a garbage can, Patrick," his father said quietly.

Patrick picked up his litter, a sheepish tone in his voice. "I *know*, Dad. The only thing I'm supposed to leave behind are my footprints."

Smiling, Natalie shifted so she could look at Adam. "I am impressed. Now if you can only house-train him."

Patrick grinned and made a face, then darted away when Doc called him. Adam watched his son run up to Doc, and as he handed him the knife, the old man affectionately ruffled the boy's hair. A very strong bond had developed between the two, and nothing could have pleased Adam more. It reminded him of his own youth, and how he had become Doc's shadow when he wasn't much older than Patrick. And he had a hunch that his son's presence had as much to do with Doc's improved health as Natalie's care.

Pete had been watching Patrick, and he turned to face Natalie and Adam. "I don't think I've ever run across a kid that's so keen on learning. Is there anything he isn't interested in?"

"Yes," said Natalie dryly. "Washing."

Adam laughed as he looped his arms over her shoulders. "What a nag."

Stretching out on the ground, Pete propped his head on his hand and gazed out across the lake. "This is really beautiful country. I can sure understand why you've decided to use this as a home base, especially with that house you're building down there beside Doc's. And this place here—man, it's fantastic."

Adam rested his head against Natalie's as he stared into the deepening dusk, his expression suddenly sober. "Yeah, Pete, it is. It feels pretty damned good to put down roots after being on the move for so long."

Grinning broadly, Pete looked at Natalie. "You talk about house-training—I'd say you done a fair to middlin' job on ol' Adam here. A wife, a house, a kid. Next thing, you'll have him changing diapers." He glanced over at the bonfire, an almost embarrassed look on his face as he got to his feet. "Think I'll try my hand at those marshmallows—haven't roasted one in years. Second childhood, I guess."

"Ah," said Natalie gravely. "What you need is a wife, a house, a kid."

Pete nodded, his eyes glinting with humor. "I think I could just about handle that." He turned and started to walk away. "But I think I'd better wait and see how ol' Adam hangs in there."

Natalie's voice was rich with amusement as she asked quietly, "And how *is* ol' Adam hanging in there?'

"I'll survive," he responded, a husky tone in his voice.

She turned to look at him. "You haven't told him yet, have you?"

Adam gently lifted a loose curl off her face and tucked it behind her ear. "No, not yet," he answered quietly, his touch lingering as he slowly smoothed back her hair. "This is something that's very special for me, Nat. And telling a bunch of freewheeling single guys that we're going to have another kid seems so out of context with what I'm feeling." His eyes darkened and became even more solemn, his tone reverent. "It's such a miracle, and this time I'm going to be around to watch it happen."

The depth of feeling in his words made Natalie's throat ache, and her voice was uneven as she whispered, "Being able to share all this with you this time makes it so special, Adam. I missed that so much when I was pregnant with Patrick—having you there."

Adam's arms tightened around her, his voice taking on a new intensity. "I can't wait for the house to be finished. The day we can move all your stuff out of storage and into our home can't come soon enough."

Natalie smiled as she rested her head on his shoulder, a faraway look in her eyes. "It's going to be so nice to be able to stay home with this one. I'm going to love every minute of it."

"Come on you two. Enough lollygagging around. Your mother and I are challenging you to a game of horse-shoes."

Adam smiled at his father. "You can't even see the pegs. How can you play horseshoes in the dark?"

Gordon Rutherford chuckled. "The way your mother plays, it may as well be dark."

Natalie laughed, then gave her father-in-law a narrow look. "I'm going to tell her what you said, Gordon, and then you'll be in big trouble."

"Now Natalie. You know for a fact I spend half my time in trouble with that woman already."

"Sure, Dad. Sure," Adam said, without an ounce of conviction.

Hilda Rutherford came up behind Gordon and slapped him affectionately on the rear, then grinned. "Be nice to me, Father, or the next time they come to visit, I'll lend them your brand-new boat."

He chuckled again. "You're a terrible woman, Hilda. Terrible."

Getting to her feet, Natalie dusted off her jeans, then reached down and caught Adam's hand, her eyes dancing. "Come on, Adam. Don't just lie there like a big lump. Show these people what you can do in the dark."

He shot her a loaded look, then came smoothly to his feet, his own eyes flashing. "You're a terrible woman, Nat-alie. Terrible."

Hand in hand, they followed the senior Rutherfords. A gas lantern was suspended from the branch of a tree, cast-ing a soft light on the group at the picnic table. Stella and Doc had joined them, and Stella had a pile of small pebbles heaped in front of her. Adam laughed. "You've just about got enough to start a gravel company, Stella."

"Wouldn't you know it. I get hot and the ante is a bunch of damned rocks."

"You're always hot," Doc said slyly as he puffed on his pipe.

"Cute, Doc. Real cute. Now ante up. I'm going to win that damned drugstore off you tonight or die trying."

His eyes were twinkling. "I don't know why you want it, lass. It would never be open with you off gadding around the country playing poker."

"Such a nice friendly little game," Adam said.

Natalie spoke just loud enough for him to hear. "I *like* friendly little games."

He had been standing behind her, and he slipped his arms around her waist and drew her back against him. His head against hers, he laughed softly. "If that's the case, why don't you let me show you what I can do in the dark?"

She laughed and leaned her head against his shoulder. "Later, Adam."

Patrick propped his head on his hand as he gazed contentedly up at his mother and father, a tone of satisfaction in his voice. "I really like it here. It makes me feel—I don't know—fuzzy inside."

And Adam and Natalie knew exactly what he meant.

Joanna Ingalls has had a secret for five years—
a brown-haired, blue-eyed secret named Casey!

A SUMMER KIND OF LOVE

Shannon Waverly

CHAPTER ONE

FROM THE STERN of the huge white ferry, Joanna watched the wharf at Woods Hole gradually recede and the picturesque southern coast of Cape Cod open out. The hot, sunny afternoon was fragrant with sea smells—fish and diesel fuel and salty spume. She took a deep breath and told herself to relax, that everything was going to work out for the best. But the effort was futile.

Leaning on the rail, she stared down at the churning water. Suddenly she became acutely aware of a weightless feeling in her stomach, a feeling of swiftly sliding backward, of water deepening perilously beneath her. Overhead, the large curved horn blared an ear-shattering farewell to the mainland.

Beside her, five-year-old Casey jumped, startled by the sound. But his fear passed quickly, and soon his attention was back on the sea gulls wheeling and swooping over the boat's wide wake.

Joanna could see excitement in her son's bright blue eyes. She could see it in the heightened color of his already tanned cheeks. And she smiled, remembering her own excitement the first time she made the six-mile journey across Vineyard Sound eight years ago.

But for her, that breathless feeling of being on an adventure was just a dry, detached memory. She wished she could recapture a little of it, and maybe she would in the restful, restorative days ahead—but for now she gazed at the sunglitter on the water and felt nothing.

But then, she was used to feeling this way, this being stuck in neutral . . . finding no pleasure in the taste of food, making no emotional connection with music or sunsets or soft dewy dawns.

There was only Casey, the light of her life, the only reason she even bothered to get up in the morning these days. She had made innumerable mistakes in her life, but Casey would never be counted among them.

At the moment, he was holding half of a hot dog bun in his slender hand, wide blue eyes fixed expectantly on one particular sea gull. The gull, tame and trusting from following the ferry out to Martha's Vineyard every day, hovered over the outstretched morsel as if suspended by invisible puppet strings.

"Careful for your fingers, Casey," Joanna said softly. "Better toss it up to him."

She turned and looked for an empty deck chair, but it was early July and, as usual, the ferry was jammed with vacationers bound for the island. There were families of all sizes and ages, adventurous young people with knapsacks on their backs, a few unmistakable honeymooners.

Joanna sighed wearily. She had nothing in common with them. She felt isolated, exhausted, and so very old. Could it be that she was still just twenty-four? She felt a tide of apprehension rising through her nervous system. Was she doing the right thing? Six years ago, she had vowed she would never set foot on the Vineyard again.

But her father's invitation had sounded so tempting. . . .

Dear Joanna,

How's my girl doing these days? Viv and I are fine—except for the fact that our lives have become rather hectic lately. My firm is opening a branch office in San Francisco, and I was told just last week that I'll be needed there to get the accounting department on its feet. I'll be leaving Boston the last week in June, which, alas, is just one week away. Viv has already gone—flew out to her sister's in Palo Alto as soon as she heard the news and, I hope, is pulling together an apartment for us somewhere.

We may be gone for as long as four months, which leaves us with a problem—namely, our cottage on Martha's Vineyard. We thought of renting it out, but neither of us really cares for the idea of strangers staying there. And a place left empty during the summer is just too much of a target for break-ins.

So I'm offering it to you, Jo. Though I haven't had time to discuss the arrangement with Viv, I'm sure she'd feel as relieved as I to know you were there watching over the place. Besides that, I think Casey would really enjoy it. My little grandson has never seen the ocean, has he?

But most of all, it would be a break for you. Phil's long illness and death last November were hard on you, maybe more than you realize. When I saw you in March, you didn't look well. You need a rest and a change of scenery. Staying in New Hampshire, living in the same apartment you shared with him, meeting friends who think of you only as half of a married couple—that can't be good for you. It only prolongs the time of mourning, which, in my opinion, you should begin to put behind you.

Think it over, Jo, and let me know your decision soon. I hope it will be yes.

Love, Dad

P.S. Our phone has already been disconnected so you'll have to write. Hurry.

The letter had come at a time when Joanna had been thinking along startlingly similar lines herself. Though Phil was gone, the visible framework of her life had changed very little. She still occupied the same apartment they'd moved into as newlyweds. She still went to work downstairs in her father-in-law's clothing store, which she and Phil had managed together. She still visited with the same family members and friends.

At first she'd considered this sameness a blessing, a reassurance that life would go on as usual and the transition wouldn't be too jarring for Casey. But recently she'd come to see it from an entirely different perspective. Everyone and everything in her life was now a reminder that Phil was gone. Ironically it was the very sameness of her surroundings that underscored the fact. At the shop, in the apartment, around her in-laws' Sunday table, someone was obviously missing.

And she was tired of it. As much as she had loved Phil, she'd finally got over the first, sharp pain of his death. And now she was afraid that the almost-comfortable sadness that had replaced the pain would never go away. If only she could make a break from it, get away from the people and places Phil had been so integral a part of. If only she could cut herself and Casey loose.

She'd hoped her son would be more resilient, but he and Phil had been too close. Usually a happy, talkative child, Casey sometimes became so sad these days, quietly sad. He occasionally wet his bed at night, sometimes cried disconsolately over the most trivial matter, and at times his chatter reverted to speaking about Phil as if he were still alive. "When Daddy gets home... Ask Daddy if we can..."

Joanna tried to take it in stride. She told herself it would pass. All he needed was time. But there were nights when it worried her to tears. How could she help her son through this traumatic time in his life? How could she be sure it would leave no emotional scars?

And then her father's letter had arrived. Her surprise was too obvious to hide. Her mother was visiting at the time and Joanna felt compelled to read it to her.

"Well, are you going?" Dorothy's lips tightened out of habit.

"Are you serious? I can't leave the shop now. The summer tourist season is just picking up. It sounds great but..."

Dorothy was pensive a long time. "Your father-in-law can survive without you for a few weeks," she finally said very unexpectedly.

"Maybe. But what about me? I can't afford a vacation!"

"How about the insurance money Phil left? Couldn't you dip into that a little? Your only expense out there would be food." Dorothy was a tireless, stiff-backed Yankee whose own life had inspired Joanna to be strong and independent, but it was obvious that even she believed her daughter needed a rest. And why shouldn't she? Joanna's hands shook so much, the teacup in them actually rattled.

"A vacation's just what you need," Dorothy continued. "It'll clear your head and calm your nerves. Even though I hate seeing you take anything from your father, I think you should go. Have a good time, too. You'll find everything easier to handle when you get back—Casey, your job, everything. I'm sure of it."

Everyone Joanna talked to agreed. Her father-in-law not only gave her the entire summer off, but he even insisted she take a small vacation bonus to help tide her over.

But now as the ferry chugged farther away from the mainland, she began to fear she had made the wrong decision. Not that her family was wrong in suggesting she get away from the sad tedium of her life. She knew they were absolutely right. But why here? Why did it have to be this particular island?

Of course, it wasn't their fault. Their intentions were good. How were they supposed to know about the devastation she had felt when she'd fled the Vineyard six years ago? She had hidden it so well. She'd returned to New Hampshire and acted perfectly normal, or as close to normal as she could muster under the circumstances. Then with her marriage to Phil following soon after, surely there was no reason for anyone to suspect that she was anything but perfectly happy.

And, truly, she *had* been happy! She'd had a wonderful marriage. She had become a successful working mother and an active member of the community.

With each passing day, the Vineyard had become more and more remote until there came a time when it seemed almost unreal, part of a dream she'd once had. She felt detached from it, detached from the naive girl she had been and, blessedly, from the people she had known. After that summer, she rarely saw her father and Viv anymore—only on those rare occasions when they chose to drive north to visit her—and she never again saw Michael.

Of course, she knew she'd be kidding herself if she said she never thought about him after that. Not that she chose to, or that it meant anything significant. But every so often a memory would blossom from nowhere, take her by surprise, and carry her back before she could push it down into the shadows of the past where it belonged. She didn't care about Michael or the Vineyard anymore. They meant nothing to her, and hadn't for years.

But now, as the outline of the island took shape on the horizon, fear began to whisper around her heart. What if this island proved not to be the cure for the dead weight in her soul? What if, after all these years, she discovered that it was capable of opening old wounds?

"Ma! Ma! He caught it! I threw it up and he caught it!" Casey's clear, sweet voice dispelled her dark thoughts. She looked down at his lean, angelic face, followed his gaze to the sea gull gliding away, and felt his excitement as her own.

"What a lucky sea gull, getting a hot dog for lunch!" Joanna laughed. "Okay, time to find ourselves a chair. We still have at least a half-hour ride."

Good-naturedly, he nodded and slipped his hand into hers. He was a slender but sturdy little boy with a meditative seriousness about his handsome features. Yet beneath that seriousness lay an engaging, congenial personality that had developed from spending so much time at the shop back home. Customers, leaning over to admire him, were more often than not drawn into conversation with him. A natural charmer, that was Casey. Just like his father, she sometimes thought.

They found an empty chair on the starboard deck, and Joanna lifted him onto her lap. "There it is," she said, pointing. "That's the island where Grandpa Scott's house is."

Casey leaned forward, eyes alive with curiosity. "It's so big," he exclaimed, causing Joanna to wonder if he was struggling with a cartoon preconception of what an island should look like.

"Yes, it is. Over twenty miles long."

"And there are trees . . . just like at home."

"That's right, babe. Houses, too. Whole towns of them. And there are farms and forests and beautiful windswept moors. I hope you weren't expecting palm trees and grass huts," she said with a gentle laugh.

Casey shrugged sheepishly, then leaned back. He snuggled closer, placid with tiredness. But that was only to be expected; he hadn't got much sleep the previous night because of his excitement. Joanna rested her chin on his silky brown hair and gently rocked him back and forth. Time passed, and when she looked down again, his long, dark lashes lay motionless on his cheeks. Softly she kissed him and returned her gaze to the approaching island.

It was going to be a wonderful summer, she told herself adamantly. They would sleep late and eat well and turn as brown as berries on the beach. And at the end of August, she would return to New Hampshire revitalized and ready to pick up the reins of her life once again.

Still . . . Joanna felt a tremor in her nerves, a tremor that had nothing to do with the engine's vibrating grind. That sense of gray-green water deepening perilously beneath her filled her soul. And though she knew perfectly well that the boat was moving forward, there was that unshakable feeling of sliding back....

JOANNA MADE HER FIRST CROSSING over Vineyard Sound when she was sixteen, just out of her second year of high school, all legs and arms, with a thin silver brace across her teeth, and her blond hair cropped too short for her gangly height of five feet eight.

She was nervous and quiet and perhaps a bit angry, too. Her parents had been divorced when she was four, and she barely knew the handsome man beside her who was her father. Jim Scott had initiated the separation, leaving his wife, Dorothy, in New Hampshire for a glamorous socialite named Vivien Malone whom he had met while attending a business conference in Boston.

Although Dorothy had been upset by the divorce, she was a proud, stubborn woman who bottled up her pain and refused to let the world see that she was made of anything but fierce independence. She never remarried and never took support. She worked doggedly and raised Joanna alone, allowing her "conceited, playboy husband" very few visitation rights. And never with "that woman"!

"I don't know what ever possessed me to fall for a man like that," Joanna remembered her mother complaining even when she was too young to fully understand. "He was too handsome for his own good—that was the trouble." Dorothy would slap her steam iron onto the board with brisk, angry thrusts as she spoke, and the impressionable Joanna, sitting by the fire with her books, would take it all in. "Handsome men get used to women coming easy. If they get tired of one, they can just toss her aside and go find another."

Then, putting down the iron, she would lean over the board in the same way their minister leaned over the pulpit when he was about to warn the congregation about the snares of the devil. "Watch out for the really handsome ones, Joanna," she'd say, her thin lips tightening until they disappeared. "They'll break your heart every time."

Physically Joanna was like her father. She had, as her mother phrased it, the same wild, Irish green eyes and thick yellow hair. She had his saucy cleft chin and clever little smile. "But, thank God, you don't have his reckless nature, Jo. You're a good girl, a sensible girl. I've seen to that."

Jo was also a very perceptive girl, and though her father went out of his way to give the opposite impression, she knew that his new wife, Vivien, couldn't have been more pleased by Dorothy's refusal to let him visit or support his daughter. Joanna sensed that Vivien wanted him to make a clean break with his past and immerse himself completely in his new life in Boston. There he had everything a man could possibly want—a beautiful wife, the right country club, an established circle of well-to-do friends, even a son from her first marriage. As far as she was concerned, Joanna and Dorothy had simply dropped off the face of the earth. Joanna often heard a hesitation in her father's voice when he called, just enough uncertainty to convince her that Vivien treated any reminder of their existence with cold displeasure.

Considering the bitter feelings harbored by the adults in her life, Joanna was amazed that she got to meet Vivien and Michael at all. But she did, finally, that summer when she was sixteen. In addition to their home in Boston, Jim and Vivien owned a vacation cottage on Martha's Vineyard off the Massachusetts coast. That particular year, Jim had four weeks in July free and called quite unexpectedly to see if Dorothy would allow Joanna to join them.

"Do you want to go?" Dorothy had asked.

"Not very much."

Dorothy controlled a smile of satisfaction. "Well, I guess it doesn't matter then. Perhaps you ought to—show him what he's missed out on all these years."

Joanna arrived prepared to have a bad time. She knew Vivien didn't like even the *idea* of her, and she knew she wouldn't like Vivien. And she didn't. Vivien was so unlike her mother. She was youthful and tanned and energetic. But then, why wouldn't she be? The most strenuous thing she did all day was play golf with the other uppity people from Boston who summered on the island.

And her father? Joanna made an honest effort to like him. But her mother had been right. He was a bit taken with himself, and he flirted embarrassingly with every woman he met.

But Michael, Vivien's son? Michael had elicited feelings from her that made the rest of her feelings pale in comparison. She'd always resented this unknown Michael for usurping her place in her father's life. But now she was glad she could hate him simply for what he was—which was everything her mother had always warned her about in the opposite sex. He was too ridiculously good-looking for words, and he obviously knew it. He was smug, self-assured, and willful. Why, when she arrived, he was on the phone with one girl making lame excuses for having been at the beach that day with another. And the way his blue eyes glittered, she knew he didn't feel a bit of remorse for the deceit.

In his bare feet and blue swim trunks, with a towel flung negligently over one shoulder, twenty-year-old Michael stood about six feet tall. Though not the muscle-bound type, he evidently took pride in keeping fit. From the corded muscles of his legs, Joanna guessed he did a good deal of running. And he was tanned to the smoothest, deepest gold she had ever seen.

His hair, thick glossy brown, curled around his face with attractive abandon. Although he was indoors, he wore a pair of amber-tinted glasses—for effect, Joanna decided, eyeing him with open contempt. His mouth was smugly turned into a small, rakish smile, and when he spoke his voice was a deep, soul-moving baritone.

"Michael, get off the phone. Joanna's here," Vivien said. Then she sighed in mock exasperation. "My son, the lady-killer!" Joanna had no doubt he believed it.

From the very first day of her visit, Joanna and Michael argued. In retrospect, she had to admit she'd started it, but she couldn't help herself. There was something about Michael Malone that made her lose her composure and forget that she was shy. Perhaps it was the way his glittering cobalt eyes continually mocked her... or the arrogant way he went on about his precious Yale... or maybe it was simply those supercilious tinted glasses worn on the tip of his straight, suntanned nose. Whatever the reason, for the entire month she was there, they were entrenched in warfare. They short-sheeted each other's beds, sabotaged phone calls, threw jellyfish down each other's shirts, laced drinks with Tabasco sauce—in short, mocked and teased each other till Joanna was often reduced to tears and Michael was livid with cursing.

Never had she hated anyone so much in her life. He was the most infuriating, arrogant, self-satisfied chauvinist she'd ever met! To make matters worse, girls seemed to find him irresistible. The phone rang constantly for him, and some long-legged beauty was always "just pedaling by." Joanna couldn't stand it! How could such stylish, mature girls be so dumb? What disgusting line was Michael feeding them?

Before she realized it, though, her month on the island was over.

"Well, did you have a nice time?" her father asked as they waited at the dock for the ferry that would take her back to the mainland.

"Yes." Much to her surprise, it was the truth. Michael, who had opted to join them, looked up sharply from his book.

"Nice enough to come back next summer?" her father continued.

"Yes, I'd like that very much."

She didn't know why, but she felt oddly drained of the resentment that had filled her on the trip out. Not that she felt any real closeness had developed between herself, her father, and Viv, but they'd managed somehow to get along fairly well. She hadn't planned on matters turning out that way; they simply had—naturally, spontaneously.

And suddenly she knew the reason. Michael! She'd spent so much time conniving ways to get back at him that there hadn't been any time nor energy left to resent her father and Vivien. Michael had monopolized all her waking thoughts, become the focus of all her emotions, and without realizing it, provided a vent for all her pent-up anger. And now, as she stared into those clear cobalt eyes, she saw a joy and a caring that she hadn't detected until then, and she knew he had let himself be that vent all along.

The five weeks Joanna spent on the island the following summer were as different from her previous visit as day is from night. By some unspoken agreement, she and Michael called a truce to the teasing and pranks that had characterized that other stay. Now was a time for them to get to know each other and become friends. They swam together nearly every day, rode bikes over hot, lazy back roads, paddled the old rowboat around the pond, dug for clams, shopped, cooked together, read, talked—especially talked!—out on the sun porch late into the night, about literature and astronomy, music and politics.

Ironically Joanna felt she knew Michael better than anyone else in his life did, including the girl he dated most often these days, Bunny Wilcox. Because she lived with him, Joanna had time to discover his serious side. Michael was not just the lady-killer his mother liked to dub him; he was also a very intelligent and intense person, an idealist, a dreamer. That summer, Joanna grew in utter awe of him.

Yet as close as they were, there was one subject they just couldn't discuss in any depth. That was their love lives. After all, she had seriously dated only one boy back home, her best friend and devoted admirer since the fourth grade, Phil

Ingalls. And her relationship with Phil had never become more heated than a few innocent sessions of kissing at the drive-in. While Michael...well, Joanna had a hunch that Michael was sleeping with Bunny Wilcox...maybe had even slept with some of his admirers the previous year. It was a hunch that lingered even after he'd laughingly told her she was fantasizing, even after he got angry and accused her of confusing him with her father.

Joanna tried to be cool and mature about it; Michael *was* twenty-one, after all, and such behavior *was* commonly accepted. But she found it hard. Michael was the most attractive, intelligent, virile young man she had ever met. And late into the night, as the sea rocked outside her window, she would lie on her bed awake, wondering where he was, what he was doing. And her body rocked with a hunger so deep and inexplicable it brought tears to her eyes.

Again time passed too quickly, and again she found herself saying goodbye on the Vineyard Haven dock.

"Goodbye, dear," Vivien said, giving her a cool peck that mostly missed her cheek.

Then her father hugged her. "Write often," he said.

And finally there was only Michael, standing a little apart, watching her with a sad stillness in his eyes. His thick, dark hair, sun-streaked lighter brown across the brow, tossed in the breeze. She stepped up to him and held out her hand, swallowing a flood of emotion she didn't quite understand.

"Well, knock 'em dead at school this year," she said, feigning a lighthearted spunk she hardly felt.

He took her hand and held it tight. His blue eyes, dark with confusion, raked over her smooth, suntanned face, over her white-gold hair that now reached her shoulders, into her bright, Irish green eyes. In one year, he'd told her recently, she had grown from an awkward girl into a beauty.

He nodded and whispered, "You, too, kid." Suddenly he took her by the shoulders and kissed her cheek. She hugged him briefly, self-consciously, then turned as the deep horn on the ferry blasted its warning to come aboard. She grabbed her suitcase and ran, blinking away tears.

"Watch out for the real handsome ones, Jo," her mother's words had echoed through her mind. "They'll break your heart every time."

Michael wrote to her all that winter. Dorothy was furious and threw out the letters if she happened to get to the mailbox before Joanna did. But Joanna salvaged most. They were long, well-written letters, even poetic at times, filled with detailed descriptions of his last days at Yale. Joanna looked forward to them as if they were new installments of a serialized novel coming to her through the mail. In them she could almost hear his deep, melodic voice, feel the summer sun as if he were talking to her on the beach, smell the clean dampness of his hair.

Joanna was, of course, in love with Michael. The fact could no longer be denied. She loved him and probably had from the moment she'd laid eyes on him. And all the warnings from all the wise women who'd ever been jilted could not change her feelings one iota.

And then his final letter arrived and her joy was almost too much to bear....

Dearest Joanna,

This will be brief since I have to be out of the dorm tonight and still have my packing to do. Just wanted you to know I've won the fellowship! So it's off to Virginia in the fall, graduate work, a teaching assistant's position ... life is too good at the moment.

Best of all, though, is that in a few weeks we'll be at the cottage again. Please stay the whole summer this time. I've missed you—more than you know or I'll ever understand.

No, I haven't seen Bunny, not since Christmas vacation when our two families went down to St. Thomas. She's written, though, and called a few times. I'm afraid she still isn't taking kindly to our breaking up. But there's no going back, and it's high time she realized it. Though I admit she once was a serious girlfriend—my *first*, let me repeat—I now realize my feelings for her were at best only tepid, lukewarm compared to what I'm beginning to discover with you.

Please, Jo, stay the whole summer. This one belongs to just you and me.

And so they'd had their romance. Joanna had loved Michael deeply that summer, and for some strange reason she'd let herself believe he loved her, too. And why not? He had told her he did, time and time again. He said he'd never felt closer to anyone before in his life and that he'd never let her go. He felt married to her—wasn't that how he'd put it?— married in a spiritual, mystical way that was far more binding than a civil license.

Now, as Joanna stared ahead at the approaching island, her heart swelled with contempt. What a pack of lies that had been! What a manipulative sham! But by then Michael had had years to practice his lines. He'd become a master at it, smooth-talking her into the most ego-shattering experience of her life.

She had turned a deaf ear to all her mother's warnings, had ignored her own hunches, too. All she'd heard that summer were the words "I love you," and she had let herself believe their summer, hers and Michael's, would never end.

But it did. Oh, lord, did it ever! In one bitter, definitive night. In spite of the calm perspective she had acquired over the years, Joanna still felt a little sick when she thought about it....

It was already the end of August, and she and Michael were facing yet another separation. Soon he would be heading for Virginia, and she'd be starting college in Vermont. She was sad—but hardly worried; after all, Michael had assured her it would only be a temporary separation till the day when nothing would keep them apart.

They were playing a game of Scrabble out on the porch when her father put down the phone.

"That was Peter Wilcox," he said, coming to the door.

"Bunny's father?" Joanna asked casually. The Wilcoxes were long-time friends of Vivien's from Boston who also summered on the island.

"Mmm. He wants us to stop over for a visit tonight."

"I'll beg off, if you don't mind," Michael said, catching Joanna's eye meaningfully. He had been right about Bunny's not taking too well to the idea of their breaking up.

"Mike, don't argue. He requested that you come along. It's 'imperative,' he said. You know how he talks." Jim tried to laugh, but there was no mirth in his eyes.

Michael took a deep breath of irritation. "Jo, do you want to go?"

But Jim cut in before she could answer. "I think Joanna had better stay here."

Joanna was too worried to be hurt by the snub. Something was wrong. She felt it in her bones.

By the time they returned, hours later, she was beside herself with worry.

"Where's Michael?" she asked warily.

Jim's brow was deeply furrowed. "He's...I think he went for a walk."

"At this hour?"

Vivien looked a bit more composed. "Jim, this is really none of Joanna's business. It's a private family matter."

"Vivien!" he admonished softly. "Come on, Jo. Let's go sit where we can talk more comfortably."

When they were seated in the living room, Jim wasted no time. "Joanna, Bunny Wilcox is pregnant."

"Bunny?" Joanna gasped. She'd first met the girl two years earlier...a spoiled, fiery-eyed brat, Joanna had decided then, an opinion that time had only confirmed.

"She claims the baby is Michael's."

It took a while for the words to sink in, but when they did, Joanna laughed. "That's preposterous!"

Vivien sighed resignedly. "I wish it were. But Bunny is definitely pregnant. She went for a lab test last week."

"Is that so!" Contempt sharpened Joanna's tone as she recalled all the times she and Michael had just happened to bump into Bunny that summer. "And how does she intend to prove who the father is, anyway?" She shook her head in disgust. "That's the oldest, stupidest trick in the book! She'd do anything to get her mitts on Michael. Boy, I thought she had nerve before, but—"

"Joanna, please! Have some compassion. The poor girl is distraught over her situation!" Vivien said.

"Oh, I bet! I can just see her now, crying in front of you people and then laughing up her sleeve. Tell me, what did Michael think of all this?"

Jim was about to say something, but Vivien caught his eye sharply. "He's going to marry her, of course," she answered smoothly.

Joanna's mouth opened but suddenly she felt so sick her words withered on her lips.

Jim drew himself up with a deep sigh. "Honey, I know there was something between you and Michael this summer. You tried to hide it, but we're not blind." He was compassionate but still he sounded as if he were talking to a child, as if he didn't consider her "something" significant. "Right now you're probably feeling as if this is the end of the world. Believe me, Viv and I understand."

Joanna shot the woman an alarmed glance. There was a strange, satisfied curve to her mouth.

"Though you may not believe it now, you will recover. Life *will* go on," her father continued. "Before you settle down with the man of your dreams, you'll have a dozen summer romances. You're so young. There's a whole world out there waiting for you. Forget about Michael and don't look back."

Joanna stared at her father stupefied. "What are you talking about, forget about Michael?" she whispered shakily. "He and I love each other."

Jim shook his head sadly. "No, honey. Michael is going to be a father. Don't you understand what that means?"

Joanna continued to stare. "But it's impossible. He can't be the father. He broke up with Bunny ages ago—last fall! *We're* going to be married!" she said feverishly. "We've got it all worked out. In a few years after he finds a permanent teaching position, I'm going to transfer to his school. Then..."

Vivien dropped her hands in exasperation. "Jim, this is too much! The girl is talking nonsense now." And then turning to Joanna, "Listen, I don't know what that son of mine led you to believe, but the idea of you two getting married... why on earth... I mean, I'm sorry if he led you on...." she stammered.

"He didn't!"

"Let me put it to you bluntly then. Michael and Bunny have dated for years," Vivien insisted almost impatiently. "I'll admit he's seen other people from time to time, but he's always gone back to her. The Wilcoxes are close friends of ours. We saw this coming long ago. I can't say I like the conditions under which they're getting married, but I know they'll make a go of it. They're such a wonderful match!"

Joanna was shattered with grief. She ran to her room and cried the night away. How could such a dreadful thing be happening to her? It had to be a mistake. She and Michael loved each other. They belonged together as no two people on earth had ever belonged before.

But evidently it was no mistake. Bunny was pregnant and Michael had agreed to marry her. Evidently he'd still been seeing Bunny on the sly, even while pretending Joanna was the only girl in his life. Evidently he had lied when he said he loved her. Joanna had meant nothing to him, nothing but a casual summer romance. How could she have been so blind?

She felt betrayed and defiled. All the times they had been together came flooding back to torment her. She felt used, degraded—and ultimately enraged.

She waited all night but he never came home. Too cowardly to face her, she decided. At five o'clock she washed her puffy face and packed her bags. She refused to stay on the island even one more day. In fact, she hoped she never saw the place or Michael's loathsome face again!

As she packed, her hands trembled. Inside, she knew something innocent and vital had died. Yet, oddly enough, she felt new strength rising from her desolation. In one night she seemed to have grown years older and wiser. Even her face, she thought, had lost its youthful openness and become more cynical.

She would go home to her mother now, back to a woman who had known all along what life was all about, back to Phil whom she had ignored too long, back to the friends and town where she belonged.

"CASEY! Casey, honey, wake up," Joanna coaxed gently.

The child lifted his head from her shoulder and looked around in momentary confusion.

"We're almost there, on Grandpa's island. We have to go to the car now. The ferry will be at the dock in a few minutes."

Casey slid off her lap and she rose. Her legs felt like rubber but she refused to admit it was anything but fatigue.

The car bin of the ferry resounded with the thunder of starting engines. Slowly Joanna inched her red compact forward, keeping an eye on the other cars also pressing toward the dock ramp. Casey had forgotten his tiredness and was now bouncing in his seat with excitement.

Before long, they were out in the bright sunlight and driving up the main street of Vineyard Haven. Passengers who hadn't brought cars were already crowding into bicycle and moped rental shops or gathering at the corner to wait for the tour bus.

Joanna paused at the intersection, unsure of which route to take. She loved the long coastal road, but Casey had done enough traveling for one day. She shifted the car into gear and set off on the quicker route through the quiet, rolling midlands.

How well she remembered her way—the roads, the old houses, the stone-walled fields and woods. Everything seemed so unchanged, so unfairly timeless. The knot of apprehension she had been denying all day tightened in her stomach.

As they got closer to the ocean side of the island, the air became slightly cooler and damp. She turned off the main road and down a narrow, rutted lane.

"We almost there?" Casey inquired, stretching his seat belt until he was kneeling up.

"Almost."

They dipped into a hollow, then climbed the crest of a hill. Suddenly a breathtaking vista opened out. Breakers were rolling in on a white sandy beach devoid of people as far as the eye could see. Casey gasped.

"That's South Beach, Casey. Isn't it super! And that's the Atlantic Ocean."

South Beach was a barrier beach, its surf-pounded sands holding in the waters of great inland ponds. The cottage stood on a gentle rise above one of those ponds. It was a typical 1920s New England summer cottage, with deep screened porches front and back, shingles weathered to a soft silver-gray, and wild roses spilling over its fence. All around it, the land dipped and swelled in meadows of beach plum, bayberry, honeysuckle, scrub oak and wildflowers. The air was heavily scented with their perfume.

Joanna pulled into the driveway and stopped at the front steps. "Well, this is it."

Casey leaned on the dashboard and looked up at the house. "I like it very much," he said with adult seriousness. Then his face broke into a smile. "Does Grandpa have a sailboat?"

Joanna followed his gaze out to the pond behind the house. A dozen white sails glistened in the late-afternoon sun. She smiled. "No, babe. He only has a rowboat, and I'm not even sure if that's in the water this summer."

Her gaze returned to the house . . . to the porch . . . to the front door that waited for her to enter. It had been six years since she'd been here, six happy and full years. Why, then, was she letting herself get so upset? Why these nameless anxieties?

So what if she and Michael had had a fling here once upon a time? So what if it had ended messily and she'd been hurt? All teenagers had to expect some heartache along the way. Big deal! She got over it.

She had started life in earnest after that—marriage and motherhood and working in the adult world. And now she was coping with widowhood. Michael was insignificant compared to the rest of her life.

He and Bunny had married that autumn and moved down to his campus in Virginia. A perfect match, Vivien had said . . . as happy as could be. And, of course, he was brilliant. And, of course, they had the most darling house and, of course, an exciting circle of friends. Joanna was sure if it hadn't been for a slip of her father's tongue, she never would have found out about the miscarriage.

After that, there was no more news. Dorothy, intercepting a phone call one day right after Casey's birth, had ordered her ex-husband not to bring up that "family trash" anymore; Joanna didn't need it.

Joanna supposed she could have asked how Michael was doing. But she never did. Her stubborn Yankee pride would not allow it. Besides, it wasn't too long afterward that Phil's condition was diagnosed and she had more pressing matters on her mind.

Well, it didn't matter now. One brief summer her life and Michael's had become entwined, then they'd gone their separate ways. Six years had passed, and time had put things into wonderfully calming perspective. She refused to let futile memories resurface and interfere with the healing she and Casey so badly needed. This was not a summer for looking back. It was the beginning of the rest of their lives.

"C'mon, Casey. Let's grab our bags and go inside."

Up on the porch she rummaged through her purse for the key her father had mailed her and inserted it into the lock. But suddenly, just at the touch of her hand, the door swung in.

Joanna stood on the threshold dumbfounded. "What on earth?" she whispered. With a frown creasing her brow, she stepped into the hall. All was quiet, everything in its place—the yellow rain slickers on their pegs, the fishing rods in the corner. Still, that did little to alleviate her fear that perhaps someone had broken in. She edged into the kitchen. "Anybody here?" she called timidly. Casey glanced up, sensing her apprehension.

"It's okay, Case," she soothed. "Want to take the grand tour?"

He nodded but reached for her hand as a precaution anyway.

"You're going to get a kick out of this place. Look, here's the living room," she said, leading him into a large, comfortable room paneled in knotty pine. A brick fireplace, at the center of the house, flanked one wall. Over it hung an antique ship's bell that chimed every hour. A glass-topped lobster pot served as a coffee table in front of the deeply cushioned, sand-colored couch. Carved water birds graced a shelf under the windows.

If someone had broken in, surely those birds would be missing. But, no, the room was the same as it had been the last time she saw it. The very same.

Joanna found herself staring at the club chair where she'd sat that long-ago night while her father and Viv told her about Michael's cruel deception. Suddenly it was as if she could see through time, see herself sitting there, confused, vulnerable, and utterly crushed. She shook her head and with a conscious effort brought herself back to the present.

"And through this door we have the dining room—my favorite." The room contained a large oak table and eight Windsor chairs, a Victorian sideboard cluttered with as many seashells as dishes, and walls hung with a dizzying assortment of barometers, bells, and seascapes painted by local artists. As she passed the phone table under the stairs, Joanna's memory inadvertently flashed a picture of Michael talking endlessly to some girl. Her smile wavered. Damn these ghosts from the past! They were everywhere she turned.

"And see this door, Case?" she said. "It leads right back to the kitchen."

Big blue eyes looked confused. He let go of her hand and crept in. Soon he discovered the pattern, that the rooms were clustered around the fireplace and that he could skip from kitchen to living room to dining room and back to kitchen again in an endless circle.

While he was getting acquainted with his surroundings, Joanna opened the door that led from the dining room out to the back sun porch. Facing the pond, the porch was a cheerful, breezy place, filled with an extravagant collection of wicker. But as Joanna glanced around, her apprehension sharpened. There were a couple of geraniums in one of the ferneries, and they looked vibrantly healthy. Could her father have arranged for someone to come in and water them? A neighbor perhaps—the same neighbor who had carelessly left the front door unlocked? That was the most probable explanation. She breathed a little easier and rejoined her son.

"What do you say we take our bags up to our room?"

"Okay!" Casey answered enthusiastically.

They went up to the room that Joanna had used as a teenager, a lovely room with a marvelous view of the ocean. It contained two single maple beds and two matching bureaus. A lavender flower-print paper covered the walls.

Joanna opened the windows and checked the bed linens. Then she gave her son a glance. He seemed thoroughly at ease. He'd dumped all his clothes onto the floor and was sorting them into the various drawers of "his" bureau.

Seeing that he was happily occupied, Joanna slipped out to the hall and peeked into her father and Viv's room. A shadow of apprehension still lingered in her heart. But the room appeared to be in perfect order.

She tiptoed down the hall to the room that had been Michael's. The door was closed. She touched the knob, then backed away at the sudden wrenching onslaught of memories.

But this behavior was all so silly, she chided herself. Michael no longer existed for her. Where was the uncaring, independent attitude she had lived with for six years? She closed her eyes, deliberately slowing her breath for a few moments.

She turned the knob and opened the door.

Suddenly every nerve in her body jerked as if an electric current were shooting through it. Her heart stopped beating altogether.

There, asleep on the bed, wearing nothing but a pair of cutoff jeans, was Michael Malone in the flesh.

CHAPTER TWO

"MICHAEL!" Joanna shrieked.

He woke with a start, his dark head snapping up in alarm and confusion.

Her legs were so weak they buckled, and she clung to the door for support.

He bolted into a sitting position, his body instantly tensed and ready to spring. "What...? Who...? No...it's not—" His voice registered a shock that matched her own. He shot to his feet and rubbed his eyes. "Joanna?"

They stared at each other for what seemed an eternity, lips slightly parted as if they wanted to speak but couldn't find the words. This wasn't happening to her, Joanna thought. This had to be a dream. Any minute now she would wake up and find it was just her mind playing a trick, just a memory suddenly become too vivid.

"Joanna?" he repeated incredulously. "Is it really you?"

No, this was no dream. That voice...that face...

"Michael?" her thin voice quaked.

They had not run into each other once during the past six years. Neither had they talked on the phone or written. In all that time, not a single word of explanation had been exchanged between them, not one word to justify his cold betrayal of her after so intimate a summer. Not even a measly, "Gee, I'm sorry you got hurt, kid."

And as Joanna stared at Michael now, she realized those words could never be exchanged. It was far too late. The appropriate time was past, buried under years of leading separate lives.

"What are you doing here?" she cried tremulously, her pulse racing with emotions too confused to sort.

The sleep seemed to pass from his body even as she stared at him, and he suddenly looked at her with a clear, cool control. "What am *I* doing here? Oh, no, the question is, what are *you* doing here?"

"M-my father asked me to stay here and watch the house. He and V-Viv are on the West Coast this summer."

Michael's eyes narrowed. "Is that so? Well, for your information, my mother happened to invite me here for the very same reason." His eyes were still the same brilliant cobalt she used to admire so much, but something about them had changed. Now they harbored a coldness she wasn't used to, a cynicism...

"But that can't be!" she gasped. Did he think she had just taken a notion to barge in uninvited?

"The hell it can't!" He yanked a shirt from the back of a chair and whipped it on. "And since neither Jim nor she would be so insensitive as to invite the two of us here at the same time, one of us must be lying." He started to button the shirt, but oddly his fingers kept fumbling ineffectually and he finally gave up the effort.

"So it seems," she retorted, vaguely wondering why he should consider anyone who brought them together "insensitive." You'd think he was the one who'd been used and two-timed.

In the heavy silence that followed, Joanna studied his broad, rigid shoulders, the long, corded stretch of his legs. He'd grown heavier over the years, but all the weight was muscle. And if such a thing were possible, he'd become even more handsome. His face had taken on character. He seemed so mature. Not that his hair wasn't still the solid rich brown it had been six years ago; it was. And his body remained firm and lean. But there had been something almost coltish about the Michael she had known, something youthful. Now he was all man.

"Well?" she prodded.

"Well what, Joanna?" he snapped.

"What are we going to do about it?" she asked, making an effort to lift her chin.

"Well, I'd say we have a little problem on our hands, wouldn't you?"

"Then I suggest you leave."

Michael tossed back his dark head and laughed scornfully. "Not on your life! *You* leave."

"I will not! My father invited me here, I've been on the road since dawn, I'm exhausted, and I'm not budging!" She paused abruptly as a sudden thought struck her. She glanced around. "Where's Bunny?"

Michael's brow lowered in a thunderous scowl. "What!"

"I said, where's Bunny? I was just wondering if your wife was suddenly going to waltz in here and try to throw me out, too." She flicked back her long, pale gold hair, pretending the ice in his eyes wasn't disturbing her.

"You're not serious, are you?" he asked quietly.

"Serious? Why, yes. About what?" she said in confusion.

"Bunny. You're not trying to pretend you don't know?"

"Know what?"

"We're divorced!" His eyes flicked over her with palpable derision.

Joanna felt herself paling. "Divorced?"

Pinning her with a cold, incisive stare, Michael began to applaud, giving slow, loud claps. "Bravo, Joanna! A wonderful performance!"

His attitude quickly turned her shock into anger. The man was insufferable! How could she ever have loved him? "What are you talking about, Michael? This is the first news I've heard about any divorce of yours." Then a bit more hesitantly, "When did it happen?"

He glanced up at the ceiling in exasperation. "Joanna, I'm hardly in a conversational mood at the moment. This situation...you showing up out of the blue...*dammit*!"

With that, he strode across the room and, being careful not to touch her, hurried out to the hall.

But within seconds, his footsteps came to a halt. "Joanna!"

"What!" she snapped, spinning herself out of the room.

Michael was standing by her room. From around the door, a pair of large, teary blue eyes was staring up at him.

She ran across the hall and knelt beside her son. Immediately he flung his arms around her neck and buried his face in her long hair. She glared up at Michael, feeling like an enraged lioness with her cub.

"Now see what you've done."

"Me? I... How was I supposed to know?"

"Oh, just go away! Go away and leave us alone!" She rocked Casey in her arms, soothing him with a kiss.

"Is that your son?" His voice was hollow and flat, his eyes dark with unreadable emotion.

Joanna nodded and pried Casey's arms from around her neck. "It's all right, babe. No need to cry."

But the child nuzzled back and sobbed into her ear, "But you and that man were fighting, Ma. Make him go away."

Michael's mouth tightened and he thrust a hand through his hair. "Will you tell the kid I'm not going to hurt you?" he said with only the briefest of glances downward.

"The 'kid's' name is Casey, and you can tell him yourself!" Joanna hissed, hugging her son closer.

Slowly, reluctantly, Michael lowered himself to the floor. As his eyes narrowed on Casey, it occurred to Joanna that he had never been allowed the joy or sense of fulfillment that comes with being a parent. She also realized that Casey was the same age his and Bunny's child would have been.

"Don't be scared," he began. "My name is Michael. I... I'm your uncle, sort of."

Casey peeked up from Joanna's shoulder. "My uncle? Mom's never told me about you."

Michael stared down at his long, graceful hands and smiled ruefully. "No, I don't suppose she has." After a thoughtful pause, "You know Vivien, don't you? The woman who's married to your grandfather?"

Casey nodded cautiously.

"Well, she's my mother."

"Oh." Casey stood up straighter. "I like Grandpa Scott and Viv. They took me for a ride up Mount Washington."

"Yes . . . well, I'm Viv's son," Michael repeated.

Lights began to go on behind Casey's eyes as he made the connections. "Do you live here, too?" he inquired, wiping his nose on the back of his arm.

"Yes, this summer anyway." Michael shot a quick glance at Joanna, daring her to refute him. In spite of the trembling that still racked her body, she managed to glare back with convincing contempt.

Casey nodded thoughtfully. Then, much to Joanna's dismay, his face broke into a smile of acceptance. "When do you have supper in this house?" he asked with his usual congeniality. "I'm starved. I had a hot dog on the boat, but a sea gull ate it."

Michael rose abruptly. Obviously he had no desire to get any closer to this child. Perhaps he even resented him.

"Don't bother Michael about supper, Casey. As soon as you've washed your face and hands, I'll take you out for a bite."

The child looked up uncertainly from one adult to the other.

"That's not necessary, Jo. There's food in the kitchen."

But Joanna looked away as if she couldn't stand the sight of him. "I'd rather starve first."

"Suit yourself." Disdain reentered his demeanor. "I just thought you might want to consider the boy first." He turned to leave. "But then, you never were the type to think of anyone but yourself. I guess it was stupid of me to expect you'd changed." He strode back into his room and slammed the door.

Joanna stared at the closed door in a maelstrom of confused emotion. What in heaven's name was he talking about?

Shakily she ushered her son into the bathroom and helped him wash. "Now, go back to the bedroom and change into a clean T-shirt. I want to freshen up, too. Then we'll go out to a restaurant, okay?"

Casey nodded, stumbling tiredly over his new, thick-soled sneakers.

Left to herself, Joanna gazed into the mirror over the sink. Her cheeks looked fevered. Her eyes were wild. She thought she might actually vomit. And to think, she'd come here to relax, find inner peace, give her life direction!

No wonder she had felt such deep misgivings on the ferry. She'd been concerned about bad memories—but now Michael himself was here. She should have listened to her intuition.

Joanna put a trembling hand to her heart. It was racing so fast she grew frightened. What was happening to her? And, why had she reacted to Michael that way? Such anger! Such contempt! She'd been like a stranger to herself, saying and feeling things that were totally foreign to her. Sure, Michael had hurt her, but that was a long time ago. She'd recovered from the pain and anger and moved on...hadn't she? Of course she had, she assured her pitiful reflection.

At that moment, she heard Michael's footsteps in the hall. She tensed, but he continued on down the stairs. At the bottom, he picked up the phone and began to dial. She looked up and was horrified to see how wild her eyes had turned again, just at the sound of his step.

She washed her face with cold water and patted it dry. The towel smelled disturbingly of a musky aftershave or perhaps a soap. Quickly she draped it back over the bar.

She supposed it was reasonable to think they could meet again, although she'd honestly come to believe they never would. After all, she had thought that he and Bunny lived in Virginia. What were the chances of their ever crossing paths, especially since Joanna never visited her father where Michael, by coincidence, might be visiting his mother? But who would have guessed they would meet here, at this particularly difficult time in her life?

She knew she hadn't handled the meeting well. Seeing him so unexpectedly had stripped her of all the defenses she'd constructed over the years. Anger had flared, emotion flowed too spontaneously—which still came as a shock to Joanna, who considered herself empty of emotion.

But that behavior had to end right now, she reprimanded her image in the mirror. She didn't know where the anger had come from, or why, but it was stupid and inappropriate, and it had to end. She didn't need any more problems. She had to return to a sense of calm, retreat behind her safe wall of pride and independence.

She gave her clothes a quick check in the full-length mirror. Her denim skirt and blue knit jersey were rumpled from the journey, but they would have to do. She didn't want to spend any more time here than she had to, not even to change. She needed to put a little distance between herself and Michael before she confronted him again. Perhaps after a meal she would feel better. Maybe then she'd even be able to discuss the cottage rationally.

She brushed her hair, which shimmered in a golden cascade of waves to midback, then applied a touch of lipstick and a dusting of blush. She didn't look all that bad considering how distraught she felt. Perhaps a bit too pale and thin, but time in the sun would cure the first malady, and as far as the second went, her recent loss of weight seemed finally to have carved cheekbones into her face. It had sculpted the womanly curves of her body, too, in a way that made them more obvious, alluring even.

For one treacherous moment, she wondered if Michael had noticed. Had he studied the changes in her the way she had studied them in him? She doubted it. While they'd been arguing, she'd had the feeling that he was completely immune to her as a physical being, totally disinterested and disenchanted in her as a female. Disenchanted? Why, the man had barely been able to contain his contempt.

But that didn't make any sense! What reason did he have to be so angry? Her showing up unexpectedly at the cottage? Now that he was single again, was he planning to use the place to make up for lost time? Had her arrival scuttled his plans?

Or... or was it guilt lying heavily on his heart? Did Michael Malone actually have a conscience?

No, she wouldn't let herself worry about it any further. Michael meant nothing to her. Less than nothing! And any sort of feeling, even loathing, was just so much wasted energy.

"Casey?" Joanna called, leaving the bathroom. "Casey, are you ready to leave?"

When she received no reply, she pushed open the door. Her son was sprawled across the bed, fast asleep. The child was obviously exhausted. At the moment he didn't need food. What he needed was sleep, and it had been self-centered of Joanna not to notice sooner. She'd been so hell-bent on getting out of the house and away from Michael. She paused abruptly. Michael had called her self-centered, too, had said she thought of no one but herself. Was it possible? Had Michael noticed Casey's tiredness when she, his own mother, hadn't?

She tiptoed in and covered him with an afghan. Then she pulled down the shades and stood at the foot of the bed wondering what to do next. Michael was still downstairs; she could hear his angry pacing. She also knew she couldn't hide out in her room all night. And though she dreaded the very thought of it, she was going to have to face him once again.

CHAPTER THREE

JOANNA TOOK A DEEP BREATH and remembered her resolution to stay calm and civil. It was the only course to take. Becoming angry would only work against her. It might lead Michael to think she was still hurting from the pain he'd inflicted six years ago. Which, she reminded herself, she definitely was not. He might even, heaven forbid, get the notion he still had some control over her.

She found him in the kitchen, buttering a slice of pasty-looking white bread. He had changed into a pair of tan denims and a cream-colored shirt that revealed a shadow of dark chest hair beneath. He'd brushed his thick, curling hair into a semblance of neatness, too, yet he still exuded an air of just-bridled sensuality.

"You've changed your mind about going out?" he asked, letting his cool blue eyes graze hers briefly.

Joanna forced a smile. "How'd you guess?"

"I saw the kid asleep when I left my room."

Joanna ignored the resentment she felt over Michael's reference to Casey as "the kid." She replied with amazing equanimity, "I guess the trip was too much for him. He's out cold."

Michael looked thoroughly disinterested. "Do you want some of this?" He gestured toward a pot of glutinous canned soup on the stove.

"No. No, thanks."

"You should eat something." He tugged open a cupboard door. "Here, help yourself." His face seemed cast in stone. She couldn't tell what he was thinking. It was as if he, too, had had time to reflect on his reaction to her arrival and was regretting the harsh words. She grew uneasy at his solicitude.

"I called my mother a few minutes ago," he said, going back to stirring his soup.

"Oh?" Joanna turned with a can of beef stew in her hand.

Michael shuffled to the refrigerator and took out a bottle of wine. Wine and canned soup?

"I had to find out what was going on here—you know, both of us being invited to the cottage..."

"And?" Joanna prompted impatiently when he began to rummage through a drawer for a corkscrew.

"She apologized for the mix-up. It was simply a matter of crossed wires. Evidently she invited me to stay here, Jim invited you, and neither of them told the other what they'd done until it was too late and we'd both accepted."

Joanna stared at him dumbfoundedly. "Just like that? Crossed wires... and she's sorry?"

"That's what I said. But it was obviously an honest mistake. She'd flown out to my aunt's, and your father was busy in Boston. They didn't have a chance to check with each other." Michael's voice was suspiciously level and calm.

"It's a pretty lame excuse, if you ask me. Want to know what I think? I think my father deliberately didn't tell your mother he'd asked me here because he knew she wouldn't like the idea of my being here for the summer. In fact, I bet she didn't know that he'd invited me until you called." Michael suddenly made a great production out of opening the wine. "I'm right, aren't I?" When he failed to respond, Joanna turned and slipped the can into the automatic opener. "So what are we supposed to do now? Does she have a solution?"

"Sure. She suggested you go back where you came from."

Joanna sent what she hoped was a malevolent glance over her shoulder.

"And then Jim jumped in and suggested I find a motel. Then . . . well, I hung up in mid-argument."

"Great! So what now? I was planning to stay the whole summer."

"So was I." They stared at each other, locked in impasse.

"Well, I'm not leaving," she said a little too adamantly. "I've been telling Casey about this place for weeks. He'd be crushed if I suddenly told him we were going home. You can't imagine how he's been looking forward to this . . . all the toys he's packed to play in the sand . . . the list of souvenirs he wants to buy." She also remembered how much he needed to be here, away from all the people and places that constantly reminded him of Phil. The more she thought about it, the firmer she grew in her conviction. "I'm not leaving," she repeated.

"Well, I'm not, either," Michael shot back. "I'm not here just to get a suntan, kiddo. I have some very important work to do." He clunked the wine bottle down so hard some of its contents sloshed out. Immediately he seemed to regret his open display of tension and forced a quick, tight smile.

"I'm not here to get a suntan, either, kiddo," she mocked, forcing a smile as phony as the one he'd just dealt her.

"You could use one. You're as pale as a ghost. All skin and bones, too. Don't you ever eat?" His eyes traveled over her in a way that made her terribly self-conscious.

Suddenly she felt the strangest urge to throw the can—stew, opener, and all—right into his dark, cynical face. But she didn't. "Thank you," was all she said. "You always knew how to make me feel so wonderful." She scooped the stew into a pot and slung it onto a burner.

Joanna hated their standing so close. There seemed to be a field of electricity crackling between them. And when their arms brushed by accident, they both jerked away as if they'd just been burned.

Finally Michael broke the silence. "So, how have you been, Jo?" he asked with a heavily mocking slur.

"Terrific!" she spat. "Yourself?"

"Great!" he returned with waspish sarcasm.

She scraped her hasty meal into a bowl and lifted it off the counter. "So, you're great and I'm terrific, but that still doesn't solve our problem, does it?" With that, she pivoted on her heel and bolted for the dining room.

A minute later, Michael joined her, pushing a serving cart so recklessly the china and silverware on it nearly clattered off. Joanna glanced at the cart and then at her muddy stew. Neither of them was having what could be called a decent meal.

With quick, impatient moves, he set his bowl on the table, poured a glass of wine, and sat. But he didn't eat. He just stared at Joanna in brow-furrowed concentration. It was unnerving.

"A-aren't you going to eat?" she asked.

He didn't answer, just went on staring. Her eyes darted nervously around the room.

"Jo, listen. This sniping is getting us nowhere," he finally said in a conciliatory tone.

"I agree completely."

He sighed a long, thoughtful sigh. "So, how about if we share the cottage?"

Joanna dropped her spoon. "You can't be serious."

"Dammit, Jo! I don't know what else we can do. We both have legitimate reasons for being here, and neither of us intends to leave."

Alarm swept like fire through Joanna's nerves. "Impossible!"

"Why? We're both adults."

"And what's that supposed to mean?" That they were no longer the star-struck youngsters to whom sharing a house would have meant the world?

"It means we should be able to work out a daily routine that keeps us from getting in each other's hair. Of course, the kid might be a complication we'll have to work on, but—"

In spite of her resolution to remain civil, Joanna exploded. "My son has a name, you know! It won't kill you to say it!"

"All right, Jo, back off," he snapped. "I didn't mean anything by it."

"Like hell you didn't!"

The room vibrated with anger for a moment, then, like dust settling, gradually went calm again. But Joanna was now positive it was a shallow calm. Each of them was as tense as a live wire with the effort to be amicable. And that scared her.

Lord knew she'd had reason enough to be angry at him six years ago. He had acted unconscionably toward her, the way he'd played at love so convincingly, promising her the sky, all the while knowing how inexperienced and impressionable she was. Unconscionable and heartless, leading her in some kind of grotesque dance of the emotions when all the while he was secretly seeing Bunny. The lies, the deceptions cloaked in such sincerity, the lack of respect for her—that was what got to her most. Yes, she'd been crushed when she found out what Michael Malone was really all about. She couldn't remember ever crying as hard as she did that night. But when the sun rose she also discovered that she was angry. Furiously angry.

She supposed she was lucky to have found anger so quickly. It had been a great defense, keeping her from falling apart altogether. But the pain and humiliation never went away completely, either. They were always there, all mixed up with the anger in a turbulent sea of emotional confusion. But it was the anger that saved her. It kept her from wallowing and got her walking, albeit resentfully, into the future again.

But all that had passed. She couldn't have gone on living with such bitterness and pain. There was Phil and her job, learning to cook and keep house—and then there was Casey.

So many good things to fill her life, to replace the anger. Only now she wondered if her new life had really replaced the anger or merely covered it over. Did unresolved feelings really ever disappear just because a person wanted them to? Or did they lie in the shadows of one's personality, ominously ticking away...?

She took a spoonful of stew, which turned to sawdust in her mouth. In cold silence, Michael picked up his bread and ripped off a bite.

"I think I'm going to live to regret this," she murmured grudgingly, "but all right, we'll share."

Michael stopped chewing and something strange and unreadable flickered across his expression.

"But I'll buy my own groceries," she went on quickly, "of which I already owe you a can of—"

"Forget it."

"No way. I don't want to owe you anything." She noticed one dark eyebrow arch. "As I was saying, I'll handle all my meals, you can handle yours. That goes for laundry and cleaning, too. In other words, I'll go my way, you go yours. Understand?"

"Perfectly. And as I was saying before I was so graciously interrupted, I'd appreciate it if you'd keep the...your son from being disruptive while I'm working, especially in the morning."

"Casey is never disruptive! He's the most well-behaved child you'll ever meet!"

"But he *is* a child." Michael's tone presumed to end the argument.

"You needn't worry. I'll keep him as far away from you as humanly possible."

The corner of Michael's mouth lifted fractionally. "Good. Then we shouldn't have any problems."

"Let's hope not." Joanna picked up her bowl, lifted her chin and retreated to the kitchen.

There, after hastily rinsing off her dishes, she collapsed onto a chair and lowered her face into her hands. An uncontrollable shaking racked her body. It had happened again. In spite of all her coolly reasoned intentions, Michael had still been able to make her blood boil. She didn't understand it. She harbored no grudges against Michael for the past; she suffered no recriminations.

Joanna dropped her hands limply into her lap and sighed defeatedly. Of course she begrudged Michael. In fact, at this moment she hated him! And if she begrudged him and hated him, it could only mean she was still carrying around all the other emotional baggage as well. The loss and regret; the pain and humiliation, too. She had thought she was over all that. She'd thought she was free. But obviously, she wasn't.

This was incredible, so unfairly incredible! After six careful years, how could Michael be back in her life? He'd stopped existing for her, or so she had thought. How could he be sitting in the very next room?

Oh, why did Phil have to die? She should be home with him now, lingering over dinner, quietly talking about their day at the shop. *Share?* Had she actually agreed to share the cottage with Michael? Was she out of her mind?

No! She wouldn't let herself get all worked up. Michael wasn't worth it. She had contained the anger and pain once before, when it was fresh and far more searing. She could do it again, she was sure. Besides, she refused to let Michael see that he could still upset her. Where was her pride?

She took a few calming breaths and got to her feet. By the time she was on her way back through the dining room, she had regained her composure.

"Not going to bed already, are you?" he asked, still sitting at the table.

She turned slowly from the stairs. "Sure. Why not?"

"It's not even eight o'clock yet. Besides, we've hardly talked." She hesitated. "Come on," he laughed. "I won't bite."

Joanna moved to the table reluctantly.

"How about a glass of wine? You didn't have anything to drink with your supper."

"And you didn't have anything to eat with yours."

Michael grinned and pushed his untouched soup aside. Then he reached into the liquor cabinet for a glass. He poured it half-full and slid it to her side of the table, then refilled his own.

"So, how have you been, Joanna?"

"You asked me that already."

"Yes, I know. But I don't think your answer was very honest. This year must have been pretty rough on you."

"Are you referring to my husband's death?" she asked coolly though her hand shook as she lifted the wine to her lips.

"Uh huh."

She studied his face and saw nothing—no compassion, no curiosity, not even satisfaction that she had suffered. The man was as emotionless as stone. That, or he had become used to masking his feelings, too. Well, two could play at that game. "Yes, Phil's death was rough, but it wasn't as if I didn't know what was coming."

"Leukemia, wasn't it?"

For a moment, Joanna's expression crumbled and a sorrow she thought she'd overcome filled her heart. "Yes."

"Are you managing all right?"

She stared into the cold blue eyes across from her and her pride rekindled. "Very well. Phil was young, but he was very responsible. He left us with no bills, a roof over our heads, and...and enough savings to get us through life without too many problems." Joanna had all she could do to keep the shock she was suddenly feeling from registering in her expression. Why was she lying to him? Where had that statement come from?

Michael stared back, a man who once had known her better than she knew herself, yet he seemed totally unaware of her deceit. "Sounds like you're doing okay financially, but what about, you know, socially, emotionally?"

Joanna couldn't figure out what he was getting at. Did he want her to say she was desperately lonely and unable to function? "Well, I'm usually too busy to worry about social or emotional problems, which probably means I don't have any to begin with. I'm the—the manager of a clothing store in North Conway." She had almost claimed to be its owner. "It's a nice little place, very trendy, yet not so upscale that the locals won't come in." She took a long sip from her glass.

Michael's eyes narrowed and she looked away, afraid her own eyes might betray her. She knew it didn't make sense, but she would be damned before she'd let Michael know that she'd been anything but perfectly happy after *he* had dropped out of her life. Phil's illness had been long and emotionally wrenching; his funeral had wrung her out. Litigation over confused property settlements had embattled her for months. Then there had been the loneliness and fear, the financial problems and the worrisome changes in Casey. She could tell Mr. Malone a lot he didn't suspect about her life. But she would *not*!

"How's Casey taking his father's death?"

"He's doing very well. He's a resilient child. But, naturally, he still misses Phil at times. They were very close." She sipped her wine and gazed boldly at the stone face across from her. "Phil was a wonderful father, right from the start, always there to change a diaper or sit up with Casey when he had a cold." She was amazed at the amount of satisfaction she derived from bragging. It was sort of like thrusting small, cold knives into Michael's heart, satisfying a strange, deep-seated need in her for—for what? Revenge? She didn't really understand it, but the longer she and Michael talked the more she felt like . . . like hitting him!

"He must have been a great help to you," he commented with cloying politeness.

"Yes, he was. But enough about me. What have you been up to? Are you still teaching down in Virginia?"

She watched his brow lower, his thoughts racing behind his eyes. "No . . . yes. What I mean is, I'm taking a leave of absence this year."

"Oh? Tired of teaching so soon?" she asked with a perverse desire to have him admit he wasn't as happy or as brilliant as Vivien had always implied.

"Not at all. I've loved every minute of it," he asserted, taking a huge swig of wine. "I've been very lucky, too—the right place at the right time. Just as I was finishing the dissertation for my Ph.D, the head of the Literature Department retired and I was offered his position."

"You're head of the department? And...and you have your doctorate?" Joanna sipped her wine slowly, thoughtfully. Strangely a part of her wanted to congratulate him, but another part held her back. Instead, she looked up with a sardonic little smile. "How prestigious! *Dr.* Malone! Bunny must have loved that." There was a moment of silence. She could almost hear ice crystalizing in the air between them.

"Yes, she was very proud of me. But she especially loved all the entertaining we did because of my position. The president of the college said she was the best hostess the faculty ever had."

Joanna was sorry she'd introduced Bunny into the conversation. Now her beautiful image was etched into all the shadows of the darkening room. She would have fit so well into that milieu, too, coming as she did from a home where so much entertaining had gone on.

"Do you mind if I ask why you two got a divorce?"

Michael hesitated, his brow creased. "We were both deeply upset by the separation, but it was a mutual decision agreed on only after months of agonized discussion. You see, Bunny is a very talented person. She studied fashion design in college and wanted to pursue a career of her own. Naturally she wanted to move to New York to be at the center of the industry, but that was impossible for me because of my job. I finally realized I had no right to hold her back, and she didn't want to hinder me, either, so..." He raised his eyebrows with a sad, resigned look.

"Oh, so it was a career choice that split you up?"

"Yes, that alone."

Joanna studied him carefully over the rim of her glass. There was no reason to doubt him, and yet there was something about his voice she didn't trust, a bravado that matched her own a little too closely.

"I guess things worked out for you in the long run then— the fact that you had no children, I mean."

"Oh, I don't know. I miss not having children. We were really looking forward to the baby she miscarried." His eyes were now so hooded he seemed to have withdrawn into a deep, dark cave within himself.

"I know what you mean," Joanna commiserated. Her head was beginning to feel like a balloon. "A child can bring so much pleasure to a marriage, bring two people really close."

"Yes, I can imagine. It . . . it would have been a boy."

"You knew?" She watched him refill their glasses.

"Uh huh. They told us at the hospital. We'd planned on calling him . . . uh, Peter. After his Grandfather Wilcox."

Joanna digested this bit of information slowly. Then, perhaps because of the unrelieved tension, the fixed smile on her face began to quiver. For a moment, she was afraid she was going to laugh right out loud.

"What's the matter?" Michael emerged from the deep privacy of his thoughts, and was suddenly defensive.

"Oh, nothing. But with a mother named Bunny, could you have named him anything else?" She gulped down a huge mouthful of wine to cover the irreverently giddy leap her voice had taken. And if they'd had other children, she wondered, would they have named them Flopsy, Mopsy, and Cottontail?

Remorse gripped her almost immediately. How could she be so cruel, finding humor in someone else's tragedy?

Michael shifted his weight as if he were sitting in a nest of burrs. "Speaking of which, your son has an interesting name. How did you come up with the name Casey?"

"M-my son?" Joanna's spine straightened as a shaft of emotion shot through her from an unexpected angle. Though she didn't understand it, the air around her now seemed to bristle with vague, undefinable danger. Suddenly she felt defensive toward Casey. Protective.

"Phil and I took a trip down to Florida right after we were married. We went on AmTrak and, to the best of my knowledge, our son was conceived on the journey down."

"Oh, I see," Michael murmured darkly. "Casey. Trains. I see."

It was a total fabrication. Joanna had simply been fond of the name. She sat back, shocked at having caught herself lying again. But the words had spilled out so instinctively. For one unfathomable moment she had been gripped by fear, and without any forethought, that story had tumbled out. She wasn't controlling this game of duplicity anymore. Some other force was doing the controlling for her. She had to prove that Michael had not hurt her, that she had survived him and even thrived. She wanted to rub his smug face in the fact that she had been happy, that her marriage had been perfect. She knew it had a lot to do with her strong sense of personal pride. *That* she could understand. But it also seemed to be yoked to something else, a disturbing, indistinct fear of what might happen if Michael found out that she'd lied. And *this* she didn't understand.

Michael stared out into the darkening night beyond Joanna. His face was like granite.

Are you simmering, you unconscionable, two-timing louse? she thought. *Are you remembering how much I loved you? Are you thinking it could have been us on that train? Are you sorry you missed out on the life I could have given you?*

But when he focused on her again, his eyes told her he didn't give the slightest damn. She meant nothing to him—just as she'd always suspected. For all he was affected, they could have been two strangers making idle conversation on a bus.

"Bunny and I went to Florida, too, a couple of times. It's a wonderful place, but nothing beats Jamaica. That's where we went on our honeymoon. Jamaica's incredible in October."

A montage of images flashed through Joanna's mind—Michael and Bunny running through a tropical surf, Michael and Bunny sharing an intimate dinner at a luxury hotel, Michael and Bunny making love! And all just weeks—weeks!—after they themselves had talked of getting married.

Suddenly Joanna didn't want to continue this game. It was getting out of hand. If she continued, she suspected she would come out of it the loser. She usually had whenever she'd tangled with Michael. She rose abruptly.

"Well, if you don't mind, I'm ready to call it a night. I'm really bushed." She yawned. "And Casey's an early riser. But I'm glad we took this time to talk. It's been ... really nice."

Michael's glacier-blue eyes stabbed her with sudden mockery. "Sure. It's been a ball."

"Good night" was all she said. She even managed a smile.

He laughed softly, leaning back in his chair like a dark, avenging devil. "Sweet dreams, Joanna."

She hurried up the stairs, but even before she reached her room, tears of frustration were clouding her vision.

CHAPTER FOUR

AT THE OUTER MARGINS of Joanna's consciousness, there was a soft, rapid tapping. Rain hitting the windows of her New Hampshire home. But when she opened her eyes, sunlight was fanning around the edges of the window shades, washing unfamiliar furniture with pale, impressionistic light. On a swift wave of sickening awareness, she remembered where she was.

Again the tapping. She lay very still and listened harder. It was coming from across the hall—from Michael's room—from a typewriter. He had mentioned he was doing some work here at the cottage this summer, though he hadn't explained exactly what it was. Work toward another degree perhaps? An article for a professional journal? Joanna yawned and pushed the question out of her mind. She really didn't care what Michael Malone was doing!

In spite of the fact that she'd been exhausted the previous night, it had taken her hours to fall asleep. She had listened to house sounds—Michael's footsteps pacing through the rooms downstairs, the occasional burble of the propane tank below her window, Casey's soft breathing in the adjacent bed. Around eleven she had heard Michael leave. Where he went, she had no idea. All she knew was that sleep eluded her until he came in hours later. And during that time she'd kept thinking about everything they'd said—and everything they hadn't. Especially that. It was so ironic. She felt sure that their last summer together was as much on his mind as it was on hers; it had to be. Yet neither of them had dared broach the subject, as if they refused to acknowledge it had ever happened. Ah, well. Probably all for the best. No, definitely for the best. She really preferred to ignore that time in her life. She had enough problems these days and she certainly didn't need to compound them by dwelling on the past.

She pushed back the long veil of her hair and glanced at the clock. Good heavens! It was already quarter to nine! Casey usually woke up around seven.

She spun around. His bed was empty and toys were strewn on the floor. But he was nowhere in sight. Joanna jumped out of bed and not bothering with robe or slippers, went running out to the hall and down the stairs.

"Casey?" she called, trying not to panic. "Casey, where are you?" She would never forgive herself if he had wandered off and hurt himself while she was sleeping. At the edge of the backyard, a wooden stairway led down the bluff to the pond, and at the bottom there was a dock where a few neighbors moored their boats. What could be a more alluring spot for a curious five-year-old—or a more dangerous one if he couldn't swim?

She raced out the back door, heart pounding furiously, then came to a sudden halt. In a nook of the yard, where the scruffy lawn gave way to sand and honeysuckle, Casey knelt playing with his cars and trucks. Joanna walked over and knelt beside him.

"Casey, you had me scared to death. I didn't realize you'd left the bedroom. Why didn't you wake me?"

The child shrugged. He was still dressed in pajamas. "Brrrm!" He pushed a miniature tow truck up a hill of sand.

"Well, next time I oversleep, wake me, okay?" He nodded. "Which reminds me, don't ever, ever wander out of this yard alone, you hear?"

"Uh huh." He looked up with a cherubic smile, and Joanna couldn't help hugging him and kissing his smooth cheek.

"Poor lamb, you must be starved, skipping supper last night and all."

"I had two cookies."

"Cookies! For breakfast?" She groaned and glared up at the house to a second-floor window. The curtain swung as if someone had just let it drop. She didn't expect Michael to feed her son, but at least he could have wakened her.

"Listen, I'm going to make us a nice big breakfast. You can stay here and play if you like. I'll call you in about fifteen minutes."

As soon as she and Casey had eaten, they packed a picnic lunch and set out for the beach, leaving the house all to Michael. It was a perfect day, sparklingly sunny and hot. They drove out to Katama Point.

Casey had never been to an ocean beach before and at first found the surf intimidating. But he soon got used to it and was dunking and splashing as if he had lived on the island all his life. He and Joanna built castles from the fine white sand, searched for pretty rocks and shells, and after lunch went swimming again.

By midafternoon, however, they'd had enough. Not only was the sun too strong, but without companions his own age, Casey had exhausted the beach's possibilities.

But Joanna wasn't ready to return to the cottage just yet. The air bristled there; emotions ran too high in spite of her efforts to keep them in tow. Feeling rather like a fugitive, she drove Casey to Oak Bluffs.

At the turn of the century it had been an elegant resort town. Now, crammed with souvenir shops and fast-food joints, the elegance had faded. Yet, Joanna loved Oak Bluffs. She loved the tiny cottages that lined the winding streets, with their gingerbread trim and Gothic windows, their tiny balconies and flowers spilling out of window boxes. Even Casey was fascinated by the dollhouse image these cottages presented.

But his eyes really lit up when Joanna led him to the attraction that had been her destination all along—The Flying Horses, a gaily painted carousel, one of the oldest in the country.

When Casey was securely buckled onto one of the horses, Joanna hopped onto one herself. Together, they rode until the music ended. Then they rode again, around and around, in never-ending circles.

Joanna could hear her son's shy laughter and was glad he was having a good time. But as for herself, she was growing unaccountably sad. The pain of losing Phil had lessened remarkably over the past couple of months. But there were still times when it came back for no reason. Was that what this sadness was all about now? For some reason she didn't think so. No, it had something to do with this place... this carousel. Michael had brought her here for the first time when she was sixteen and full of resentment.... And yet the feeling was like a feeling of grief for something lost.... And it was here the following year that Michael, half hanging off one of the horses, had recited a Byron poem to her—She Walks in Beauty—one line for each spin past the spot where she stood laughing.... Grief, then, for someone gone... And here that Michael had lifted her onto a horse the final summer and with knightly tenderness kissed her fingertips before handing her the reins. Suddenly Joanna realized her eyes were misting over as they rode around and around, going nowhere.

She was relieved when the ride finally ended. She and Casey walked down to the waterfront and found a restaurant with tables on an outdoor deck. They ordered delicious-looking hamburgers and fries, but knowing she would eventually have to return to the house and face Michael again robbed her of her appetite. She lowered her head and massaged her throbbing temples. This arrangement wasn't going to work. She'd been out of her mind thinking it would.

"Joanna? Joanna Scott?"

Joanna glanced up, responding unthinkingly to her maiden name. Walking toward her was a buxom, freckle-faced redhead in her mid-twenties.

"Meg?"

The girl nodded and laughed. "Good Lord, it *is* you! I thought I was seeing things. How are you, Jo?" Meg was a native islander whose family lived along the same pond as the Scotts. She was unquestionably one of Joanna's pleasanter memories of summers past.

"Okay. Yourself?"

"Great! But what are you doing here?"

"I'm staying at my father's. He and Viv are in California for the summer."

"That's terrific!" Her face beamed merrily while her red hair, as ebullient as her personality, puffed around it in a cloud of curls. "Oh, Jo, is this your little boy?"

Joanna nodded proudly. "Uh huh. Casey, this is an old friend of mine, Meggy Trent."

"McGonigle's the name now, Jo—has been for five years. Oh, he's adorable. Hi, Casey," she greeted, bending over. He gave her a ketchupy grin. "You look just about the age of my little boy, Paul. Are you four?"

Casey shook his head. "Five!"

"Oh, my! A much older man!"

"Meg, I didn't even know you were married. And you have a four-year-old son?"

"Yup. And a three-year-old son. And a nine-month-old daughter." Joanna couldn't help laughing at Meg's expression of mock exhaustion. "Do you remember Steve McGonigle? That's who I married. He and I were already dating the summer you and Mi..." Her words thinned to a whisper and her already florid complexion flushed.

"No, sorry, I don't remember him," Joanna intervened quickly. "Do you still live here?"

"Uh huh. Steve and I bought the house right next door to my parents'. It works out great for baby-sitting." She let her gaze wander over the boat-specked horizon a moment. Her face became pensive. "Mind if I sit awhile?"

"Please do."

"I won't be long. I'm just waiting for my brother, Nathan." Her head inclined toward a shop near the restaurant. "That's his place. He has another over in Edgartown. He was just closing when a customer showed up. You remember Nathan, don't you?"

"Of course." Joanna smiled.

"Thought you would. He was nuts about you when we were kids." She paused and laughed. "You wouldn't give him the time of day, though, as I recall." Their eyes met briefly. "So, have you heard from Michael lately?"

"Believe it or not, I saw him yesterday for the first time in years. It turns out that he's planning to spend this summer at the cottage, too."

Meg's expression shifted with speculation, but, to Joanna's undying relief, she made no comment. "Jo, I heard you became a widow recently. It was last winter, wasn't it?"

"Yes, November." Joanna screwed her attention on a swirl of spilled salt and ran a pattern through it with her finger.

"I feel so bad for you. It was a tough break," Meg whispered.

Joanna shrugged, managing a wan smile. "Every day's a little easier."

"I hope I'm not prying, but what did he die of?"

"Leukemia."

Meg shook her head and made small, sad clicking noises with her tongue. "Then it wasn't a sudden thing, an accident or anything like that?"

"No, he was in and out of the hospital more than half the time we were married."

Meg reached over and squeezed Joanna's hand, her eyes filled with compassion. "Do you still live in New Hampshire?"

"Uh huh."

"And are you working?"

Joanna hated talking about her life. She wished Meg wouldn't ask. Nothing about it seemed right. Since Phil's death, it was all fragments running in purposeless directions.

Just at that moment, Meg began to wave and spared her the agony of answering. "Over here. Nathan!"

Joanna's gaze followed Meg's with a mild sense of anticipation.

"And you complain about the way I talk," he said, grinning. He gave Joanna a cursory glance then immediately did a double take. "Joanna! What...?"

She couldn't help laughing at his surprise. "How are you, Nathan?"

"As of this moment, terrific!" He was a handsome man, though short and slightly stocky. He had thick red-brown hair, a shade darker than his neatly trimmed beard, warm brown eyes and a sensitive mouth. It all added up to an engaging appearance that somehow reminded Joanna of a cuddly teddy bear.

"What are you doing here?" he asked.

"She's come to spend the summer," his sister cut in excitedly. "She's staying at her father's."

"Great!"

"I take it you're still living on the island?" Joanna asked.

"Oh, sure. In fact, I just finished building myself a new house."

"If you haven't already guessed, my brother's doing pretty well for himself."

"Sure looks that way. Meg told me you own a couple of shops...."

"Yes. Clothing stores."

"Really? I work in a clothing store back home."

"Well, well. Small world." His eyes sparkled warmly.

"And is there a Mrs. Trent these days?"

"Nah!" He paused and looked down at Casey. "I used to know somebody I thought I could settle down with, but evidently somebody else beat me to her."

Joanna laughed with a dismissive wave of her hand. "Nathan, this is my son, Casey. Casey, another old friend, Nathan Trent."

The child swallowed the last of his food and held out a hand. "Hi. Nice to meet you, sir."

Nathan's eyes crinkled. "Nice to meet you, too, Casey."

"Well, Nate, what do you say we hit the road," Meg suggested. "We're disturbing Joanna's meal. Besides, you still have to get over to the other shop to see how the new girl did today."

"Uh . . . right."

Meg rose. "Jo, it was really good seeing you again. We'll have to get together soon. And if you ever need a baby-sitter, don't hesitate to call. I'm home almost all the time, and if I'm not available I have a list of sitters we can share."

"Thank you."

"I mean it."

Joanna laughed. "I believe you do."

"Well, so long." Nathan waved and gave Joanna one last incredulous look. "Bye, Casey."

The next minute they were gone, and the smile they had brought to Joanna's face began to crumble. She could put off returning to the house no longer.

The sun was riding low when they arrived. It splashed gold across the pond, into the high leaves of the trees, over the silver-gray shingles of the commodious old house. Joanna showed Casey the outdoor shower her father had rigged up on the side of the house, and together they screamed and giggled as the cold downpour hit their backs.

"There, that ought to get the sand off us," Joanna said, still laughing.

Michael was at the small kitchen table when they came through the door, their wet hair plastered to their heads, towels wrapped tightly around their shivering bodies. He was hunched over a half-eaten TV dinner and a copy of *The New Yorker*. He looked tired and his eyes were red.

"Hey, Uncle Michael," Casey called through chattering teeth. "We went to the beach today."

"That so?" Michael continued reading.

"I went into the ocean," the child continued, nonetheless, pronouncing the word "ocean" in three distinct syllables.

Michael finally looked up, drawn by the boy's charming speech pattern. Joanna grew uneasy. Alone, she knew she could avoid Michael pretty well, but Casey was another matter. He could be such an open, friendly child, he was bound to get in Michael's way eventually, and she feared the encounter wouldn't be a pleasant one. Michael had made it clear that he did not want Casey underfoot.

"We don't have an ocean where we live," Casey continued, his blue eyes gleaming with excitement, undaunted by Michael's disinterest.

"And is that the first time you went swimming?"

"Yes, in the o-ce-an," Casey stated, small teeth chattering. His hair stuck up in dark, wet points all over his head. "We have a river near our house. I been swimming there plenty of times. You gotta be tough to swim there, though."

Michael put down his magazine with a slight huff. "Oh? And why's that?"

"'Cause it's so cold. My dad says the water comes from the top of the mountain, from the snow."

Michael shot Joanna a swift, inquiring glance at Casey's use of the present tense when referring to Phil.

"Let's go, Casey," Joanna said quickly. "Michael is trying to have his dinner. I'm afraid we're disturbing him."

"See you later, Uncle Michael," the boy called sweetly.

"So long, kid." His eyes were already back on the magazine.

On the way up the stairs, Joanna paused. "I wish you wouldn't call him *Uncle* Michael, Casey. He isn't really your uncle."

The child looked up, confused. "What is he then?"

"He's . . ." Joanna's heart suddenly seemed to turn into a hard ball of fire. "Nothing. Nothing, babe. Hey, come on. Let's go find a good ol' Dr. Seuss to read before bed."

The day was just a glimmer of lavender on the horizon when she again descended the stairs. She'd had trouble getting Casey settled. But after three stories and a glass of warm milk, he had finally fallen asleep.

Joanna had showered and was now ready to relax with a good magazine. It really hadn't been such a bad day after all, probably because she'd been away from the house—and Michael—for most of it.

She padded out to the darkened sun porch in bare feet and a green silk kimono and stood at the screen door watching the lights from other houses shimmer across the pond. She had no idea she had company until Michael cleared his throat. She jumped. Immediately her heart was pounding crazily.

He was slouched in one of the old wicker chairs at the far end of the porch, his feet propped up on the windowsill. His long fingers were casually linked around the base of a wineglass resting on his belt. He was looking at her intently, a soft breeze ruffling the dark hair over his forehead. Somewhere in the night, a foghorn sounded.

"The kid settled for the night?"

Poor Casey! Michael had evidently taken a real dislike to him.

"Yesss." She turned her gaze back to the pond, her hair swinging silkily over one shoulder and down her breast.

"It took long enough," Michael murmured. "Why do you pamper him so much? Why not just put him to bed and say good-night?"

Joanna's head swiveled around. "And why don't you mind your own business?" Immediately she was kicking herself for rising to his bait.

"Don't get all huffy again," he said with infuriating calm. "I was just asking a question."

"Well, I'd appreciate it if you'd keep questions like that to yourself."

"Fine. I go my way, you go yours. I remember."

"Right. Which reminds me, I used more of your food this morning. But don't worry, I'm keeping a careful list. I'll replace everything as soon as I get to a market."

"Fine." He continued to stare, his eyes cutting her with the intensity of a hot laser.

Joanna felt extremely uneasy, full of emotion, yet at a loss for words.

Suddenly the telephone rang.

"Ahh, saved by the bell!" Michael droned sardonically.

Joanna hurried into the dining room. "Hello?"

"Hi, Joanna? Nathan."

"Oh, hi. How are you?" She switched on the table lamp.

"Not bad, except for feeling rather like a jerk."

"Oh? And what brought that on?"

He sighed heavily. "Well, this afternoon when I bumped into you—Jo, I completely forgot to extend my condolences to you. I heard about your husband's death last winter, but it slipped my mind completely. I guess I was just so surprised to see you I couldn't think of anything else."

"Oh, for heaven's sake, Nathan! The thought never even crossed my mind."

"Still, I wish I'd said something. I hope you won't hold it against me."

"Of course not!" She looked up and saw Michael's dark, muscular form leaning against the doorjamb.

"I hope you mean it," Nathan continued, "because I want to ask you something. Since it's been quite a while since your husband's death, I thought perhaps...have you started going out socially yet?"

Joanna's nerves suddenly pulled tight. "With men?"

Nathan laughed his deep, hearty laugh. "No, with Martians."

She laughed, too, uneasily because Michael was watching so intently. "Not really."

"Well, how does the thought strike you now?"

"It's a little frightening. The thought of dating again, when I already feel so old and matronly—it isn't just frightening, it's positively ludicrous."

A muscle in Michael's jaw tightened, and she shot him an irritated glance.

"You, old and matronly? Never! All kidding aside, would you care to go out some time?"

Joanna ran a hand over the banister, staring at her ringless third finger. She had finally put away her wedding band in April, but so far she hadn't found any incentive to start stepping out. Perhaps Nathan was just what she needed. With a leap of courage, she said, "Sure, I'd love to."

Michael retreated into the shadows of the porch.

"If it'll make things easier for you, I can get my sister and brother-in-law to come along."

Joanna's breath trembled with relief. "That would be great. When?"

"Tomorrow night? Or is that too soon?"

"No, tomorrow's fine."

"Good, I'll be by around seven then."

Joanna hung up the phone in something of a daze and wandered back out to the sun porch. Michael was standing at the far end, scowling like thunder.

"Well, that certainly was an unexpected call." She was smiling, proud of the step she'd taken.

"You have a date tomorrow night?"

"Yes, with Nathan Trent. Remember him?"

Michael's laughter was a low, mirthless rumble from the shadows. "Yeah, I remember him. Boy, you don't waste much time."

Joanna bristled with offense. "I don't recall asking for your opinion."

"You're right." He raised a hand in concession. "But can I ask just one more question? What are you going to do about your son?"

Joanna dropped into a wicker chair, casually draping the silky green folds of her robe around her legs. "Hire a baby-sitter, of course."

"And where are you going to get a baby-sitter on such short notice? You don't even know anybody here."

Joanna felt her breath coming short. Still, she managed to smile. "I have connections."

Michael looked at her narrowly. "Good. I was afraid that because I'd agreed to share this place with you, you were beginning to assume you had a built-in baby-sitter."

"What?" Joanna stared across the room for a few stunned seconds. "Michael, let's get one thing straight right now. I don't want anything from you, not a single thing."

Michael glared down the straight line of his nose at her, eyes cold and fierce. "And evidently you never did." With that, he strode out of the room.

Joanna felt weak with reaction. Her head fell forward into her hands and she closed her eyes. From the dining room, there came the sound of dialing. There was a pause, and then Michael dialed again.

"Operator," she heard him say impatiently, "there's some trouble with my line. I'm trying to reach a number in New York but the line keeps going dead. Could you ring it for me, please?"

Joanna didn't want to eavesdrop, but . . .

"Hi, Joyce? Michael . . ."

Joanna opened her eyes. Her back straightened. But of course. Michael was single again and undoubtedly as foot-loose as ever.

"How was your flight? I was a little worried when you decided to go back on that private plane. Next time, take the regular shuttle. It's a lot more reliable than . . ." His words became muffled, and Joanna found herself rising from her seat to get closer to the doorway.

When she picked up the conversation again, he was dis-cussing something about a plumber. Evidently the woman he was talking to had a cottage on the Vineyard and wanted him to call a plumber to fix a leaky faucet. Who was this Joyce anyway? The familiarity in his voice as he spoke to her produced a sudden unexpected uneasiness.

Joanna reprimanded herself for cowering in the shadows. After all, Michael had listened without compunction to her phone conversation. She strolled into the dining room with a nonchalance she hardly felt and started searching through the collection of old records in the stereo cabinet.

"Yes, that's all I called about," he continued, his voice deep and lingeringly sexy. "And to say thanks for last night." He laughed quietly at something the woman said.

Last night? Was that where he'd been till three in the morning?

"See you next weekend, Joyce."

Joanna threw a scratched copy of Tchaikovsky's *1812 Overture* onto the stereo and jerked on the switch, and only the fact that Casey was asleep upstairs kept her from turning the volume up full blast.

CHAPTER FIVE

AFTER ANOTHER RESTLESS NIGHT, Joanna dragged herself out of bed, wondering how her nerves would hold up to the tension of yet another day. Of course, she had shopping to do this morning, and this evening she would be out with Nathan. Now, if only she could do something about the rest of her time, the time she was forced to spend at the house with Michael.

She slipped into her favorite shopping dress, a teal-blue, cotton-knit shift with small cap sleeves and a belt that nipped in her waist. She brushed her hair up into a loose top-knot and applied a little lipstick. Fortunately she hadn't burned as badly as she'd thought the day before. Her skin had merely taken on a red-gold tone that was actually rather attractive.

By eight o'clock, when Michael came down to the kitchen, she had the washer whirring, and she and Casey were digging into a hearty breakfast of pancakes and sausages.

"Morning," he greeted coolly from the doorway.

She turned. "There's coffee made." She had decided to try treating him as she would any other housemate, someone who deserved at least common courtesy.

One dark eyebrow lifted questioningly.

"Owe me," she replied with a small smile of concession.

He looked a little surprised. "Seems like it's going to be another nice day." He walked into the room and stared out one of the sunny windows.

"The radio says it'll be in the eighties." Joanna sipped her coffee and gazed at his profile, feeling a sudden, almost palpable awareness of his presence. He was still the most attractive man she had ever met—thick, dark hair looking as if some woman had just run her fingers through it, the mouth with the slightly debauched droop at the corners, the body that moved with the slow easy grace of one assured of his virility.

And it dismayed her that after all he'd done she could still see him this way. Not that those good looks actually affected her emotionally or physically, she reminded herself. Oh, no! She was definitely over that! It was just that she had never met anyone more handsome, and she wished she wasn't quite so aware of the fact, as objective as that fact was.

"So what are your plans for the day?"

"Grocery shopping. Laundry. The beach maybe. Yours?"

He said something about having to go into town, too...and seeing to a repair at a friend's cottage. But somehow, as he talked, Joanna lost track of his words and found herself watching the play of morning sun on his dark hair instead, the slant of it across his broad chest...

It was so odd, she thought. Once this man had been the soul and substance of her life. Once they'd been desperate to spend every minute in each other's arms. And now all they could talk about was the weather.

Well, perhaps that was best. She couldn't bear talking to him about anything more serious. Last evening's conversation had left her in a bad mood, all bottled up and wanting to scream for reasons she couldn't fathom.

Thank goodness for Casey. In his innocence, he filled the void with his chatter, giving the household an appearance of harmony.

Michael was scrambling a few eggs, and Casey, contentedly fed, was dredging out the clothes from the washer when Joanna went to the phone.

A few minutes later, it was all settled. She'd got the number of a local girl from Meg, called and arranged to have her come and stay with Casey that night. Not only that, Meg had insisted Joanna bring Casey over to play with her children instead of taking him to the market.

Pleased with her efficiency so early in the morning, she returned to the kitchen smiling. But at the door, she realized that while she'd been on the phone, Casey had finished his chore and gone out to the porch for his sand pail. Now he had the middle of the kitchen floor strewn with the seashells and rocks he'd collected at the beach the previous day and was chatting excitedly to Michael about each and every one.

"This big white rock—we're gonna use it for a doorstop, Mom says. And this is my favorite." He scrambled to his feet and went to the table where Michael was having breakfast. He held out a shell. "See? Isn't it beautiful? The pink and the gray and the purple—just like a rainbow."

Joanna was touched by her son's sensitivity, and his facility with words. Michael ought to appreciate that. But Michael seemed completely disinterested, even when one of Casey's small hands casually drifted onto his shoulder. Joanna's stomach knotted at her son's unthinking affection.

But then she saw the fine stream of sand drizzling down from the shell onto Michael's toast, and she clapped a hand to her mouth to stop a cry.

To her undying relief, Michael said nothing. His eyes just lifted icily to hers.

"I'm sorry," she mouthed quietly. "Come on, Casey. Help me hang the laundry." She took her son's hand, the hand that held the shell, and coaxed him away. "Meg, the lady we met yesterday, has invited you over to play with her children today."

Casey tried to pull his hand free, a slightly rebellious look in his eyes. In the process, the shell slipped from his fingers and hit the floor. Before he could check his step, his foot descended right on top of it. He jumped back, but too late. The shell was shattered. Suddenly his lower lip began to tremble.

Joanna stooped and quickly swept the pieces into her hand. "It was only a shell, Casey. We can find lots more like it."

Casey had always been the sort of child who took disappointment in stride. But since Phil's death, he'd sometimes had difficulty accepting other, smaller losses. Today he would not be consoled. He raised a hand over his face and began to cry, quietly, sadly, barely making any noise. Only his shoulders shook.

Joanna clapped the shell dust into the wastebasket, then scooped her son up into her arms. "Shh! Shh!" she soothed, carrying him out to the front porch. "We have a whole summer to collect shells, love. We'll find lots more, hundreds of them. We'll have to rent a trailer just to carry back our shells."

She decided to forget about the laundry. She could always hang it later. "Why don't we take a ride over to Meg's right now and meet her little boy Paul? I hear he collects Matchbox cars just like you do." It took a full five minutes before she succeeded in getting Casey's mind off the shell. But finally she was able to set him back down on his feet.

"Okay, you go wait in the car. I'll be right back. I just have to get my bag and shopping list from the kitchen."

Joanna ran back inside. Michael had left, undoubtedly disgusted by Casey's behavior. He'd also left the shells littering the floor.

CASEY AND MEG'S SON had little trouble getting acquainted. Joanna left them engrossed in a game of Chutes and Ladders, then drove to the market to buy her share of the week's groceries.

Two hours later she was back at the cottage. Michael's car, a surprisingly sensible Volvo, was gone. She put away the groceries, picked up the shells and hung the laundry. With that done, she went upstairs to make the beds.

The door to Michael's room was open. His bed had been made but with masculine haste and ineptness. For a moment she felt the urge to go in and straighten it out. In fact, her foot was already in the room before the shock of what she was doing hit her. What had ever possessed her? Michael didn't deserve the slightest gesture of help or kindness from her.

Joanna leaned in the doorway and let her gaze wander around the room. Inadvertently her memory wandered, too—back to the night her father and Viv had told her about Bunny's pregnancy. Some time during that awful night, she had crept across the dark hall from her room to this one, and in her desolation had crawled into that bed. What a pathetic little thing Michael had reduced her to, hugging the sheets to her sob-racked breast as if she might extract a bit of him from the cold material. She had stayed there until the sky lightened—and she began to realize he was not coming home. Then she'd risen and carefully remade the bed, erasing any traces that she'd been there.

Michael hadn't even had the decency to come home and face her that night. He hadn't called to offer even a minimal apology. So why had she just felt that appalling urge to go in and straighten his bed?

Joanna felt a throbbing behind her eyes and knew her face was probably pinched with worry. Were there feelings she didn't know about, didn't even suspect, lying beneath the surface of her life along with all the unresolved anger and pain? At the moment, however, the last thing Joanna wanted to do was start asking herself uncomfortable questions. She closed the door to Michael's room and ran down the stairs as if pursued.

THOUGH SHE HAD THE HOUSE all to herself and could have sat and read a book or gone out to lie in the sun, Joanna was still too edgy to relax. To get her mind off Michael and their untenable living arrangement, she hauled out the vacuum cleaner and dust cloth and gave the house a thorough cleaning.

Meg brought Casey back around three, and Michael returned shortly after that. Evidently he'd been shopping, too, for typewriter ribbons and paper. He set his bag down on the gleaming dining-room table and gave the place a slow appraisal. He was scowling when Joanna came down the stairs, lugging the vacuum.

"You've been cleaning," his rich baritone rumbled.

"How perceptive!"

"The whole house?"

"All but your room." The day was hot and muggy, and Joanna's topknot had fallen out. The ponytail that resulted was now sticking to her neck. Her navy shorts and white tank top clung uncomfortably.

"What happened to doing our own chores?" he asked derisively.

"I couldn't figure out how to divide the downstairs rooms. We all use them. So I decided we can alternate their cleaning."

Michael chuckled scornfully. "Nice to know you still like to make all the rules."

"And what's that supposed to mean?"

"Not a damn thing, Joanna." The heat was getting to him, too. A few dark curls clung to his forehead and he exuded a musky male scent that was not unattractive. He picked up his purchases and headed for the stairs. Halfway up, he turned and leaned over the banister. "Are you still planning to go out tonight?"

"Yes."

"Did you find someone to stay with Casey?"

"Yesss! Don't worry about it."

"Oh, I'm not worried. I just wanted to remind you that I won't be available."

"I know that!"

"Okay, okay. I don't want to get into another target shoot." He raised a hand as if warding her off—now that he'd succeeded in riling her thoroughly. "Just so long as you know." With that, he continued up the stairs and disappeared into his room.

"Ma?" Casey called timidly. She turned, startled. He must have been on the sun porch during the whole exchange.

"Ma, how come you and Uncle Michael fight so much?"

The question caught her off guard. Casey was obviously more aware of the tension in the house than she'd thought.

"Don't worry about what Michael and I say to each other, love. We're just...just teasing most of the time." She bit her lip, hoping he would accept the excuse.

Children were so perceptive. She had thought she and Michael were masking the tension between them well, at least in front of Casey. But she was beginning to fear that it had been evident all along—and worse, that it was growing, day by day, like a head of steam.

NATHAN CAME BY promptly at seven. They picked up Meg and Steve and then went on to Edgartown. Joanna was nervous at first but soon realized her apprehension was totally unfounded. Nathan was an easy person to get along with, and his humor was dwarfed only by his sister's. They ate at an elegant little restaurant, then went on to the Hot Tin Roof, the popular night spot owned by singer Carly Simon who, like many other celebrities, had a home on the Vineyard.

Joanna had a lovely evening. For the first time in months, she even felt attractive. She had worn her white sundress with the red piping and white T-strapped heels. She'd swept her hair up into a loose twist and applied makeup with a careful, delicate hand since her complexion was already glowing from the sun.

All in all, though, she was glad it was a weeknight and the men had to get up early for work the next day. They were back at the cottage by eleven o'clock.

"Would you like to come in for coffee?" she asked politely. Nathan was opening her door. He had brought her home first, and she suspected it was a deliberate move to ease any fear she might have that he would pressure her for a good-night kiss. His sensitivity was touching.

"I'd love a cup," Meg sang, feeling the effects of too many rum-and-cokes.

"Honey, do you know what time it is?" Steve asked. He was a mild-natured man, as quiet as Meg was outspoken.

"Yes, I do. It's early and I'd love a cup of coffee."

"So would I," Nathan added.

"Good," Joanna laughed. "Come on in."

Meg literally danced up the stairs, singing the song the band had been playing when they'd left the bar. On the porch, she threw her arms around Nathan and Joanna. "Have I told you yet how cute you two look together?"

Nathan shot Joanna a quick, amused look. "A few times."

"I mean it. Don't you think they make an adorable couple, Steve?" She slurred her words slightly as they entered the kitchen. Her husband groaned.

"Don't be embarrassed," Joanna said. "That's what I like about Meg. You always know what's on her mind." Suddenly her smile froze. Michael was sitting at the small Formica table, deep in a game of cribbage with the babysitter. There was no way he couldn't have heard their entrance.

"Michael!" Meg exclaimed, rushing over and giving him a hug. "It's so good to see you again." From the corner of her eye, Joanna could see Nathan tense.

Michael put his cards down slowly. "Good to see you, too, Meg." His eyes swept over the others, stopping to linger on Joanna. He hadn't seen her before she'd left. He'd stayed in his room, door firmly shut, all the time she was getting ready. Now those eyes swept over her with a thoroughness that caused a rushing in her ears.

"How w-was Casey tonight?" she asked quickly.

The baby-sitter rose reluctantly. There was a flush to her complexion that gave Joanna the distinct impression she already had a crush on Michael.

"Oh, just fine. We played for a while, then we put him to bed. No trouble."

We? Joanna searched Michael's face, but it remained impassive. She opened her bag and dug out her wallet to pay the girl.

"Can I give you a lift home?"

"Oh, no thanks. I brought my moped," she replied. But if Michael had asked, Joanna thought with amusement, she would've forgotten she even owned such a thing.

Once the baby-sitter was gone, Joanna put on a pot of coffee and invited them all into the living room. Much to her relief, Michael rose and excused himself from their company. A moment later she heard the back screen door clatter.

They moved into the living room and Joanna had barely settled herself into the club chair next to Nathan's when Meg said, "You know, seeing you and Michael together there in the kitchen really brought back memories."

Suddenly the walls seemed to close in on her.

"Memories? What memories?" Steve asked.

"Oh, Michael and Joanna mostly. They were quite a pair the last time I saw them."

Steve looked perplexed. "Did you two date? I thought you were related."

Dread gripped her heart. She and Michael were a subject Joanna definitely did not want to delve into with these people.

"Did they date?" Meg exclaimed. "Why, those two were so much in love—sorry, Nate—that I could feel the heat from this house clear across the pond." She turned to Joanna laughingly. "There were more girls around here who wanted to tear your eyes out! But then..." A puzzled look filtered into her slightly unfocused eyes. "All of a sudden you were gone without even saying goodbye to anyone, and the next thing I knew, Michael was marrying that awful Bunny Wilcox and you were marrying a guy up north. Boy, if that didn't have the island buzzing!"

Leave it to Meg, Joanna thought with a silent groan. In her guileless way, Meg had brought up the very issue she'd been trying to avoid for the past three days—maybe even for the past six years, if she were perfectly honest. But, of course, she'd been thinking about little else, arguing with herself in the dark recesses of the night, trying out expressions, rearranging answers. What attitude should she take if the subject came up? What reasons could she give if she bumped into an old friend?

She took a deep breath and tried to relax. After all, it wasn't as if this were the first time. There had been her father and Viv...and Phil's parents...and her mother, of course. But that all seemed so long ago...

"What a memory you have, Meg!" she said, laughing as casually as she could. "I'd nearly forgotten about all that." She rolled her eyes as if suffering mild embarrassment over some minor girlhood experience.

Nathan fidgeted uncomfortably in the other easy chair, glowering at his sister, who didn't notice it.

"We were just kids, Michael and I," Joanna continued. "I was just one of his many dates, and he was just one of mine. All in all, considering the entire scope of our lives, it was a rather insignificant few months."

"Didn't seem all that insignificant at the time." Meg laughed uneasily.

"Good grief, if a girl married every guy she thought she was in love with, the world would be in a state of bedlam."

"As if it isn't already." Meg's eyes still looked troubled. "I suppose you know best what you felt but—it was just strange. There was a rumor that Bunny..." She shook her head and let the thought trail off.

"That Bunny was pregnant?" Joanna said quietly, fighting the tightening in her chest. Meg nodded. "And if Bunny was pregnant, then I must have married Phil on the rebound? Yes, I imagined there would be rumors like that."

"Meg, why don't we forget the coffee?" Nathan said, smiling sympathetically at Joanna. "I'm sure Joanna doesn't want to dredge up—"

"No, really, it's all right," Joanna said almost adamantly. "It was nothing like that. Nothing at all. Actually my marriage to Phil was as inevitable as night following day. I don't suppose any of the rumors included the fact that I'd been dating him for four years."

Meg looked up. "Four years! Really, Jo?"

"Really," she emphasized, feeling the ache in her chest tighten even more. But her pride was at stake; she couldn't let down her guard now. Besides, there was Casey—and Phil's memory—and she loved them simply too much to let them appear a cheap consolation prize she'd turned to at a low swing in her life. "Michael was just a . . . a summertime kind of thing. A lot of heat, but over in a few months—if you know what I mean." She tried to laugh lightly. "Phil was the constant in my life all along. When I went home after that summer here, I realized how much I'd missed him, and we decided to get married right away. Maybe Michael was good for me—you know, someone to test my love for Phil. But that's all he was. My marriage was definitely not something I rushed into on the rebound."

"I see," Meg said. "I should have known."

"That's all right. How could you?" Joanna sensed her audience was convinced. She sat back, exhausted, realizing only now how tense she had been.

But somehow she had survived the ordeal. She'd reconstructed the past and made her company see only what she wanted them to see. She was amazed, if not a little horrified, at how thoroughly she had done it, too. There had been moments when she'd almost lost track of the truth herself.

She rubbed her eyes tiredly. At times, she sounded so like her mother—that same cold pride and uncompromising independence that stemmed from being hurt by a man. It was frightening.

"What did you say?" Joanna lifted her head, suddenly realizing that Nathan had been speaking.

"...about you two sharing the cottage this summer. Let's face it, if what people said was true, you and Michael certainly wouldn't be able to live here now without bitterness, right?"

Joanna caught the drift of his words and felt her face flushing. "Oh, right. Of course. That coffee smells about ready," she interjected quickly, rising from the chair.

"Let me help." Nathan was immediately on his feet, too.

Conversation seemed a blur of inanities to Joanna until her company left, which, blessedly, was soon after the coffee was drunk. When they were gone, she put the cups in the sink. Then she tiptoed back through the living and dining rooms, turning off lights as she headed for the stairs. She longed for the refuge of her bed. The conversation tonight had taken more out of her than she'd realized. Maybe tomorrow she would be able to ignore what Meg had forced her to remember. Maybe tomorrow she would be able to go on pretending that the lies she'd told them were the truth. But not tonight. She was as aware of her love for Michael and the devastation it had brought her as if the years that had intervened were just a matter of days.

In a way, she thought, it was a shame she and Michael had never had the opportunity to confront each other. Maybe if she'd been able to vent her anger, spill out her feelings, get him to admit he was wrong—maybe all of this would be out of her system by now. But they hadn't. Nothing had ever been resolved. It had just been buried under the happiness and the busyness and, yes, especially the sadness of what followed.

But she couldn't tamp down those feelings any longer. Not tonight anyway. Here she was on Martha's Vineyard again, sharing the cottage with a very real Michael Malone, and as if that weren't enough to bring the past to life, to-night she'd had to endure Meg's recollections.

She was sure she'd be all right in the morning. All she needed was time to mend. Somewhere in the night, she would find the uncaring, independent attitude she had donned after leaving here six years ago. All she needed was rest, and then no one, not even Michael, would be able to make her feel this vulnerable again.

CHAPTER SIX

JUST AS SHE REACHED the stairs, Michael's tall frame detached itself from the darkness of the sun porch. Her heart leaped to her throat. She had been under the impression that he'd gone out.

"Sorry, I didn't mean to startle you."

"You didn't," she lied. He looked dark and ominous and unfairly huge. She wished she could get her feet to move but they suddenly seemed paralyzed.

"Did you enjoy yourself tonight?"

"W-what?"

"On your date."

"Oh, that! Yes." Her fingers played fretfully with the folds of her skirt. "We went to... to the Hot Tin Roof."

"Well, he seems a nice enough guy." Michael's hair was rumpled over his forehead. The dim lamplight cast shadows into the hollows of his cheeks. "He used to have a crush on you, didn't he?" His voice was liquid with a predatory sweetness she didn't trust.

"I guess." She shrugged.

"You guess? And are you aware that he still does?"

Silence shifted uneasily between them.

"I don't think it's fair to jump to that conclusion," she said defensively.

"It wasn't much of a jump. His eyes kept following you like a mindless little puppy's."

Joanna stared at Michael, unable to control the turbulent feelings rising inside her. "I don't appreciate your talking about Nathan like that. He and I had a wonderful time tonight. It did me a world of good to get out, and if he decides he'd like to go out again, I'd feel honored." In her agitation, she had taken a step closer to Michael, close enough to smell the clean, warm fragrance of his body.

He raised his hands in mock surrender. "Okay, Jo. I'm sorry. It doesn't matter to me what you do or who you go out with. You go your way, I go mine, etcetera, etcetera."

"Good!"

"Fine!"

Joanna's chest rose and fell like a bellows. If she knew what was good for her, she would get up to her room right now. She didn't want to start anything with Michael now, not strung out the way she was from that dreadful conversation. She felt out of control, stripped of her defenses. She wasn't sure what she would say or where her feelings might take her.

She had turned and climbed two stairs when Michael's smooth, sardonic voice cut through her resolve.

"If you want to go out dancing and carousing so soon after your husband's death, that's entirely up to you."

Joanna's feet froze to the stair tread. She closed her eyes and groaned. For some unfathomable reason, Michael seemed determined to keep them on a collision course.

Well, maybe he was right. Maybe they'd been playing their silly game too long. Maybe it was time she gave him an honest piece of her mind!

She stomped down the stairs and pushed him out to the sun porch where their voices wouldn't carry up to Casey. "For your information, Michael Malone, my husband died nearly eight months ago! What am I supposed to do, dress in sackcloth and ashes all my life?"

"Of course not. But isn't it traditional to wait at least a year? Or doesn't that stuff matter to you? Maybe this wasn't even the first time you went out."

Joanna's fists tightened at her sides. "I have no idea what your problem is, but my affairs are none of your business."

He lifted his head and laughed contemptuously. Starlight, coming through the windows, streaked the bridge of his arrogant nose and deepened the furrows of his brow. "Isn't that a revealing choice of words!"

Joanna stared at him dumbfoundedly for a moment before she felt the color drain from her face. Then she grabbed up a pillow from a chair and flung it at him with all her strength.

But Michael's reflexes were quick and he deflected the missile easily. "Stop it, Joanna!" he ordered, taking a threatening step forward.

"Apologize for that insinuation first!"

"Why should I? Evidently affairs are your specialty. You admitted it to your friends in the living room just a few minutes ago."

"What?" she shrieked incredulously. Had he been in the sun porch the whole time? Suddenly the conversation with her guests took on nightmarish proportions.

"Oh, I'll admit, you had me fooled that summer, but then I didn't know what a good little actress you were." Though his voice remained level, his fingers tightened on the back of a chair until they turned white.

"What are you talking about?" Joanna whispered frantically, wishing she could transport herself to the safety of her room.

"Don't play the little innocent with me, Jo! I've seen that performance before and frankly, it's getting a little stale. I'm talking about the summer before you got married. You *do* remember that summer, don't you? The summer you and your friends just had such a laugh over? Or did it mean so little that it's slipped your mind already?"

The shadows of the room swam before Joanna's eyes until she thought she would faint. "I . . . I remember," she whispered weakly. "But I seem to recall it as the summer before *you* got married, Michael."

Michael's eyes swept over her disdainfully. "May I ask what the hell you thought you were doing that summer?"

She averted her eyes, remembering what she'd said to Meg and the others.

"What did you think you were doing?" he repeated. With each word, his voice rose until it was a nerve-shattering explosion. Joanna clapped her hands over her ears, but he tore them away, glaring at her with a coldness she had never dreamed him capable of.

"What were you trying to prove, pretending you were in love with me," he continued, "when all the while you were planning to marry someone else?" He pointed out the window as if that someone else were just beyond the nearest bush.

Joanna's eyes opened wide with shock. Not only had she convinced the others about the shallowness of her feelings that summer, but she had convinced Michael, too. Incredible as it seemed, he believed every last word. And he was furious!

It didn't make any sense. Somehow, everything had become twisted around over the years. She hadn't the foggiest idea why it should matter to him now—unless his ego was so big he couldn't stand the idea of learning, however late, that he'd once been made the fool? But it didn't matter. Late or not, Michael was genuinely upset.

For a moment she felt the wildest urge to tell him the truth and set things right. But she would be a fool to do that. Why shouldn't he feel some of the pain of rejection *she* had felt six years ago? Let him think she'd walked away from here unscathed. Whatever he felt, it would be nothing compared to what she had suffered.

"What were you doing all those times we made love?" he continued to demand, leaning so close she could feel the angry trembling of his body.

She stared into his cobalt eyes and was suddenly overwhelmed by the memories she saw reflected in them. Just as suddenly, she was gripped by an incomprehensible sadness, a grief for those profoundly happy days that had been snuffed out by his treachery. She tore her eyes from his and turned away, weak and trembling.

"I'm serious. I'd like to know." He gripped her arm and swung her around again. "Were you unsure of yourself as a woman? Were you trying to learn about lovemaking with me so you wouldn't disappoint the guy you were really planning to marry?" With his free hand, he again pointed out the window. "Or were you just looking for a summer of kicks before you settled down?"

The conversation was turning into a nightmare of distortions. Where did he get such notions? And why was he probing so cruelly? Why couldn't he just let the past rest in peace?

"Michael, I don't want to talk about this anymore." She made a move toward the door, but his hand tightened on her arm.

"What's the matter? The truth too hard to face?"

Joanna winced. Suddenly something inside her seemed to shudder—and snap. "The truth? The truth? Michael, you wouldn't know the truth if it hit you between the eyes." This time when she tried to yank free of his grip, she succeeded. But instead of backing away and heading for the door as she'd intended, she took a bold step closer, her face tilted defiantly toward his. She was trembling from head to foot with newfound anger.

"The truth is you've never been capable of loving anybody but yourself, Michael. You've always been that way— irresponsible, self-serving, drunk on your own appeal. I knew it the first time I met you, and I was only sixteen at the time. You never gave a damn about me. I just attracted you because I was an innocent kid. And the only reason you're angry now is that your pride is hurt. You're asking yourself, 'Gee, why couldn't I break this girl's heart the way I broke so many others? Why didn't she fall to pieces when I threw her over for somebody else?' "

Michael's eyes narrowed. He went very still. "Is that what you think of me?"

"That's what I *know* about you, buster!" she returned, her strength continuing to rise. "Oh, I'll admit, I let down my guard for a while that summer. But then, I was a little out of my league tangling with you. In fact, I didn't have a chance. There I was, an inexperienced country kid, and you...you were a past master at seduction." Her words seemed to have a mind of their own, as if they were all spilling out after years of being repressed.

"Seduction?"

"That's right. With your slick lines about feeling married to me, and all those grand promises about our future together." For a moment, her strength failed her and she felt herself swaying. "No, Michael, I wasn't experimenting with sex and I wasn't just out for kicks," she said sadly, feeling that inexplicable sense of loss again. "You seduced me into making love. It's as simple and tragic as that."

Michael's eyes widened and he gasped a halfhearted, bitter laugh. "Is that so? Well, if it was seduction, you certainly didn't give me much of an argument."

Rational thought abandoned her, and all the feelings she had denied since leaving here came roiling to the surface.

"Are you trying to say I—I was *easy*? When you were out behind my back sleeping with Bunny Wilcox—sleeping with half the girls on the island, for all I know!" She could feel her nails digging painfully into her palms. "You have a nerve to stand there and criticize *me* the first time I see another man after being faithful to my husband and his memory for five and a half years!" Emotion was mounting so rapidly, she was actually seeing red spots in front of her.

Michael continued to glare down at her, his expression so cold and derisive she wondered if he was really the same person she had once loved and found so charming and compassionate.

"Faithful? You don't know the meaning of the word, Joanna! Tell me, how soon will it be before you let ol' Nathan give you a tumble?"

Without realizing what she was doing, Joanna raised her hand and sent it cracking across his face. The derisive smile dropped from his lips and his eyes went black and fiery. A split second later, she felt a hard palm come smacking across her own cheek.

Tears sprang to her eyes and a voice within warned her that she should be frightened. But she wasn't. She was merely seeing his appalling treatment of her with deeper clarity, feeling the pain of his deceit with renewed sharpness—and falling further and further into the depths of her pent-up fury.

"Don't you dare hit me!" she fired back, green eyes flashing. She pushed his chest hard, wanting to knock him down and pummel him with her bare fists. She could almost taste the satisfaction it would bring.

But her efforts were meaningless. Michael caught her wrists and pinned them behind her back.

"Let me go," she rasped. She struggled against him and temporarily lost her balance, tottering on her high-heeled shoes.

"Not until I'm damn well ready to, my love," he taunted, crushing her against him.

Joanna couldn't stand feeling so helpless, being imprisoned in his arms, feeling the heat and powerful strength of his body trembling through hers. She could hardly think coherently anymore. She was simply a mass of nerve ends and pumping adrenaline.

With all the desperation of a cornered animal, she raised her foot and jammed it down along the inside of his shins.

He winced and his body felt heavy against hers, as if it were momentarily boneless. Again she felt herself tipping out of balance. This time, however, Michael was unable to set her right. This time her knees buckled and she fell backward, Michael's heavy weight going with her.

She hit the floor with a bone-crushing thud. She gasped, first to catch the breath that had been knocked out of her, and then in reaction to the pain that nearly paralyzed her body. Fresh tears filled her eyes.

Michael had fallen, too, Joanna cushioning much of his fall. As if his weight weren't bad enough, one of his arms was still wrapped around her, digging agonizingly into her back. She tried to move to free his arm but every ounce of strength seemed to have left her.

"Get off me. I can't breathe." The words were difficult, made breathless by her suppressed sobs.

Michael slid his arms out from under her and slowly lifted himself up onto one elbow. Still stunned, he shook his head, then rubbed his forehead. Joanna began to wonder if he had knocked it on the floor when he hit.

"Are you all right?" she whispered.

He nodded. "You?"

"I don't know. Yes . . . I guess."

Michael's eyes swept over her. She could feel tears trickling down the sides of her face. With a low moan, he lowered his head and buried his face in her long tangled hair.

"What have we done to each other, Joanna?" he whispered raggedly. "What have we done?" He lay very still, with an exhausted heaviness throughout his body.

Joanna lay beneath him, sobbing quietly.

After a while, he dragged himself up and without looking at her, held out a hand. She noticed it was trembling. Slowly she lifted hers and let him help her up. Her dress was twisted and torn. Her hair hung like a tattered mop.

"Michael?" she whispered tremulously.

He looked up and starlight silvered his handsome, anguished face. It lit his dark, wavy hair, made sensuous the sad, drooping mouth. His long eyelashes were wet.

Joanna felt a thousand emotions in that moment—most of them illogical. But the one that disturbed her most was the compassion she suddenly felt. This was no casual case of a womanizer's wounded pride. Michael had been hurt. He had genuinely suffered. Though she still didn't understand it, he was wrestling with a pain, an anger, that very

much resembled her own. At that moment she felt so unutterably bad for him her heart ached.

''Uh...nothing.'' She drew back, alarmed. This was no
time to start feeling sorry for Michael Malone! She had
come too far. She couldn't allow herself to lose ground now.
It was...too late!

She turned on wobbly legs and went up to her room.
There, she pulled her suitcase from under her bed and in the
dark began to empty her dresser.

CHAPTER SEVEN

"JUST GET IN THE CAR and stop asking questions," Joanna
snapped uncharacteristically the next morning. Her son
glared from under the veil of his dark lashes and obeyed.
Joanna bit her lip guiltily. She had been bullying him all
morning—rushing him through breakfast, barking at him
when he'd tried to sneak up to Michael's room.

"But where are we going?" he asked, trying to tie his
sneaker as the car lurched down the driveway.

She didn't answer—couldn't answer—knowing the disappointment her reply would bring.

Fifteen minutes later, she was standing inside the Steam-
ship Authority, reading the ferry schedule on the wall.
Good. There was a boat leaving at one, which would give
her plenty of time to pack the rest of her things.

"Ma, why are we here?" Casey persisted, tugging at her
hand.

Joanna glanced down at his wary face. She knelt down
and took him by the waist. "Casey, I'm ready to go home
now. I . . ."

Before she could say anything else, his lower lip began to
tremble. "But I don't want to go yet."

"Casey, please don't argue. We can't stay here forever."

"I know, but we just got here."

Joanna sighed impatiently. "Stop it! We're going and
that's all there is to it."

"No!" he wailed. A few people nearby turned and gave
Joanna censorious looks. "I didn't buy Grandma a present
yet. And we never went out to the other island."

"Nantucket?" she said, remembering a promise she had made before they'd come. "Some other time, babe." She tried to soothe him, but he wriggled away.

"Leave me alone!" he hollered.

Joanna's face flushed. Casey had never pulled a tantrum before, at home or in public. What was the matter with him? What was he doing to her?

She paused abruptly. What was he doing to *her*? The question was, what was she doing to *him*? Had she taken leave of her senses? Did she really want to take him away from all this—the lazy timelessness of the sea, the joy he found playing in the sand, wandering through meadows of wildflowers, meeting new playmates who bore no association with the grief he had suffered?

Then why was she running away? And running it was, she realized. Did Michael still hold so much power over her that he could send her fleeing for the nearest ship even now? Well, Michael Malone could go straight to hell! Even if he tormented her to skin and bones, she would not leave. Casey meant far too much to her.

"Yes, may I help you?" the ticket agent asked.

"Oh, no thanks."

He looked at her quizzically.

"Come on, Casey," she said, scooping him up. "Sometimes I think you have more sense than I do."

"Are we going home?"

"No, we're heading back to the cottage."

Casey flung his arms around her neck and pressed his wet cheek to hers. "That's what I meant, Ma!" He giggled with trembling relief.

There was a large manila envelope on the kitchen table when she returned. It was addressed to her, with her mother's return address in the corner. Evidently Michael was up and stirring and had gone out for the mail.

She poured herself a glass of lemonade, then opened the envelope. Inside was a short note from her mother and a copy of the weekly hometown paper, which Joanna had asked Dorothy to forward. She sat down and opened the paper to the job ads.

"Good morning," a husky voice called from the door.

"Nathan! Hi, come on in."

"What are you doing?" He collapsed into the chair opposite her.

"Just browsing through the want ads."

He reached across the table and lifted the drooping front page so he could read the masthead. "You interested in a new job?"

She shrugged. "I'm thinking about it."

"Good Lord, why? Hasn't your life been crazy enough this past year?"

"Can I get you something to drink?"

"No, thanks. So why are you looking for another job?"

She sighed wearily. "To put it in a nutshell, money. Don't get me wrong, we're getting by, but just barely. I'd like to do so much more for Casey."

Nathan scratched his thick beard and stared at her thoughtfully. "Come work for me then."

Joanna nearly choked on her lemonade. "What?"

"That's right. I'm looking for someone to fill a managerial position at my Edgartown shop, and I think you'd be perfect. You have experience, you're career minded, and you like retail work, don't you?"

"Yes," she admitted hesitantly. "But that would mean I'd have to live here permanently."

A smile lit Nathan's rugged face. "That's the basic idea."

She laughed. "I'll have to think about it."

"All kidding aside, I'm really strapped for help. And I'd pay a good salary, with medical coverage, a pension plan, and lots of other fringe benefits." He leered comically.

"Thanks. I mean that," she said, hoping her voice conveyed her appreciation. "But I was thinking of something—well, more professional, something I might have to go back to school for."

"You're thinking about returning to school?"

"Possibly." And before he could remind her again how turbulent her life had been, "What brings you here today? I thought you'd be working."

"I fully intended to, but it's too nice a day. How would you like to go out for a boat ride?"

"You have a boat?"

"A small cabin cruiser. I keep it docked at Menemsha."

Joanna smiled, having discovered something to keep her out of the house for the day. "Sure, why not?"

"Great. Go grab your gear and your son, and we'll be off."

"Casey?" Joanna called as she hurried up the stairs. He had told her he would be up in their room playing with his Lego blocks, but when she looked in, he wasn't there. From across the hall, his high, thin giggle sent a shiver down her back. *Michael's room.*

She pushed open the door and there he was, perched on Michael's lap at the desk. Neither of them heard her enter.

"Good. What comes next?" Michael's head was bent close to the boy's.

"*H*. I know, it's *H*," Casey said, his voice brimming with boastful delight. "But I can't find it. Oh. Oh, here it is!" His finger hovered over the typewriter, then clumsily smashed down a key. He leaned his head back against Michael's shoulder and laughed with the pride of accomplishment.

"Now *I*," Michael prompted.

"I *know*. *I J K L M N O P*," he recited in a rush.

Joanna wondered how long Casey had been with Michael. She hoped he hadn't said anything about their trip to the ferry landing.

"Casey, what are you doing in here?"

He turned in surprise. "I'm typing, Ma. Just like Uncle Michael."

Joanna hadn't seen Michael all morning, and even now he didn't turn toward her. She wondered if he felt as embarrassed about last night's battle as she did.

"I've told you a dozen times not to disturb Michael while he's working." For a moment she wished she had her son's vantage point and could see what that "work" actually was.

"I know. What do you want, Ma?" Casey wound an arm around Michael's neck and rested his chin on the man's shoulder.

"I want you to come over here right now and stop bothering him."

"I'm sorry." But he still didn't move.

"Nathan's going to take us for a boat ride today."

"A boat ride?" He considered the proposal, then slid off Michael's lap and walked to his mother.

"Sorry he disturbed you," she said curtly to the back of Michael's head.

"No bother."

Joanna's eyes snapped wide open. It sounded as if he almost meant it.

IT WAS A WONDERFUL AFTERNOON, and the boat was a dream, a sumptuous forty-foot cabin cruiser with all the amenities of a home. It was just what Joanna needed to forget the clash of the previous night.

But it was impossible to forget completely. Now that she was determined to stay, she would have to face the dilemma of living with Michael all over again, and this time on a new plateau of difficulty. Last evening the polite facade they'd been hiding behind since she'd arrived had finally been stripped away. Now their feelings were out in the open, all the raw wounds and accusations. Where had she stored all that anger and hatred during her happy marriage? How had she ignored the pain for so long and convinced herself she felt nothing for Michael?

It still startled her to think that Michael was hurt and angry, too. After all, *he* had two-timed *her*; there was nothing for him to be angry about—except that he really believed *she* had two-timed *him* while Phil waited in the wings, or some such nonsense. But even more puzzling was the fact that it saddened her so much. This strange pity stealing over her, this compassion for his anguish—where was it coming from? And why? He didn't deserve it.

She spent the afternoon lounging in a deck chair—and trying not to think about Michael—while Nathan piloted the boat through the Elizabeth Islands and around Buzzard's Bay. They docked at the old whaling city of New Bedford and had lunch at a restaurant overlooking the modern fishing fleet. Later, they strolled the narrow, cobbled streets of the newly restored historic district, stopped into an antique shop, and even found time to tour the whaling museum.

"Can I take you two out to dinner?" Nathan asked as they docked back at Menemsha. The sun was already riding low on the horizon.

"Thanks. It's been a wonderful day, but I'd like to get home."

"Mmm. I understand. Bouncing around in a boat can be awfully tiring."

Joanna smiled, glad for the ready excuse. Actually she wasn't tired at all. In fact, her whole body was running on overdrive now that she was heading home and back to Michael. All day she'd been worried about returning to the house and risking a repeat of last night's argument.

Suddenly she thought of a solution. It wasn't a permanent one, but at least it would get her through one more night and buy her a little time.

JOANNA AND CASEY pitched the old canvas tent in the sheltered hollow of a dune. Then they walked the dusky beach, gathering driftwood. As night sifted down from the gold and pink clouds, they sat by a cozy fire roasting hot dogs on the ends of long sticks. The thicket of beach plum rustled with a slight wind. The tall grass whistled. And over it all, the sea murmured its incessant low roar.

They didn't say much. Casey just sat watching the flames, and Joanna sat watching Casey. How she adored this child! No one could ever come close to guessing.

And yet there were times when she knew he couldn't fill all her emotional needs. Like now. There was an empty spot inside that she didn't fully understand, a need to share her thoughts and problems, her anxieties and joys.

Oh, why did Phil have to die? Why did her safe little world have to fall apart? It had been such a comfort and a refuge.

But what had it been a refuge from?

The evening was growing cool and damp. She zippered Casey's sweatshirt and tugged up the hood.

"Aw, Ma!" he laughed, shrugging away. Something pulled at her heart strings. He was growing too quickly, maturing from her baby into a boy. Day by day, she could see changes in him, in his increasingly complex speech patterns, in the growing agility of his body.

But lately there were changes that disquieted her, too... like his stern refusal to cuff his jeans because Michael's had no cuffs... like the way he slouched in chairs, his feet barely reaching the windowsill, again because of Michael. And he had been under Michael's influence how long? Four days?

It wasn't that she begrudged Casey's admiration of another adult. There were lots of adults he loved and admired—his grandparents, aunts, uncles. It was just his admiring *this* adult that bothered her. Michael paid almost no attention to Casey. It was obvious he considered him a disturbance in the house. And the way he called him "kid," as if he had no name—as if Michael were trying to deny his very existence!

Then, what was this instinctive attraction Casey felt for Michael?

"Ma, your hot dog's burning," Casey cried.

Joanna shook herself out of her reverie. "Oh, it's all right, Case. They taste better this way. Will you get the buns, please?"

The child stood up and went to the picnic basket. The breeze, coming over the lip of the dune, caught his hair and whipped it back.

"Hurry, come sit," she said, feeling suddenly possessive and protective.

No, she didn't begrudge the wind, either—just what was blowing in the wind. No matter how hard she tried to avoid it, Michael was breezing his way back into her life. And Casey's.

Casey was exhausted and fell asleep before nine, but Joanna lay awake, staring up at the dark peak of canvas long after that. Her eyes were wide and restless. Finally she lifted herself out of her sleeping bag and unzipped the door. Outside, the night was still faintly luminescent, the air alive with rushing shore sounds. She wrapped her arms around her knees and listened.

She heard the crackle and spit of the dying fire, the soughing of the wind blowing sand over sand. And beyond the ridge of the dune, down the flat, damp beach, the waves rushed forward and back, forward and back.

She knew the beach was deserted, yet she had a feeling of something breathing out there, something immense and wonderful and eternal. It was a feeling she used to get when she was a girl, staring up at the stars or gazing across the mountains. But she'd always felt it most here, on this island of such varied and dramatic beauty.

Especially at Gay Head. She must take Casey out to Gay Head someday soon. The terrain there was wild and recklessly beautiful. It was a place of windswept moors, hills and hollows, and of course, the famous clay cliffs that rose 150 feet from the sea in dramatic striations of pink and yellow and mauve.

She and Michael used to love to drive out there in the evenings. In fact, it was the first place they went when she arrived that third and final summer. Inadvertently her mind drifted back... They had slipped through a gap in the fencing that was supposed to keep people off the eroding cliffs. Then they'd picked their way along a narrow path and sat at the edge of a steep drop, listening to the murmurous rush and retreat of the sea far below. A beam from a lighthouse stroked over them with its steady pulse.

"We shouldn't be out here," Joanna whispered guiltily. "This area's restricted."

"Good. Then we won't be disturbed."

"Michael, is this supposed to be a date?" She still wasn't sure if he meant what he'd written in his letter.

She felt his hand on her back, running up under her long, silky hair to her neck, his fingers stroking the smooth downy skin at her nape.

"If you want it to be," he answered softly, seductively.

She stared into his dark, languid eyes and felt as if she were tumbling off the cliff. Yes, she believed it; this was going to be their summer.

"I'd like that," she whispered.

He smiled. His head lowered and his lips found hers. His kiss was gentle, tentative, making no demands. But much to her alarm, she began to feel things, like the fluttering of tiny bird wings in her stomach. And when he drew away, she felt a wave of dismay.

He rose abruptly, the wind raking back his hair, and silently stared out over the ocean. Had she done something wrong? Had she disappointed him? Dear Lord, was he already getting bored?

He dug his hands into his pockets. "Joanna, this isn't right. Our parents are going to have a fit."

"Frankly I don't care."

"It's not only that. You're . . . you're too young."

"I'm eighteen!" All the love inside her was crying out in her anguished expression. If only he'd turn around, surely he would see it.

"A very young eighteen." His eyes narrowed as if against a deep pain.

"I know you're used to girls with more experience . . ."

"Not as much as you seem to think." He hung his head. "Nevertheless, I still don't deserve you. But I can't help myself. I can't get you out of my mind...."

He looked so distraught, Joanna had to laugh. "Michael?" This time he did turn. She lay back and raised her arms to him, imploring him to come to her. "I'm not a china doll, you know." She smiled adoringly, her long blond hair fanned out on the ground. "I'm not going to break."

Even now, Joanna could still remember the way Michael had caught his breath, the look that had come over his face. He'd lowered himself to his knees and gathered her into his arms. This time when he kissed her, there was no holding back, and she responded with a passion that was unlearned. It was as if the floodgates of womanly emotion had been locked up tight until that moment.

Joanna shook herself out of her reverie. She couldn't imagine what had started her thinking about that now. Granted, there were some very lovely memories...but she had to remember Michael as the cold, self-serving two-timer he was at the end of that summer, not the person she had adored at the beginning.

Suddenly there was a flicker of white outside the unzipped door. She jumped. What on earth...? A sea gull perhaps, flapping too near the tent?

It came again, and now she recognized it for what it was. A man's handkerchief tied to the end of a stick.

"Joanna?"

"Michael?" she cried. It was as if her thoughts had conjured him up bodily.

He laid down the white flag and peered into the tent. "Is Casey asleep?"

"Yes."

"Good, I'd like to talk."

"Go away!" The night was suddenly pulsing against her ears like the beating of a huge heart. It was difficult to breathe. She couldn't see his face; the fire was behind him, but she knew he was exasperated. She heard his impatient huff.

"Joanna Scott, get out here!"

His voice held so much authority she decided to obey without argument. The air was cool against her burning cheeks, the sand beneath her damp as she scrambled toward the fire. She huddled there sulkily and drew her sweatshirt closer.

"How did you know where to find us?" she asked as he placed another piece of driftwood on the fire.

"This is where you and I always came when we wanted to be alone." The ease with which he referred to their past took her by surprise. In fact, it was the first time either of them had referred to their past at all, apart from the distortions of last night.

He clapped the sand from his hands and settled across the fire from her. Light flickered over his face, a face so handsome Joanna sometimes felt an ache in her heart when she looked at it. It seemed unfair that one man should possess so much appeal.

He flipped up the collar of his windbreaker. "You must be crazy camping out on a night like this. The weatherman says it might even rain."

"Thanks for the warning, but you shouldn't have trekked all the way out here just for that."

"I didn't trek all the way out here just for that, and you know it." Their eyes locked, and Joanna's breathing went shallow. He was up to something but she didn't know what.

"Not another brawl, I hope. Listen, Michael, if you think I get a thrill out of being mauled and manhandled—"

"Will you be quiet?"

"What?"

"Please."

Joanna's mouth dropped open but nothing came out, so deep was her surprise at the gentleness in his voice.

"Jo, I'm really sorry about last night. I've wanted to apologize all day, but either you've been out or I just haven't had the courage. I—I hope I didn't hurt you."

With a start, Joanna realized he was nervous. She shook her head. "No, I wasn't hurt."

"Good." He sat without speaking, and yet she sensed there was something trying to reach out from behind his eyes.

Joanna cleared her throat. "Apology accepted. I wish I could also say forget it, but..."

"No, I don't want to forget it. What happened last night was too important to forget. I don't know what got into me. By the time your friends left, I was so angry at you I just couldn't control myself any longer. But rest assured, it won't happen again." His voice was becoming a lot more familiar to Joanna. It rang with the sincerity that belonged to the Michael she'd known years ago, one short eternal summer.

"You see," he continued, "ever since you arrived, I've been so tied up in knots trying to stay cool, I could hardly think. I guess overhearing that conversation with Meg was the last straw. But today..." He laughed with amazement. "Today I feel so much better. Lighter. You know?" His eyes raked over her, imploring her to understand. "It's as if last night was a necessary exorcism of something I've been carrying around for years. And today I've been going around with the strangest urge to talk."

"We talk."

"No, we don't. We hit and run. I don't think we've really talked since you got here."

Joanna's golden lashes fluttered nervously. Michael was looking at her, and his eyes were not hooded and flinty with deceit. They were clear and honest and imploring, and a bottomless feeling opened up in her stomach.

"Sooo!" He drew up his shoulders and dug his hands into his windbreaker pockets. "How the hell have you been, Joanna?"

She was reminded of all the other times he had asked her that same question and she'd either lied or lashed out. But she knew she could do no such thing now. It wasn't fair that he could make her feel so exposed, so vulnerable, especially after last night's argument. But then nothing that he had ever done was fair. Her shoulders slumped with defeat.

"I've been miserable," she confessed. "Really miserable."

Michael's smile broadened until his eyes crinkled, and suddenly Joanna couldn't keep from smiling, too. Being honest with him wasn't all that hard after all. In fact, it felt like a kind of release. Perhaps she'd exorcised a few demons of her own.

"Me, too," he admitted.

"No kidding?"

"No kidding."

She hesitated. "Is it . . . your divorce?"

"My divorce..." He sighed reflectively. Then, "Hell, no! Getting Bunny out of my life was a relief! Our marriage was a farce. Besides, that's ancient history. We split up five years ago."

Joanna fell off the elbow she was leaning on. "You mean you were married only one year?"

"Less. What's the matter? Are you really all that surprised?"

Joanna could only laugh incredulously.

"No, what's really got me crazy is what I'm doing now. I—I quit teaching."

"You quit?" Joanna was still having trouble digesting the fact that Michael had been free for five years.

"Uh huh."

"But what was all that about a leave of absence?"

"I took a slight liberty with the truth."

"Wasn't it working out for you?" Suddenly she was sorry she'd ever wished failure on him. It had been such a small, mean-spirited sentiment.

"It was going very well."

"And are you really *Dr.* Malone?"

"Yes."

"Head of the Literature Department?"

His lips twitched with a small sheepish smile "That too." Though Joanna knew it was absurd, she felt a bubble of pride swell inside her.

"Things were going great. The school's literary journal was becoming nationally recognized...."

"Under your direction?"

He nodded again. "And a student-exchange program I'd been working on was finally gelling. I would've been traveling to Russia next year..."

Joanna rested her chin on her knees and let her imagination paint a picture of him as a college professor. He'd probably worn denims and tweed, she thought, and he'd probably left every female student starry-eyed by the end of the first lecture. Dynamic, passionately in love with his subject, humorous in an intellectual, offbeat way—yes, she could see him, his moves, his facial expressions. Could see him so clearly, in fact, that she felt a sharp pang of something absurdly akin to jealousy.

"And you quit?" she asked.

He nodded stolidly. "In May, as soon as the semester ended. It was one of the toughest decisions I've ever made. I really enjoyed academic life. But—but I love writing more."

Joanna's back straightened. So that was what he'd been working on up in his room!

"I finally realized I couldn't write and teach at the same time. Each one's too time-consuming. So I took the plunge."

"Writing?"

"Hmm. I know it doesn't make much sense, giving up the career I had. That's why I said I was on a leave of absence. But look at it this way, I now have only two choices. I can either succeed or I can fail, and I don't take too kindly to failure."

Joanna laughed incredulously.

"It isn't funny, Jo," he said, playfully swatting her leg. "I haven't a clue where I'm supposed to go from here if I don't succeed. I have a limited amount of money. I gave up my apartment in order to cut expenses. I even sold my furniture. The only things I kept were my car and my clothes. That's why—" he lowered his head "—why I need the cottage so badly this summer. The money. And because I need an environment of peace and tranquility in order to write."

Suddenly the full scope of his situation became clear. "Oh, Michael! I had no idea. You should have told me."

"It's really not so bad. Actually..." He began to smile. "Actually it's pretty incredible. I'm finally doing what I always dreamed of doing, which is more than most people can say."

"If I ask you what you're working on, will you tell me?"

"It's...a novel. Is that answer enough?"

An unexpected warmth swept through her and she smiled softly. "I should have known. You always were such a wonderful writer."

His eyes glittered in the firelight. "Wasn't I just!" They both laughed quietly. "I never thought it could be so hard, though. This piece is going slowly. I'm even beginning to wonder if I'll finish it on time."

"On time?"

"Mmm. I have a deadline. The beginning of August."

Joanna's nerves began to leap with excitement. "Does that mean...do you have a commitment from a publisher?"

He nodded, his smile growing. "Only because I have the most incredible agent. Her name's Joyce Sterling. She's with the Miles Carson Agency. You've probably heard of them. Really high-powered...?"

Joanna cocked her head warily. "Is that the same Joyce you talked to on the phone about a plumber?"

"Oh, you overheard?"

Joanna blushed and was glad of the cover of darkness.

"We met last fall at a writer's conference. She spends her summers here, too. The weekends, anyway. The rest of the time, she's in New York running the publishing industry—or just about."

Joanna stared into the flames with oddly turbulent feelings. "So, this Joyce of yours—she's actually sold your novel for you?"

"Yes, to Gateway Books, and finagled a sizable advance for me, too, even though the thing's not even done yet."

"Oh, Michael, that's wonderful!"

"Not wonderful. But it'll tide me over till royalties come in—or I sell something else."

"I guess Casey and I really threw a monkey wrench into your plans, showing up out of the blue. I'm sorry."

He tossed a hand dismissively, though she noticed he didn't deny it. "Things'll work out."

"When do you expect this novel to be on the market?"

"In about a year, if I ever get around to finishing it."

"I'm sure you will."

"Sure." He fell into reflective silence. "But will it be as good as if I had unlimited time?" Joanna was pierced by the depth of concern in his eyes. "Jo, I *am* a good writer, and this novel—all my instincts tell me..." He looked away in sudden embarrassment.

"...that it's right on target?"

"Yes. Oh, yes!" Joanna couldn't help hearing the breathlessness in his voice. "I just want the whole thing to be good, beginning to end. But these last few chapters... I hate having a gun to my head." He paused. "I sometimes get these crazy visions of a roomful of editors reading the last chapters and keeling over with laughter."

"Fat chance! If they bought your book just on the strength of the first few chapters..."

"Joyce says that, too," he interrupted a little too eagerly. Joanna could feel her own enthusiasm momentarily flicker. "If you listen to her, I'm going to be rich and famous within a year."

"Since when does Michael Malone have such doubts about himself?"

"Oh, I don't have any about *myself*. I wouldn't have quit the university if I did. It's just that I've been publishing for years—poetry, short stories, essays. This isn't even my first novel."

"It isn't?"

"No. My first wasn't so bad, either. It even got into print, but it didn't go anywhere. I didn't know Joyce at the time."

Joanna forced a smile. "So, you expected to be rich and famous overnight? You were just paying your dues, that's all."

"Actually I never expected to be rich and famous at all. I just wanted to be good. But now..." He shuddered and laughed as if the idea frightened and amazed him all at the same time.

"You must be very happy."

"Yes. Yes." His vision seemed to turn inward. "But there are times... well, it could be better."

"What do you mean? How much better can it get?"

"Well... look at me! Here I am nearly thirty, and I no longer have the security of a regular job. I don't have a home. I don't have a wife, kids, a dog. You name it, and I don't have it! I feel sort of like a boat without a rudder."

Joanna chuckled. "Oh, really! Tell me about it!"

"You, too?" Again that tentative smile. Joanna felt her heart jump. A companionable warmth had stolen over her while Michael had been talking and although she didn't know how or why, his revelations had dispelled her own stubborn refusal to talk.

"Becoming a widow is pretty much the same. All of a sudden, all my reasons for being who I was and doing the things I did vanished. Without Phil, I have to build a whole new life for myself. Of course, there's still Casey." She closed her fist as if hanging on to an invisible lifeline.

"And you still have your job."

"Y-yes. But it's not like a career I chose on my own. I went to work there only because it was a family business and our apartment was right upstairs."

"Oh, I see." Mist was thickening the air now, and Michael's hair was beaded with tiny silver droplets of moisture.

"I don't think I want to keep that apartment much longer, either. There are too many memories there. It's not doing Casey any good."

Michael's attention intensified. "I thought not."

"It really worries me, Michael."

"Give him time."

She nodded. "That's why I brought him to the Vineyard. He...we both needed to get away." Even if talking didn't actually solve anything, she felt so much better having Michael there to hear her out.

"Lately I've been thinking about looking for another job, too...or maybe going back to school, getting a degree."

"Great!"

"No, not great. It'll be an expense I can't afford. And I'll hardly ever see Casey. But maybe with a degree I'll be able to find a job that will allow me and Casey to live a little better."

Michael's face grew grim. "I guess I've never thought of you as head of a household before. Has it been rough, Jo?"

"We've managed," she tossed off, then made the mistake of looking into his eyes. "All right, at times it's been rough."

"What are you planning to study if you go back to school?"

"I don't know. Computer Science?"

His look sharpened and went right through her. If ever there was a touchstone in her life, it was Michael.

"I have to think of the present job market," she said defensively.

"I haven't said a word!"

"Yeah, sure, but I know what you're thinking. You're thinking I always hated math. But we all can't be as idealistic as you and write novels, Michael. Some of us have to compromise." At that moment, she felt so lost that her lips quivered. "Actually I don't know *what* I'm doing. My life is just so gray and fractured right now. And that's why *I* need the cottage so badly this summer. I really need to rest, think clearly, find out what I'd like to do with the rest of my life." The immensity of her statement made her groan. She dropped her head to her knees and shook it from side to side.

Across the fire, Michael laughed quietly. "Aren't we a pair, though!"

She lifted her eyes. "A couple of champs." And they both laughed.

"I think what we need is a stiff cup of coffee," she said. "Do you have any?"

"That's the first thing I packed." She crept into the tent and took the thermos out of the picnic basket. Back at the fire, she poured out two cups. When she handed one to Michael, their fingers brushed. Their eyes met nervously.

"Michael?"

"Hmm?"

"I'm sorry about last night, too. I said a lot of things that were unfair, but my anger was leading the way. I seem to have had a whole lot of that stored up inside me."

"It's all right. I came out here offering an apology, not looking for one." He sipped his hot coffee pensively, and she knew he was thinking about the previous night again, as she was.

"I really am sorry," she said. "I hope you don't have any bumps or bruises from that fall."

"No. Not from the fall." He sipped his coffee and stared into the fire. Then, probably knowing that she was staring back with deepening curiosity, he slowly lifted the hem of his jeans.

Joanna bit her lip.

"Barbarian!" he whispered.

Joanna's gaze lifted from the raw scrape on his shin to his face and realized he was trying to suppress a smile.

"That was a pretty stupid move...."

"The whole argument was. Idiotic!"

Suddenly they both began to laugh, releasing whatever tension still lingered between them over the incident last night.

Michael set down his coffee mug and stood, looking like a huge idol in the distorted shadows thrown by the fire. "As long as we've managed to strike this truce...I'll be right back. Don't go away."

Joanna watched him clamber over the dune and disappear into the darkness. But within a minute he was back, a sleeping bag riding on his shoulder. He swung it to the sand and reseated himself.

"Actually the real reason I came out here was I didn't like the idea of you two camping out all alone."

"Oh, and did you come to protect us?"

He grinned endearingly. "Sort of. You don't mind, do you? I haven't done any camping in years."

She shrugged. "It's a big beach."

"Yeah, you *would* make me sleep out on a night like tonight."

"You should've brought a tent. The weatherman says it might even rain."

"Very funny." He picked up his mug and drained its contents. They became quiet, and their silence gradually deepened into private thoughts.

"Jo, I feel like a total heel for not having extended my condolences to you yet, and well, you must know how sorry I feel about your loss."

"Yes, of course."

"I know Phil's illness was a burden—your father kept me informed—and you probably don't need me dredging it all up again, but I want you to know I thought about you a lot and prayed for you to have courage." His voice was hushed now, and at times Joanna confused it with the plaintive sighing of the wind.

"Thank you. That means a lot to me. But I wish you could have been upset about Phil's dying instead of my having to cope with it."

"Sorry, but I didn't know him, except for the little you told me. Was . . . was he good to you, Jo?"

"Yes. A good father to Casey, too."

"Good. I'm glad you were happy." The corners of his mouth drooped strangely. "Bunny and I were never happy." The driftwood crackled and broke, sending up a yellow spiral of sparks. For a while, the whole world seemed consumed by its heat.

"You don't have to tell me about your marriage."

"But I want to. I feel like talking. In fact, talk is just what you and I seem to need most right now. I just can't go on letting you believe that fairy tale I told you the other night, all that nonsense about Bunny loving our life together. She hated it. We fought constantly about how little money I made and about my writing. She actually used to laugh when I said I wanted to be a writer. What she wanted me to do was quit grad school and join her father's brokerage firm in Boston."

"Michael, please!" Joanna closed her eyes. "You shouldn't talk about her. It's like spreading gossip about the dead."

"But it's the one thing we *have* to talk about. We've stored up too much anger for too long, and we both know what's at the bottom of it."

"No!" she snapped decisively. "I don't want to hear it."

Dismay sank furrows into Michael's handsome face. "You're probably right." He seemed deflated, but Joanna didn't care. She didn't want to hear about his marriage. As comfortable as she'd begun to feel with him, there was still a proud little voice within her that made her pull back. She didn't want to be appeased with tales of how unhappy he had been with Bunny. She didn't want excuses now. Nothing could amend the fact that he had coldly, deliberately lied to her, used her, and then dumped her for Bunny.

The night suddenly seemed to grow damp and cold, as if the wind had stirred the warm spell of the fire and spiraled it away.

"Maybe we should call it a night," she suggested, and before Michael could protest, she got to her feet.

Inside the tent, she crawled into her bag and snuggled down, searching for some warmth. Casey was still sleeping soundly. Outside, she could hear the rip of a cord and the flop of a bedroll hitting sand. Suddenly Joanna felt awful. Michael was camping out at the foot of their tent like a sentry at a castle gate. He was too worried to leave them alone; he had apologized for last night, initiated a truce—and she was indeed feeling better for it—and now she was making him sleep out on a raw, misty night.

"Psst! There's room in here," she called.

A moment later, Michael was in the tent, carefully spreading his sleeping bag on the other side of Casey. "I'm usually not this much of a pushover. I usually play hard-to-get, especially on a first date, but under the circumstances . . . just promise you'll respect me in the morning."

Joanna felt a smile tugging at her tightly pressed lips. He had always been able to do that, no matter how dark her mood.

"Hush up and get settled. Lord! You're as graceful as a rhinoceros!"

"Ahh," he finally sighed. "Heaven!"

Outside, the wind buffeted the sand and flung it like rain against the tent. There was barely a glimmer of light now from the fire, but she could still make out Michael's eyes fixed on her over Casey's small body.

"Jo, I don't want you coming out here just to avoid me." She tried to protest, but he reached over and put a finger on her lips. "Shh. I saw your bags, too. You were planning to leave, weren't you? I don't blame you. I said some pretty nasty things last night, and I'm sorry. And for all it's worth,

I'm glad you didn't leave. The house feels empty without you." His voice died on a whisper, but it took Joanna's breath away.

She turned and stared at the canvas peak overhead, not knowing why there was such a tightness in her throat.

"Jo, I have to keep on talking. Somehow we've connected tonight, and knowing how proud and stubborn we can both get, this moment may never come again."

Joanna swallowed with difficulty, her throat so hard and dry it ached.

"Jo, what I was trying to tell you before . . . I never loved Bunny. Our marriage was a farce."

His words pressed down on her, stopping the breath in her lungs. So, what did he expect her to say in answer? She rolled over with her face to the wall. A tear trickled from her eye over the bridge of her nose.

"Jo," he whispered. His voice sounded as if he were desperately trying to keep in touch with someone slipping away into the sky. "Jo, I married Bunny because she said she was pregnant, and I was too young to fight all the people telling me what I was supposed to do—Bunny's father, that crazy Wilcox woman, my mother, even your father. I was hemmed in.

"But that didn't matter to me. Even if they'd doubled their pressure, I wouldn't have married Bunny if you hadn't run off and left me the way you did." He paused and Joanna thought she heard his breath catch on a sob. "But in the end, I married Bunny because you went home and married Phil. I didn't have anything left to live for.

"What I still don't understand is why you married Phil. *Was* it because you'd planned to all along? Or . . . or did you marry him on the rebound? I've lived with speculation for so long I don't know what to think anymore. Didn't you love me, Jo? Weren't we so crazy in love with each other we couldn't see straight? Or did I dream the whole thing up?"

Joanna's pulse was pumping so hard her temples hurt. She was rigid with terror. Perspiration broke out on her face.

"Jo," he called insistently. "Why did you marry Phil?"

His question pressed on her like a gigantic boulder, crushing her bones. There was no way she could answer—no way she *would* answer. It was too late. The lie had gone on too long. And so she didn't.

The silence in the tent became oppressive. The question hung there unanswered until he must have finally thought she'd gone to sleep. She heard him sigh with resignation and, a moment later, roll over, too.

CHAPTER EIGHT

JOANNA WOKE to a damp, chilly dawn. She turned her head and looked at Michael and Casey, still asleep in the thin gray light. Unexpectedly her heart swelled with emotion. For once, she stopped fighting herself and admitted that it felt good to be with Michael again. It was a joy to wake up and realize he was there, not hundreds of miles away. To know she'd have the chance to talk to him today, see his face, his eyes, his smile, hear his deep, soul-moving voice.

Michael's long black lashes fluttered and he opened his eyes. "Good morning," he whispered.

She smiled peacefully, her gaze linked with his. They said nothing for a while, just listened to the wind gusting over the beach. Joanna had thought sleep would elude her. For a long time, she'd lain awake, face to the tent's wall, turning over Michael's words in her heart. She had tried to make sense of them, but it had been like trying to put together a puzzle with too many pieces missing.

Had he really loved her as much as he'd said? It was possible. But her thoughts had invariably come back to the same dead end. If he had loved her so much, how could he have been seeing Bunny at the same time? And he must have been for Bunny to be pregnant.

He'd also said he never would have married Bunny if she hadn't married Phil. Well, she hadn't married Phil for four weeks. In the meantime, why hadn't Michael tried to contact her? If he'd loved her so much, why hadn't he even called? And what about his responsibilities to Bunny and to their unborn child?

There were lies snaking through his story everywhere, and she'd be a fool to think he was doing anything but rationalizing his way out of a bad conscience.

Joanna had finally fallen asleep, weary with unanswered questions. Unanswered? They'd never been asked. Michael had wanted to talk. Maybe if she had simply asked...but she had turned her back on him, pretended to be asleep. She had deliberately blocked all channels of communication. But she'd felt so panicked at the time, she hadn't known what else to do.

It was quiet now, peaceful. Maybe the issue could be broached again.

"Joanna?" He spoke before she could frame the right words.

"Yes?" She searched his face expectantly.

"About our conversation last night..." He rolled onto his back, releasing himself from her gaze. "I'm sorry if I probed where I shouldn't have. I've had the night to think about it, and I guess you were right. It was inappropriate to talk about Bunny the way I did, and I had no business asking you about Phil. Maybe some things *are* best left in the past. I thought it might straighten out some misunderstandings if we talked, that maybe we could relax around each other a little more if we cleared the air. But obviously you feel better letting sleeping dogs lie. Fine. I guess it doesn't make any difference anymore. It's all over and done with—water over the dam, so to speak. No amount of talk is going to change it. Right?"

Joanna swallowed with difficulty. "Right," she whispered, staring at his finely chiseled profile. All of it, water over the dam.

"All right then. I won't bring up the subject again. Only..." He turned, his long black lashes shading his eyes. "Let's put an end to the sniping, Jo. We both desperately need a summer of peace."

"Yes, let's, *please*."

He reached across Casey and gently tucked a strand of her hair behind her ear. As his fingers lingered on her cheek, Joanna became aware of a pleasurable warmth stealing over her. It puzzled and dismayed her, and she was relieved when he drew away.

"I know things aren't completely right between us, and maybe they never will be, but as I said, maybe it doesn't matter. We can still call a truce and go on from here, share the house amicably..."

"Or at least without murdering each other."

"Oh, I hope so," he laughed. "Maybe we can even learn how to be friends again. We were great friends at one time, weren't we?"

Joanna eased onto her back and closed her eyes, remembering. "I'll stay at the cottage. I'll try not to snipe. But we're both carrying too much emotional baggage to delude ourselves into thinking we can promise more."

Michael's lips worked wordlessly. "I know," he finally said.

Suddenly there was an ominous tapping on the canvas overhead. They were both silent, listening. Within seconds, rain was pelting the roof with a deafening beat.

"Oh, no!" Joanna groaned. "Michael, it's raining!"

"No kidding."

"What are we going to do?"

"I haven't the foggiest. Think we're here for the duration?"

"Oh, Lord!"

"How much food did you bring?"

"Just enough for breakfast, but—"

"Hey! What...you...Uncle Michael!" Casey cried out.

"Morning, kid." Michael smiled.

"How did you get here?" the child asked excitedly. "Hey, it's raining. Ugh! It's all wet under me! I didn't do it, Ma, honest!"

Joanna laughed at his energetic flow of chatter. Much to her surprise, Michael was laughing, too.

"How do kids wake up so fast?" he said. "I usually need two cups of coffee before I can gear myself up to that kind of enthusiasm."

Casey crawled out of his sleeping bag and before either adult could stop him, undid the door flap. A shower of rain came gusting in. They all screamed, and Michael scrambled to his knees to zip up the opening again. Joanna expected him to be a angry—or at least a little miffed—but she was wrong.

"Isn't this fun!" he cheered. "Let's have some breakfast."

"Are you crazy?" Joanna laughed, amazed at how quickly the mood in the tent had changed.

"No, just famished. What do you have that's edible?"

"Bananas."

"Oh, boy, Casey! Bananas!" At that moment, a drop of water plinked him on his unshaven cheek. Everyone looked up and noticed the stain of moisture spreading across the canvas over his head. *Plink!* Another drop hit his eye. In the distance, thunder grumbled angrily.

Unexpectedly, a giggle rippled up through Joanna's ribs. How absurd they were, caught in a thunderstorm, in a tiny, leaky tent, a mile's walk from the cottage! How utterly absurd! She fell back and laughed harder.

Michael tried to ignore the rain now dripping rapidly on his head and asked with dignified calm, "What, may I inquire, are you laughing at?"

Joanna couldn't answer. All she could do was point.

"Laughing at me?" he said with affronted innocence, all the while reaching stealthily into the picnic basket. A second later, he was wielding a large banana and flogging her around the shoulders with it.

"Stop! Stop it!" Joanna cried, laughing raggedly. She grabbed up her knapsack and swung it at his head.

Casey caught the silly mood of the two adults and jumped to his feet, looking for a weapon of his own.

"No, Case..." Joanna cried in alarm, but too late. Suddenly the roof of the small tent came folding in and the walls buckled.

"Do you suppose we'll ever learn to do anything right, Joanna?" Michael's muffled voice drawled from somewhere under the toppled mess.

They finally made it back to the cottage, cold, drenched and gritty with sand. But they were exhilarated. It was as if they'd been on a great adventure and were dying to tell someone about it.

Their good mood persisted throughout the rainy morning, too, although it later sprang from a sense of well-being derived from a steaming shower, dry clothes and a cup of rich, hot chocolate.

Joanna was curled up on the couch, sipping from her mug, while Michael and Casey adjusted the logs on the fire.

"There, that ought to break the chill." Michael gazed at the crackling fire. "Keep the mildew down, too."

"Ma, can I watch TV?"

"Sure, *Sesame Street* will be on in a few minutes."

Michael clapped ashes off his hands. "*Sesame Street*. You know, I've never seen that show. Heard a lot about it, though."

Joanna pinned him with a look not unlike the one she usually reserved for Casey when he was trying to squirm out of a chore. "Don't you have some work to do?"

Michael dug his hands into his pockets and nodded boyishly.

"Well?"

He sighed. "I'm going. I'm going."

Joanna liked this new atmosphere of calm. It sure beat what they'd lived with before. Everyone seemed so much more at ease. And yet she couldn't help thinking it was a fragile calm and that it didn't run all that deep. True, they had dispelled a lot of their anger the other night, but she couldn't help fearing that they were merely floating on the surface, pretending the water beneath them wasn't still deep and perilously dark.

EARLY THE NEXT MORNING, Joanna got a call from Nathan. He had just stopped by his sister's on his way to work, and Meg had reminded him of a concert they'd bought tickets for months ago.

"It's this weekend. Would you like to go?"

Joanna hesitated. Nathan had taken her out to dinner Monday night, out on the boat Tuesday, and here it was just Thursday and he was asking her out again. Was Michael right about Nathan still carrying a torch for her? At the time, she'd thought he was just clutching at straws to start an argument.

"Can I let you know tomorrow?" She cringed as he waited for a reason and she came up with none.

Finally, "Sure, no problem. I'll call again tomorrow. Oh, before I go, my sister would like to talk to you."

Meg came on the line then and asked Joanna what plans she'd made for the day.

"Well, I've been dying to get into Edgartown, do some browsing, shopping..."

"Great. How about doing me a favor and bringing your son over here? He and Paul played so well the other day I hardly knew they were around."

Joanna considered the proposal. No matter how Meg phrased it, she knew Meg was doing her the favor. "All right. But one of these days, I'm going to have to reciprocate."

Joanna spent an enjoyable morning wandering through shops and strolling the streets of Edgartown. It was a lovely, warm morning, the air fresh and sunny after the previous day's storm.

Though Edgartown had been settled in 1642, it really hadn't flourished until the mid 1800s. Those were the golden years of whaling, and the streets facing the harbor were lined with the stately homes built by the money that had flowed in. Driving by, you simply could not appreciate their beauty. You had to walk, stop, admire their elaborately fanlighted doorways, their prim fences spilling over with roses, the widows' walks crowning their peaks. And Joanna did just that, snapping nearly two rolls of film in the process.

By early afternoon, however, she was anxious to leave. Meg had offered to give Casey lunch, but Joanna didn't want to take advantage of her hospitality.

"Meg?" she called through the kitchen screen door. "Will you tell Casey I'm back?"

"He isn't here, Jo." Meg turned from the counter where she was rinsing dishes. "Come on in."

"What? Where is he?"

"With Michael."

"Michael!"

"Yeah, you know, that guy with the deep sexy voice and bedroom eyes who lives at your place," she mocked laughingly. "He came by for Casey at least half an hour ago... said something about going fishing."

Joanna's green eyes widened with confusion. "Where'd they go?"

"Down to the pond, I think."

"Thanks."

"Hey, don't you want to stay for some iced tea?"

But Joanna was already in her car.

She could see them even before she reached the cottage. They were sitting at the end of the dock, legs dangling over the side. On their heads, to protect them from the sun, were identical sailor hats of light blue poplin—Vivien's and her father's.

Joanna jumped out of her car and ran across the yard. She didn't understand her sudden mood, but she was both frightened and angry. What did Michael think he was doing? She didn't mind the fact that under the new truce he had become quite civil around the house, but she'd never asked him to go this far.

An irrational possessiveness filled her. She was desperate to rescue Casey from a harm she could not name but genuinely felt, when something made her pause. A laugh. Casey's laugh. In spite of her anger, Joanna started to watch them.

It was nothing short of a calendar picture—a boy and a man, sitting at the end of an old wooden dock, their lines bobbing lazily on a blue, rippled pond. It was a scene straight out of Norman Rockwell. *Summer Idyll* it should be called.

Then she noticed something else, something amazing considering the difference in their ages. It was the similarity in the lines of their shoulders, in the long stretch of their backs. Casey not only had hair the same texture as Michael's and eyes the same dark blue, but he was going to grow up to have his build, too.

At that moment, Michael leaned over and in spite of the distance, Joanna heard Casey's laugh again. Unexpectedly her eyes filled with tears, and the summer idyll blurred and swam out of focus. It took her well over five minutes to compose herself.

"Damn you!" she cursed, wiping her cheeks with the back of her hand. By the time she set foot on the dock, every trace of sentimentality was gone from her face.

"Michael, you could have let a person know about this!" She walked down the dock with brisk, aggressive strides, her soft, flowered dress swinging around her knees.

Michael turned calmly and squinted up at her from under the brim of his hat. How blue his eyes were, here by the water and open sky! How much depth of character was added by the small creases fanning out from their corners! For a moment, Joanna's heart skipped a treacherously quick beat. Her fear deepened.

"What's that?" he asked languorously.

Casey turned, too. The brim of his hat had been secured with a safety pin to clear his eyes. "Ma, I caught a fish!" he cried exultantly, scrambling to his feet.

"Really?" For her son's sake, she momentarily set aside her emotions.

"Uh huh." He nodded vigorously and his hat fell forward.

"Let me hold your pole, Case," Michael offered.

With his hands freed, Casey lifted a heavy bucket. "See?"

Joanna peered down at a small silvery fish, one eye coolly staring back at her. "Very good!" she laughed. But when her eyes linked with Michael's, her smile dropped again.

He gave Casey back his pole, propped his own against a piling, and stood up. Then he and Joanna moved out of Casey's earshot.

"I'm sorry if I've put you out," he said. "But I didn't think Casey would mind getting out of that house. It's full of strangers and noisy as hell and—"

"Don't make excuses," she whispered with a vehemence she didn't intend. "I just drove miles out of my way but you did nothing wrong. You didn't even—"

"What did you want me to do?"

"You could have let me know!"

"How? Mental telepathy? I didn't get the idea till after you were gone." He was leaning so close Joanna could feel the heat of his body and smell the clean, spicy fragrance of his after-shave. His closeness was oddly disturbing.

"In any case, what harm's been done? What's the big deal?"

"Well...well, there are all sorts of things to consider." Her eyes darted across the landscape searching for something, anything. "You can't just take a five-year-old fishing without preparation. For instance, have you bothered to put sunscreen on him?"

"Joanna, the boy's skin is browner than mine!" he retorted, his blue eyes beginning to flash.

"Did he go to the bathroom before he left Meg's?"

"Guys don't have to worry about such things. Besides, the cottage is just up the hill."

"Well...do you realize it's nearly two? I always give Casey a snack in the afternoon. Have you packed a snack? And what if I'd already made plans for him? How would I drag him off this dock now after you've...after you've..."

"What is it, Jo? What's really bugging you? So far, I haven't heard a single protest that holds water."

She was speechless, devoid of answers, knowing only that some instinctive fear was driving her to act this way.

"And I actually thought I was doing you a favor bringing him fishing. I do have more important things to tend to, you know."

"Well, why don't you go do them and leave us alone?" Her tone was unintentionally caustic. Michael's mood had changed, too. She could see it in the tightening of his jaw.

"What is it, Jo?"

"Nothing," she answered sullenly.

"I don't believe it. You just don't like me spending time with him. That's it, isn't it?"

"Yes. No! I mean..." Joanna bit her lip, suddenly realizing that he was right.

Michael nodded self-righteously. "Sure. I can see it in your eyes. In spite of everything you say to the contrary, you're determined to keep that boy aware of his father's memory. You're so determined that you can't stand the idea of his spending even one afternoon with another adult male."

Joanna was stunned by his misinterpretation of her motives. "No! That's not it at all!" But he wasn't listening.

"Can't you see how futile it is?" Michael went on. "It's downright stupid, too. It'll do more harm than you think. The boy needs men in his life."

"Oh? And what makes you such an authority on child rearing?"

"It's just common sense."

"Michael, do us all a favor and stop inventing problems he doesn't have."

"He *will* have them if you keep isolating him."

"I'm not isolating him!" Joanna spat defensively. "We've managed quite well so far without your sage advice, and I'm sure we'll manage in the future."

"Yeah," he drawled, "I don't know why I should even give a damn."

"You? Give a damn? Michael, until yesterday you barely said two words to the boy. You'd think he was carrying some contagious disease or something."

"That's not true."

"It is, too! What's wrong, Michael? What is it about Casey you don't like? Is it the fact that your son died and Casey lived? Do you resent him because he's the same age yours would have been? Does he remind you of what you lost?"

This time it was Michael's turn to be stunned. His face suffused with dark color. "Where did you ever dig up such a stupid notion?" he whispered incredulously.

Joanna immediately felt tactless as she studied his reaction. How callous could she be?

"If I kept my distance from Casey, and I admit I did at first, it was only because he was a living, breathing reminder that you deserted me to marry somebody else. You had this child with someone else, you had this life I wasn't a part of..." His voice rasped with emotion. "I certainly don't resent Casey, Joanna. I think he's a terrific little guy. I only resent myself for being such a damn fool when I was young. Now, if you'll excuse me..." He started to move away, but Joanna clutched his arm. Her fingers tingled as they came in contact with the warm, hair-coarsened skin.

"Then it had nothing to do with Bunny's miscarriage?"

Michael thrust his hand through his thick, unruly hair and squinted out over the water. "There was no miscarriage," he said bitterly.

Joanna blinked confusedly. "W-what?"

"Look, Joanna, I thought you wanted to leave all this in the past. I thought we weren't going to bring it up again."

"But how can I just...*what* did you say?"

He turned to her, an empty sadness in his eyes. "There was no miscarriage. Bunny pretended to have one. She came out of the bathroom crying and weak, but when I took her to the hospital—against her wishes, I might add—the doctor who examined her said she was fine. In fact, she'd never even been pregnant."

Joanna felt herself swooning. "But . . . your mother told me she went for tests . . ."

"Bunny said she did. Her parents believed her, and without anyone bothering to confirm it, it became an accepted fact."

"Then there was no pregnancy?"

"How many ways do you want me to admit it?" he said icily. "Does it amuse you to hear I got duped—me, the guy you thought was such a hotshot with women! Are you glad I got caught and was made to pay for my sins?"

Joanna stared at him for a few long seconds. Then, slowly, she pulled herself out of her shock. "No, I don't find it amusing, and I'm definitely not glad." How could he even think such a thing? She felt only sadness and an incredible frustration. All that unhappiness . . . all those years lost to them! And all because of a lie! Joanna was so overwhelmed with sadness she couldn't even be angry at Bunny.

"She must have really loved you to make up a story like that and to suffer the embarrassment of gossip—just to get you to marry her."

"You call that love, trapping an innocent person?"

"Innocent?"

"That's right." He spun away and glared out over the water.

"Michael, what are you trying to say?"

"Forget it, Jo." Under his knit shirt, his shoulder muscles tensed.

She lifted her hand to touch him but instantly thought better of it. "Well, I'm sorry you had to go through that. It must have been awful." He wouldn't look at her, and she didn't blame him. She wasn't getting across even a fraction of what was in her heart.

There was obviously no place to go with this conversation, and she didn't try. "Better get back to your fishing. Bring Casey up to the house—whenever," she finished vaguely.

He nodded and she left him standing there on the dock, his chin lifted proudly. But she noticed a decided slump in his usual confident stance.

CHAPTER NINE

JOANNA WAS SORRY she'd been so harsh with Michael. He obviously had more pain in his past than she'd ever imagined. Besides, he wasn't going to do her son any harm, not if she was careful. The summer was too short. She should have controlled those defensive feelings before she'd gone out on the dock and acted so irrationally. She had upset the companionable mood they'd recently fallen into, and she deeply regretted it. She returned to the cottage determined to set things right.

By the time Michael and Casey came up from the dock, she had made a potato salad, baked a chocolate cake, and prepared the grill for hamburgers. She was quickly coming to the conclusion that cooking separate meals was ridiculous, as ridiculous as trying to divide the air each of them breathed. So much wasted energy! Besides, she'd noticed that Michael was usually too busy to cook and didn't eat well. And though she tried not to think too much about it, that worried her.

Michael looked at the cheerful yellow plates set out on the picnic table. Then he looked at Joanna, poking the hot coals with a long-handled fork. She had changed out of her dress into a bright pink halter and matching satin running shorts. She knew she looked far more rested than when she'd arrived, and her skin was now a healthy gold. What she didn't expect was the sudden headiness she felt when Michael's eyes registered the fact.

"And what are we supposed to do with all these fish?" he asked, setting down the pail. He stood with legs aggressively apart, one fist on his hip, the other gripping a pole.

Casey peeked up at him and struck the same pose. Joanna looked from one to the other and laughed. If she didn't, she was afraid she might cry.

"We'll have them tomorrow," she said. "Let's go put them on ice and wash our hands. Boy, what a catch!"

On Friday morning, Nathan called again. He was at his Edgartown store. Having come up with no believable excuse overnight, Joanna agreed to go with him to the concert Saturday night, chiding herself for being so reluctant in the first place.

Then, to provide a morning of undisturbed quiet for Michael, she took Casey out to Gay Head. When they came back, hours later, Michael was still at the typewriter.

"Are you still working?" Joanna asked, peeking into his room. He turned stiffly.

"Uncle Michael!" Casey burst into the room. "I talked to a Indian!"

Michael's tired eyes crinkled as the boy ran up to him. "'A Indian'?"

Casey scrambled into his lap. "At Gay Head. They live there."

"Is that where you got this?" Michael lifted an intricately beaded necklace from the boy's chest.

"Uh huh. They were selling them. I got these, too." He spread out a fistful of postcards on Michael's manuscript—colorful pictures of the Gay Head lighthouse, the steep clay cliffs, a family of Wampanoag Indians, the Menemsha fishing village at sunset.

"On the way back we saw a mother turkey, too."

Michael shot Joanna a quizzical look.

"A wild turkey. I couldn't believe it. I thought those things were extinct. She was just walking along the side of the road with a couple of chicks, so I stopped the car and got out to get a better look."

"But it chased Mommy," Casey finished for her, laughing merrily behind his hand.

"Damn thing scared me half to death!" Michael laughed, too, she was glad to notice.

"Sounds like you had quite a morning."

"We did. And you?"

"I got a lot written, but I sure could use a break. Anyone here feel like going for a swim?"

Casey slid off his lap and did a little dance across the rug. Joanna couldn't help laughing. She hadn't seen him so happy in months.

Her bathing suit was a simple black maillot with a deep, plunging neckline and high, cutaway legs. It made her legs look twice as long and revealed the entire inner swell of her bosom. She felt self-conscious wearing it and wished she hadn't bought it, but at the time it had seemed such a bargain.

Standing on the dock, she unzipped her terry robe with grave reluctance. Michael, who was buckling an orange life jacket around Casey, looked up from where he was kneeling. Instantly she yearned to pull the robe back on. His eyes held a glitter she knew only too well.

"Wow! Look at your mother in that suit!" he said, leaning conspiratorially close to the child. Casey cupped a hand over his mouth and giggled. "Mothers aren't supposed to look like that. How come yours does?"

Joanna felt her face flush. She suspected Michael was just making fun of her and tried to look unruffled. She dug into her canvas carryall for a brush and proceeded to tie her hair back into a ponytail. Then, still feeling his eyes on her, she walked to the edge of the dock. She wanted to leap off immediately and conceal herself in the water, but suddenly an unexpected playfulness overtook her shyness. She looked over her shoulder with a confident smile. "If you've got it, flaunt it!" she said, wiggling her bottom. Then she jumped off the dock, none too gracefully, she had to admit. The cold water rushed over her ears, drowning out Michael's deep, raucous laugh.

It was a hot afternoon and the water felt glorious. For over two hours, they swam and dived and played a game of water tag. Too often, however, Joanna found herself just treading water beside Michael, talking about inconsequential matters. Too often his hand came drifting to her waist to keep her afloat. Too often she felt the cool brush of their legs.

How it reminded her of that other summer, when Michael would touch her that way and the touch would be to much too handle! He would pull her into his arms and cover her mouth with his and in his reckless passion invariably take her under, coming up only when it seemed they might drown. There was a soft humor in Michael's eyes that made her wonder if he was remembering those days, too.

When they'd finally had enough, Michael hoisted Casey onto the dock. Then he leaned over to give Joanna his hand. As she swung up, his arm wrapped around her waist to steady her balance. But his hold on her lingered a moment too long, and she felt the hardness of his wet thigh pressed against hers.

She went weak so quickly she didn't have time to halt her reaction. She leaned closer, and the hand that had unthinkingly come to rest on his chest became alive and aware of the flesh beneath it. A wave of heat coursed through her, and from the serious expression around Michael's mouth, she was sure he felt it, too.

They moved apart abruptly. Joanna scooped up a towel and rubbed it briskly over her burning skin.

They walked back up the path talking as if nothing had happened, and perhaps, she thought, nothing had. Her imagination had just run wild. Certainly, after all the resentment and hurt they'd carried around for so long, there couldn't still be any physical attraction left! Could there?

Instead of dwelling on it, she turned her attention to the fragrant tangle of bayberry and honeysuckle along the path.

The bushes were humming with summer insects. Overhead, a wheel of gulls cawed loudly against a cloudless blue sky. The smell of marsh grass rode the air, and all up and down her arms and legs was the tickle of salt water drying. Joanna took a deep breath and smiled. It had been years since she'd felt so alive, so sensually aware of her surroundings.

They decided to make a supper of the previous day's catch.. But first the fish had to be cleaned. With Casey watching intently from the end of the picnic table, she and Michael scaled and cut. As they worked, she noticed that they laughed a lot—giddily, comfortably, as tired people often do.

Just as they were finishing up, however, there was the sound of a car door slamming in the front yard.

"Oh, no! Look at me!" Joanna cried with a nervous giggle. Her still-damp hair was matted and snarled from swimming. Innumerable silver scales dotted her arms and legs, and her terry robe was soiled where she had been wiping her hands.

Michael strode off to the side yard and broke into a smile. He waved casually, and suddenly Joanna felt a shadow of dread falling over her good mood.

A moment later, the visitor appeared—a tall brunette in high-heeled sandals and a smart, perfectly crisp dress of cool navy-blue. Every strand of her long, luxuriant hair was in place, not a millimeter of her nail polish chipped.

The feeling of dread deepened as Joanna watched her and Michael embrace... the familiar fit of her arm around Michael's neck, the casual kiss on the cheek as if she were confident there would be time enough later for deeper intimacies.

"Jo, I'd like you to meet Joyce Sterling," Michael said with what Joanna thought was a bit too much pride. "Joyce, this is Joanna."

Joanna made a hasty pass at her robe and shook the woman's hand. So this was Joyce Sterling, Michael's high-powered literary agent. She should have known. Joanna guessed Joyce to be in her mid- to late-thirties, but her age was hardly a liability. In fact, Joyce's age only added a dimension of mature intelligence and cosmopolitan sophistication to her already obvious assets.

"Nice to meet you, Joanna," Joyce said, her keen dark eyes quickly sweeping Joanna from head to feet. She smiled.

Joanna smiled back, warmly she hoped. Bunny had been attractive in much the same way, she remembered—tall and cool, with a sense of style that had left Joanna feeling cloddish by comparison. Joyce should come as no surprise. What did surprise Joanna were the growing knots of hostility she thought she'd outgrown along with her braces.

"I didn't even know Michael had a sister till he told me about you last Saturday night."

They had talked about her last weekend? "Oh...I'm not his sister."

"Excuse me. Stepsister."

Yes, whatever. It obviously didn't matter.

"I hope I'm not disturbing anything," Joyce continued, her voice a deep, melodic lilt. "I should have called."

"Don't be silly." Michael swung a lawn chair around and invited her to sit. "You're not disturbing a thing."

Only the best time you and I have shared in six years, Joanna thought peevishly.

Michael glanced at his watch.

"I left New York early," Joyce explained, reading his gesture. "I thought I'd beat the weekend traffic at the airport." Her dark eyes were fixed on Joanna's legs now, at the scales clinging as tenaciously as barnacles, at the dirt shading her toes.

"If you'll excuse me, I'd better take this fish inside." Joanna gathered up the food and utensils and took them into the house. She slung the fish into the refrigerator and dropped the rest of her burden into the sink. Then she ran upstairs, tearing off her grimy robe as she went. She drew a hasty washcloth over her arms and legs and brushed out her tangled hair. Then she slipped a long shirt over her swim-suit.

Michael was sitting next to Joyce when she got back downstairs. His arm lightly draped the back of her chair. Casey was standing in front of them, regaling Joyce with his fishing adventure of the previous day. Joanna paused at the sun porch door to listen.

Joyce's dark head turned, eyes glittering with a hard luster. "So, you went fishing, huh?" she teased Michael, though Joanna sensed an undercurrent of reprimand.

"And we went swimming today," Casey boasted. "All afternoon!"

Joanna could have sworn the woman's nostrils flared.

"Don't sweat it, Joyce," Michael said softly. "It'll get done."

Joanna opened the screen door. He turned with a look that oddly resembled relief.

"Where have you been?"

"Just making myself more presentable."

"Joyce, would you like something to drink?" he asked.

"A gin and tonic would be glorious."

Michael rose. "Joanna?"

"Anything."

He disappeared into the house and, uneasily, Joanna sat down in the chair beside his.

Joyce plunged into conversation right away. "While Michael's gone, I'd like to have a word with you, Joanna."

"About what?"

"As I understand it, you and your son have decided to spend the summer here."

"Yes. It was the craziest coincidence. My father wrote to—"

"Yes, I know all about that," Joyce cut in impatiently. "Michael explained the mix-up to me last Saturday night. All I want to say is, perhaps you don't realize how important it is for Michael to be here." She sat coolly, calmly, totally in command.

"Of course I do. He told me. He's writing a novel."

"A damn good novel! It could be an important piece of literature. Michael is a very talented person."

"Yes, I've always known that," Joanna said tightly, bristling at Joyce's condescension.

"Listen, I'm not asking you to leave, but please could you give him some room? Stay out of his way? Keep the house quiet? That's all I'm asking." Her eyes wandered to Casey.

"I'm doing what I can."

"Well, it's not enough. Michael's written practically nothing this week. Nothing!" Angry color climbed to Joyce's cheeks. "I can't believe he spent all yesterday afternoon fishing! And today—today I show up to find he's been romping at the beach! Joanna, *please!* I can only do so much. He's got to write the book himself, and fast. He has a deadline, you realize. It *has* to be done in three weeks."

"I hope you're not blaming me for his going fishing yesterday. It was his idea entirely."

Joyce said nothing but she was breathing heavily. Her eyes darted condemningly from Casey to Joanna as if their mere presence were cause enough for Michael to fail.

"Well, for heaven's sake, dissuade him the next time he gets a notion to go fishing. He can't waste a minute. Maybe you can even turn this living arrangement around into something positive—cook his meals, do his laundry, that sort of thing. Those of us who are close to him have to do what we can to launch his career."

Joanna could feel a vein at her temple throbbing. Was that the image she gave to strangers? Is that what she'd let herself become? Only good for cooking, washing, "that sort of thing?"

"Joyce, if you're so concerned about Michael, why don't you offer him your place? You're gone most of the week."

"I did. He was so upset last Saturday night after you showed up I didn't know what else to do. But he declined. I even offered my apartment in New York. He's always been comfortable enough there in the past..."

A fist closed around Joanna's heart. It was all very silly, of course. What did she care if Michael was seeing this woman? It didn't matter. She'd stopped loving him the day she left this island six years ago. Their lives had gone separate ways.

Just then, the screen door opened and Michael stepped out into the late-afternoon sunlight. Joanna's eyes narrowed as if in pain as they traveled over his dark, curling hair and long muscular torso, down the corded length of his legs and back up to his eyes. And even while she was telling herself it didn't matter, her heart went soaring on an unexpected flight and she knew she was only kidding herself. It did matter—more than ever.

"Will you stay for dinner, Joyce?" Michael asked as he set their drinks on the picnic table.

"I'd love to. I'm famished," Joyce answered, lighting a cigarette.

The cogs of Joanna's mind began to whir. And who was going to cook that dinner? Her eyes grew mutinous. She downed her drink with unladylike speed and shot to her feet. "Casey, come on, sweetheart. Time to wash up."

"JOANNA, WHAT GIVES?" It was half an hour later, and she and Casey were just leaving their bedroom, both of them freshly showered and dressed.

She lifted her eyes with icy contempt. While she'd been dressing, she'd heard him come up to his room—him and his "agent!"

"Bye, Michael. Have a nice dinner."

"Hey, wait a minute." Suddenly he was angry, too. He strode across the hall, gripped Joanna's arm, and propelled her into her room.

"Casey, your mother and I have to talk. In private. Wait out in the hall, okay? She'll be right with you."

The boy nodded, trusting Michael unquestioningly, and skipped toward the stair landing. Michael closed the door and turned, as tense as an animal about to spring.

"Listen, I can put up with your grousing when we're alone—" he pointed a finger in her face "—but I will not put up with your being rude to Joyce. Grow up, for pity's sake!"

Joanna tossed her hair over her shoulder and glared at him. "But that's just the point. I have grown up, and I've developed a sense of self-esteem along the way. I will not put up with being cast in the role of chief cook and scullery maid for you and... and that woman!"

Michael opened his mouth to protest, but she went right on with her well-rehearsed harangue. "I've also developed a set of values that will not allow me to put up with your disgusting little bedroom games. Not under this roof! Not while Casey and I are still here!"

A muscle jumped in Michael's jaw. "I seem to recall a time when you didn't consider my 'bedroom games' all that disgusting."

Joanna's cheeks burned. "We all learn from our mistakes, don't we?"

"Yes, we do," he returned with matching conviction.

She raised her chin, hurt and proud. "Well, it's always nice to find out what people really think of you."

Michael gripped her arms, his fingers digging into the soft flesh. "I suppose you think you didn't have it coming?" He groaned. "Why do you make me say such things? Dammit! Why do you still make me so angry?"

Tears sprang to her eyes before she could stop them because she'd been asking herself the very same question. And at this particular moment, she didn't have the strength to face the answer she kept coming up with. She turned her head and fought for composure. "This is getting us nowhere. I'm simply going out to a movie with Casey to leave you and Joyce alone."

"No, you're not. You're angry because you assumed you'd have to cook us dinner."

Yes, she thought. That, and also because *their* dinner together, hers and Michael's, had been ruined. But she couldn't very well say that now, could she? That admission would be an act of incredible stupidity!

"I just thought you'd appreciate a little privacy, you and Joyce. But apparently my being here doesn't seem to matter."

His grip tightened and she winced. "Right now, Joyce is in my room because that's where I happen to work and keep my manuscript. She's reading what I've done this week—as she does every weekend. That's all. So you can spare me your narrow-minded lecture on ethics." His breath fanned hotly over her face, his taut body pressing hers. "But even if she weren't, even if she and I were about to engage in a session of wild, abandoned lovemaking, it would still be none of your business. If we're going to share this cottage like two rational adults, you've got to understand that point right now."

Joanna looked hard at his face, loathing it and admiring it both in the same confused moment. "Over my dead body!"

His mouth twitched, suppressing a smile. "That can be arranged, you know."

"Oh, you'd love that, wouldn't you? If I weren't here, then you and your...your little tootsie would have the run of the place." His amusement deepened. "But tell me, Michael, does she realize you're just using her to further your career? How long will it be before you dump her?"

Now he laughed openly. "Is that a serious accusation, or are you just fishing to find out how involved we are?"

"I couldn't care less how involved you are." Joanna was trembling and knew he could feel it; he was standing so close. "You can sleep with every woman from here to Mexico for all I care. But not in this house!"

Michael's hand moved to the back of her head and dug into the heavy thickness of her hair. She was sure he was going to yank. But instead, he sighed and dropped his forehead to hers.

"Joanna, Joanna! Why do you still have the power to burrow so deep under my skin? After all this time..."

She tilted her head back in amazement, her lips parting as she did. On a wave of white heat, she realized what they were doing. He was holding her in his arms and their lips were just inches apart.

His eyes became intense and smoldering as if the realization had just struck him, too. A moment later, he had lowered his head and his mouth was touching hers. She gave a cry, but it was only halfhearted. She felt his arms enclose her more tightly, imprisoning her against the warm, hard length of his body, and his kiss deepened. Her body went weak under his bruising hunger; her bones turned to water. Michael's kiss affected her the way nothing else ever had. It was as if all the years that had separated them had never existed, and she responded with an ardor that was humiliating.

Slowly Michael lifted his head. They were both breathing erratically, their eyes glazed with desire. Joanna felt dizzy and rested her head on his chest. His fingers trailed along her spine.

"Jo, I'm not sure I know what's happening here," he whispered unsteadily. "I'm not sure I want to find out, either."

She swallowed with difficulty and drew back. She couldn't look at him. "Then you'd better go. Joyce will be wondering what's become of you."

He nodded and opened the door.

CHAPTER TEN

IT WASN'T LATE when she and Casey returned home, yet Joyce had already left and Michael had gone to bed. The sleep clearly did him good because Joanna awoke the next morning to the sound of his typewriter. Quietly she got Casey breakfast, then they left to pick up Meg and her children for a day at the beach.

When she got back in the middle of the afternoon, she was relieved to hear Michael still up in his room. Her reaction to him the previous evening was still disturbing her tremendously. How could she have let herself lose control like that? After the humiliating, hurtful way he'd treated her, after all the years of simmering resentment that had followed, was it possible she could still feel physically attracted to him?

Obviously he wasn't immune to her, either. The kiss had been unpremeditated, unexpected, and she could still feel the heat of it.

But really, did it mean anything? Michael was a physical person. He always had been; he probably couldn't hold *any* woman without reacting that way. She'd simply been the woman he happened to be holding at the moment. And as far as she was concerned, well, perhaps she'd just been living without a man's touch for too long.

They had made a mistake last night, and not an easy one to forget, but now she was forewarned. She was sure that with a little vigilance, it would never happen again.

She was staring into the refrigerator wondering what to fix for dinner when she heard Casey's excited chatter up in Michael's room. With a groan, she left the kitchen and went to fetch him.

"Sorry about this, Michael," she said as Casey shuffled slowly out to the hall.

"No problem." He went on typing.

"Aren't you going to take a break?" she asked, pausing in the doorway.

"Can't afford to. Joyce read me the riot act last night."

"She's a tough lady."

He pushed away from his desk, revealing the clutter before him—a mountain of crumpled paper, a coffee mug and two TV dinner trays.

"I know," he said. "But she's good for me."

She'd been right. The kiss really hadn't meant anything to him. Without another word, she made her exit.

Downstairs, Joanna checked the refrigerator one more time before finally grabbing her car keys and heading for the nearest seafood market. She knew buying lobster was an extravagance, but she was sick to death of scrimping. Besides, indulging oneself occasionally was good for the ego—therapeutic even. And when it came to benevolent indulgence, she was certainly overdue.

As she returned to the cottage, however, she couldn't help recalling Joyce's suggestion that she do Michael's cooking. Sitting on the back seat, clawing menacingly against the thick paper bag, were three large lobsters. Three, not two.

But Joanna dismissed Joyce's words immediately. Before she'd even met Joyce, she'd already come to the conclusion that cooking separate meals was a waste of time and energy. Besides, she was *not* doing this for Michael. She was doing it for herself.

When Michael finally came down the stairs, rubbing his aching neck, the table was all set—the baked potatoes, the crisp salad and warm garlic bread, chilled white wine, hot melted butter, and the platter of steaming red lobsters.

He paused in midstep. "A-are you having company?"

"No. Come and eat before it gets cold," she answered brusquely, not wanting him to read anything into her efforts.

He approached the table hesitantly, as if he still didn't believe her. Then, "What a wonderful surprise!" He smiled softly and the strain and fatigue eased from his handsome face.

Joanna was sure it was the most delicious meal she had ever cooked. She cleaned her plate, every last succulent, buttery mouthful. Michael evidently felt the same. He even finished off what Casey left. She was glad. And, though the admission came slowly, she finally realized that it *pleased* her to make him happy—Joyce be hanged; it was not just some altruistic concern for his health or burgeoning career. It pleased her, deeply.

Finally they sat back, replete, smiling at each other over a heap of empty red shells. Peace pervaded the room.

"Thank you for a lovely dinner," Michael said, leaning over to touch his napkin to the corner of her mouth. She was embarrassed to find herself leaning into his touch, longing for it to stay. All through the meal, she had felt a growing awareness of him, until at times she'd been unable to concentrate. At times she'd found herself listening not so much to his words but rather to the rise and fall of his deep voice. She had been caught up in the myriad expressions of his face, utterly fascinated by and lost in his personality.

"A far cry from our dinner last Saturday." She shuddered at the memory of his oily chicken soup and her muddy stew.

His mouth lifted in an endearing, crooked smile. "What a difference a week makes!"

"Yes, well…" She looked away uneasily. Had it only been one week? How much had changed! How much she had discovered locked up within herself—and him!

"I'd better get moving. I'm supposed to be going to a concert with Nathan tonight."

Michael's long, dark lashes lowered over suddenly troubled eyes.

"Sandy is coming to stay with Casey again."

He nodded, his finger tracing an invisible pattern in the tablecloth. "Go on. Go get ready. I'll clean up."

"Thanks." She rose quickly, afraid if she lingered even a moment longer, she wouldn't go at all.

NATHAN KISSED JOANNA at the door that night. She had sensed he would all evening and didn't discourage him. She was curious to see what her reaction would be.

She shouldn't have wondered. Though she was sure Nathan was quite adept at what he was doing, his advances left her cold. As he drove away, dismay settled heavily on her heart.

Much to her relief, the next few days passed uneventfully. She couldn't forget the kiss she and Michael had exchanged. And she couldn't imagine Michael forgetting it, either. Just thinking about it sometimes rocked her to the foundation of her equilibrium. However, the more unsettling her emotions, the harder she worked at hiding them. Evidently Michael had also decided to ignore their encounter. If he thought about it—and from the way he occasionally looked at her, she was sure he did—he never said anything. After a few days, she felt immeasurably better.

Michael worked on his book from morning to night now, and Joanna usually took Casey out to the beach all day. In the evening, she cooked a healthful meal for them all, fearing that if she didn't, Michael would forget to eat altogether. These days, he was working as if driven.

One morning she found him out on the sun porch. His face was drawn and serious.

"Taking a break?"

He looked up slowly. Dark shadows deepened his eyes. "Jo, I don't know if I'm going to finish it."

Joanna knew Joyce had been calling regularly, but her pep talks only left him keyed-up and pacing the floor.

She lowered herself onto the cushioned settee beside him. "And if you don't?"

"Gateway will have every legal right to cancel my contract."

"Will you get serious! They wouldn't do anything as drastic as that."

"Maybe not, but Joyce's credibility will be damaged. She really went out on a limb for me."

"I wish you were as concerned about your own career as you are about hers."

Michael fell back tiredly against the nautical print cushions. "I am, I am. That's just it. I've just been wondering if I'm going to finish it at all. It's just not . . . coming." He closed his eyes, his last few words sounding so desperate.

Joanna looked at him, and though she'd been running from her feelings for days, her heart now filled with a yearning to reach out to him. For once, she stopped fighting herself and admitted she wanted to take him in her arms and hold him close.

But she didn't dare. All she said was, "I think you're working too hard."

"Oh?"

"You're forcing it. You've got to relax, get some physical exercise."

He cocked open one eye. "And what would you suggest?"

"Well . . . jogging, swimming, rowing. I put my dad's old rowboat in the water this week, you know."

"Aw, hell!" He snapped his fingers. "And here I was thinking you had something more interesting in mind."

She swatted his leg in mock exasperation, though inwardly she was glad to see his spirits lifting. He caught her hand and drew the palm to his lips. Their eyes met and Joanna felt a surge of excitement that made her head spin.

"Maybe you're right. Joyce's way obviously isn't working."

Self-consciously, she drew back her hand, aware that the brief touch had left her tingling all over. "Michael?"

"Hmm?"

"Why don't you bring your work down to the dining-room table? There's more room. Besides, I'll be able to watch Casey better from there while I'm helping you."

His eyes widened. "What did you say?"

"I'm no speed demon, but I type a heck of a lot faster than you do."

His expression brightened, and a smile lit his blue eyes. "Yeah?"

"Yeah."

"Be right down." He took the stairs two at a time.

They immersed themselves in their collaboration that very afternoon. Though plot-wise Joanna couldn't make much sense out of what she typed that day, since she was starting with chapter seventeen, Michael's writing still stunned her. After dinner that evening she sat on the sun porch and began reading at the beginning.

Joyce was right, she thought. Michael really was a gifted writer, and this, this was an extraordinary novel—funny and lyrical and driving. About halfway through, a lump tightened in Joanna's throat and nothing she could do would make it go away.

It was an introspective story, a contemporary drama of a young divorced man trying to cope with his disheveled life. Michael? she wondered. The main character was, after all, a teacher.

Michael joined her on the porch just as she was starting the chapter she'd typed that day. Tears were trickling silently down her cheeks.

"That bad, huh?"

At that moment Joanna didn't think she had ever felt so melancholy, or so inspired, or so proud in her entire life. She tried to say something but her lips trembled too badly and the tears kept pouring from her eyes. All she could do was raise her hand toward him.

He walked over and let her wrap her arms around his waist. He leaned down and kissed the top of her head. Slowly he lifted her from the chair and folded her close to him, rocking her back and forth. It was almost as if he were consoling her, she thought.

Did he know how defeated she felt just then, how dazzled by his style and sensitive insights? Did he realize how aware she was of his strength of character? He must. Reading his novel had been a startlingly intimate experience, like living inside his skin, thinking with his mind. And she had been alive for every second of it, alive in a way she had never been before. And the fact that she could no longer hide her feelings behind a facade of pride or independence—or anger—made her feel so very, well, *defeated!*

Michael eased away from her a little and smoothed back her hair. His hands were warm and secure, cradling her head. He was smiling, and his eyes were glittering over her face as if he had, indeed, finally conquered something. Then he kissed each eyelid softly, drew her closer, and kissed her lips. Joanna felt a weightless, bottoming-out sensation in her stomach, a dizziness in her head. And then the warmth began, that wonderful, debilitating heat that made her press closer...

Only to be cut off when Michael pulled back abruptly. He took a deep, fortifying breath and looked away from her. "You'd better get some sleep. I'd like us to get an early start tomorrow."

Joanna was startled to feel disappointment crashing down around her. Yet she managed a small smile and a nod before heading for her room.

The days soon fell into a routine. All morning long, sometimes till two or three in the afternoon, Michael would write and pace the porch, then write some more, and Joanna, at the dining-room table, would type. Then they would break for the rest of the afternoon and take Casey swimming or rowing or hiking. Sometimes they simply took long rides in Michael's car. Then in the evening, after a meal they usually prepared together, Joanna would do the dishes and laundry while he sat in his favorite corner of the sun porch rereading and revising what they had done earlier that day. Joanna had never realized what a tedious back-and-forth movement this business of writing was.

Oddly enough, he seemed to be making more progress now than he had when he'd been working longer hours. Not only that, his skin was turning the smooth, deep gold she remembered envying so much when she was a girl. His appetite was ravenous, too, from all the exercise he was getting in the salt sea air.

Casey behaved extremely well while they were working, especially as they were able to give him very little attention these days. Most of the time he played contentedly in the yard where they could see him, building imaginary roads and bridges in the sandy soil for his cars and trucks to travel. And one afternoon, Michael came home from a mysterious shopping trip with a small inflatable pool.

Joanna couldn't help laughing at the purchase, considering how close they were to the beach. But since Casey couldn't venture off alone, it only made sense. At times, in fact, he seemed to enjoy the pool much more than the beach. It was an ocean just the right size to launch his fleet of toy boats.

He was doing so well these days, she thought. There wasn't a single reference to Phil that didn't indicate a complete acceptance of his death, not one unreasonable tear since the incident with the seashell. Perhaps the island was working its healing magic after all.

On her, too, she realized. She was unquestionably happy, happier than she'd been in—yes, if she was really honest—*years*.

Nathan called nearly every evening, but Joanna made polite excuses when he asked her out. She could have found the time, she supposed, but she was afraid he was jumping to conclusions about their relationship. Probably, she thought with a pang of guilt, because of the kiss that had ended their last date. She didn't claim to understand her reaction. Nathan Trent was considered quite a catch. He was personable, good-looking, had his own thriving business, a beautiful home, and he was family-oriented. Yet, he just didn't . . . fit! They were gears that didn't quite mesh.

Only once in her life had she felt that way—only once. That deep abiding harmony . . .

There were moments when she paused in her typing and wondered if Michael ever thought about that time in their lives, too. He looked as if he did. At times, a disconcerting warmth entered his eyes. As he passed her chair, she sometimes felt the touch of his hand. . . .

And then she'd think of those unguarded moments of affection they'd recently shared. And her heart would start wondering what it all meant.

But these were dangerous thoughts, insidious thoughts. Michael was seeing Joyce Sterling these days, a woman who seemed to take nothing casually, least of all a personal relationship.

But even if his relationship with Joyce was just a casual affair, was she wise in letting herself speculate about Michael and herself? She knew what he was like from bitter experience. The past could not be changed. And the truth was that Michael could not be trusted or believed.

The only trouble was . . . she was afraid she was in love with him again. No, not *again*. Her love had probably never ended. Like all the other emotional baggage she'd been carrying around since she'd run away from here, her love had probably always been with her, way down there under the surface of her life. Otherwise, why had she still been so hurt over Michael's deceit? Why had she still been so angry? Those feelings didn't make sense anymore. No, it was precisely *because* she still loved him that she'd felt so devastated and enraged.

One thing was clear, though. She had to keep this insight to herself. If Michael found out she still loved him, she wasn't sure exactly what he'd do. But he'd used her once before, and as far as she was concerned, once was enough for an entire lifetime.

CHAPTER ELEVEN

IT WAS THE MIDDLE of the following week, five days before
his deadline, when Michael finished the novel. He was
leaning over Joanna, reading the last few sentences as she
typed them, and he made the announcement.

"That's it. I'm not going to fuss anymore. That's it."

She half turned and looked up at him. "What?"

"I'm through with revisions. Just type 'The End' and let's
be done with it."

She did as she was told and sat back. Michael had strolled
to the sun-porch door and was staring out toward the pond.

It had been quite an experience for Joanna, tiring and tedious but oddly exhilarating. Even though she looked forward to spending more time with Casey now, she was still
sorry her job was done. She could only imagine what Michael was feeling.

"What happens now?" she asked, lifting her long hair off
her neck. The weather had turned hot and oppressively humid. Her T-shirt and shorts clung to her uncomfortably.

"I'll give Joyce a call and let her know," he said distractedly.

But of course. Always Joyce. She should be used to it by
now.

"She'll be here in a couple of days. I'll drop the manuscript off with her, and she can take it back to New York on
Sunday."

Joanna's tired shoulders slumped with a sense of anticli-
max. Michael had just finished his novel, yet he was acting
as if it were just an ordinary day. She had expected a little

more excitement, a few unrestrained whoops of joy, maybe even a "Gee-I-couldn't-have-done-it-without-you-kid." But—nothing?

Michael scooped up the phone, sat on the stairs and dialed.

"Joyce Sterling, please."

Joanna picked up a few crumpled papers from the floor and stuffed them into an already full wastebasket.

"Hi, Joyce? Michael." He was smiling.

She moved the typewriter to the floor, the manuscript to the sideboard, and then polished away the coffee rings and eraser crumbs accumulated over the past two dreamlike weeks.

"Yes, that's why I'm calling," Michael's deep voice rumbled on, warm and sexy.

Joanna sprayed and polished again. The room was beginning to look as if nothing had happened there.

"I'll leave it with you Saturday. You are coming to the Vineyard this weekend, aren't you?"

Joanna glanced up from the polished table. He had a look on his face that was all too familiar. She really should take a picture of it and hang it on her wall as a constant reminder. She could caption it "Michael Malone on the Make."

"A party? You don't have to do that . . ."

She put away the dust cloth and told herself she didn't really want to cry. So what if Michael didn't want to celebrate with her? Joyce deserved to share that special moment much more than she did. Joyce was his agent. She had gone to bat for him on a partial manuscript. She had negotiated a terrific contract.

"Excuse me." She tried to pass Michael on the stairs, but he looked up and motioned for her to wait.

Then covering the receiver, he told her Joyce wanted to talk to her. "She's having a celebration party this weekend, and she'd like you to go."

"Me?" she mouthed silently.

"Yes. Here. She wants to talk to you."

Joanna sat on the step above Michael's and took the receiver. Of course Joyce wanted Joanna to go. And bring along a friend. It would be just an informal gathering of friends and business associates.

Joyce was actually very gracious. But then, she had no reason not to be. She was undoubtedly quite confident in her relationship with Michael. If she suspected anything about Joanna's past, she certainly didn't fear it.

As soon as she got off the phone with Joyce, Joanna called Nathan. She was glad Michael had wandered out to the kitchen. Unfortunately he returned too soon.

"You can make it?" she was saying. "Oh, great! I really didn't want to go to something like that alone. Thanks a million."

Oddly, Michael's smile vanished. "You asked Nathan Trent to Joyce's party?" he asked when she was off the phone.

"Y-yes. Joyce said I should bring a date."

"So?"

"So, who did you expect me to ask?"

He gave her a look she couldn't explain, and yet it shook her to her very soul. Only as he was turning and heading back into the kitchen did she notice the bottle of champagne and the two glasses in his hand.

JOANNA RODE to Joyce's cottage the following Saturday evening in a quietly distracted state, but Nathan hardly noticed. He parked in the circular driveway and got out to open her door. Quickly she glanced in the mirror. She had taken such care with her makeup and clothing, but still she felt insecure.

She was wearing a new, ice-blue silk dress with a softly gathered skirt and halter top. It had been last year's stock at her store and she'd bought it at a fraction of the original cost. It was the most alluring dress she owned, but she'd never worn it before, and Michael had left too early for her to get a critique. Of course, Nathan's eyes had registered total delight. But then they always did, whether she was wearing an alluring dress or simply a pair of old jeans.

The front door was open and people were gathered in small groups around the living room, talking and laughing lightly as ice cubes clinked in their glasses. One of them was Michael, looking tall and attractive and utterly masculine. In fact, he dominated the room with his air of authority and his stunning good looks. She was surprised by this facet of him. He looked so...so urbane! And it occurred to her that she'd never seen him dressed this way before, in dress pants, shirt and tie.

As soon as he saw them, he walked over, his eyes sweeping her like a searchlight, swift and brilliant. "You're looking very nice tonight," he said with a polite smile. "I don't think I've ever seen that dress before." He quickly turned to Nathan, cutting Joanna off before she could say anything in reply. "Joyce is out back with the rest of the guests. Let me introduce you around."

He led them through the tastefully modern living room to glass sliders that opened onto a flagstoned patio. A dozen people were mingling there, but Joanna saw only Joyce. Tonight her rich brown hair was coiled at her nape and she wore a silk caftan in butterfly colors, which, on anyone else, might appear gaudy but on her became a masterpiece of design. Her bearing was regal. She talked with an ease that Joanna envied.

Their eyes met and Joyce's smile froze. She cocked her head and glanced speculatively over Joanna and the two men by her side.

"Joyce, I'd like you to meet Joanna's friend Nathan Trent," Michael introduced smoothly, every inch the social counterpart of his hostess.

Nathan shook the woman's hand and smiled. "It was very nice of you to invite us."

"Very nice of you to come." Still smiling, she flicked another cool glance over Joanna. "I hear you're the owner of those charming little boutiques that carry all those wonderful English wools.''

Nathan was flattered and talked for several minutes about his shops. But eventually another couple arrived and Joyce's keen eyes captured Michael's. He nodded, communicating on a level that needed no words. Joanna's chest tightened.

"Excuse us, please," Joyce said, taking Michael's arm. "I have to introduce Michael to someone, but do make yourselves comfortable. Help yourselves at the bar." She drifted off, with Michael at her side.

At first, Joanna found mingling difficult. While Joyce's gathering wasn't large, it certainly was illustrious. Several writers and artists who lived on the island were there, as were politicians, magazine people, and business associates from New York. But once they discovered who Joanna was, or rather who her housemate was, they opened up to her in a way she found almost amusing.

It didn't take long to realize this was no ordinary celebration among friends. Joyce had deliberately gathered these people together as a public-relations move. She wanted these influential people in the arts and media to get to know her dashing young client. Joyce had orchestrated the whole thing for his benefit. She had even invited Douglas McCrory, the publisher of Gateway Books.

Joanna was sorry she'd come. Joyce was not only beautiful and intelligent, but she was also a vital force in Michael's career. They made a perfect couple, blending in a way she and Michael never could.

Joanna drank liberally, but it did little to dull her senses. No matter where she was or who she talked to, she remained aware of Michael's presence in the crowd. Aware, too, of his disapproving frown whenever their eyes met. She tried to talk to him once, but after a few desultory remarks, he excused himself and walked away. Was he ashamed of her? Did he not want to be associated with her in front of these people?

Well, she would be damned if she'd allow him to intimidate her. Even if she wasn't part of this crowd, she had nothing to be ashamed of. She had always been considered fairly intelligent and creative herself. And she certainly hadn't been locked in a vacuum the past six years. She had read nearly a book a week and she'd been on a committee at the library that organized lectures and slide shows. Even working at the store had had its advantages; she had met and talked with people from every walk of life, from the farthest corners of the globe.

By ten-thirty, however, she'd had it! "Nathan, do you think we can leave now?"

"Sure, honey. Let's go say our goodbyes."

They found Joyce on the fringe of the gathering talking with Mr. McCrory. Michael was by her side—as he had been nearly all evening.

Joanna lifted her chin and dredged up yet one more smile. "Joyce, we're going to be leaving now." She avoided Michael's cool gaze.

"What, so soon?"

Nathan grinned and his hand drifted to Joanna's waist. "Well, I haven't seen this little lady in nearly two weeks. You know how it is."

Joyce laughed, giving Michael a quick glance. "I certainly do. Oh, before you go, I'd like to thank you, Joanna."

"Me? For what?"

"For helping Michael. I hear you've been quite the busy typist."

Joanna looked at Michael. Yes, she had certainly typed—but she'd done more than that. She had encouraged him, cajoled, even made some fairly candid remarks that had inspired a few important pages.

And then there were all those wonderful, golden afternoons rowing on the pond, and the giggles that accompanied cooking dinner, and later the quiet, peaceful talks on the porch... Somehow she sensed they had helped even more than the typing had.

But Michael's eyes returned none of this. No defense, no gratitude. She might have been a stranger to him.

Fighting back a new wave of rejection, she smiled valiantly. "Well, it's nothing compared to what you're doing for him."

Joyce smiled like the proverbial cat with the cream.

"Good night," Nathan said. "Again, thanks for having us."

Joanna turned and walked away, feeling the bitter sting of tears in her throat.

LATER THAT NIGHT, after Nathan had gone, Joanna wandered out to the front porch. Casey was sleeping over at Meg's tonight, and she had the whole place to herself. Undoubtedly she wouldn't be seeing Michael for a while tonight—if at all!

A gigantic moon was glowing in the sky, its light sparkling across the crushed seashells in the driveway. She sat down on the top step and carefully folded her silky skirt around her ankles. There was an unearthly luminescence on everything, all the low brambles from here to the sea. Even insect sounds seemed silvered with the light.

She leaned her head against the rail and sighed, thinking back to Joyce's party. She was still hurt by the way Michael had ignored her. Hadn't she fit in with this crowd? Or was Joyce so fascinating that he hadn't even been aware of the way he'd snubbed her? Maybe she just didn't exist for him outside this cottage. Maybe that's how it had always been—a limited, summer-cottage relationship.

Joanna blinked at the stinging in her eyes. She loved Michael so much at this moment, and the truth was she wanted him to love her in return. She wanted to be a part of his life. She didn't want to go back to New Hampshire. She wanted to stay here with him—forever. And it hurt so much knowing that she couldn't, knowing he didn't want her.

Joanna listened to the low thunder of the waves, feeling more and more bereft. Their hypnotic rhythm carried her over the dunes and away, back to a night six years ago when Michael had not been so immune...

It had been a night much like this one, a night so still and sultry the air felt like velvet on their skin. They'd gone down to the beach after dinner and were lying together within the folds of a thick blanket, staring hypnotized into each other's eyes...

"Joanna?" she remembered him whispering.

"Yes?"

"Nothing. I just wanted to say your name. I love the sound of it."

And she had laughed and told him it was an awful name, so plain and old-fashioned.

But he'd shaken his head. "To me it's the loveliest word imaginable. Joanna. Three little syllables that can turn me completely inside out..."

A tear trickled down Joanna's cheek as she remembered that night, how his eyes had seared into hers with such drugging intensity, how their arms had wrapped so tightly around each other, their damp legs entwined. Even now, she could feel his hard masculine strength over every inch of her body....

"Jo, do you realize how deeply in love I am with you?" he had whispered. "It's different from anything else I've ever felt. We're so close I feel...I feel married to you."

"I love you, too, Michael. I'll always love you."

"Forever," he'd vowed. "We *are* married, Jo, in a way that's far more binding than a civil license. I really believe it. In a spiritual, mystical way, you and I are husband and wife."

"Oh, Michael! If only it were true!"

He'd smiled softly and then got to his feet.

"What are you doing?" she'd asked.

"Here, this will have to do." In his hand was a clump of seaweed.

"What?"

"Your flowers, ma'am." He'd bowed elegantly. "Well, you said you wanted to get married . . ."

When she'd continued to stare at him, he'd pulled her up and thrust the brittle bouquet into her hand. Then he'd draped the sandy blanket over her shoulders "for a gown."

"Michael, sometimes I swear you're crazy!"

But he was undaunted. He even waxed poetic, exaggerating his gestures comically. "The ocean's murmur will be our music, my love, this sacred beach our church."

"And the minister?" she'd asked.

Joanna still remembered the serious look that had overtaken his expression, eyes wandering over the moon-glittering sea and up to the stars. "He's here. He's listening."

He'd taken her hand then and held it in both of his, close to his heart. "Joanna, I don't know exactly how the words go, but I think it all comes down to this—I love you. You're my soul, my body's breath, my life's joy. And I guess I'm yours from this day forward, completely and forever."

Joanna had stared into his eyes, eyes so deep and sincere and loving she almost couldn't speak. "And I'm yours, Michael, completely and forever. Wherever we go, whatever we do, apart or together, throughout time into eternity, we'll be as one."

On that hot, languid night six years ago, Michael tenderly and sensitively carried her over the threshold of full womanhood on a wave of emotional and physical ecstasy she had never dreamed possible. Their lovemaking left her limp in his arms and sobbing quietly, but she was happier, she was sure, than anyone else who had ever walked the earth before her. She was irrevocably his, branded by him, indelibly molded by his body and his love.

Now as Joanna gazed out over the moon-washed landscape, tears streamed silently down her hot cheeks. Why did she have to remember that silly ceremony now? Such flowery, formal vows! Such hopelessly idealistic nonsense! It had meant nothing! Michael had mocked those vows within weeks—indeed, had been mocking them all along.

Then, why did she remember the details of that night so vividly? And why, after all that had intervened, did she feel even now this vital, unbreakable bond?

Joanna was startled out of her thoughts by the beam of a headlight bouncing up the driveway. She wiped her wet cheeks quickly, recognizing the sound of the engine.

Michael's Volvo came to a skidding stop and he vaulted out, slamming the door angrily. He took two long strides before he noticed her curled up on the stairs.

"Oh. You're alone?"

"Yes." She was alarmed at the sudden sense of excitement shooting through her nerves.

Slowly he loosened his tie and undid the top button of his shirt. "Good. We're going to have to talk."

CHAPTER TWELVE

MICHAEL LOWERED HIMSELF to the step beside her. All of Joanna's senses were alive and ringing with an awareness of him.

"What do you want to talk about?"

"You and Nathan."

"Michael, did you come rushing home just to give me another lecture on how a respectable widow should behave?"

"Yes...no! Of course not! Listen, I know I get pretty upset when you butt into my affairs—or at least I used to—and I have no right butting into yours, but...dammit, Joanna!" He thrust a hand through his hair, raking it back from his forehead. "I just want to warn you to watch out for yourself. You're going through a transitional period in your life and you're vulnerable. I'd hate to see you get hurt."

Considering her emotional state, Joanna turned a remarkably calm stare on him. "Oh? And what makes you so sure I'm going to get hurt?"

Michael shrugged. "I'm not. I can't tell how serious you're getting or what Nathan's intentions are." And when she didn't answer, "Well?"

"You were right. It's none of your business."

"Dammit, Jo! Will you level with me!"

"Why? You didn't level with me when I asked about Joyce."

He subsided with a guilty look. "You're right, and I should have. I detect a little misunderstanding where Joyce is concerned."

"I doubt it."

"Well, you're wrong. There's nothing between me and Joyce, nothing except a business relationship. We're not lovers and never have been. I won't deny that we've gone out together socially a few times, and maybe she was hoping it would turn into something more. But it never did. And I've never led her to think otherwise."

Relief and joy swept through Joanna even while she was trying to remind herself to be careful. "Then why the big fascination with her tonight?"

Michael's brow furrowed. "What do you mean?"

"You know what I mean. You never left her side for a minute. And me...? You treated me as if I had leprosy." She tossed her hair over her shoulder, feeling it swing heavily against her back.

Michael leaned his elbows on his knees and stared broodingly down the road. "You didn't suffer by it. You managed to make your presence felt."

She glared at his moon-washed profile. "I refuse to let you bully me into thinking I did anything wrong. I looked as presentable as anybody else. I didn't say anything dumb or uncouth—"

"Will you shut up for once and listen? That's the trouble with you! You go on and on about how *you* see things, and you never listen to what anyone else is saying."

Joanna laughed mirthlessly. "And why should I? Whenever I listen to you, I hear insulting things, like I'm a lonely ol' widow who's letting men take advantage and—"

Michael didn't give her a chance to finish. He grabbed her arms, pulled her to him and silenced her with a kiss. Joanna gave a muffled cry and went stiff with instinctive resistance.

When he finally let her go, she gasped, "Michael, you're out of your mind!" So he kissed her again. This time, however, she knew her willpower was abandoning her.

She could feel the firm pliancy of his lips as they moved over hers, could feel what his warmth was doing to her body.

Her heart was beating against his chest like a hammer, and her blood was turning to fire. When he attempted to draw away, it was she who clung and held him close.

"You don't play fair," she moaned as his lips brushed hers with tantalizing softness.

"I learned the rules from you, love." His lips left hers to trail along her cheek to her ear. "Why did you have to look so beautiful tonight, hmm? If I hadn't stayed away from you, I'm afraid I would have done this right on Joyce's patio. This, or broken a few bones in Nathan's body."

Again he kissed her, long and deep, and Joanna didn't try to protest. She loved the feelings he was arousing in her.

"Michael?" she whispered. "Just for the record, there's nothing between me and Nathan, either. Not on my part anyway. I asked him to Joyce's party simply because I didn't know who else to ask, and I didn't want to go without an escort."

Michael shook his head and laughed. "You're hopeless! I just assumed we . . . I mean, after the way we've been getting along lately . . ."

"That we'd be going together?"

"Of course. That's another reason I was so ticked off tonight."

So, it hadn't been just her imagination! Something really had been happening between them these past two weeks while they'd been working on the novel. Wasn't life strange? she thought vaguely as he pulled her close again. Wasn't it awfully, wonderfully strange!

This time when he kissed her, his tongue began a hot exploration of her mouth. She cried out softly and dug her fingers into his hair, drawing him even closer. She was dizzy with the masculine fragrance of his skin, mindless with the ecstasy of knowing he wanted her—and had, even at Joyce's party.

He tipped her back onto the floor of the porch and lay alongside her. His hand caressed her with gentle intimacy, yet there was an underlying urgency in his touch that was exciting, igniting a fever wherever it went.

When he undid the strap of her halter, however, her old doubts surged to the surface one more time. Hadn't she learned anything from the past? Hadn't all her troubles started just this way?

"Michael, don't." She sat up, fumbling with the loosened ties.

But he sat up behind her and kissed the side of her face, lifting her hair to brush his lips over her neck. She closed her eyes, dropped her hands and surrendered to the delicious heat washing through her. Michael must have felt the slackening of her body, because his lips moved more persistently to her ear, exploring its sensitive curves with a sensual slowness that soon had her weak and breathless again.

"Michael, stop. This is madness," she said, her voice hoarse with longing.

He turned her around in his arms. "This isn't madness, Jo," he said against her soft, responsive mouth. "This is the sanest, most honest thing that's ever happened between us, and it's too beautiful to keep fighting."

Joanna didn't want to fight it, either. Holding him, kissing him—that was what she longed for with every fiber of her being.

"Jo, I don't want to want you as much as I do," he whispered raggedly. "I wish I could get you out of my system. You've never been anything but trouble to me. But you're like a fever in my blood. You're driving me crazy...." His last words were muffled against her mouth, and when Joanna began to kiss him again, he shuddered through his entire body.

"You've grown so beautiful... it's been pure torture being with you and not being able to hold you this way. If only you knew how many times I've wanted to do this—to stop whatever we were doing and pull you into my arms..." Again he kissed her, and again the effect was like a minor earthquake through her nervous system.

"Jo, I'd come to think I'd never hold you like this again," he said huskily. "I'd never feel your wonderful body or see your beautiful face…" He pulled her closer, the heat of his body seeking the heat in hers. "You make me feel so alive again…as if all these years I've been dead…" He slid down the soft material of her dress and the moonlight bathed her breasts.

Somewhere at the back of her mind, a small voice was trying to say she was being reckless, that this could lead to nothing but pain. She had to make him stop, had to make herself stop. But the voice was so faint and what it was saying seemed irrelevant now. Michael wanted her; something was still there between them, something beautiful and strong and enduring. Maybe in the few weeks they had left, they could build on that. Maybe this time things would work out for them after all. She couldn't think of past hurts anymore. There were too many other feelings crowding out the pain—love and joy, and most wonderful of all, hope.

Her mind swimming through a haze of passion, she was vaguely aware of being carried into the house and up the stairs to his room. Moonlight, slanting in through the window, washed over the bed. Michael laid her down and for a moment just stood there gazing at her. So much was in his eyes, Joanna thought—desire, sincerity, admiration—no, it was nearly an adoration.

"Are you sure you want to do this, Jo?" he asked softly.

She smiled and raised her hand to him. How she loved this man! And she would go on loving him till the end of her days. There was nothing she could do to stop it. This was *right*; it was an acknowledgement of their future, not just their past.

He sat on the edge of the bed beside her. Slowly Joanna removed his tie and tossed it on the floor. Then she unbuttoned his shirt and ran her fingers through the crisp, dark hair of his chest. Michael closed his eyes and moaned softly.

He took her hands and kissed their palms. Then he leaned down and captured her mouth with a savage sweetness that scattered the very last fragments of her doubts or inhibitions. With a gentle tug, her dress slipped silkily over her legs and off the bed. A moment later his trousers followed.

"I want you so much, Jo." His voice was breathlessly urgent now. Lying close beside him, she could feel his body trembling with tightly controlled passion. "It's been so long since I've been able to do anything except conjure you up in my mind. I can hardly believe you're here...." He took a deep, shuddering breath. "Oh, my beautiful Joanna..."

Emotion reached too high a pitch for any further words. Soon they were soaring to new heights of sensation, and when sensation finally peaked in ecstasy, Joanna felt certain she and Michael had melded inextricably, body, mind, and soul into one person.

JOANNA WOKE LATE the next morning. She had slept soundly, wrapped in an inexplicable feeling of well-being. When she opened her eyes and saw Michael asleep beside her, she smiled and remembered why. She leaned up on one elbow and stared down at his devilishly handsome face. Even in sleep he managed to look sexy, she thought with a laugh.

His absurdly long eyelashes fluttered. "Oh, hi there." He smiled sleepily, rolling toward her and nuzzling her hair. "What time is it?"

"After ten."

They lay for a peaceful moment, without speaking. Joanna couldn't help feeling secure this bright morning, cherished and ... complete! She wondered if she should be disgusted with herself for succumbing to him so easily, if she should be sick with worrying where this step was taking her. But she wasn't. She couldn't be. Michael had been right: their lovemaking really was the most honest part of their long and muddled relationship. It was natural and beautiful, and Joanna no longer wanted to drown out what it was trying to tell her.

"When's Casey due home?" Michael's eyes were gleaming, a small, teasing smile on his lips.

"Not till around noon." She began to smile, too, exquisitely aware of the hard length of his body alongside hers. He leaned over her, his tanned, muscular shoulders made golden by the morning sunlight. He kissed her long and deeply, then raised his head in order to look at her again. Joanna couldn't tell which was more arousing—that incredible, debilitating kiss of his, or the look in his eyes.

She wrapped him in a tight embrace, loving him so much that tears sprang to her eyes.

Suddenly the sound of the phone shattered the cool morning stillness. Michael groaned and his head fell heavily on her bare shoulder. It rang again. They looked at each other questioningly.

"Forget it," Michael said. "Let it ring."

"But it might be important."

"So is this." Michael lowered his head and kissed her into silence.

From the bottom of the stairs, the phone shrilled again. Joanna raised herself onto one elbow. "No, Michael. We should answer it."

Muttering darkly, he swung his feet to the floor. When he was gone, Joanna sat up and pulled the sheet around her. She felt cold and hollow with his absence, however momentary. Still, she gave her reflection in the mirror a quick smile. Incredible as it seemed, Michael wasn't seeing anyone else. He wanted *her*. His whispered love-words still thrilled along her spine. And in a few minutes he would be back and they would continue to make love.

Of course, he hadn't actually said anything about the future, but she refused to let that concern her. She simply wouldn't let anything get in their way this time. She stared at her radiant reflection and her smile broadened. Yes. Yes! In the few weeks they had left at the cottage, she was sure they could turn the past around.

"Jo!" Michael called urgently as he ran up the stairs. "Jo, get dressed."

"What's the matter?" she demanded as he burst into the room.

"Don't get alarmed but Casey's had an accident."

CHAPTER THIRTEEN

MICHAEL WHIPPED A SHIRT from his closet. "That was Meg on the phone. She's at the hospital with him right now."

"The hospital?" Adrenaline started pumping through Joanna's body. She jumped to her feet and ran across the hall to her room. "What kind of accident?" she called, jerking open her dresser drawer.

"Meg took the kids to some damn park this morning and apparently Casey fell off the top of a slide." He entered her room as she was still dressing.

Joanna's hands were so shaky she couldn't get the front of her dress buttoned. She had never felt so panicked in her life. Well, maybe once before, she thought as she gazed at Michael helping her button up. Poor man! He looked as frightened as she felt. He'd gone white under his tan.

"Ready?" he asked.

"No, but let's go."

Meg was sitting outside the emergency room with her three children. She looked pale and nervous. When she spotted them, she shot to her feet, swinging her littlest one onto her hip.

"Where's Casey?" Joanna burst out.

"Inside." Meg tilted her head toward one of the many doors along the corridor. "They're preparing him for X-rays."

Joanna started off, but Meg held her back a moment. "Jo, I'm really sorry. I was right there, honestly. It wasn't as if I let them run around unattended."

Joanna could see the anguish she was suffering. She would have felt the same. "Stop that right now. Accidents happen and there's nothing we can do to stop them."

"I know, but I was so careful. I don't know what happened. He moved so fast."

"Stop feeling guilty, Meg. It's not your fault."

The baby began to whine and squirm.

"You'd better take these kids home. There's nothing else you can do here."

But Meg shook her head. "Steve's off-island, but I called Nathan to come get them. I'd like to stay."

"No, I insist you go, and I don't have time to argue." Joanna looked around. Michael had already disappeared.

"Well, I gave the doctor all the information I could, which wasn't much..."

"Then goodbye." Joanna was adamant.

A moment later, she was standing by Michael's side, looking down at Casey's small, inert body. There was a large gauze pad on his forehead and several scrapes on his arms and legs. Splayed out on the harshly lit table, he looked so small and vulnerable.

"Casey, Mommy's here," she whispered, wishing with all her heart that she could gather him up and return him to some sort of protective womb.

"He can't hear you, Jo," Michael said.

"Are you the boy's parents?" the doctor in attendance asked.

Joanna looked up, distracted and frightened.

"This is the boy's mother," Michael answered for her.

The doctor was forcing Casey's eyelids open and shining a narrow flashlight into his unseeing irises. "Uh huh," he murmured. "Uh huh. Casey's had a bad fall." He lifted the gauze and replaced it quickly. Joanna winced at the sight of the gash. "He may have a sprained wrist, maybe even a fracture, but we aren't too concerned about that at the moment. I'm more concerned about his head." Joanna reached for Michael's hand. "I believe he's given himself a walloping concussion." The doctor was middle-aged, gray-haired, and smiled sympathetically. "Don't worry, he'll be all right. Children come in with concussions all the time."

Joanna stared at him numbly. Yes, but not *my* child! she wanted to shout. But she didn't. She felt too weak even to move.

"You said something about X rays before Mrs. Ingalls came in?" Michael reminded him.

"Yes, we'll take him up in a few minutes. In the meantime, would you be so kind as to fill out a few forms, Mrs. Ingalls? I'm sure it's the last thing you feel like doing right now, but it's hospital policy."

"Yes, of course." Joanna turned confusedly.

"At the desk in the lobby."

She nodded, giving her son a hesitant glance.

"I'll stay with him," Michael reassured her.

She nodded again, feeling like a puppet whose strings were being manipulated by some cruel fate.

She took a seat out in the hall and started to fill in the lines—Casey's name, his age and address, her name, phone number, employer... The print was swimming under her trembling pen. She found her insurance card and jotted down her identification number. Childhood diseases... Immunizations... Date of last tetanus shot? Joanna was afraid she was going to cry. Was there no end to this form? And where were they wheeling Casey?

Suddenly she was aware of someone standing beside her. She looked up, dropped the clipboard and rose to her feet.

"Oh, Nathan! Casey—"

"I know. I heard all about it." He folded her into a warm embrace.

Joanna tensed and was glad that he released her quickly.

"Have the doctors been able to give you any news on his condition?"

"Most likely he has a concussion. They're taking him up for X rays now."

Nathan's hands were still on her arms, stroking them comfortingly. "I'm sure he'll be fine."

Suddenly she remembered why he was there. "Oh, Nathan, you shouldn't have come. Meg's already taken her kids home."

"Oh, has she? Well, good. Now I'm free to stay with you."

"That's very thoughtful, but Michael's here."

The expression on Nathan's rugged face fell. "Oh, I see."

"He's with Casey now."

His warm brown eyes avoided hers. "I guess you really don't need me then."

Joanna swallowed hard. She didn't want to hurt Nathan. She liked him so much, but only as a friend.

"I'm sorry, Jo, I know this isn't the time nor place to bring up the subject, but I was serious about wanting you to stay here on the Vineyard. You may not have noticed, but I happen to be crazy about you." His voice strained with emotion.

She lowered her head. She wished she could love this man in return. Life would be so simple then.

"I'm sorry, too. We had such a good time going out together. You made it easy for me to get back into the swing of things. But I never meant to lead you on."

Nathan still looked hurt. Impetuously she added, "Who knows? Maybe sometime in the future..."

He sighed resignedly. "Yeah, maybe." He paused and glanced away. "He doesn't deserve you, y'know."

Joanna followed his gaze down the corridor to where Michael was talking with the doctor. "Who? Michael? There's nothing between..." But the words died of their own weakness. Was her love for Michael that obvious to others?

Nathan shrugged. "Oh, well, I'll be around if things don't work out."

Joanna embraced him. "Thank you. You're quite a friend."

He winked and disappeared in the dazzle of sunlight outside the glass doors.

Joanna turned with a pensive frown. Michael was hurrying toward her.

"We can wait for Casey up in his room. He'll be out of X ray soon."

"His room?"

Michael nodded grimly. "They'd like to keep him overnight."

Joanna picked up her handbag and began to follow.

"Mrs. Ingalls?" the secretary at the desk called. "The admission forms?"

"Oh." Joanna paused. "May I take them with me? I'd like to be with my son when he gets to his room."

The woman hesitated. "I guess it'll be okay, but please bring them down as soon as possible."

"Thanks."

Casey drifted into unconsciousness once or twice more that long afternoon. Mostly, though, he just lay there, dizzy and nauseated, his head hurting so much that sometimes he cried.

The doctor came in as supper trays were clinking down the corridor and said that Casey was lucky. "No fractured skull, Mrs. Ingalls. Just a concussion. But it's a mean one. That's why we decided to keep him overnight. I'll check on him again tomorrow, bright and early. Most likely he'll be able to go home then." In the meantime, he assured her, the nurses would take good care of him.

"May I stay?" She didn't know why she was bothering to ask. Nothing was going to pry her from Casey's side.

The doctor sighed heavily. "We can't provide a bed . . ."

"I know. A chair's fine. I'd really rather be here."

"So would I."

Joanna shot Michael a glance and knew there would be no dissuading him, either.

"Sure." The doctor nodded. "I understand."

When he was gone, Michael said he was going in search of the cafeteria. "What can I bring back for you, Jo?"

Though she wasn't the least bit hungry, she suddenly realized she hadn't eaten all day. "Soup and crackers, tea, anything."

"I'll drop this off for you at the desk, too."

Joanna looked up sharply, remembering the admission form. "Oh, don't bother. I can go down later."

"Don't be silly." The clipboard was already in his hand and he was halfway out the door. Joanna fell back into the chair, closed her eyes and whispered a silent prayer.

Joanna and Michael didn't say much as the night ticked on. They just sat and listened to the sounds drifting in from the corridor—the metallic repetition of doctors' names, the small ping of bells.

"I hate hospitals." Joanna shuddered, gazing at Michael for comfort. She was so grateful he was there.

His lips pressed together in what appeared to be a smile, but no emotion reached his eyes. He seemed lost in thought, distracted. Lines creased his brow.

"There's no need for you to stay," she said.

"I'll stay, if you don't mind." His eyes avoided hers. He had been acting strangely ever since he'd returned from the cafeteria. Still, he hadn't said anything... He was probably just as tired and worried about Casey as she was. At least, she hoped this was the reason.

They dozed in their chairs and the night passed. Casey woke shortly before dawn, crying, and a nurse gave him an injection to ease the pain of his bruises. Soon afterward, carts laden with breakfast trays rattled down the corridor. Outside the sun was growing hot and life was resuming as usual, but not in here. Joanna felt time had stopped within these sterile walls.

She gazed at Michael. His shirt was rumpled, and his cheeks were shadowed by a day's growth of beard. He did indeed look tired and worried, yet every time she'd asked him how he was, he'd said fine. Evidently his fondness for Casey ran deeper than she had ever suspected.

A nurse came in and for the hundredth time, it seemed, checked his pulse and eyes. "Nothing we can do really. In a situation like this, the body mends itself in its own good time. Let him rest. He's doing fine."

"Where am I?" Casey asked when she was gone, his blue eyes looking too large for his tiny face.

"At the hospital, kid," Michael answered softly, leaning close. "Do you remember what happened yesterday at the park?"

Casey shook his head and winced with the sudden pain it caused.

"You fell off a slide, honey," Joanna offered, worriedly.

"Oh, yeah. I wanted to go down on my stomach, so I stood up to turn around and—"

"Oh, Casey!" Joanna admonished softly.

"I won't do it again, Ma."

"I'm sure you won't." Michael leaned over and kissed the boy's head tenderly.

Joanna ducked into the bathroom so Casey wouldn't see the tears that were welling in her bloodshot eyes.

When she returned, Michael was reading Casey a story from a book borrowed from the playroom down the hall. He leaned heavily on the bed, his eyes half-closed.

"You look worse than he does," she said, trying to sound cheerful. "Why don't you go grab yourself some coffee?"

Michael didn't protest. In fact, he didn't say anything to her at all, only to Casey. "I'll be back soon, kid. Don't go out dancing while I'm gone." The child giggled weakly.

Casey was released that afternoon. Despite her exhaustion, Joanna felt almost light with relief. He would have to rest quietly for a few days, and she would have to watch for any signs of recurring nausea or blurred vision, but the worst was over. He would soon be as good as new.

Michael carried him into the living room and laid him on the couch. "Would you like me to turn on the TV?"

Casey nodded.

"Okay, you and Bugs keep each other company for a while. I'm going up to shower, and then I've got to go out, but I'll be back real soon."

"Where are you going?" Joanna stopped him as he headed for the stairs.

He turned but didn't quite raise his eyes to hers. "Just to pick up a few things." He had been unusually quiet since Casey's accident. He'd said so little to her directly that she was sure he was avoiding her on purpose. She wished she could attribute it to tiredness, but she knew it wasn't that. He had simply retreated into himself and was brooding on...on something. It hurt to be cut out of his life this abruptly, especially after the intimacy they had come to share. But where was that closeness now when she needed it most? Was their relationship so fragile that it had already broken? And why? What had she done?

Meg dropped by some time later with a platter of macaroni salad and slices of ham and cheese. "I figured you wouldn't be in much of a mood to cook," she explained. She also brought get-well cards from her children.

Joanna was glad of her visit. After the tension of the past two days, she needed someone as talkative and jolly as Meg. When she left, Joanna felt immeasurably better.

After an early supper, she tucked Casey into bed with a favorite stuffed toy, then lowered the window against the damp ocean breeze. Twilight obscured the road until it was just a trench of darkness cut into the jungle of beach plum and bayberry. In the distance, faintly luminescent, was the twisting path of sand that cut through to the beach. The ocean was calm tonight, the low breaking waves just a murmur.

Her vacation was more than half over. The sun was already setting noticeably sooner than it had just a few weeks ago. There were brilliant bars of vermilion streaking the evening sky. Somewhere over the rolling meadows, a robin trilled his last plaintive song of the day.

Joanna felt her heart swell with emotion. How she loved this place! And how dearly she loved the man who was sharing it with her. If only the summer didn't have to end....

But end it would. In three short weeks her vacation would be over. And then what? Would Michael ask her to stay on with him? For a moment she felt a surge of optimism, the same hope she had allowed herself to feel only days ago. But it soon crumpled under the weight of doubt. Michael was acting so strangely...

Suddenly Joanna felt depressed and frightened. She dreaded going back to New Hampshire. She hadn't the slightest inclination toward returning to the store or becoming a computer programmer. At that moment she saw herself with a clarity that was startling. What she wanted most out of life was to be Michael's wife, to be his mate till the end of her days.

It really didn't matter where they lived or what they worked at—just as long as they were together. Everything else was secondary and would fall into place.

But living here on the Vineyard would be ideal. In a house not too different from this one, only larger to accommodate the other children they would surely have. And there would have to be a study where Michael could get away to write... and a garden where she could grow her flowers.

Joanna smiled ruefully. In a world where women were battling to free themselves from the role of housewife and mother, here she was wishing desperately for just the opposite.

Not that she ruled out the possibility of working, too, as long as the work was satisfying and meshed with her family life. Work like the typing she'd done for Michael. Yes, she'd enjoy working at home, making her own hours, setting her own goals. Maybe she could start a typing service; with a good word processor, maybe she could even get into small publications...

But, of course, she was letting her mind wander ludicrously. She was dealing in dreams, dreams made possible only in some uncomplicated and ideal world—and the real world was anything but! In fact, she had bowed to expediency so often in the past that her life was now a mud hole of complications. And if she knew what was good for herself and Casey, she would go on sloshing through.

"Night, Casey. If you need me, just call. I'll be down on the porch." He smiled dreamily, his eyelids lifting slightly then falling again into sleep.

Michael was sitting at the top of the wooden stairs that led down the bluff to the dock. Joanna hadn't been aware that he'd returned. She hesitated for a moment, then gave in and joined him.

She settled down on the step beside him, drew up her knees, and tucked her midcalf skirt around her ankles. "Hi," she said nervously.

Michael continued to gaze out over the dark water, his long, graceful hands pressed to his lips in thought.

"Have you eaten?" Joanna hoped she could somehow draw him out of his sullen mood.

But he probably hadn't even heard her. "How's Casey?"

"Fine. Asleep."

He nodded pensively, dropped his hands between his knees and took a deep breath. "Jo, may I ask you a question?"

"Sure."

"How much did Casey weigh when he was born?"

"What?" she laughed. Just as abruptly, however, she went very still. "I don't remember."

Michael turned his head and pinned her with a cold, laserlike stare. "All right, let me put it this way—was Casey premature?"

Joanna suddenly felt numb. She had a sense of everything in her past rushing up on her, all the days and months and years since she'd run away from this cottage leading to this appointed place and time. *Lie!* she told herself. For heaven's sake, lie!

But Michael was looking right through her, and she couldn't even breathe.

CHAPTER FOURTEEN

"ANSWER ME, dammit!" Michael exploded.

Joanna jumped. "All right! All right!" she snapped, his anger grating on her already traumatized nerves. There was nowhere to run, nothing to do but face the moment she'd hoped would never come. Somehow he'd found out anyway. "He wasn't premature. Casey was a perfectly healthy seven pounds, ten ounces."

"Then . . . he was conceived that summer?"

She swallowed hard. She couldn't answer but Michael could read her expression. He covered his eyes with his hand.

Joanna was beginning to feel sick. She touched his arm but he flung her off and turned away.

"H-how did you find out?" she asked shakily.

It took a while before Michael could speak. He cleared his throat. "I saw his date of birth on the hospital admission form you filled out."

Joanna nodded. She'd known that was a mistake, letting him take that form to the desk. Up to now she'd been so careful . . .

"So, little Casey is my son. *My* son." He stared up at the grayness of approaching night as if searching for something that would help him understand what he'd just said. His expression hardened. "Jo, how could you keep him from me all these years? How could you do that to me? All this time . . . Did I mean so little to you? Did you hate me that much?"

Joanna had feared this would be Michael's reaction, right from the day she had decided to keep Casey's paternity a secret. Over the years her fear had only grown. The longer she kept the secret, the angrier he would be when he found out. *If* he found out. But he never would, she had thought.

"Michael, once a deception is started, it's awfully hard to go back," she began vaguely. "Besides, there was Phil. He wanted to raise Casey with no interference from another party."

Michael turned. "He knew?"

Inside, she felt as if she were dying. "Yes. He asked me to promise I'd never tell. And then there was Casey himself," she added quickly. "I didn't want him growing up torn and confused, like I did."

"Still, you could have found a way," he persisted. "Even if you never told him I was his father, you could have had me meet him and get to know him." He wasn't just angry; Michael was hurting, hurting deeply. "You can't imagine how frustrated I feel right now. I'm so angry, so sad...and there's nothing I can do...all that wasted time! And the saddest part is, that time's gone forever. Nothing can bring it back. It's lost to me."

Joanna nodded. Now, when she loved him more than her own life, Michael loathed her. And she didn't blame him. Keeping a son from his father, concealing the fact of that son's very existence, robbing the father of all the joy of those infant and toddler years, that was unforgivable—an enormous wound that refused to heal.

Michael continued to stare out over the water. "Why didn't you tell me you were pregnant?"

Joanna didn't know what to say.

"Damn you, Joanna! Why didn't you tell me?"

His renewed anger startled her. "I didn't know it myself, not till after I left here."

"Why didn't you get in touch with me then?"

Joanna gasped in disbelief and felt anger rising inside her, too. "I might not have been too smart, but I wasn't a masochist. You already had a pregnant girlfriend, or so we all believed at the time, and you'd made the decision to marry her."

"No, I hadn't." Then he paused and looked at her questioningly. "But I hadn't! Who told you that?"

"Everybody. My father. Your mother. Don't try to rationalize your way out of it now. Furthermore, if you weren't planning to marry Bunny, why didn't you try to contact *me*?"

"I did! For weeks!"

They stared hard at each other. Joanna felt angry and hurt, but all at once she realized she was also very confused. "I'm getting a bad feeling about all this, Michael," she whispered, sitting very still.

"Me, too. Me, too." The pensive lines returned to his brow. "*Where* did you say you went after you left here?"

"Home, of course. But my mother suspected something had happened here. She kept asking me questions and started going through my things. So I left for school."

"School?"

"Yes. You remember. I was supposed to be going to college that fall? Classes weren't starting for another week, but the dorm was open and I moved in. I had to be alone."

"Is *that* where you were?" He turned to face her more directly. "I called your house so many times, but your mother just kept saying you weren't there."

Joanna's eyes widened. "You really called?"

"Mmm. I guess I shouldn't have told her who I was. She didn't think she owed me any favors."

"Not with you being Vivien's son!"

"Boy, you people know how to hold a grudge!"

"You really called?"

"Of course. Joanna, did you actually think I wouldn't?" She shrugged and Michael's look narrowed. "You mean, all these years your mother never told you?"

"Never breathed a word."

He stared at her incredulously. "What could you possibly have been thinking? Don't answer that. I think I know. Get back to your story. You were in college..." But again he paused. "Why the hell were you in college if you and Phil were planning all along to get married?"

Joanna dropped her head to her knees. "We *weren't* planning to get married," she wailed. "I just happened to be pregnant and in need of a husband, and you...you were too busy marrying somebody else to bother." Tears burned in her eyes. She could feel her composure slipping.

"But..." Michael looked confused.

"But what, Michael? You had one hell of a summer for yourself. Hell, not one, but two ladies pregnant as a result. Sorry if I don't congratulate you, Michael, but I happened to be the pregnant lady who got left out in the cold."

"Shut up!" He gripped her arm and dug his fingers into the soft flesh. "Let's get one thing straight. I loved you, loved you more than I'd loved anyone before in my life, and God only knows why but I've never loved anyone in quite the same way since."

Joanna couldn't breathe. She stared at him, tumbling dizzily into the turbulent depths of his cobalt eyes. "Well, you sure picked a fine way to show it!"

His grip tightened. "Joanna, I *never* cheated on you! Never!"

"Sure. I know. Bunny wasn't really pregnant but you thought she was—and you married her. Doesn't that sound a little fishy to you?"

Michael let her go and turned his eyes back on the dark rippled pond. "Not even you believe me," he muttered. "Don't you realize how in love with you I was? That winter before we got here...I should have known...all I lived for were your letters. And then that summer, that was the most incredible time in my life. You were so—*beautiful*."

"I was very young and naive," she bit out.

"Yes, you were. But so was I."

"Michael, you were never young."

"I was only twenty-two."

Joanna glanced away at the lights shimmering across the water from other docks and houses. "Well, whatever you felt, it was nothing compared to what I felt for you. You had me right there!" She thrust her palm forward. "Right there! I was riding so high that summer because of you I...I..."

Suddenly her angry confession conjured up images that were too vivid. A sob choked her. Then another. She broke down under the weight of all they'd confessed and cried uncontrollably.

Michael stroked her back gently, then finally pulled her closer. She buried her face in his shirt.

"Oh, Joanna, how could we have been so stupid! How did we let all this happen?" His hand caressed the side of her face. "Will you please tell me exactly what happened that night? It's time we straightened this mess out."

"Whi-ich night?"

"The night I had to go over to the Wilcoxes. The night you left. Start at the beginning."

"Oh. Well, I waited for you to come home. I suspected something was awfully wrong, otherwise I would have been included. But then only my father and Viv came back, around eleven-thirty..."

"And they told you the news about Bunny, that she was pregnant and had accused me of being the father?"

"No, they told me you *were* the father."

"Damn! I told them not to say anything to you. I knew they'd distort things."

"Then why didn't you come home?"

"Obviously, I should have. So much damage was done..."

"You're darn right!" She drew back. "Do you have any idea how I felt? Can you even begin to imagine how hurt I was?"

Michael's face constricted.

"I was devastated, Michael. I was so hurt and angry I wanted to die. I kept thinking of how close we'd been, about the plans we'd made to get married, and I couldn't understand how you could be so deceptive, so cruel. I ended up hating you that night. I never wanted to see you again. So, before the sun was even up, I packed my bags and left the island."

"You should have waited for me," he answered, his voice rasping with a matching pain.

"Why? What was there for me to wait for? Vivien had already said you'd agreed to marry Bunny."

"But I hadn't. She had no right to say that. It was she and Bunny's mother who brought up the subject of marriage. My mother always was a little too impressed by those people. Her fondest dream was to see me marry into that family." He drifted into a moment of reflective silence before continuing.

"I sat on the beach most of that night thinking about my predicament. The deck did seem stacked against me, Jo. You see, I'd... been with Bunny once, earlier in the summer."

Joanna sent him a look of pure dismay.

"It's not what you're thinking, Jo. Granted, Bunny and I had dated the summer before and, yes, I'd even made the mistake of sleeping with her. At the time, though, I thought I was in love. But, believe me, the moment passed quickly. We broke up that fall. The relationship was over well before you and I came to the Vineyard that summer. She was a part of my life before I started loving you."

"Then how do you explain that *one* time you were together? A slip of memory?"

He raked a hand through his hair in frustration. "It was early June. Like me, she'd just graduated from college, and her parents were throwing a big party for her. I didn't feel like going. I'd tried to make a clean break with her, but I knew she never really accepted it. As far as she was concerned, we were still an item, and I would come to my senses eventually and agree.

"I'd like to think she was still just infatuated with me, that her attitude sprang from purely romantic notions, but it didn't. Truth was, she just couldn't tolerate the idea of someone breaking up with her. How dare I! Nobody dumped Bunny Wilcox!

"So, anyway, there was this graduation party. I hadn't seen nor heard from her in months and I really didn't want to go. But my mother insisted. She said the Wilcoxes would be hurt if I didn't. As it turned out, I should have listened to my instincts.

"The evening began with Bunny hanging all over me as if we were long-lost lovers. Then our parents, in front of half of Back Bay Boston, started making not-so-subtle comments about how we were now free to make plans for the future. And then, I swear, Jo, I only had two drinks, but I got really sick...dizzy, headachey. I probably shouldn't have had even one drink. I'd really pushed myself studying for finals and still hadn't recovered. In fact, I'd been so concerned about it that I'd gone to the doctor's that day to see if I had mono. But I didn't...just old-fashioned exhaustion.

"I asked Bunny if she could get me some aspirin, but after I took it I continued to feel sick. Worse even. To make a long story short, the next thing I remember is waking up in their guest room the next morning—with Bunny lying beside me. I got up and left immediately.

"I didn't see her again till we were on the Vineyard. I was positive nothing had happened that night in her guest room, so even though I was pretty ticked off, I wasn't worried about it—not till I got called over to their cottage at the end of the summer and she accused me of being the father of the baby she was carrying. I told her she was crazy, I'd been too sick to make love to anyone. There was no way that baby— that fictional baby—could have been mine. But nobody believed me. I don't think they wanted to. I finally stormed out and, as I said, spent the night on the beach.

"In the morning I went back to Bunny's house all fired up again and ready to tell her to find some other sap to marry. I'd just remembered that when I'd woken up that morning in their guest room, I was still wearing all my clothes. It was a foolhardy thing to do, knowing how explosive her father can be, but, as I said, I was young and far from prudent. Anyway, he and I argued and before I knew what hit me, I was on my back in the middle of their living-room rug with a broken nose."

Joanna let out a small cry. "Oh, no! The two of you fought?"

"Oh, yes!" He smiled ruefully. "Mrs. Wilcox insisted on driving me to the hospital, and by the time I was bandaged up and back here, you were long gone. I couldn't believe it—you, abandoning me, heading for high ground when the water was running up to my chin! I figured you just didn't care enough to help me through my trouble."

"Michael, how could you think that?"

"Well, what was I supposed to think? Nobody said otherwise—your father, my mother. They were obsessed with Bunny and the fact that I *had* to marry her; I *had* to do the proper thing.

"There was nothing for me to do but leave. I packed and went back to Boston. After stewing in my anger for another day, I called your house, but your mother hung up on me. I called night and day for the next two days, in fact. Then, frantic with worry, I drove up to New Hampshire."

Joanna closed her eyes against the throbbing darkness. She didn't think she wanted to hear this. A truth was emerging, a truth she didn't want to face. If only she'd stayed and waited, the smoke would have cleared eventually. And how different her life would have been! How different it would be now! She should have trusted Michael more. That's what marriages were built on.

"I went to your house and encountered the iron lady you call your mother," Michael continued with a grimace. "Though I don't suppose she told you any more about that than she did about my phone calls?"

Joanna shook her head. "She hated everything associated with my father and Viv, and that included you."

"I guess I scared the hell out of her, too." He laughed bitterly. "I hadn't shaved in about five days, hadn't slept. I looked like a derelict, with a bandage over my nose and two black eyes. The first day I showed up at her door, she told me you'd gone away for a while and couldn't be reached. The second day, she told me in no uncertain terms to buzz off. The third day, she had the telephone in her hand and threatened to call the police.''

In spite of her misery, Joanna chuckled. "She would have, too."

"I didn't doubt it even then. At that point, I was already a day late for my presemester curriculum meetings, so I drove back to Boston, packed up, and headed down to Virginia."

Joanna calculated the days on her fingers. "That was just about the time I was calling Phil."

Michael's dark head tilted, and she could see the pained curiosity in his eyes,.

"As I told you, I was living in the dorm waiting for classes to start and...and I was beginning to suspect something was wrong. So, I went to a clinic and had myself tested. Sure enough, I was pregnant. Well, let me tell you, I didn't know which way to turn. I wasn't about to tell my mother. She would have had a stroke, especially if she found out you were the father. And I certainly couldn't go back to my father. So I called Phil. He was my best friend."

"Was he only that? I know you two had dated."

"Yes, we'd dated. I . . . I think he always loved me."

"And you?"

"I liked Phil immensely. He was kind, steady, gentle. We practically grew up together. But I didn't always love him. That didn't come until later...after we were married. When I called him from school, he was just a friend.

"Well, as soon as we got off the phone, Phil drove up to school with a solution to my problem. He offered to marry me and raise the baby as his own. When it was born, we would simply tell our folks it was premature."

"Did he know I was the father?"

"Yes. He was aware of the whole situation right from the beginning."

"That explains it then." Michael chewed thoughtfully on his lower lip.

"Explains what?"

"I went back to New Hampshire as soon as my preliminary business at school was straightened out."

"Again?"

"Mmm, I had a few free days before the actual start of classes. I went back to see your mother, and this time she told me where I could find you. I couldn't believe it. She gave me an address, and I went racing over to an apartment above a store."

Joanna's lips parted mutely.

"That's right. She sent me over to your apartment. Or rather to what would be your apartment in a couple of weeks. Someone was there, all right, but it wasn't you. It was Phil. He was painting a ceiling." Michael paused and his eyes grew sad. "I introduced myself and he gave me the strangest look, but, of course, now I understand it. You had told him all about me and what a rat I was."

Joanna didn't deny it.

"I asked for you but he was evasive—said you were out shopping and didn't know when you'd be back. Told me he was getting the apartment ready for you. And then he hit me with the news that you were going to be married. I was knocked off my feet. I didn't believe him at first, not till he showed me around the place and I saw your things."

Joanna's head was swimming. Michael had once been in her apartment?

He grew quiet, pensive. "Can you imagine how I felt, seeing boxes of your clothing . . . the blue sweater I loved so much lying across the bed . . ."

Joanna touched his arm, but he wouldn't be comforted. He turned away from her instead, hunched forward as if protecting a pain he'd grown accustomed to.

"What could I say to him? I felt like such a damn fool! So I said nothing, not about you, not about our summer or our plans for the future. Nothing. I just stood there, confused and bleeding. . . ."

"Please don't be angry at Phil. . . ."

Michael dropped his head and shook it side to side. "No. Of course not. He undoubtedly saw himself as your knight in shining armor, fighting to rescue your pride. And me—I was the villain.

"I told him I thought your marriage was rather sudden, and without taking a second to think, he contradicted me. Not at all, he said. The two of you went all the way back to the fourth grade. You had always intended to get married." Michael's expression became sad and wistful. "He must have really loved you, Jo, the way he covered for you, knowing I was the father of the baby he was going to raise! I told him I thought you two were awfully young to be getting married and that it was a mistake. But he was ready for me again. He said age had nothing to do with making mistakes and at least you were making yours out of free choice. That hit me like a ton of bricks. I realized then that you must have told him all about me and Bunny, and maybe you were laughing at my predicament."

"No! Never!"

"Well, I was so confused I didn't know what to think. I wished the two of you well and left the apartment. I never went back after that. I figured there was no use. The Wilcoxes, meanwhile, were making arrangements for a wedding and, well, I went along with them. Bunny needed a husband, or so I thought, and maybe I had slept with her after all. I wasn't sure of anything at that point. And, well, it just didn't matter anymore what I did. It didn't matter..." His voice trailed off into a thin thread of remembered despair.

Even while Joanna watched him, though, his expression hardened. "But of course, I hadn't slept with her. After her pretend miscarriage, I forced her to level with me. She had made up the whole story. And the reason I don't remember being put to bed in their guest room—those two aspirins she gave me were really her mother's Valium! Ten milligrams of the stuff, on top of alcohol and exhaustion!"

"That idiot! She could have done you so much more harm!"

They fell into a long, sad silence. Finally Joanna looked up, smiling wanly. "Do you know who we remind me of?"

"Who?"

"Romeo and Juliet. We were running on blind impetuosity, missing each other at all the most crucial moments."

Michael began to nod.

"We were surrounded by well-meaning people, too," she continued, "just like they were, who in the end did more damage than good."

Now he shook his head. "When it came to us, nobody was well-meaning. They were too caught up in their own myopic bitterness. And the damage they did runs so deep it can never be repaired."

The weak smile on Joanna's lips quivered. No, it probably never could. In the same moment she also realized that their whole conversation had revolved on the love they *used* to feel for each other. "I loved you more than anyone else," he had said, but not once had he said that he loved her still. They could clear the air, iron out misconceptions, illuminate the past till everything was perfectly explained. But the fact remained: whatever love he had felt for her, however true or passionate or exclusive, it was all a part of the past.

CHAPTER FIFTEEN

"DO YOU WANT TO MOVE inside?" Michael suggested, noticing Joanna shiver. "It's getting a little damp."

"Yes. I'd like to be closer to Casey, too."

In the sun porch, Michael settled into his favorite chair while Joanna lit the candle in the hurricane lamp between them. Its steady glow drew them into a circle of intimacy carved out of the warm, dark night.

She sat and folded her hands. There was nothing more to say about their disaster-riddled past. But the conversation wasn't over yet. They still had to face the issue at the heart of it all—Casey.

She chanced a look at Michael. He was holding his hands to his mouth, prayerlike, his stare never wavering from her face. Candlelight flickered in his eyes and cast shadows over the planes of his high-boned cheeks.

"So, Casey is my son," he said finally, his voice contemplative and slow. Joanna nodded, barely able to swallow past the tightening in her throat. "You've done a fine job of raising him."

"You think so?"

"Sure. He's a wonderful child. Bright, happy, well behaved..."

"He looks exactly like you." Immediately she wished she'd kept the thought to herself. Michael's expression crumbled into a look of raw grief. She knew he was thinking again about all the years he had missed with Casey.

"You could have found a way," she thought she heard him mutter before he got up from his chair. For a long time he stood at the screen door, lost in the blackness of the night.

Joanna felt unutterably miserable. Those missing years evidently canceled out everything that had happened between them this summer—the happiness, the working together, the glorious lovemaking. How stupid it had been of her to start hoping, to start thinking they had a chance! Michael loathed her for keeping Casey a secret! Had she thought he would never find out? And even if he never did, did she think they could be truly happy with such a grave deception over their heads?

"I guess it's silly to say we can make it right," she murmured sadly. "As silly as trying to turn back time."

"Yes, it is. The past is lost to us," he agreed. "But I'd like to do something about the future, Jo."

Joanna's head snapped up. "What did you say?"

"I'd like to see Casey regularly from now on."

She smiled—until his words registered. "Oh, I see."

He turned. "Is that all right with you?"

"Yes, sure. He's grown very fond of you." Why had she just let herself think he might want to include her in that future? She knew how deeply he was hurt.

"You don't have to worry about my confusing him, either. I won't breathe a word about our relationship till he's old enough to handle it."

Joanna nodded woodenly, feeling bereft. She pushed herself up from the chair with a sudden longing to be alone. "Sad, isn't it?" she said softly.

"What is?"

"That we have the capacity to understand how and where and why we went wrong—but not the capacity to forgive." Her chin sank to her chest as she stumbled into the house.

If only she'd introduced Michael to Casey sooner, perhaps by now the sting would be gone. But that would have been impossible. How could she have arranged to have Michael visit without turning her marriage into a battleground? For that matter, how was she going to cope with his visits now? How would she greet him at the door? What small talk would they make? How could she bottle up all the love inside without letting it tear her apart? And what if he came to see Casey with another woman—or worse, a wife? How would she smile and wish them well?

No, she couldn't do it. She'd have to arrange it so that Michael came to visit Casey when she wasn't around. She couldn't bear to see him anymore. It would kill her slowly but surely if she did.

In the dark, she slipped out of her clothes and into a long cotton nightgown. Casey was sleeping restfully.

She glimpsed her wan, dejected reflection in the bathroom mirror and thought again about going home. This time she meant to go through with it. There was a sense of morbidity to the cottage now. As long as she and Michael remained here together, grief would be with them. She had to leave.

Michael had just reached the top of the stairs when she left the bathroom. She looked down at the floor as he walked past her on his way to his room.

"Michael?" she called impulsively. "I'm thinking of going home tomorrow."

He turned to gaze at her, his eyes narrowed. "That's not necessary, Jo."

"Yes, it is. Trying to share this place now would be a farce."

He swallowed, looking uncomfortable. "Is Casey ready to travel?"

She shook her head. "I was wondering if you'd like to keep him here with you for a few weeks."

"Just the two of us?"

"Uh huh. It'll give you guys a chance to make up a little of that lost time." Though she smiled, she could feel her jaw trembling. "I'll come pick him up at the end of August."

Michael nodded slowly. "I'd like that." He took a step away from her, then paused again. "What are *you* going to do in the meantime?"

She shrugged. "Go back to New Hampshire, look for a new apartment, work . . . same old grind."

He nodded again, and they continued to move apart, but more slowly.

"Oh, by the way," Michael added, "Doug McCrory loves my novel."

Joanna's eyes flew wide open. "What?"

He nodded without emotion. "I called Joyce today while I was out. She gave him the finished manuscript Saturday night at her party and he read it the next day."

"The publisher?"

"Mmm. He had to find out what Joyce was raving about. Raving, apparently, isn't her normal mode of doing business."

"And he loves it?"

Michael nodded.

Joanna studied his crestfallen face a moment. "What's the matter? Aren't they paying you enough?"

He laughed ironically. "They're paying me quite well, thank you."

"Then what's wrong?"

"Nothing you'd understand." He sighed as he reached for the doorknob, but then he paused. His mouth tightened and he began to blink rapidly. "Joanna, don't go."

Her breath caught in her throat. "W-what did you say?"

He rested his head against the door, as though he were drained of strength. "Please. Stay here."

Joanna hesitated, wondering if her heart still remembered how to beat. Surely he couldn't be saying what she thought he was!

Slowly he lifted his head and looked at her, a man disarmed. "I should be really happy now. I've finally established the career of my dreams, I've become financially independent. . . . But something is still wrong." His deep baritone wavered. "I still feel incomplete, as if half of me is missing. Joanna?" He lifted a hand, reaching out to her. "I need you with me."

With clamoring heart, she ran into his arms. He gathered her close and held her tight. They were both trembling.

"Jo, we've made a lot of mistakes in the past and we've both been hurt, but that's no reason for us to go on punishing ourselves the rest of our lives." They clung to each other as if they were afraid to let go. Finally their trembling subsided; their bodies relaxed and they drew slightly apart.

Michael caressed her face, stroked back her tangled hair. "There's still so much between us, Jo."

She wanted desperately to believe him, but how could she be certain he wasn't going to hurt her again? "What you mean is, there's still a physical attraction between us."

He surveyed her fearful expression. "Oh, yes, there's still that."

Joanna swallowed painfully. Should she tell him she was sorry, but a physical relationship wasn't enough? Or should she be silent? Didn't she love Michael so much she would take him on any terms?

"But a physical attraction isn't all there is between us, and you know it!" He guided her into his room and closed the door, pinning her against it with his body. "I love you, Joanna. I *love* you. You're... you're my soul, my body's breath, my life's joy."

Joanna wound her arms around his neck and drew his head down so that their eyes were level. "Wherever we go, whatever we do..." She could feel her throat tightening with tears. "And I love you, Michael."

His lips quivered for a second. "Good. That's all that really matters, you know—not how many years we've spent apart, not who we've been with or who hurt whom—just our love, now and in the future." He kissed her forehead tenderly. His hands stroked her arms and came to rest on her hips. He urged her closer. "Jo, will you marry me?"

She melted into his embrace. A tear spilled down her cheek.

"You probably think I'm an awful risk. I mean, a man who loves writing so much he gives up his job and apartment for it, lives on the beach like a transient. But—"

Joanna placed a finger over his lips. "I'd marry you if you were a pauper."

"But that's what I'm trying to explain. I'm not a pauper. Gateway is offering me a contract for my next three novels!"

"Are you kidding me?" she shrieked, forgetting Casey was asleep across the hall.

"No! And the terms are phenomenal! I already have an outline for one story, and I have . . ." Suddenly he paused. "Hey, what did you say?"

"About what?"

"Did I hear you say you *would* marry me?"

"Sure did." She felt a smile tugging at her mouth. She began to unbutton his shirt. "When would you like to do it?"

"Tomorrow? Or is that too soon?"

"Don't you want to plan a reception or anything?" she asked. "Invite a few people, like our parents?"

"No! Especially not them!"

"Michael, they're our parents. Besides, they're responsible for our getting together this summer."

"By mistake."

Joanna's hands roamed over his chest, her fingers sliding through the mat of his coarse, dark hair. "The loveliest mistake they ever made," she whispered huskily.

"Yes, I suppose you're right." He began to smile. "We'll have them here for a visit—but not until we've tied the knot good and tight. I'm not taking any chances this time!"

Joanna smiled too. Her hands glided down to his hips and rock-hard thighs. She could feel desire rising through his tautening body, and it thrilled her to know she had the power to move such a virile man as Michael.

"Oh, well," she sighed, abruptly drawing away. "Now that's settled, I'd better be getting back to my room. If Casey wakes up, he'll wonder where I am."

Michael's eyes gleamed with desire for her. A smile tilted his mouth. "You're not going anywhere and you know it. And as far as my son is concerned, he's just going to have to get used to looking for you in my bed in the morning because that's where you're going to be from now on, every morning, for the rest of our lives."

JOANNA FELL into a deep peaceful sleep after they made love, but she woke again just before dawn. Thin gray light was easing through the open windows. Gulls were beginning to caw above the ocean's soft murmur. She gazed lovingly at Michael, still asleep beside her.

She felt incredibly content. It amazed her to think that she had come to this cottage on Martha's Vineyard just five weeks ago feeling drained of every ounce of hope or enthusiasm. Everything important in life seemed to be behind her. And now, here she was, profoundly happy, realizing that life was just beginning. So much lay ahead of her.

She and Michael had rediscovered their summer love, and this time she knew nothing would ever come between them. Theirs was a special kind of love, an enduring love, one that would take them through all the seasons of their lives.

cause there's where you're going to be from now on, every morning, for the rest of our lives."

Kristen fell into a deep peaceful sleep after they made love, but she woke again just before dawn. Thin gray light was seeping through the open windows. Gulls were beginning to cry above the ocean's soft murmur. She gazed lovingly at Michael, still asleep beside her.

She felt incredibly content. It amazed her to think that she had come to this cottage on Martha's Vineyard just this week, ... draped of every ounce of hope or stillness. ... everything important in life seemed to be locked far... And now, here she was, profoundly happy, realizing that life was just beginning. So much lay ahead of her.

She and Michael had each survived their separate loss, and she thought, she knew nothing would ever come between them. Theirs was a second kind of love... an endurance love, one that would last them through all the seasons of their lives.